Simon Butterworth completed his education in West Sussex, England before pursuing a career in the travel and tourism industry that took him to many colourful places around the UK and beyond. In 2008, he moved to Ireland and made his home in County Cork where he started to find inspiration for writing. *The Rents* is the first novel of what he hopes to be a long and successful career as a fiction writer.

The Rents

Simon Butterworth

The Rents

Vanguard Press

VANGUARD PAPERBACK

© Copyright 2016
Simon Butterworth

ISBN 978 1 78465 1 206

Vanguard Press is an imprint of
Pegasus Elliot MacKenzie Publishers Ltd.
www.pegasuspublishers.com

First Published in 2016

Vanguard Press
Sheraton House Castle Park
Cambridge England

Printed & Bound in Great Britain by CMP (uk) Limited

Acknowledgements

Mr Chris Brennan whose help and support has always been appreciated, that and the coffee...

Contents

CHAPTER ONE   13

HOLIDAY IS COMING

CHAPTER TWO   21

AN ALARMING START TO THE DAY

CHAPTER THREE   30

ISLAND OF DREAMS AND A WORST NIGHTMARE

CHAPTER FOUR   38

A DISTRACTION FROM REVENGE

CHAPTER FIVE   47

SETTING THE RULES

CHAPTER SIX   55

DINNER FOR TWO

CHAPTER SEVEN   63

BREAKFAST CALL

CHAPTER EIGHT   71

TO THE BEACH

CHAPTER NINE   79

THE PERFECT GIFT

CHAPTER TEN   87

VOLLEYBALL

CHAPTER ELEVEN   96

AN INNOCENT MISTAKE

CHAPTER TWELVE   105

AVOIDING THE ISSUE

CHAPTER THIRTEEN   115

THE MESSENGER RETURNS

CHAPTER FOURTEEN   124

REUNION

CHAPTER FIFTEEN   133

STATUS UPGRADE

CHAPTER SIXTEEN   142

AN AWKWARD ENCOUNTER

CHAPTER SEVENTEEN   152

THE LEAP INTO NATURE

CHAPTER EIGHTEEN   161

A NATURAL DISASTER?

CHAPTER NINETEEN   170

THE VILLAGE TRIP

CHAPTER TWENTY   179

GOLFING AROUND

CHAPTER TWENTY-ONE   188

PARENTAL CONSENT

CHAPTER TWENTY-TWO   196

A TRIP TO TURTLE BAY

CHAPTER TWENTY-THREE   204

CHECKMATE

CHAPTER TWENTY-FOUR   213

PICASSO WOULD BE PROUD

CHAPTER TWENTY-FIVE 221

THE VOLLEYBALL REPRISAL

CHAPTER TWENTY-SIX 230

A HUNTING DISTRACTION

CHAPTER TWENTY-SEVEN 238

THE UNAVOIDABLE CHORE

CHAPTER TWENTY-EIGHT 247

THE LONG WAY HOME

CHAPTER TWENTY-NINE 255

AND THEN THERE WAS ONE

CHAPTER THIRTY 263

RETURNING TO REALITY

CHAPTER THIRTY-ONE 274

THE END OF THE BEGINNING

EPILOGUE 283

Chapter One

Holiday is coming

Every year Jim had waited patiently for the end of the school year to arrive so he could look forward to his summer holiday and this year had been a particularly difficult year with the added pressure of exams. This year he had earned his summer and making it even better, he knew he wasn't going back to school. His entire school career was about to be decided by a group of people who had probably never even met him and he knew there was nothing he could do about it. Thankfully while he waited for his future to be decided he had the family holiday to look forward to.

Now his school days were over he knew the amount of family holidays he had left to look forward to were limited, so this year he was going to make it special. Every year he was sure he had been the model of a perfect child while on holiday because the rents* had never pulled him up for anything when they returned home. This year he had decided there were no rules, no one was going to tell him what he could or couldn't do because they couldn't exactly send him home – could they?

There was one thing that was bugging him about this year's holiday – one more thing to aggravate him as if he didn't have enough stress with the exam results looming over him. This year he hadn't been told where they were going, he had been given the dates and told specifically to mark them on the calendar – as if he was going to forget them, but whatever, he had done it to amuse the rents anyway.

He had taken the standard precaution of prying out of them that they were going abroad but that was as much as they had disclosed. If there had been any inclination that they were spending two weeks in England as it would be 'just as much fun' Jim had the fuel to remind them of the last UK summer holiday. Strangely enough the two week stay on a holiday centre with cheap discos still playing classics from the 80s had been quickly dismissed as a learning experience.

Even at the age of twelve Jim was sure the cheaper option of a UK holiday was a direct reflection of his Dad having changed jobs. This theory was confirmed when they had returned and the first thing Dad had done was plead with his ex-boss to take him back. Even with the assurance that their family holiday was abroad it hadn't fully settled Jims mind, how was he supposed to gloat to his friends about his forthcoming trip when he didn't know where he was gloating about going to?

*rents was Jim's adopted word for referring to his parents

The more he had been asked by friends about his summer holiday the more difficult it had been to convince them he was going away. They needed more than just his word that he was going abroad this year, why wouldn't they? He had never been vague before even the year he had endure the English summer break. Some of them had taken to digging him in a non-aggressive manner by hinting that he was going camping this year and he was too shy to admit it. These digs had put him on a defensive foot but he had nothing to back up his story of a trip abroad.

He had made desperate searches throughout the house for evidence of a foreign trip. A discrete brochure or a guide book, he would even settle for an invoice that showed details of where they were going. He had searched everywhere except the rents bedroom, which was a known no-go zone. Not even his friends would expect him to enter that territory without a life or death situation forcing him to do it. A few times he had been tempted to cross the border into their room but the thought of what may be inside that room had always prevented him.

Holiday shopping had been sublime as well this year, the rents clearly had no idea how bad it would look if he was forced to wear the same clothes repeatedly during his holiday. He had resolved this by taking on an after school job for a couple of hours a day three times a week and claiming he had been studying with friends. The rents had accepted his story and he had successfully managed to build up a collection of essentials for his trip.

Thankfully, as well as his playfully mocking male friends he had a strong contingency of female friends that had been happy to drag him from shop to shop and show him items that suited him. The cringe-worthy moments were when they picked up shirts holding them against him and trying to work out if they would look good on the boyfriend. Being a living model for a person that in some cases he wanted to be himself was a small penance for being able to put together a good holiday wardrobe.

Jim found that he was giving himself a mental pat on the back, despite the inconvenience and pressure put on him by the rents playing their game of guess the destination he was ready to go with nearly two days to spare. His dad had given him the usual pre-holiday warning of an early night being imminent due to their four a.m. start which hadn't sat very well with Jim due to his allergy to mornings.

This allergy hadn't affected him in his early childhood but had seemed to develop around the time he turned thirteen and now it seemed it would be with him for life. It was a seasonal allergy that seemed to know when he was at school and when he wasn't because he only seemed immune to it on days he didn't need to get up early. In recent years he had been victim to a few close shaves when it came to making the allotted departure time but somehow – usually through his mother's persistence he had made it with seconds to spare.

This year he had it all planned out, there would be no last minute rush for him, he was going to spend the night catching up with his gaming buddies around the world. His father had made repeated his recommendation of an early night and suggested ten p.m. as a target time. Such an early nocturnal retirement would usually have been cause for protest as that hadn't been bed time for four years but on the pre-holiday night it would be accepted without question. From experience he knew the alternative to questioning it would be to lead a one man campaign trying to justify his ability to get up and be ready in a shorter time but that would be answered with the new standard response.

'If you're not ready on time, we will leave without you'.

The difference between having made that response when he was thirteen or fourteen years old and now was that legally he could now be left alone and the rents knew he was able to look after himself if needed. There was also the risk of them having a back-up plan of friends and relatives that could conveniently check up on him if he was left at home. The elements were against him, usually an educated decision could be made as to whether it was worth the risk of oversleeping but as he didn't know the destination he had no idea what he might be missing out on. He also had to take in to consideration the fact that this year due to the 'guess the destination' game he had spent his hard earned (and unknown) money on clothes for this trip.

An all-night gaming session was not only fully justified but was the only fail safe way of knowing he would be up in time.

Taking advantage of his last normal night before travelling Jim had stayed up until after midnight to encourage his body to have a lay in which to his surprise had worked successfully. Instead of waking to an alarm clock he found he was awoken by an alarm shout from his mum announcing that Dad and she were going out for a few 'bits'. With less than twenty-four hours before a holiday, the word 'bits' could only mean one thing in Jim's opinion – the tickets.

There was something more significant than the idea that they were finally going to collect the tickets and that was the fact that he would have the house to himself. If he could do everything he needed to get done before they returned he could disappear to his room for most of the day allowing him to avoid any last minute conflicts.

He was careful not to respond to his mother's voice announcing they were going out. Feigning sleep meant he could avoid extra chores being added to the list he was sure would be waiting for him when he got downstairs. He listened carefully for the front door shutting and waited an extra ten minutes before getting up. He had learned from experience that the door shutting doesn't always mean they have gone – sometimes they return for a forgotten wallet or bag. Many times he had been caught out by getting up as the door shut only to receive the non-negotiable invitation to join them. Even though he was sure that today's trip was one they wouldn't want him to go on it wasn't worth the risk.

Keeping a stealth-like approach, he crept along the upstairs corridor toward the top of the stairs, listening closely with each step for any sound of the front door being opened. Each step took him further from the safety zone but he was confident that he could make it from his room to the top of the stairs before they got back in the house if needed. He started his way down the stairs, from here there was no return – he was out of the safety zone and in to vulnerable territory. At the bottom of the stairs he was completely exposed to anyone that might decide to come in to the house and there on the coffee table propped against a glass of juice was his list of chores.

There was no way of escaping the chores; if he had got up when they were home they would be issued as gradual instructions whereas now he was faced with them all on a numbered list. Empty and refill the dishwasher and deal with the washing were the main items on his agenda. Deal with the washing left a range of possibilities as to what needed dealing with. It would be one of three phases and until he got into the kitchen he wouldn't know if it was filling the washing machine, transporting the items to the dryer or worst of all – ironing and folding.

Before completing the rents assignments he had an agenda of his own to complete. An agenda he had dreamed up in his head in the ten minutes he was lying in bed waiting to see if anyone returned to the house. It occurred to him that despite weeks of policing the post and scouring the usual locations around the house for clues there was still one place he hadn't looked. He knew his dad fairly well and he knew that he would be itching for information on the place they were staying. Despite this he couldn't see any logical way that the rents would have got physical information in the house without him knowing.

That left only one option for a source of background information on the quickly approaching holiday. The internet, Dad wasn't very clever with computers but if he tried hard enough he would eventually get to what he was looking for. There had been a few awkward moments with his online pursuit's one that involved him looking for pictures of cats and one when he was looking for a new web camera and had shortened the word to cam. Eventually Mum had accepted they had been genuine errors and allowed him back on the computer.

Since being let off he had taken more caution and even bought a new office style chair for the computer desk that sat catching the afternoon sun through the patio window. Somewhere on the computer Jim had decided he would find the evidence he had been looking for. It surprised him that he hadn't considered the idea of the computer before but he put the oversight down to the stress of exams.

He sat himself in the comfy chair – Dad had made a good case for buying it, saying it was something the family could enjoy. Jim had never used it because he had his own computer in his room and mum had given him the stern nod to say she would go along with what he was saying even if she knew in her heart that it would be dad using it most of the time. With a rush of adrenalin he flicked the power button and stared at the screen waiting impatiently for the computer to boot up. Oblivious to his anticipation it casually displayed a message saying welcome and waited for the password.

There was no secret amongst the family as to what the password was, sometimes it seemed pointless having one, but Dad had insisted it was for security reasons. He watched the screen load up and quickly pointed the mouse at the icon to access the internet tapping the fingers of his other hand as the screen opened. Quickly he pointed the mouse up at the browser and clicked on it staring at the screen eagerly as he looked for the browsing history. To his dismay he was met with a blank reply from the computer filling him with frustration that he took out by hitting the table and causing the keyboard to jump.

Of all the things that his dad could remember how to do on the computer, all the little helpful hints he had asked for repeatedly why was it the only one he had remembered was how to clear the history? He cupped his head in his hands and looked up at the screen trying to will it to take pity on him. Staring didn't change the blank box that was mocking him, the box that should have held a list of sites that had been visited. In desperation he checked the bookmarks and favourite websites lists but they offered no evidence either.

He couldn't understand it – when had the rents got so clever at hiding stuff from him? Had they been taking night classes in how to outsmart your teenager or something? The only thing he hadn't tried was asking his sister and that was not an option he was willing to give in to.

Chloe didn't live at home anymore it hadn't taken her long after the disastrous family holiday to Wales to announce she was moving in with her boyfriend who called himself Jay. At such a young age it had been a little bit confusing to hear that his sixteen-year-old sister was moving out but Jim had shrugged it off. The rents had different thoughts on it and had decided it had to be discussed further.

Dad had never liked Jay. It wasn't just the dreadlocks and twisted gesture he made that vaguely resembled a hand shake that distressed Dad. The thing that had made Dad cautious, more than anything else, about Jay was the clear plastic bag that had been bulging out of his pocket with what had looked to Jim like grass seeds when he had first met the rents.

Adding to the frustration about the person Chloe had decided to date was his choice of 'career' as he put it. Even if the rents had overlooked the other characteristics that they didn't like about him the fact that he was making a living as an artist made it worse in Dads eyes. He wouldn't have minded so much if he was a successful artist, or even if he was trying to be successful with the vague talent he had, but he wasn't trying. His idea of being an artist was filling the house with canvasses of coloured work that needed a full day's explanation of what they were. He openly admitted to having never had an exhibition of his work and was quite happy to let the government fund his projects in every way possible.

Dad's request for a family discussion had been calmly agreed upon in between Chloe's repeated protests that she loved Jay. It had been arranged for a Sunday lunch which suited everyone involved and Chloe had reluctantly agreed not to bring Jay along to it. They had waited until the main course had been served before any mention of her moving out and as if she knew the best timing for her second announcement she made it. Dad had just scooped a fork of peas into his mouth after a calm and collected lecture on how young she was that in his mind was Oscar worthy when she burst his illusion. 'Dad, I'm pregnant' were the only words needed to send one of the peas like a missile towards Mum's head as she choked down her glass of water at hearing the same three words.

Nine months later and the rents now had their first grandchild and it didn't take long for Chloe to watch Jay decide to follow his calling and disappear to travel the world, leaving Chloe holding their daughter. The note he left saying he was going away didn't give her much choice in the matter. It took her two years to find a man to replace the delinquent Jay and, in complete contrast, this one was approved of as he was apparently a 'keeper' (according to Dad).

Chris was well dressed, highly focussed and polite around the rents which appealed to them. His only downside was that he was ten years older than Chloe; however, Mum pointed out that the age difference may be an advantage with a young child to look after. It didn't take too much convincing for the rents to accept Chris and on more than one occasion they referred to him as their son in law. As he watched, Jim found himself wondering how much that opinion would change if they ever saw the comments he made on social media. Apparently a steady job and a clean cut look was all it took to win the rents affections.

The only advantage to asking his sister if she knew anything about the holiday was that it was likely she had an idea as she would be on house watch during their time away. There was no real reason to have anyone looking after the house, and the more he thought about it Jim couldn't recall having a house sitter before Chloe had moved out but dad insisted it was better to be safe. There were no plants inside that might need attending to and no pets that would need feeding or watering but the house sitter was still put down as a security feature.

On the negative side asking her would show a weakness in that he hadn't been able to find out for himself. As he considered the option of bringing his sister on board to find out the secret he reminded himself that he had to securely hide anything that she could use against him.

Despite the fact that she was no longer a resident at the house and she had two children now, one from each of the known partners she had been with since moving out, she seemed to have plenty of time to uncover his secrets. Somehow she seemed to know where to look for stuff that would incriminate him in some way or another to the extent that she was able to find things he didn't even know he still had.

Leaving her with full access to the house for two weeks and no distractions gave her plenty of digging time. For two years he had been developing more and more ways to hide the things he didn't want found. He knew that if he wanted he could probably question why she was in his room when he wasn't there but usually the stuff she had on him was far more awkward to explain than why she might be in his territory. The more he contemplated the scenario the more he was sure that it was better to go without knowing than to ask her and give her unnecessary fuel Jim let out a loud huff as he carried out the other chores he had been allocated to him. He knew there was no one around to comment on his frame of mind but huffing seemed to make the household chores easier to bare. Quickly he admired the work he had done and checked that he had left no evidence to say he had used dad's computer. Satisfied that he had covered his tracks, he grabbed a few random items out of the fridge that could vaguely make up a snack and headed back to his room.

By the time they had returned, he was deep in online chats and passing emails between his usual crew of online mates as he arranged his night session. Their announcement of 'We're back' seemed fairly pointless given the fact that he had heard the front door being opened and closed but they seemed to feel the need to say it. He replied with the standard grunt to acknowledge he had heard them and continued his search for a team for later.

Lunch time came and went without any major issues except a request from mum to collect the suitcase for traveling. Since his first memory he had used the same case for his holidays and it showed that in the tattered corners and dated tweed colouring. At first this case had been the one he shared with his sister but by the time she was hitting the age of thirteen she was demanding her own case.

She had made her request in plenty of time before their booked trip which as Jim recalled was to Majorca that year and after weeks of protesting the rents finally caved in. Her new case was much smaller than the shared one that Jim now appeared to have full claim to but she seemed happy that it gave her more privacy. It wasn't until the day before that holiday that the extra space in Jims newly acquired case had become home to some of the rents luggage which at the age of eight years old didn't matter to him.

Gradually over the next few years he gained more and more of the territory until by the age of fourteen he had the case to himself. Carefully he reached under his bed to the hidden bags that contained his newly acquired clothes purchased with his own hard earned money. It was like having a second Christmas although he knew exactly what was in each of the bags. Some of the bags had stories behind them that linked them to the person he had been with while shopping but most of the stories involved him sitting in a café in a shopping centre while his chosen shopping partner told the latest tale of their boyfriends bad ways.

By dinner time, his presence was requested by the rents and he reluctantly took himself away from the computer to join them. Nothing was mentioned about the holiday except a casual reminder that they had to be out the door by four a.m. They seemed to know there wasn't much point in asking him if he was looking forward to the trip as it would just spark comments on not knowing where he was looking forward to going.

After being recommended for the third time to get an early night he confined himself to his room and drowned out the noise with a set of headphones as he prepared to join his crew online. When he was in a game it was like he was part of a different world, an elite force that did things that would be considered impossible in the real world. This was his escape from reality; here he could be anything – the commander of a large army, a pirate on the seas in search of treasures or a lone ranger trying to defeat an army of zombies. Most of his crew he had never met before although a few familiar voices had become regular gamers with him.

He had mental pictures of what they might look like that he had built from their voices but he knew that sometimes the voice doesn't match the person that could be created by an imagination. The players that he did know in real life were proof of that however it didn't matter who the person behind the onscreen avatar was. Nothing real mattered no one would ask him questions about where he was going because nobody cared about anything except the player's ability and winning the game.

Chapter Two

An alarming start to the day

Jim wasn't completely sure if it was the gentle knock on the door or the dead weight of his arm giving up the battle against gravity and sliding off the desk that woke him up. The only thing he was certain of was that he was still at his computer desk and someone was outside his room trying to get his attention. He felt his skin peeling its way off the keyboard as he lifted his head up to check what the time was. Without any remorse his alarm clock that had not been set in anticipation of an all-night gaming session was calmly advising him that it was 3.45 a.m.

For the few moments it took for reality to set in all he could hear in his mind was his father's voice reminding him that they needed to leave the house by four a.m. That was followed by warnings he could remember from previous years that if he didn't make it they would leave him behind. He made note that the warnings hadn't been issued to him this year, well not yet anyhow, but then with only fifteen minutes to get out the door he knew there was a possibility that it would be yelled through the door at him.

Staring back at him on the computer screen was the image of his character standing patiently waiting for a command. He could vaguely remember one of his team suggesting returning to the safe zone and a debate starting about the next plan of attack but he couldn't remember what the plan was or if it had been executed. As his character was still in the safe zone he had to assume that any planned attack had been carried out without him. He flicked the keys to check for other players and noted that he had been abandoned so presumably someone in his team had pointed out that he wasn't responding. Shrugging to himself he turned the monitor off to hide the incriminating evidence from whoever was waiting outside his room.

Quickly he grabbed a robe and stripped to his boxers to give the impression that he had just got out of bed. The indentation on the side of his face told a very different story to the one he was trying to convince whoever was waiting behind his door was the truth. Rubbing his cheek to try and hide the keyboard shaped chequered pattern he reached out for the door and opened it. Waiting patiently with a soft smile on her face and her hand poised ready to knock again was his mum.

It was at this stage that he realised how grateful he was that he had remembered the small bit of advice the rents had drilled in to him for years about packing the night before. Instead of trying to make excuses for his dishevelled state he could now just calmly hand his case over to her and make his way to the bathroom.

She acknowledged his offering of a suitcase with a soft and amicable greeting of good morning before making her way back downstairs. Jim had often wondered why it seemed ritualistic for a person to lower their voice when they were talking in the early hours of the morning. Fair enough if you were in a group environment and the only two people awake were you and the person you were conversing with but when everyone in the house was up at the same time it seemed pointless. Maybe the lowered tone was to save disturbing any birds that were sleeping on the window ledges.

With a steady but quick pace he made his way along the corridor and into the bathroom. The tiles were cold under his feet which came as a surprise to him with it being the middle of the summer but then again it was early in the day too. The bathroom window looked out over the street which at ten to four in the morning was still bathed in darkness apart from the few working street lights. Nearly directly below him was the car and he could see his dad standing patiently at the boot waiting for the luggage to arrive.

Jim had never worked out why Dad was the designated car packer and Mum the collector of cases when it was always Dad that contested to being the man of the house. He was sure there was logic somewhere behind it but he found it hard to see when the cases would be heavy and therefore a man's job to carry. Mum had never argued the position – and, he felt sure at this stage, never would – and she seemed happy to be the one dragging the family's bags to the car. In many ways Jim was pleased it was Mum that did the case collection because he felt sure Dad would have been much less amicable about this oversleeping than Mum was.

He gazed down at Dad through the darkness and with almost perfectly timed synchronization Dad looked up towards the bathroom. The worried look on his face coupled with the frantic pointing at the space that should be occupied by his watch acted as a stern reminder to him of the time.

Every day of his working life Dad wore a watch – the same watch for as long as Jim remembered. It was a leather strapped watch with a gold casing and roman numerals telling the time. When it came to time to go away that watch was abandoned and safely stored in a location only Dad knew. For the next two weeks he would buy himself a temporary watch that would cost anything from the equivalent of one pound upwards but never more than ten pounds. This watch was usually a digital watch with plastic straps that was purchased under the provision that it was only meant to last two weeks. After the return from the holiday it didn't matter what condition the watch was in it was consigned to the holiday watch drawer and condemned to remain there until the end of its time.

Jim had analysed this several times and always come to the same question of why he didn't use an old watch the following year. He asked Dad one year and was reminded that a new watch was cheaper than a replacement battery.

In a quick response to his Dad's gesture, Jim ran the cold tap and splashed himself down with water. Suddenly his senses were alert and he was aware of the urgency of getting out the door. Thankfully all he had to do was to get dressed; he ran back to his room and threw on the clothes he had arranged the night before and shut his computer down before checking he hadn't left any plugs in. Racing back the bathroom he moulded his hair in to some sort of fashion, not that anyone would take much notice at four a.m. but it felt like the right thing to do. In his mind, the ultimate thing to be doing at such an early hour was sleeping, but today was the big day.

Grabbing the hand luggage bag he had packed with items that might come in handy, he skipped his way down the stairs while mentally preparing himself for a lecture about timekeeping. Slipping out of the door he checked his phone, he had two minutes before the deadline but was that enough time to avoid any pre-holiday lectures? He couldn't be sure. Like a chauffeur Dad stood holding the door to the back seat ready for him to slip in. He hesitated for a moment wondering when to expect the first comment about his time keeping.

"Morning, son," Dad said as he closed the door.

Just two words; was that a good thing or a bad thing? He realised it could be either, he had been allowed access to the car so he was not being lectured about being left behind but now he was in an enclosed space. The rents raced around the house as he sat waiting, he knew they would be performing their final checks on everything. Remaining in his seat was definitely a good plan during these crucial few moments. The clock in the car agreed with his phone that they were now a few minutes later than scheduled – potentially this could be turned around and used against him.

Dad glanced through the mirror at him as he sat in the driver's seat and started the engine. Jim looked up trying to get some idea from the eye contact in the mirror as to what was going to be said. They pulled away without even a comment, something wasn't right; surely he must have done something to antagonize the situation. Now it was a game of patience, there was no point bringing it up too soon because they were still close enough to home for him to be threatened with being left behind. On the other hand if he let it go until he got to the airport he was then in a public place which would make it more humiliating. Maybe that was what they were waiting for – somewhere they could make him feel bad in the eye of witnesses.

After a short consultation with himself, during which time he weighed up the options, Jim decided it was best to tackle his oversleeping in the car. At least if he did it in the car the options were limited to just lectures and evil eyes through the mirror unless mum got involved then she could turn round to have face to face contact. He decided that the best idea was to wait until they were a reasonable distance away from the home, that way he could brace himself for the response and reduce the risk of the 'we will turn around and go home' scenario.

The only problem with an in car confrontation was that there was no easy way to escape. Any adult to child confrontation at home could be diffused by one or the other electing to leave the room. This wasn't possible in a car; even though on TV people seemed to jump out of cars on a frequent basis Jim was sure it wasn't as easy as it looked. There was also the fact that Dad would be likely to use the middle lane on fast roads which meant the possibility of landing safely was severely reduced.

"Sorry 'bout this morning," he muttered in the hope that if he said it and no one heard at least he could say he had apologised.

"What about it?" Dad responded as expected but his response was jovial and calm but also vague which threw Jim off balance.

There was no way that Dad didn't know what he was talking about, he knew how this worked. Mum who had played the part of his friend by knocking on his door would have told Dad he had just got up when she got to the car. Dad had also made the pointing at the invisible watch gesture so he knew that Dad was aware.

"I overslept, forgot to set my alarm." He gazed up at the mirror; he could see a knowing expression in Dad's eyes, but how much did Dad know? Had mum worked out that he hadn't actually gone to bed and added that in to the equation meaning that both of them knew he was lying his way out of trouble?

"You got to the car on time, no harm done," Dad responded, shrugging under his seat belt as he kept a calm tone in his voice.

What was going on? He had just confessed to oversleeping which may have been seen as a lie but the rents were letting him off? That wasn't how it was supposed to go. He glanced up at the mirror again but Dad's eyes had re focussed on the road and seemingly lost interest in his confession. Part of his mind wanted to continue pressing his apology to ensure that any wrath was encountered en route instead of at the airport or even worse on the plane but the logic side of his brain told him to drop it.

The dawn was just breaking through the night sky as they reached the airport entrance. Jim had spent the remainder of the journey gazing out of the window while keeping a casual eye on his dad's facial expression in the mirror. To his surprise he hadn't let his guard down and let the rant that Jim was sure was building up inside him explode. Casually, he pulled up at the taxi rank and turned round towards the back seat, waving a rolled up twenty pound note at Jim.

"Did you want to go get some food while I park the car?" he asked with a casual expression.

Jim hadn't noticed how hungry he was – maybe it was because his body hadn't fully woken up yet. There was the possibility he could hold off until they got on the plane but there was the risk that there wouldn't be inflight meals offered and it could be a long time until he got to eat again. Smiling back at his dad he grabbed the money and acknowledged the gesture with a nod as he got out of the car.

No matter what time of day it was there always seemed to be activity around the airport. The check in desks had a continuous stream of people patiently awaiting the announcement of which desk to use. That was when he realised what had happened, check-in, by sending him off for food the rents had cleverly distracted him from knowing where they were going for a few more moments. Of course, he could wait where he was under the premise of officially needing to check his own bag in for security purposes. However, if he had got away with over-sleeping, he didn't want to antagonise them.

It always seemed a bit strange asking a person checking-in if they had packed their own luggage. Surely it was only a complete idiot that was going to say no the neighbour packed it for me or anything remotely as stupid. He could imagine the reaction of the people on the desk if a person said no they hadn't packed their own bag. Surely there was a protocol for it that included systematically unpacking the person's bag and repacking it or something like that but Jim had never seen anyone answer that question incorrectly. He felt sure that on this occasion instead of confessing to not packing his bag the rents would assume his packing was safe and answer on his behalf.

Just before the security gates a large self-service cafeteria style restaurant provided the last chance to eat before crossing in to no man's land. Jim had used this restaurant before and although the prices were reasonable the food quality was sometimes questionable. Breakfast, however, should be a safe option; there wasn't much that could go wrong with cereal and the cooked food was a take it or leave it option. With the unknown adventure ahead of him as long as the hot food didn't look too alien he decided he was going to risk it.

He queued up behind a woman who had a young child on what looked like a lead. The child seemed content to pull his mother's arm in as many different directions as possible including nearly tying her legs together as she walked and selected items for them. Jim watched with subtle amusement as he grabbed a tray ready to start the collection for his family.

A tap on the shoulder distracted him from his in queue entertainment forcing him to turn around. His mum had decided to join him, now he would have to ignore the young mother being tied in knots and concentrate. Slowly they edged toward the hot food counter with their trays carrying only a couple of portion sized boxes of cereal.

The woman serving the hot food seemed surprisingly chirpy considering the time of day but then again she had probably been at work a few hours by the time Jim had got up.

As they carried the tray over toward the table that Dad had managed to secure with a series of coats and hand luggage items, Jim noticed how surprised his Mum looked as she counted the change for the third time before putting it into her pocket. Dad's ability to mark chairs as taken on a table that could comfortably seat more than four people had always amazed Jim; however, he could understand it had been done as a precaution to prevent strangers joining them for their pre-flight meal. There was always the possibility that the spare chair could be acquisitioned by a young foreign exchange student that Jim would be quite happy to practice his broken French with. Then again the chances of that happening were very slim; it was more likely to be a man in his late seventies who knew as much about where he was going as Jim currently did.

Jim took the opportunity to sit opposite Dad for the meal, from that position he could try to get a sneak peak at the tickets. He was still uncomfortable at how the rents had managed to get him to this stage and still no closer to knowing where he was going except the fact they were clearly getting on a plane. He glanced up at the departures board; there were too many options to choose from. Flights were taking off to several places that would seem appealing as a summer holiday destination to anyone and others that wouldn't appeal to the majority of his school friends. The one that caught his eye was a flight to Florida, could it be that he was finally going to America? The rents had talked about it as if it was a pipe dream but a destination like that would explain the secrecy.

Jim kept one eye on the departures board while they made their way through their breakfast. He had mentally noted a few of the destinations as personal preferences for this mystery trip he was going on. One by one he watched the list dwindle down with a few of his preferred destinations still in the running. Florida seemed to be taking a good place as it was still comfortably on the list when they made their way to the security gate.

Maybe it really was Florida they were going to, but if it was he actually felt angry that the rents hadn't told him. That would be an amazing place to be able to tell his friends he was going to despite the fact a lot of the attractions were aimed at younger kids. As they walked through the shopping area Jim took another peek at the board, Florida hadn't announced a gate yet but then again a number of the destinations he had earmarked hadn't.

They sat in an area that in Jim's opinion was very non-committal as it was fairly central to all the gates. The anticipation in his mind grew stronger as more destinations popped on and off the board. Suddenly Florida's gate was announced – he looked over at his Dad almost willing him to stand up but he didn't. That was another hope cancelled; one of his prime targets was being pulled away from him.

A noisy group of women ploughed their way into the waiting area in synchronised outfits that hinted towards them being a party of some kind. He prayed to himself that they weren't going the same way he was. Thankfully his prayers were answered quite quickly as he watched them wobble on their heels towards their gate. A group of backpackers followed with a person ahead of them that looked like he must be in charge ushering them like sheep toward the gate for Prague.

Jim sat back relieved at the crises that had been averted by the rents not choosing those two destinations. Muffled announcements echoed through the departure area giving verbal instructions that matched the changes on the television screen. Lost passengers were requested to their gates and still there was no movement from the rents. They seemed to have played another clever trick in making him believe they were heading to their gate when clearly they weren't. Accepting that he was going the be the last one to know where they were going he sat back and pulled his MP3 player out of his hand luggage.

Beyond the hustle of the airport he could absorb himself in a pre-made play list that he knew would probably be repeated several times during the holiday. He found himself breaking down the logical choices of destination in his head. In his mind he could picture the list of departures that had been showing when he started his music. The cities were hopefully not in contention; he couldn't imagine the torture of two weeks in or near a city. The cities in England were stressful and he knew that cities abroad could be much more fun but two weeks seemed a bit excessive. UK destinations were definitely out of the question because passports had been shown at the security gate.

Suddenly out of nowhere he felt a hand on his shoulder; he jumped and glanced to see his mother pointing into space to tell him it was time to go. Finally he was going to find out where they were going, but he hadn't heard a destination or gate called. He watched the signs frantically as they passed the corridors leading to gates 1- 10 and then 11 – 20. His father was hurrying them along, maybe they were under pressure and had missed the first call for their destination.

Gates 21-30 came and went and they entered another moving platform that ushered them towards the next exit. In his mind Jim could see a use for these travelling walkways in everyday life but he was sure there was a practical reason they hadn't been installed in shopping centres to carry people. Maybe it was because there would be too many exit points needed to accommodate the shops. He did however admire the fact that by using them in an airport it gave a true perspective to how large the building actually was.

At the end of the next walkway Dad took a sharp left leading them down the corridor for gates 31 – 40. Jim hadn't noticed which flights were boarding from these gates but he knew now that they were within ten gates of the plane that was going to start his holiday. The answer to the question that had tormented him for weeks sat at one of the next ten desks.

One of the now familiar screens stuck out from the wall giving a brief overview of which flights were available. Jim took a snapshot in his mind and systematically ruled out the ones that were either doubtful or definitely not his flight. Three of the gates had no destination listed which reduced the options to just seven different flights. One of them was a domestic one making it doubtful unless it was to connect to another flight. That was a possibility he hadn't considered – maybe this was just the beginning of the journey, maybe he was getting on a plane here to connect to another destination.

Taking that into consideration any city flight was a possible starting point for his onward journey. Ahead of him he could see the group of women from earlier still patiently waiting to board their flight – obviously they had been delayed he decided. What if the delay was his family not hearing the call, his heart raced with fear that he might be spending the next few hours trapped on a plane with them. Thankfully Dad walked passed them without even a glance, his heart slowed down to a much more normal pace.

Gate 32 was home to the flight from hell with the gaggle of girls in matching costume and Gate 33 was empty. Gate 34 was a flight to Edinburgh but the chances of them going to Edinburgh to change planes he felt confident was minimal. Gate 35 was offering a trip to Paris, a number of his female friends had drooled over the possibility of being taken there on romantic weekends but to Jim it was just another city.

Gate 36 was another one of the empty gates, leaving just four gates that were home to his flight. He had decided that no matter how many people were on this plane this flight was his by default of how much effort he had put in to trying to work out where it was going to. Gate 37 got him excited when he realised it was another American destination and quite possibly a connecting flight but Dad continued moving them past the possibility of a trip to New York.

Gate 38 held the name of a place that Jim had seen on the board and had wished to go to for many years. He remembered mentioning it to the rents before a previous holiday but he wasn't sure exactly why he wanted to go there. When he had seen it as a destination option he had dismissed it as a lost cause resigning himself to the fact that if he was going to go there it would be on his own merits not as part of a family holiday. His heart nearly leapt out of his body when his Dad stopped at the gate and took a seat waiting to be called to board the plane. He couldn't believe it was actually going to happen; he wanted to grab the tickets and make sure it wasn't one of Dads tricks but he was definitely preparing to board the plane.

No wonder they had kept it secret from him, they had known he wouldn't stop going on about it if he knew, finally after years of wanting he was going to Zante.

Chapter Three

Island of dreams and a worst nightmare

For the first time in years, Jim felt the memories of childhood Christmases come flooding back. Since the plane had taken off he had been watching out of his window at intermittent intervals for the first sighting of Zante. In his mind he knew it was hours away but the anticipation of actually going to the place he had spoken about was overriding the rational side of his brain.

In many ways the destination the rents had chosen was better to him than a trip to Florida. The initial let down he had experienced when he realised that a transatlantic trip was out of the question had left his mind. He still held some frustration at not being told where he was being taken because he hadn't been able to prepare any research. Then again he could also see the reasons the rents had held it from him, if they had told him he wouldn't have concentrated at school and with the exams that concentration had been crucial this year.

From his memory one of the biggest attractions on the island was the area that was known as 'Turtle Bay'. It wasn't seen as cool for a boy of his age to want to go and see turtles so he had kept his interest quiet. There were a million questions he had that he wanted to ask the rents but part of him said that if he did ask them their answers would be vague.

At least with his mind distracted with thoughts and anticipations he was able to avoid his father discretely chatting up the stewardess. Just like most of the events in the lead up to the holiday this was a yearly ritual. Even with the increase in male flight attendants somehow Dad always seemed to find a female steward to pass bad innuendos to. When it had first happened, Mum had responded with one of a few subtle gestures that seemed to be designed to cause Dad immediate pain without anyone else noticing, but now even she accepted it.

Somehow despite all the years of flirting once they got off the plane Jim didn't recall any mention of it. He knew there was a chance it was discussed when he was out of sight but to him the main thing was the rents were still married. He was lucky in that sense, a lot of his friends lived with one parent while visiting the other at a designated time during the week. That was the lucky ones, there were also a few that didn't see one or the other of their parents for reasons he hadn't enquired about.

Jim gripped on to his MP3 player as they travelled over the European mainland wondering every few minutes how far they were away. He was tempted to ask the rents if they were there yet but he knew the reply would be no. As a child he had relished in that question, his sister had used it a lot, possibly to antagonise the rents but she seemed to get pleasure out of it. To him it would have made more sense to ask if they were nearly there yet because if they had been there (wherever there was) they wouldn't be travelling anymore. It was strange that she only seemed to feel the need to ask that question in a car, it never came up when they were flying.

Three times during the flight the fasten seat belts lights flickered on which to Jim was a sign that the plane was due to land. Each time they had flickered back off again within a few minutes draining the pent up excitement from his body. He decided that no one was doing it on purpose, the light had gone on for a reason but unless he heard the captain announce they were landing it was a false alarm.

After what seemed to be an eternity, Jim finally heard words of reassurance echoing over the internal PA system. With a tone that sounded like a tour guide he could hear the voice of a man claiming to be the captain announcing they were entering their final descent into Zakynthos. Hearing the local name for the island threw Jim at first but then he settled as he realised that he had read somewhere in the past that Zante was just the English name for it. He felt sympathy for the islanders as he considered how he would feel if he knew another country had changed the name of where he lived just to make it easier to pronounce. Part of him wondered if the inhabitants of the small island were aware of the name adaptation but he knew it was best not to enquire.

If he had been a dog in a car he would have had his head hanging out of the window and his tongue hanging out as they made the final descent. As it was he peeked out through the porthole to try and capture the first glimpse of the island. What he could see was amazing, not only was Zante in view but he could see the outline of other neighbouring islands. Just witnessing such a view made him realize how spread out Greece was, people had told him it was made up of several thousand islands but he had taken that as an exaggeration, now he could see it was true.

Finally he stepped out of the plane and into the intense heat to make his way through the airport. He could imagine what it must have felt like to be the first person to place foot on the moon because for him setting foot on the tarmac runway was just as exciting. Even though he knew technically the place he was standing was classed as a no man's land he dismissed that as being ridiculous, these were his first steps on Zante.

Quickly he made his way to the luggage collection point and waited eagerly for his case to arrive. Like a showcase display of the latest range of suitcases one by one the bags appeared on the carousel. This process was a frustrating one because there didn't seem to be any order to the bags. He wasn't even sure if the people offloading the bags distinguished between first class and economy bags on bigger flights. Just to make things more difficult a number of airlines now had a super economy class. People in this class paid more, got a few inches more leg room and still sat in the same area as those paying the standard economy fare which seemed pointless.

Jim found himself hurrying his family through the airport once their luggage had arrived. He was relieved to see that queues at the customs gate were minimal due to the fact there had only been one flight landing. After that it was a straight run to the gate and into the airport terminal where he anticipated looking for a coach. The plane he had travelled on had not given anything away as it had been chartered by several companies so he wasn't sure which sign he was looking for. He pushed his way through the electronic door and along the gangway watching for his Dads reaction and was surprised when he saw a small man holding a board with his family name on it.

He had never considered himself important enough to have his name on a board so seeing this made him both confused and shocked. This little man was clearly waiting to take them somewhere but there was no holiday company written on his board just their name. Jim watched as his Dad introduced himself and confirmed his identity with his passport as if this sort of thing happened all the time.

Trusting his Dads judgement he followed the man out of the airport and towards a black Mercedes style car. Even at this early stage his holiday had been full of surprises, some of them orchestrated by the rents amazing ability to keep secrets and others by their casual response to things he had done. With this in mind he decided not to question the fact they were not getting in to a coach to go to their hotel.

Coach transfers were always risky, the people you encountered on a transfer bus could well be either on the return journey with you or staying at the same hotel as you. Depending on the type of people a chosen destination attracted it was these small things that could make or break a family holiday. The representative that stood patiently waiting for a coach transfer party to arrive would inevitably be bright and cheery. Jim had decided this was possibly due to a heavy prescription of legalised drugs. Then there was the inevitable family that couldn't be found, no matter how big the sign was for the holiday company there would always be someone that the coach was waiting for. In some of the bigger destinations there was also the possibility that the coach would be waiting for more than one flight to arrive.

Once the representative had managed to account for all the names on their list of arrivals, there would be the announcements on the coach. Depending on the person making the announcements these would take the form of either a cheery greeting and a long spiel including some bad jokes or it would be a formal list of hotels. Either way there would be the standard 'we hope you enjoy your stay with us and if you have any questions please ask'.

Coach transfer crowds could go either way too, in the ideal world everyone would be going to the same hotel and there would be a good mix of families and sensible people. This very seldom happened because the chances of everyone going to the same resort were remote and the people getting on the coach were all on holiday. Being on holiday had the effect of bringing out the best and worst of people depending on the age and the reason for the holiday. Luckily holiday companies avoided putting families on the same coach as the 18 – 30s brigade.

Jim had read the stories and seen parts of some of the documentaries about the late teen and early adult style holidays. Even at the age of sixteen, he didn't see the attraction to some of the activities that the average holiday maker of this type got up to. Maybe it was something that would become attractive at college but drinking to a state of unconsciousness just didn't appeal to him.

By travelling in a Mercedes they would avoid all of that hassle, there would be no waiting while the entire airport was searched for the missing family, no countdown until you finally arrived at the hotel you had selected just to find it wasn't the way it looked in the brochure and no choruses of holiday songs or screaming babies as they made their way from one hotel to the next. In between all these positive points Jim could also see a negative side in that no one was telling him about the island as they travelled and he didn't know who to go to if he needed anything while on holiday. Suddenly he began to appreciate the role that the person checking people on to the coach played in his usual holiday.

Jim decided maybe the rents would become his tour guide in the absence of a person in uniform that was paid to help him. He felt sure that once they got to their hotel everything would become just like any other holiday. Despite how clever they had been in hiding information from him on where he was going he knew that somehow they would have found out all about the island and the hotel before booking their trip. It was at that stage that he realised he still hadn't managed to get all the pieces of the puzzle.

More to the point, the only thing he knew was the island they were staying on, it seemed the private transfer had acted not only as a distraction but a clever tool to keep the actual location of his holiday away from him. There was no point in asking now; it wouldn't take long for the rest of the puzzle to reveal itself. Finally he could leave some comment on his social network pages telling his friends where he was. He would have to make sure that the first thing he did when he got to the hotel was to take a photo to post proving he was actually abroad.

In the meantime he could at least ask some questions about the one thing he knew about that happened on the island. The turtles were finally going to prove themselves useful even if it was only to break the silence of the journey. He glanced at the front seat where his Dad was sitting as the passenger, something in itself that rarely happened. Dad's left hand was gripping the back of the chair, a movement that his sister had pointed out to him was possibly because he was not used to not driving.

Mum was sat next to him and seemed relaxed as she gazed out of the window at the fresh Grecian scenery. He knew there was a possibility the relaxation was actually tiredness. On previous holidays it hadn't been unusual to find mum sleeping on the coach a long time before they had left the airport. Jim pondered his options for a second, if he asked Dad he might either get a vague or a single word answer even if the question begged for more. It was definitely a better idea to ask Mum any questions; if Dad added any answers, all the better.

"Are we staying anywhere near the turtle area, Mum?" he asked casually, making sure it was loud enough to allow Dad to participate in answering if he wanted to.

He had been clever with the wording of the question in as much as it left the door open for them to tell him the hotel name or resort name without him directly asking it. In his heart he knew the chances were they wouldn't mention in but at least it was worth a try.

Suddenly mum seemed to start glowing; a new found energy had made its way into her body in response to the question. Jim waited patiently for her to compose herself whilst wondering if her excitement was because she had been asked the question or because of what the question was.

"That's a very sweet question, Jim. Yes, Laganas is just down the road from our hotel," she responded, smiling, as she placed her hand on his forearm, stroking it lightly to show how pleased she was with him.

Jim cringed inside as he heard her reply, he had prepared himself not to receive the final pieces of the puzzle with her answer but the word sweet stuck in his throat like toffee. Girls used that word when they wanted to let a boy down gently with their reply and now his mother had used it on him.

Words like sweet had become the bane of his life throughout his time at high school so much that he had banned it from his vocabulary. It was words like sweet that were the reason he was not only single but considered a permanent member of the friend zone by the strong contingency of female friends that he had. Some of them had become female friends by failed attempts at asking them on dates, only to receive the 'That's sweet of you' let-down.

A response like that's sweet of you was usually followed by a line about either an imaginary boyfriend or a story about not wanting to ruin the friendship. Both of these get out clauses annoyed him but he had learned to accept them rather than question them. The imaginary boyfriend get out clause was usually quite easy to exploit if he had been the type to do that but he wasn't he preferred to cut his losses and gain a friend.

Ruining a friendship by becoming a couple had in many ways confused him. He wasn't sure how getting closer to a person could ruin a friendship – surely it would make them stronger as a couple because of their friendship. Despite years of friend zoning and knowing some of the most intimate secrets of a number of his female friends he had never successfully had a real girlfriend. When he got to college he was determined to rectify that as quickly as possible even if it was only to prove how good he could be as a boyfriend.

On the positive side as a result of his brief chat with Mum he had achieved two things. Firstly he had reaffirmed his interest in the island so that should settle the rents mind as to whether he was going to enjoy the trip. Secondly he had worked out vaguely in his mind where they were staying. He had read up quite a bit about Laganas but only the beach area because that was the area known for its turtles. He had visualised the golden sands and felt contented that the rents had done well in their choice of area at least. All that remained now was the hotel and he knew they wouldn't choose anything too bad because they liked to be comfortable.

Despite the lack of commentary and the much quieter atmosphere Jim decided he liked the private transfer. It was a much more efficient way of getting to the hotel than the coach and he noted that it took much less time than he had expected for them to pull down a quiet road toward the entrance to what must be their home for the next two weeks. The gate way stood proudly open and there was nothing else in sight down this secluded road. Its location wasn't the best for getting into the small resort but his first impression was that the complex they were entering was a nice one.

A clean looking but simple white building stood at the end of a long drive with Greek lettering above it in bold blue letters and the translation in three different languages below pointing out this building was the reception. Jim was busy gazing at the olive trees that lined the path as his Dad got out and followed the driver to the back of the car to rescue the luggage. Acknowledging a subtle gesture that appeared at first to be a hand shake but turned into Dad handing over a folded bank note to the driver who smiled before getting back into the car and pulling away.

Jim waited patiently outside the building with his mum while Dad collected any valuables from them and walked in to check them in to their rooms. Another advantage to travelling to the hotel by car instead of coach had suddenly and discretely made itself known. If they had arrived by coach there would be a group of them all trying to check in to their rooms at the same time. Jim often admired how the receptionist seemed to manage this with a calm expression while drowning in a sea of tourists.

It took less than five minutes for Dad to return with key cards and safety deposit box keys before leading them round to the other side of the building. Sprawled out in front of him Jim could see a large and well maintained holiday complex. A second, much larger building sat down a small hill like the centre piece of the complex. Beyond that was an outdoor pool that seemed surprisingly quiet compared with some of the pools he had seen on previous years.

Towards the back of the main building Jim could see some roof top tennis courts. He had always watched the sport with great interest, as he got older his interest became more pronounced in the women's game than the men's. People had frowned at him for this but he had proclaimed it was because the women's game was more graceful. On one of the courts he could see two couples darting about athletically chasing the ball. One of the couples seemed to have a distinct advantage physically over the other but it wasn't that that caught his attention. Maybe his eyes were tired or maybe the sun was deceiving him but as he looked down he thought it looked like they had no clothes on.

"Dad, check the tennis courts out," he commented. "Looks like they're naked, doesn't it?" he added with a chuckle in his voice.

There was nothing he could think of that could prepare him for the response he received. Even in his wildest dreams he had never predicted hearing the words that his dad used next.

"They probably are, Jim, this is a naturist resort."

Jim blinked in disbelief; he was sure his ears must be deceiving him, maybe the sun had got to him or maybe it was tiredness. Slowly he digested what his Dad had just said but was still unable to accept he had heard the words correctly so he asked his Dad to repeat himself. The same sentence was repeated to him 'this is a naturist resort.' He had heard of them before. His heart sank as he tried to make sense of what he had just been told; the rents had bought him to a naturist resort.

"What!" He scowled angrily, stepping backwards, away from the view.

"We thought it would make a nice change to have a holiday that we wanted this year." Mum had joined the debate and she was clearly on Dad's side.

All the time it hadn't been the destination that had been the secret from him it had been the hotel. Jim felt like he had been double bluffed, deceived and lead into a false sense of security. Everything was clear now, the calm expressions, the lack of reaction to his bad time keeping and even the private transfer. Why would they do this to him, surely they didn't expect him to run round naked for two weeks. Worse still surely they didn't expect him to be happy with them running round naked for two weeks. He felt the bile at the back of his throat as he wrenched at the thought of seeing the rents with no clothes on.

"I ain't doing it," he grunted, folding his arms to enforce his words.

Mum looked at him with a calm expression; he hadn't expected her to look so casual about it.

"What are you going to do? Go home?" She asked with a slightly mocking tone.

Check mate, Jim didn't have much to say about that, there was nowhere he could go. The road to the complex had not shown any other hotels, but then again he knew why now. He could go back to the airport but he would be waiting there for two weeks, alone. He didn't have any choice, it was here or nothing all he could do was make the most of it and avoid them.

"You have your own apartment, Jim, and there is an envelope of money here for you with another one due next week; we aren't going to force yourself to enjoy your holiday, but you're not spoiling ours," Dad added.

He was like a rabbit caught in the headlights; they had closed the door on his main objections by giving him his allowances and his own room.

"Fine. I'll stay in my room for the two weeks, room service all the way, then," he retorted, trying to push the argument back towards the rents.

"It's all inclusive, Jim." Dad smiled as he spoke. "Do what you like; it's not going to cost us anything extra."

He contemplated his Dad's words for a few moments; usually he was good at strategic moves. He had his own room, money to himself and the place was all inclusive no matter what he did he couldn't play a card that was going to upset them. Maybe he could try using a guilt trip by reminding them they wouldn't be seeing him for the entire holiday but what good would that do – they had already told him it was their holiday as much as his.

If they were going to be condemned to two weeks here he may as well get on with it. The longer he stood outside the more chance there would be of someone random walking past him with their bits hanging out.

"Fine!" he said, presenting his hand to the rents for his key.

Smiling softly in contrast to his scowl, his mother handed him the key card, a key to the safe deposit box and the envelope his Dad had mentioned.

Cupping his hand to the side of his face to avoid seeing any unwanted naked flesh, he followed quickly behind them to the apartment, huffing at them as he continued on to his shutting the door quickly behind himself.

Chapter Four

A distraction from revenge

Jim reeled with frustration as he paced round his bedroom, no matter which way he turned the rents had cleverly found a legitimate reply to his objections. He felt sure they had done it on purpose; they knew he wanted to go to Zante and they had booked a trip there. They had hidden the trip from them and let the distraction of finally learning where they were going act as a tool to stop him asking about the hotel.

In the corner of the room his suitcase laid where he had dropped it, still unopened while he tried to devise a plan. All he had on him was the money envelope he had been given and the key to the safe deposit box. If he tried to get away from the complex he would have difficulty finding somewhere to stay and more than likely it would only take a few days for someone to come in pursuit of him. If there was one thing the rents were good at it was finding him when he didn't want to be found. He couldn't even get revenge on them with room charges; they had made it clear that everything was paid for.

Frustrated he threw himself on the bed feeling it bounce him slightly as he landed. These four walls were going to be his home for the next two weeks, he was out of options – even his threat to remain indoors had fallen on deaf ears. It was clear to him that they didn't care how miserable this holiday was going to make him.

It startled him slightly when he heard a creak from the living area that he recognised as the front door being opened. Even though he had managed to shut it when he came in it was obviously not locked. He made a mental note to learn how to lock it once he had dealt with his visitor.

"Told ya, Mum, I ain't going out with you guys naked!" he shouted with a tone of hostility through his closed bedroom door.

He felt sure that his tone would generate one of two responses from them, either they would stand in his apartment and conduct a debate through the door or they would burst in on him. Which part of his argument outside hadn't they understood? He had made it clear that he was going to spend his holiday in his room. They had even acknowledged his objections and given him money and his keys so he could do what he wanted. He grabbed the pillow ready to shield his face from their anticipated rampage on his bedroom.

In past years they would have shrugged off his anger as a tantrum and teamed up to coax him out of his room. When he was younger they had even gone to the extent of lifting him by his arms and legs and transporting him manually to wherever they required him. Now he was older he was beyond the age of being comfortably carried so verbal battles had replaced physical confrontation. After a few moments of waiting for a reply finally a voice carried through his door into his room but it wasn't the voice he was expecting.

"Well, I'm not ya mam, but if ya don't want to say hello, it's grand," a younger female voice responded.

At first it caught him off guard, was this some clever trick set to make him investigate and leave the safety of his room? He had established that the rents were much cleverer than he made allowance for but this was surely beyond their abilities. His heart beat fast as he tried to work out what to do, he was curious to find out who was in his room.

"No, sorry; hold on, I'll come out," he responded in a much softer tone as he slowly got up.

He waited as he heard the creaking of a door again and heard the click as it was shut. Patiently he waited unsure if his mystery visitor had heard his reply and was waiting for him or not.

"I'll wait so," the voice returned again.

He felt relieved that whoever it was had heard his apology and decided to hold on for him to make an appearance. Maybe this was the holiday rep he had been expecting to see at the airport, maybe he had locked the door and she had a master key to allow her to introduce herself to newcomers. No that was crazy, why would a rep let themselves in to a room, she wouldn't know who or what she might see. If it wasn't a rep then who was this stranger who he now knew was waiting?

Quickly he glanced in the mirror, patted his hair down and brushed his shirt off to make himself look presentable. It would be wrong of him to leave whoever it was that was waiting for him too long without him appearing. He rehearsed words in the form of excuses for his hostility but none of them made any sense. This stranger must know it was a mistake and his scowl had been meant for someone else. She, whoever she was, had clearly heard him address his comment at his mother.

Taking a deep breath he walked out of the bedroom and stopped in his tracks as he looked over at his visitor. He could feel the blood rush to his face and his jaw dropping as he tried not to stare at her. Sitting casually in the plastic chair that had been idle next to the front door was a girl about his age. He was used to greeting girls but this one was different because unlike his female friends this one was sat there naked.

Mortified with shock he quickly turned away and occupied his hands by brushing his shirt down again. In the anticipation of finding out who it was that had invited themselves in to his room, suddenly he remembered the type of complex he was staying at. He stopped himself as he felt the blushes filling his cheeks; maybe he should be taking his shirt off not brushing it down. A light finger tapped his shoulder making him jump slightly with shock, she was stood behind him.

"S... S... S... S... S... Sorry," he stuttered nervously. "This will sound stupid but I didn't expect to see you naked," he added, feeling his heart thumping at his chest as he spoke.

He had seen nude girls before but only ever in films, they weren't real, this one was very real and standing behind him. Maybe he should just turn round and make the most of the fact that she was naked and he hadn't had to do anything to get her to that stage. No, that was wrong; he had learned much more respect for girls than to just do that. In his head he had role played seeing a girl naked and how he would react but each time it had started with getting to know the girl first and maybe seeing flesh after a few dates.

She giggled politely behind him; she had never seen such a flustered response before. Quickly she looked round the room; over the back of the couch a light cotton throw covered the cushions. Running over to it she grabbed it, wrapped it round herself and tied it loosely under her arm. She noted to herself how sweet his response was as she returned to her spot behind him and tapped his shoulder again.

"It's safe to look now," she said. "I've covered up."

Jim felt the tension in his muscles release itself as he let out a deep breath and turned round. She stood coyly watching him as he turned to face her keeping his head low at first but lifting it as he realised she was actually covered and hadn't just said it to make him relax.

"I'm Sasha," she said, smiling at him as she extended a hand towards him.

Jim could feel the rigidness of his body, he must look like a soldier ready to go on parade but what could he do. His body was still in shock at being caught off guard firstly by her appearance and then by her lack of clothes.

"Jim," he responded, grabbing her hand softly and shaking it like it was a fish that he had just caught.

An awkward silence followed their first physical contact, Jim knew in his head that he didn't want the silence but it was there mocking him. He had never been caught like this before, usually he had no problem speaking to girls but then again normally they were fully dressed. He knew in his head that most boys his age would jump at the chance to be where he was now. Surely there must be something he could find to say, if he didn't she was going to leave and he would probably never see her again.

"It's your first time here, I guess," she said, breaking the awkwardness between them.

Like a naughty school child he stood fixed to his spot and nodded. It must be glaringly obvious that he didn't know what to do but thankfully she had taken sympathy on him, or so it seemed. He hadn't decided if he should start undressing in front of her or not, it could be taken either way if he did. Maybe for now it was better that he remained dressed, she had covered herself after all and he didn't want to give a worse impression than he already had.

"Are ye going to invite me to sit down or will we just stand here?" Her tone was much more authoritative this time. However, the soft Irish lilt made her statement much easier to listen to.

Trying to keep his body calm which was defying everything his mind was telling to do he gestured over to the couch mumbling the words "please sit" as he choked.

Acknowledging his gesture Sasha took herself round the couch and made herself comfortable while she watched to see what Jim was going to do. She felt slightly put out when instead of joining her on the couch she watched him choose the seat she had been using while she waited for him to appear.

Casually she stared round the apartment trying not to show that his distancing had upset her. She tried to put herself in his place, if she had been the newbie and he a fully-fledged regular guest at the complex she could see that she might not know how to handle the situation. Naked person in your apartment, someone you hadn't met before, looking at him he was about her age so unlikely it was his first time seeing a girl naked but all in all she could see his nervousness.

She distinctly remembered her first time at the complex; she had been much younger than her new acquaintance was at just eleven years old. It had been a family holiday just like the one she was now on but seeing her parent's nude had been a little strange. There had been mention at school of the difference between boys and girls and even some childhood games amongst other people she knew which included the exposure of body parts but she had never seen a man nude.

Once she got over the fact that her first experience of an adult male without clothes on was her father and the differences between herself and her mother were things that she still had to look forward to she just got on with her holiday. She tried to put herself in the same situation five years later, if Jim was about the same age as her that would be a good timeframe to work to. Now she could see that accepting nudity would be more difficult, seeing her parent's nude might not be as easy and then extending that to a stranger would definitely be more of a task than a pleasure. Nodding to herself as giving herself a mental pat on the back she smiled softly over at Jim.

In her opinion, coming to this complex had completed her education and matured her a lot quicker than her school mates. She had watched them chase around trying to catch the attention of the lads at the neighbouring school. She had seen the uniform skirts getting shorter and the blouses getting top buttons discarded in an attempt to attract boys.

She has also seen the boys that she had grown up around turning into clumsy teenage idiots as they tried to win the girls. She wasn't immune to it, a few of the lads had tried to talk her into house parties that she knew would end up with people being coupled off or games that involved clothes coming off. Immune wasn't the right word to use in her opinion, she was wiser to it and therefore not getting involved in it.

By distancing herself from the after school activities she had in some peoples opinion suffered the consequences by not having a real date for communal school activities including her junior cert disco. She didn't see her situation as one of suffering because she had seen the outcome of some of the partnerships that had formed. She had escaped the tears of a broken heart as the high school crush found a new love and had decided when she did date someone they would have to be special.

Her only regret was that for five years she had not been able to share her holiday experiences with the few people she classed as friends. For fifty weeks of every year, she has to act like she had no idea what a man looked like; they all knew she hadn't dated anyone. If the boys had found out that she spent two weeks comfortably walking round naked she knew the circumstances would be unbearable. The most awkward moment was when friends asked about her holiday and she had to keep the details vague before distracting them by asking about local gossip. Thankfully, the need to spread the word as to what was going on locally outweighed her holiday.

She glanced back over at Jim who she noticed was still struggling to find the right words to use. It couldn't be easy for a textile* in a naturist world and he was clearly struggling while trying not to make her feel unwanted. She smiled at how innocent he seemed, who knows what he got up to back home, maybe he was just like the lads she had left behind but somehow she couldn't see him being like that.

He appeared to be more of a charmer, a real ladies man, someone who was possibly confident around girls and knew how to treat them. Quite possibly he had left a beautiful girlfriend at home who was patiently waiting to hear that he had arrived safely. Then again at his age surely he would be allowed to bring his girlfriend with him on holiday – assuming he was with family of course so maybe he was more similar to her than she took him to be.

"So, did I catch you at a bad time?" she asked sweetly, trying to hint that he hadn't said much since she had arrived.

Jim felt his face fill with redness, he must look terrible to her, there she was trying to be friendly and all he had done was sit speechless.

*textile is a term naturists use to describe a person who prefers to wear clothes

"I... I... I just don't know what to do." That stammer, which had caught him before, had returned to plague him as he spoke. "I don't want to give the wrong impression by sitting dressed, but I don't want you to think I'm after something by getting undressed." He cringed as he heard the words he had said filling his mind.

Filling the room with noise, Sasha burst into a melodious chorus of laughter. causing her body to bounce in the chair. Recomposing herself she fixed the single knot holding the drape around her body and looked at him smiling. He wasn't like the other boys back home, in that single sentence he had shown her that he was a thinking type, conscious of what he did and said.

"You're grand," she giggled.

Her accent was intoxicating to him, sometimes difficult to understand, but it carried on the air like a melody as she spoke.

"I heard the door slam as you arrived in your apartment and said to myself, you know what, I am going to go meet my neighbour."

Even when the words she put into a sentence didn't fully make sense to Jim he loved hearing them.

"So you seem a nice lad, maybe we could hang out together?" She hadn't ever had a friend of her own age on holiday and it would be nice to show a new person how things were while getting to know them.

Jim felt the colour drain from his face, hang out together would mean going outside. Going outside would mean being in the same place as the rents and being in the same place as them meant possibly seeing them naked. Then again hanging out with Sasha meant he had someone he could enjoy time with while he was here – maybe she was the distraction he needed.

"Knock for me tomorrow morning," he said, trying to sound as friendly and confident as he could. "But," he added, knowing he was putting conditions to their hanging out together, "I can't do the naked thing. Not yet, anyway."

Sasha nodded, she had in her mind expected him to either say something like this or make an excuse not to hang out. Casually she stood up gripping the knot under her arm as she walked over toward him. Jim watched her like it was a slow motion movie and he was waiting to see what happened next. He stood up as she presented herself in front of him, it seemed more practical than remaining seated.

"C'mere," she said softly as she opened the door with her free hand, propping a foot behind it to keep it from closing again. "I've a secret to tell ye," she added, validating her request for him to get closer.

Puzzled but not wanting to question her request he leaned in towards her, her skin smelled of sun lotion.

"See ya at ten, then," she whispered softly before kissing him on the cheek. "Oh, and I think this is yours."

Jim felt something flop on his opposite shoulder and looked up to see her streaking out of his door as the throw she had worn landed clumsily at his feet.

Bewilderment filled Jim's mind as he tried to recall what had happened in what had clearly been the most awkward moment of his life. If his friends at school had seen him they would have enough fuel to mock him for weeks over his behaviour. Somehow within an hour of entering his room a complete stranger had entered his life and not only befriended him she had convinced him to go outside. There was of course a possibility that it was all a cunning plan, a plot orchestrated by the rents but he couldn't see any way they could have arranged it so quickly after arriving.

All he was sure of now was that he had just one night to prepare himself for whatever might happen as a result of his agreement. Bending down he picked up the cloth that had fallen to the floor as Sasha left and folded it neatly choosing not to replace it on the couch. He could still smell the aroma of her sun cream sealed within the bundle which reminded him of how cleverly she had distracted him with a cheek kiss as she left.

He had been blessed with cheek kisses from girls before so he was used to them, several of his female friends had endorsed him with them for helping them with their messy break ups. Cheek kisses were a friendly gesture, there was no way in his opinion they could be anything else. After the way he had responded and made Sasha feel less than welcomed in his apartment it was a miracle that she even wanted to see him again.

He wasn't sure if he could cope with walking round the complex with her, maybe it was a bad idea to agree to meet her. Fair enough she had accepted that he wouldn't do the naked thing but that didn't mean that she was going to be dressed. Part of him wanted to cancel the arrangement, slip a note under her door saying sorry but I can't meet you. He sat and analysed his concerns about meeting her, most of them led back to the same thing – nudity – not so much her nudity but seeing others including the rents nude. He lay across the couch, questioning in his mind if he had made the right decision in saying yes to her – was the risk worth it?

****

Sasha slouched back against the door of her apartment as she closed it behind her. What a funny experience she had endured in meeting the person that was temporarily her neighbour. She giggled to herself as she reviewed how shy and sweet Jim had been and how nervous he had been about seeing her. Across the back of her couch was a throw that nearly matched the one she had worn for her visit. Never before had she even considered covering herself with it but in emergency circumstances it had done the necessary job.

She was pleased she had taken the time to meet him; even though his first reaction had been hostile he had quickly changed his tone. Within moments he had gone from being aggressive towards his parents to unsure around her. It hadn't taken her long to see that he wasn't like the boys she knew back home, he was a thinker and that appealed to her.

Pushing herself upright she walked past her couch lightly brushing it with her finger tips as she made her way into her bedroom. She glanced into the sparsely filled closet that held the minimal few items she had bought with her for the evenings. At night the complex changed mainly for comfort in her opinion as Grecian nights were renowned as chilly. This was the one time of day when nudity wasn't allowed in the main communal areas.

Suddenly she had an idea that in her mind was perfect, Jim didn't like nudity and at night nudity wasn't allowed so the evening was the perfect time for them to hang out. With new motivation, she flicked through her range of flimsy dresses, selecting a light blue one. She stood in front of a mirror and slipped it on over her head watching as the silky material hid those parts of her that in normal society were taboos.

Its length truly left little to the imagination and she made note that if she bent over it rose over her buttocks making her giggle. She had never worn this dress at home for the same reasons that she liked wearing it on her holiday, it barely covered anything. If she had worn it to a party with her friends she knew the boys would be salivating and trying to see up it. Here maturity was at a different level, no one cared how short a dress was because everything it hid had been on display just a few hours earlier. Jim would love it she decided, questioning herself as to why his opinion had any validity in her choice. Then again it was him she was planning on spending the evening with so he had to be comfortable with her.

She flattened it down checking again that everything that needed to be hidden was hidden. Maybe she should wear panties – she had some with her but begrudged wearing them if it wasn't necessary. No the dress was enough cover, Jim could either accept her as she was or not at all she had no reason to go out of her way for him, if he didn't want to go to dinner with her then they still had their meeting the next day to look forward to.

Nodding approval at her decision she slipped a little bag over her shoulder that she kept for evenings. She had learned that carrying a bag over the shoulder during the day was more of an inconvenience than anything else because it left a red mark where the strap had stuck to the skin. Of an evening though – when the skin was covered and the sun not an obstacle it didn't matter. Checking that she had everything she needed she made her way to the door.

"Jim, I hope you're ready," she muttered to herself. "Dinner is waiting for us."

Chapter Five

Setting the rules

Sasha was quite concerned when she got to Jim's door and realized she had butterflies in her stomach. The excitement of actually having someone near her own age to have dinner with was overwhelming her. When she had first started going to the complex meal times had been with her parents but in the last two years they had let her get on with her own holiday. She felt complimented by the fact that they allowed her so much freedom but she had noticed the number of people close to her age had dwindled.

Her parents hadn't really noticed the decline in people for her to group up with but why would they? They trusted her more than most parents would trust a teenage girl and she had proved herself worthy of that trust. At the age of fifteen, she had been one of only two teenage girls that were regular visitors to the complex and the other one was too busy trying to chase the boys to qualify as someone she wanted to be seen with. Janace may have only been six months younger than her, and the closest to her age by a few years, but Sasha felt relieved not to see her when she arrived this year.

Thankfully, as a distraction from the other lone teenager, she had associated herself more with a small group of young adults who were not interested in her in any way except to be sociable. Being treated as a young adult at the age of fifteen suited her as it proved to her parents that she was able to look after herself. As a bonus she had been given an apartment to herself this year which felt a bit strange at first but she knew her parents were only a doorstep away if she needed them for anything.

For now she had her own little project to deal with which was Jim, if she was careful she might be able to gain a friend her own age and make him like naturism. She peered through his window as she got to his door and saw him lying casually across the couch. His feet were comfortably crossed at the ankles and she could see something in his hands that resembled a menu or information leaflet. Either he was reading up on the complex – which wasn't a bad thing or he was choosing dinner which as she wanted to take him to dinner wasn't a good thing.

She paused for a second and contemplated how to put the suggestion of dinner to him. She could go with the polite way of just asking him to join her to dinner but he might take that the wrong way. Then again if she told him he was going to dinner with her that could sound bad too. There wasn't an easy option – she just had to choose which option was less hazardous and go with it. Taking a breath she prepared herself for any objections he might put up and knocked at the door.

After his pleasant but awkward meeting with Sasha Jim had decided to make the most of his first night by keeping his word to the rents that he was going to spend the holiday in his room. He had come to terms with the fact that his actions couldn't financially affect them but if they didn't see him for at least the first night then he could at least show some rebellion. Given that he had agreed to meet Sasha the next day his rebellion was going to be short lived and in some ways seemed a little pointless but it was the principal of it.

He flicked through the room service menu, casually trying to decipher the grammatically incorrect English translations for the various dishes. Seeing chips mentioned as accompaniment for a sandwich confused him slightly at first but he soon realized it was the Americanism and they were actually referring to crisps. He was still contemplating his main course when he turned to the Dessert page and heard a knock at the door.

Slowly he gazed at the only clock in the apartment except the alarm clock and saw that it was about dinner time. He felt sure that this time his visitor would be the rents trying to convince him to join them. Maybe if he stayed quiet they would go away, then again shouting at them through the door that still wasn't locked would make him feel better. Slowly he swung his legs round pulling himself into an upright position and took a deep breath ready to launch a volley of growls when a familiar voice entered the room.

"Jim, it's me; Sasha. Can I come in?"

For the second time in one evening she had startled him by appearing at his apartment. He found himself questioning what she might want, maybe she had decided to cancel their meeting in the morning, if she had that would be okay because he could continue his 'stay in hiding' vigil. Maybe she had left something behind; quickly he started scanning the room before realising it was a stupid thing for him to think. She had arrived in his apartment naked; it wasn't as if she had any pockets to have dropped something out of. Then again, it could be an earring.

"Sure. Give me a second," he responded.

Logically he wasn't going to find out what she wanted by sitting here thinking about it. He knew it was bad manners to leave a girl waiting at the door under normal circumstances. Leaving a naked girl waiting at the door was definitely not acceptable even on a naturist resort. Quickly he flattened the throw she had worn previously back over the couch sensing a whaft of her scent as he watched it settle in place. Then he thought, she will be naked – even if he couldn't go all naked he should show at least some effort. Quickly he pulled his shirt off and kicked his shorts gracefully across the floor leaving just his boxers covering himself. He folded his shirt over the back of the plastic chair and opened the door to greet her.

His nervousness and anticipation quickly drained from his body as he realised she wasn't naked after all. Standing in front of him was the same girl he had met before but now she looked as normal as the rest of his female friends in her light blue mini dress. It was nice that she had made allowances for his shyness from before but now he felt vulnerable in just his boxer shorts.

"Come in, love the dress," he said through a vague smile as he waved a gesture inviting her into the apartment.

Sasha paused for a few seconds she was unsure whether his comment was actually a compliment or an observation. She was sure that when she peeked through the window he was still fully dressed so seeing him in boxers caught her off guard.

"I'm here to take ya to dinner," she announced.

She wasn't sure if she had been too forward in the way she had said it but It was said now there was no way of changing it without looking foolish. She watched patiently as she decided to invite herself to sit down in the absence of Jim offering a seat to her. His face seemed distraught; she could see he was trying to find a way to talk his way out of it. Maybe she should just put him out of his misery and retract her offer but now she was curious as to what he was going to say.

"That's nice but I can't," he said, quickly grabbing for the room service menu that she was sure he hadn't used.

There was a small feeling of anger in her as she looked at him, he was clearly making excuses for not going and she was sure she knew why. She looked over at him as he awkwardly tried to hide his own body behind his arms. They twisted and turned in front of his bare chest like snakes as he tried to cover as much flesh as possible without seeming obvious. She wasn't going to let him get away with it, now it was her mission to get him out the door.

"So you would prefer to eat here alone than join me, would you?" she asked as she stood from her seat and started slowly walking indirectly toward the door.

"Well, no, but..." He was cut off by her voice telling him to cancel the room service.

What was she doing to him? She knew he wasn't confident with nudity and now she was ordering him about. She barely knew him and yet she seemed to have decided it was her place to organize and arrange his holiday. He had to stop himself from saying anything nasty, it was his gut instinct to defend his decision but he liked her.

"Read this," she continued, thrusting the welcome pack into his hands.

Jim looked up at her with a puzzled expression; he had seen welcome packs before at hotels. They always had the same boring stuff in them about fire exits, meal times and opening times. Once you had got past the first few pages talking about the history of the place you were then bombarded with information of different attractions in the local area. None of this was going to be of much use to him as he was planning on spending as little time as possible in places that he could see other people except Sasha.

Huffing slightly he complied with her demands and opened the front cover to see the standard 'Welcome'. He looked up at her; she had her arms folded patiently as she waited for him to turn the page. Page two was just boring stuff about the on-site shops and their opening times and the standard where to go in the case of a fire. Flicking the page he looked at page three, it gave a sample menu and stated the restaurant opening times – nothing he hadn't seen before. He grabbed the corner of the page in preparation to turn it but was stopped by her finger directing his eyes to a note below the opening times:

Although the restaurant supports the naturist way for breakfast and lunch, we request clothing to be worn during the evening. A dress or top and skirt for ladies and a shirt and pants/shorts for men. Footwear is recommended but not compulsory. Thank you.

Slowly, he looked up with a vague grin on his face that said he knew he had been caught out.

"Go on, get dressed, I'll cancel your room service." She emphasised the word 'cancel' as she snapped the menu shut and threw it over her shoulder towards the couch.

Scuttling past her he grabbed the clothes he had removed to let her in and ran into the bedroom. He wasn't sure how it had happened but somehow she had not only seen through him she had also gone out of her way to get what she wanted. At the moment what she wanted was to take him to dinner, surely this was a good sign. They had arranged to meet the next day and although Jim wasn't comfortable with the idea he wasn't going to let her down. Still regardless of this she had bought forward their meeting to that night and now he was here getting ready for her.

He couldn't remember the last time a girl had been so pushy with him, more than likely it had been his sister at some stage but that wasn't the same. This girl was not related to him, until less than an hour ago they had been complete strangers and now she was in his front room, waiting for him. Maybe that was a sign, one of those signs that he kept missing, the sign that she liked him. If he had been at home and this had happened he would have played it casually, tried to find out from others if she liked him or not but on holiday all the rules changed.

He had seen this sort of thing happen before on previous holidays within the groups of holiday friends he had encountered. A girl shows interest in one of the boys, the boy makes a quick response and within a day or two they were a holiday couple. This time it was his turn to be the lucky guy, he had to put the past behind him and go for it.

Quickly he kicked off his boxers feeling a breeze of air tingling against his body from the air conditioning. Still conscious of his nudity he grabbed a pair of thin pants and a shirt slipping them on before checking himself in the mirror. He had never gone out without boxers before and the feeling of not wearing them left him feeling uncomfortable. He gazed over at the pair he had discarded; they had been stuck to his body for more hours than he wanted to count and, now they were off, he wasn't going to put them back on.

Shrugging to himself he decided to leave it as it was, nothing else had been normal about this holiday so far maybe the change would be a good move. He looked at his hair which was showing the signs of a day's travel, something needed to be done about it. Quickly he shuffled into the bathroom, flattening it as well as he could with his hands before giving up the fight and digging through his case for his comb. He looked over at his shoes, he couldn't remember if Sasha was wearing anything on her feet or not – he hadn't noticed – he had been more shocked by her wearing a dress.

The problem with shoes on holiday was that the rules changed as to what was acceptable to wear. On a beach visit it was quite okay to wear sandals as long as it was without socks. Trainers could be worn with or without socks but, during the day, they would feel uncomfortable and usually end up being carried, in the evening socks and trainers would be okay – even white socks.

Completing his dress up he looked again in the mirror, the rents would say he looked at least respectable which wasn't bad. He took a deep breath and told himself that he was ready for what was hopefully going to be his first date with Sasha. Filling his head with confidence, he left the bedroom and looked over at the couch where Sasha was sat waiting patiently.

Sasha heard the bedroom door open and looked behind herself with a soft smile as Jim entered the room. His stride was filled with self-confidence and the way he walked resembled a peacock on parade. Her heart sank as she found herself looking at him, the boy she had met had disappeared and now looking back at her was something that resembled the boys she had left behind in Ireland. Part of her wanted to just disappear out the front door and never be seen again but she had made the invitation to dinner and it would be bad of her not to go through with it. There was one way she knew she could find out if this was all going to be a big mistake or not.

Thinking quickly she excused herself to the bathroom and cringed as she watched him walk past her and sit on the couch. She could nearly feel a tear in her eye as she scuttled out of the lounge trying to keep her composure. What she had in mind was completely insane and in some ways maybe a bit risky but it would give her the answer. She couldn't believe that in just a few moments the shy and withdrawn boy who had caught her eye with his polite and gentle ways had turned into the creature she had just seen.

Taking a deep breath to calm herself down she slipped her dress off and bundled it in her hands. Carefully she crept out of the bathroom glancing round what she knew to be his bedroom. She looked round it, there was nothing that gave away too much, all his clothes were still in the suitcase where she had expected to see them as it was his first night.

She gazed at the door gripping tightly on to the silky bundle she had just removed before slowly and carefully making her way back to the lounge. Thankfully she saw that he hadn't heard her return, his head was still looking towards the window.

"Okay, I'm ready now," she announced calmly.

Jim flicked round in the couch and felt his jaw drop and the colour drain out of his face as he stared at her. The silk dress was gone and replacing it was just her soft slightly tanned skin, her hands were behind her back hiding nothing and her casual expression gave away nothing. He gulped hard feeling the lump passing down his throat as he crouched down hiding himself into the couch.

He couldn't understand it, he knew he had read the text in the guide correctly, it clearly said evening meal was a dressed occasion. If it was a dressed meal why was she now standing there with no clothes on? It didn't make any sense. Surely she wasn't that forward that she had decided to skip dinner and just get close with him.

If she had wanted to do that he felt sure she would have done something when he was wearing just boxers. He didn't want to have a girl like that, he wanted to get to know the girl, holiday or not he wanted more than just a quick fling.

He felt a shiver rush down his spine as he felt a familiar finger tapping him on the shoulder.

"Jim, it's okay, I'm dressed again." She said the words softly.

Slowly he turned in the chair keeping his eyes closed as he reached out desperately trying to confirm the validity of her statement. Gently, she took his hand, placing it on the bottom seam of her dress and holding it there as he ran the material through his fingers and tugged lightly as if trying to confirm it was attached to her body.

"Easy, tiger, you'll rip it," she snapped, pushing his hand away. Making her way from beside the couch, she grabbed the plastic chair, placing it in front of him.

He felt his muscles relax as he slid his feet back down to the ground and carefully opened his eyes. Sitting in front of him on the plastic chair was Sasha, as he remembered her in the thin blue dress she had been wearing before. The stern look on her face told him that she wasn't happy but he didn't know why.

"Jim, I did that for a reason," she said softly, reaching out and grabbing his hands by the fingertips.

"The first time I saw you, I liked the shyness and gentleness you showed me," she continued, "but when you came out of the bedroom just now – what I saw was a monster, the type of boy I've been avoiding." He could hear the sincerity in her voice. "Which one are you, Jim? Which is the real you? Because that monster can have room service while I have dinner alone."

As she spoke Jim found himself drawn in to what she was saying, the sincerity was intense and he could almost hear her crying as she spoke. He knew instantly that he had completely misread things with Sasha, she did like him but she liked what she had seen not what he was trying to be.

All his efforts to try and impress her with his display of confidence had been shot down with what he could only describe as shock treatment. By presenting herself in the one form that he hadn't expected to see her in she had knocked anything that resembled self-confidence back into the box he stored it in and locked the door on it. He hadn't realised how close he had been to losing a friendship he had only just gained by acting like something he wasn't. In complete contrast to everything he had seen done by others to win a girls interest his attempt had nearly lost her to him.

He couldn't help but wonder what would have happened if she had just taken him to dinner as he was. He knew some people would be too polite to point out that they didn't like what they saw and consequently they had wasted hours with a person they really didn't want to be with.

He knew that he had a lot to be thankful for with Sasha, she had shown him that more than once. She could easily have made excuses and disappeared for the evening leaving him to his room. If she had done that he was sure she wouldn't have come back the next day and he would have put it down to a misadventure. Instead of that she had chosen to tackle the situation in the most diverse way he had ever seen.

"This is the real me, Sasha," he said with a solemn voice; "the shy person is the one that is real."

Never before had someone seen through him and called his bluff so quickly and in such a diverse manner. If he hadn't blown his chances already, he knew that he was going to enjoy whatever time they spent together.

His words were like a fresh rain shower on a hot day to her, they had told her exactly what she wanted to hear. She felt sure that in seeing his false display she had seen what she considered to be the worst of him. Although she had taken a big risk she was fairly sure that he was telling her the truth.

She had heard stories from friends about guys that adapted their story to get their way with a girl but she hadn't made any promises to Jim. They weren't actually going on a date they were just going to dinner and hopefully now he knew not to expect anything more.

She knew she had the option to walk out the door and let him feel the consequences of his actions. By doing that she felt she would leave a bad impression with him and make any future meeting on site awkward. There was sincerity in his eyes and the way he spoke that convinced her that he wasn't just saying these words. Anyone can just say something to please the others around them but the tone he had used and the speed he had responded was too instant.

Jim could feel tension in the silence as he waited for her to respond to his confession. If he said anything more to try and justify his words it could look like he was trying too hard to sell his story. It was like being on trial, the awkward feeling, the regret for what he had done and the anticipation of what was going to happen next.

Sasha stood up slowly letting go of his fingers so she could straighten her dress back to where it should be.

"Come on, then, let's go," she said with a carefree tone as she walked the chair back to its place.

"No," Jim responded softly.

His response made her pause as she squared the chair off to the wall. She turned to face him slightly confused and slightly startled and saw he was now picking himself off the couch.

Jim could see her expression soften as he gazed over at her, his reply had caught her off guard. He had made sure to say it as softly as he could so she knew it wasn't meant in an aggressive manner.

"Let me take you to dinner," he added, smiling.

She angled her head at him as a smile slipped its way on to her face. A little confidence wasn't too bad, she decided. This was more like the sort of gesture she had expected of him.

"C'mon then."

Chapter Six

Dinner for two

Jim felt undecided about which way his holiday was going as he shut the door to head for dinner. Without trying too much Sasha had changed his outlook on a number of things that others around him at home would take for granted. As he reviewed the situation he found himself astounded that he was actually in her company still. If he had acted as foolishly around others as he clearly had around her, he knew she would be a distant memory by now.

His biggest problem was that the most recent incident had come as a result of following what he thought to be normal behaviour when a girl had shown interest in him. Knowing the signs wasn't a subject that had been bought up at school, it was something that had to be instinct. The lads that made themselves out to be experts in the field of courtship seemed to comfortably know what to do and how to do it. It was by careful observation of how they acted that Jim had drawn his conclusions about where things were going with Sasha.

He had often thought someone should write a book about the different signs a girl might make and what they could possibly mean. Eye contact, hand gestures and even stances all seemed to have certain meanings but it appeared that the same gesture might have more than one meaning depending on the girl making the gesture. Then again, none of his male friends had been put in a situation quite as unique as the one he was in.

Even if the lack of dress code was taken out of the equation the fact that she had come looking to take him to dinner put a completely different sway on things. Gestures that he was sure would mean 'I'm interested' if he had been pursuing her didn't necessarily mean that when he was the one being pursued. Then again it could just be that Sasha was not like other girls, maybe it was a cultural thing. Maybe the gestures he was accustomed to seeing in England had quite different meanings to people where she came from. The more he thought about it the more he realised it wouldn't be a book it would be an encyclopaedia in several parts.

Sasha had taken his hand as she walked past him and out of the apartment. She was conscious that such a gesture could be taken in many ways but after the risk she had taken in the apartment this seemed trivial. He held on to her hand lightly barely even looking at her as they started to walk toward the main building.

Jim had been a party to hand holding gestures several times despite his status as firmly in the friend zone. Girls seemed to use a hand hold in the same way that a toddler gripped a blanket – it was their way of knowing he was still there. Sasha's hold had too many similarities to the hand holds he experienced at home for him to take it as anything more than her way of knowing he was still there.

This was the first time he had taken note of the grounds from close quarters and, despite knowing that, during the daytime, anyone that he might see would be (in his view) underdressed, he felt safe. Over toward the centre of the complex he could see the ridge that lead down to the outdoor pool. He was in many ways relieved that the pool was at a lower level than his apartment because that meant he wouldn't end up looking at nude bathers from his window.

The silence between them didn't seem to worry Sasha too much, he could sense that she was possibly glancing over at him but she hadn't disturbed him from taking in the view around him. Despite the atmosphere between them not feeling like a bad one he decided it would be bad to keep looking away from her and turned to face her. A vague smile passed between them without even a word being said but her expression was calm and soothing. All the drama of their first two meetings had, it seemed, been left behind and she was happy to move on and get on with her holiday.

Ahead of them, travelling toward them he could see another couple who from a distance looked like they had their hands locked too. Maybe they were just like him and Sasha, or maybe they were a real couple. Either way, they looked like a long distance mirror image. Jim hadn't interacted with anyone except his family and Sasha so far during his stay so this was going to be a new experience for him.

He wondered what would be the best way to greet them, would Sasha know them already and would it be a long conversation or just a passing hello. Mentally he tried to prepare himself for his first real interaction on what could now be a nice holiday.

As the couple got closer he realised they looked familiar, it wasn't going to be a new experience after all. He didn't need to worry about if Sasha knew them or not because he knew who they were. He mumbled to himself under his breath, cursing his luck that of all the people he could meet on his first outdoor adventure it had to be the rents.

As soon as they recognised him they would know he had backed down on his threat of staying in his apartment for two weeks. What made matters worse was that they had the perfect opportunity to capitalize on it by showing him up in front of Sasha. He didn't need anything to help him on that front he had proved he was quite capable of making a fool of himself already. He felt his body tense as they got to within a few metres of each other and then felt a sharp pain in his forearm.

He looked down and pulled his arm away quickly in response catching a quick glimpse of what had caused the pain. Two subtle nail imprints where forming a temporary tattoo on his arm where Sasha had pinched him.

"What's that for?" he grumbled in protest.

She stopped walking and slowly lifted up her clearly crushed and reddened hand that was slowly returning to a natural colour.

"Either that or lose my fingers," she replied softly with a light smile.

He blushed realising what he had done, that was his third strike if he counted their awkward first encounter. Smiling softly he started to apologise and try to explain himself just in time to hear his father's voice.

"Are you going to introduce your girlfriend, son?" His tone was playful and friendly as they stopped directly in front of Jim and Sasha, blocking the path.

Sasha realised there was no need for an explanation; it was clear what had happened. She smiled lightly gripping his arm and rubbing the place her nails had nearly pierced the skin.

The similarities between Jim and this man that had given her the label of girlfriend were too close. Even if he hadn't used the word son to refer to Jim it was clear the tension in his hand had been caused by encountering his parents. She had seen this sort of atmosphere many times before and was used to parent and child rivalry. She glanced over at Jim and could see his expression hardening as he tried to come up with a reply.

"Sasha," she announced before he had time to speak.

She launched her hand out towards his parents in a friendly manner and was greeted by two handshakes.

"I'm his neighbour. As for his girlfriend; not yet, anyway." She turned and winked at Jim playfully as she completed her reply.

Jim was speechless; her words blotted out anything he had even began to think of saying. He had heard that the Irish were eloquent but he had never been witness to such a perfect reply. He waited and watched silently as his parents introduced themselves cordially in return to her gesture.

Fiona and Paul seemed just as surprised by the polite but forward response they had received from a girl that to them was a stranger. In some ways it relieved Paul that it had been her that had responded not their son. He knew he had taken a risk in making a remark about a girlfriend after the hostile chat they had endured the last time they saw each other.

Fiona was the first to break the quad formation they had made for their unplanned reunion and introduction. Quickly she leaned across and beckoned Sasha to join her for a private girl to girl chat. Tentative but curious about the invitation Sasha obliged leaning in while words were whispered in her ear. She let out a vocal but girly giggle as she returned to her spot next to Jim straightening her face to a subtler smile.

"I will, of course." Her words seemed like a song as she jabbed Jim softly in the ribs before grabbing for his hand again.

She gazed at Jim who was heavily over emphasizing the pain that had been caused by her elbow jab. Poking her tongue at him playfully she dragged him away from their impromptu meeting acknowledging his parents again as they continued their walk towards dinner.

In some ways she could see advantages to meeting his parents so early in their holiday. If things went well and Jim and she continued to get on then at least she would know who they were if she saw him with them. It also meant that if she got invited to join him and his parents for any activity she wouldn't feel uncomfortable. Then again now she had seen his reaction to his parents she was fairly sure any future interaction with them would be coincidental.

She paused as they got to the glass door leading in to the main building waiting to see if he was going to offer to open it for her. Whether he did or not it wasn't going to change her current opinion of him it was just an additional point to his credit. Patiently she fiddled in her bag pretending to be looking for something before they went in. As if he was reading from the same script as she was Jim moved toward the door pulling it open and turning to her to beckon her to enter the room. Smiling at his gesture she dropped her bag down by her side and thanked him as she walked past and into the atrium.

Even in the early evening walking in to the building from the humid weather outside was like walking in to a different atmosphere. The cool breeze let off by the air conditioning brushed over the exposed parts of their skin refreshing and rejuvenating them. The marble floor that would usually feel cool against bare feet shone from its most recent polishing.

Jim gazed up at the patterned roof as they walked down a narrow passage and in to the heart of the building. In the centre of the roof a glass dome presented the night sky to anyone that cared to take the time to notice it. The walls themselves were sparsely decorated with the white paint only broken by intermittent posters. It seemed to Jim like whoever had designed the building had decided that visitors were going to spend their time looking upwards rather than where they were going.

The central area was filled with arrangements of low level tables and couches that seemed to be an upgrade from the ones in the apartments. Opposite the couches a panelled glass door lead into the main bar area that then disappeared into what seemed to be a club style room. Jim peered nosily into the bar, the lighting was still minimal but he felt sure it would get brighter as more people wondered in. He could see basic pub style tables and chairs disappearing into the back room where they seemed to be arranged to allow a dance area.

The bar reminded him of similar entertainment complexes from previous holidays. One that particularly came to mind was the complex they had stayed in on their one UK holiday. He remembered watching as a group of children had been paraded in by one of the hosts to endure party dances before being ushered back to their parents.

Similar children's clubs had been available at most of the places he had stayed but the one in the UK seemed to be in bigger demand than any other. He had put it down the fact that British people on a British holiday knew that the weather was unpredictable so in order to make the most of the holiday the children's club was free child minding. He smiled as he thought of it then began to feel a mixture of curiosity and horror as he wondered if such a facility was available here. There was no logical reason why a children's club wouldn't be available – everything else seemed to be, but then again he knew he would feel a bit self-conscious at a naturist kids club.

At intervals around the couch filled central area were the shops and stalls that Jim had seen listed in the welcome guide. Most of them were closed but he did notice the pharmacy and a small shop selling jewellery still had lights on. Timing was everything, there was no mystery that people on holiday would need sun cream and after dinner he was sure some people got into a romantic mood and started looking at jewellery. He admired how these two shops had adapted their opening times to suit the demands of the clients.

Sasha made a quick bee line to a set of elaborate double doors choosing to avoid the temptation of window shopping. In a way Jim was pleased that she had focussed on dinner and not spending the money he didn't have on him. That reminded him; with all the confusion of the night so far he hadn't opened the envelope the rents had given him. It had felt well-padded so he had taken the assumption that it was more than just ten or twenty Euro. Surely they couldn't expect him to go a week on holiday on such a small amount.

The smell of different styles of cooking filled his lungs as they entered the restaurant. In the centre a large circular buffet style counter took pride of place and was surrounded by a swarm of people. Jim could see chefs behind certain parts of the counter telling him that it wasn't fully self-service. Signs above the counter announced the style of cuisine that was being offered at the different segments. Jim glanced round trying to work out which one of the options he might be interested in trying.

Pulling him away from the buffet Sasha led him over to an area of the restaurant that was laid out differently. The tables were dressed with cutlery and glasses and there were several staff patiently waiting to take orders. The concept amazed him, this complex had truly thought of everything when it came to dining experiences. In this area they could eat without trying to co-ordinate the buffet and negotiate with the chefs as to what size portion to give them.

Sasha was quite excited about eating in the served area of the restaurant; it was the first time she was going to do it. She had seen the area a few times and commented to her family that it would be nice to be served the food one evening. Dad had politely acknowledged her request before telling her that in the buffet area they could eat as much as they wanted whereas over there the portions were set.

Tonight was going to be different though, she didn't want to make it look too formal but she also didn't want to spend half the meal getting up and down out of her seat when her main goal was to get to know Jim. Her mind told her that possibly buffet was a better idea as it was more casual but this might be her only chance to get waited on.

Carefully she made her way through the tables swerving her body to avoid the waving arms of a person graphically explaining something in a foreign language as she walked. It proved difficult to find a table that she felt was suitable; all the tables for two were in booths along the restaurant wall and the larger tables were not appropriate. The last thing she wanted was to make it look too much like a date by taking one of the secluded tables but she also wanted to avoid someone else joining them. Finally she opted for a table that was set for just three people deciding that they would be very unlucky if someone else chose to keep them company.

Strategically she grabbed one of the chairs that would give Jim the opportunity to choose to sit next to or opposite her but was gently prevented from moving it by his hands crossing in front of hers. She watched him as he pulled the seat out, feigned brushing it off and then presented it to her before clumsily pushing it toward the table. Never in her wildest dreams had she anticipated him even role playing such a gesture but she was happy to go along with it. Making herself comfortable she watched as he moved round the table choosing the seat opposite her.

Jim patted himself mentally on the back for going beyond the call of duty in his over exaggerated show of hospitality. He had remembered playing restaurants as a child and somehow he always ended up being the waiter to Dad and his sister. He couldn't believe that such a repeated exercise from childhood had actually been put into a real world situation and hopefully made a good impression on his dinner partner.

"Not bad, but ye didn't pass me a menu," she commented with a cheeky grin as he settled down.

Jim picked up the menu quickly to hide the smug grin he could already feel cracking the sides of his face. The last thing he wanted was to give the impression that he was returning to the over confident person that Sasha had already reprimanded. He was however fairly proud of himself, after the worst start in history he now felt like he had a chance to make a good friend out of Sasha and after her comment to the rents maybe more. He knew it was best not to assume the maybe more but in a way a holiday romance would be nice.

He wasn't sure how he would deal with a holiday romance and the more he thought about it the more he realised that he would feel bad if he started something just to end it in two weeks' time. That was too far in advance to be thinking, for now he had to focus on getting to know her and keeping his approach at the same level he had done. She seemed to like the gentleman's approach and as much as she didn't ask for it or demand it he had learned how to do it and now seemed to be a good time to practice it.

"So where are you fr…" His words stuck in his throat as he lowered the menu, now that his grin had retired.

Sasha was sat casually across from him with her elbows on the table and her hands cupping her head. She had a deep look in her eyes and a poker face that didn't give away why she was gazing in his direction. He leaned back trying to avoid her deep stare but making sure he didn't look too obvious. Something had distracted her, either that or she was frozen in time but that seemed unlikely as it only happened in films.

"It's okay," she said, breaking what could have become another silence. "I was just wondering if I was going to spend the meal talking to a menu or to Jim." She gave a big grin as she finished her sentence.

Her words seemed slightly cutting but he could see her point, he had started speaking from behind a barricade. Had he really lost any credibility he had gained by just one small error? Surely not, she had let him get away with so much more under much worse circumstances. Maybe he hadn't realised he was on thin ice and that was the breaking point she was waiting for – if that was the case he may as well go home now.

Quickly she reached across the table grabbing his arms that had fallen like soldiers on to the cotton cloth. She had over reacted and she felt sorry for him, the deep gaze had been unnecessary and he had been doing so well. She gripped his arms lightly stroking them with her finger tips trying to reassure him. She could feel clamminess in his skin as she over emphasized her touch making sure not to grip too hard but enough to let him know everything was okay.

"Ireland," she said softly. "But ye probably guessed that. I'd tell ye the town too but it wouldn't mean a lot to ye," she added.

Her voice and her reactions settled him again, her touch was so soft on his arms and her grip so tender. She was right, his geography of Ireland was limited to the fact it was across the sea from England. She could have said any random place in Ireland or even made one up and he wouldn't know the difference. In fact his geography of his own country wasn't that good, he knew what was north and what was south but some places he was sure he would have to ask for directions to. The more he thought about it the more he realised how little he knew of his home land.

He knew he could play out that he knew something about Ireland but he knew that she would trip him up if he tried to act clever. The last thing he needed was to be humiliated again by her catching him out. She had already shown him that she wasn't easy to outsmart twice in one night and now he seemed to be making some positive steps he didn't want to put that in jeopardy.

Taking the alternative, much safer and without doubt much more sensible route he acknowledged her point. He hesitated briefly as he responded to her wondering if she would be any more familiar with where he was from than he was of her land. Mentally he shrugged his thoughts off; challenging her knowledge of England would be as bad as trying to convince her he knew Ireland.

"Maybe you can tell me more about it over dinner," he said softly, smiling at her. Where had his common sense been hiding? That was without doubt a perfect answer. If he had been in a debate and given such a well thought out response he was sure he would have received a round of applause.

She gazed at him deeply, she had expected a quick remark from him, something witty possibly, maybe even an ice breaker. Instead of all those she had been hit with a comment that showed genuine interest and it had caught her off guard but in a nice way. She nodded politely glowing as she decided that whether he actually wanted to know or not she was going to tell him a little about her town while they ate.

There were worse things than discussing a person's home town over a first meal together. She could only imagine what image he might have of Ireland as a person that had never visited. In some ways it was frustrating that the only two things a number of people knew about were leprechauns and Guinness but she knew she couldn't change that. At least having a topic would make the conversation easier than asking questions about each other. She knew the basic rules, no discussing sport or politics on a night out, talking about home wasn't ideal on holiday either but it was a start.

Glancing round the restaurant she quickly flagged down a waiter.

Chapter Seven

Breakfast call

Since the first time he had been left to entertain himself on a family holiday Jim had memories of varying degrees of success as to how his first night of freedom had gone. As he lay in his bed taking into account all the factors he decided that his night with Sasha had been amongst the more successful first night experiences. Not only had he spent the night in the company of a girl who he felt confident was about his age despite her comfort with alcohol. He had also spent the evening in what would be classed as a communal social area rather than the games room.

He made a mental note that even if it was just to settle his curiosity he should at least find the games room but there was no rush to do that. Games rooms in hotels or at holiday centres didn't have a set standard that they adhered to. Most of them had common features like the air hockey and a pool table or two as well as a range of video games. The age of the video games was usually a good indication as to how well maintained the games room was.

Depending on the interest of the person that had been left in charge of running the facility the games available may be dated to a time before he could remember. The strange thing was that he noticed that even if the game was from before his lifetime the price of the game was usually reflective of modern day living. Dispersed in between the games would be gambling machines that would be heavily attended to by older teenagers and young adults that all seemed to have the same opinion that they could outwit the machine.

It had been these games that had started Jim's interest in the PC gaming world that he was now a well-established member of. He had evolved to the PC when he realised the same game that he was spending countless hours staring at in a loud room and spending money on he could buy straight out and master in his own time in the comfort of his own bedroom.

The biggest factor that was holding him back from finding the games room was the dress code this year. Suddenly all the clothes that he had spent time and effort buying and organising for his holiday would have no significance. There was a good chance this year that if or when he decided to find the games room its residents wouldn't even have a towel on. There was something sinister about trying to play a game of pool against a person who would without doubt end up mooning at you involuntarily.

Even worse than the thought of someone's rear being presented as he graciously conceded another defeat at pool was the thought that if there were table tennis tables they would probably be in use by oldies. It was bad enough seeing people pretend to be good at table tennis under normal circumstances, the thought of it being done nude disgusted him.

Then there was Sasha to consider, the chances were that she was not the type of girl that would be into staying indoors. If he was going to be trying to spend time with her while he was on holiday there was a good chance she wouldn't have any interest in the games room. As a long term plan he decided that he would tackle the games room at a time when she wasn't available and when he had mentally prepared himself for what he might see.

He glanced over at the pre 1970s analogue alarm clock that was pointing its two thick black plastic hands at the numbers twelve and eight. It was far too early to get up considering he hadn't actually got home until gone two a.m. He didn't even successfully manage eight a.m. on a school day so why was his mind already awake? Huffing to himself he curled back over turning away from the clock and drifted back towards a half sleeping mode.

With his eyes closed he felt his mind start to wonder to reminiscent thoughts from the previous night. The thoughts he was getting were not ones that he wanted to have but they had been bugging him since he first met Sasha. He knew in his mind that what he was contemplating was too far-fetched to be accurate but it appeared his mind was determined to have the debate with itself. Was there a chance that everything that had happened with Sasha could be an elaborate plot arranged by the rents?

It seemed far too convenient that within an hour of arriving he had told the rents that he wasn't going to leave his apartment and she had arrived to change his mind. If it hadn't been for the new level of cunning that they had shown he was sure his mind wouldn't even give it a second thought but the facts were all there. They had managed to outwit him more than once in the lead up to the holiday and even on arrival they were prepared for his objections – could it really be that Sasha was in on a plot?

It wasn't something he was willing to tackle her about, if it had been a plot then surely it would come out on its own eventually. If Sasha was really working with the rents then all he had to do was work out how to react when he found out, for now it was better to push these thoughts out of his mind and enjoy her company. Creating sinister scenarios that involved everyone he knew plotting against him would only dampen any fun times that he could have with her. He snorted as he dismissed the bad thoughts and felt himself sink into the crater he had formed in the bed.

A tapping sound slowly started making its way into his ear as he felt himself slowly drifting toward sleep. He paused and half opened one eye as he listened trying to hear where it was coming from. Opening an eye didn't seem to make much sense when what he was trying to detect was the location of a sound but he was reluctant to move. The noise stopped leaving the silence that had been there before it filling the room again only for the same noise to return but this time louder.

Lifting himself up on to his elbow he peeked through the curtain to try and work out what was making the noise only to find the morning sun streaking into his eyes and blinding him. Quickly he dropped the curtain and rubbed his eyes trying to recover from the temporary blindness that had been inflicted on him.

"Jim, I know you're there. Will ya come to the front and let me in?" Sasha's voice called through the window.

Quickly he found he was able to forgive the inconvenience of the sun that had temporarily impaired his vision. Blinking a few times he gazed back over at the alarm clock wondering how he had managed to miss it going off. Relentlessly it stared back at him telling him it was only eight thirty, it wasn't that he was late it was she that was early.

Shielding his eyes he pulled the curtain back and slowly allowed the light to enter the room again before peering out at what was the back of his apartment. Sasha was not there, maybe he had dreamed it all but why would he imagine her knocking on his bedroom window. There was no way he could imagine the sting he had received from trying to see who or what was outside but there was no one there. He was sure he had heard her voice, it didn't make sense that her voice could be there but she wasn't.

As a precaution he decided it was safer to check at the front door to see if he had just been too slow. He pushed his legs out of the bed and twisted himself into an upright position as he yawned. How ironic, he hadn't been tired when he had been gazing at the clock but now he had a reason to get up his body just didn't want to do it.

He pushed himself off the bed and stood stretching in front of the mirror as the realisation of what he was about to do struck him. Sasha was potentially at his front door, she had been there before but this time she was there during the day time. Normally having a girl at the front door during the day wouldn't be a cause for concern but on this complex the day time meant there was a good chance she was naked. He had seen her naked before but that had been the cause for awkwardness and embarrassment. He had also accepted that she would be meeting him in the morning even though he knew nudity was a possibility.

Even if he could accept and act normally around her nude he was sure that he wasn't ready to be seen nude. Even if it was just the two of them at the start and they spent a while in the apartment together before adventuring to the outdoors once he was out there anything could happen. He glanced down at the boxer shorts that he had chosen to wear to bed; she would have to accept that he was only going as far as that for now.

Forcing his hair into a reasonably tidy place on his head he adjusted his shorts so they looked like they had been just put on instead of worn for hours and walked out of the bedroom. Quickly he brushed past the couch and prepared himself for what she might look like. He realised very quickly that picturing her naked at the door wasn't the best idea and cleared his mind as he adjusted his shorts again. Slowly he opened the door hoping that there was no sign of the thoughts that had started off as innocent in his mind but his body had taken in a very different way and prepared to greet her.

Standing patiently waiting for him with a calm smile on her face was Sasha, he was pleased and in many ways relieved to see that she had a light peach coloured wrap around dress on. The cool early morning breeze was teasing the gap where the dress was held on by some flimsy ties and casually flashing glimpses of flesh at him as he stood mostly out of sight behind the door. For the second time he felt relieved that he hadn't tried to surprise her by greeting her at the door nude. Somehow his reserved mind was actually working to his advantage and he was proud of it.

He watched as she sat down and pondered over whether he should complement her dress. He knew from past experience that girls liked to hear compliments on what they were wearing. He had commented on her choice of dress before going out for the evening and he couldn't recall how it had been taken. Was it seen as good protocol to acknowledge how nice a person's clothes looked if you knew they would prefer not be wearing them?

"Morning," he said with a yawn in his voice. "You're earlier than I expected."

Sasha gazed over at him as she sat down in the same spot on the couch she had used for her first visit. This was going to become her spot on the couch for future trips to see her neighbour. Then again that would depend on how often she planned to come and see him in his apartment – she didn't want to make too much of a habit of it in case he got too comfortable being indoors with her. Mentally she noted to make sure the next meeting was done outdoors to break the consistency.

When she had awoken that morning she knew she was early but she decided that as she was alone she might as well have company for breakfast. It had taken time for her to decide whether to dress or not, her preference was to go out as she was but then again being covered would make it easier for Jim. She could always go and have a nude breakfast and enjoy her freedom before meeting him but eating alone was never fun and as she saw it he had to eat as well so there was no harm knocking for him.

Deep inside she had known that he would be most likely to be in bed as she left the apartment and although there was a chance his front door might be unlocked she had given him a fairly comprehensive demonstration in how to lock it. She recalled how it had made her giggle that he had been transfixed by the little light that changed from green to red as the door was locked. Simple things like that seemed to be cause for amusement to quite a lot of people after a few drinks and although they hadn't drunk too much in the early hours of the morning small pleasures like that were acceptable.

Taking an educated guess on his whereabouts she had decided it was better to head towards the back of the apartment. Thankfully she was aware that next door apartments mirrored each other so his bedroom would be next door to hers. In some ways it felt strange to be analysing his apartment from outside and the realization that the gap between their apartments and two walls was all that separated them was curious.

Picking up a wraparound dress and some matching panties she decided to be a little rebellious and not dress immediately. From the outside his window would be too high for him to notice if she was dressed or not if she crouched down a bit. It didn't matter to her but to him it could make the difference between a warm welcome and a nervous grin.

As expected she had found his curtains closed when she arrived at the window but she knew that didn't necessarily mean he was still asleep. The likelihood was that he would be as they had only parted company a few hours before hand but she felt it was a waste of a day to lie in when the weather beckoned you outside. Her first tap had received no response but then again it had been fairly quiet against the glass so she tried harder and this time caught a flicker of the curtain, he was awake.

She found herself skipping round the building once she had almost invited herself in again. Maybe she could try the door but then again appearing in the front room for a second time would be a little bit creepy. She stood patiently at the front door anticipating him opening it as she looked down at the bundle of clothes in her hand. Quickly she tied the dress round herself watching as the door handle rattled as he tried to master the unlocking technique. With seconds to spare she slipped her panties on and fixed her hair so she didn't look like she had rushed as the door opened.

"Before ye get ideas, this is for your benefit, not mine," she commented with a grin as she pulled at the top of the dress.

Jim smiled; it was nice that she had taken his conservative nature into account before meeting him but that didn't explain why she was so early.

"My folks are out and I'm alone for breakfast," she continued. "I said to myself, who would I like to join me, if yer man enough to?" She winked playfully at him as she made the subtle dig.

He could see the playfulness in her expression as he looked up at her ready to respond to her challenge. In his mind it wasn't about how manly he was it was what he might encounter outside that concerned him. He knew he had made arrangements to see her later in the morning but room service breakfast was a much safer option than encountering the rents in their flesh. He couldn't imagine a scenario where he could keep food down so early in the day if he saw them without clothes on.

Then again breakfast with Sasha sounded like a nice idea, the cool breeze and morning sun had seemed inviting. Maybe it was time to face his fears, if he was going to be taken outside by her it may as well be earlier in the day than waiting round nervously after a breakfast alone. Apart from anything else the fact that she had challenged him stuck in his throat. It didn't matter if it was a playful challenge or not, it had been a legitimate challenge and he took pride in himself on not backing down on challenges.

With a subtle shrug he looked over at her trying desperately to hide his concerns from her.

"Give me five minutes to get ready," he said with a soft but meaningful voice as he stood up and walked toward the bedroom.

"If you take too long, I'll leave without you, and you can bring this back to me when you meet me after," her voice carried towards him as he reached the bedroom door.

Turning in fascination he could see her hand reaching over the back of the couch dangling the dress she had been wearing like a puppet. He stared at it briefly as it danced in her hands trying not to picture what she might still have on as he slid into the bedroom shutting the door.

Even as she had called out her message to Jim she had been aware that her nudity might not have the same effect that it had done before. She knew that after their night out together Jim was starting to get comfortable around her but it was worth a try. She also knew that he was not aware that although she had no dress on she was still partially covered by her panties but if she left the dress she could get rid of them at her apartment – no need to wear them if she was dining alone. She was in some ways relieved to hear him disappear into his bedroom; at least she still had some control over him.

Jim gazed into the mirror, she had been very clever with her dress manoeuvre, he wasn't afraid of seeing her nude anymore he had seen it all before. It wasn't her nudity that had inspired him to get ready it was the idea of having someone to share breakfast with. Deep down he wondered if he could convince her that they should eat at his place but he didn't want to antagonise the situation. She had made her thoughts on the room service menu clear the night before and now he wanted to build on the bond they had started not ruin it.

The figure staring back at him was showing the signs of tiredness, the pasty skin made it obvious he hadn't seen much of the sun and the shorts looked crumpled after a nights wriggling in bed. He heard her voice carrying through the door advising him he had four minutes left. Was she really timing him? Could she really be serious about leaving her dress for him? Surely no one took a reference to five minutes seriously did they? Quickly he kicked his shorts off and ran into the bathroom jumping under the cold shower which revived his senses immediately.

Towelling himself off he heard a faint shout of two minutes from the front room. She was seriously timing him, but how? He thought back as he dried himself trying to recall if she had a watch on, he couldn't remember seeing one but somehow she was able to tell him how long he had left. This was no time to reflect on how something was happening; his only safety net was that if he missed her now he was still meeting her. He didn't envy the task of carrying her dress to their meeting point because that would mean she wasn't wearing it and they would be outside. Walking through the complex alone left all sorts of possibilities including running into the rents.

So far in his one adventure outside independent of them he had still somehow managed to bump into them. At least on that occasion they were dressed but if he bumped into them in the morning they probably wouldn't be and that would probably scar him for life. He skipped out of the bathroom throwing the towel back into the bathroom as he dug through his half unpacked case. Swimming shorts were a good option because then he was prepared for anything. He found a casual pair and hopped around while trying to slip them on before glancing at the bed and wondering why he hadn't just sat down.

The one minute warning rang into the room as he tripped his way back into the bathroom again to fix his hair. If Sasha was in effect fully dressed, or he hoped she would be, then maybe he could get away with wearing a shirt as well as shorts. He grabbed one from the case slightly ruining his hair again as he pulled it on as she called out a thirty second warning. He took a quick glance in the mirror noticing the damage he had done in choosing a shirt after doing his hair and shrugged he didn't have time to sort it out now.

He ran out of the bedroom with his heart in his mouth not knowing what to expect waiting for him. Standing opposite him with her dress pressed against her body Sasha was waiting by the front door. Her eyes seemed to show a mix of emotions as he appeared somewhere between happy to see him and frustrated that she now had to keep her end or the bargain. Subtly she huffed as she pulled the dress back around herself and tied it in place under her arm.

As much as Jim's good timing impressed her Sasha was in some ways disappointed that she had to redress. Dressing wasn't something she was used to doing during the day time on her holiday unless it was a special occasion. There had been a few times on previous holidays when her parents had taken her out for a day to see some of the island but each time her main focus had been on getting back to the complex.

When they had first found this complex a whole new world had been opened up to her, one that had none of the rules of modern society, one where it didn't matter who she was, what she did or what she looked like. In her younger days day trips while she was abroad had been something to look forward to but now she had found something much more adventurous and much less standard she wanted to spend as much time without clothes as possible. Then again she was starting to like Jim and although he had hang ups about nudity she had a game plan to gently make him comfortable with it. Spending one day in a light dress was a small burden for having company to enjoy her holiday with.

"I know a spot we can sit; it's pretty quiet, you probably won't see many people," she said softly as she tied the last bow in her dress.

Jim's face beamed as he heard those words, she had thought of everything even somewhere he could hide away from nude rents.

"Great. So we aren't going in to the restaurant, then?" he responded with a tone of relief.

She gazed at him somewhat amazed by his response but then again she could understand his relief. How did he think they were going to eat if they didn't go into the restaurant to get the food? Maybe she could take pity on him and bring the food out to him this once.

"Your Da called me your girlfriend, not your waitress," she giggled as she spoke, "but I'll take pity on you and get the food this time."

Jim felt his face flush with embarrassment, in the moment of relief at her saying about a quiet spot he hadn't thought of the practicalities. She was right, it was completely mad to think they would have food served to them outside the restaurant. He assumed her quiet place was on the outside of the restaurant, he couldn't think of any hidden corners that might be available inside the building but then again maybe there were.

Sasha walked towards him slowly, watching his face change as he realised the madness of his comment about not going in to the restaurant. Poor Jim, so much focus on avoiding nudity it had clearly clouded anything that resembled common sense. She reached out grabbing both his hands and pulling him slowly toward the door.

"C'mon you, I'm hungry."

Chapter Eight

To the beach

The more Jim reviewed it the more he realised considering all the factors that were against him his first day on holiday had been fairly successful. Sasha's hidden table had made the perfect breakfast spot, the bushes between them and the footpath sheltered them from any onlookers and the picnic style table was set at such an angle that one side of it couldn't be seen from the window that led into the restaurant. It hadn't come as a surprise to Sasha when Jim had chosen to sit on the hidden bench leaving her the option of next to him or opposite him. She had chosen opposite him so she could enjoy the sun rising over the coast line that was only a matter of meters away.

For the morning Sasha had agreed to stay in areas where they could just 'chill out' as Jim called it. It seemed a little strange referring to it as chilling out when the weather was in the mid-thirties (centigrade) but she went with it. She even avoided the temptation to expose herself to the warmth of the sun despite fighting every urge in her body to just give in and let Jim deal with it. As a compromise that he wasn't aware of she had chosen a moment when he had disappeared to the men's room to lose her panties. What he didn't know wouldn't hurt him and it made the midday heat that bit more bearable.

Jim had kept to his word and reluctantly joined her in the restaurant at lunch time but only for as long as it took to choose food and escape quickly back to their hidden table. She had noticed him admiring the floor tiles for most of the time in the restaurant and cringing every time he heard an English voice just in case it was the rents. Sasha found it a bit peculiar how he also avoided the salami and sausage based dishes but maybe that was just a coincidence. She teased him on the way out of the restaurant by trying to make him look in directions that she knew he wouldn't be able to avoid seeing human flesh but after the first glimpse he managed to avoid her attempts.

The afternoon's activities hadn't been much more exciting than the mornings but they had spent a lot of time getting to know each other so it hadn't been too bad. Sasha had left Jim to get on with his own plans for the evening as she had promised to spend time with her parents and despite his reluctance he had made the effort to eat dinner with the rents. They had spent the time asking him about this mystery girl he had been seen with and getting limited response but then again what did they expect? He hadn't fully forgiven them for what they had done but Sasha had definitely made the holiday easier.

For their meeting on the second day Sasha had asked him to meet her outside instead of at his apartment. Her main reason was that she didn't want to keep calling round for him as if she was a ten year old looking for a play mate. Also it would prove to her that he could make the effort to get out of the apartment on his own.

Jim had been happy to meet her the next day in fact after an evening with the rents he was looking forward to it; the only thing he didn't like was the time she had asked to meet him. Nine a.m. wasn't a nice time to be meeting someone on holiday but she had explained that they only had the morning together so he had accepted it. He woke up at eight which seemed to be becoming a regular thing since he had arrived for some reason.

With ten minutes to spare, he left the apartment and started making his way up towards the main building. Standing near a post he could see silhouetted figure that looked like it could be Sasha. He decided it had to be her, that was where they had agreed to meet and the chances that it was anyone else were pretty slim. Questions started to enter his head, he knew she had made allowances for him during the previous day but today he knew she might not do. He paused for a second and mentally tried to prepare himself for spending the morning with her nude.

In some ways he had started to get used to nudity around him, as much as he had tried to avoid it he had seen quite a few bodies on his first day. Thankfully the ones he had avoided included the rents, he wasn't ready for that yet, but then again was he ready to see her nude again? Seeing her without clothes on wouldn't be the same as it was with the other people on the complex because he knew her.

Taking a deep breath he continued his walk at a modestly slower pace as he tried to assess the situation. As he got closer the sun disappeared briefly behind a passing cloud that took the shadow away from the figure. Jim was relieved to see that it definitely was Sasha he was walking towards and not only that she was wearing something. Admittedly it wasn't as much as he had hoped, she had a sarong tied around her waist, but from there upwards she had nothing on. All he had to do was cope with her being topless, that wasn't too bad he could probably manage that.

"Ye made it, then," she chirped as he arrived next to her.

Trying to focus on her face Jim nodded and smiled briefly before discretely glancing away from her to compose himself.

"After breakfast, we are going to the beach," she added.

Jim liked trips to the beach when he was on holiday, they were so much better than the beach trips at home. Even on a good summers day the beach was too far away from where he lived to enjoy at just a few moments notice. He could vividly recall many occasions from his childhood when a day trip to the beach had been arranged.

The ritual was quite well set and in many ways well practiced, it started off with Dad checking the three day weather forecast. That would lead to him passing a cryptic comment to Mum – these comments had in early days taken the form of spelling the word beach, but as both the children grew up that wasn't an option. This was just the start of the process, the seed was now planted, there was no logic behind following a three day forecast but Dad seemed confident.

There had always seemed some irony in Jims mind about following the advice of a person on TV. His sister had pointed it out to him as he hit ten years of age by commenting that mum and dad told them not to listen to strangers and yet here they were taking a strangers advice. Neither of them had ever contested this with the rents, it was safer to just go along with it.

The next stage in the ritual was the announcement to the kids, this step was easy. A simple announcement under the pretext of them being on their best behaviour for two days. There was an element of tactics in this, by requesting best behaviour it meant him and his sister would spend two days trying not to antagonise each other unless mum and dad were out of ear shot. After this stage nothing more would be said about the trip until the day, unless one of them misbehaved, then they were threatened with being left behind.

Depending on how things went the big day itself had several angles to cover. The first of these was Dad, on the day that had been allocated beach day he would stand in the window staring at the sky. His eyes would be focussed on any clouds that were disputing the weatherman's predictions. The aim of this ritual seemed to be to break any clouds using the powers of his mind.

The second angle was mum; while dad was busy cloud breaking she would be busy packing beach essentials. These essential would include sandwiches that had been prepared the night before, sun cream and in the early days the buckets and spades.

The third angle was him and his sister, beach meant one thing to them – swimming – this meant they would appear downstairs in their swimming costumes and some form of sun hat. This gave mum a new ritual – redressing the kids for the journey and packing the swimming costumes for them to awkwardly change into under a towel.

The towel changing ritual was an art form in itself; this form if performed correctly preserved your dignity. If you failed at any stage it left a red face and glances from other beach goers as if you intended to flash your body at them. As a safety precaution the car had frequently doubled up as a changing room as they got older preventing the awkwardness. While mum was allocating clothes to the kid's dad would be packing the essential bag into the car. During this time he would still momentarily be cloud breaking with his eyes as he juggled the bags and car keys.

With the preparation tasks over all that remained was the journey and the on-going weather willing by dad. On arrival at the beach one of two things would happen. The first possibility was that they would spend a few hours hopping in and out of the car recharging their body temperatures while grabbing a sandwich before heading home. The second option was a much more beachy option, swimming costumes out, running up and down to the sea and dad buried up to his neck in sand as a reward for all the effort he had put in to getting them there.

Even if the beach at home had been easier to access there were other factors that made the beach abroad a more pleasant experience. The thick brown stodgy sand of home was replaced with soft white powdery sand abroad. The cold grey sea water was replaced by a warm azure blue sea and the pasty skinned families made way for deep tanned Europeans.

Using the same tactic he had deployed over lunch the previous day Jim managed to avoid as much human contact as possible over breakfast and was relieved when Sasha returned with beach towels from reception. Quickly he ushered her away from the complex towards the coast allowing her to take over and guide him to the spot she wanted. She pointed out a large permanent net that was set out on the beach advising him that she would meet him there the next day for the weekly volleyball match.

Jim took advantage of the opportunity to look away from her making note of where it was and grunting in agreement as they walked. She pulled on his hand lightly as she turned towards a more secluded spot and flicked her towel out creating a perfect cover on the ground. For a second Jim contemplated trying the same manoeuvre but he felt sure if he tried it he wouldn't have the same success. Opting for the safer option he knelt down and flattened his towel out next to her before lying down.

The warm sun felt good against his skin as he lay chatting casually with her uninterrupted by other beach goers in their hidden spot. Jim felt like he had impressed himself in his ability to finally accept that she was topless. This had been a necessity more than something that had come naturally to him. It had taken time and several reminders but after a very stubborn first half hour Jim had accepted that Sasha really was telling the truth. There had been the need for a bit of convincing but eventually his mind accepted that, no matter how much he spoke to them, her breasts were not able to answer him but her face could.

At first it had seemed worth trying to communicate with them and she had taken his fascination with her breasts in good humour. Every time his eyes wondered downwards she had just smiled and given him a light tap on the chin. Out of embarrassment and courtesy he had apologised every time for his involuntary gaze downwards and she had acknowledged how hard he was trying to avoid the distraction. Thankfully his mind had given up with its protest and was now allowing him to keep eye to eye contact with her as they spoke.

Sasha had given Jim time to adjust to her semi-nude state and although it was frustrating having to keep reminding him to his credit he had apologised for his peering eyes. One of his apologies did seem to be directed at the body part he wasn't supposed to be staring at but she let that go. Now he was comfortable with her topless all she had to do was re-introduce him to her without clothes and she could get on with her holiday the way she was used to doing. As they only had the morning together taking things to the next step would wait for another day.

Tomorrow was as good opportunity as any because everyone playing volleyball would be nude so he wouldn't have much choice but to accept it. The sun was getting warm against her skin, the sea looked inviting so with a quick motion she stood up.

"I'm going for a swim," she announced, looking over at Jim who seemed comfortable on his towel. "Are ya coming?"

Jim looked down at the ocean, it did look tempting but he had just got comfortable and someone should look after the towels. He gazed up at Sasha who was patiently waiting for him to reply to her invitation.

"Nah, I'll stay and watch the towels," he said calmly.

Watching the towels seemed a lame excuse not to go swimming but the rents had taught him never to leave things unattended. Shrugging at him she dropped her sarong to the floor revealing a light blue bikini bottoms under it and ran down to the sea. She waded into the cool water until she was waist deep and duck dived showering her whole body with the water. Flicking her hair out of her eyes she glanced back and saw Jim was propped up on his elbows presumably watching her.

About fifty metres away from her was a jetty, she knew the water depth changed dramatically but she was a strong swimmer and she fancied the challenge. Diving downwards she pushed off from the sand and started out towards the man-made island. The tide was fighting against her the whole way but she knew that meant that the journey back would be easier. Reaching for one of the ropes holding it together she pulled herself up and flopped on to the plastic base to catch her breath.

From here she could barely see Jim but she was sure the little dot on the beach was him. She pondered for a moment, out here she could do as she pleased and he wouldn't know. The temptation was to get a few moments of nude bathing in before returning to shore but then again, what was the point? Her goal was to get him comfortable with it. She could of course slip her bottoms off and wave them at him playfully but he wouldn't know if she was doing that or not. As a compromise to herself she chose to just stand and wave in his direction and see if he responded

Like an off duty life guard Jim sat watching Sasha as she frolicked about and started to swim away from the shore. He knew that he couldn't do much if anything happened but he felt like he was at least keeping an eye on her. Smiling to himself he watched her climb on the jetty and stand up waving frantically at the shore and just in case she could see he sat up and waved amicably back. In an unspoken response to his wave he watched her dive gracefully back into the sea and make her way back toward the shore.

Sasha waded through the last few metres of the sea deciding that to try and swim all the way to shore would be messy. She could imagine that if she tried to kick her way up to the dry land she would end up looking like a beached whale. That combined with the amount of sand that would become matted in her hair was not a very attractive picture.

Standing next to him she wrung her hair out over Jim's chest as she arrived back at the towels and watched as he squirmed under the cold water. He scowled at her for giving him the second shower of the day and then laughed it off as she winked back at him. Gracefully she leaned over picking her sarong off the towel and wrapped it around herself before sliding out of her bikini bottoms and laying them out on the sand to dry. Jim felt a little disturbed by her disrobing but settled again once he saw the practical side of it. Wet clothes on skin weren't nice at any time even in the best of weather so letting them dry made perfect sense. He glanced over discretely at Sasha as she lay warming herself under the sun, he didn't want her thinking he was staring at her breasts again. Casually he admired the way the sun caught the droplets of water on her mildly tanned skin, it was almost hypnotic.

Suddenly without warning and contrary to any plans he was rehearsing in his head Sasha stood up and brushed herself down. Jim had always found it fascinating how no matter where a person lay their towel and how careful they were the sand always seemed to mock them by intruding on the space they had allocated for bathing. With her sudden burst of energy it didn't seem the right time to be dwelling on such trivial thoughts. Shielding his eyes so he could see her he craned his neck and looked at her with a puzzled expression.

"Jim, I have to meet my parents for lunch." She frowned slightly as she looked at him.

In the excitement of the morning, it had slipped his mind that she was going to be abandoning him for the afternoon.

"I'll see you tomorrow, yeah?" she added reminding him that they had arranged their next meeting already.

Reluctantly Jim forced a smile as he looked up at her and nodded silently in response to her question. Sasha leant down gripping his shoulder as she winked at him before walking slowly away.

As he leaned up on his elbow to watch her walking away Jim noticed something out of the corner of his eye. He reached over casually to pick it up and realised immediately what it was he was looking at. Dangling from his fingers was the bikini bottoms that Sasha had discarded after her swim.

"Sasha, I think you forgot something," he called out after her, too lazy to get up.

Hearing his voice, Sasha stopped and turned to face him. What could she have possibly forgotten? She knew she had left the towel behind but surely it wouldn't hurt him to return that for her. Her face flushed as she saw him casually swinging one of her items of clothing at her. So many times she had gone swimming in the sea while she was on holiday and not had to think about what she was wearing. She hadn't given it a second thought when she slipped out of her bikini bottoms as she returned to the towel. If anything it had felt unusual covering herself in the virtually see thru sarong that was clinging to her waist.

She giggled discretely glancing up at him to make sure he hadn't noticed her involuntary fit of laughter. If only he knew the irony behind the item he was dangling for her to collect she was sure he would laugh too. Less than twenty-four hours previously she had waited for him to be out of sight to relieve herself of her panties and now she had accidentally left her bikini bottom with him.

For a few seconds she contemplated going back to him for it but something took over her inhibitions. In a way it was laziness stopping her retracing her steps back to the towel. She had nothing to hide, her parents wouldn't expect her to be wearing anything when they met up anyway. If anything they might wonder why she was wearing a sarong but they wouldn't question her. Most women wore something light at some stage during their holiday for reasons only they knew so it wouldn't be a big issue.

"Dry them for me, would ya?" she called back. "Ye can bring them with ye tomorrow."

There weren't many men she would trust with an item of clothing on holiday, especially something of an intimate nature. There was even less chance she would let a boy at home look after even her jacket. Leaving items with some of her home acquaintances was all the reason they needed to assume that the person leaving the item had some interest in them. She had seen girls use this to their advantage on countless occasions with mixed results. Normally the boy would make an attempt to ask the girl out and would become deflated when he was turned down. Once in a while the opposite would happen, the girl would be asked on a date and would accept – but that seemed to be the exception not the rule.

In some ways this was going to be a test for him, a show of confidence and trust. She knew there was no way of knowing what he was going to do with them when she wasn't around but that was for him to decide. As long as they came back to her in one piece and in good condition she had nothing to lose. Even if they didn't come back to her there was a good chance she wouldn't need them again during her holiday. There was no way she was dressing up for the volleyball game she played that every year and had never worn more than a pair of sunglasses. When Jim arrived for the game tomorrow she hoped maybe being in a crowd would encourage him to join their naturist ways only time would tell.

Jim stared between Sasha and the discarded item that was dangling limply from his finger. It seemed a strange request but there was no harm in him drying them for her. Hanging an item of clothing in his bathroom wasn't going to cause him much inconvenience when he got back to his apartment. Glancing at her he made a failed attempt at a friendly wink as he shouted out his agreement to complete her request as she dashed away.

He had a lot of experience of looking after things for his female friends but usually it was a coat or a bag. Normally the request became a distraction – delegation of responsibility while they went off dancing or trying on something in a shop. He had never before been issued the responsibility of an item of clothing overnight and definitely never an under garment. Then again was a bikini considered an undergarment or not? It was hard to tell.

Jim found it amusing how women were happy and in some cases exhibited their bodies when they wore a bikini but if the wind caused a wardrobe malfunction it was a different story. He often wondered if it would be possible to sell underwear as a bikini and then send a message out revealing what it actually was how would the buyers react?

No matter what the answer was he was now left in charge of Sasha's accidentally forgotten bikini bottoms. Their temporary appearance in his life wasn't cause for alarm, they weren't going to become the topic of conversation for him and anyone because only he knew about them. Even if anyone else had known about it a discarded bikini didn't seem like a major event under any circumstances.

Jim folded the item and laid it neatly next to himself before laying back to enjoy a bit more of the sun.

Chapter Nine

The Perfect Gift

With Sasha unavailable for the afternoon Jim found that he was left with a tough decision to make. He was growing to like her and he wanted to find some way of showing her without making things awkward. He was good at buying gifts for girls; his band of female friends had usually commended him on the little things he bought them. There had been a few occasions when his gifts had been met with hostility but that was usually the boyfriend not the girl the gift had been going to.

Just like anything else buying gifts for female friends had its rules and restrictions most of which Jim was happy to comply with. The gift wasn't allowed to be an item of clothing as that was showing knowledge of their measurements. A number of them he did know the measurements for but he decided to allow the partner to make the mistake of buying the wrong colour or style – he was happy not to have that burden. Buying jewellery was also limited to simple or generic items like a brooch; if it was non-committal, a necklace was okay but not recommended. Bracelets, earrings and rings were definitely out of the question for similar reasons to clothing.

Other items had to be chosen with care as they could cause offence to the recipient or their partner. Plush items like cuddly toys had to be non-affectionate or not seen as threatening. If a cuddly toy was won during a day out at either a machine or on a stall at a funfair that was acceptable. If it didn't fit into one of these categories it had to come under the heading of not desirable to be taken to bed.

With Sasha, buying a gift had fewer restrictions. Firstly, unless she was hiding her boyfriend or she had left him at home, there was no hostility to worry about. Secondly, it wouldn't be practical to buy her an item of clothing even if he had known her sizes because she probably wouldn't wear it. Jewellery-wise, he wasn't sure if she wore earrings; her long raven hair had hidden her ears for most of their time together. Nodding to himself, he acknowledged that, even if she had short hair, there was a chance that he wouldn't have noticed with all the other distractions that her body was giving his eyes. Buying her a ring was far too heavy as she could take it in too many ways and he didn't know her ring size anyway.

This left the options as bracelets or necklaces, but as he hadn't seen her wearing one he wasn't sure if she had any allergies. His sister had what he classed as an expensive allergy meaning that she could only wear gold. One of the first challenges in dating her seemed to be whether the partner had taken that into consideration in gifts they bought. Jay, the guy she had moved in with, hadn't been one to take risks and as a result he had made sure jewellery wasn't made with precious metal of any kind. He justified this by saying that even something that looked like it was gold might be fake.

Before he could consider buying her a gift he had to firstly work out how much money the rents had given him in their mystery envelope. He had briefly assessed it when he received it and concluded that it seemed to have reasonable bulk but that could mean small denomination notes. His second challenge was where to go to buy the gift, the shops on site were the obvious location but that would mean potentially having to deal with naturists. The other problem with using the on-site shops was that Sasha might see him browsing.

If as an alternative he chose to go offsite shopping he wasn't sure how far it was to the shops or what type of shops there would be. He felt sure he hadn't seen any retail outlets on the street leading up to the gate but that didn't mean the village didn't have anything. Then there was the possibility of sellers on the beach which although risky had a certain appeal to him.

He knew from the tales he had been told on previous holidays that it wasn't wise to hand money over to a person that was selling without a shop. He had always visualised short men with thick moustaches, trilby hats, sunglasses and long coats as the ultimate beach seller. Their appearance would be completely out of place on a warm sunny beach but a long coat would give plenty of places to hide stock. The stock itself he imagined would have brand names that made them look expensive even if they weren't.

The biggest problem with these types of sellers was that it wasn't possible to know where the stock was coming from. Even if you could trace the source of the stock there was a good chance the seller wouldn't be there when the item broke. Adding to the problem was if an item needed replacing for any other reason tracking down the seller would be nearly impossible. The last thing he wanted was to buy her something that wasn't suitable and have nowhere to take it back to.

Having accepted that his choices were limited to either the shops on the complex or wasting time and money getting into town he opted reluctantly for the on-site option. He sat up propping himself on his arms and gazed out to the ocean remembering the way Sasha had athletically shown off her skills and contemplated a quick dip before returning to his apartment.

Next to him, neatly lying on the sand, were the bikini bottoms that he decided she had accidentally left with him. These had now become his responsibility having agreed to dry them for her before they met again the next day. If he went out swimming and came back to find they had gone he would feel guilty, it was safer to just head back. Carefully he bundled the discarded item in the towel making a mental note that he had to try and work out where the towel needed to be returned to. Maybe the fabled welcome pack would provide the answers just as it had on his first night.

Even though the journey from his current location to the apartments wasn't a long one he found himself mapping it out for the safest route to avoid flesh as much as possible. There were obvious places to avoid like the outdoor pool and at the current time, the main building, then again lunch would be a nice idea maybe it was worth chancing the restaurant. He contemplated his state of hunger for a moment deciding that he could wait for dinner.

Between the pool and the main building was a large area of mainly open grassland with a few trees dispersed offering intermittent shaded areas. With this area having very few hidden places he could easily avoid walking too close to any sun worshippers. This also meant he could avoid the path for over half of his journey which meant there was less chance of bumping into the rents. The route was as perfect as it could be and given the time of day, it would have to do, either that or he was stuck where he was until later in the day.

Although the beach looked like a tempting option and his hidden spot felt like it was ideal he had now set his mind on buying the gift. Jim found it impossible to carry a towel bundle without looking awkward in one way or another. Tucking it under the arm was far too stereotyped by TV animations and holding it to his chest would look messy. Normally he would drape the towel across his shoulders but as it was carrying an item of clothing that wasn't practical. Shrugging to himself at the limited options he chose the chest bundle – no one apart from him was going to worry about what it looked like.

With the sun overhead it was difficult to know which of the items on the ground were people and which were just random mounds created by the contours of the land. Carefully and quickly he walked at an angle that met with the foot path only a few metres from the beginning of his block of apartments. The gravel path felt warm under his bare feet as he walked with more urgency up to his apartment door and let himself in.

Jim realised, as he closed the door, that he had never been alone in his apartment during daylight hours since his first day. Since meeting Sasha, the rents had thankfully left him alone to get on with his holiday. He got the impression they weren't going to make too much fuss over what he was doing after the first day protest however seeing him with someone had settled their mind.

He reminisced over the last couple of days as he walked through the front room towards the bedroom. How things had changed in such a short time, when he had first stormed into his apartment he had been determined to minimalize the amount of daylight he was going to see, now the apartment was more of a safe haven. He decided it had been lucky that Sasha had decided to come and meet her neighbour because there wasn't much to inspire entertainment in the apartment.

The standard old and basic TV was secured to the wall on a metal arm in the corner of the room. The angle it pointed into the room at was only practical from one side of the couch and even then the viewer would need to be lying across both cushions to see it. Jim had put it on at one stage and fought with the remote for hours trying to find a channel that was in English only to find the news was his only option. Reading material wasn't much better; it consisted of the welcome pack, a room service menu and a bible which was coincidentally in English. There was also a copy of what looked like a telephone directory but that didn't count.

On the dressing table in his bedroom the envelope that he had been handed when he arrived was still unopened. To him an envelope of money that had been in his possession for so long and still hadn't been opened was a miracle in itself but then again there had been no reason to open it yet. He squeezed the contents between his fingers trying to work out how much might be in the mystery package.

Preparing himself for either a pleasant surprise or a shock he sat on the corner of the bed and peeled the envelope open. Shaking it he watched a neatly wrapped bundle of notes fall out and hit the bed. Thankfully there were no coins obvious, although being as there was nothing major to spend stuff on he had half expected to be presented with a bundle wrapped in a single note. Casually he discarded the envelope by throwing it towards the woven brown waste bin in the corner. His accuracy impressed him as the scrunched up envelope bounced off the wall and into its intended target.

Picking the notes up, he flicked through the ends, checking to see if they were all the same denomination. It didn't come as much of a surprise to him that every one of them was a five euro note. Jim decided that must have been mum's idea, she always took into consideration how difficult it was changing big notes on holiday. The other reason for giving him all low denomination notes was that it made the bundle look bigger.

Jim paused for a moment; he wasn't sure how much he should take with him for his gift. As much as onsite shops were convenient they did have the advantage of a captive audience. On this complex being in a location that appealed to residents would be more appealing than on in a normal hotel due to the dress code. As much as a captive audience was appealing to a shop owner it was unappealing to a consumer as the prices might not be as competitive as they would be in town.

It was while he was contemplating how much to take with him that Jim realised he didn't know where his wallet was. Since leaving home to go to the airport he hadn't had any need to find it and now he had doubts as to whether he had packed it at all.

Quickly he sprang off the bed and knelt down to check through his main suitcase which was still open on the floor. Two days into a holiday was a long time for him not to have fully unpacked but it seemed pointless if he was going to be wearing very few clothes.

Suddenly he found himself contemplating whether there was a launderette on the complex. There didn't seem to be much need for one but he had noticed on previous holidays it seemed to be a feature. Launderettes on holiday had been a frustration of his for many years; he didn't know anyone that enjoyed doing the washing at home so why would they want to do it on holiday. Doing it abroad was a scenario he didn't want to visualise; it seemed too much of a randomly insane thing to do.

As he dug through the neatly packed clothes he contemplated unpacking, even if he wasn't going to wear many of the items it seemed to be an appropriate ritual. Unpacking a suitcase on holiday was one way of staking a claim to the room that was temporarily his. Thankfully most of his clothes were foldable as the complex didn't make a lot of allowances for clothes to be hung. Normally this would be a frustration to him but on this occasion he could understand the reasons behind it. One by one he unpacked his items and placed them in the various drawers and closet spaces that were available. Each time he took an item out he stared at the next item hoping to see his wallet appear.

It wasn't until he reached the bottom of the suitcase and found that his wallet wasn't to be seen that he realised it was probably in his hand luggage. It had been crazy to think of it being in his main case, why would he put it in there? Maybe the heat was getting to him. Quickly he shuffled the case into the closet space and grabbed the much smaller bag that was sat next to his bed. Most of the contents had been emptied out of it into the security box at reception but there next to his sunglasses was his wallet. Relieved at the discovery he pushed the bundle of notes in and walked out of the bedroom.

From here onwards the afternoon was going to take on a much more complex feeling. Firstly he was going to be willingly entering a public space that would be potentially filled with nudists alone. Secondly with it being around lunch time he might encounter the rents which he knew was inevitable but he was happy to put it off as long as he could. Thirdly and much higher on his concerns list was the idea of bumping into Sasha or being seen by her browsing the shops.

Carefully he peered sideways out of his window trying to see if there was anyone on the path. The angle he was looking from made it hard to tell and the path led slightly uphill but the first few metres seemed clear. There wasn't much point in worrying he decided, sooner or later he was going to see someone, he had seen people before but Sasha had been a good distraction and this time she wasn't there.

He padded the wallet that he had just placed in his pocket as reassurance that it was still there and closed his eyes preparing himself before opening the door. Peering both left and right he saw a couple coming towards him from beyond Sasha's apartment. Turning away from them, he made out that he was looking for his key card, hearing them amicably talking in a foreign language as they walked past. He paused for a few moments to let them get far enough away that he wouldn't be forced to follow their nude buttocks.

Peeking toward the building he was pleased to see the path was clear and quickly started walking. For safety he kept his head tilted downward peering upwards every few seconds to make sure there was no one coming towards him. There was one thing he dreaded more than seeing random nudity and that was accidentally walking into someone that was nude. It was embarrassing enough walking into a stranger that was dressed but clashing flesh with flesh was an experience he didn't want to have to experience.

Jim couldn't believe the relief that ran through him as he reached the door to the main building. He had managed to successfully dodge the small number of other path users with clever ducking motions between apartments. Inside the building, it was going to be harder to avoid people and more likely he would see someone he knew. He didn't have much choice, if he wanted to surprise Sasha with a small gift he was going to have to do it. With a deep breath he walked in and made his way towards the atrium where as he had expected several people were wondering around.

He took a quick scan around the room making note of places he could disappear if he saw the rents or Sasha. There were a few doors but none that were easy to get to and even fewer that he knew led to somewhere he was allowed to go to or that were safe. Settling his mind he decided that behind one of these doors was the games room at least if he had to hide there was a chance he might find that.

Unlike in previous trips into the lobby style area this time the shops were fairly busy with people. Most of them he guessed were taking their time window shopping before heading back out to the sun. A man selling chiffon scarves seemed to be popular, maybe that was a good place to find something for Sasha but he couldn't picture her wearing a scarf. After the morning they had spent together it was becoming difficult to picture her wearing much at all. He could see a pattern forming to her dress code, gradually it was becoming less and less, tomorrow there might not be anything hiding her body.

The next shop looked like a pharmacy of some kind, selling hygiene products, cosmetics and sun burn prevention items. That was definitely not the place to look for a gift, admittedly sun cream would be a nice gesture but it wasn't what he was looking for. He questioned make up for a few moments, he hadn't seen Sasha wearing any, there were two possibilities, one was that she had run out and the second was she didn't like it. She didn't seem the type to run out of anything so the chances of her running out of makeup were limited.

Even if she had run out there were too many traps that he could fall into with makeup, girls had often commented on having the wrong shade bought for them. Jim hadn't often noticed much difference, red was red and pink was pink just because it was given a fancy name didn't make it a different colour. Makeup was too risky – if she wasn't a fan of makeup buying her some could become the end of what was looking like becoming a great friendship.

The next shop seemed out of place as it sold clothing; then again t-shirts were always popular as souvenirs. After that a news agent's type shop offering postcards and confectionary had a few younger customers wondering round inside it. Jim paused for a few moments, maybe he should send a postcard to his sister telling her the usual lines of how sunny it was and how he was having a great time. Surely the rents would deal with that and just add his name to the bottom of the card for him.

Although he had never received a post card from the rents his sister had shown him some of the ones she had received. The format remained the same no matter where they had gone for their annual holiday. The top line had simply said the name of the recipient, the second had advised them they had arrived safe and the third mentioned the weather. After the standard formalities there was a list of places they planned to visit during their stay.

Dad had always made a point of sending the post cards off within the first few days of their trip. His theory was that if he sent it early enough the recipient would receive it before they returned home. It didn't seem to matter if the post card had arrived or not when they got home the same questions would be asked over an evening of photographs and stories. Jim wondered what would be said about this trip, he felt sure that any post cards would be very brief considering there were no planned excursions.

Jim's mind wandered from the thought of postcards to the idea that the rents might have gone on excursions without him. The fact they had given him his own room meant he had no way of knowing where they were. He stopped himself before he got to deeply consumed by potential sinister plots and scanned the room again. The crowd that had been there as a post lunch gathering was now doing as he expected and disappearing outside.

Feeling slightly more vulnerable to being seen but less imposed upon by the lower number of naked bodies Jim moved on to the next shop. This shop seemed to be more like the sort of place he was going to find something that suited his needs. In the window a tidy display held decorative items of jewellery to suit most occasions. He felt sure he even saw rings that would be suitable as wedding rings if anyone wanted to go that far.

He glanced at the prices, they were reasonable considering most of the items appeared to be made of high quality metals. All he had to do now was work out what he wanted before he went in to the shop. He knew from experiences that he had been told about that this type of shop wasn't the type a person went into just to browse.

He peeked through the money in his wallet and took a quick glance around the room again. There was still no sign of Sasha and more importantly no sign of the rents although at this stage he hadn't decided which one he wanted to avoid most. On a normal occasion it would be the rents that he would dread seeing but under the circumstances maybe it was Sasha that he would prefer not to see him.

He could imagine how it would look for her if she saw him gazing in the window of a jewellery shop. Just the fact that he was stood there could conjure any one of a number of ideas in her head. The worst of these would be that she could assume he was buying for a girlfriend that he had left back home. Even though Sasha hadn't taken the role of being his girlfriend it would be difficult to convince her that he was single if the moment arose.

Peering over his shoulder one last time he slipped into the safety of the shop and smiled over at the shop keeper. He was a small man with a well groomed moustache who smiled pleasantly as Jim entered the shop. Jim looked over and acknowledged the gesture with a forced grin that he felt sure made him look like he was up to no good as he turned to look at the glass cabinet on the wall. In his anticipation to escape the atrium he had forgotten the words of his friends back home that once you entered a jewellers it was assumed you were buying something.

A part of him wanted to try and explain that for now he was just looking but he wasn't sure if he would be understood. Just looking might also inspire the shop owner to try and make recommendations to encourage a sale. As he wasn't sure exactly what he was looking for he didn't need anyone trying to get rid of last year's stock on him. He glanced over at the man relieved to see that he hadn't moved and was now looking at a book studiously.

Calming the tension in his body he resumed his glance around the shelves, admiring the vast display of items available to him as he calculated how much of his budget he could spend. Suddenly one of the items caught his eye, it was perfect, the design, the price both seemed to match what he had imagined buying her. With slow steps he approached the man and waited until he looked up showing the same pleasant grin he had before.

"I'll take that one, please," Jim said with assertion in his voice as he pointed at the wall display.

Chapter Ten

Volleyball

Jim stretched his arms out pressing his fingertips against the wall as he woke from a heavy night's sleep. He was pleasantly surprised at how well he had slept but glancing over at the clock changed his mood. Almost mockingly the clock that he had chosen not to set was telling him that it was 8.40 a.m. He cursed himself for not setting it; there was no logical reason for him to have forgotten. After getting home from his shopping adventure he had been cornered into spending another night with the rents. In the excitement of not being caught shopping by Sasha and not seeing the rents during his time in the atrium he had forgotten to be cautious passing their apartment. If he had done things right he had been ready for a night to himself, probably not in his apartment but maybe finding the games room. He had decided the evening was the safest time to go looking for it because of the casual clothing rule.

Admittedly outside the restaurant he was aware people might not follow it but at least there was a chance. Consumed by his thoughts and busy crediting himself for his achievements he hadn't seen his Dad until it was too late. Acting as casually as he could Dad had appeared at the window that Jim was thankful at least hid the lower half of his body. Jumping in shock Jim had quickly tucked the boxed item he had purchased into his pocket as if it was something he shouldn't have. Waving amicably Dad had then insisted on them spending another evening together which Jim had started protesting to. The finishing blow was when Dad had called for Mum, the fear of seeing her topless had been enough for Jim to quickly agree to meet them before disappearing to his apartment.

Deep down he knew that his late start wasn't their fault but in the absence of someone else to blame he was now cursing them. Next to the alarm clock on the bed side table was the boxed gift that he had placed proudly before turning the lights out. Opposite the end of the bed hung carefully over the door handle was the bikini bottom that Sasha had accidentally left behind. He knew there were hundreds of places that would be much more practical for them to hang and dry but their current location was one that he knew he wouldn't forget to pick them up from on his way out.

Kicking his way out of bed he picked up the box as he struggled into a pair of shorts. He had contemplated the idea of going down to the game nude as a way of acknowledging all the time she had accommodated his shyness about naturism. He wanted to show her some effort but he wasn't comfortable doing it in such a crowd –

especially when he didn't know who else might be there. Even though he was fairly sure volleyball wasn't the sort of activity the rents would involve themselves in it wasn't worth risking.

Grabbing Sasha's discarded item of clothing he tucked it into the spare pocket as he walked toward the front door. He peered left and right still conscious that he wanted to avoid unwanted sights for as long as possible. With an air of urgency he walked down the path away from the main building toward the beach. Even though he was late and the trip was slightly longer it felt like the safer way to go.

Jim wasn't surprised to see that the swimming pool was already starting to get busy. This was the same on most of the holidays he went on, no matter what time of day and no matter what the signs said there always seemed to be a healthy arrangement of bathing spots reserved by towel. Even though the pool was fenced off with a waist height aluminium rod style fence, the gate had most likely been open for a couple of hours.

As he reached the sand dunes, he paused to catch his breath and rehearsed what he was going to say and do in his head. He peered down at his shorts, he could possibly risk taking them off but then again that could complicate things more. Digging into his pockets he pulled the box and the bikini bottoms out and transferred them both to the same hand. This was a tactical manoeuvre as much as anything else because it left one hand free to offer her a hug in apology for his late arrival. Beyond the dunes he could hear the sound of people cheering and clapping reassuring him that the game was still on. His heart filled with nerves as he climbed through the wiry grass toward the top of the dune.

Just as he had anticipated, below his position on the beach was a sea of activity as people made their way toward the net. On one side, a few people stood around with hands on their hips as if they were waiting for something to happen. On the other side, elated figures were jumping up and down, celebrating what he assumed was winning the game. Jim lifted his empty hand to shield his eyes from the sun as he scanned the ground for Sasha. His heart stopped as he spotted her raven hair, he found himself frozen to the spot as he witnessed her being pulled into an embrace by another man.

The shock that had sent his body into a frozen state released him and allowed him to drop her panties and the box he had spent hours choosing. He felt like he heard the thud as both items fell in what seemed to be slow motion from his hand to the floor. A rage like he had never felt before filled his body as he pivoted on the spot and started to run.

Consciously he knew what he had dropped had monetary value but to him it was now just money wasted. Even though she hadn't said she was his seeing her in another man's arms had been more than his mind could take. He could feel the anger filling his face as it twisted forming wrinkles in his nose and exposing his teeth.

So many times he had been the outsider on a relationship, the third wheel and the friend to fall back on. Each time it happened it had been because of the category he had by default been placed in. The category of the friend zone, every girl's best friend, the guy she could tell anything to but never do anything intimate with. He had never asked to be categorized as the friend but somehow it kept happening. With Sasha it was different; she hadn't known him long enough to place him in the friend zone. He acknowledged that she hadn't asked for anything more than friendship but that didn't matter – she hadn't mentioned any other man.

He nearly forced the door down as he got to his apartment and scrambled around closing the curtains. His safe zone was temporarily not safe, she knew where he lived and he knew there was a chance she might come to find him. He didn't want to wait around for an explanation, an excuse or a reason why she had been cuddling this man he had never met before. He didn't want her telling him it was all a mistake, he wasn't meant to see that or it wasn't meant to happen.

Quickly, he grabbed a shirt and his wallet before running back out of the apartment again. He glanced in the direction of the beach; there was no one obvious following him. He knew that, even though he hadn't seen anyone, it didn't mean he wasn't being followed on an alternative route. Quickly he ran behind the building and followed the direction of the main path along the grass between him and the wall until he got to the main building. He glanced over, it wasn't safe to be there either, the rents could find him there, and Sasha might see him there.

Through the rage that was occupying his minds he could see only one logical solution. He had to get off site and he had to do it fast, there was no time to wait for taxis he would have to walk. Keeping a quickened pace he made his way to the reception and out of the main gate as he pulled his shirt on. The small town of Vassilikos was going to be his safe haven for the rest of the day, he grunted to himself as he started walking.

****

Sasha had arrived at the beach early for the game; she hadn't slept well due to the excitement of catching up with some of her other friends and introducing them to Jim. She was nervous for him because she was unsure how he would react to being in such a large group of naturists but she was also excited at seeing him again. Her mixed emotions scared her in many ways because consciously she was aware that she barely knew him but somehow he made her feel safe.

The crowd for the game settled as the organiser started pointing people towards different sides of the net. Sasha glanced over at the path she had shown Jim that led to the beach and was disheartened to see that he wasn't there. Maybe he had just over slept; surely there wasn't any other reason for him not to have turned up. She had got the impression that he wasn't great with mornings from him as they had got to know each other and now she was going to use it as a playful dig.

After the game she would simply go to his apartment and knock on the door and window until he woke up. From there on in it was a simple case of digging at him a few times during the day about being sleepy. She felt sure he wouldn't get upset about something like that especially when it was true. Shrugging his absence off she prepared to enjoy the game glancing at every opportunity at the path just in case.

The game went well, she had a good group of players around her and between them they managed to secure a comfortable victory. Elated by the result she ran around congratulating her team mates with friendly gestures that finished with a huge hug for her friend Greg. She had known Greg for years and although he was a few years older than her it had been her initiative that had united him with his long term partner Alice.

Even with her youth and inexperience of relationships she had seen their attraction for each other long before they had. The sneaky glances that Greg had thrown toward Alice were in some ways painful to watch. He always seemed slightly distracted when she was around but in a sweet way. He hadn't acted foolishly to try and catch her attention just watched from afar as she mingled with her own social group.

It was during a planned social event that Sasha had noticed that Greg's glances over at her were being returned in a similar shy fashion by Alice. Taking charge of the situation Sasha had managed to orchestrate a situation where they were placed in an event together. She was lucky that she had known one of the hotel staff that year and had pointed out her observations to them. The staff member had discretely placed them as a couple for a competition forcing them into a situation where they only had each other to talk to. Sasha had watched as they started getting to know each other and had made her excitement known when they arrived on holiday the following year as a couple.

At first she had tried to play down her part in bringing them together but Alice had been quick to catch her out. She had referred to it as female intuition but what she really meant was that she had seen Sasha plotting their ice breaking meeting. Sasha hadn't been sure how to respond when Alice told her that she knew what had been done, she knew that it wasn't always seen as a compliment when someone interfered in other people's business. To her surprise and relief Alice and Greg had not only thanked her but had complimented her on how well she arranged the whole thing.

As she had been in her amicable embrace with Greg Sasha had found herself glancing away from him. Her gaze had not been towards the path which from her position was impossible to see but it had been toward the sand dunes where a few spectators were gradually disappearing back to the complex. Normally the dunes wouldn't be of any great interest to her but as she looked over she saw a familiar sight. There standing on top of one of the dunes was a lone figure that she recognised from their build as Jim – he had made it at last.

She had mentioned Jim to Greg and Alice at the beginning of the game and had received what she decided was a response similar to that of his parents. Greg had been the first to use the term boyfriend but Alice had been quick to join in as she told them more and more about this mysterious boy. They had seemed quite surprised when she had explained how nervous he was about nudity and questioned why he was at the complex if he didn't like it. Luckily Sasha had asked him the same question on his first night and could now explain it without the scowling he had used when referring to his parents.

"That's Jim," she whispered in Greg's ear as she tipped her head toward the dunes. Greg looked over just in time to see the figure that Sasha had been trying to point out to him disappear. He felt Sasha's arm drop down his back releasing him as the look on her face changed from the happy Sasha he knew to a more confused Sasha. Her eyes were still fixed at the spot that had now been vacated by Jim as she tried to work out where he had gone. Maybe he was making his way round to the path but why would he do that when there were only a few steps from the dunes down to the beach.

It hadn't taken long for instinct to kick in and Greg to realise what was going on in this young man's mind. He could easily see himself in the same position that this boy was in. There was more to Jim's feelings for Sasha than he had told her and, just at the moment that he had prepared himself to express his interest in her, something had got in the way. Like a younger version of himself, he knew how it must feel to see the girl that he had an interest in hugging another man. Thankfully, this figure on the dunes had acted in the same way that he would have done and retreated from the situation rather than antagonise it. Cautiously, Greg looked back at Sasha as she made her way towards the vacated area where Jim had been standing, trying to make sense of his disappearance.

Alice grabbed his arm and walked with him behind Sasha allowing her the space she needed to realise what had happened. They watched as she climbed the dune and bent down to pick up the item that Jim had dropped. She recognised the item as being her bikini bottoms from the previous day but there was something more with them, a box. She realised as she picked it up and examined it that the box was a jewellery box, possibly a present his parents had bought him.

Out of curiosity she opened the box and felt her shoulders twinge as she saw what was inside. Lying against a soft red velvet cushion was a fine gold necklace with a diamante letter "S" hanging from it. She knew instantly that the chain hadn't been a gift for him; the initial made it obvious that it was meant for her. She ran her fingers under the decoration, mimicking the design with her fingertip as she felt her body start to shake.

By this one single, thoughtful and beautiful gesture he had confirmed to her that what Greg and Alice had been joking about was something he had wanted. She had been denying it to herself but with the sensitivity he had shown her in their brief time together she was growing to like him too. She had never considered any of the boys back home as worth liking in the way she was beginning to like him and she knew none of them would have shown such generosity without wanting something in return.

Clasping the box close to her chest she felt a mix of sadness and joy fill her body as she realised the implications of what had happened. For the first time she had actually won the attention of a man that wasn't just looking for one thing and now because of a simple gesture she may have lost him in the same heartbeat. She looked up with a sharp stare realizing what she had to do, she had to tell him he had made a mistake, she had to explain herself to him even if it was just to clear her name. Glancing behind herself she saw her two friends waiting patiently for her to tell them what was happening.

"I've got to go find him," she announced with a lump in her throat as she waved the box at them.

Clutching the box tightly in her hand Sasha ran through the complex towards the apartments. Her head ached with thoughts of what she was going to say when she saw Jim. Although she could understand his actions when he witnessed her hugging Greg she felt shocked that he hadn't waited for her to explain. She felt sure that once he heard the truth everything would be fine and they could get on with enjoying their holiday.

Even if he didn't want to accept her story and see her again she wanted to see him to at least try to clear her name. Until she saw the contents of the box she hadn't given the idea of Jim being her boyfriend a second thought. He had been sweet and fun to be with and she did like him but it didn't seem practical. Behind her Greg and Alice were following her; she could hear them but didn't stop to let them catch up. They were proof that couples could meet on holiday and make a future but then again they lived in the same country as each other Jim wasn't anywhere near local to her.

She reached his apartment and took a deep breath trying to compose herself as she desperately looked into the windows. The curtains blocked her view; maybe he hadn't opened them before he left. Desperately she wrapped her free hand on the door shouting his name as she felt her eyes filling with tears. She paused leaning against the door waiting to hear any movement even a shuffle to confirm he was there. Silence filled her ears; she pushed herself upright and ran to the window that led to his bedroom. Once again the curtain blocked her view into the room; surely he hadn't forgotten to open that one too. With urgency she tapped on the glass and then the frame pleading with him to answer her but again was greeted by silence.

Slowly she walked back toward the front door, across on the grass she could see the figures of her friends waiting for her. Maybe he was in the main building, it was after all breakfast time, without hesitation she hung her bikini bottom on the door to let him know she had tried to contact him. The box was not going anywhere, if she left that he would think she had rejected him when it was quite the opposite. She walked slowly toward her friends curious as to why they were still there when they must have better things to do.

"Any sign of him?" Alice enquired softly.

She knew the answer but it seemed to be the correct protocol to ask the question anyway out of politeness. Sasha had been a good friend to both her and Greg over the years and they had watched her grow into the young woman she was. Without her they wouldn't be a couple and now they had witnessed something they didn't think would ever happen. Sasha who had always seemed content to be herself was falling apart over a boy she had just met. Even if he didn't know it this Jim was the first boy they had seen her talk about with any excitement in her voice.

Shaking her head slowly, Sasha looked up at them. Greg's eyes showed the guilt he felt for his part in her situation. He hadn't done anything wrong, and she was sure he knew it, but the company would be nice, at least for a little while. Smiling softly she started to walk up toward the main building glancing down any gaps between apartments as she walked.

For the first time since coming to the complex all those many years ago she felt anxious as she pushed the door open. The shops around the atrium were being opened and had the regular few people looking casually in their windows. The bar area was closed off and filled with darkness so he wouldn't be in there. The couches were empty except for one couple who seemed to be contentedly cuddled up after breakfast. Shuffling her feet slightly she made her way toward the restaurant in case he was in there.

As she walked round the tables she made a point of looking through the window at the bench she had shown him on their first morning together. She wasn't surprised to see it was empty; no one else seemed to bother using it except her; and now him. She gazed over at the central buffet monitoring every person to try and recognise him.

Her stomach ached as she checked every table and kept an eye on the entrance door in the hope of seeing him.

Outside the building Greg stood with Alice watching the door in anticipation for her appearing. Even though he had only caught a short glimpse of Jim he felt fairly sure he would recognise him if he appeared from the building. He wasn't sure what he would say and he wasn't sure if Jim would talk to them if he did appear but it was the best idea he had. At least from their position they could give Sasha directions as to where he had gone if they saw him.

Every time the door creaked open Greg felt his body tense as he looked over to see who it was. Eventually he saw Sasha re-appear; she looked so lost standing there alone with her arms hanging by her sides. He wanted to go over and give her a reassuring hug to tell her everything would be ok but Alice pre-empted his reaction and stopped him.

"Hugging her isn't a good move, hun," she said softly as she smiled at him.

Greg stopped himself; Alice was thinking with a much clearer head than he was and he knew she was right. He turned back waiting in anticipation to see what Sasha was going to do next, expecting her to update them on the situation that they knew was still unresolved. Without warning Sasha ran, not toward them but away from them and round the side of the building.

As she moved out into the sunlight Sasha had seen her friends patiently waiting for her. She knew the correct thing to do was to tell them that she hadn't found him and she was going to keep looking but her head was full of emotions as she looked over at them. She needed time to herself before she could do anything and she knew there was a bush to the side of the building that she had hidden behind as a younger girl.

Without any word she dashed round the corner hoping they wouldn't follow her as she slipped in behind the greenery to a place of solace. She heard a noise from the path as she crouched out of sight near the wall of the building and peeked through. It wasn't anybody important just one of the other guests that was immune to her situation. She settled against the wall and held the box tightly in her hands as she pushed her back against it.

Where could he be?

She was determined to find him – somehow – and to tell him that she reciprocated the feelings which he had so silently felt for her. To see if they could resolve this mess she was in because of a non-committal gesture of victory that had been taken badly.

She closed her eyes, trying to clear the bad memories and focus on what she needed to do next.

Slowly, Greg pulled away from Alice heading toward the corner Sasha had disappeared round. Leaning out Alice grabbed his arm stopping him and pulling him back forcing him to look at her.

"I have to help her," he pleaded with Alice, who knew what he wanted to do.

Alice smiled softly; his kind hearted nature had been part of what had attracted her to him in the first place.

"We have to help her," she corrected him, "but first, give her time to herself," she added as she clasped his hand.

Greg nodded allowing a vague smile to cross his face; he knew Alice was right, she always was.

Chapter Eleven

An innocent mistake

Recomposing herself slowly Sasha lifted her head out of her hands, and pushed the last few tears across her cheeks using her wrist. Carefully she brushed her hair out of her eyes and sniffled hard as she caught her breath trying to push the emotion that had kept her paralysed behind the bush to the back of her mind. Lying clumsily next to her on the ground propped between a small stone and her skin was the little box that she had watched fall from Jim's hand.

This small box represented so much to her now but two points stood out prominently. Firstly it represented an insight into how Jim had felt towards her up to the fatal volleyball game. Secondly this box represented the reason she wanted to find him again, it was like the starting point of a quest – the quest to let him know what he thought he had seen wasn't what it looked like. The frustration that such a small, innocent, friendly gesture had become the cause of such a misunderstanding was eating away at her.

By his clever disappearing act Jim had made it clear that he didn't want to be found any time soon. She knew in her heart that there was a chance that he was going to try to avoid her for however long was left to his holiday. Losing him over something so trivial almost mocked how close they had become in such a short time. She knew that he couldn't avoid his apartment forever but keeping a twenty-four hour vigil over it seemed non-productive. She could always try to bring his parents into the equation but the complications that could cause far outweighed the advantages. She could visualise in her head how the conversation would start if she was to try and get his parents help.

"Hi, remember me? You met me with your son two days ago. Well, um, I've lost him. Do you know where he is?"

She could clearly see the look on their faces as she explained, a look that would be sure to appear, it would be somewhere between confusion and concern. Confusion because they wouldn't understand why she was asking them where their son was and concern as to where he actually was. Then again, at the age of sixteen, they might not be too worried about where he was as long as he was enjoying himself.

Being parents they would possibly try to make the matter light hearted with comments like 'where did you last put him'. Under normal circumstances she would see the humour but they wouldn't know how she had lost him unless she explained the whole story. Trying to explain what had happened was going to be difficult enough when she found him there was no way she wanted to tell someone else what had happened. She paused momentarily in her thoughts, yes she had just implied she was going to find him, at least she was staying positive mentally even if her body told a much different story. Approaching them was not a good idea, the least they knew the better if she wanted any chance of seeing him again.

She found herself visualizing what this situation would be like if she was back home in Ireland. If there was a boy she wanted to get to know and he had seen her in a casual embrace with another man. On the assumption that the boy she liked also liked her he would without any doubt run home and tell of how evil she was to his parents. The end result would be stories about how she had played with his emotions and treated him badly and bans from going anywhere near him again – more than likely the ban would be imposed by his parents. As she wasn't at home at least she could avoid that unnecessary drama because nobody at the complex would be interested enough to worry about what had happened – except those that were involved.

Making it worse she knew if she approached his parents he wouldn't look favourably on her getting them involved. He had made it quite clear from the beginning that his relationship with his parents wasn't harmonious at the moment. She hadn't asked the reason why, maybe it was an on-going conflict with them, the source of years of frustration. Then again it could just be something to do with the holiday they had bought him on, the possibilities were endless. Whatever the reason was the chances of him going running to them to vent his frustration at what had happened were minimal.

Resigning herself to the fact that it wasn't going to be an easy day she took a few deep breaths refocusing her mind. Looking down at the box she grabbed it with committed but gentle fingers as if she wanted the contents of the box to feel her anxiety. She picked it up and gripped it cupping it tightly in her hands holding it close to her chest before carefully crawling out of her hiding space.

This little haven behind a bush had been her refuge for the last ten minutes, no one had found her there, her friends would have surely gone by now. There was no point in them waiting for her, especially when they didn't know where she was. Apart from anything else, this was her problem to sort out, fair enough Greg had been as much part of the hug as she had been but it wasn't as if they had anything to hide. Alice and he had their own holiday to think about, she had hidden from them not the other way round.

Hindsight told her she should have not played the game, she should have missed the first half and gone to knock his door but then again he knew what time the game started. If he had been there on time he would have met Greg and Alice and would know there was nothing sinister in the hug. This mess was as much his fault as it was hers; surely he knew that – didn't he? She paused for a few moments before heading back towards the apartments, she had to try to see it from his side, he wouldn't have accounted for being late. All he would see was the hug; she had to accept that he would see nothing except the circumstances he had walked in to.

Why were boys so hard to deal with? Even when there were less boundaries than under usual circumstances, their mind worked so differently to girls. Then again, if she had been the one arriving on the dunes and seeing him hugging a girl, she would possibly have reacted in a similar way to him. The big difference was she wouldn't run off away from the scene, she would have gone in with her guns blazing to tackle the offenders. Maybe she should be grateful for his reaction being so submissive; at least it hadn't caused a scene. If he had caused a scene, she wouldn't be looking for him now; she would have sorted it out with him and probably left him alone to work it out. She decided that neither scenario was ideal, one she would have felt hostile toward him and the other was the one she was now in.

Coming to terms with her new found reasoning she turned back to the main building. Sat on the soft grass outside the building she saw a sight that sent a warming glow through her body. Despite her assumptions the two friends that had accompanied her in the initial pursuit of Jim were patiently waiting for her. Part of her conscience wanted to tell them that they hadn't needed to wait but a greater part of her mind was telling her that the extra help would be useful. Even if they weren't here to help she knew in her mind that she could do with friendly faces round her.

She couldn't help herself smiling as she saw them; whether they were here to help or not didn't matter at this precise moment it was more important to know she had friends round her. She hoped it wasn't an awkward guilt pushing them to stay, she had known Greg for years, he must know that the fateful incident had been a mutual thing. In her left hand she gripped tightly to the box, if she had lost Jim she wasn't going to lose that. It would stay with her as a lasting reminder of her time with him and a warning to her to be careful of her actions in future – no matter how innocent they were.

"Ye didn't have t…" she started saying softly as she approached them only to be hushed as she spoke by a hand gesture from Greg signalling her to stop speaking.

"We wanted to, Sasha," he assured her.

For the first time since meeting Jim she suddenly felt the vulnerability that came with both her youth and her emotional position. Looking back at her were two people who were together because of her intervention but now they were here to repay a favour that hadn't been asked.

Her shoulders dropped as the tension that had built up inside her body drained from her muscles. She hadn't cried so heavily since she had been a young girl when the family pet had passed away and now a single man had inadvertently caused her the same state. Was this what it felt like to love and lose? She contemplated. She wasn't used to losing, having always had a very competitive streak and a high level of motivation.

Coming second had never appealed to her throughout school. Team events she had pushed her fellow team mates on towards victory and individual events she had always forced herself to play to the best of her ability. The result of this drive was a series of trophies and achievements littered around the home and in amongst them a few disappointments that had spurred her on to try harder next time.

Here before her she had a team that had chosen to join her to some extent, she had to establish how far they were willing to go but that would come with time, for now she had two people backing her up. This was going to make things easier for her even if it was only from a view of moral support. The only thing that sill nagged in her head was how to tackle the problem she was faced with.

Alice broke the silence between them

"Come and join us for something to eat Sasha, plans are better made on a full stomach."

****

The small resort of Vassillikos made a perfect haven for Jim; it had taken him about half hour to walk into the main resort which he decided was understandable. He could relate to the locals not wanting a place filled with naked body's right on their doorstep. More to the point the distance in to the town made it less likely that the rents or anyone else would come looking for him.

The walk had also given him time to calm down and relieve his frustration at what had happened. He was still mad at Sasha for leading him on but he was used to being let down by girls. More annoying was the fact that he had dropped the surprise gift he had for her, maybe he could go back and recover it later if he was careful.

His parents were a long way down his list of people to go running to, they wouldn't understand what he was going through, why should they? They had been married for years so they didn't know what it was like surely. Apart from anything else he didn't want a lecture about how things were different in their day or a heart to heart chat about girls from his mother. He had managed to avoid that chat with the distraction of his sister falling in the family way. Once they became grandparents his naivety seemed to take a back seat.

He didn't consider 'the talk' as he had heard it referred to by others as something that he needed anyway. It was bad enough imagining his parent knowing that stuff, then there was the reality that at some stage they had done that sort of stuff. Thankfully any time they had tried to sit him down he had mentioned that the internet was able to fill in any gaps that had been created by educational videos at school.

Despite his adversity to 'the talk' he knew he could do with someone he could tell of his experience – but who? How could he ever explain that he was on a nudie holiday? Even if he could explain that bit how would he explain what had happened? He knew none of his friends would believe him – he would get one of two reactions. The girls would tell him how sweet he was and how there were plenty of fish in the sea; he definitely didn't need to be considered sweet. The lads would be more interested in what she looked like and tell him how lucky he had been to see her naked without asking followed by telling him that all girls were the same and to find someone else.

The resulting message was the same whichever way he looked at it – he had to put it down to an experience, all be it an unpleasant experience, and move on. No one had told him how difficult moving on was though, then again what was he moving on from? They had never been a couple. He knew in his heart that he wanted more than a friendship but that seemed ages ago, now all she was to him was a person he wanted to avoid.

Easier said than done, he didn't know how long she was there for, they had to use the same restaurant and the site was too small to hide. Sooner or later he would have to create a story to appease the rents.

'Where is your girlfriend?' his father would surely ask, that was easy to answer all it took was a mumble about her not being his girlfriend. That would then be followed by his father pretending it was a play on words before mum shushed him. Jim would then have to convince them that either she had gone home or she had a boyfriend and he wanted to let them have space. The first option wasn't practical because they knew what she looked like and they were bound to see her around the site. The second option was easier; it would incur a 'That's sweet of you' from his mum but he could take that on the chin. The bigger problem would be the long-term effect.

If he wasn't going to be hanging round with his friends they would expect him to hang around with them. Jim loathed hanging round with the rents at the best of times but hanging round with them naked was beyond his acceptance. Then it occurred to him, there was a games room, he could hide away in there during the days. But what if she came in with her boyfriend? Once he was in there he was trapped. There would be a series of awkward hellos as he slipped out pretending to be busy or in a rush. Slipping past girls was easier than spending time with the rents but what if her boyfriend stopped him? He hadn't seen much of this mystery man but what he had seen looked fairly tall making him harder to slip past.

Jim stopped in the street and heard a mumble of something foreign as a couple shuffled round him. He scanned the street and saw a little café, reaching into his pocket he pulled the envelope of money out of it that Dad had given him on his first day. He felt quite impressed with himself, he was half way through his first week and his finances were good, quite a comfortable feeling when put into comparison with past years. Hopefully the café would understand him if he spoke slowly, if not soft drinks usually had universal names. The hot sun was blazing and he needed time to think.

Time to experience the hospitality of the locals.

****

By lunch time, Sasha found herself sat at the table that would in her mind usually belong to Jim and her. Her mind wondered over the short memories she had of their times eating in this spot together while he tried to avoid spotting his parents. Although she had been determined all morning to try and find him there had been little progress made between herself and her lunch companions Greg and Alice mainly because she didn't know where to start looking for him.

During the time they had spent together there were very few places they had visited – except the beach and the spot she was sitting. She was fairly confident he wouldn't go to the beach as that would be seen to him as the scene of the crime.

During both breakfast and lunch she had kept extremely vigilant when entering the dining room pausing and staring a few times towards people that bared a vague resemblance to him but each time finding herself disappointed when she realised it wasn't.

She had also taken one trip back to the apartments mainly because she felt over exposed for the first time in her life and wanted to cover up. She had taken the time to glance at Jim's apartment and felt her heart skip a little as she saw the curtains open and her underwear missing from the door handle. After a thorough search through every window, including noticing the new location of her panties laid across his bed, she had concluded that the change of appearance was due to housekeeping paying their daily visit and not Jim's return.

Allowing time for her disappointment to settle she returned to her friends and decided not to tell them the moment when she had seen a glimmer of hope. She now sat with them as the odd one out wearing the little dress she had worn for Jim on their first night together. There was a sentiment to this dress now; it wasn't just any dress it was the beginning of a friendship she had hoped would last. A friendship she was now determined to rekindle and possibly progress if she had the chance.

Greg had noticed her change of attire but used his discretion in not making any fuss about it. It was the first time he had seen her dressed in the years they had known each other, she was sure it must look strange to him but he knew there were extenuating circumstances. Alice had commented on how pretty she looked in the dress but that was more out of politeness and to make her relax than out of need to make a comment.

As they sat eating and discussing a plan of action for the afternoon Sasha found her mind wondering to more awkward thoughts. Her panties on his bed would look bad when he returned; he would wonder how they got there. Maybe she could try and retrieve them, but how could she do that when the door was locked? And even if she could it would look worse if she was in his apartment when he returned. She pondered on it for a moment deciding it was fate that had put them there and not her, maybe it would become a blessing in disguise and force them to talk again.

Refocusing on the discussion she watched as Greg clumsily mapped out the main complex on a napkin using a pen he had borrowed from one of the staff. Although the detail was rough it was clear that he knew the layout of the complex. He had even pointed out a few spots that Sasha wasn't familiar with highlighting that they would be good havens for a person not wanting to be seen.

The main advantage they had was that hopefully Jim wouldn't recognise Greg and he definitely wouldn't know who Alice was. This meant that although he might be defensive with Sasha, there was a chance that the other two could get him talking. The biggest problem was that apart from a description of him neither of them knew who they were looking for either. The whole situation seemed hopeless.

How do you go about finding a boy that doesn't want to be found on a complex where you couldn't even confirm who he was by what he was wearing?

Was it better if they just stayed on guard at his apartment? Watching for his return? If they did that they might look too suspicious

Sasha cursed herself for not having any pictures, or even a camera to have taken one of them together.

His parents were the key, but how to use them without raising alarm?

She knew she had to get a picture of him to show her friends but if she approached them how could she avoid raising suspicion?

More to the point – they were on holiday, why would they have a picture of him? In a sudden moment of inspiration she realised she did have access to a picture of him – if she was lucky. On their first night together an onsite photographer had taken pictures and she had coaxed him into posing with her. She was nearly 100% certain he wouldn't have bought it. All she had to do was get the picture and the search could begin.

Leaping to her feet in a moment of jubilation she excused herself from her friends and ran into the atrium.

Greg and Alice sat patiently waiting, the only words they had caught were "I have a plan, don't go away."

With a spring in her step Sasha returned to the table clutching an item to her chest. The photographer had listened to her story and taken pity on her handing her the picture without payment. Eagerly she displayed the picture on the table, the happy pose of what to anyone would seem a couple stared back at them from the image. There was a depth in the gaze between the two of them as the picture had been taken. For the first time Sasha could see the chemistry between them had started on their very first night, even if they hadn't admitted it.

Finally they knew who they were looking for, the search could begin.

****

It was getting dusky before Jim returned to the complex; he had spent an enjoyable time wondering the narrow streets and was now feeling hungry. The restaurant was far too risky, anyone could find him there, Sasha, the guy she was with or the rents. He wasn't sure which would be the worst, now her secret was out she had no reason to hide this other man and he didn't really fancy seeing them together.

Tonight he was going to treat himself to the room service that he had promised himself on his first night at the complex. The circumstances that had led to his first experience of room service were leagues away from those that he had first browsed the menu under. Maybe this was going to be the first of a number of repetitive meals from the menu that was the only way to be sure he wouldn't see her in the restaurant. Then again he hadn't done anything wrong to lead to his confinement to his apartment so maybe once the dust settled he would go back to the restaurant again.

With watchful gazes he made sure there were no unwelcomed figures around as he made his way back towards his apartment. It wasn't safe to go into his room yet, he knew she could see his apartment from hers and there was a chance she might try to confront him. He gazed over and could see light streaming from her front windows, she was in her room. Casually he sat and waited until he saw her door open and watched her walk to another apartment. Maybe that was her mystery man's apartment; maybe she had met him on holiday too.

She didn't enter the new apartment choosing to stand outside until two other people appeared. That must be her parents he decided, she must be going to dinner with them which was perfect. Keeping himself hidden from view he watched the trio walk past his apartment, he convinced himself that he saw her gaze toward his window as she passed. He waited until they had gone all the way up to the main building before dashing down to his apartment and slipping quickly inside.

The curtains that he had made sure of shutting before he left were now open, presumably by the cleaners, he decided, as he slid the key card into the door. On tip toes he walked in and shut his door pausing after a few seconds and questioning why he was sneaking in to his own apartment. No one except Sasha and possibly her parents knew he was avoiding her and he had just watched her walk away. Taking every precaution he could he closed the curtains again and turned on the light before grabbing the menu.

He sat comfortably on the couch tracing his finger down the list of options and reminiscing on the last time he had looked at this menu. How much fun that night had become afterwards, a night that now seemed like a lifetime away. He could now see her in his head, a meal with the family then the evening in the arms of the mystery man she had been with that morning, the thought made his stomach knot.

Changing his mind and deciding dinner could wait he placed the menu carefully on the couch and wondered through to the bedroom, shower first then he would eat. Casually he flicked the light on and turned to the bed. There lying on the bed was a site he thought he had removed from his life, an item that seemed now to be haunting him. How they had got into his apartment was one thing but why they were here was another. He felt his body fill with frustration, anger and astonishment as he blinked in disbelief.

Sasha's panties were laid out on his bed staring back at him

Chapter Twelve

Avoiding the issue

Sasha's panties making a guest appearance back in his apartment after he had kind of ensured returning them to their owner had startled Jim slightly. It hadn't taken him long to put his initial thoughts of her somehow gaining access to his apartment to rest by deciding the cleaners must have put them in his room thinking they were his. The bigger question was how they had ended up in such a place that the cleaners had assumed they were his in the first place. He distinctly remembered taking them with him to the beach to meet her and was sure he had dropped them with the boxed gift, which now could be anywhere, before making his prompt escape.

It felt like they were mocking him, a lifeless inanimate object was subtly jabbing him in the side as if to say 'I told you so'. There was an outside possibility that somehow Sasha had got them to his room, maybe she had followed the cleaner in and left them there herself. But why would she want to be in his apartment? Maybe she hadn't seen him appear at the beach, maybe she didn't know that he was avoiding her, maybe she wasn't aware that he had seen her with her other man.

Calling this stranger her other man seemed unnecessary; their embrace had told him that it was him that was the other man. Then again she hadn't asked him to be anything more than just her friend; she didn't know how much he liked her. Now there was no point in telling her how interested he was in her anyway even the present he had spent his holiday money buying was insignificant to him. If he took it home he wouldn't have had anyone to give it to so maybe it was for the best that it was possibly now buried in the sand or had been picked up by someone else.

Thoughts of the mysterious reappearing panties had kept him awake until the early hours of the morning when he eventually drifted off to sleep on the couch with the TV in the corner humming away to itself.

Barely four hours had passed since he had finally drifted off before he found himself being woken by a banging and shouting noise. He felt his body jump with the shock launching one hand towards the floor to stop himself falling off the couch. Recomposing himself he twisted his head trying to work out where the noise was coming from and realised it was coming from his bedroom.

Slowly he dragged himself into a seated position; through his bedroom door he could hear a muffled voice. He recognised the accent straight away but the voice seemed to be one of sorrow and desperation. Quickly he glanced toward his front door, the curtains were closed, he had thankfully remembered to do that before settling on the couch.

"Jim, we need to talk, I know you're in there."

Sasha's voice was almost begging for his attention; it didn't make sense, why was she so desperate to see him?

Maybe she genuinely didn't know he was avoiding her, maybe she was worried for him and didn't know that he knew her little secret. Maybe he should go to her at the window and tell her to go away, that he didn't want to see her anymore. He thought about it for a while, if she hadn't seen him at the beach maybe she just thought he wasn't feeling very well.

"C'mon, Jim, just give me five minutes, I can explain everything."

Her second statement confirmed to him that she knew he was angry with her, he had heard lines like that before. One of the advantages of having so many female friends was that they told him the lines that they had heard from their boyfriends when they wanted to try and appease them with an excuse. 'I can explain everything,' what she meant was that she had worked out what to say to try and win him over, convince him everything was ok and try to keep things as they had been

In a way he was glad she had used such a cliché to try and get his attention because now he was sure he didn't want to entertain her cries at his window. He waited on the couch, unsure if it was safe to move, holding back the urge to use the bathroom. Clearly his body wasn't aware of his need to remain unseen and was protesting against him in the only way it could. He clenched his stomach hoping that he could restrain natures needs long enough for her to get bored and give up.

After a few tense moments of wondering if it was safe to move or not Jim got his answer. A heavy slap at the door told him she had given up trying at the back and was now trying to get his attention at the front of his apartment. Quickly he stood up and tip toed his way toward the bedroom door opening it quietly before dashing into the bathroom.

"Jim! Please!"

He could almost hear her crying through the door, this was unexpected unless it was her way of making a last ditch attempt to get his attention. Even if he wanted to answer her cries he couldn't, the room service meal was disagreeing with him and there was no way he could move from the toilet now.

Hearing her cry penetrated through him, her performance was award winning, she really didn't like losing but he wasn't going to let her win this time. He pondered and reflected on things for a moment as his bowels relieved themselves.

Jim had accepted that for reasons he couldn't understand Sasha liked running around with no clothes on but could that mean the hug he had seen wasn't what he

thought? There was a chance that it was her brother or father but he felt sure that there were very few circumstances that would make a hug with a relative in the nude acceptable. He ran through what he had seen in his head, the guy was older but not old enough to be her dad. He was fairly sure she hadn't mentioned a brother but even if she had – hugging your brother or sister naked seemed wrong even as a naturist.

If she was going to pursue him and try to convince him that the guy she was hugging was a relative he needed to stay out of the way. He had seen the village and as much as he liked it he didn't know if he could manage two days in a row there. He wasn't sure how much longer Sasha was going to continue her attempts or how long she had left of her holiday. One relief about holidays was that sooner or later people went home and he was fairly sure she had arrived before him so her time left was probably shorter than his.

The problem was that unless he went to his door to see if she was there he was potentially trapped. Years of gaming had taught him that if a person was waiting for you to appear the likelihood is they would wait near the front door so his escape would be better planned out the back window.

He stared at the garment he had that belonged to her wondering how or when he should attempt to return it. Daylight wasn't the ideal time especially considering that she had already made an attempt to contact him and it wasn't even eight a.m. yet. No matter what else she was he couldn't fault her on how keen she was to try to piece together her story.

Then again he didn't want her clothes littering his apartment for any longer than they had to. This left him with two options; the first was full of risks but involved handing them in to the reception as lost property. Reception was completely the wrong way to the direction he wanted to be travelling so not only was it impractical it was inconvenient. The second option was to discretely place them somewhere near her apartment in the hope that she would see them. This option although the more obvious solution came with its own risk because the last place he wanted to be seen was near her apartment.

Reluctantly he grabbed the offending article and a few essentials and made his way cautiously toward his bedroom window.

Peeking from the corner of the bed he scoped the area behind the apartment to ensure the coast was clear. Slowly he opened the window and threw a towel and a few other items out on to the ground listening for the thud telling him it wasn't far to jump. Carefully he climbed up on the window sill and slid out tipping the air beneath his feet until he found the ground.

Sneaking behind his apartment he felt like a character from one of the war games that he played online with his friends. He peeked at the corner and saw an empty footpath between his apartment and Sasha's. The obvious place to leave her panties was at the front so she would see them when she got to her front door but that was too risky. Slowly he moved toward her apartment gazing up at the back window which he could see had open curtains.

If he was clever he would be able to slide the panties on to the back window ledge without her noticing. Slowly he made his way along the back of her apartment keeping his back to the wall until he was underneath her window. From here he needed luck to be on his side because if she was near the window she would be bound to see him and the game would be over.

Turning himself to face the wall he edged backwards until he could see diagonally into her bedroom. There was no obvious movement, no one looking out of the window but that didn't mean she wasn't somewhere near the window so it was still risky. Gripping the panties in a ball he positioned himself against the wall and beneath the ledge and took a deep breath.

In a singular fluid movement he swung his hand up slamming the panties against the window ledge and dashed on crouched legs to the corner sliding out of sight. Breathing fast as he rested against the wall and listened for the sound of the window opening as he looked toward the path for anyone appearing. The coast was clear and no shouts or sound came from the window so he slowly peered back to confirm the garment was in position.

Relieved he noted that it was and let out a long deep breath.

So far everything was going as he had hoped, he had escaped his apartment, her panties were back in the proximity of her apartment, now all that remained was to make himself scarce for the day. Keeping as close to the line of the back of the apartments as he could he made his way towards the beach dashing in to the dunes as soon as he could to conceal his position. Now all he had to do was make his way toward the normal beach and find something to eat.

****

Sasha had woken up intentionally early, she had been frustrated by not being able to find Jim and resolve things with him but knew she had done all she could. It was clear that he was avoiding her and it annoyed her that he hadn't let her clear her name but she knew in her heart that if the roles had been reversed she would probably react in a similar way. Tucked under her pillow was the box that she had not let out of her sight since picking it from the ground. This box stood as a trophy in some ways, it was something she had to either try to achieve or something she had to accept she was not worthy to have.

She grabbed it as she slipped out of bed and held it close to herself; taking a deep breath, she contemplated her next strategy. She didn't know Jim too well but there were a few things she was fairly sure of about him. Firstly he was not good with mornings; his late arrival at the game had confirmed that. Secondly he wasn't comfortable with naturism, not yet, so if she was going to try to see him she would need to dress. She glanced over at the bikini she had laid out for herself and pondered whether it was worth the risk to confront him.

At this stage if she had lost what they had started to build up between them, even though it was hurting her, she would get through it with her friends. She didn't want to lose him completely; this gesture in her hands was in its nature the sweetest singular gesture a boy had made without expecting anything. Maybe he did expect something but he hadn't pushed her for anything which made him different to other boys. Losing him had made her realise that she might want more if she could just get him back but the first task was talking to him.

Nodding to herself she slipped the bikini on and looked in the mirror, was she really doing this for a man? Yes she was. She glanced over at the clock, it wasn't even seven thirty yet there was very little chance he was out of his apartment, the timing was perfect. She had agreed to meet Greg and Alice for breakfast, they seemed determined to make sure they helped her as much as they could whether it was in finding Jim or to keep her mind off him. She smiled vaguely, her first smile in nearly twenty-four hours, as she thought how great it would be to be able to meet them with Jim.

Gripping the small box she made her way out of the apartment and glanced over toward Jim's apartment. Logically the place to find him would be in his bedroom; quickly she slipped between their adjacent buildings and round toward his bedroom window.

She peeked in through the open curtain; the bed was neatly made and looked like it hadn't been slept in. She paused for a second, surely he wasn't already out, it was far too early, maybe he was at his parents but that didn't make sense. It wasn't worth dwelling on the apparently unused bed, this was her best opportunity to catch him and right the wrongs.

"Jim, we need to talk, I know you're in there"

She tapped hard on the window as she spoke, her words seemed a bit presumptuous but she wanted to seem positive.

She waited silently staring into the empty room waiting for him to suddenly appear from wherever he was hiding. There was no way he would know she was coming to his apartment so where was he?

"C'mon, Jim, just give me five minutes. I can explain everything."

She shouted with desperation in her voice, enough of the games she just wanted to get this sorted out now and get on with her holiday with or without him. She hoped that by telling him she could explain everything he would give her the time and they could get things back on track. Still she found herself greeted by silence from the empty bedroom, maybe he was in the front, she decided to check there, it was on her way toward meeting Greg and Alice anyway.

Shuffling round to the front of the apartment she noticed the curtains were closed. Adrenalin poured through her body, he was in there somewhere, the curtains must have been closed by someone and hadn't been opened again yet. She didn't particularly care why he hadn't made it to bed – there could be a million reasons, the fact was he was in there.

"Jim! Please!"

She almost whimpered the words as she beat her hand against the door.

She stepped back defeated, whatever was stopping him answering the door she couldn't try anymore. Her heart sank, he was clearly not going to make it easy for her, maybe he was in his parent's apartment, maybe he had confided in them after all, if he was there it was too early to go randomly trying another apartment. All she could do now was continue to try and find him after breakfast, surely he would eventually appear and they could sort things out for better or worse.

****

Greg was patiently sat with Alice waiting for Sasha to join them for breakfast. In all his wildest dreams he had never expected to be spending his holiday on a wild goose chase for his young friend. He didn't begrudge her the time, without her he wouldn't be happily in a long relationship with the girl he was sat next to. All he could hope was that somehow between the two of them they could either find this mystery attraction of hers or convince her that there were better things to do than to be chasing someone that didn't want to be found.

Sasha had spent the previous day continuously referring to him and how different he was to other boys. She had talked about how he didn't want to spend time with his parents and how funny it seemed to her that he wasn't comfortable in his own skin. It seemed strange to Greg that a person that didn't like naturism was at a complex dedicated to it but that had given him an idea. He had suggested to Alice that it might be sensible for him to try going further afield to try and track this boy down. While he was looking She could take Sasha for some girly time and try to prepare her for the worst while not saying it directly. Admiring his initiative Alice had agreed to his scheme and hugged him tightly to thank him for his dedication to his friends.

They had been sat waiting patiently for less than half an hour when Alice noticed the familiar figure of Sasha wondering up the path. The slow pace she moved with made it clear to them that she was still not ready to let go of Jim. She arrived and stood in front of them clutching tightly to the box she had not let go of throughout the previous day. Greg smiled at her vaguely, he wanted to hug her and assure her that everything was going to be alright but in his mind he couldn't be sure if it would help or not.

Somehow between them they had to bring this to a conclusion today.

****

Greg didn't waste any time after breakfast in making his excuses and leaving Alice to deal with Sasha. He knew exactly what he was going to do, his logic made perfect sense the more he thought about it. A teenage boy on holiday that didn't want to get found was either going to sit in his room or find somewhere away from the complex. If Sasha was correct about him not liking naturism it didn't make sense for him to stay around a complex full of it but logically the beach was going to be a lure for him.

Quickly he made his way to his apartment and picked up a towel and some shorts. He reflected on how strange it had been seeing Sasha dressing on the complex, in all the time he had known her he had never seen her do that. Maybe it was her way of holding on to her thoughts of Jim while she tried to get over him.

He waited until he got to the beach before reluctantly becoming part of the textile world for what he hoped was only a short time. On the complex's part of the beach was the volleyball court that was being used by a group of people that were probably having a private tournament. He reminisced for a few moments about days gone by, days before Sasha was even interested in boys when she would join Alice and himself in a fun knock around in that very spot. How ironic it seemed that a place of so many lovely memories was now the spot that had caused the current predicament. Shrugging off his memories he slowly walked past the sign marking the end of the clothing optional beach.

The sign itself was in some ways a cause for humour between seasoned travellers to the resort. On one side it gave a polite but stern warning that nudity might be encountered beyond that point and on the other it reminded residents that they had to wear clothes beyond the same point. There was a boundary marked by intermittent signs that separated the two parts of the beach. Officially a textile family could place themselves just centimetres away from the sign and be faced with a naturist family only a signpost away. Most people from either side of the boundary had the sense to use discretion and stay out of view in the first few metres but after that it was a free for all.

Greg kicked the sand lightly as he strolled down into the textile side of the beach. It was still early in the day but a few tourists were already making their way down to catch the day's sun. He gazed around without commitment making note of those around him while consciously looking out for a boy that fitted the photographic description Sasha had shown him. He was careful as he looked not to avoid larger groups of teenagers because he knew it was easy to befriend a group. If Jim had joined a group it would be a little bit harder to get his attention but somehow he felt sure he would manage it.

After about fifteen minutes of walking, he noticed a lone figure huddled up, gazing out to the sea. The closer he got, the more he realised that this figure bore a resemblance to the boy in the picture. Stopping close by, he gazed over and smiled vacantly before settling himself down in the warm sand. The boy acknowledged his greeting with a customary teenage grunt; if this was him, he hadn't recognised Greg. He would have to investigate further.

"Lovely day again," he remarked with a light-hearted expression. The boy smiled politely back and nodded.

"Is this your first time here?" He continued his meaningless conversation in a non-committal fashion.

"Yer, here with the rents, they got me staying at that place over there," the boy remarked, nodding in the direction of the complex.

Okay, Greg thought, that's a good start: he has indicated toward the complex. He tried to remain calm as he continued the conversation. Best way to play it was to confirm that he meant the same complex; there weren't many hotels in the area but it was worth being sure.

"You mean the naturist place?" Greg continued. "Yer," the boy scoffed.

"You're not into it, then, I guess," he commented.

The boy looked at him with an inquisitive nature, he paused before responding, it seemed strange that someone would ask such a random thing of him.

"No, it's weird," he grunted.

Casually Greg nodded and turned to look out to the sea this was far too coincidental, the boy looked like the picture, was staying at the complex and hated naturism. He contemplated his next move, he could either come straight out with it or make 100% sure first that it was him.

"I'm Greg, nice to meet you." He smiled as he reached toward the boy, offering a friendly handshake. It didn't take long for the boy to throw his hand back and shake his fingers limply.

"Jim," he answered.

Greg couldn't believe his luck, less than an hour off site and he had found the boy that he had been looking for since the previous morning. Part of him wanted to grab the boy and shake him hard as if to say why are you avoiding Sasha but he held back his urge. He gazed out to the sea again while he composed what he wanted to say in his head. Whatever he said he knew he would have to say it quickly, the boy might decide to move and there was no way he wanted to spend the rest of the day trying to find him again.

"Jim, can I talk to you about something? You look like a good listener."

Jim huffed; no matter what he did or where he was, he always seemed to take on the role of listener. There must be something about the way he dressed or the way he looked that drew people to him to tell their stories. He wasn't in the mood to become a counsellor for some stranger but he was curious about what this guy might have to say. For all he knew this guy's story might distract him from everything that had gone on over the last couple of days.

"Sure, why not?" He shrugged as he responded

Greg smiled casually and pulled himself back until he was closer to Jim so he didn't have to crane his neck as he talked.

"See, Jim, it's my girlfriend."

Jim heard the words and froze, he had promised to listen to this guy but this sounded like it could be a story he couldn't cope with right now. He contemplated leaving but felt bad making a sad excuse when he hadn't been asked for advice, just to listen.

"I have left her back at the hotel dealing with a mutual friend who is in pieces over losing a guy because of a misunderstanding."

Suddenly, Jim found himself feeling sorry for this mystery girl. Some guy had left her over a misunderstanding? That was terrible. He didn't even know the girl but he felt compelled to try and help with advice if he could.

"Turns out the guy she likes saw her with another guy and got the wrong conclusion and now she wants to find him and sort it out."

Jim looked at Greg with a puzzled expression; he could see some similarities to his own predicament creeping in.

"What would you suggest for her to do?" Greg asked trying to involve him in the chat.

Jim looked at him silently, this was a tough thing to respond to, he knew it was easy to make an innocent mistake. Too many times he had been confronted by the boyfriends of his friends who thought he was looking to get together with them. He looked at Greg with a pensive expression as he tried to work out what he would advise this girl to do.

"She needs to try and find the guy and sort it out, I guess." His answer was as vague as the question had been but he hoped it pointed in the right direction.

"I hoped you would say that, Jim" Greg continued casually. "My girlfriend is called Alice, her friend is called Sasha and the guy you saw her with was me."

It took Jim a few moments to register what had been said, that this was the guy he had seen Sasha hugging.

"That hug was completely innocent, Jim. I love my girlfriend and I think, if you give Sasha a chance, you will realise how much she likes you too."

Greg hadn't given him time to comprehend what was being said, he had pre-empted the objections perfectly. He could see Jim trying to take it all in, the tension that had built in his shoulders was starting to relax as he ran through what he was hearing in his head.

"She has a box from you, Jim; she hasn't let it go since yesterday."

Dumbfounded by this statement, Jim felt both his stomach and his jaw drop, Sasha had his box, at least it hadn't got lost. Everything he thought he knew had just been blown apart in a few moments of conversation with a guy that wasn't a stranger but the guy he had up until that moment wanted to hit.

Silence filled the air between them as Greg allowed Jim to work out what was going on. He didn't want to push him too far but he felt confident in the fact that not only was Jim still sitting down he hadn't burst into a volley of abuse over the whole situation.

"Would be great if you joined us for lunch Jim, we will be in the main building at about one p.m."

With his last statement made, he got up to walk away. He glanced over at Jim, who was looking up and nodding.

Chapter Thirteen

The messenger returns

Greg couldn't help feeling a sense of accomplishment as he casually walked away from Jim. Mixed in was a sense of relief that if Jim responded to their little chat in the way he was anticipating he would hopefully get to see his friend Sasha happy again before he went home.

For five years since she had first come to the complex he had stayed close friends with her and her family. He had watched her grow up from the age of eleven to the young lady that he now knew. He had a lot to be grateful to her for over the years including his relationship with Alice. Even if he hadn't have finally got together with Alice he couldn't ever see Sasha as anything other than a friend.

She was more like a sister to him than anything else and it had been a pleasure to be a small part of her life. They had stayed in contact briefly over the years through emails and she had always told him when her family were booked to visit the resort. Since moving in with Alice they had both shared light conversations with Sasha and knew her opinion of boys.

It hadn't come as a surprise to him that Alice had encouraged Greg to book their holiday to coincide with Sasha's family. It was always nice to know that there would be someone they knew and could get along with on their holiday.

Greg gave a second passing glance at the volleyball net, the group that had been playing when he set out were now resting across the makeshift court. He gazed down at his shorts; it felt like he had been punished for the last hour by having to wear them in the morning heat. He gripped the waist band and paused before sliding them off. As much as he wanted to get back into the naturist way of life he also wanted to make sure that if Jim arrived for lunch he didn't feel awkward about joining them.

Alice was bound to question him remaining dressed when he caught up with her but he could discretely update her on his good news and hopefully encourage her to follow suit. He glanced down again, a couple more hours of wearing clothes and then it was back to normality, it was a small sacrifice in anticipation of the reunion of Sasha and Jim.

****

Jim watched as the stranger who had in some ways counselled him and given hope back to his holiday walked away. It was refreshing to see that he was going to be left to his own devices and not frog marched back to the resort like a naughty child. If he had been escorted back he felt sure that despite his interest in meting up with Sasha he would probably find an excuse not to just to prove a point. His back-up plan would be to somehow get news to her at a later stage and see how things went from there.

All his careful considerations of back-up plans seemed irrelevant as he realised that everything was there for him, it was up to him to either seize the opportunity or else let it go. He watched until Greg disappeared out of sight before lying back in the sun to contemplate what he was going to do. There was no doubt in his mind that he was going to be there at one p.m. but he wasn't sure how he was going to handle the meeting.

Going into the main building full of confidence seemed like the wrong way to approach the situation. He decided that would give too much of an 'I knew it all along' impression to his appearance. Going in cautiously with a well-rehearsed script was also too rigid, that would look like he was being bribed into turning up just to please someone. Somehow it seemed that the best thing to do was to turn up and see what happened.

Picking himself up he looked around the beach, this may be the last time he would see a normal beach during his holiday. Normal people wearing clothes and just enjoying the beach running in and out of the sea or bathing in the sun were unlikely to feature in his future. If things went well with Sasha he felt sure she wouldn't want to bother with the clothed side of the beach.

Then again there was a possibility that things might not go well with Sasha and that what Greg had told him wasn't fully true. He felt sure after his early morning visit from her that she wanted to sort things out with him but maybe it was just to clear the air. Maybe she had already given up on him after he made it obvious he was ignoring her. If it all went wrong at least he had an idea where he could hide but for now he wanted to remain positive.

Slowly he wondered back toward the complex, even though he knew Sasha was there and hopefully waiting for him the idea of being back in a place full of nakedness still sent shudders down his body. He stopped for a moment as he reached the border between the textile and the naturist side of the beach. What if Sasha didn't know that Greg had arranged to meet her for lunch? Would that mean she wouldn't be wearing anything?

Suddenly he realised not only was he possibly going to be having to deal with seeing her naked Greg and his so far unknown girlfriend would possibly be naked too. Why had he agreed to meet at lunch time? Why couldn't he have asked to make it dinner time when they would have to be dressed? Too late to be worrying about it now, the arrangement had been made and although he knew he could try to arrange meeting her on his own later it seemed like a lot of unnecessary effort when a meeting had been handed to him on a plate.

If the chances were that Sasha and her friends were going to be naked maybe he should try and make the effort too. Maybe this was the opportunity he had been hesitantly waiting for to let her know that he was willing to try it. He pondered for a minute pulling the waist band of his shorts forward and peering down at himself. No he wasn't ready to let his genitals make a guest appearance, not quite yet – there were too many factors that could go wrong to risk it.

He continued slowly down the beach until he could see the dunes that lead back to the complex and the volleyball court. A few people were casually laid around the court in a noncommittal fashion. Volleyball was currently not his favourite sport, but then again sport had never really been his favourite subject at school anyway. It seemed more like torture than exercise, especially in the colder months during which for some reason outdoor sport seemed to be a favourite.

First part of school sport was the popularity contest that was conveniently named team picking. As he wasn't amongst the best players of any sport but thankfully not one of the least liked people of his year Jim was always somewhere in the middle of the pecking order. He felt sorry for the last few players because even if they were anywhere near as good as he was their level of being liked always got in the way of their being selected. Sometimes to prevent the burden of being picked last the teacher would number people off but this was more the exception than the rule.

Once teams were picked came the challenge of how to define one team from the other. Shirts vs Skins seemed to be a favourite amongst the teachers when it came to the boys sports. Jim had been reprimanded many times during geography classes for gazing out of the window while the girls were playing hockey in the hope that their teacher might choose the same team definition. Experience, extra homework and a few detentions had taught him that, during the girls' PE time, the teacher could always conveniently find sashes to define girls' teams.

Jim found himself wondering how teams would be defined in a naturist environment. Would one team be forced to wear shirts? Or would they find an alternative way to work out who was on which team. He tried to imagine soccer being played on a professional basis by naturists' team. Companions would obviously know who was who but the commentator's job would be a nightmare. Maybe stick on numbers could be used they would be far more practical and easy to remove than a permanent tattoo. Not only were tattoos impractical for player definition but it would make team transfers much costlier and more painful.

Refocusing himself Jim decided that it made sense to stay out of the way until lunch time. Even though he was excited about the possibility of sorting things out with Sasha he liked the idea of doing it with others around just in case it all went wrong. Retracing his steps he walked back to his apartment pausing briefly outside Sasha's bedroom window when he noted that the garment he had left there was still on the window pane.

Maybe he could hand it back to her in person, use it as some kind of icebreaker to start talking to her. He thought for a moment but decided it wasn't a good move as presenting an undergarment to someone was possibly the worst thing to do under any circumstances.

'Here, I think you left this with me' with her panties dangling off a finger was possibly the worst thing he could ever think to say. The only circumstance that would be acceptable in was one in which he didn't care or didn't want to see her again. With Sasha it was quite the contrary, after his unexpected talk with Greg he wanted to see if he could rebuild their relationship not destroy it.

****

After looking round the complex for half an hour with no luck Greg decided to head back to his apartment. Time was now of the essence if he was going to have everything in place for his planned reunion between Jim and Sasha.

Running in through the front door, he made his way quickly to the bathroom to refresh himself while he tried to work out what he was going to do. In reality he knew it didn't really matter if he didn't get to see the girls before lunch, their arrangement was already in place and agreed but it would make thing easier if everyone was covered discretely just in case Jim arrived.

He had to think positively, he had spent the entire journey back from the textile beach hoping that Jim would arrive and the more he thought about it the more likely it was going to happen. Jim hadn't become defensive when he had been told about what had actually gone on between Sasha and himself he had actually appeared to be interested. Even when Greg had left him on the beach he seemed quite positive about meeting them. Greg knew that sometimes a nodding gesture was non-committal and in effect could be used to just get rid of an unwanted person but intuition told him it was likely to happen.

He breathed a sigh of relief as he splashed the cold water on his face, even in the early part of the day the heat was intense and walking into the morning sun for half an hour had left his cheek feeling sore. He stared into the mirror, there was a redness appearing just below his eyes which he knew before the end of the day would become irritating but it was all in a good cause. Grabbing a towel he made his way into the bedroom and saw a hand written note waiting for him on the bed.

Greg,
Sasha sorted, we are in the sauna, look forward to seeing you soon Love
Alice x

Suddenly his day had hit a complication; there could be a thousand different implications to the words 'Sasha sorted'. All the good fortune he had had so far could be in vain if Alice had said the wrong thing while he was away. He knew Alice wouldn't intentionally do or say anything to her to change her opinion but Sasha was very influential and strong minded. He had seen her before when she had made a decision to do or not to do something; there was very little chance of changing that. Grabbing the note he gazed up as if he was looking for divine intervention and ran out of the apartment and up to the sauna.

Trying to keep a casual approach Greg walked through the door into the sauna and saw Alice and Sasha casually sitting and talking as if nothing was wrong. He glanced at Sasha's hands and noticed the box she had been cherishing was missing but then again it wouldn't make sense to have it in a sauna. What concerned him more was that she had discarded the bikini that she had been adamantly wearing when they met for breakfast. Keeping as positive as he could he also put this down to being in a sauna and smiled over at them as he walked in.

"Hi, girls," Greg kept his voice amicable as he glanced between them, conscious that he was the only one who was partially dressed.

Sasha waved over at him with a warm smile as she saw him appear. She didn't seem either upset or surprised that Jim wasn't with him.

"Alice, can I speak to you alone, quickly?" He was getting more concerned about how carefree Sasha was.

He needed to discretely fix whatever had been said without getting her hopes up too much. Smiling and leaning over to whisper something in Sasha's ear that made her giggle politely Alice got up and walked over to Greg kissing him lightly on the cheek as he guided her out of the sauna. Excitedly she grabbed Greg by both hands and jumped up and down gently as she looked at him.

"I think she is finally getting over him," she said with a chirp in her voice.

Greg looked at her, this couldn't be any worse timed than it was, if he hadn't accidentally found Jim this would be great news but all his plans would be in vain if he couldn't reverse whatever Alice had done, quickly.

"That's great, but I have found him and sorted everything with him."

Alice stopped jumping and her expression weakened to a less positive smile. In all her wildest dream she had never expected Greg to come out with such a statement. Suddenly she had to try and think of a way to undo everything she had carefully done to get Sasha back to her happy self. Before she did that she needed to know more about how he had found Jim and what exactly had happened.

Quickly he explained all about the surprise encounter with him on the textile beach. With a serious look he told her about how he had tentatively arranged for Jim to meet them at lunch time before adding in a request for her to grab something to wear before lunch. Alice's expression got deeper and deeper as Greg revealed the contents of his morning adventure.

"But," Greg said abruptly, "there is a slim chance that he won't join us so whatever you do, don't get her hopes up."

Alice ran through everything she was being told in her mind and nodded vaguely at Greg as the door into the sauna opened and Sasha appeared. In unison they smiled at her and pulled her into a three way group hug before Greg made his excuses and left them to their sauna. He glanced back at them briefly making sure that there was no suspicion and was relieved to see that both the girls had disappeared.

Alice sat casually close to but not fully next to Sasha, suddenly the game had changed but she had to see how easy it was to revert the main player to the original rules.

"Just wondering, if you were to see Jim again, what would you do?" she asked casually carefully watching Sasha's reaction

Looking up she smiled meekly, she hadn't expected such a trivial question after being told that it was better to enjoy her holiday than to dwell on it. Wrapped neatly in her bikini in a locker was the box that she still hadn't opened from him. It was now a shrine, a memory of what might have been if things had gone well for her and Jim. Around her wrist on a feeble looking elastic band was the key to the locker, she had never had to use them before but she felt sure it was secure. In her heart she knew that eventually she would open it and remind herself of what he had bought her but for now she wanted to keep it as a memory.

"I don't know," she responded quietly. "He was a lovely guy, so kind, so shy and just great fun," she added as she tried to maintain the brave face.

Referring to him in the past was understandable; Alice had tried to gently convince her to get on and enjoy her holiday. The words she used when she thought of him were kind words, not aggressive. She wasn't blaming him for what had happened, the chatty and happy impression she had shown since Greg had disappeared after breakfast was going to be easy to break if Jim appeared at lunch time.

"Never lose hope, Sasha," Alice responded calmly placing a loving hand on the knee of her young friend. "Sometimes it's worth holding on for a short while but don't let it get you down," she added.

Sasha gazed back. In some ways, this statement contradicted what Alice had said to her before but she liked what she heard.

"Greg is taking us for lunch," Alice said, trying to show she was changing the subject. "He has found a little place off-site so you will need that bikini," she added as she remembered what Greg had said about being dressed, just in case Jim appeared. Standing up to lead the way out of the sauna Alice casually held the door and led Sasha out before confirming that they would meet her at twelve thirty in the atrium.

Left alone for the first time that day Sasha wondered casually back to her locker pondering over the question Alice had put to her. No matter which way she thought about it, it seemed to be a strange question to ask after having spent so long telling her to just enjoy herself. Pondering on the statement as she opened the locker door, she accepted that, no matter what she did, it was probable that she would see him on the complex again. He couldn't hide for ever – that was probably what Alice had meant. Shrugging it off, she looked at her bikini; the clock on the wall told her it was nearly midday and Alice had asked her to meet them at twelve thirty, so it seemed practical to put it on now.

Carefully she unwrapped the box and looked at it. It was still too soon to look at its contents again; seeing what Jim had bought would just bring back memories she wasn't ready for yet. Draping her towel over her shoulders she grabbed the box clasping it in both hands as she made her way slowly to the atrium to meet her friends.

Sitting at a table that faced the bar and the doorway, Sasha saw Greg and Alice snuggled up together. They looked so contented it seemed a shame to disturb them but as soon as Greg spotted her he released Alice and waved over, beckoning her to join them.

Alice shuffled away from Greg freeing up a space between them for Sasha to sit down. She paused as she walked up to them wondering why they had beckoned her to sit between them but shrugged it off and nestled in the vacated space just in time for a waiter to appear with coffee for all of them precariously balanced on a tray. Greg glanced up at the clock, it was exactly half past, Alice had updated him on the situation with Sasha and now he felt more confident that if Jim appeared things could go well. All that remained was to wait and see if he was going to do as his expression had implied on the beach.

Sasha felt comfortable in between her two friends, even though she knew she was like some kind of human barrier between them they had invited her to that spot and she was happy to take it. She placed the box on her leg and watched it slip between her thighs as she leaned over to grab the coffee that had been bought over for her. Sipping at it, she was surprised by how nice and welcoming a hot drink was even on a hot day.

Nestling back in between them she picked the box back up and started to play with it, teasing it open slightly and letting it snap shut almost catching her fingers. She was careful never to open it enough to reveal its contents but found the snapping noise calming.

Greg glanced discretely up at the clock a second time as he sipped on his coffee, quarter to one and still no sign of Jim. Admittedly it was early but he was sure that if he was keen to sort things out with someone he would try to be early. Maybe fifteen minutes was too soon, maybe Jim had been delayed, maybe he wasn't the type to be too early or maybe he just wasn't coming at all. The only relief was that if Jim wasn't coming Sasha wouldn't be let down but Greg had decided that if Jim didn't appear he would make sure to hunt him down and challenge him about it.

Sasha had given up with the snapping the box open and shut and was now gazing round the room. She was getting impatient and hungry but didn't want to pester Greg into how long until they were going for lunch. It seemed pointless sitting in the atrium drinking coffee when they would have to walk to wherever they were going. She couldn't work out why he had chosen to take them off the complex to eat when there was a perfectly good restaurant available and it was free.

Impatiently Greg found himself staring at the door before glancing back up at the clock to find that only five minutes had passed since the last time he looked. He and Alice were making small talk about things that didn't make much sense to Sasha as his foot started to tap up and down. Ten minutes before an arrangement was still early in some people's eyes but he clearly remembered arriving to meet dates ten minutes before the set time only to end up waiting twenty minutes for them to either arrive or let him down.

He was tempted to suggest that Alice and Sasha went to look at the shops before lunch but that carried two flaws. Firstly there was a chance that Jim would turn up and if he did that and Sasha wasn't there he might disappear again. Secondly there was no logical reason to send them looking round the shops when they had got Sasha here under the impression they were going out for dinner.

Suddenly the door creaked open and with eagle eyes Greg looked over to see if it was Jim appearing. He felt let down when he saw the new arrival was an elderly couple who quickly made their way toward the restaurant. He slouched his shoulders just as the door creaked again, staring over at it again he saw the familiar figure of Jim walking in slowly. He glanced over at Alice who smiled and nodded back having recognised him from the picture she had seen. Sasha was busy rolling the box up and down her leg out of boredom as she waited to be told to go to lunch.

Jim looked over and was greeted by a silent smile from both Greg and the woman he assumed was the mystery girlfriend. Sat in between them with her head pointing toward her leg was Sasha pushing a little plastic box up and down her thigh. Just as Greg had told his she was not letting it out of her sight and was using it as a distraction.

"Can I give you a hand with that, Sasha?" The first words that had broken nearly two days of silence between them felt clumsy but seemed appropriate.

He watched patiently to see how or if she would respond to his random and trivial question that was only meant to announce his presence. He decided that even though she was partially dressed she probably wasn't aware of him being invited to lunch. Greg had obviously chosen not to tell her for reasons only he knew, surely he had made it clear by nodding in response to Greg's offer that he would be joining them but never mind.

Standing the width of the coffee table away from her he watched as she stopped rolling the square box. Her hand seemed to grip it tightly as she lifted her head and threw her hair back so she could see him. Slowly a smile started to form on her face as she clenched the box unsure what to do with it. She glanced left at Alice and then right at Greg who both smiled silently at her.

"Go get your man," Alice whispered softly in her ear, placing a hand lightly on her forearm to show encouragement.

With a vibrant bounce she lifted herself off the chair and threw herself towards Jim narrowly missing the coffee table with her shin. Landing clumsily against him she knocked him backwards slightly as she flung her arms around his neck. Natural instinct told Jim to catch her as she fell into him stepping back to balance himself as she pushed herself into his arms.

"I missed you, Jim," she whimpered softly as a single tear pushed its way between her cheek and his.

"Missed you too," he mumbled back as he looked over at the couch, grinning with relief at the man that had bought them back together.

Chapter Fourteen

Reunion

It didn't take long for Greg and Alice to make their excuses and disappear into the restaurant. Discretely Alice tapped Sasha on the shoulder muttering words that Jim could just about make out as being "We will catch up with you later." Sasha responded with a small nod that bounced off Jims shoulder as she whispered thank you. Left alone with Jim she pulled him toward the empty couch and directed him into the corner before gently sitting next to him and clamping him down with her arms.

Jim had been pinned into seats before but only as a child and even then it had been by the family dog. He had been told it was a comfort thing, a way of telling you they were there and you weren't allowed to leave. The position benefitted both parties to some extent because the person being pinned could benefit from the dogs warm coat adding a layer of heat to the chosen leg. In the summer this wasn't as nice but as with a lot of gestures pets made it didn't seem to matter to them if it was summer or winter.

Having their owner on such close quarters seemed to pacify a dog and allow them to fall into a deep sleep. This was the kind of sleep that often resulted in snoring or heavy bouts of canine flatulence. The end result of such unannounced passing of wind was that the owner felt compelled to try to escape the seating predicament which then led to a mournful look from the dog. Either that or the flatulence encouraged the dog to move first, unable to cope with the aroma produced by their own body.

With Jim having been put into the 'clamped to the seat position' by Sasha, he felt confident that it wasn't going to result in flatulence but there was a possibility that it may result in sleep. Her arm pressed across his body and her head resting on his chest had made it impossible to know if she was sleeping or just resting. Making the predicament awkward for Jim was that she had clamped him down in such a way that his left arm was trapped behind her.

Moving the arm he was sure would cause an element of discomfort to either her or him. Even though there was a soft leather effect cushion between his arm and the frame of the chair it didn't feel very thick with the dead weight of a body pressed on his bicep. If he moved his arm upward he would end up with everything from the elbow down to his hand flailing helplessly outside her body. Sliding it downward was just as risky, he could already feel clothing material in his fingertips and with the angle of his arm he was sure it wasn't her bikini top.

Lower clothing items when they were attached to the owner were risky to touch if you weren't sure of your status with that person. Even if the finger tips brushed the item by accident it could cause any level of dramatic response depending on how the girl attached to the item felt about it.

Jim had been unfortunate enough to have been on the receiving end of minor drama involving an accidental touching incident. He had been out with a girl and even though he liked her they had mutually agreed to be just friends. They had met several times under this agreement and this time it was to comfort her while she bitched about how the latest boyfriend had left her. He was used to this type of day out; he had endured it several times with different girls, each time ending with the 'just friends' hug.

After a couple of hours of shopping they had decided to take a rest and had found a bench to have their takeaway lunch on. Jim had been gazing around with nothing on his mind except the bus times to get home when he reached out to grab a handful of chips. Unfortunately for him his sense of direction had betrayed him and he had ended up with a handful of thigh.

The resulting feud had alerted the entire shopping centre that something was happening and he had been left with a startled expression and a volley of abuse. Thankfully after letting off steam, a few scowls and one threat to slap him she had calmed down and was suspicious but accepting his story of it being an accident. Jim decided there and then that the lessons of the day were to always watch what you were doing and exercise caution when in the vicinity of a woman's body. This didn't seem practical when sooner or later he was going to want to get into a relationship with a woman but for now it seemed a good rule. Following these steps had saved him a high five to the face on several occasions and kept him on the right side of friends and their boyfriends.

Even with all this experience he had not been able to avoid being in a position where his hand was currently in an area he had told himself was a no go zone. The ache in his arm told him that he was going to have to take a risk and move it soon just to keep circulation going. He pondered his options for a moment; both of them had unappealing sides to them. The moving the arm up and outwards was by far the least risky but it would leave his hand looking like it was lost as it waved out to the side beyond her back. Sliding it downward, although that was the more logical solution meant that he might lose her again if she took it the wrong way.

He gazed down, a sea of raven black hair greeted him, she seemed fairly sedate and calm against him. If she looked up at him he knew he would end up with a whip of that hair in his face and he was sure that if she didn't like where his hand was a hair sandwich was imminent. Taking a deep breath he closed his eyes as he slid his hand into a much more comfortable position slightly lower down her back. Moving his shoulder had allowed him to find a void between her buttock and the couch and gave him a much more acceptable position for his arm.

He waited cautiously to see if she noticed his arm had moved and how she reacted to it. Surely she would be aware that his hand was now hovering close to her bikini bottoms and would make the necessary adjustments. Her body started to wriggle; she remained silent placing her arm down on his waist as she moulded herself to the revised arm position. To his surprise she didn't protest about his offending arm, she didn't even comment on it, in contrast she felt like she was actually pushing her body closer to it.

This was new territory for him, he had expected a much more aggressive response but instead she had greeted it with a welcoming gesture. It was too soon to see how far he could push his luck but for now having the mound of her buttock practically in his hand was a good start. He heard her breathe a deep sigh of either relief or tiredness as she nestled deeper into his chest.

Feeling more comfortable and more positive that he wasn't going to be presented with a slap he started reviewing things in his head. He was relieved to be back on good terms with Sasha for more than one reason. Experience had told him that on holiday it was important to be part of a social group of some kind in order to avoid lengthy time with the rents. It was bad enough being forced to sit with them at the pool side or for meals during a normal holiday but the element of nudity made it even more important to avoid them.

He would have been happy if his social group had just included Sasha and himself but now fate had intervened and he knew that he was part of a wider circle. Greg and his as yet unknown girlfriend were now aware of who he was and would make efforts to be sociable with him. He had a lot to thank them for; without them, he would still be wondering aimlessly around the beach trying to spend as little as possible while making sure he ate substantially enough before hiding away in his apartment for the evening. Sasha had given him a taste of the outside world and with a few adjustments he felt sure he could avoid the rents and enjoy the evenings as long as he wasn't trying to avoid her as well.

The biggest problem with the introduction of two people that had reunited him with Sasha was that Greg now had a virtual upper hand. If he needed help with a crisis of some kind it would fall on Sasha and him to help out. Greg also had the 'don't forget it was me that got you where you are' status attached to him now. This was a status that Jim was familiar with as he had been the one picking up the pieces of a relationship at home on more than one occasion, who knew he would be on the receiving end of such a status while on his family holiday – no one could have predicted that.

Adding to his dilemma was the fact that although so far Sasha had accommodated his need to be dressed he was fairly sure Greg and his girlfriend probably wouldn't be as accommodating. Even if he spent the rest of the holiday covering himself there was no reason for them to do so. Jim was no stranger to female nudity but his limited experience of it hadn't been very positive.

His first encounter was when he was just twelve years old and during a session of homework in his bedroom had felt the need to use the bathroom. He had got all the way to the toilet and started relieving the pressure when he noticed his sister was cowering in a vague attempt to cover herself with the shower curtain as water cascaded down into her eyes and mouth, drowning out the blood-curdling screams. Making matters worse the flow of urine seemed to go on forever so he had no choice but to see the ordeal through to its bitter end.

His next taste of female nudity came just a year later when he was using the local swimming pool. Jim loved to swim and spent most of his time in the pool underwater where he felt the freedom of a fish. Unfortunately on this particular day the pool caretaker had been fairly heavy handed with the chlorine causing his eyes to sting. Taking care he stumbled from the pool into the changing room with his eyes mainly closed due to the severe stinging sensation. He followed the wall into the shower room and stripped his shorts off before fumbling for the pressure timed shower button on the wall. As the water started to cleanse his eyes he eventually opened them to find himself surrounded by middle age naked women.

On the positive side having more people that knew him meant there was less chance that he would be without friends for the full duration of his holiday. The biggest problem with befriending people abroad was that sooner or later they went home. This meant the group you attached yourself to had to have a good regular turnover of new members to cover the full duration of your stay. Without this constant flow sooner or later you became a group of one and that left room for the rents to try and make a summer holiday a family bonding experience.

Family bonding was okay in small doses; he didn't really begrudge the rents their attempts to build the family bond but he didn't really envy the idea of bonding with them naked. That type of bonding was a special kind that he didn't want to become part of. He had heard of special bonds like that before and was fairly sure some of the children at school had been the result of special family bonds.

Jim glanced round craning his neck to see the clock on the wall that was telling him they had been sitting here for fifteen minutes. The time didn't bother him, he was happy to be in such a position with Sasha but his stomach had been promised lunch and it was ready to start a protest. He peered down at the mound of hair that hadn't moved much since they had readjusted themselves and wondered if Sasha actually was asleep. If what Greg had told him had been correct there was a possibility that the whole fiasco had left her restless. He ran over the brief but significant conversation with Greg, the correction of the misunderstanding and the box, where was the box. She had been playing with it when he arrived and now he could feel her hands firmly attached to his body.

Pushing himself forwards slightly he could just about see it sat on the table in front of them nestled between two empty coffee cups. Since their reunion the waiter had decided it was better to leave them in peace than to try and clear up in front of them. Jim acknowledged this decision accepting that it must be difficult to know where to look when two people were in such an intimate embrace. The waiter probably knew that if he waited long enough eventually the table would be vacated and he could complete his job.

He grabbed Sasha's shoulder gently squeezing it to try and get her attention he felt safe doing this as she clearly was okay with him having his hand in much more intimate locations. Sleepily she looked up at him, a soft smile lit up her face as if she had been presented with an award she had worked all her life for. He nodded his head and pointed at the table with the hand that was propped over the arm of the couch.

"Time we put that on, don't you think?"

Sasha brushed her hair to one side as she heard his voice and felt a tear forming in her eye as she registered his words. She knew instinctively that even though his comment to others would seem cryptic he was referring to the gift she had been protecting for two days. The box had only been fully opened once since she had found it hidden under her panties on the beach. From that moment it had become a symbol, a penance, a trophy she was yet to achieve authority to own. In the excitement of seeing Jim reappear in her life she had forgotten all the setbacks and casually put the box down for the first time in two days.

Even when she went out with her parents for dinner and the evening no one had questioned her obsession with it. Although he had been disgruntled by its appearance at the dinner table her father had taken her mother's advice and not made an issue of it. As only mothers can do she had discretely debated the item with her father using a series of signs and mouthing words to him until eventually he had backed down.

Even after the meal when they had gone into the bar area her father had managed to withhold the temptation to ask her where she had got it from. Mum had hinted that it must be something special and Dad had paused before accepting that mother knew best. As an only child Sasha had been watched over and almost smothered with affection but both her parents knew that she was of an age when these sorts of gestures were going to start appearing in her life.

Brimming with excitement she leaned forward but felt Jim grab her shoulder to stop her getting the box. Confused she looked at him but realised that it was his to give her not hers to take. Freeing him from her clamping grip she moved across the couch to let him pick the box up. She didn't need to restrain his movement anymore, she felt confident that he wasn't going to run away. Smiling softly at her he pushed forward in the chair, his body ached as it moved from being held in the same position for so long. Twitching his shoulders he picked up the box and casually sat back glancing over at her.

He held it between his fingertips as he questioned in his mind whether he should open it or present it to her to open. Offering it toward her with a grip that looked like he might be handing over an armed bomb or perhaps handling his mother's best china he watched as she tentatively reached out toward it. Gripping the bottom of the box he waited as she slowly lifted the lid and peeked inside. Resting on a tightly packed bed of foam that had been designed to imitate velvet sat the decorative letter "S." Its chain had been threaded through the felt to prevent it moving around in the box.

Sasha pulled the chain delicately from the box and hung it over her hand watching the small decoration dangle beneath her fingers. As it swung gently from side to side lights caught it giving it an almost hypnotic sparkle. Jim watched Sasha as she examined it moving it to different angles so she could see the diamond effect stones shimmering. Carefully she gestured it toward Jim waiting until he had it hanging off his hand before she stood up.

Carefully she shuffled the table away from the couch cringing every time it screeched over the floor. She gazed back at Jim gesturing him not to move as he tried to stand up to help her. Gently she leaned over him pushing his legs apart with her feet as she separated his knees with her hands. Content that she had everything in the right place she gracefully knelt on the floor in front of him tucking herself into the gap she had just created.

Jim leaned forward, getting a brief attack of hair as she flicked it out of the way, presenting her neck and tucking her chin down she waited patiently for him. Jim looked at her; this was the moment he had waited nearly two days for, he knew how important this must be to her. Despite the seriousness of the moment he couldn't help having vampiric images popping into his head at the sight of her neck being freely presented to him. He wondered if Dracula had ever thought of giving a girl a necklace as a way to get her to show her neck to him.

Sasha could feel the cold of the tiled floor under her knees as she waited patiently for the necklace to be put on. She had her hair carefully bunched into her hands to prevent it from getting caught in the chain. One of the setbacks of long hair was that it could easily get caught in neck decorations. If a person was unlucky enough to be caught by this fate the struggle to free the neck decoration from the hair could be both a painful and time consuming job. Somehow hair seemed to have a mind of its own when it came to these situations and even the simplest of mechanisms such as the clasp of a necklace could become the cause of such disasters as split ends or hairs being unintentionally pulled out.

Even though she wasn't big on fashion and didn't really see the need for piling layers of makeup on she was passionate about her hair. She had been careful from a young age to look after it; she had never dyed it and always made sure to keep it clean and tidy. It was the one thing that had on some occasions delayed her going out to parties, not that she went to many, but if she did go to one she wanted her hair to look good.

There was a tingle of cold on her chest as the necklace fell into place; it was an exciting moment in her eyes because it marked the reunion of Jim and her. As she reflected back on it if she had been brave enough to put it on before reuniting with him she felt like she would have been even more determined than she had been to find him. Determination hadn't been lacking in her search for him but she felt like she would have been less willing to accept Alice's talk about preparing to move on with his gift around her neck as a reminder. She stood up clasping the necklace against her skin, it almost felt like it was meant to be there.

"Jim, I love it, it's a very sweet gift, thank you." She smiled, sitting gently back next to him as she spoke and rested her head against his arm.

Suddenly out of nowhere Jim had heard a word that to him was a nemesis: 'sweet'. He had heard that word so many times before, the last of which had been his mother as he tried to show an interest in Zante. On that occasion he had managed to hide his disliking for the word behind a nodding expression as he listened to his mother talking. He knew there was no way of getting the word removed from the English language but that didn't give one word the right to burden his life did it?

This time it felt like it was being used as some sort of penance for the misunderstanding that had pushed him towards avoiding Sasha. Surely he hadn't misread the signs with her had he? There was no denying that for fifteen minutes he had been trapped under most of her body but that word was making him wonder if it had been intended as a 'nice to see you again' cuddle. In the past he had only ever heard it used as a get out clause to ensure a friendship was maintained and to ensure that the 'sweet' boy would still be there if the girl using the word needed him. A gift had never been referred to as sweet unless it had been given as a birthday or Christmas present but this one had been neither of those two things.

His curse had followed him onto his holiday and was now being used to describe a gift that he had spent time picking out. Admittedly he hadn't expected a necklace to change things significantly between Sasha and him but in the same way he hadn't expected the word sweet to be used to describe his gift either. Maybe in this context it meant she liked the present but had hoped it was something more elaborate, or maybe it was too elaborate and she wasn't sure what he might want as an implication of getting her it.

The deeper he considered her statement the more he realised that his little gift might hint that he expected something in return. That wasn't the intention at all when he got her it, admittedly he would like her to become more than just another friend but he wouldn't use something like a necklace to say that. Buying a gift in anticipation of more seemed almost seedy, like an advance payment for their future development. Maybe he should try to discretely rectify the situation with her before it made things awkward.

"You're welcome," he responded with a vague smile.

Sasha nodded acknowledging his response as she continued to play with her new necklace. Distracting his thoughts from the whole situation that had occurred with the use of the word sweet his stomach finally gave in to its needs and let out a noisy growl. He glanced over at the clock trying not to make a big issue about his involuntary reminder that they hadn't eaten. It was 1.45 p.m., the restaurant didn't have long left before they would stop serving lunch. If that happened they would have to find somewhere else to eat which would mean going off site again. He didn't mind the idea of going off site, at least he would have company this time but he would much rather just relax with Sasha for the afternoon.

Sasha giggled politely as she heard his stomachs protest.

"Think someone's hungry, don't you?" she commented as she sat up to face him.

Leaning in toward him she kissed him gently on the cheek, this was a thank you for the gift as much as anything else.

"Maybe it's time I took my boyfriend for lunch, what do you think?" she asked, biting her bottom lip as she waited for his reply.

She had never used that word on anyone before, and she had never imagined it would be her making the suggestion. All her friends had told her of how the boys they had dated had asked them out not once had she been told that a girl had asked the boy. She knew of some girls that had chased the boy they were with but sooner or later the asking out part was always done by the boy.

She watched Jims as he relaxed into a smile and his face glow as he registered what she had said. It was clear to her that he hadn't expected it; she wasn't sure why he was so surprised when she had made it as clear as she could that she wanted him.

Surely he didn't think she would sit smothering just anyone, she certainly wouldn't have done it with just a friend.

"No, Sasha," he responded calmly, "your boyfriend should take you to lunch." He stood quickly and grabbed her hand to walk with her proudly into the restaurant.

Chapter Fifteen

Status upgrade

Just like a lot of phrases that he had heard adults using, Jim had often pondered over the idea of being like a dog with two tails. He understood that the expression was meant to show a state of happiness and it was common knowledge that a dog's tail was used by the dog to show happiness. They were as far as Jim knew the only animal that used their tail in such a way which begged the question of whether it was actually being used to show happiness or not. Regardless of the possibility of having misread the signs Jim wasn't sure if having two tails would make the dog happier.

He could see several disadvantages to having the second appendage presumably poking out of the same place as its original. Firstly there was the co-ordination issue, fair enough the brain would probably handle that with ruthless efficiency but two tails had a good chance of clashing with each other. As a rule tails of dogs seemed to be fairly skinny, in fact if they hadn't been blessed with the movement ability you would swear they were just a long collection of bones covered with skin and fur to make them aesthetically pleasing.

The second disadvantage in his eyes was that when a dog wasn't wagging his tail in an assumed expression of pleasure he or she was chasing it. As the child of a dog owner Jim had spent several of his younger days laughing at the family pet chasing and on some occasions catching his tail. Once caught the tail was usually tugged at and then released presumably due to the pain that would be caused by biting on part of one's own body.

With all that in mind, Jim had woken up happy to refer to himself mentally as being like a dog with two tails. He had pushed the vision of a beagle with its two tails wafting the air in perfect harmony from his mind and was now focussed on his latest promotion to the status of boyfriend.

He had never been promoted to this status before; his road had always stopped at the best friend or sometimes best friends forever. Both of these were titles he had been relieved to have on more than one occasion. But having stopped at the best friends station it had proved to be a dead end with no one willing to reverse the engine and change to the relationship track.

Sasha had changed all the rules, she had given him the status as her boyfriend and even if it was only a holiday thing he was happy to be trying out the new position with her.

Thankfully, his years of experience of clearing up the mess that had been left by others had left him in a good position for this new and challenging role. He had witnessed a number of the pitfalls and traps that could cause stress and in some cases end a relationship and he felt confident he could avoid most of them.

The problem with relationships was that they seldom followed the same path as each other. What had bought one couple together had in some cases spelled the end for another couple. There was no correct thing to do or say to ensure the solidity of a relationship, every day was in some ways a new challenge. Like a hunter out in the thick of a forest he would have to be careful with every step just in case someone had set a trap for him to fall into.

His face ached from the smile that seemed to have been a permanent fixture since their lunch together. He wasn't sure but he had a good idea that he might have actually been smiling all night - if that was possible.

He could see advantages to his first experience of having girlfriend being one he met on holiday. The first advantage was there was no complication as to where you were going to meet that person. There was also no need for a phone meaning the chances of miscommunication were limited. Even with all the advantages he knew one of the biggest disadvantages was that holidays didn't last forever.

That left him wondering if he should try to limit how close he got to Sasha, surely she was aware that their time together was going to be limited. It was too soon to decide which way they were going to take things after they went home but he felt confident that if they stayed as close as they seemed to be getting they could arrange something.

"Stop thinking negative," he mumbled to himself, giving his head a virtual slap and telling it to just enjoy what he had and take things as they go.

Despite teasing his way past a negative spell he could still feel part of a smile stuck to his face. He decided this part smile was what the oldies referred to as a smirk, something he had never been fully aware of doing but clearly had done before.

'What you smirking about?' was a common question fired at him by the rents from the age of five upwards.

He didn't have any way of knowing what a smirk was at such a young age but it seemed clear that whatever it was he shouldn't be doing it. His first reaction was to try and clarify what a smirk was but that would be followed by questions of what he had been up to. This was where life got complicated as a five year old, normally all he had been doing was playing in his room but convincing the rents of that was difficult when their focus was on his 'smirk'. If he did confess to having done something that could be seen as even mildly bad he would be reprimanded for it, but saying he hadn't would be deemed as a cover up so there was no way of winning.

He felt lucky that he wasn't sharing his apartment with the rents, if they saw him with this permanent grin they would be bound to ask why. This time he had a genuine reason to be happy and he knew they had met Sasha but they would still give him a hard time if he said he had a girlfriend. He had endured it before with girls that they thought were his girlfriend so he couldn't imagine it being any different now he actually had one.

Peeking over at the clock, he could see it was only seven thirty a.m., a time he seldom saw when he was at home and yet he was awake and ready for the day. The morning sun was already peeking through the curtain and dancing on his shoulder as he contemplated staying in bed a little longer. Shrugging off the temptation to remain in his man made cocoon of covers he flopped his feet out of the bed and on to the cool floor.

Lifting himself out of the bed he stood briefly looking in the mirror and noted redness on his shoulders that was slowly giving in to a healthy tan. In contrast his legs still seemed pale which didn't make sense because they had seen as much of the sun as his upper body. Pulling his shorts down a bit he made note of the break in healthy tan and pale unexposed skin. This holiday held a unique opportunity for him to get an all over tan if he wanted to do so.

Even if he did get an all over tan there was no real advantage to it when he got back home. Friends would joke with him about having one and expect him to laugh back making out he hadn't been walking around naked even if he had. Then again if he said that he had gone for it and stripped bare to make the most of the sun none of them would believe him. He had no way of proving his claim without actually showing them and he was fairly sure his friends wouldn't appreciate him doing that.

His female friends would probably turn away in disgust at seeing his parts naked. Not that there was anything wrong with his parts but they would consider that the boundary between friendship and wanting more. In the same way they wouldn't expose themselves to him to prevent crossing the border, underwear was the least he had seen any of them wearing. The male friends would make out that they had no interest in seeing his body but he knew a few of them would want to confirm that he wasn't overly large or small beneath the boxers.

Now Sasha had given him the pass to cross the line into being a boyfriend rather than just a friend he wondered how it was going to affect things. Cuddles would still be allowed, he was fairly sure about that but was there a way of cuddling a person that could possibly be naked without it causing arousal? He wasn't sure. He hadn't spent much time watching how other couples handled the intimacy of a cuddle. Then there was kissing, he was used to kissing on the cheek, even relatives did that, but now he had entered the realms of on the lips kissing something he had made failed attempts at just once before.

Lucy Sheldon had been the first girl to accept his offer of meeting up outside school. He had waited until his friends had confirmed she was single and had even been told she was interested in him which boosted his confidence. Tentatively he had mentioned taking her to the cinema and was grateful when she agreed but cringed when she said it had to be a chick flick. As it was his first date it didn't matter to him, the main thing was that she had agreed to go on a date with him.

He had arrived at the cinema early to avoid being caught out with the 'I was there but you weren't' trap. She had arrived a few minutes late but still, she had arrived and that was what counted. They sat through the movie and as he had suspected she had used his shoulder as a handkerchief more than once. Afterward he had done the gentlemanly thing and walked her to the bus stop and waited with her for the bus.

On its arrival she had moved in to hug him and that was when he had misread the signals. He should have been quicker to realize when she kept referring to him as sweet but he wasn't thinking straight. As she tried to pull away from the hug he went in for the kiss, he couldn't even claim it as a good night kiss as it was the middle of the afternoon. She was quick to stop him with a volley of abuse and a heavy slap to the left cheek as she released herself from his grasp and ran on to the bus. They avoided each other at school for the rest of the year and thankfully she moved away before school started again.

Since that fateful night he had made attempts at the sort of kissing he associated with relationships but only with the help of romantic films and the back of his hand. There seemed to be a lot of eating motions involved in the advanced stages of partner kissing but it seemed to work in the movies. On one occasion he had kissed his hand so hard that he ended up with a sore looking red mark. Making note of it he decided that was enough practice and had stuck to just watching the different techniques on film.

There was a possibility that he wouldn't get to the big kissing with Sasha, maybe that wasn't what she had in mind for them when she had referred to him as her boyfriend. He shrugged at his reflection in the mirror, he wasn't going to find out what she wanted until the time was right and he was fairly sure she would let him know what she wanted as their holiday progressed. One thing he felt sure about with Sasha, she wasn't the type to hide her feelings, if she wanted something he was sure she would do everything she could to make sure she got it.

"Just go with it, Jim," he mumbled to himself and he smiled into the mirror and made his way into the bathroom.

While she was on holiday Sasha liked to sleep with the curtains slightly open, the feel of the morning sun tickling her skin was so much nicer than the grey skies she was used to at home. Feeling the first rays warming her head she turned on to her back and stretched under the thin blanket that was covering her body. Despite the day time being comfortably warm enough to embrace the naturist way of life the nights had a chill to them that would force the stubbornest naturist to cover up. Refusing to bring night clothes on her holiday the blankets were the only thing available to her against the cool of the night.

Brushing her stomach gently like a person contented by a large feast she slid her hand up her body until she reached the necklace that she was now officially able to wear. She kept her eyes shut as she traced the delicate outline of the initial that was pressed lightly against her chest. She had won the right to wear this but it had taken the help of her friends to get her into that position. She knew without any doubt that if it hadn't been for them she would not be where she was now and the necklace would probably still be in its box.

Once they had been reunited she had felt it important to let Jim know how much he meant to her and had been happy to react to his nervous touch as they sat together. She had noticed how delicate he was about holding her close but she didn't care, he was hers and he had to know it. The presentation of the necklace had been the ultimate confirmation that he was interested in her and although it had been a bold move she had been confident in labelling him her boyfriend after he had given her the gift.

Having spent time without Jim through a terrible misunderstanding she felt like she knew and understood the phrase absence makes the heart grow fonder. She had denied to herself that she was falling for him but his shyness and amazingly chivalrous ways had grown on her. So many times in the past she had got on with boys on holiday but had gone out of her way to stay clear of anything deeper than friendship.

On holiday it was even worse than at home because boys would go after just one thing knowing that if it didn't happen they probably wouldn't ever see the girl again. At least back home they would have to put up with the rejection and live with the fact that they would probably end up seeing that person every day, small villages made bumping into people unavoidable. Jim hadn't tried anything which made him different; he hadn't pushed her into her decision to call him hers. If anything he had actually seemed happy to keep her as a friend and she did wonder if they would be a couple now if it hadn't been for the incident. Something inside told her that they would have got together eventually regardless.

It was a happy coincidence that she had actually been on the complex this year, she had hinted to the parents about finding another place to visit but they were set in their ways and now she was thankful for it. She hadn't wanted to find anywhere as elaborate as Disneyland or Terra Mitica in Spain. She knew most girls would love to be part of the magic of Disney but to her it was important that the holiday allowed her to be the naturist she loved being.

Although she enjoyed nature she hadn't wanted something cultural like the mountains of Italy. Nature and heat were important parts of her holiday but she liked being able to explore both without the burden of having to dress and she was sure in the Italian mountains she would get arrested for not wearing clothes. All she had asked for was to see what it was like on a different naturist resort like maybe one in Croatia or Playa Vera. Mentally she noted that on this occasion she had to thank her parents for not changing their mind.

Even though, in her mind, she had never had a real boyfriend back at home, she had endured a few false starts. The most memorable was her date with Michael O'Riordan he had been nearly forced upon her by both of their parents. Reluctantly she had agreed to go with him to the village fair that was around for two weeks every year. Makeshift rides and stalls appeared overnight in an unused field that probably earned the landowner his salary for the fifty weeks it was empty.

She had been pleasantly surprised at how the date had gone; he had not let her pay for anything, even buying her candy floss. When they got to the roller coaster he had promised to keep her safe which seemed to be a brave statement considering it was him that rushed to the bathroom afterwards to throw up but the thought was there. She had been forced to stop him when he had tried to get more out of her than a kiss on the cheek but she was used to that.

The real deal breaker was the next day at school when she accidentally heard him talking to his friends as she left the library. Something inside told her to keep out of sight and just listen which she was glad she did. She heard him graphically telling his friends lies about how forward she had been and how keen she had been and even creating stories about getting to second base with her. Patiently, she waited until she heard him mention that they were definitely an item before walking out of the library and challenging him about his bad stomach. The silence that followed seemed to be an appropriate time to land the palm of her right hand across his face before walking off. She heard from one of her friends that the hand print was still vaguely visible three hours later when the school bell rang.

Slipping gracefully out of bed she looked over at the chair that held her small selection of swimwear. If anyone had told her at the beginning of her holiday she would have worn it so many times in her first week she would have laughed at them.

Draped over the back of the chair was the silky dress she had worn on the first night she had met Jim, that dress held some lovely memories but it was too formal for day wear. She pondered for a second whether she could risk going with the naturist dress code but chose not to risk it. Jim hadn't been comfortable with naturism from day one and even though she longed to get him into it so she could enjoy her holiday the way she liked to she had to entertain his need for clothes a little while longer first.

It was important to her that today went well for them; it was their first day officially as a couple. No one knew that they were a couple yet which took the pressure off them a little bit and gave them time to get used to each other. The best way she could think of to do that was to go somewhere that would potentially be unused or at least quiet. In a moments inspiration she remembered there was a small Jacuzzi near the indoor pool, no one used the indoor pool unless the weather was bad and it was early morning too so the chances were it would be empty.

Selecting a bikini she reluctantly put it on looking at herself in the mirror as she tied the bra strap. She looked like a normal teenager on a normal holiday and as much as she despised the idea of it she knew it was for a good cause. Choosing not to wake Jim she quickly wrote a note telling him where to meet her and slipped out of the door.

****

Having decided that it was pointless going back to bed now that he had made the effort to get up Jim wondered through to the front room of his apartment. He contemplated as to why he hadn't taken the time to make arrangements to meet Sasha today but knew that one way or another they were bound to find each other. It wasn't as if either of them was trying to avoid one another now in fact it was quite the opposite. Nearly every day since first meeting they had either arranged a place to meet or Sasha had knocked at his door. Today he was up early, possibly too early but he had decided as they hadn't arranged anything he should make the effort to meet her at her apartment for a change.

Casually, he slumped on the couch having decided it wouldn't be good manners to knock on someone's door before eight a.m. when they were on holiday unless it was an emergency. Browsing through the menu he remembered his previous attempt at room service that hadn't agreed with his stomach. Maybe he had just been unlucky; then again if he was going to have room service again it hopefully wasn't going to be a dining experience for one. He heard a shuffling noise and peered round to see something slowly appearing under his front door. Although he was tempted to get up and see who was pushing it through he knew there was a chance it was the rents and decided not to bother.

Inch by inch a folded piece of paper made its way in under his door and then stopped as if it had run out of energy. He waited a few moments before quietly making his way over to investigate into what his mystery gift was. Bending down he noticed it was a piece of paper similar to the ones he had seen somewhere in his apartment and realised it was a note from someone on the complex. He paused for a moment realising that the likelihood of it not being someone on the complex was a million to one and mocked himself for ever thinking it could be.

One thing he was sure was that it wasn't his allowance from the rents; it was too early in the holiday for them to be giving him that and knowing them they would want to hand it to him. Then again it might be a note to meet them somewhere in the hopes of presenting it to him. He had dreaded having to meet them for any reason during this holiday, especially during the day, but he knew it was inevitable. Bouncing down onto the couch he relaxed back into the soft cushion and opened the note.

"I'll meet you at the Jacuzzi, if you're not too late getting up Love S x."

At first seeing a note from Sasha came as a surprise to him, why hadn't she knocked for him? She always had in the past. Maybe she was in a rush to get up there and wanted to make it a surprise for him when he got there. It didn't matter, the main thing was that now he had an arrangement made and he knew where to meet her.

He peered at the time and noted it still wasn't eight a.m. yet, barely anyone would be around, maybe a few early breakfast people but the complex wouldn't start getting busy for at least another half an hour. Maybe this was a good time to try naturism for the first time, it was only a few minutes' walk up to the main building and he could surprise her when he got there. Then again he had to walk past the rents apartment and knowing his luck they would appear just as he passed their door. Keeping the risk factor in mind he decided it was better to wait until he was in the main building to decide whether he was going to go for it or not.

Grabbing a towel he ran out of the front door and looked over at the rents apartment. No sign of them, quickly he locked his apartment and jogged past their apartment and up to the main building. He had found the swimming pool once before and felt fairly sure the Jacuzzi must be somewhere near it. Sliding through a door near the restaurant he made his way excitedly past the windows of the indoor pool. He peeked in and saw that there was only one person swimming up and down doing his pre breakfast laps.

Opposite the door into the pool was an unlabelled wooden door, to him it made sense that this door would lead to the Jacuzzi. He took a deep breath and looked down at his shorts, there was never going to be a better time to try naturism without anyone except her knowing. Less thought more action he muttered to himself as he slid them down and pushed through the door.

"Morning, Hun, bet you didn't expect this." The grin that had been fixed to his face overnight had returned to its place as he slid through the door.

"Morning, Jim," a chirpy voice came back to him.

The voice that he heard wasn't Sasha; he stood frozen to the spot as he realized he wasn't in the Jacuzzi but some kind of steam room. His surprise for Sasha had backfired on him in the worst way he could think possible.

Sitting casually, looking back at him, was his worst nightmare. The Rents.

Chapter Sixteen

An awkward encounter

'It's okay, son, we have seen it all before' was one of those things a teenage boy should never hear his parents say. Them seeing him naked was one thing but him walking in to a room with them sitting there naked made the situation even worse. This was the sort of situation that came under the heading of worst case scenario. Kids at school had talked about worst case scenarios and most of them had been so extreme it would be pretty hard to imagine a case where they would happen. If he had mentioned a worst case scenario where you walk into a room with no clothes on and the rents happened to be in that room and they also had no clothes on it would definitely hit the top of the list of worst case scenarios.

Worst case scenarios were similar to those moments that the rents put their children through that a child never wanted to go through. The one that all children had to go through that was unavoidable was when their mother or father decided it was time to have THAT talk. Usually by the time the parents chose to have the talk the child had already either been taught the basics in class or self-taught through the power of the internet or with the help of a friend that was happy to play show and tell. For some kids that talk was just one of the moments they had to endure from their parents. Much worse than that talk was the talk about the rents getting separated or divorced. Not only did separation mean they wouldn't get to see both parents at home it also meant you were put into an unofficial category at school.

Children of broken homes seemed to have some teachers that sympathised with them and some that didn't. In contrast to that a child whose parents were still married were scrutinised by the teachers equally.

Children of parents that were happily married had a very different problem to deal with at home. Intimacy between their parents, these were the sort of things that as you got older you knew your parents did but didn't want to see them doing. Parents holding hands was borderline acceptable, all couples did that whether they were married or not. Seeing the rents kissing was a sight that firstly couldn't be unseen and secondly was cringing material for all children. If the intimacy went any further than that whether knowledgably seen by the children or not it could scar a child for life.

Stuttering loudly as he tried to cover his embarrassment with his shorts in one hand and scraping the door in search of the handle with the other, Jim had endured a full range of emotions by the time he managed to escape the room. He stood in the corridor aware that he was still naked but happy to be out of the sight of the rents before one of them decided to get up to welcome him into the room with them. Quickly he threw his towel over his head and hopped awkwardly into his shorts as he hyperventilated and tried to clear his mind.

Lifting the towel off his head and allowing it to rest on his shoulders he slowly walked over to the window that overlooked the pool. It made sense that the Jacuzzi was somewhere round here and now he knew much to his horror that it wasn't in the room he thought it would be. He peered through the window, the lap swimmer was still gliding gracefully up and down the length of the pool immune to anyone that might be around. At the far end of the pool he could see a second much smaller pool with a lone figure sat in it.

He had thought that second pool was a paddling pool for mothers and children but seeing a solitary person sitting calmly in it made him review his opinion. In a lot of ways it made sense to have a Jacuzzi in with the main pool, they were at the end of the day both water based facilities. If he had thought it through properly and gone into the pool first he would have saved himself a lot of embarrassment.

Keeping his focus on the far end of the pool he pushed through the glass door and into the pool room. Like a whale coming up for air the lap swimmer puffed out a breath glancing over at him before resuming his swim. Jim had seen this type of swimmer before at his local pool and always wondered where they got the motivation to bounce aimlessly from one end of the pool to the other. Swimming to him had always been a group recreational activity and had not actually included any real swimming at all.

As he got closer he could see the person in the smaller pool had long dark hair and even though they had their back to him they seemed to be female. After the most recent disaster he wasn't going to take any chances, he knew he could just call out her name but the echoing sound seemed pointless when there was less than fifty metres between them anyway.

He could always take the risk and just slide in next to them but that was one risk too far. He could see it now, slides in casually leans across to either kiss or cuddle the person in the pool only to find out it wasn't Sasha but some strange woman or even worse a very feminine looking man. Making it worse if it wasn't Sasha and she caught him in the arms of another woman or even worse another man that would be much harder to explain than her volleyball incident. The phrase 'it's not what it looks like' would take on a whole new meaning in either case. He kept walking hoping that the person he was walking towards would eventually move or turn around so he could identify them.

"Sasha? Is that you?" he muttered in a low voice to prevent the words echoing around the room.

Whipping the water with her hair the Sasha turned to face him; she had recognised the voice and had waited patiently in anticipation of his arrival. In hindsight it would have been more practical to have made arrangements to meet but thankfully her little note had worked. She pulled herself up feeling her legs battling against the onslaught of bubbles as she held out her arms inviting Jim to join her.

Seeing Sasha's face had started a series of reliefs on different levels, firstly there was the relief that the person in the pool was her. He knew in his own heart that ensuring he had the right person was the safest move. Even without the possibility of him getting in the water and surprising both himself and a complete stranger he didn't want to risk leaving Sasha doubting his interest in her.

His second relief came when he saw her standing up, the bikini she was wearing was different to any that he had seen so far which surprised him but he shrugged it off. He had wondered how many different items of swim wear a person on a naturist holiday bought with them but chose to accept that some people probably wore swimwear as part of their evening attire. The fact she was wearing a bikini was a bigger relief to him than what colour or style she had chosen to wear.

Gaining confidence he made his way with quicker steps toward the pool and waded in throwing his towel toward the side. The warm water danced around as he made his way toward Sasha who had followed him with her embrace and now stood opposite him. He wrapped his arms round her feeling her pulling him close into her body until her breast was pressed close against his skin. She touched his nose against hers and leaned in kissing him softly on the lips closing her eyes as their lips met.

It came as a small surprise to him that their kiss had none of the tongue tying action he had seen in so many films and even accidentally seen friends doing. He preferred this sort of kissing, the deeper more intense kiss seemed messy and in many ways unnecessary. He wasn't in any doubt that as time progressed there was a possibility that Sasha would want to progress to this type of kiss but for now slow deep lip to lip kissing was perfect.

"What took you so long?" she whispered softly as she guided him to a sitting position and nestled between his knees.

Jim was sure that she was only joking and making small talk with her passing comment, there had been no time frame put on meeting up but he felt compelled to tell her of the night mare he had endured before meeting her. She listened intently as he dramatized his appearance in the steam room opposite the pool and felt comforted when he mentioned that he had tried to surprise her by appearing naked. She couldn't help but bite her lip to prevent giggling as he told her that he had found himself stood in front of his parents.

Hearing his admission to trying out naturism came at first as a shock to her but a pleasant one. She could see his logic that in a Jacuzzi there wouldn't be many people and once he was sat down he would be hidden anyway but it was the fact he was willing to do it that shocked her. Hopefully the experience of coming face to face with his parents hadn't put him off trying it again. Maybe she could coax him into it, show him that naturism wasn't as bad as he thought it was.

Resting against his chest she could feel his heart beating gently, the dull thud reassuring her that it was a person she was laying against not a wall. She had guided his arms around her waist and initially clamped them against her stomach to show him where she wanted them but now she was curious about what he would do. Releasing his hands she focussed her energy on lightly stroking his arms waiting for the moment when he would start to explore her body with his fingertips.

He remained motionless not showing any intention to move from his position, only his breathing telling her he was still there. Maybe he was asleep, but then again if he was there would be more chance of wondering hands. In an unconscious state she was sure a person would have less control of where limbs ended up so she felt sure he was still awake. Subtly, she moved his hand higher up her body, resting it at the top of her abdomen to see if he gave in to temptation and targeted her breasts. In contrast, he slid his hand back to her stomach deciding it was more comfortable lower on her body and deeper in the water.

If she hadn't witnessed his doing this she wouldn't have believed it, she knew that most of the boys back home would have attempted a quick grope but he hadn't. She had been confident of his kind nature and felt sure he had experience of women before meeting her. This was all too good to be true, an open invitation to grab a handful of breast and he had not only silently declined it he had actually moved away from it. In a way she was tempted to see what he would do if she pushed his hands down her body but that was far too forward and risking too much.

"Have you had many girlfriends, Jim?"

She felt sure she wasn't the first girl he had been with; he was too comfortable with her in his arms. At the end of the day, he was the same age as her at sixteen years old and, although she didn't class herself as having had any relationships, it was doubtful that he was in the same position. If she had been determined to save herself for someone at home, her selection was fairly limited and, even then, most of them were only interested in one thing and that didn't suit her. Most guys seemed to think that a girl agreeing to go out with them was the start of a target to see how far they were willing to go and how soon they were willing to go there. She knew it was a lot to ask but she wanted more than that – she wanted a boy who wasn't just after her body.

Even if the number of girlfriends he had was high she wasn't going to be put off him. Everything they had lost out on with him she now had and could experience with him and that meant a lot to her. If he had dated a lot of girls she would be left wondering how many of them he had taken to bed. Maybe asking him such a direct question wasn't a good idea but she had said it now so all she could do was wait for his answer.

"You're my first," he answered solemnly.

His answer seemed too convenient; the fact that he could get on with her so easily hinted towards there being at least one previous girlfriend. In a way she could understand him telling her she was his first girlfriend but surely he knew he didn't have to impress her. At the end of the day it was her that had made the first move toward making him her boyfriend. She squeezed his hand intentionally tightly until he had to pull away from her grip.

"What's that for?" He scowled as he flinched.

She had him firmly backed into the wall of the Jacuzzi, he knew it would be difficult to get out without causing either of them injury. Releasing himself from her grip he hissed between his teeth as he plunged his hand into the water to soothe the pain. Maybe her grip was just being playful but he wasn't sure if he liked this game and he wasn't aware they had started playing. In compliment to her she had a good firm grip that a man would be proud of, her strength was a bit of a surprise to him.

"Jim, it's sweet of you to make me think I'm your first but I'm a big girl; I can handle the truth," she muttered as she bounced her head lightly against his chest.

He had been hit with the 'S' word again, the second time in two days. This time in a much more serious context, it frustrated him how one word could be used in so many different ways and have so many different implications. In the context she had used it this time it implied that she doubted him but didn't want it to cause a major argument. Whatever he said next it had to be said the right way to squash the debate without leaving any casualties.

There was certain logic to what she had said, he realised how much of a cliché it must have seemed that he had told her she was his first. In a way it was a compliment to him that she thought him more experienced in relationships than he was. He knew from his experience with his friends that some guys used the same line to give a false innocence to a new girlfriend. Maybe mentioning he was friendly with a few girls would explain things to her. Then again bringing the implication of other girls back at home may just fuel the fire. There was no easy way to respond to her subtle implication without possibly incriminating himself further.

"You are my first girlfriend, Sasha," he said with a pleading tone. "I know it might seem difficult to believe but you are," he added, hoping he had said enough to settle her mind.

Sasha pondered to herself for a moment; his response had seemed genuine enough. She doubted he would try to continue a lie he seemed intelligent enough to know that eventually lies get caught out. It didn't need to be him that stumbled, his parents might say something to squash any stories he was trying to cover.

Could it really be that she, Sasha O'Callaghan, was the first girl he had been in a proper relationship with? The more she thought about it the more it made sense, it would explain his shyness around her but surely she couldn't have been that lucky. Surely she hadn't found a guy that she was comfortable enough with to call her boyfriend and become his first real girlfriend had she? She reached over grabbing his stray hand that was being soothed in the bubbles and dragged it back across her stomach holding it firmly but tenderly in place with a dominant but not heavy grip.

"You're my first, too," she responded, relaxing her shoulders and pushing her head back into his chest.

In just a few words Jim could see why his statement had caused such an aggressive response. He knew that if he wanted to he could have questioned her in the same way as she had questioned him but he didn't want to. He liked the idea of them both treading the same unknown path together, blindly leading each other into the realms of a relationship.

They sat in silence, both taking in the reality of what had just been confessed by each other. Sasha returned to stroking Jim's arms gently, flattening the soft hairs against his arm as she gazed up at the plain clock. Unlike anything else in the main building the clock seemed extremely bland with its almost metallic looking face filled with roman numerals and two thick hands that obeyed the instructions of a needle like second hand.

With the chunkiness of the hands it was easy to see that it was nearly quarter to nine. She had been sat in the pool nearly an hour and could feel her fingers forming the pruned effect that was common after lengthy exposure to pool water.

"Fancy some breakfast?" She turned her head slightly as she posed the question at him.

Since joining her in the pool Jim had forgotten that they hadn't eaten, even his stomach seemed to have made allowances for his absent mindedness. In a way he was quite comfortable where he was and mentally wanted to complain to the complex for not offering a poolside service. Logically he knew that his mother had always told him not to swim for an hour after eating but that rule seldom lasted when they were on holiday.

Even the thought of the rents sent his mind hurtling back to the last time he had seen them which was sitting wearing vacant smiles and nothing else. That grim sight seemed reluctant to move out of his subconscious, all he could hope was that in time it would fade into a distant memory that he could pretend hadn't happened. In a way it was fortunate that he had seen them sitting down, the amount of flesh that a child should never see on their parents had been limited to just breast, he felt sure if he had seen any more he would have been put off women possibly permanently. Then again being sat in such closer quarters to Sasha his mind told him he would probably get over the shock eventually.

Releasing her from his arms he watched Sasha gracefully stand up and hold her hand out to pull him out of the warm water. He followed her out to the tiled floor and shuddered slightly at the change in temperature as he walked over to get the towel he had bought with him. Peering round he noted that there were no real changing rooms in the pool, in one corner a door marked with the word "toilets" and in the opposite corner an open shower. In a way he could understand there wasn't much need for a changing room on a naturist complex – very few people were going to be getting dressed.

As he peered round the room he noticed Sasha was suffering with the cold much more than he was. Without thinking he wrapped his towel around her shoulders and made his way over to a bench holding additional towels presumably supplied by the complex. He wasn't sure how long she had been in the Jacuzzi before he arrived but it was obvious she was having a worse effect to the temperature change than he was.

The fitness swimmer that had been making his way up and down the pool when he arrived had disappeared leaving the pool empty except for Sasha and him. Neither of them had noticed him disappear, he certainly hadn't used the showers near the Jacuzzi but one way or another he had made his escape. Casually Sasha dabbed her body dry before handing the towel over to Jim and walking to the edge of the pool.

Bending over the water she wrung her hair out over it, Jim had seen this routine performed several times. Each time he saw one of his friends doing it he had pondered about how much more efficient it would be if the wet hair could be put in a tumble dryer and a spare set of hair used while the owner waited. Girls he knew loved long hair and in a lot of ways he admired it too but it did seem like a lot of maintenance. He had grown up around long haired women and had never really accepted that overly short hair suited a woman. In the same scale he often found it strange seeing a man with long hair, surely they knew how high the maintenance was on so much hair – didn't they?

Since his confession to having never had a girlfriend before Sasha had decided to test him a little bit. She had devised a plan that she knew was quite daring but she wanted to see how he responded. Intentionally she walked behind him as he set off down the length of the pool toward the door. With the pool deserted now was as good time as any to try her little plan out.

"Jim, can you hold this a minute?" she questioned calmly.

Without questioning Jim glanced backwards as he stretched out his hand to take whatever it was Sasha was offering him. It seemed a strange question as she didn't have a towel with her, maybe it was her way of saying she wanted him to hold her hand. He stopped in his tracks when he was presented with her bikini top instead of her hand. It seemed to be a strange thing to be doing on the way out of the pool but smiling vaguely he took her top and wrapped it in his towel before continuing his way toward the door.

Sasha contemplated his response, he had seen her topless before so there was no surprise in seeing her topless again. Also she had made the mistake of mentioning food and she had always been told the way to a man's heart was his stomach. Hopefully his lack of interest simply meant he was too hungry to question her reasons for handing her top to him. Maybe step two would get a bigger reaction; there was only one way to find out.

"And this too, if you don't mind." She kept her voice calm, as if this was just an additional statement to her first request.

This time Jim stopped walking and thought before turning to see what she wanted him for. Surely there wasn't anything else she could be giving him to carry into the restaurant. As far as he knew there was only one thing left she could be giving him to carry. He closed his eyes taking deep breaths before holding his hand out behind him unsure what to expect.

Sasha huffed to herself, she wasn't letting him get away with this, she could tell he had worked out what was going on and the shyness she had expected had come back. Grabbing his hand she pulled his arm forcing him to turn and face her. Not realising her own strength she pulled him so hard he fell toward her grabbing her shoulders as he tried to balance himself.

Looking up at her she could see his face was red as she steadied him supporting him in her arms and pulling him closer. Despite the potential for an accident her plan had gone almost perfectly, not only was he facing her he had been given no option but to grab her to prevent falling. She gripped his waist, pressing her body against his as they stood looking into each other's eyes. She trusted him and she felt like even if she had met him at home she would be comfortable with him seeing her like this. The advantage was that on this complex her nudity would not be seen as out of the ordinary.

Grabbing his arms she placed them around her waist encouraging him to pull her closer to him. With nervousness he stood rigid not wanting to show his fear but in the same time not wanting to let her down. He could feel her hands on the waist band of his shorts; he had mentally prepared himself to be naked for her today and now seemed to be an appropriate moment.

Taking one hand off her waist he awkwardly manoeuvred his shorts down over his hips feeling the springing motion of his hardened manhood as it freed itself from them allowing them to fall to the floor. She gazed down his body vaguely, in all her time of visiting the complex she had seen so many naked men she had stopped paying attention to them but now she had one in her arms. His member was pressed against her showing his excitement at them being so close to each other.

"Don't let that stop you enjoying naturism, Hun." She smiled softly, nodding down his body.

Jim blushed at her words, he was conscious that his body had let him down but at least it was only Sasha that had seen it this time. She had read his mind perfectly, these involuntary motions were the main reason he was conscious of running around naked. He didn't expect it to happen every time he saw a woman but he knew he couldn't control when or if it happened.

As much as he had tried not to notice other men during his holiday so far it was difficult not to notice something as significant as part of the body that is usually covered being let out. It was like trying not to comment if you saw someone walking a cat or a rabbit in the park. The fact that it was happening and you weren't used to it made it something that caught your eye.

In all the brief glimpses he had caught of men he had never once seen one suffering from the effects of arousal. It was as if someone had anaesthetised all the men on a daily basis to ensure it didn't happen. In his heart he knew that wasn't the case because if it was surely he would have been advised about it by someone even if it was the rents – yet another thing that should never be heard but just as essential as the birds and the bee's talk.

"I can't promise you, but I am fairly sure that you won't have that happen every time we are nude together," she added softly, trying to reassure him and encourage him to consider naturism.

Despite her innocence sexually she was aware of the visible problems that boys could suffer from. She knew there was a possibility that Jim might be unique and have this happen on a regular basis. She hadn't risked stripping off in front of him to see this happen, she just wanted to try and coax him towards naturism. As much as she cared for him she didn't want to spend the rest of her holiday hiding her body and she hoped that he knew it.

Jim could see the sincerity in her eyes as she gently took her bikini back and started redressing. Quickly he bent down pulling his shorts back up to hide the source of his frustration. Sasha had been so patient with him for so long; she had even kept her faith in him alive during his absence. He knew that he had to return the compliment by trying to enjoy naturism with her. He wasn't ready yet but soon he knew it was going to be make or break for them. It was wrong of him to expect her to keep entertaining his fears and he knew eventually she would give in to naturism leaving him to either accept it or embrace it.

"Breakfast time, then?" He smiled at her, holding his hand out.

She gazed over at him leaning in to kiss him softly to acknowledge his first attempt at naturism as she accepted his offer. Small steps, next time she would try it without the intimate cuddle and somewhere more secluded maybe.

Chapter Seventeen

The leap into nature

Having Sasha's hand tenderly gripping his own was the only real consolation Jim had of his first experience of naturism. He was in many ways relieved that she had chosen a place where they were alone to try to coax him out of his shell. In addition he was impressed with himself for taking the step into it and although it felt foreign to him he was pleased he had tried it.

Every year previous to this he had been able to tell his friends about where he was going on holiday before going away. Not knowing the destination had caused unrest among his social group who had decided he was actually being sent to some form of summer camp. Thankfully after months of trying to prize the information from the rents he had finally confronted them about the idea of summer camp and been given a definitive no.

Some of his friends had experienced 'summer camp' in the past and although they had learned some fun new activities to him it was just a cop out to get rid of the kids. Many times a trip to summer camp had resulted in the abandoned child being told the news of a new brother or sister on the way. This bordered on the edge of too much information as they got older because that indirectly told the camper what their parents had been up to in their absence.

Some of his friends actually seemed to like staying in their own country for their summer holidays but to Jim that seemed pointless. Summer holidays were the one time in the year you had the chance to change the pasty skinned look of life in the UK for a much healthier bronzed look. Admittedly the bronzed look didn't last but it was one of the highlights of the year.

On the other side of the extreme were the acquaintances he had – people he didn't quite count as friends because the only time they spoke to him was when they had something that they wanted to try and impress him with. These people would be taken on their annual cruise by their more affluent parents and spend two weeks drifting between destinations.

Even though Jim spent a lot of his time on holiday in the close proximity of the hotel he was staying in he liked having the option to explore. The idea of being able to say yes I have visited Italy, I was there for six hours on one cruise seemed almost as pointless as the UK holiday but at least on this style of trip the traveller would get the coveted suntan. Cruises also had the difficulty of postcards, these were hard enough to write at the best of times but how did a person firstly write them without a set location and secondly how did they post them? Did the post man drop in at night by helicopter to collect the consignment? At least he had a destination and a suntan to bring back from his holiday even if he did have to skim over the concept of naturism.

Reflecting on Sasha's latest attempt to introduce him to naturism he conceded to the fact that even if he wasn't willing to embrace it he had to be ready for Sasha to want to. Logic told him that this holiday was probably the only time she was able to be a naturist. Even though he had never been to Ireland he felt certain that the rules on running around naked would be similar to those in the UK. He couldn't imagine a country that was so close to the UK being so diversely different but then again maybe it was.

On the basis of this being her only opportunity he felt bad and complimented that she had made allowances for his adversity to it. Every time they had spent time together she had gone to the effort of ensuring she was at least partially covered. Somehow, he had to let her know that it was okay if she wanted to strip off; however, he felt like he would feel more awkward as the clothed one if she did that.

Back at home he knew that once a girl was in the category of being someone's girlfriend she was classed as not to be looked at by others. He had been the shoulder to cry on more times than he could count as a result of a boy lashing out unnecessarily at someone who had (usually accidentally) brushed past the girl.

He had been the victim of such rivalry at one stage and that occasion stuck in his mind. It was the school Valentines disco and although he didn't have a proper date to go with he had gone along with one of his female friends. He wasn't a big fan of school run disco's they quite frequently led to drama once the glamour of them had faded back into the class room.

He had been minding his own business while the girl he had come with tried to impress the boy she liked with semi raunchy dance moves when one of his other female friends approached him to say hello. She had chosen to greet him with the standard hello and hug around the neck which he returned with a similar non-committal hug. Unfortunately, her boyfriend, who appeared to have been lacing his own drinks with vodka, took the hug badly and launched himself at Jim.

Being the more alert of the two of them Jim had been able to comfortably move out of the way of the unprovoked attack sending the attacker falling into a table. Several drinks were lost as he made his ungraceful landing the last of which came from his now ex-girlfriend who threw her drink at him as he was escorted off the premises. The end result was Jim's adopted role of the shoulder to cry on again as she regaled stories of his ongoing jealousy and how she was better off without him.

Jealousy and Alcohol 1 – Boyfriend 0, and relegation back to single life for his troubles.

Over the years Jim's ability to get on with girls better than boys had taught him a lot but also penalised him from a lot too. He wasn't sure of exactly how he had been chosen as a reliable male friend but it seemed to stem back to when he was eleven years old. At such a tender age even unknowingly he was showing girls a respect that other boys hadn't done. At that age that simply meant he wasn't spending his break times trying to peek up their skirts or making attempts to flash their panties at groups of sniggering friends.

By the time he reached twelve and was settling into secondary school he found himself watching as the latest group of recruits went through the same torturous process and tried to work out who was going to be singled out. His first official female friend had also been his neighbour as a child making it easy for her to get to know him. As the years went by she had drifted away a bit but still remained an acquaintance coming to him for advice on the odd occasion.

It took until he reached the age of fourteen for his male friends to start drifting away in pursuit of girlfriends. This drifting left him with a steady flow of female friends that told him secrets that sometimes came into the category of too much information. In some ways if he could have turned back time it was probably somewhere between the age of twelve and fourteen he would choose to go back to so he could tell himself not to trust friendship as a gateway to relationship.

During the next year he watched and listened as his male friends checked in with him updating him on their progress. There seemed to be some clear goals to achieve in the road of a relationship the first of which was the kiss. He had now thankfully achieved this goal for himself even if it was two years later than some of his friends. After this goal it was the signs of public affection, some of which looked to him like they were grooming procedures.

Stroking the girlfriend's hair, fingers following the line of their chin, straightening their collar and brushing off imaginary crumbs. Jim knew the crumb brushing tactic was also an excuse to unintentionally pass the hand over the breast. In order to officially get away with the breast touch you had to get the girl's permission and that was easier to do in private than public.

Once this boundary had been established and crossed it took the relationship to the next level. Touching girl's intimate parts was only the beginning of the journey the next stage was being permitted to see them. In a diverse sense Jim had bypassed the permission to touch stage and gone on to the permission to see them stage with Sasha but that was by default.

He was sure without any doubt that if they had met in a normal environment he wouldn't have seen her nude. There was a good chance that if they had met back at home she wouldn't have classed him as a boyfriend but he would never know that. Even if she had classed him as a boyfriend he wouldn't expect to be at the see her nude stage for a long time. He wondered how he was ever going to explain meeting her to his friends back at home.

Trying not to show how much his mind was wondering and the debate he was having with himself about naturism he glanced over at Sasha squeezing her hand slightly. Almost as if she knew he had a lot on his mind she turned to face him stopping their walk through the atrium. She turned to face him grabbing his free hand and lifted herself up on her toes to kiss him softly.

Her response implied that she too had been contemplating how to tackle his fear of naturism. If only there was a way of finding out what was on her mind without asking her, some way of seeing her thoughts. Then again if he could see her thoughts he knew she would be able to see his and not all of them were ideal for her to see. Maybe psychic powers were not the best of ideas in his confused and concerned state.

"Morning lads." A cheery voice came across the room, breaking the silence between them.

Jim was thankful that he recognised the voice and that it wasn't the rents but in the same way he was aware that this voice was owned by someone who knew the brief and awkward history between Sasha and him. Casually walking up to them from the restaurant was Greg and Alice, both of them nude as had been expected but, in Jim's head, not the best timed reunion with them. Trying to avert his eyes Jim smiled vaguely and tried not to focus on the couple as they made their way up to him. He lifted one of his hands clasping the back of his head as a nervous reaction to distract from the redness he could feel hitting his cheeks.

He had been warning himself since the beginning of his holiday about a situation like this. Socializing with nudes was something he was trying to avoid but just like an oncoming train there was little or no stopping it arriving. Mentally kicking himself he accepted that these encounters were going to be part of his ongoing holiday and tried to look like seeing them was normal to him when clearly his face said it wasn't.

Greg nodded silently at Jim almost acknowledging his efforts to try and make out that their dress sense didn't affect him. He was impressed that Jim wasn't cowering away but could see the pain in his eyes as he tried not to react too adversely to the situation. Thinking quickly he decided not to make an issue of it, treat this as just a normal chat with Sasha and her new boyfriend and make his excuses to leave before the situation got too tense.

"We won't keep you now," he said with a jovial tone, "but maybe you will join us after lunch for a game of tennis?"

A casual invitation for a planned meeting seemed to be the logical way to handle the situation. If they agreed to it Greg and Alice could decide during the morning whether they wanted to accommodate Jims embarrassment or not and at least a physical activity like tennis would give him a distraction if they chose to stay nude.

Sasha looked at Jim with excitement in her eyes, it was clear to him that she wanted to join her friends for the game. He knew it would be wrong to refuse to join them for more than one reason, he had already decided to try and do things for her and this was his first opportunity to do that.

"See you at two at the courts?" Jim responded calmly still avoiding full eye contact but glancing in their direction.

He felt Sasha bounce slightly in his hands as she acknowledged his reply and commitment to meeting them. Greg smiled at him relieved and pleased that he had taken the initiative and confirmed the arrangement. Nodding at Jim he placed one hand on his shoulder gripping it lightly as if to say well done we are all proud of you before walking away with Alice.

It didn't take long for Jim to realize what he had talked Sasha and himself into doing for the afternoon. Male friends had warned him that once a man is in a relationship with a woman he starts to do things that are out of character to either impress or to please her. He was fairly sure that none of them had arranged to meet a couple of people that were likely to be naked for a mixed doubles game of tennis though.

He thought back to when he had first seen the tennis courts; they had been his first indication of the naturist element of the site. He had jokingly mentioned that the two couples playing tennis in the distance looked like they had no clothes on and the rents had confirmed his suspicion instead of laughing along with what he thought was a joke.

Immune to his thoughts about what he had done Sasha had decided to take him back to their little secluded part of the beach. She was proud of him for making the arrangement with Greg having anticipated that he would make an excuse not to join them. After her risky adventure with him at the pool she intentionally had waited to see how he responded to the amicable invitation but couldn't hold her excitement back when he confirmed they would attend.

Jim lay down next to her on the soft sand having passed her the only towel they had between them to lie on. In all their time on the complex sunbathing was one activity he hadn't given much time to yet. Maybe now everything was starting to settle down he could concentrate on just enjoying the weather. Making this option better than it would be on a normal holiday he had Sasha to enjoy it with.

He glanced over at her half expecting to find her bikini lying next to her but was pleasantly surprised to find it still attached to her body. Maybe this was a good time to experiment with naturism, the morning sun would be able to make a good start on his all over tan and there was no one about. Questioning it in his mind her gave the idea some consideration before turning it down. Knowing his luck he would just start relaxing and enjoying it and the rents would turn up adding to his series of naturist disasters.

Instead he set himself a target to have at least tried it before the end of the following day. He put rules for his introduction to naturism in place so that he couldn't use an excuse like using a shower as having been nude. This process was quite a common one for him, he used the rules process for anything he didn't like doing but knew he had to do.

The rules for this were in effect quite simple;

1. Being nude in his apartment didn't count even if Sasha was there at the time.
2. Being in a public area alone didn't count – it had to be with someone.
3. The rents catching him making him feel the need to cover up disqualified the attempt.
4. Sasha had to be there and it had to appear like it wasn't forced on him.

Even as simple as these rules seemed to him he still had to get over the idea that it was wrong to be nude. He had been on this complex for long enough now to accept that it was the way of life here. In many ways it was only coincidence and fate that had prevented him from being in a situation where he was surrounded by nudity.

Sasha looked so tranquil next to him, the necklace he had bought her hung at an awkward angle pointing toward her shoulder as she lay on her side facing him. Carefully he reached across to her touching her fingers as they hung limply down as if they were guarding her body from him. He watched as she woke and made small talk with her as they lay there, this was what he imagined it would be like to have a girlfriend.

Effortlessly they remained on the beach resting and taking in the sun until lunch time when they made their way back toward the complex. Jim knew the time of meeting Greg and Alice was getting close and felt his stomach knotting in anticipation of the possibility of them playing tennis on the rooftop together.

Keeping tennis courts on a rooftop seemed strange, the logistics were all wrong. All it would take was one heavy handed ball and some random passer-by would surely be bombarded by a green bouncing ball shaped missile. This seemed hazardous from the point of view of the other residents and non-productive from the point of view of the player that had fired the ball having to then retrieve it.

Jim's experience of tennis was limited; they had tried to teach him how to play it at school but not been very successful. This lack of success was down to two factors; firstly it was only a substitute sport that was thrown in instead of another activity that some school board had decided wasn't as educational so the teachers had limited knowledge of the game. Secondly the great British weather made it difficult to teach with six out of the eight weeks allocated to it being cancelled and changed with yet another activity.

When he was a child Jim had made a failed attempt at playing it against his father during a previous holiday. The first year they attempted it the racquet had been nearly as big as he was so that experience didn't last very long. The second time they had felt inferior as players because the people next to them were able to maintain a good consistency where they found it hard to keep the ball in play. They endured it for about half an hour on that occasion before deciding to abandon real tennis for the table tennis.

It fascinated Jim how the skills from one version of tennis were not interchangeable with the other. Both games had racquets, a bouncing ball and a net to attempt to get the ball over in order to score. Both games even had areas that were counted as either in or out – admittedly in table tennis a ball was in as long as it hit the table whereas tennis had lines to guide the player. Maybe it was the larger scale or the holes in a proper tennis racquet but no matter how hard they tried his dad and he always looked better playing table tennis to real tennis.

Jim peered up at the roof as they got to the feeble looking iron ladder that led up to the tennis courts. The first thing he noticed was that the designers had taken into account the lack of ability of the average holiday tennis player and enclosed the courts in a wired metal fence that seemed to be about three metres high. Even the worst player would find it hard to launch the ball over the top of that. He looked over at Sasha who was still smiling softly at him as she started making her way up to the court.

"I'll be back in a couple of minutes, just need the bathroom," he blurted out, grabbing her arm as he tried to assure her he wasn't running away from their arrangement.

Nodding, she blew him a kiss as she disappeared up the steps.

Jim wasn't sure what had got into him as he ran to the main building and disappeared into the bathroom. Quickly he looked at himself in the mirror trying to ensure he was thinking straight. At the top of the steps he was sure Greg and Alice would be waiting and Sasha would be joining them. He knew instinctively that the chances of them being dressed were minimal; it made no sense for them to go to such lengths.

They had been dressed when he had first met them but having encountered them again this morning he knew they felt better as naturists. Sasha had tried earlier in the day to introduce him to naturism and apart from his body acting badly he had done it. Now was the time to prove to her that he could do it again and this time without her coaxing him into it. On the top of the roof there would only be a few people, he knew the rents weren't tennis players so they were out of the equation.

From his memory there were only two tennis courts he had seen when he first noticed the courts on arrival at the complex so that meant a maximum of about eight people including him. Out of the other seven potential people, he knew three of them and one of them was his girlfriend. This was his best opportunity to give naturism a try without being exposed to too many strangers.

Taking a deep breath he made his way to back to the steps that led up to the tennis courts. He felt like a man that had been convicted and this was the walk to the electric chair. Even though consciously he had made the decision that this was the best time to do it the act of stripping naked in a public place still scared him. He closed his eyes trying to calm himself down, he was doing this for Sasha and that was the perfect reason to do this.

He knew what he had to do; he had to make it so that he had no way of backing out. His shorts were the only thing separating him from the world of naturism and they weren't one of his best pairs. If he was going to do this he should leave them at the bottom of the steps there wasn't much chance of them being stolen on a naturist resort. He glanced along the path, there was a couple heading toward him, quickly he turned to face the wall avoiding social interaction.

Along the wall was a flower bed that was neatly tended, that was the place to tuck his shorts, no one would take any notice of them there. One last look up and down the path to be sure there were no additional strangers, a last deep breath and he slid them down his legs kicking them in amongst the flowers. Taking the first step he started to climb the ladder style steps toward the top of the wall. As he got closer he could hear Sasha chatting amicably with her two friends, she seemed to be telling them how happy she was.

Hearing her voice gave him the encouragement he needed; he looked up and could see the wire door into the courts was partially open. Quickly he scaled the last few steps and slipped inside the gate closing it behind him before turning round. Like a slow motion scene from a movie he saw Greg and Alice, both nude as he had suspected, Greg pointed in his direction triggering Sasha to turn and face him. The pointing finger was not an accusing one or a mocking one it was clearly to let her know he had arrived.

Sasha reacted with shock at first at seeing him stood there naked but didn't take long running over to greet him with a huge hug. He watched almost bemused as she ran to him throwing her bikini a piece at a time over toward the side of the court before landing on him.

Skin to skin contact felt better this time than it had in the pool and he felt sure his body wasn't behaving like it had the last time they had been nude and in an intimate position. She lowered herself down his body slowly and gently and gazed deep into his eyes. This was a big moment for her, she had not forced him into doing this but she had wanted him to at least try naturism. Carefully she glanced down his body reassuring herself that there was nothing that could cause him embarrassment. She smiled and kissed him before turning to face her friends and leaning back against him.

"Anyone for tennis?" She couldn't hide the beaming smile as the words flew out of her mouth.

Chapter Eighteen

A natural disaster?

As he reflected on the tennis game Jim found himself wondering why he had taken so long to convert to naturism. After the initial discomfort he had quickly realised that none of the people he was with had commented on his lack of clothes. Logically there was no reason to comment on it as none of them were wearing anything. For over an hour they had enjoyed jokes and fun just like he would do with his friends back at home.

It was humorous to him how so many people did things on holiday that they wouldn't dream of in everyday life. Tennis was one of those things he wouldn't dream of doing at home unless he was forced to do it. He wasn't sure if this new energy was due to being in a place that they didn't care about how bad they looked or if it was that they just didn't have time at home. For him tennis just didn't appeal as an activity but as he was now trying something he hadn't done before it was a welcome distraction.

Having to focus on a tennis ball being fired across the net made it less awkward and gave Jim less time to look at those around him. Staring at people in a state of undress wasn't acceptable behaviour in a clothed environment so he felt sure it was looked at unfavourably in a clothing optional environment.

Jim thought about the careful wording of the type of complex this was – clothing optional seemed to be a loose reference. Even though there had been nobody except Sasha trying to push him toward naturism he knew that if he had kept up his silent protest he would feel odd. To him the word optional meant you can take it or leave it but on this complex it seemed to mean if you choose to stay dressed you will be in the minority.

Despite trying his best to focus on the tennis game fate had got in the way and put him in a position where the sun had blinded him for a split second. He had been playing against Greg at the time while the girls sat talking – he decided it was probably about Greg and him. Somehow he had successfully returned the ball to Greg's side of the court for the fourth time in a row but this time it had bounced extremely high.

As he had expected Greg had jumped and stretched to reach the ball putting all his effort into the return shot. At that exact moment the sun had made its attack on him causing him to try and shield his eyes while attempting to watch for the ball. His defensive action against the sun had left his racquet a long way from the oncoming ball which made its way without remorse toward his groin.

The resulting stinging pain had caused Jim to fall into a crumpled heap on the floor gripping on to himself as he mumbled expletives. Sasha, Alice and Greg had all responded in split second timing, Greg being the last to get to him as he had to get round the net first. After moments of trying to prize him out of the ball he had huddled himself into Sasha had positioned herself at his side level with his waist.

She gripped his leg pulling it gently until it was flat on the ground as she tried to assess the damage. Unexpectedly his hand wasn't covering the area she had expected it to but was clamped to the top of his leg. Gently she pulled his hand away trying to calm him down and tried to see what had happened. An angry looking red tennis ball shaped mark sat on the top of his thigh that she was sure was going to bruise.

Caving in to her attention and conscious of the crowd of three people around him Jim relaxed taking deep breaths as he came to terms with the stinging pain. Even if he had been wearing clothes there was no way he could avoid the mark that he knew was now part of his leg. The force of Greg's shot that he knew wasn't intentionally aimed at him would have needed armour to have stopped it causing a mark on his flesh.

Even with all this in mind Jim felt positive about his introduction to naturism, he could understand how it would appeal and wondered why it wasn't more readily accepted. He had seen places in Africa and South America where natives wore nothing or next to nothing and they seemed quite happy about it. Maybe it was just the weather stopping people in England adopting the way of life but he doubted it.

If naturism had been a normal thing back at home he felt sure it would make his life a lot easier. He had lost count of the hours he had spent waiting for his female friends to get ready for a night out only to appear wearing the shortest skirt and the smallest top possible. Surely if that was all they were going to wear they may as well wear nothing but who was going to tell them that?

Then there were the hours he had spent playing the unpaid escort to clothing shops. This role was not only time consuming it was in some ways humiliating because it involved him sitting in the women's clothes department. His friends seemed immune to the fact that he was male and would pop in and out of changing rooms showing off the items they planned to buy to impress their boyfriends. Meanwhile his role was to sit and give them honest opinions as to how it looked, he had learned very quickly that honest opinion meant to tell them it looked nice on them.

Telling a girl something looked bad on them was cause for a debate unless you could see that they actually didn't like it and then it was a risk just in case they were showing signs of not liking it but actually did. All this running of the gauntlet could be easily resolved if his friends could just embrace their body in the same way that he had now done.

Maybe he could introduce them to naturism by telling them about his holiday, being honest about where he had been. He could picture their reaction; it wouldn't be greeted with understanding and interest. According to his friends their body was only for their partner to see and appreciate and that rule stuck no matter how many partners they had been with. Surely as life went on and more and more people had seen their body it became less important who had seen them and who hadn't.

Even though tennis wasn't among them Jim knew certain sports had started off as nude events. At school they had avoided telling him but the internet had informed him that major events like the Olympics had originally been nude. At first this had surprised him because he had found himself wondering how they knew one countries competitor from another but then again the Olympics had probably been very different when it was first ran.

Some sports would work out better than others if clothing was optional to compete in them. There were obvious sports where it would be a bad idea, like rugby – he couldn't imagine scrums being a great experience if the players were nude. Any sport that involved the wearing of pads or guarding equipment would also be hazardous but then there were sports that clothing really didn't matter for. The most obvious of these was any sport that involved being in a swimming pool.

There seemed to be little point in going into a changing room and getting undressed just to cover up the essential areas with a bit of fabric that was neither warm nor waterproof. Essentially these swimming costumes were just used to entertain the need to hide certain body parts. No one actually took any notice of a person in the water unless they were swimming under water and then it was just to avoid collisions. Most leisure pools even got referred to as 'baths' which hinted to them being large communal bathing areas. At home people would use a bath without clothes on so if it wasn't for society he felt sure swimming costumes could be classed as optional.

Jim had learned the hard way that naturism had its downfalls as well as its up sides. From a male perspective he was well aware of the danger of arousal at the most inappropriate time but so far that hadn't been a problem. His one experience of that had been in a very intimate setting with Sasha and she hadn't made any fuss about it.

Much more serious than obvious arousal was dealing with whatever the weather threw at you. While he had been addressing his sporting injury it had come to light that the tennis ball hadn't been the only thing that had attacked his skin. Unknown to him the sun had been making an impression on him in more ways than one.

In a way it was his own fault, it was unusual for him to do anything unprepared but in his rush to get over his fears of naturism he had let his attention slip. He knew he had no one but himself to blame but it was something he never really thought about before. While he was gazing down at the spot that had been assaulted by the tennis ball a second reddened area had come to his attention and this one was a much more tender location.

He tried discretely to place his hand over his manhood to try to avoid bringing attention to it but the action of covering it had the opposite effect. It was stupid of him to think that covering the one part of his body he had been hiding for a week would make it less obvious but that was instinct.

No sooner had he placed his hand on it than Sasha had looked up at him with a puzzled expression. Covering himself after an hour of running about the tennis court naked seemed not only pointless but trivial. She didn't have to say anything for Jim to know why she was looking at him. Slowly he pulled his hand away revealing the second red part of his body causing looks of discomfort from Greg.

"You did remember to use sun cream, didn't you?" Sasha asked as she tried not to smile at his misfortune.

The rents had always told him how important sun cream was when they were on holiday. There wasn't enough good weather at home to worry about it too much but while they were abroad it was an essential part of the daily ritual. In the early days both he and his sister had been smothered in the stuff from head to toe but only the parts of their body that were going to be exposed.

Jim had continued this ritual into his teenage years and although his shoulders had caught a bit of sun he could handle the discomfort there. The problem was that the area below the short line wasn't an area he was used to covering with cream so it hadn't occurred to him when he made the decision to kick his shorts off.

After being helped off the courts by both Sasha and Greg who felt a sense of guilt for the injury Jim had been happy to spend the rest of the afternoon with Sasha alone. She had seemed relieved when even though he picked up his shorts he hadn't rushed to put them back on. Even with the events of the afternoon so far he had made the commitment to try naturism for her.

He liked the sense of freedom, the not worrying about getting his clothes dirty and the idea that fashion really didn't matter. He wasn't sure about the lack of pockets but he could handle that. The deciding factor for him was how happy Sasha seemed now she could enjoy naturism without having to deal with his embarrassment.

****

Sasha appreciated that Jim's first experience of naturism hadn't been without its fair share of drama but she wasn't willing to let him off so easily. It was nobody's fault he had forgotten the sun cream, and the injury could have happened whether he was dressed or not. After they had been left alone she had subtly pushed him until he had agreed to give naturism a chance.

It hadn't taken long to convince him all she had mentioned was the amount of time she had spent dressed for him and he had buckled.

At first she had thought it was some kind of decoy when he had said he wanted to take her into the village. He knew she had to dress to go there making it look like a cleverly placed suggestion of a day out. She had questioned his choice but had soon been assured that he had suggested it because he had been there before and he thought she would like to see it. She pondered for a moment while she tried to accommodate his suggestion and keep her push on naturism prominent in his mind.

"Okay, we will go after breakfast," she had finally responded.

Jim looked pleased when she agreed to the trip but seemed a bit put out when she added her own conditions to it. The first condition was that they spent as much time as possible as full naturists before they went; dressing could be done just before leaving. Her second condition was that they got back for lunch time. In a way this made sense because staying out for the day would mean eating out and it seemed pointless when food was free to them. He knew there was more than that reason for her request but it suited him so he agreed to accommodate her.

Slipping out of bed she wondered over to the wardrobe, there was quite a healthy amount of storage space for clothes when she thought about it. The only time most people would need them was of an evening or at arrival and departure and yet there was a wardrobe and a large set or drawers. Casually she flicked through her hung clothes, the most casual thing she had was her wrap around dress but that was too revealing for a day out. Dismissing it as an option she walked to the set of drawers and opened it trying to remember what she had packed.

In some ways she was relieved when in amongst her assortment of bikinis and underwear she found some shorts and a vest top. She vaguely recalled packing them for the journey back to the airport but hadn't given them a second thought after slipping them in her small luggage case. Although she knew these wouldn't be anywhere near suitable for when she got back home they gave her an opportunity to catch the last of the good weather before going through to catch the plane. Selecting a bikini too she added it to her selection for their trip off site, if she decided to bathe while they were out at least she could get a half decent tan.

The biggest problem with the arrangement she had made with Jim was that she had very few options for carrying the clothing. In all her wildest dreams she hadn't expected to be preparing to leave the site during the two weeks she was away. Digging through her case she pulled out a carrier bag that had somehow found its way into the side pocket. In contrast to everything else she had packed this bag advertised a local store back at home – it was the only reminder of the weather that would be waiting for her that she had with her and she was grateful not to have any additional reminders. Stuffing the items she had selected into her bag she added a light pair of sandals that she used for the evenings before leaving the bedroom. Swinging the bag carelessly beside her she passed between her apartment and Jims taking in the early morning sun. She had tactically arranged to meet him quite early for breakfast in order to make the most of her morning time before she had to burden herself with clothes.

Although she knew he had overslept before this time she was meeting him at his apartment so if she needed to she could wake him up.

Knocking gently at the door she called to him through the plain wooden panel anticipating that she would need to make what was becoming a fairly regular trip to the bedroom window before she would see him. If this had been their first morning she would have taken his oversleeping as a sign but she felt like this was just part of the routine now. She found herself pleasantly surprised when the door started opening without even having to knock twice.

"Morning," she chirped, sliding through the door as soon as it was open wide enough.

She pulled herself to her tiptoes as she passed Jim giving him a quick peck on the cheek before settling into the couch. Taking in her surroundings she found her happy demeanour fading as she looked over at him. Slowly she picked up the bag clutching it close to her body trying to hide the scowl that was replacing her smile.

She knew they had made their agreement to enjoy naturism during their evening together. She had even made sure his sun burn was OK before she made the ground rules. She even remembered how willingly he had agreed to what she had said before mentioning taking her to town. Everything they had discussed had been about spending as much time enjoying naturism as possible. The more she ran through their conversation the more she couldn't understand why he was stood there looking like nothing was wrong but wearing boxer shorts.

"What's that about?" she grunted harshly, pointing over at him.

Jim had barely been awake for more than ten minutes when he had heard the knock at the door. It had surprised him that she had chosen the front door for a change but he wasn't going to question it. It was much easier to let her in the front door than try to pull her in through the window.

Windows seemed like a very unglamorous way to let someone into a person's home under any circumstances. He had heard of friends using windows when their presence was to be kept secret at a partner's home but it had always seemed sneaky. The only other time he had ever heard about people getting in a house through a window was when they had locked themselves out or when they wanted what someone else had in the house. It didn't seem right to sneak someone you were supposed to care for in through the window.

With Sasha's interest in naturism it made the window even more difficult to negotiate. It was difficult enough to imagine trying to pull someone in through a window when they were wearing clothes but when they weren't where did you put your hands? There was too much scope for badly placed hands when there was nothing to hold on to like a belt – it was truly hazardous.

In his half-asleep state he couldn't work out what was making her scowl so much, she had seemed so happy as she came through the door. Maybe he had a mark on his body she didn't recognise, a scratch that he had given himself or something that she had decided shouldn't be there. He peered down his body, he was only just out of bed surely he hadn't done anything wrong. That was when he noticed it, the only thing that could be upsetting her was what he had worn to bed – his boxer shorts.

Jim could see how bad it looked as he kicked them off flicking them awkwardly into his hand. Sasha had made sure he was comfortable with naturism, re-enforcing how much fun it could be several times after the tennis game. She hadn't known her appeal was unnecessary because he had already decided to give it a try for her. He had tried his best to reassure her he was okay with it but then he had mentioned taking her off the complex which contradicted his assurances.

Quickly he hinted toward them being his nightwear and had a subtle dig at her asking her what she wore to bed. His joke was quickly shot down by her reply that she found a smile and skin was the best thing to wear to bed. He had never met a person his own age that slept naked; then again he hadn't discussed night wear with any of his friends – that crossed the line of too much information. In many ways Sasha's reply suited her passion for naturism and at least he had got her smiling again by working out what he was doing wrong.

Making his way to his bedroom he gathered up some items of clothing bundling them together in a pair of soft shoes that would be comfortable to walk in. The arrangement was specific, naturism for as long as they could and then dressed to town and back for lunch. Handing his bundle over to Sasha he quickly offered to take the bag from her and was taken up on his offer as they left the apartment for breakfast.

It didn't take long for Jim to realise that by walking up the path during daylight hours there was a higher risk of bumping into the rents. At least this time he would have advanced warning of their appearance unless they approached from behind. Conscious of the thought they could appear from any angle he discretely looked around trying not to arouse Sasha's suspicion. Thankfully she was too focussed on their journey to the main building to pay much attention to where his eyes were.

Jim knew the risks of being caught looking around when in the company of a woman. Even though he had been out with a number of girls on friendly terms they never appreciated him not giving them full attention. Some of them had come to him in tears after they had seen their boyfriend looking at another woman only to find out the reasons were trivial in most cases. A wondering eye was one of the hardest things to explain under any circumstances but he felt fairly certain Sasha would understand him watching out for the rents.

Keeping to his word he followed Sasha into the restaurant, his first time in this room naked. There were more people than he had expected but then again it was foolish to think it would be empty at a peak time. Trying hard not to consciously stare at anyone while also trying not to show that he was conscious of his nudity was difficult. The experience was made even more harrowing when he got to the meat counter and watched the chef calmly slicing the breakfast sausage.

Sasha grinned sheepishly as she watched him flinch at the large cleaver preparing the meat. In a way it amused her that such a daily activity could cause discomfort to someone but she chose not to comment. She led him over to a table, choosing to eat inside today not at their usual table. This was going to be an ultimate test for him, if they were outside they would be secluded whereas in here they were at the mercy of the much busier restaurant environment.

While they sat calmly eating their breakfast Sasha slid the bag over toward her side of the table and started digging through it for her purse. Discretely she removed a small packet and slid it over to him tucking it under the plate before pulling her hand back. It wasn't until she had her hand back on her knife that she realised how bad her gesture could have looked to anyone watching. A young woman digging in her purse and offering a small packet to the man sat opposite her could be taken as anything – it was only her that knew it was sun cream.

Jim watched carefully as Sasha's hand had made its way over to his side of the table. It seemed a bit late in the day to be trying to hint toward him holding her hand; they had already established themselves as a couple. As her hand slid back to her side of the table he noticed she had placed something under his plate, it was a packet or a note of some kind. Curiosity told him to find out what it was and without thinking he pulled the packet out.

"Just in case ye forgot," Sasha smiled at him, referring to his sun incident from the day before pointing her knife casually towards him.

Instinctively he glanced down at himself; a red line blazed its trail down his manhood as if he was gaining stripes on his body. He had forgotten to put cream on again but that was because he had rushed out of the house this time. Unlike the day before he hadn't actually put any cream on today and he was sure the small sachet wasn't going to cover all of his body. Gracefully he accepted it wondering when he should mention that he hadn't used any cream at all today but decided not to pursue the subject.

After breakfast, they disappeared quickly to the main atrium. Sasha ordered two coffees without asking him if he wanted one. Even if he didn't she felt sure she could drink them, the cups were only half the size of the ones she had back at home. It didn't take long for Jim to admit he hadn't used any cream and rush off to the pharmacist store to buy a small bottle. Sasha looked up at him as he returned; it would be nice to have an extra layer on her back, which was the one place she found hardest to cover. "Do my back for me while you're at it, would you, Jim?" she asked softly, turning her back to him as she spoke.

Gently he applied cream on her soft skin wondering how she managed to do this by herself normally. He had quite often neglected his back concentrating on his shoulders, chest and legs but then again he would usually spend a lot of time with only his front exposed to the sun.

"You know, Sasha, I think I like the outfit you have on most of all," he commented cheekily as a dribble of cream ran down her spine.

She glanced over her shoulder, intentionally whipping his face with her hair in retaliation for his comment. Smiling as he brushed her hair out of his eyes, he could see she was just being playful.

"If you're a good boy, I will wear it just for you one day too." She winked at him cheekily, turning her head to let him finish her back for her.

Chapter Nineteen

The village trip

It came as no surprise to Jim that Sasha had kept to her word completely and waited until they were nearly at the gate to put her clothes on. In the same way as soon as she had mentioned leaving Jim had taken himself off to the bathroom to get dressed. Sasha had at first wondered why he had made such an occasion of it by using the bathroom but decided not to mention it. She knew that if she had got to change clothes back at home she would do the same.

As much as she had no problem with her body being on display she knew that disrobing in front of anyone that wasn't used to her naturist side was a bad mistake. Her friends back at home would have mixed reactions to her not hiding away. The male ones would be caught somewhere between wondering what she was doing while trying to make out they weren't looking and enjoying the show as they would put it.

In her mind the expression to enjoy the show when a girl was trying to discretely get changed cheapened the whole thing. There was no show to speak about; none of them had paid to see it and in most cases they would be too embarrassed to pay to see such a show. There were places available in Dublin if they wanted to enjoy the show – all they had to do was convince the doormen that they were over eighteen.

Adding to her frustration was the fact that if by chance a girl did accidentally show some flesh when getting changed it was usually nothing more exciting than maybe a thigh or the strap of her bra. Most of the girls she knew had more sense than to disrobe completely in a place that boys could see them. There was even one corner of the changing room at the local swimming pool that was avoided due to a crack in the wall. No one knew where the crack led to but as a precaution no one went near it when they were removing their swimming costume.

She had sometimes been tempted to "accidentally" show a bit too much just to see what sort of reaction it got but in a small village environment it was risky to do such a thing. One moment you would be victim to an accident and within a week you would have boys queuing up to take you shopping for clothes just in case it happened again. In some ways this sort of accident could be beneficial to a girl that liked clothing but she wasn't that sort of girl.

Jim waited patiently for her as she slipped her shorts on wondering at first why she hadn't put anything on under them but quickly realised there wasn't really any need. Girls back at home had talked about how daring it was to go commando before telling him they had worn shorts which in some ways squashed the adventurous nature of doing so. He had never been brave enough to point out to them that the whole thing about going commando was the thrill of maybe being caught out.

If he had at any stage told them to make it real they would have to wear a skirt of some kind he was sure it would have been greeted with hostility. People that hinted at seeing what was hidden under a girls skirt had frequently been condemned by girls soon after. It wasn't as if telling them to wear a skirt was saying that they had to perform handstands to prove it but either way it wasn't seen as acceptable conversation material.

He was thankful but didn't comment when Sasha tied a bikini top on before covering it in a small top. He knew there was an irony in him wishing this girl to wear more clothes but they were going into town and clothing wasn't optional there. If he had told his friends that he had to pester the girl to get dressed he would have been mentally tortured for days or possibly weeks before something else came up to distract them.

Jim felt like he was too familiar with the narrow road that wound its way toward the town. It had only been a couple of days since the last time he had been walking down it. This time though he was in a much more positive state of mind and able to take in his surroundings. He also had Sasha gripping his hand firmly but tenderly making the trip a much more pleasant experience.

Unlike his first journey into town this time he had found the fifteen minute walk back to civilisation a pleasant one. He put the more positive experience mainly down to being in Sasha's company but elected not to tell her. In a way he felt bad dragging her away from the complex when that had meant dressing but he wanted her to see what he had seen in her absence.

Quickly they turned the corner on to a notably busier street; unlike the first winding road this one actually had cars on it. Each side of the road had residential properties that reminded him how unspoilt Vassillikos was in comparison to other resorts. In contrast to the towns that he was used to from previous holidays this town had kept its charm and its heritage. Even in what he assumed was the middle of the town the use of languages that were not the local language was rare. Jim had only seen one other property that bared a resemblance to being a possible hotel but he was sure others existed probably hidden down the streets that pointed back toward the coast. A scattering of shops had embraced the need for tourists to the locality and had attempted to advertise facilities in a second language but Jim had noticed that even this wasn't English.

Leading Sasha across to a small green that looked like the centrepiece of the town Jim invited her to find somewhere to sit. Like an excited school child she kissed him on the cheek and scurried off to find the best spot for the sun leaving him to look round the shops. To Jim this was like a role reversal on what happened back at home, usually it would be him sitting waiting. On this occasion there was a hidden agenda behind what he classed as his way of distracting her.

Making a beeline to the far end of the park Sasha looked around, she could see Jim casually walking down the line of shops in pursuit of 'snacks', as he had put it. Getting food seemed pointless when she was determined to get back to the complex before lunch but it wouldn't hurt to have a small picnic while they were in the town. Slipping her top off she sat on it cursing herself for not wearing the full bikini so she could remove her shorts too but at least her legs would get a bit of sun.

Lying back on her tiny top she stretched her arms up and felt the sun catch her body as she took a deep breath. It didn't take long before she found the sun being blocked by an overcasting shadow. She propped herself up on her elbows half expecting it to be Jim but found herself looking at a stranger of about her age. She could tell that the boy was either local or of Mediterranean upbringing by the healthy tan that seemed quite permanent. She could tell from his height that even though his face looked young he was probably somewhere around her age. As if she was swatting an imaginary fly she waved her hand trying to hint to this boy to move out of the way.

Edouardo acknowledged the gesture and responded accordingly by moving to a position by her side. As far as he was concerned by signalling at him she was making contact and that meant that she knew he was there. Carefully he made an assessment deciding that this raven haired girl looked like she was English. He had seen English tourists before and had vaguely learned a few words of their language.

"I sit?" he commented, pointing at the ground next to her.

Sasha had seen and heard about this before, when her family had been on normal holidays she had seen older friends dealing with the befriending of a stranger. Shrugging casually she waved her hand trying to hint to him that she didn't care what he did as long as he got out of her way. Edouardo took he hand gesture as an invitation and peeled his shirt off placing it as close as he could to her before sitting down.

From here on in she knew that his next move would be to try and make conversation with her. This conversation could go one of many directions, there was a possibility that he was trying to sell her something but she doubted that theory. More than likely he was going to make an attempt to get to know her in what would turn into something similar to a speed dating event. He was likely to ask her a series of badly worded questions in an effort to find out where she was from, her name and how long she was there.

During this time she already knew she was going to attempt to let him down gently by mentioning Jim as many times as possible. In her mind this was the much more polite way of handling him, the other option was to tell him in no uncertain terms to go away. She had learned that getting aggressive with boys like this was pointless as it caused an unnecessary scene. On the positive side at least this mystery boy would keep her entertained while Jim was on his adventures around the village.

When he had come into the town the first time Jim had subliminally made a note of some of the shops before he had found a cafe to while away a few hours over a glass of coke. Now he needed to try and remember where he had seen the sign referring to trips to Laganas beach. His mother had confirmed something about the turtles on the way from the airport and somehow he had remembered it.

Going to see turtles was the sort of thing that would have appealed to a lot of his friends back home which was why the sign had caught his eye. When he saw it he had cursed it because of the grave outlook of the situation he was in with Sasha but now he wanted to surprise her with it. The only thing that was holding him back was that it would mean another trip off the complex which he felt sure she wouldn't be happy with but hopefully the enticement of turtles would make it okay.

After a few desperate moments of scanning windows, he finally found the card, taking note of the bad grammar before entering the shop. It was clear to him that even if there were tourists in this area English wasn't considered to be a priority as a language. Along the narrow walls of the shop was a selection of small souvenir type items mixed in with local delicacies. He decided the range of sweets would make a good distraction when he got back to Sasha and picked a couple of bags that looked edible before approaching the counter.

Patiently looking back at him was a boy who looked like he was about twelve years old. Jim gazed at him before glancing over at the shop and making a mental note of how the long narrow corridor like building with only one way in and out would make an ideal location to trap someone. If he was going to make this transaction he had to make it quickly before his mind played too many tricks on him. He could almost hear the door being bolted in his mind as he smiled and took the final few steps to the counter.

One of the difficulties he had seen before when dealing with a person whose knowledge of the English language was limited was their assumption that the person they were speaking to was American. At first Jim had tried to correct the boy by referring to London but after the first few attempts he gave up agreeing with whatever the boy was saying when he mentioned New York and the big Apple. Focussing on the reason he had started this conversation was much more important than correcting geographical errors. Several bouts of sign language and finger pointing later Jim seemed to be making progress and have got to a stage where the small assistant was writing out a receipt for the trip he was trying to book.

Mentally noting what was left of his first weeks spending allowance Jim added a couple of cans of what he hoped was some kind of soft drink before looking at the boy to thank him. Just as he was slipping the voucher into his pocket an elderly woman appeared behind the boy placing her hand on his shoulders. Jim took the assumption this new arrival was some kind of relative and waved at her graciously thanking her for what she hadn't done before turning leave the shop. He cringed as he heard the woman shouting 'Ah, American', increasing his pace and slipping quickly out of the door.

He glanced over at the green which was quickly becoming populated with a mixture of what he felt sure was both tourists and locals confirming his suspicion that somewhere hidden in the village were more hotels than he had seen on his travels. Vassillikos wasn't the first resort that came to mind when a person mentioned Zante but clearly it had an attraction to more than just naked people for a holiday. As he scanned the crowd he found himself wishing Sasha was a blonde haired not the dark haired girl she actually was. With a healthy mixture of Mediterranean's all with similar looking dark hair and varying degrees of sun tans it was hard to tell one person from the next.

He tried to remember which way she had gone after he had made his excuses to go to the shop but then again her first direction of travel wasn't guaranteed to reflect her actual position. Using logic he ruled out a number of people due to their age and finally spotted her leaning on her elbows sitting next to someone he hoped was a man. The long hair of the person sat with her made it hard to tell if it was male or female but the fact the person was clearly topless made him hope it was male. As much as he was now getting used to seeing nudity as part of his holiday he had hoped that their short time off site would prove to be among what he classed as normal people. As he got closer he realised that his assumption of masculinity was correct but he didn't know who this stranger was. In a way it seemed too coincidental that it might be someone she knew from a previous holiday but he couldn't rule out the option.

He was determined to be careful not to make any rash assumptions or jump to the wrong conclusion this time. The chances were the situation was much more innocent than he expected just like it had been the last time he had seen her with a man. Apart from anything else he didn't want to fall back to where he had been before and he didn't want to increase the number of people that were familiar with who he was if this man was from the complex.

Walking casually around the Sasha's side and tactically avoiding the area taken up by this mystery person he smiled over at her as he put the bag with his newly acquired sweets and drinks down. The look of relief as Sasha saw him spoke volumes to explain who this mystery man was.

"I missed you," she whispered softly as she sprang to her feet, throwing her arms round him.

The energy she put into hugging Jim was similar to the hug she had presented him with when they had first been reunited. As unprepared as he had been before Jim found himself knocked back by her enthusiasm. In some ways although it was nice to be welcomed in such a warm way he wasn't sure if his body could handle her throwing herself at him every time he left her side and returned. Turning proudly she pushed herself into Jim until she could feel his heart beating through her back. She grabbed his arms wrapping them round her waist as she looked casually down at the bewildered Edouardo.

"This, my boyfriend," she announced, clamping her hands against Jim's and pressing his hands into her stomach.

Jim pressed his face into her hair trying to hide the smile that was forcing its way onto his face. He had heard of dogs marking their territory and cringed when he had been told how they did it. Marking the territory was something the male did as a deterrent to other males to stay away. What he had witnessed Sasha doing was something like the human version of this, she wasn't marking her territory she was just telling a stray male to stay away because she was already taken.

Jim watched as suddenly Edouardo realised he had somewhere else to be, trying not to giggle at the broken English. Like the intruding dog in territory that didn't belong to him Edouardo quickly jumped to his feet grabbing the top that he had been sitting on and waved a vague goodbye before disappearing across the green. While they were in town it seemed like a good time to let her know about his surprise purchase but timing his announcement was important too. He felt certain he was going to face a few objections to the trip he had arranged firstly because it was another trip off the complex but that was easily resolved by the second issue.

From what he had understood of his conversation with the young counter assistant, the trip was early morning. He knew Sasha was okay with early morning but this was really early, he had even checked the voucher just to be sure he had heard the time correctly. According to this twelve year old expert the best time to see the turtles was as the sun was rising and that meant meeting the guide at four in the morning. On the positive side such an early start did mean they wouldn't miss any of the day time activity so she couldn't complain about it too much hopefully.

Guiding her back to the ground so he could sit with her he waited until she had finished positioning herself before assessing the dangers of mentioning the trip to her. She had decided for reasons only she knew that it was a good time to lay with her head on his legs. Maybe this was something to do with the territorial display she had just demonstrated, he wasn't sure. Carefully he placed one arm across as if he was trying to hold her close but tactically he knew this arm was now a barrier against her sitting upright. The choice now was whether to tell her or let her read the voucher for herself and carefully monitor her reaction. He thought over the voucher for a few minutes trying to picture it in his head and realised very quickly that it had the price on it which he didn't want her to know.

"Have you ever heard of the turtles of Laganas?" he asked casually, trying to keep his question vague while judging her level of interest.

Sasha peered up at him through one half open eye trying to focus on his face and avoid the sun blinding her. She was familiar with the story of the turtles that used Laganas as a breeding ground; her father had told her about it before their first trip out to the island. His question puzzled her as it seemed unrelated to anything they had discussed before and the chances of Jim having spoken to her dad were minimal.

"Yeah, they come here every year. Dad told me about them, why?" Her response seemed both comprehensive and precise.

In some ways Jim was relieved that she knew about them but he had hoped she might give him a hint as to how interested she was in them. Instead her response was similar to the type of reply he would expect if they were playing poker, straight to the point. Jim had never played poker but he had heard that a good player didn't give away anything in their eyes it was only when the cards were revealed that the truth was known.

Without another word he dug his hand into the bag and found the voucher deciding it didn't really matter if she saw the price. Carefully he placed it on her body watching it subtly as it balanced across her breasts before falling toward her neck. Lifting his arm to allow her to move he watched as she picked it up and sat upright to read it. This was make or break time, if she liked it he had got away with it but if she didn't he was sure she would let him know physically of verbally.

Sasha caught the card that Jim had placed on her body and was curious as to what it was as she grabbed at it and sat up. She knew there was a chance it was nothing and he had just placed it there for fun but if she left it there she would end up with the imprint of it on her skin. Angling it so the sun wasn't hiding the words from her eyes she glanced over it. In the top corner was an outlined image of a sea turtle and a company name that had clearly not been thought out but had been designed for the American tourist market. The date on the card was two days away and the next line down said that the voucher was for two people, but whoever had written it had used the incorrect spelling of 'two.'

Glancing down the page she could already tell what this was, Jim had booked for them to see the turtles which meant another day in textile land. In her mind she had always wanted to see them but was reluctant to leave the complex. She smiled as she read through the card a second time; it was a lovely gesture, very thoughtful of him and truly reflected why she liked him so much. At the bottom of the card was the pickup time: four in the morning. Surely this wasn't going to be a full day, she decided.

"Jim, I love it." She pulled him into a warm hug, gripping the card in her hands. "I guess we will have to stay together tomorrow night so we don't oversleep," she whispered, softly maintaining her hug.

In all his wildest dreams he had never expected Sasha to suggest spending the night together. He knew in his heart that such a suggestion didn't mean anything other than they would be in the same place as each other overnight and in many ways it made sense. Jim had been invited to sleepovers before by groups of friends but something about being the only male in a room full of girls that thought of you as one of their own didn't appeal to him.

He had seen scenarios where men were left at the mercy of women in movies and on TV; as much as he hoped they were far-fetched and outlandish, he knew that being the only male in the room was a vulnerable position to be in. In a girls bedroom there were far too many things that could be used against a man in the long run. Makeup was one of the biggest problems that could be used as a weapon against him. If makeup was suggested he knew that could lead to makeovers and from there to pictures of the makeover which could then leak on to social media, ruining his credibility as a straight male.

It didn't take long after the presentation of the voucher for Sasha to decide she had seen as much as she wanted to of the town and suggest they made their way back. Jim glanced around as he stood up he could see the back of what looked like Edouardo sitting in amongst a new group of girls. Clearly his less than subtle rejection from Sasha had not deterred him and he had decided that he had a better chance with a group than with one individual. One of them appeared to be playing with his hair already – that was a clear sign to Jim that a makeover was likely, if only Edouardo knew what he was letting himself in for. Keeping a good distance between themselves and Edouardo's new harem Sasha and Jim made their way back out of the town.

In a way it surprised Jim that the walk back to the road that led to the complex seemed to take less time than it had to get to the town. The more he thought about it the more it made sense because he knew that Sasha was keen to get back to the environment she loved. After the adventure with Edouardo he couldn't really blame her for being eager to return. Slipping down the quiet lane he knew he was less than fifteen minutes away from the complex again and Sasha's smile told him she thought it was a good thing.

For reasons she couldn't explain suddenly now they were on the road back to the complex Sasha was in a mood to do something outrageous. This had never happened to her before, but then again she had never been off the complex before nor had a boyfriend before, so today was a very unique day. Part of her knew that it was a curiosity to see what reaction she was going to get from Jim. She hadn't had a shocked reaction from him in a while and as much as she didn't like torturing him she didn't want him feeling like she was going to let him off the hook either.

The biggest problem she had was how to implement the plan she was forming in her head and how soon to implement it. She needed to be alone for a few moments to put the plan into action and although the road had proved itself to be quiet she didn't want to risk too much. She knew vaguely how long the road back to the complex was, it was too early to do anything adventurous just yet just in case a car appeared.

She knew that in order to carry out her plan she had to distract Jim into letting go of her hand so she could disappear out of sight for a few moments but how could she do that without raising suspicion? There was the obvious option that she could claim an urgent need to answer the call of nature but that seemed too tacky. A close alternative was that she felt ill but with Jim being the gentleman he was he might offer to hold her hair for her. If she used a less subtle option like just disappearing into the bushes he would probably follow her which was still no good.

"Wait here a minute for me," she blurted out as they walked past a larger healthier looking bush.

She wasn't sure if he would do as she had asked but they were within about sixty metres of the complex and she had no idea how to make her excuse to disappear off the path. Hopefully her random statement would be all she needed but she knew he would be suspicious of why she had disappeared if she took too long. Peering from her hiding place toward the complex she confirmed the rough distance in her mind before peering up the road again and confirming there was no oncoming traffic. What she had in mind was completely insane but she wanted to add a bit of adventure to her life and she felt like now was the time to do it.

Jim found himself stood at the side of the road holding a carrier bag full of the meaningless snacks he had bought and the voucher for their trip as Sasha disappeared behind a bush. Her request seemed vague but she seemed like she was in a hurry to disappear and looking at the bush lined path he decided it was better not to follow her. There was after all no way he could know why she had suddenly run off, sometimes things had to be done and he wasn't going to question that.

Curiously he tried to peek round the side of the bush that Sasha had disappeared behind. Wherever she was she wasn't in clear view so all he could do was wait just as she asked. Ahead of them, in clear view was the entrance to the complex, it puzzled his as to why whatever she was doing couldn't wait the few minutes the remainder of the walk would take.

From her concealed location Sasha made her way carefully and slowly round the bush. As the branched thinned out she could see Jim stood patiently waiting at the end of the bush she had disappeared through. Peeking down the road she could see that, as she expected, there was still no traffic, it was like the only people using this road were coming to the complex. Slipping back on to the road she felt her heart beating fast as she walked as calmly as she could up to Jim.

"Okay, I'm ready." Her voice startled him as he had been expecting to see her reappear from the same place where she had disappeared.

As Jim turned to welcome her back and offer his hand so they could complete their journey he nearly dropped the bag. Sasha stood smiling calmly at him her arms stretched forward clamping a neat bundle for him. Pressed neatly between her hands was the bikini top and shorts she had been wearing all morning leaving her wearing only the smile. He felt himself breathing heavily as he looked around conscious that they were not on the complex yet.

Suddenly the urgency to get back to the complex had hit a new level for Jim. He wasn't sure if Sasha had lost sense of where she was or there was some other motivation behind her doing what was. Ultimately he knew and felt sure she knew it was illegal but she didn't seem too worried about it.

"The complex is this way, Jim, are you coming?" she asked with a casual smile on her face as she dropped her clothes into the bag and walked past him.

Two could play this game, she clearly wasn't worried about being caught and if she was going to get in trouble he was as well. Quickly he slipped his shorts off and kicked them at her watching as they caught her on the back and fell to the ground. Sasha stopped in her tracks and turned to see Jim tucking his clothes into the bag and picking it up.

"I'll race ya to reception." He poked his tongue out as he ran past her with the bag in his hand.

Chapter Twenty

Golfing around

Having a naturally competitive streak Jim hadn't made the race back to the complex easy for Sasha. He had comfortably reached the finishing point of the reception wall ahead of her and was now trying to control his breathing. At first he hadn't been sure why he was breathing so heavily after such a short distance. From start to finish he estimated the entire run to be less than 200 metres which even with his little interest in sports was still minimal.

One of his neighbours at home was a daily early morning jogger and had even almost convinced his dad to join them at one stage. Dad had seemed quite keen to participate until he heard what time the guy left the house and how far he ran. Something about jogging for about an hour put him off the concept especially as it was a pre work activity. As an alternative he decided to maintain his weekly routine of a trip to the local pub but make an effort to walk to it instead of driving.

There was more than one advantage to walking to the pub, his new found urge to get fit meant he could also drink more. To Jim these activities seemed to cancel each other out but dad justified it with one of his usual sarcastic responses. This time it had been that he got enough exercise running around after the kids and the walk to the pub was just a top up.

In contrast to the fitness regime that was embraced by his neighbour there were a number of people in his road that insisted on going to the local shops by car. The common excuse was that the car was handy just in case you bought more than you expected. At first this justification made sense but as Jim became more aware of what was around him he realised that it was just an excuse. The local shops comprised of a newsagents, a chemist, a travel agents, a bookmakers and not forgetting the pub. None of these shops would seem to have sufficient stock choices to make a person's shopping load too heavy to walk home with.

The thing that aggravated Jim more than anything was that the rule about driving to the shops changed if the person was going to the pub. The distance from his house to the pub was the longest out of all the commercial premises which added to his argument about walking to the shops. Not only did he set an example by walking the short distances to the shops he had also in recent years taken to walking to school which was notably further but in a different direction.

This decision to make his own way to school had been more of a tactical one than anything else. It was really all about damage limitation rather than maintaining a level of fitness but that didn't matter. He had the get out clause that if the weather was too bad for considering the walk he knew his mum would be happy to drop him there on the way to work.

Being dropped to school by the rents was a skill in itself that for many took years to perfect. The problem was that in a car you had no control over certain things like how close to the school they parked to let you out. You could make suggestions or recommendations of parking spaces but there was always the argument of there being somewhere closer to park.

The proximity of the parking space to the school was a vital aspect because as the passenger you had no way of refusing any requests the driver made of you. Protesting against favours could result in future lifts being made less available to the child. The worse of these requests was the famed goodbye kiss that was a favourite amongst mothers. As a teenage boy got older this kiss became less appealing due to the nature of it. Worse still was the fact that no matter how close you were to the school the moment of the goodbye kiss frequently coincided with the appearance of one of your friends.

Conclusively Jim ruled out the idea that his heart was beating at the rate of knots due to lack of fitness the more likely option was an adrenaline rush. It didn't really matter if the distance from the start of the run to the finish line was five metres or fifty kilometres there was something about running naked that was invigorating. He felt sure that such an activity would be seen as normal behaviour – maybe even an organised event on the complex but he hadn't started his run on the complex.

Taking into consideration that what they had done was for all intent and purposes illegal made it all the more exciting. He wasn't sure that he was ready to repeat the activity any time soon but that didn't take away from the thrill of having done it. He had been a little bit unlucky in as much as that he had seen something fall out of the bag and he was sure it was one of his items of clothing as they had been the last things into the bag.

In fact, not only was he sure it was something of his, by process of elimination the last item he had put in the bag had been the shorts he had kicked at Sasha so it was likely to be them that he had lost. In a way he could have stopped to pick them up but that wouldn't have been practical as Sasha was behind him and would have more than likely collided with him. His shorts were probably by now being considered as part of a home for some small animal – a rabbit possibly.

The idea of a small creature getting comfortable in his shorts concerned Jim a little bit. He even felt his skin crawl at the idea but that was because he had heard of some towns in England where shoving a live animal down a person trousers was seen as a normal activity. Thankfully Jim had never been to the places where this activity was apparently popular.

Now they were back on the complex Jim was aware that he was back in a place where he could bump into the rents at any stage. So far he had been fairly lucky having only encountered them during the evenings and on that one unfortunate occasion in the Sauna. Sasha had mentioned to him about making them officially known as a couple to both his and her parents on the way back from the town.

That would mean meeting them and actually talking to them in a civilized manner for a short time. He had tactically suggested they leave it for another day because he wanted to arrange it with them and that was best done in the evening. He was hoping that maybe he could arrange to meet them of an evening too but Sasha had insisted that the meeting needed to be before they went to Laganas for the turtles. That gave them just over twenty-four hours for her to officially meet his parents and him to meet hers.

Jim had met girls' parents before but only under the heading of being a friend and although it had taken some convincing he had always managed to assure the suspicious father that all he was to them was a friend. This time it was going to be different for a number of reasons; firstly there was the environment they were in. Sasha had briefly met the rents on their first night and although his dad had labelled her his girlfriend they had corrected the error.

They had agreed to pace the meetings of parents out during the course of the day. Jim realised as soon as Sasha mentioned the word 'day' that one way or another they were going to be in the company of either her parents or his while they were potentially naked. Having already endured a brief run in with the rents naked he discretely suggested he should meet her parents in the evening which thankfully she had agreed to without questioning his reasons.

Without realising it Sasha managed to successfully distract Jims mind from the thought of meeting her parents by suggesting a game of golf. Jim had briefly caught professionals playing this game and had often wondered about how much fun it actually was. Unlike other individual sports where you hit a ball, like tennis, with golf nobody actually returned the ball to you. Instead the person hitting the ball then endured a long and normally quite casual walk to wherever their ball had landed.

He wasn't sure if it was just a cynical side within him but he failed to see the logic in hitting an object just to chase after it. Adding to the complexity of the game was the fact that whoever had created the course seemed to be of the impression it would make it more fun by putting sand pits intermittently on it. Jim knew these sand pits were referred to as bunkers but whenever he heard the name he could only think of the holes that were used for hiding in during times of war.

Bunkers however were among the more sensible terms used in the game, it could in some ways be categorised along with the green and the fairway. All of these terms actually seemed to make a lot more sense than some of the other terms he heard being used. He had enquired with people that found the game interesting and had established that reference to a birdie was a good thing and a bogey was a bad thing but then nobody wanted a bogey in any context.

The clubs had unique names too, a putter he could understand and he could even understand a sand wedge which seemed to be the preferred weapon against bunkers. After those two clubs he got lost in the others which seemed to be referred to as either woods or irons. He accepted that their names probably referred to something historical and if he had the inclination to find out he could probably track their names to a certain event. However researching such a thing seemed pointless to a person whose interest in the sport was minimal.

Several times he had heard people asking each other what their handicap was and sometimes the quick reply of 'the clubs'. The first time he heard this it had made him chuckle but the more times it got used the less fun it became. Presumably the handicap was again something a person learned if their interest was high enough. In comparison handicaps seemed much harder to explain than the offside rule in football which he had a vague knowledge of.

Thankfully he had mentally decided to focus on doing stuff that Sasha wanted as a way of acknowledging he had unintentionally restricted her so far. This meant that he would have little chance coming face to face with any of the bizarre fashions associated with golf. The caps he could understand as they shielded the sun from the player's eyes but some of the other items seemed over the top. Maybe there were more advantages to naturism than he had accounted for, at least without clothes there was no clash of colours.

Sasha had highlighted that this wasn't normal golf but mini golf which to some extent was a relief to Jim because that meant they wouldn't be walking too far to retrieve their ball. As a child his dad had taken them on pitch and putt courses and allowed him and his sister to have a go with one of the clubs. Both of them had adopted similar awkward grips on the club holding it a bit like the pole that was used for support on a moving bus.

Rigidly they had turned their body instead of swinging the club as they hit the ball in the general direction of the hole. Every so often one of them would get lucky and actually get the ball to its desired destination but more often than not it took a subtle kick from dad to get in anywhere close. No matter how far the ball travelled Dad had always treated it like the best shot ever and applauded whichever one of his children had played it.

Without showing his reluctance to play the game Jim followed Sasha to the reception desk to get the equipment. He was familiar with reception as a location to pick up equipment for a sporting activity but also aware that usually a deposit was required. Luckily on this occasion he had money on him just in case but the more he thought about it the more he realised expecting a deposit on a naturist site was not practical. Maybe they would take a key card or something but then again if equipment was lost what were they going to do – lock you out of your room? He could imagine that eviction for a lost item of sport equipment was far too harsh as a penalty.

Waiting patiently for their request was a petite girl that seemed not much older than Sasha and him. Being the novice at requesting equipment and wanting to stay as far out of sight as he could from their young receptionist Jim pretended to be looking at the pictures on the wall while Sasha asked. He stared blankly up at what turned out to be a map of the island with large red arrows pointing out areas of interest dotted across it. In one familiar corner was a larger arrow that may as well have said 'you are here' but instead just had the name of the complex plastered above it.

Sasha tapped him on the shoulder with the end of one of the clubs hiding a smile as she saw his right hand cupping his chin. This was obviously his attempt at looking like he knew what he was looking for on the map and maybe he did but she doubted it. Next to the large arrow advertising the complex was a picture of a turtle and an arrow pointing to Laganas. In less than two days' time she would be going there with him and she was really looking forward to it even though it meant time off the complex again.

The cold metal against his warmed flesh sent a chill down his back as he turned preparing to receive the clubs. Much to his surprise Sasha only had two clubs in her hand that he recognised as being putting style clubs. This slim selection of clubs surprised him, he knew it was only mini golf but with just a putter each the game was going to be a long one.

Grabbing his club and a ball that was bright yellow in colour he followed her out of the building. In his few attempts to watch golf on TV he had never seen the players using balls of such a vivid colour. Admittedly with the sometimes outlandish fashions luminous balls had a high risk of clashing with their clothes or those of their opponent but he was sure that wasn't the reason for it. A more logical explanation was that the bright balls were a hotels way of saying – we know your crap at the game but we will humour you by letting you play.

He could visualise a professional golfer on holiday being presented with one of these balls. In his mind they might either take it with a pinch of salt or they would get upset at either not having been recognised or not being given the standard white ball. Then again it would make sense for a golf professional to bring their own balls with them in a way – as long as they could get them past the security gates at the airport. The logical answer of course was to put them in the check in bag but then again as he had no intention of becoming professional or asking a professional it didn't really matter.

As Jim followed Sasha round the front side of the main building he realised that he had never actually been past that particular part of the building before. It occurred to him that despite the time he had been on the complex he had only ever approached the building from this side on his way in through the main gate. Even on the rare occasions that he had approached it from this side he had avoided the path they were now on as it led away from the apartments.

Tucked down the far side of the building was an area that was enclosed by healthy looking bushes. An arched wire gate announced in moulded letters that disappeared into the gates surround if you didn't look properly were the words 'Mini Golf'. They walked through and Jim looked down toward the sea wondering how big this course was. He had worked out that if they had been on the correct side of the building this area was hidden from them by its high bushes but it was somewhere near their path down to their favourite part of the beach.

Suddenly the realisation as to why they only had a putter hit him with a huge sigh of relief. Somewhere lost in translation between Anglo-American and Greek the name mini golf referred to what he knew as crazy golf. This was a much easier and in a number of ways much more fun game than anything that resembled normal golf. This revelation also explained why Sasha had been quite casually referring to being able to achieve the coveted hole in one on several occasions.

Jim had seen and played on crazy golf courses before and admired the imagination of the person who created the courses. On the odd occasion that he and his family had ventured down to the beach they had seen and more than once played on a course near their regular beach. That particular course had holes that seemed to vary in the skill level required and in some cases challenged their mathematical skills too.

It was almost as if the person that created the course had run out of ideas for fun challenges and had decided the play with angles instead. One of his particular favourites on that course was a hole that had a large house built in the middle. The front door of the house was the direction to play the ball and the back door was its escape onto what would be the green on a normal golf course.

The challenge was what happened to the ball in between entering the house and exiting it. Depending on the speed the ball was played more often than not it returned to you at the front entrance instead of appearing out the back door. Jim was the first of his family to successfully navigate the ball to appear at the back of the house. His father had spent hours working out what was inside the concealed area stopping the ball from continuing its journey and eventually joined Jim as a successor of the hole. His mother and sister both came under the category of having gracefully given up on the hole and moved on – a category that had more members than the elite group Jim was a part of.

This course he was now looking at seemed to have a theme of Grecian mythology and history running through it. Jim recognised a few of the characters that stood in between the player and the hole they were trying to complete. His knowledge of Greek history was minimal but the designer seemed to have taken into account that most visitors had a limited knowledge and had worked with that.

Just like the course he remembered from his childhood this one had some holes that played on angles and others that had obstacles to clear. The first hole seemed too easy, the scale model of the Parthenon gave several possible routes toward the hole. Casually Jim lined his ball up and took aim at the gap between one of the many rows of pillars. The tricky bit was that if the ball got stuck half way down the row it would be difficult to retrieve. Keeping his tactics in mind he chose one of the outer rows and hit the ball directly at the gap between the first and second rows.

To his amazement the ball bounced off what looked like thin air and returned to him. Sasha smiled at him politely; she had made a similar error on her first attempt at playing this game. After several failed attempts she realised the only real gap was between the central set of pillars all the rest were closed off with clear Perspex. Placing her ball, she cleverly aimed it at the central passage and tapped it gently. She watched it idly wander down between the pillars on to the slope, which allowed it to clear the far end of the building and land within a short distance of the hole.

Hole number two presented a different challenge, this one started at the entrance to a tunnel that had been shaped to look like a snakes tail. Once inside the snake the ball disappeared out of view dropping down a slope and appearing randomly out of one of the heads of hydra. Unlike the first hole this one was based on how lucky the player was, getting the ball into the snake was easy but there was no control of where it would appear. The only guarantee seemed to be that it would make an appearance somewhere near the hole.

Having won one hole each thanks to a lucky break causing his ball to appear from the middle head Jim took the first strike at the third hole. Just like number one this one appeared far too easy with a clear gap between the legs of what seemed to be a model of Colossus. The knees of Colossus disappeared into a blue painted surface that had been ripples to make it look like the sea. Jim could see that this hole wasn't going to be as straight forward as it looked, hundreds of bumps sat between the start point and the hole. He hit the ball and watched it bobble between the mounds as it clumsily trickled through the gap toward the hole.

Jim inspected the next hole carefully, in a central location there was a box that was opened to look like a treasure chest. Inside the chest concealed under a glass cover was an ornate design that seemed to be a track of some kind. At the beginning of the course the words 'Hope lies at the end of Pandora's box' were written in several languages. Sasha tapped her ball first getting it to the entrance of the box before lightly hitting it in. The ball rested against an invisible wall preventing it from falling in one direction on the track.

Quickly she skipped to the side of the box and fiddled with a series of levers manoeuvring the ball around the delicate design. Jim watched intently trying to map her movements in his mind; she knew the course and therefore had the advantage. After a few moments the ball seemed to disappear into a hidden area before appearing at the other end of the box ready to be putted. Mentally he acknowledged the engineering as he followed her lead bringing them to two holes each as they went on to number five.

Pandora's Maze

Awaiting them next was a carefully designed mountain with a flat plateau at the top. From this point the ball had to be carefully tapped on to a path that led it like a helter skelter down the side of the mountain and toward the hole. The first problem Jim could see was if the ball was hit too hard it would end up using the mountain as some kind of elaborate ramp before possibly hitting someone over the other side of the bushes. Thankfully he followed Sasha's advice and played the hole with extra care preventing any unnecessary disasters.

Hole six was a play on angles that had been very cleverly shaped to represent a trident. Two starting positions were offered one on the left and one on the right prong of the fork shape. Conveniently the middle prong was unavailable as from there it would have been a straight shot to the top of the handle where the hole lay. Along the handle of the fork images of Poseidon had been delicately painted to remind the player who this hole was representing. If a person played it carefully they could make the ball follow the edges of the trident but if a shot was too heavy they would spend hours trying to get in a good place to hit the shot to the hole.

An oversized foot faced them at the next hole, with the toes pointing toward the starting point. Sasha allowed Jim to take the first shot at the obstacle successfully hitting the ball in through what would have been the little toe only to see it reappear from the middle toe. He looked down at the ball puzzled at first but realising that he had to choose the correct toe. Cleverly he offered to let Sasha play the next shot but wasn't surprised when she politely declined. He was two holes ahead of her and she needed to use any advantage she had – her knowledge of the course was going to pay off, it seemed.

Choosing the big toe next he felt frustration but didn't let it show as his ball again reappeared. This time it appeared from the toe nearest the little toe making his next attempt easy. Process of elimination meant the only likely option was the toe sitting next to the big one. How or why this one had been chosen as the way to the back of the foot he didn't care.

Jim admired the work that had gone into the next hole; it combined both angles and mechanical bits. A carefully mapped out path that could not be completed in one shot led through scenes of an eerie and morbid nature. Waiting at the end of the path a little river crossed the course with a barge looking vehicle passing up and down it. On the barge a ghoulish looking modelled figure sat motionless as if he was guiding the barge up and down. On the other side of the river the course had been painted with black, red, yellow and orange to look like flames licking. The word Hades was on a sign across the back of the course with the hole in the opposite corner to the start point. After a very difficult time getting to Hades, Sasha finally beat Jim by one shot on the penultimate hole. Together they walked up to the last hole, Sasha knew that they were tied up until this point, Jim had played well and her competitive nature and experience of this course had served her well. Facing them for the final challenge was a short but steep ramp leading up to a dominant looking head of a figure Jim recognised as Zeus.

After several attempts each finally Jim watched his ball disappear into the open mouth and the eyes of the character light up with a red glow. Sasha's ball followed quickly behind leaving them both holding their clubs but with no luminous ball to return. Above the model a sign in many languages advised them to return the clubs and thank you for playing.

Sasha turned to Jim, she knew in her heart she had beaten him on the last hole but it wasn't something she was going to hold against him. She grabbed his hands climbing to her tiptoes to kiss him softly

"Shall we call it a draw, then?" She smiled as she led him off the course.

Chapter Twenty-One

Parental consent

Introducing girls to the rents was something Jim was comfortable doing; he had even introduced them to Sasha accidentally on their first day. The difference was that usually when he introduced a new girl to them she was only a friend and he had to convince them of that. At first this had been a frustrating and in some ways embarrassing process especially for the girls he knew that had boyfriends. After a few narrow escapes he now had it done to perfection, the key was to ensure the girl knew.

There was nothing worse than bringing a girl home for what was usually one of his comforting consultations just for dad to label her his girlfriend. If it was a consultation the likelihood was that the girl was actually in a vulnerable state and wouldn't appreciate the labelling. There had been one occasion when the girl had had to hold back from lashing out verbally but by that time Jim was an expert at returning fire in such a way that dad lost any momentum in his questioning.

After the golf Jim had done something unique and actually arranged to meet the rents for dinner. It had been a tricky thing to do because it involved going to their apartment and avoiding seeing too much naked flesh. The obvious solution would be to stand at the door with his eyes closed but then he wouldn't know when the door had been closed. Checking the doors status could potentially involve waving a hand in front of him and if the door wasn't closed that was too risky.

The second option was to knock and then turn his back on the door which would cause friction. He had always been told not to have your back turned toward the person you were talking to. If he tried this method he may end up with whoever answered the door coming out of the apartment to face him. Their appearance would make him turn round to face their apartment with the risk of the other parent being in the doorway. Even though he knew that the time until he was faced with their nudity was less than a day away he wanted to avoid it as long as he could.

Sasha had a much more difficult task, even though in principal it was the same as his. She had to talk her parents into meeting him under the heading of him being her boyfriend. He had noticed that when his sister bought a new boyfriend home the boy or man was always treated with hostility. At first he put that down to the type of social outcast she chose to date but when he was faced with the same hostility on visiting a female friend he realised it was a universal thing.

In some ways he could understand the hostility because a daughter was always put on a different pedestal from a son. It was her job to avoid getting pregnant as long as she could whereas it was the boy's job to try and find someone that was willing to have their child. Darwin had talked about natural selection in his theory and that was still valid today in a parent deciding if the boy intruding the family house was suited to their daughter. In contrast to this, men had their mind on one thing and would do anything to achieve it.

During the morning leading up to the first meeting of parents Sasha asked Jim a question that he realised he actually didn't know the answer to. He could see it was her way of trying to get some background knowledge of what type of people his parents were.

"What got them into naturism, Jim?" she had casually asked him while they relaxed together in the sun.

He hadn't thought about it before, nothing they had done to date as a family had pointed to them wanting to run around naked. He had just put it down to the result of a mid-life crisis and they didn't care who saw their bodies anymore but clearly there was more to it. He pondered over her question for a few moments casually stroking her arm so she knew he wasn't avoiding answering before casually responding.

"I don't know."

At first his reply had come as a bit of a shock to her but the more she thought about it the more it made sense. She wondered if she had asked him something more basic like when their birthdays were or how old they were would he know the answer to those questions but chose not to pursue it. Jim had seldom spoken about his parents or as she had noticed he liked to refer to them 'the rents' but this didn't help her.

Even though she had never really been introduced to someone's parents as a girlfriend before she knew it was always easier if you could at least say you knew something about them. She had prepared herself for meeting them properly rather than just as passers by one the foot path but wanted to be able to say 'yes, he has told me all about you'. Then again, if he didn't know about them, it was probable that they didn't know much about her.

Calming herself down she lay her head down closing her eyes and reminisced on when her parents had first chosen the naturist way of life. Up until the age of ten, her parents had done the same as a number of families in her town. Every summer the same holiday to the same area this in their case was the south coast of Ireland. She wasn't even sure if they had a passport but she knew that she didn't have one because she had never had the passport picture taken in her life before.

After the holiday they had made arrangements to go and see an old family friend who lived in a remote area outside the town. He was difficult to get hold of at the best of times due to phone signals but he assured them that if they sent a text he would get it eventually. The challenge was to get as much information into your message as you could so that it only needed one reply or you could be waiting days to hear from him again.

Ted was an English man that had chosen to settle in Ireland after a broken marriage in the UK. Once the arrangement was made Dad negotiated the winding road to his little cottage. Ted welcomed them with his usual smile and tea and biscuits waiting on the table. The evening was going well from what Sasha could tell, all the adults were laughing and reminiscing on their trips and she had been left to the TV. Then mum asked the question that completely changed the direction of the conversation

"Why don't you ever bring photographs to show us?"

At the time the question seemed quite normal but when Ted went quiet they knew that something wasn't quite right. After a few moments of silence during which time he pretended to be topping up the tea and biscuits he made the confession that changed all their lives.

"I am a naturist; I don't usually take pictures on my holidays."

Even Sasha stopped what she was doing when she heard him add that he seldom wore clothes at home unless he had visitors. Sasha had heard about naturists but had always associated it with places that had sun or something that people did in the 1960s. It wasn't the sort of thing that she expected someone to admit to doing with the unreliable weather in Ireland. Very quickly the subject was changed to their trip to the Waterford coast with a brief stay over in Kilkenny on the way down.

The subject of naturism wasn't bought up again until they were on the way home and mum had commented that Ted was probably already naked. By that time Sasha was dozing in the back of the car but could hear the jovial chatter between her parents that lasted most of the journey home. Somehow from light comments about where did a naturist put their purse it only took a month for her parents to book a weekend away.

Sasha hadn't realised it but that weekend away was to the Costa Vera in Spain where naturism was a way of life. She had been passed over to her Aunt and Uncle while her parents took Teds advice and gave it a try. Maybe it was the challenging way he had said 'don't knock what you haven't tried' as they left but something had inspired them to at least give it a go. They left while Sasha was at school on the Friday and returned on the following Monday which was a bank holiday and the start of her October break. By the end of the Tuesday they had booked their first family holiday abroad to the complex they had grown to love over the years.

Naturally they had been concerned for Sasha on their first time visiting; they couldn't guess how easily she would accept running around without clothes on. At the age of eleven she was becoming aware of boys and was also becoming more aware of her own body but that didn't seem to stop her. Within a week she had practically forgotten what it was like to wear clothes during the day and was nearly protesting having to wear them of a night.

Out of nowhere they saw their daughter become a happier person and much more comfortable with herself. All the normal mystery that was associated with growing up was available to her and she clearly loved it, they even started visiting Ted more but never went nude with him. The bigger problem came when they got back home and she had to be told that clothes were compulsory again. Several times she would come home from school and be in her underwear before being told to put something on just in case someone called round.

Puberty provided what her parents thought would be the next challenge she had to overcome. Not wanting it to affect their little girl too much her mother talked to her in graphic detail about what was going to happen and told her it was all natural. A few tense months between Easter and the summer holidays gave way to the major hurdles and by the time she was back on the complex the clothes had been forgotten again.

"One of our neighbours got us into it." She spoke the words softly as she gazed at Jim.

The grip he had on her hand had become much more clammy while they lay on the soft white sand. Even without him knowing it he was showing signs of tension about the first meeting of the day. He turned to face her, he wanted to learn more about her and was conscious that he hadn't asked but right now his mind was focussed on their lunch with the rents.

Like a man waiting for the verdict on a murder trial Jim could feel his muscles getting tenser as the sun got closer to midday. In contrast to any other experience of introducing a girl to the rents this time he felt sick. It wasn't the idea of introducing Sasha to them that was catching in his stomach, he was looking forward to that, it was the idea of spending an hour with their bodies fully exposed. He wasn't sure which was worse, him seeing them fully nude, them seeing him fully nude or them meeting the first girlfriend he had ever introduced them to fully nude.

Part of him wanted Sasha to get nervous too and decide that the meeting was a bad idea. He would even be happy with her deciding that she should wear something for the meeting but that was about as likely as a blizzard in the middle of the summer. There was no situation that he could imagine where nudity and introducing your girlfriend to the rents felt like a normal thing to do but he was about to do it. Sasha gripped his hand tenderly reminding him that she was there and softly whispered that it was time to go.

Thankfully they had arranged to meet them outside at the table that had been unofficially branded their table. Sasha led him up to it with confidence and placed herself facing the path that led towards the table and nearest the wall. For a moment Jim pondered about whether to sit facing her or to place himself where he could see them arrive. If he faced her he would at least have a distraction while his body knotted up in anticipation of their arrival. No sooner had he settled into his seat and put on a strained smile across the table at Sasha than he heard his Dad shout his name. Tactically he waved over at them shielding his face from them with his arm and beckoned them over.

Suddenly Jim found he was feeling nauseous, he cringed in the corner pushing himself against the cold limestone wall. There was something distinctly wrong with being forced into a position where you were face to face with another man's genitals. He felt sure it wouldn't be any better if it was a stranger but as it was his dads it felt worse. Immune to the predicament he was in his father casually stood leaning across the table and jovially greeted Sasha.

Glancing to the side of his Dads flesh didn't help because there in his eye line was his mother who was standing patiently waiting to say hello to her properly too. Casual hugs seemed to be something that was not only acceptable but expected between naturists. Both of the rents got what he classed as a friendly but don't press yourself against me hug from Sasha who seemed to be acting like it happened all the time.

Without sitting Paul turned to Jim

"Maybe we should go and get some food for all of us?" Jim could already see where this was leading but reluctantly agreed.

If his dad could choose a worse time to have a father to son talk he wasn't sure when it would be. Jim found himself stuck with his Dad as they wondered around the restaurant picking items on to two plates each. Paul kept on firing questions at his son about Sasha that awkwardly Jim realised he didn't fully know the answers to. He knew her age and that she was from Ireland and that she had been coming here for years but then Dad asked about brothers or sisters and he couldn't remember her saying anything about them.

The relevance of her having other siblings didn't really seem important unless he was planning on marrying his sister off to one of her unknown brothers. Surely that constituted as arranged marriage and even though he wasn't sure about how it was viewed in Ireland he was sure it wasn't legal in England. After a fumbled reply Paul came out with the statement Jim had been half expecting and half anticipating.

"Just make sure you're careful, okay?"

There were so many things that such a statement could mean but in the terms of boyfriend and girlfriend it only really had one meaning. Suddenly Jim felt very self-conscious; the entire restaurant seemed to go quiet at the same time as the words left his dads mouth. He could try to play out he didn't understand the comment but that would possibly make matters worse. Vaguely he nodded and smiled at his dad grunting timidly as he continued to make his way round the buffet.

Back at the table and immune to the talk he had just suffered Sasha was happily laughing and joking with his mum as if they had known each other for a lifetime. He was sure he even heard Sasha calling his mum Fiona which was a name only other adults usually called her. Deep down he felt sure that Dad had arranged the chat with mum before meeting up with them and somewhere in amongst the meal he would make some gesture to ensure she knew he had done his fatherly duty.

The meal seemed to go on for an eternity but eventually the rents decided they had to be elsewhere and stood to leave. Jim watched as the ritual hugging went on and found himself cringing as his mother offered him a hug. Sasha looked over with expectant eyes as he stood and reached over to her patting her on the shoulders as he bought his cheek in toward hers. Thankfully Dad knew better and only offered him a handshake before walking away from the table.

Round one was now over and he had a few hours to prepare himself for round two. Even though in theory meeting her parents was the harder of the two meetings they had planned at least they would be clothed.

After a restful afternoon Jim found himself staring into the wardrobe at the range of clothes he had bought with him on what was actually a fool's errand. In some ways he was grateful that he hadn't been told the place was a naturist complex because now he had a good range to choose from for meeting Sasha's parents. Then again if he had known and had for some reason still decided to come along on this holiday rather than putting up with the elder sister as a child minder he would have saved a load of packing.

One particular shirt that was beckoning him to be worn was a bright red shirt with a Chinese style imprint of a dragon running down the back. This shirt had been a birthday present from one of his friends that he had helped back on track with the boyfriend she had left four times that year alone. Although the shirt was lovely, it was at least two sizes too big for him; he wasn't sure why he had even packed it but it was there, staring back at him. The biggest problem was that the colouring was so vivid it would make him look like he was trying to attract attention. Pushing it out of sight he decided on a much safer pale blue shirt that fitted and wouldn't look out of place in the restaurant.

Neutral ground had proved to be a good thing when Sasha had officially met Jim's parents so it seemed correct that his meeting with hers was to start in the atrium. Slowly he walked through the door, not knowing what to expect as he made his way toward the couch where he could see Sasha sat with two other people. Her dad stood as Sasha gestured over toward Jim pointing him out as the one they were waiting for.

It felt almost like he was the one being singled out in a line-up of suspects and condemned for his crimes.

"Jim, nice to meet you. I'm Diarmuid and this is my wife Mary." Her dad pointed at the other woman on the couch who was sat next to a very reserved looking Sasha. "And of course ye know our daughter," he added with a wink, inviting Jim to join them.

There accent was stronger than Sasha's making it more difficult for him to understand them. He concentrated hard trying to make sure he answered their questions correctly. Sasha smiled and held back giggles a few times when he had to ask for something to be repeated. After a coffee and a short getting to know you interview Diarmuid invited Jim to join them for dinner.

The sense of relief was clear in both Sasha and Jim after her parents had left them to enjoy their night. Somehow they had both got through the official meetings without too many dramatic moments. The biggest stumbling block had been when Jim had casually announced that he had no interest in religion but thankfully Sasha had reminded her dad that Ted wasn't religious either so maybe it was an English thing. Admiring his daughters quick defence of the boy she had just introduced them to her Dad smiled and accepted her comment.

Taking the first opportunity she could Sasha made her way to the bar and ordered drinks for both of them. The relief at having such a big day finally over with was flowing through her body as the bar man placed two shots in glasses and a bottle of coke down for her. In her own little way she was proud of Jim, she knew how difficult the first meeting had been for him, his tense grip on her hand had proved that. She also knew that the second meeting wouldn't have been any easier because she had been discretely nervous but able to hide her emotions much better.

Since they had officially become a couple he had proved himself to her in so many ways. His maturity in front of the stranger in Vassilikos, the way he had handled the meeting, the way he had pushed himself into naturism and tomorrow their trip. She knew her intentions were completely insane but she wanted to share something with him that she hadn't shared with anyone before and tonight was the right time. They shared small talk and remarked on their adventurous day over a couple of drinks in the bar before she recommended they went to the apartment.

Jim opened the door and gestured for her to go in ahead of him as his guest for the night. He hadn't made any special preparations for her staying but he felt sure that somewhere in the bedroom there would be a blanket he could use on the couch if she wanted to use the bedroom. Shutting the door behind them he turned to face the room and was greeted by a long deep kiss and close embrace from Sasha as she pulled him toward the couch. He stumbled across the floor as she sat down guiding him to sit down next to her in the darkened room. He could hear her breathing heavily as she pressed her body against his and wrapped her arm over his chest and down his arm.

His eyes adjusted until he could see her hand playing with one of the buttons of his shirt and her fingers slipping onto his chest. The innocence he was showing was in some ways arousing to her as she tipped her fingers against his skin. She was sure that if she had done this to any boy at home he would have pushed for more but instead Jim was just holding her. Adrenaline ran through her body as she grabbed the hem of her dress and lifted it over her head before placing her hands on his and pushing them against her waist.

She straddled herself across him sitting on his legs and placing her hands on his shoulders. She had never put herself in this position with a boy before; she had made preparation in case the feeling inside her bought her to this place but hadn't expected herself to go through with it. Maybe it was the holiday atmosphere but if it had been just that she felt sure someone else would have been here with her before now. Something made her sure that Jim was the right person for her to be here doing this with - his innocence, his understanding, his interest in her and yes she felt like he loved her. The darkness covered his expression but she was sure from his lack of movement that he wasn't sure what to do which attracted her to him more.

"Jim, are you OK honey?" She whispered through heavy breath

His nervous reply assured her he was very happy as he leaned in to kiss her tenderly. Encouraged by his response she pressed her hands to his chest and began opening his shirt. Sitting across him wearing only panties she knew how vulnerable she was to anything but she wanted to be, she trusted him. Carefully she pushed his shirt down over his shoulders pulling it from behind him before placing her hands near the button to his jeans.

Finally a positive move from him as his hand gently caressed her breast, teasing her nipple lightly between his finger and thumb. She unbuttoned his jeans and slipped her hand inside them happy to find he had no boxers on as she touched him running her hand up and down. Pulling her hand out she leaned over to the small bag she had been carrying with her all night. She had made an unscheduled trip to the bathroom during the night and had a small foil packet for him.

"Jim, this is all I want you to wear tonight," she whispered softly as she slipped off his knees and kicked her panties off.

Chapter Twenty-Two

A trip to turtle bay

Trapped by an arm that felt somewhere between a dead weight and a comfort blanket Jim stared up at the ceiling. Resting against one of his shoulders was Sasha's head and one of her feet had decided that his shin was a good foot rest. He could hear her breathing heavily and knew instinctively that she was asleep on him.

He felt guilty and had been cursing his lack of experience for how quickly their moment together had ended. He had heard people joke before about this sort of thing but had never expected the jokes to reflect the reality that he had now experienced. Sasha had been kind and not commented on it choosing to just cuddle up to him and sleep on him after it was all over.

He had been awake a long time and could see from the thick hands of the clock that it was still too early to get up but his bladder was protesting. Lifting her arm carefully he looked down at the tranquillity in her face as he gently slid out of bed. For a few seconds he stood watching her sleep, thankful that his movement hadn't disturbed what seemed to be a restful night for her. Silently he felt the relief at having not disturb her pass through his body as his bladder reminded him why he was standing out of bed

Through half opened eyes Sasha peered silently at Jim as he stood at the side of the bed. She had sensed his discomfort as he squirmed trying to free himself from her slumped position. His chest had been a comforting pillow and heartbeat had gently rocked her to sleep. She knew that if she told anyone back at home what she had done they would tell her she was wrong to give herself to him but they didn't know him.

His attentiveness to her had been faultless since they had been reunited and although she didn't want their first night together to seem like a prize in some ways it was. His awkward fumbling had shown his inexperience but that made it all the more perfect in a way. They had both experienced such intimacy for the first time not only as a couple but on an individual level too. Her friends had whispered about their first time and now she understood what they meant when they said that now they felt like a real woman.

Something unique and special had happened between them and even though it was now too late for regret she had no regrets to worry about. He had been so careful, even asked her if she was sure before entering her but by the time he had asked excitement had taken over from logic and she had almost pushed herself onto him. The fact that he had asked showed her how special she was, she felt like a queen amongst women, none of her friends had ever told of a boy asking such a question at such a critical moment.

She watched him tiptoe away from the bed as if trying to escape unnoticed and slide quietly into the bathroom. Even though she felt almost deceptive by pretending to be asleep it seemed like that was what he wanted. The light trickled under the bathroom door after the gentle thud of it being shut and that was her queue to get up.

Sliding into a seated position she pulled the sheet round her body covering herself in its warmth. The clock told her they had time to spare before they were due to get up as she slid her hands down herself pushing the sheet away. Standing up she walked silently over to the mirror and looked at herself in the half-light that the bathroom door offered. She didn't admire her body much but even though there was no obvious change only Jim and she knew what her body had done and how it had changed.

Breaking her moment of fulfilment she heard the noise of a mini waterfall through the bathroom door. Taking long silent steps she pushed the door open and could see Jim standing with his back to her concentrating on the task he was performing. Something about seeing this man that now owned her most lovely memory inspired her even though her view was only of his naked back and buttocks.

Pausing while he completed the task in hand she snuck up behind him trapping his shoulders as she pressed her body against his back. She nestled into his neck as she ran her hands down his arms and felt protected by him even though it was her holding him.

"Wash yer hands quick and come back to bed" she whispered softly as she kissed his neck before scuttling back to the warmth she had left behind.

Surprised by the warm greeting while he tried to empty his bladder Jim found himself looking up at the wall as Sasha's lips touched his neck. By the time he had avoided any unwanted drips and turned to face her the door had shut telling him she was no longer in the same room as him.

Composing himself he washed his hands drying them thoroughly on the towel to prevent shocking her with cold hands. He knew from several experiences of shock treatment that cold hands against flesh was not nice and Sasha had asked him back to bed so it was clear she wanted to keep warm together. Walking back into the bedroom he caught a glimpse of her holding the covers open for him before he turned the light off and made his way to the bed.

It took Sasha less than a minute to place her arm back round his body, this time nearer to his waist than to his chest. With subtle passion she kissed his shoulder as she bought her leg up his thigh clamping him back to the bed. Lightly he stroked her arm tracing his hand back down the side of her body as she pushed herself against him.

Until only a few hours ago he had wondered how it felt to have a person sharing your bed that was more than a friend. He had top and tailed with friends before but that always seemed an awkward arrangement because both parties woke up with cold feet.

Stroking her hand downward she felt a bump against her arm as she reached his thigh. It was clear that his arousal had returned and wanted to redeem its bad performance but she had only prepared for it once. Her body filled with lust, wanting to be taken again by him, sample him again before the night was over. Sliding her buttock into his hand she grabbed him gently trying to relieve the passion for him and felt pleased when he responded to her needs with a similar gesture.

Almost as if it was one of their parents telling them that was enough fun for one day within what seemed like the shortest time possible the alarm clock told them to get up. Leaving such a nice cosy place seemed almost criminal but Jim knew that this trip was the reason they had chosen to share a bed the previous night. Everything happens for a reason, sooner or later possibly they would have chosen to do what they had just done but the trip ahead of them was a once in a lifetime.

Hand in hand they walked the pathway up to the main building; it wasn't a surprise to them that nobody was around. Glancing over Sasha discretely acknowledged the bush she had hidden behind before their reunion. Jim didn't know anything about that and in was now just a distant memory that she was happy to forget and happier to have moved on from. A small light shone from the reception building, the first sign that there was someone else apart from them awake at such a crazy hour.

Walking past the reception they saw a saloon style black car parked patiently waiting for them. Outside the car a portly man in a casual white shirt that wasn't dissimilar to one of Jims evening wear options stood with his hands clasped in front of him.

"Mr. Jim?" The man greeted them with broken English as Jim presented him with the hand written docket.

Nodding vaguely at it he produced a pen and scrawled a large tick across it before handing it back and opening the back door of the car. Jim had been on excursions before with the rents but they had always been in a bus of some kind, this trip felt more like getting a taxi. Gesturing Sasha to slide in first he followed her in hearing the door being slammed as he settled into the leather seating.

With an excited smile Sasha clasped his hand as the car crunched its way out of the entrance gate of the complex. In many ways her excitement confused Jim, he hadn't expected her to be so pleased about leaving the complex for a second time during her stay. Unlike any other tour that he had been on this one didn't have the holiday rep trying to explain where they were going. In many ways that was a relief to him because he had never really paid attention to what they were saying and the early hours were no time for a person to be happy about travelling – even if it was somewhere worth seeing.

The silence inside the car in many ways complimented the deserted roads they travelled along. In contrast to their previous visit the village was almost like a ghost town now with no-one even wondering the streets. Maybe that was part of the beauty of a small village; the early hours were a time when no one wanted to be out in contrast to bigger resorts where Jim had heard and seen people crawling through the streets at all hours of the day.

The few street lights of Vassilikos were soon replaced by a much darker road that reminded Sasha of the country lanes that reached to the outer parts of her town. In contrast to the ones she was used to this one seemed to be almost a main road just have no traffic running along it. Deciding to make the best use of the journey she leaned over the seat resting her head against Jims legs and let the odd bump of the car rock her into a gentle snooze.

Jim peeked down at Sasha as she nestled down against his legs, it was a skill in itself being able to sleep in a car and one that he hadn't mastered in his teenage years. As a child it had been an easy task but as he got older he had become more aware of the countryside that whizzed past him as they travelled. In a grim moment of realisation it occurred to him that if anything was to happen no one would know they were here. The driver was blissfully unaware of the fact they had family on the complex so the chances of news getting to anyone was minimal. Clearing the sombre thoughts from his mind he placed one hand on Sasha's shoulder and peered out of the window into the darkness.

After half an hour of silence the driver flicked the indicator and took the car down a narrow road that lead toward the coast. Turning the headlights onto their full beam Jim could see ahead of them was a beach. He waited until the driver had turned a corner leaving them parallel with the sea and dimmed the lights again before waking the dozing Sasha.

"Please, one hour," the driver announced, turning his head to face his passengers. Jim nodded pushing the door open and leading Sasha out into the refreshing breeze that was teasing the air. Shivering gently at the change in temperature between the heated car and the outside Sasha looked along the beach. Even at this early hour a few people could be seen hiding in amongst the lower dunes clearly waiting for the same thing they were here to see.

When he had first bought the voucher for the trip Jim had wondered how easy it would be for an inexperienced person to know where to look for the elusive turtles. The beach stretched on far along into the distance and the half-light made it hard to define the sand from the wispy grassy patches. Dispersed at random intervals along the beach were small frames that looked at first like they needed tent canvas putting over them to finish them off.

Walking carefully up to one he bent down to try and work out what they were and saw the words 'Caretta Caretta' and a series of undecipherable details. These small fortresses had been placed here not randomly but for a good reason which he hoped were the turtles. Guiding Sasha over to an area where he could see the car behind him and one of the wooden constructions in front of him he sat down amongst some of the tall, thin dry grass.

Sasha took in the view around her, the beach dotted with just a few people all looking for the same thing, the sea docile as it brushed the shore and the sun trying to climb into the sky. Nobody around here would notice her if she was to strip off before she sat down. She glanced down at Jim, he was the only one that would know and she knew he would be conscious of it if she did it.

Even though the last time she had done something so daring he had joined in she felt like it was wrong this time. Her head was caught between wanting to see how he reacted and knowing that her nudity would distract them both away from the reason they were here. Settling down between his legs she lay back against his chest and bought his ankles up around her waist taking a deep breath as they awaited the unknown.

There was something both timeless and in some ways almost meaningless in sitting staring at a wooden frame for what might be an hour of nothing but somehow it seemed to be the thing to do. Somewhere under that exact spot a nest of eggs was waiting for the right moment to produce its goods and welcome them to the world. People would spend hours waiting just in case it happened knowing that the most likely thing they were going to catch was the sun but still it attracted thousands of people each year.

In a way it was almost like the Northern lights which Jim had found out at an early age wasn't the yearly display in Blackpool but something much more spectacular. His grandparents had gone on about wanting to see them and how it was pot luck whether you were lucky enough to witness them or not and at first he hadn't argued but eventually he pointed out that they weren't really that easy to miss. That was when he had been corrected and shown images of what the real northern lights were; now he wanted to see them too.

They sat silently waiting for some sign that something was going to happen, Sasha gazed out to sea. The sunrise would have made a lovely painting if she was the artistic type and the distraction would pass the time while they waited. In the absence of canvas, she mimed drawing the image on his leg with her fingertip. She felt him jump when she brushed her finger along the inside of his calf, accidentally she had found a ticklish spot that could come in handy at a later date, she made note of it and removed her finger.

Jim found himself gazing up at the stars that were making their final struggle to stay visible in the sky as the sun won its battle against the moon. He hadn't taken much note of nature before; it had always just done its thing while he grew and moved around it. Peering past Sasha he could see the sun climbing over the surface of the sea, this was his first sunrise abroad. He was used to seeing the sunrise through his bedroom curtains at home but that was usually the result of a night's hard gaming.

The rents never questioned his prolonged lay ins and even if they had he would put it down to study. Now he had left school he had to find a different excuse to have in stock in case they asked him. College wasn't far away and that would bring back the studying excuse but for the next few weeks it wasn't going to be seen as valid.

Pulling her shoulders he felt Sasha fall against him before struggling back to her seated position. Logically, it was easier to see any activity if they were sitting up but the short spell of sleep was catching up on him and, with nothing else happening, he was starting to feel tired. Somehow, the twenty minute snooze she had taken in the car had brought Sasha to a state of readiness and in a way he was grateful that one of them was aware of what was going on.

He peered behind himself wondering how the driver was going to let them know it was time to leave. At this stage it was a game of trust that the driver was still there, a small docket wasn't really enough evidence of being stranded on a beach. The dunes behind obstructed his view but he was almost sure he could see the top of a car if he stretched his neck high enough.

Suddenly, out of nowhere, he felt Sasha lunge backwards, grabbing for him in an excited state: it was clear she had seen something and wanted his attention. Jumping himself back to an upright seated position he felt his legs pull against her as he used them to lever himself. Leaning his chin against her shoulder he brushed her hair away from his mouth and eyes as he tried to focus on whatever she had seen.

Ahead of them concealed by just the few patches of thinning grass the small canopy they had positioned themselves to look at seemed to be rippling underneath. Like a small centralized earthquake the sand below it rumbled forcing the structure to rock erratically. Watching intently at the rumbling sand Jim was almost relieved to see a small speck of black appear. Gradually the dot was joined by more and more hints of black until finally a turtle appeared.

Sasha gripped his hand pulling it round her body as the little creature made its way down the beach. It wasn't long before a second and a third appeared and within minutes it was as if a coach of them had pulled up under the sand. Like over keen tourists fighting to get to a landmark that wasn't going to go anywhere they piled out and over the top of each other in a rush to get down to the sea.

At first Jim was surprised at the volume of turtles that were appearing from what seemed to be a perfectly normal piece of beach. What surprised him more was that they all seemed to know which way to go as if they all had a little homing beacon guiding them. The more he watched them the more his mind started to wonder to thoughts like are turtles blind when they are born and will they ever meet their mother and if they do will they know it's her.

In almost perfect timing just as the last of the tiny turtles were disappearing from sight a discreet flash of light appeared behind them. Logic told them that this was the drivers way of telling them there time was up and it was time to return to the complex. In some ways the subtle but effective method seemed clever because it was silent and saved the driver trying to find his passengers. Maybe he had experienced walking in on situations before that he preferred not to repeat again forcing him to find an alternative method.

Jim pondered as they walked back to the car how long the driver would have waited for them. More importantly if they hadn't noticed his discrete light signal would he have tried something else to catch their attention. There was nothing he could think of that would be worse than being left stranded on the beach. It wasn't so much the idea of being left alone it was more the fact that no one knew they were there that concerned him. If they had come here as part of a group tour he was sure the group leader would ensure they were on the coach before leaving but they were the only two passengers this driver was waiting for.

Patiently waiting by the car door the driver held it open as soon as he saw them arrive. It almost looked like he was smiling in the knowledge of what they had seen but Jim felt sure the grin was more likely to reflect what his mind was telling him might have happened. There was no way of convincing him their own happiness was due to the spectacular they had just seen and there was no reason to try and tell him. Even if the language barrier wasn't so high between them he felt sure the driver wouldn't really be too interested in their experience.

It was more than likely that when he had got them back to the hotel he would have a family waiting at home for him. Quite possibly a wife that was still in bed and children ready to wake him up as soon as he had got comfortable and was getting back to sleep. Maybe the little boy that had served him in the shop was his son and the older woman his mother or wife. Jim wasn't prepared to ask in fear of a repeat of the American assumption all over again and this time at a much less sociable hour of the day.

Bursting with excitement Sasha was nearly bouncing in the car all the way back to the complex. She had prepared herself for a trip to nothing knowing that it was a high risk trip. Unlike any other trip she had been on the chances of actually seeing the intended event was far less on this one. No one could set a timer to tell the turtles it was time to hatch and show themselves in co-ordination with the arrival of people who had paid to see them. It was almost as uncertain as actually seeing the elusive giant panda at any zoo that advertised having one.

Sasha had visited Dublin Zoo a few times and initially she had got her hopes up at seeing the panda but in recent visits she had resided to the fact that it wasn't going to show. She was sure there were people that probably stood there for hours or in some cases returned day after day to find the shy animal. There was part of her, the negative part in some ways, but she referred to it as the realistic part that wondered if the panda actually existed. Its presence may have at some stage in the past been real but maybe now it was just a clever plot to keep visitor numbers up – marketing at its best.

The Irish were not known to miss out on a trick and she was proud of that part of her heritage. People made digs about them but to her all the things people found to comment about were just parts of the charms of the land she had grown up in. She had learned to shrug off the jokes about leprechauns and the bad impressions of the Irish saying things that they really didn't say. Maybe it was innocence or maybe respect or politeness but she had made mental note that for all their time together Jim hadn't dared once dig at her fellow countrymen. He probably didn't even know it but that was another positive point that he had earned.

Quickly dragging him out of the car she waited patiently while he fulfilled the last of his duties to the car driver and handed him a rolled up note. This gesture surprised her; she had seen people doing it before and knew it was customary but hadn't really expected Jim to do it. The only time she had ever seen tips given out was by adults and even though they were the only two passengers she hadn't wanted to assume he would. Nobody seemed to know why the driver was tipped, she had asked a few people and the best answer was that it was a thank you for him getting them home safely which in some ways made it like a ransom.

Almost dragging him down to the apartments she stopped when she got to his door. Logically it was still early enough to pretend she had spent the night in her own bed but who was going to know? Her parents had their own apartment and seldom knocked for her when she hadn't introduced them to a new boyfriend. Shrugging off the idea she waited patiently for him to open the door and ran inside before bursting out with how pleased she was with the trip he had chosen for them.

Chapter Twenty-Three
Checkmate

Waking for the second time that day disorientated Sasha as she peered around the room that shared her memories of her first night with Jim. She had fond memories of their trip off the complex but now the space next to her in the bed was empty. Still dressed from her trip she couldn't remember how she had got to her current position. More concerning was the space that in her mind should have been taken up by the man she was proud to say she was in a relationship with.

In the small hours of the day they had travelled more than she had done in the week she had been on the complex. She wasn't sure why she was fully dressed and in bed the combination didn't make any sense. Even at home she seldom wore clothes in bed but while on holiday it was less likely for her to wear clothes for more time than was necessary.

Dropping her feet out of the bed she stretched herself feeling her back creak as she arched backwards. She had two priorities to deal with before even contemplating breakfast which felt like it should have already been had. First was being over dressed for a day on the complex and second was where her man had hidden himself.

Staring in the mirror the dress that she had worn twice in the last twenty-four hours was now too creased to be useable. Brushing her hands down it she felt the static electricity between her fingers as she tried to make it presentable. She knew in her mind that she could leave it here in the bedroom but it made more sense to get it back to her own apartment.

With heavy steps she made her way out of the bedroom and into the lounge where she could see a familiar leg draped over the arm of the couch. Quietly she walked round to see Jim still dozing; the shirt he had been wearing was now a makeshift blanket. For the first time since meeting him she was better dressed than he was something she didn't intend was going to last too long. Lightly she stroked his toes and jumped backward as he flicked his foot in a light kicking motion. He grunted as he opened his eyes throwing his shirt in an involuntary motion toward the floor.

"Morning," he snorted through a sleepy expression as he pulled his feet away from her.

She smiled sweetly, another spot where he was vulnerable to tickling if needed had been exposed to her. These places were useful to her if he needed to be set back in his place for any reason. Every girl she knew had learned places like this on their partners and on more than one occasion had used them to their advantage. Most of them had been commonly known places like the back of the neck or the sides of the body which, she had yet to test, but so far she had found two which was good enough.

Leaning over him she held her dress to her chest as she kissed him lightly on the cheek. She felt strange having held clothing to her body to perform such and activity but it was instinct that had made her do it. Clothing had never been an issue until her school was merged with the boy's school. The merger happened when she was thirteen and already more aware of the ways of the opposite sex than her friends. She had her parents to thank for her awareness as part of their induction to naturism they had made her aware of the dangers of it.

There were obvious things to avoid like being nude in a place where naturism wasn't accepted but that was a legal thing. The bigger danger was outsiders that were aware of the areas where it was allowed but didn't want to join in. This type of person was frowned upon at any level of society but in places where clothing was optional they were probably among the lowest of society.

With the arrival of boys at her school several things changed including the addition of facilities for them. In addition to the facilities that the school provided for them the boys bought wondering eyes with themselves. Suddenly the need to be aware of how you bent down when you dropped a pencil became necessary. The older the boys got the more aware they got of who and what was around them meaning suddenly skirts had to get either longer or shorter reflecting the girls interest in the added attention.

Hiding a body that she not only wanted to set free but that Jim had seen several times before seemed trivial but undressing in front of him she felt sure would give him the wrong idea. Although the idea of him seducing her again wasn't beyond her intentions she didn't want him to take it as something that was available all day every day. She waited patiently while he gazed up at her and stretched like a dog that had been woken for its dinner.

"If ye don't move, I am going to sit on ye," Sasha huffed as she stood at the edge of the seat.

It wasn't so much that she wanted to sit down it was more the fact they he wasn't sitting up that was irritating her. She decided it wasn't something he was doing to intentionally antagonise her but no one had made him sleep on the couch that had been his own decision. She felt sure he had a reason for doing so but rather than pursue a string of questions trying to find out she chose to ignore it.

Jim looked at her through one half opened eye, the prospect of being sat on by her wasn't completely intimidating but the fact she hadn't said where she would sit was. He had curled up on the seat and fallen asleep after carrying her into the bedroom. Although he knew she wouldn't mind him crawling in beside her she seemed comfortable in a position that took up two thirds of the bed so he chose not to antagonise her.

In their time together she had made it clear that she didn't wear anything to bed but it seemed wrong to undress her. The early trip out had clearly exhausted her and she was practically asleep in his arms as he escorted her through to the bed. Undressing a person who wasn't fully conscious seemed wrong to him under any circumstances no matter how well you knew them. He decided a couple of hours rest wouldn't hurt either of them and lightly kissing her on the forehead had quietly taken himself to the couch.

Sitting upright he could now see she was patiently stood waiting for him and to his surprise she was still dressed. She sat beside him pushing herself effortlessly under his arm and kissing his chest as she gazed up at him. The smile in her eyes told him that she was happy as she wrapped her arms around him before leaning in to kiss him more passionately.

After just a short cuddle she pulled herself back out of the seat making her way to the door. Jim looked at her with a slightly bemused expression, was he supposed to follow her or not? He didn't know. She peered back at him as she pulled the door open and smiled at the puppy dog expression he had across his face.

"Meet me outside my place in five minutes and we will go for breakfast." She smiled as she slipped out of the door.

Staring at her own apartment for the first time in over twelve hours was in some ways a relief. She was happy with how well her time with Jim was going but it was nice to have some time to relax and think about their adventures without him being around. Even though it was only breakfast time after such an early start she felt like it was nearer to lunch time. She muttered to herself that she should have said half an hour, not five minutes, but she had melted into his eyes and hadn't thought about essential things like a shower.

Running into the bedroom she slipped her dress off, it felt like she had been wearing it for an eternity. Kicking her panties into the corner of the room she danced and jumped around the room as if she was having a private disco. The freedom of being nude again after only a few hours of being dressed was like a release from conformity.

She thought back to the trip to turtle beach, it had been so quiet there had really been no need for her to stay dressed but at the time it felt like the right thing to do. She felt naughty, like this was the first time she had been nude in her life and she was going to show herself to the world. In some ways she was a new person but the only people that knew about her intimate little secret were her and Jim, and no one else needed to know.

Pulling a brush through her hair she fought against the knots that an interrupted night's sleep had caused. It was notably more tangled than usual but then again Jim had been playing with it on and off overnight. Stepping outside she was pleased to see Jim was sitting on the grass patiently waiting for her.

Turtles seemed to be the biggest topic of the day; Sasha had been commenting on them and asking Jim about them all the way through breakfast. It was almost as if now he had taken her to see them he was meant to be an expert on them. It was nice to see her so enthusiastic about something other than naturism but with every question he found himself struggling more and more. Eventually she changed the subject to suggestions of things they could do together.

Jim listened intently to her list of suggested items; each one of them sounded like it required a lot of energy. He didn't have the heart to tell her he was exhausted and would be happy to just go back to the room and go to sleep. Somehow he knew he would find the energy to join her in whatever activity they agreed on.

"Can't we just play chess or something?" Tiredness was catching Jim as he blurted out the words.

He wasn't sure why he made such a random suggestion and he knew he had sounded harsh when he spoke but he hoped Sasha didn't get upset. Quickly he grabbed her hands holding them together in his as if they were both praying. This was a slightly tactical manoeuvre because it meant she couldn't hit him very easily but he had also seen friends doing something similar as a sign of affection for the person they were with. Looking at her with a soft smile he saw her shoulders drop into a relaxed position as he released his grip.

Jims comment both shocked and amazed Sasha, it had been abrupt enough to sound like he didn't care but his hand gesture said he did. But it had also shown knowledge of the complex that Sasha was both amazed and pleased about. Maybe he had seen more of the complex than she thought during his two day disappearance.

Near what Sasha classed as the back of the complex, beyond a maze of neatly tended gardens was a giant chess board. She had never played it and never had the inclination to do so because the average players were old enough to be her grandparents but now she had a playing partner of her own age.

She vaguely knew the rules of the game having spent many hours playing against the computer at home. She knew each piece by its name and she knew the direction and number of squares it was able to move. Strategies were not her strong point and many times the computer had comprehensively beaten her but she felt confident that Jim would show pity on her. The biggest challenge was going to be moving the pieces that were almost three foot high. Pleased that he had taken some initiative and some interest in an activity that didn't involve just lying about she eagerly agreed.

Jim was confused by her response to a comment that was only meant to stop the on-going flow of suggestions. He had been worried that his snapping remark would upset Sasha and that was the furthest thing from his mind but instead she had embraced it in a way he didn't think possible. Maybe the hand gesture had appeased her but she seemed to actually want to play the game.

Whenever he thought about a game such as chess all he could imagine was two elderly people staring at the chequered board with a timer in between them. He had never been sure what the timer was actually for because there didn't seem to be any time penalties. Instead the players seemed to be complimented on how long it took them to move a piece of sculpted wood from one square to another.

This game of strategy had no bearing on the much easier game of draughts or chequers as he had heard it called. Pieces in that game only moved in one direction – diagonally and once you were in front of another piece the only challenge was how to take the piece in front without your piece being taken as a result. A game of chequers was usually over within less than half an hour whereas he had heard of chess games that lasted days or even weeks.

Maybe it was the length of the games that aged the players, he had never seen a really young player but maybe they weren't ranked as good enough to play the professionals. Maybe unlike other sports age was actually an advantage in chess because you had nothing left to think about but the game. He wasn't sure if that was a life that he wanted to lead and he hoped that underneath all the other bits he still didn't know about Sasha she wasn't an aspiring chess player too.

One thing that he did notice was that contrary to what he had expected they were not heading toward the reception to get the board. Surely she hadn't packed it on the off chance that someone might want a game had she? He was relieved when she turned away from the apartments and started heading toward the dunes he had crossed to avoid her.

That was when it occurred to him that if they were heading to that part of the beach they weren't appropriately dressed. In fact if they were heading to that area they weren't dressed at all, surely she wasn't thinking of heading into the real world naked again was she? They had only dared expose themselves off the complex once and on that occasion they were heading back to it not away from it.

His moment of worrying was appeased very quickly when he realised she was only taking such a course to get away from the pool. To him it was a clever idea to avoid the area that might be populated by the rents, even though they knew about Sasha and him one meeting was enough.

Guiding him through the row of apartments that lined the back of the pool he found himself facing a second row of apartments that were secluded from the complex but still easy to reach. He had seen these before but never really taken much time to look at them. Quickly she guided him through them into a large green area where several families were casually throwing Frisbees and playing recreational games. Jim had never seen this area and in some ways he had wished he had because apart from the lack of clothes it resembled the park in his home town.

Directing him toward one of the corners where he could see some lovely arrangements of flowers. The scent caught his nose filling him with smells of the summer as they made their way into the square patch that they hid from view. Laid out in the centre of it was a 8 x 8 area chequered in black and white and standing along one edge were thirty-two large pieces that he recognised straight away as oversize chess pieces.

Without a word Sasha ran across the large board and started separating out the pieces handing the black ones to him. With silent reluctance he ushered his pieces to the opposite side of the board and placed them so they mirrored Sasha's layout. He knew instinctively that his king and queen had to be the opposite way round to hers and he was familiar with the rules but had never attempted a game before.

Staring at the board that had been laid out he waited while Sasha played the first move. The rule that white moved first was the only one he was fully familiar with except for how or where the pieces were able to move to. His best hope was that this game was similar to the online games he found himself not only capable of but competent with back at home.

He had to imagine this not as a board but as a battle field that he had to conquer in order to win the game. Just like the online gaming standing in between him and his goal was an opponent that was after a similar goal. The first difference was that he not only knew his opponent he could physically see her and secondly he actually had to move the pieces not just press a button and let them move for themselves.

In a way this game was similar to the game of capture the flag, the king was the flag that he had to protect. The difference was that in chess each team had one move at a time not a series of strategies and moves to complete their turn. Having only one move should make it easier but then there was the fact that the flag could move making it hard to target.

With what seemed to be minimal effort, both mentally and physically, Sasha moved one of her pawns. She pushed it two spaces forward of its starting place which at first confused Jim who was sure they could only move one space at a time but then he remembered there was a subtle variation on their first move. Of all the pieces these were the only ones that had this little variation in their moves giving them a slight level of unpredictability.

Jim knew that there were other pieces with much more flexibility, like the Bishop which could move both back and forward but only diagonally, the Knight whose move was completely unique and the Queen who could in effect go anywhere she wanted. The poor King in contrast was limited to just one square at a time but could at least move any direction he wanted if the space was available to him.

Then there was a move he had heard of once called castling this move seemed a bit like a cowards escape plan. Unlike any other move this move involved moving two pieces at the same time - the King and the Castle. If he had seen the move right it was like the king had a secret passage that allowed him to change places with the castle transporting him from a central position to a corner position. Even though strategically this seemed like a clever move there were too many conditions surrounding it so he decided not to even think about it for the game ahead.

Looking pensive Jim picked up one of his pawns before looking over at the piece she had moved. The fact she had moved it so precisely made him wonder if she knew more about the game than he was prepared to accept. He glanced to the side of the board and was pleased to see there was no timer waiting to be set going in between their moves.

Hopefully the lack of a timer was a good sign that games here were only expected to be short games. It didn't make much sense for a game to last too long when on holiday mainly because standing too long in the heat would give anyone sunburn whether they used cream or not. Then there was the fact that although eating wasn't compulsory there were meals put on for the guests three times a day. Keeping a game running would mean eating in rotation which wasn't practical due to the distance between the board and the restaurant.

The other factor hinting towards shorter games was the fact that most people were here on holiday. He didn't begrudge anyone doing what they liked on holiday and maybe there were people that came on holiday to play chess but a holiday only lasted on average somewhere between one and two weeks. Changing his mind he walked to the other side of the board and duplicated Sasha's movement of one pawn, two squares.

Barely giving Jim enough time to get off the board Sasha was back over to one of her pieces and pulling it across the board. This time it was another pawn but this one had only been granted the distance of one square before being placed. The speed of her move made Jim suspicious about her interest in the game, she seemed far too efficient for just a casual player.

Sasha watched Jim with great intensity waiting to see what his next move was going to be. Even though she knew this was not a competition she felt like she needed to make sure she played a good game if she could. In the back of her mind she had a strategy forming but it was impossible to know what the other player was going to do.

She had marvelled several times at how quickly the computer calculated its moves and out played her. Jim had mentioned this game for a reason she felt sure of it, maybe it was his way of proving himself after their mini golf game which she had declared a draw. She hadn't seen much of his competitive side but it almost felt like she was going to see it now.

The morning sun poured down and gradually more and more people came to the green each with their own agenda. Most of them ignored the game of chess that was being played but one by one a small crowd of spectators appeared. Jim found the game to be a helpful distraction from this group that was on average old enough to be his grandparents. Through one corner of his eye he could see a couple that had made themselves comfortable on a blanket and were pointing at the board. From the way they were gesturing, they seemed to be discussing their own tactics for the game.

As he moved his next piece which he decided was going to be the bishop that he had freed up he noted that one of them nodded. He would have given anything to be able to discretely over hear what they were talking about. To have their experience of the game would have been invaluable to him if this was for a prize. As it stood there was no prize just something to pass the time of day between him and Sasha. He felt like calling out to this couple to seek their approval that he had moved the right piece and that he had moved it far enough but he knew that would be cheating.

Sasha paused looking at the board, moving such a big piece so early was either aggressive or defensive and she couldn't work out which one it was. His latest move meant that she had to be careful which piece she chose to move next. At the moment his renegade Bishop had the opportunity to attack her front line of defence but surely that wasn't a wise move as it would leave his piece in amongst her troops and easy to capture.

Following his lead she carefully lifted one of her knights over the front row using its ability to jump pieces to her advantage and placed it in front of her king. This piece was much less predictable than the piece that he had out in open play due to the many different combinations of moves that it could make and seemed to get him thinking.

Over the next hour more and more random or tactical moves got played by both of them. The crowd around them seemed to be taking sides with more of them seeming to favour Sasha to win the game. After a very clumsy move Jim left his king in an exposed position whereby it was easy to attack and had very few escape routes. Sasha looked at the board for a few minutes, she couldn't believe her luck, she had seen something similar to this played against her by the computer. From where her pieces were placed one precise move left Jim's King in an inescapable position.

She glanced over at him; he seemed completely immune to how vulnerable his key piece was on the board. She paused before placing her hand on the queen waiting to see if he was aware of what she was going to do. In some ways she felt guilty because she knew that they had quite a following of supporters for their game and she didn't want to embarrass him but the lure of victory was too great. Picking the Queen up, she carried it and placed it precisely in the space she had designated to her victory.

"Checkmate, I believe." She smiled as she walked over to a bemused and out-played Jim, hugging him as the crowd applauded her.

Chapter Twenty-Four

Picasso would be proud

After breakfast Jim found himself back on the green that had been the extended arena for his defeat to Sasha at chess. He didn't begrudge her the defeat; in fact he had in some ways welcomed it because he felt like he was in an unannounced competition with her.

Friendly competitions were an on-going thing for him; he had lots of friends that, intentionally or not, tried to be better than him on things he had done. He had beaten Sasha back to the complex on their random streaking event that no one knew about and she had gracefully conceded a draw at the golf so her winning the chess bought them back to evens.

In some ways, this green felt a bit like the Bermuda Triangle; no one seemed to know it was there but, if you found it once, it was easy to find again. The difference was this green wasn't filled with mystery vessels that had never found their way home and were condemned to eternity in its existence.

Jim's recollection of the previous day's crowd was limited to the fact that Sasha's victory had been witnessed, not private. In the same way, the crowd had been a surprise to him because, even though he had been aware of being watched, he hadn't been aware of how many people had appeared until Sasha had announced 'checkmate'. Breaking out of the bubble he had placed himself in while they played had bought him back to reality with a bump. In the few seconds that passed between her announcement and her running to embrace him he had found himself surrounded by what seemed to be a naked senior person's convalescent home.

In contrast to his memories of families playing with frisbees and randomly throwing balls to each other now the main part of the ground was covered with plastic sheets. He had seen similar coverings before but only on television and they had been used to protect outdoor tennis courts from the unpredictable English weather. Beyond the plastic covering the chess board still held pride of place waiting for the next players to take up the challenge.

From his position it looked to Jim like the board still held the pieces in the place they had remained after his defeat. In some ways he wanted someone to take the initiative and move them in preparation for a new game but in a way it was a reminder of their game. Focussing his attention elsewhere Jim glanced around the area that had been covered. Several parasols had been placed around to protect any participants from the sun.

This was a tactical move because anyone that was joining the day's events had been asked not to apply sun cream. Enforcing this request a station had been set up with a man-made shower that consisted of a hose and an oversize tub to allow people to wash off their sun protection.

In the centre of the area a table was set up with one of the staff sat casually taking details from people. On both sides of him were rows of paints that were available with a display of brushes carefully laid out in front of them. It was almost like looking at a large art easel with a selection to suit the anticipated crowd.

The event he had been encouraged and brought to was body painting, Sasha had been keen to try it. She had justified the need to go by telling him that she had wanted to try it and nearly had one year but the idea of being manhandled had put her off. Even though she trusted everyone that she had met on the complex, there were certain things she had not got the confidence to let them do.

It was almost ironic that these people that she knew and had known for years had seen her grow up and had shared hugs with her but she didn't want them painting her. There was something about them having to poke every inch of her body with a brush that didn't appeal to her.

Greg had told her one year that if she did it he wouldn't paint certain parts of her but that was out of respect for her. He hadn't been with Alice at the time but there were some things that even as a naturist he felt were beyond his boundaries. She was too much like a sister to him for that sort of touching even with a brush to be something he was comfortable with.

This year it was different, this year she had Jim to take along, he had touched and been far beyond the boundaries of any man either on the complex or back at home and she felt safe with him. She didn't know how he felt about art but his abilities with a brush were the least of her concerns. Today was about the experience and she couldn't think of anyone she would prefer to experience such an activity with apart from Jim. The nice part about it was that if she registered them both as artist and model she would be able to give him the same experience he was going to give her.

When she had mentioned body painting to him in the few moments as they had been preparing to go to bed he had seemed fascinated by it. He had mentioned TV programs that had performed social experiments by sending people into towns in just body paint. He had explained how they had always used female models which she could understand – the female body was so much easier to disguise than the male would be. The experiments had had varying degrees of success but in most cases nobody had noticed a person wearing just paint walking down the high street.

Having equipped herself with a range of paints and handed a few brushes to Jim Sasha led him to one of the parasols. Already making preparations under the parasol were another couple who recognised Sasha, the man smiled over prodding his brush in a jar of water before selecting his first colour. As she lay the colours out at Jim's feet a third artist and model appeared under the parasol choosing the corner opposite where Sasha had set out her paints.

Jim was patiently standing and waiting not knowing what he was supposed to do and not wanting to get in the way while Sasha decided which colour to use first. The new arrivals chatted loudly in their corner in a language that Jim didn't understand. The volume of their voices was so high it drowned out the jovial chatting of others around them but the two girls seemed oblivious to the distraction they were causing.

Turning away from them Jim looked over at Sasha who had chosen a small plastic container of blue paint. Seeing the paint for the first time Jim was surprised that it didn't come in a pot as he had imagined. Contrary to his expectations it came in a form that was similar to the foundation pots he had seen girls using as part of their makeup routine.

As she opened the small plastic container Jim realised that in the two days they had barely left each other Sasha hadn't used make up. This was a refreshing change to him after the hours he had spent in the past waiting for female friends to apply the several layers to their face. He had never fully understood the need for it but had always been assured that it was an essential part of going out. In contrast to this Sasha had proved them all wrong by not even mentioning it to him before a night in the bar.

She knelt down by his feet and started applying a layer of the deep blue paint to his lower legs. The paint felt cold at first as she dabbed it with a thick brush in between his toes. She stopped below his knee and moved away from him toward the paints leaving him with what looked so far like a pair of blue socks on and nothing else.

Returning to him she resumed her painting this time with a vivid orange colour and a much thinner brush. At first Jim was curious about what she was doing and leaned down to try and see what was being applied to his legs. Deciding that looking down wasn't a very comfortable position he straightened his back and started looking round at the other bodies that were being turned into works of art.

Underneath a different parasol a man was painting his model in much greater detail with a gold paint. He had barely completed a shoulder in the same time as it had taken Sasha to complete the lower half of both of his legs. Beyond that a man was being painted in vivid reds and blues. Thin black lines were being integrated into the design making the parts that had been done so far look like one of Jim's favourite super heroes.

In the corner of his parasol the two girls that were still being very vocal seemed to be applying paint with no particular direction or pattern. The back of the models legs looked like a hallucinogenic dream with swirls of red and blue combining with yellow and pink. It wasn't the design that was catching Jim's attention it was the language they were using. Jim had studied French and German at school and although this sounded similar it wasn't quite the same as either of them.

Kneeling at the perfect height to intricately complete what she had decided was a beautiful scallop shell on one knee Sasha shuffled over to face his other knee. She peeked up intermittently and had noticed that he was busy watching what was going on around him which in some ways was a good thing. At least he wasn't trying to hide away from the crowd that was gradually getting larger as the day went on.

Huffing a bit that she hadn't got his attention she picked up the blue paint ready to hand it to him. Even though she was comfortable around him and knew his body in the most intimate way she could there was part of him that she felt he should paint. It wasn't so much that she was uncomfortable touching it; it was more a precautionary matter. Logically if she handled it she may end up with it doing things she didn't want it to do in public.

Discretely she coughed into her hand holding the paint up as if it was an offering to him. Clearly he was too absorbed in what was going on around him and hadn't heard her. She coughed a bit louder hoping that if nothing else he would be concerned as to why she was coughing but got no response.

"Deanabh usaid as tu fein." She announced the words as clearly as she could.

Distracted by the sound of Sasha's voice Jim looked down at her. She hadn't moved from her knelt position facing his knees that now had a very decorative design on them. Maybe it was the hum of noise around him but he hadn't quite understood what she had said. She seemed to be presenting him with the blue paint so out of politeness he took it from her looking at her blankly.

"Make yourself useful," she translated her words from her native tongue to one that he would understand as she nodded at his groin.

Irish wasn't a language that she used very often unless she was forced to or was in her Irish class at school but she was proud of it and loved the language. By speaking in a language that he wasn't aware of she had managed to get his attention and now he was prodding at his groin with the brush as if it was a dangerous animal. She looked down and smiled as she continued to add to the design on his knees. It was funny to see how he treated his own body parts when asked to attend to them instead of her; if this was how he handled them hopefully he understood why she was reluctant to do so.

Whatever language it was that Sasha had used it fascinated him, he had a vague recollection that the Irish had their own language just like the Welsh did but he had always thought it to be a redundant language. The words seemed more attractive in many ways than the language he had grown up with and he wanted to learn more but that could wait. Clearly she had a job that she wanted him to attend to and now wasn't the time or the place to learn whatever the language was that she had spoken.

He had read a lot of fiction fantasy books and they had always had made up languages in them but none of them had really caught his attention. Maybe it was that this time he had heard the words not just read them but there was definitely something more about the words that Sasha had used. Prodding vacantly at his manhood he carefully covered it with the paint that he had been issued with.

Satisfied with the job he had done Sasha continued up his body with the blue paint stopping intermittently to dot a different colour onto his skin. She peered up and noted that now she had his full attention which she found more pleasing than having him gazing around.

Just above his waist she carefully painted the shape of a lobster along the left hand side of his body. This was the first living creature she had decided to put on him; another much larger creature was going to be the central part of the design. She angled one of the large front claws toward his groin leaving it in an open position as if it was ready to attack him if he misbehaved. Jim acknowledged her design and felt his stomach tense at the thought of where this creature was aiming his claw. Even though it was only a painted design the fact that she had come up with such an idea concerned him in a way.

Continuing up his body she mirrored her scallop design from his knees on to his elbows and painted a star fish on each of his shoulders as if it was holding his arm in place. Jim shivered as the cold paint touched his chest forcing Sasha to pause and remove her paint brush. The intricacy of her work was a compliment to the time she was putting into getting the design perfect. Carefully she marked the outline of the underbelly of a shark with the mouth open around one of his nipples.

The design was reflective of the lobster he had reaching a claw toward his genitals as it appeared to be biting down on to him. The shark's body stretched its way across his body, under his arm with the tail crossing over his back completing the image. Taking care with her paints and using a much smaller brush she finished off the work with a design of bubbles up his face. Jim followed her over to a mirror where he admired her work before turning to a table that had been set up with a buffet for a light lunch.

With the afternoon upon them the onus now turned to Jim to make an artwork out of Sasha. She had set a high standard with the piece that had been dubbed 'the shark boy' by those that had admired her handiwork over lunch. It was clear from the detail that the piece she had created was one that she had imagined and now had made a reality. In contrast he had no image to work from and the canvass in front of him was physically different from the one he had given her to work with.

Adding to his concerns were thoughts of what would be seen as the correct protocol when painting a person. After her reference to him decorating certain parts of his own anatomy for her he had discretely glanced around to see how others were handling the same area. It had been difficult to look without being seen as staring but he had seen a mix of those that had decorated themselves and those that the artist had decorated. The biggest differences seemed to be that it was easier for a woman to be fully painted than a man and in some cases how important the body part was to the design.

One man had been painted with a jungle scene with the central design being an elephant making productive use of his genitalia. The man that had been painted to resemble a superhero hadn't been so easy to incorporate parts into the design and appeared to have painted himself in the same way that Jim had. Jim's main concern wasn't just Sasha's lower areas it was her breasts, he didn't want to be prodding and painting them if she would prefer to do it herself. The best thing he could do was start at her feet just like she had with him and work his way up tackling bits as they became necessary.

Jim stared down at the range of paints he had available to him and then looked up at Sasha who was patiently waiting for her first taste of being painted. He could take the easy way out and just select a colour covering her legs in that colour in the hope that inspiration would come to him as he painted but that wouldn't justify the time she had taken on him. This piece he was about to embark on had to at least look like he had made an effort even if it looked bad as a result of it.

In a moment of inspiration Jim decided to make Sasha into a garden scene with the grass growing up her legs and the Sun rising over her tummy. Taking a medium size brush he started painting green waving stripes up her legs. Feeling the tingling sensation as the first drops of paint were applied sent a mild shiver up her calves. Even in the afternoon heat the paint seemed to keep its cool feeling as it marked out the path that Jims brush was taking over her body.

She felt her body fill with anticipation as the brush strokes got higher up her leg and then the anticipation subsided as he started on her other leg. Shuffling round her body Jim moved to her back where he carefully painted her buttocks green to match the grass he had growing up her legs. Making her back the focal point he designed a serene image of the sun in a blue but cloudless sky filling the length of her back.

Moving back to her front he had finally made the decision that he was going to be brave and attempt to complete the work on her body on his own. If she didn't like him doing it he was sure she would make it known to him but he hoped she wouldn't mind.

Kneeling in front of her he carefully painted a simple leaf on to her groin and added a small red creature on one side which he decided was supposed to look like a ladybird. Sasha watched him carefully taking note of the concentration on his face as he added the delicate design to her most sensitive parts.

His consideration for her was higher than she could have ever anticipated and although she had not dared paint his genital area she was in some ways pleased that he was painting hers. It showed her a level of maturity she had always anticipated him having that was beyond that of any other boy her age that she knew. Not only was he being gentle and loving with his brush strokes he was also showing an ability to treat her body like a canvas and not make too much fuss over the particular part he was painting on. His dedication made her feel guilty for not wanting to touch him in the same area but there were more practical reasons for her choice that she knew he couldn't hide.

Moving his way slowly up her stomach he designed a series of basic hills that reached up toward her breast but didn't touch them. He contemplated adding livestock to the hills but chose not to as they would distract away from the creature he planned to place in the sky. He continued the design across her arms matching it clumsily with the level of the green at the top of her buttocks. He painted clouds across her chest that contrasted with the cloudless sky she had covering her back.

Stretching between her shoulders he painted what looked like a dragon to add a bit of fantasy to his design. Fire billowed from its mouth and the tail wrapped round her left shoulder and disappeared into her back. Leading up toward her neck its wing flared out toward her left side displaying a bold yellow underside that contrasted with the red body of the mythical beast. Finishing off his work he painted her face in a deeper blue that looked more like a night sky and added a couple of stars to her cheeks to complete his celestial vision.

He stepped back gazing upon the work he had done as Sasha slowly turned to show him the completed piece. He had never been a fan of art at school and had stopped doing it as soon as the opportunity arose. Here staring back at him was a rough design that had been created as he went along. The abstractness of his piece concerned him as it lacked the continuity of the painting she had done on him. The smile in her eyes told a different story, contesting the critical opinion that he had of his creation.

He could see in her reactions that she wanted to embrace him but she was afraid of ruining the work that either of them had done. Escorting her over to the mirror that was still in place next to the buffet that had been comprehensively depleted during the afternoon he stood next to her as she looked over his work. He could see in her reflection that her eyes were watery but it wasn't sadness filling them in was happiness.

Carefully she dabbed the tears away with a napkin before following him back to their parasol. Jim made the necessary amendments to her face paint just as a man walked into their painting area with a large professional looking camera. He looked at Sasha wondering how she would feel about being photographed wearing only paint. The man approached them waving a badge that was dangling round his neck to show that he was official and not some random person that wanted pictures for a private collection.

Looking at Jim with casual but questioning eyes he smiled back at her, somehow wearing paint seemed to make the concept of being photographed acceptable. Jim thought about it for a few moments, in a way the paint was like they were dressed but when all was said and done their bodies were still naked. There was a vulnerability to the photos that he wasn't completely comfortable with but it would make a lovely memory of his holiday even if he couldn't show the picture to his friends.

In the corner near the chess board a large white screen had been temporarily set up ready for anyone willing to have their picture taken. Standing randomly near the screen was a white umbrella with a light in it that he had seen many times in preparation for school photos. He had often wondered what the point of the umbrella was but decided not to ask. The photographer directed them into different poses that showed the back and front of both of their designs as a couple and individually. In a way Jim found himself wondering if this was what it felt like to be a photographic model.

The sun was struggling to hold its position in the sky by the time they had socialised with their fellow models. The energy amongst those that had spent hours painting and those that had been painted was one that Jim found indescribable. In many ways it was a shame that something that had taken them a full day to produce was going to be washed away before the day was finished. As they walked back to their apartments Sasha questioned Jim as to whether he was going to keep the design on for the night.

Hiding such a design under anything seemed almost criminal but in order to comply with the rules of the complex Jim knew they would have to cover up. Logically clothing on top of the paint was going to get marked with the colours as they gave in to the added warmth. He searched for the right answer in her eyes; she clearly wanted to remain painted for a while longer. It didn't matter if others were going to wash it off before dinner that was their decision. Jim could see a fun element in staying painted and watched her smile as he suggested they kept their multi-coloured skin.

Chapter Twenty-Five

The volleyball reprisal

Sitting in a half stacked pile on the table next to the bed was a collection of pictures from the body painting event. Jim had been pleasantly surprised to see the photographer with a temporary stall outside the restaurant. The amazing efficiency in how quickly he had managed to get the pictures was admirable.

Jim had noted the camera set up that had been used and despite the readily availability of digital cameras this man had chosen to use an older style camera. But somehow he had got from the event to an unknown location and managed to print and organise the day's pictures into a comprehensive display. In arranged sections a range of pictures of artists and models posing separately and together were scattered across large boards.

With relative ease Sasha found the collection of pictures that had been taken of them and constructively commented on each of them with a critical eye. She peered over at Jim who was quietly working out which ones he liked best before selecting two of her, two of himself and two of them together. Over dinner he had separated them out and given her one of each as a memento of the day.

He had discretely wanted some pictures of them to take home but had not known how to tackle the question. By not taking his camera with him into the village he knew he had already missed his best opportunity. The next option was the evenings but he really wanted something that showed them together during the day. Admittedly he couldn't show these pictures to his friends but at least now he had something. Maybe if he asked her carefully he could arrange some way he could get some pictures of her dressed during the day.

Lying in bed with Sasha's head resting peacefully against his shoulder he stared up at the ceiling. There was no easy way to ask her about pictures that he could show his friends without basically telling her they would have to go somewhere textile. The logical place was the beach which made the logical time to do it after their morning activity.

After a lot of persuasion Sasha had convinced him to go down for the second volleyball game of his stay at the complex. His memories of the first one although they were brief were memories he had pushed out of his mind. Even with Greg and Alice no longer at the complex he wasn't looking forward to the game.

In some ways he felt like he would have been happier if they were there because at least then there would be someone else he knew. Then again knowing people at team events didn't always mean that you would end up on the same team as them. School sports had proved that to him but surely it was done more fairly on a holiday. No one knew the ability of the other people around them so whoever was the team captain had minimal options of friends to pick.

There was no way around it, he had no excuse not to be there, the person that had told him they were going to the game was pinning him to the bed. He glanced down at her before closing his eyes again and trying to rest for what was left of his night's sleep.

If he had been in his own bed, he would have got up rather than lay there restlessly but he knew better than to disturb a person that was sleeping. When he was much younger he had suffered the wrath of his sister when he woke her up excitedly on Christmas morning. Admittedly, at the age of eight, he had not been aware that five a.m. was too early to be getting out of bed. Disgruntled by the awakening his sister had been quick to reprimand him and demand that he go back to his room with a range of words that he hadn't heard before.

In between the expletives and cursing she had however given him an insight to the advantages of being the younger sibling. Over the next few years Jim watched as his sister got complimented on certain things, reprimanded for others and grounded for the worst activities. By the time he had reached the age of twelve he felt like he had a good idea of what was allowed and what wasn't. He felt confident of what would push the rents to their limit and what would push them over their limit and he was sure he could avoid some of the fates that his sister had encountered.

Jim quickly learned that his sister leaving home to have a child had changed all the rules. Things that she had got away with were now seen as not forgivable and required punishing. He had even protested that she had done it before and it had been okay when she did. This sparked a question that at first instilled fear into him – why would he follow her if she jumped off a bridge? Surely the answer was obvious. Later in life he had responded with a question as to what made her jump off the bridge but that had got him grounded.

As he drifted back into a sleep that he felt had eluded him for hours at the thought of playing volleyball he felt Sasha move lightly. Gently she climbed over him oblivious to the fact that his eyes were barely closed. Maybe her nonchalant departure from the bed was the advantage of being the cuddler not the person being cuddled but he watched her disappear into the bathroom.

For the third time in less than eight hours Sasha found herself slipping into the bathroom to use the shower. Hygienically she was very proud of herself at home for her discipline of showering daily and other ablutions that were necessary but three showers was a bit excessive. She felt certain that there were some people at her school that didn't maintain the same principal. Some of them seemed to only find a shower once a week or less but she wasn't the type that was going to make example of them. Everyone had a reason for what they did or didn't do and that was up to them, as long as they didn't moan when nobody would socialise with them that was okay.

The problem was that even though she had enjoyed the body painting immensely she had felt like there was still paint on her even after a night's sleep. Carefully she rubbed her body with the sponge she had packed that she barely ever used as shower gel seemed to sufficiently know where it needed to go with some guidance from her hands. She peered down at the water as it slid off her body and down the drain and was pleased to see there was no unexpected tinting from the remnant of paint she thought still clung to her body. If she had to pick one negative from her day of painting it would be the urge to shower so many times.

As she had cleansed herself Sasha had found herself smiling quietly at how much she had enjoyed her first body painting experience. Her mind drifted to thinking about whether she had seen any signs advertising such an activity at home. She wouldn't expect it to be well advertised, it wasn't the sort of thing that most people would consider normal but now she had a taste for it she wanted it more.

Her biggest reservation was that if she did it back at home she wouldn't have Jim painting her. In fact depending on how far she would have to travel it was probable she wouldn't have someone she knew painting her. The only solution to her predicament would be inviting one of her friends to do the artwork but she didn't want them to do it.

There was something about nudity that made people blush in the little village she lived in. The only time it was accepted was when the people didn't actually mention nudity but mentioned an activity that logically involved it like having a baby. If one of the local wives announced being pregnant it was a wonderful thing, even Sasha herself felt happy for them. But if one of the wives had mentioned having to get undressed to try to get pregnant she was sure it wouldn't be seen in the same light. It was almost as if the body was frowned upon unless it had been seen by the person's partner with the intention of increasing the population.

She even found herself grinning with an evil expression when she contemplated someone trying to incorporate body painting at school. That would be far too complicated to justify, firstly there was the idea of teenagers painting each other. That could be resolved by enforcing a rule that swimwear needed to be worn but then again would swimwear be easy to paint over? Probably not. Adding to that was the complication that she was currently tackling of the shower after the painting.

In an ideal world she would meet up with Jim and they could go to a body painting session together. They both knew what to expect and they were both comfortable with each other's body. As she considered the idea she realised that nothing had been said about what they were going to do when the holiday was over and they went home. After all they had been through it wouldn't seem right to her that it ended at the airport. It was Jim's first time at the complex so she had no guarantee he would be back either. Making a mental note to speak with him about it soon but not today she stepped out of the shower.

Wrapping herself in a towel she tugged at the knots that were stubbornly refusing to leave her hair. She glanced in the mirror as she started to win the war with her tangles and noted that even though they had been under parasols or painted she had somehow managed to catch a tan. Peeking back at the shower tray, she felt happy to see that, as she had expected, there was no sign of paint trickling down the plughole before she headed back into the bedroom.

Sitting patiently on the bed, Jim had listened for the cascading water of the shower to finish. He had contemplated joining her in the shower but their first attempt at such an exercise had proved not to be practical. On that occasion it had been with a view to helping each other with the paint that was streaking over their bodies. Even though the shower in the apartment had only two solid walls and a curtain around the remaining two sides the designated area had clearly not been designed for two bodies of any size.

Even pressed tightly together it always seemed that one of them was either pressed against the wall or had part of a limb hanging out of the curtain. Jim had heard his friends talk excitedly about their showers with their partner and how sensual it was. In contrast the only things he had drawn from his first experience was a near drowning experience and cold chills as they playfully fought for prime location under the water.

He found himself wondering if sharing a bath was any nicer, people had also mentioned that to him. A standard size bath didn't seem like the right option because he knew he struggled to fit in one by himself. Then there were the abstractly shaped baths but they seemed just as impractical. Clearly this shared bath option was one that was best tried in a larger bath or cramped so tightly together that movement was barely possible. Swimming pools seemed a much more sensible option if activities such as touching were allowed.

Smiling at him with wide eyes she tiptoed over to him as if she was creeping before guiding herself on to his vacant knees. She opened her towel passing it round his back to wrap them both in the same cocoon kissing him softly as she nuzzled him to say good morning. Jim could feel the clamminess of her wet skin against his body and shivered gently as she pressed against him.

Even in her slumber she had sensed how tense he was about the game and had chosen to avoid it. This was going to be a big day for both of them as their shared memories of the last game were a heavy burden. Unlike Jim she had found an ability to put them behind her but she could tell he felt guilt and heaviness inside. In many ways that was a compliment to her as it proved to her that he had feelings for her that he had not shown until they had reunited. Now he was officially with her she could pay him the compliment that he deserved for coming back to her and trusting the words of Greg that she missed him as much as he had missed her.

Even though she knew how much she had already given to him she felt compelled to show her appreciation for him. Maybe after the game they could do something that he wanted so she could show him as much commitment as she felt he was showing her. Now wasn't the time to dwell on it, they were due down at the beach to play volleyball.

On the way to the beach Jim decided to ask Sasha about her interest in sports at school. Her answer threw him and in some ways made him regret asking her such a casual question. Up until that point he felt sure he was familiar with most team sports but he had never heard of Camogie. Almost pausing in his tracks he looked at her with a puzzled expression and was greeted with a polite chuckle. His understanding of the game didn't get any better when she tried to explain to him that it was a cross of hockey and soccer with a bit of rugby thrown in for good measure.

Trying not to picture a group of abnormally large players gathering together in a scrum formation with hockey sticks he asked her more as they got to the dunes. On the other side of the sandy mounds hidden from them a crowd could be heard gathering. He felt nervous but he wasn't sure if it was the idea of playing volleyball or the moment when Sasha mentioned to him that Camogie was only played by girls. This put a whole new vision in his head, now he wasn't picturing large men with hockey sticks in a scrum but women. If his vision was right he dreaded to think about what role Sasha might play in a game that sounded truly ferocious.

Climbing over the dunes as if they were making a special appearance at the event Sasha guided Jim down towards a small table where a man with a whistle was guiding the players to different sides of the net. Keeping a firm grip on his hand she made sure they both ended up on the same team which after her revelation about being competitive at sport he was relieved about.

After a few minutes of what seemed like male bonding and team hugs Jim found himself in the middle line of his team facing an extremely athletic opposition. Despite the randomness of the selection process their opponents seemed to be familiar with each other on a deeper level than the team he was in. Maybe there had been a tactic in the process that he wasn't aware of or maybe they had used a similar process to the hand hold that Sasha had used to denote which side of the field they wanted to be on. No matter how it had happened the end result was that the team beyond the net seemed geared up and ready for the game.

Jim stood with feet apart and hands clutched in front of himself which seemed to be the correct pose as he looked at the person opposite him. A glaze of fear and anticipation in the same expression crossed the face of the boy that was directly in his eyesight. From behind him the ball was launched with speed and efficiency across the court, the game had started. Jim had in some ways expected a starting whistle just like he had experienced at school but the holder of the only whistle was busy entertaining some young women as the ball passed between them.

The sound of cries of jubilation seemed to alert the staff member that was in charge of organising the event back to reality. The uprising shout hadn't been to signify a major event it had just represented Jims team winning the serve. Now the ball was theirs and they could play it to their advantage in an attempt to win as many points as possible before losing serve. Jumping around the court as if he knew what he was doing Jim watched the movements and took mental note of them.

Two points were gained before the ball was lost to the other team putting his team on the defensive side. Jim had a vague idea of the rules of the game; the ball could be hit three times by any one side before going over the net. If it hit the ground it either signified regaining service or scoring a point but the team had to gain service before they could score. Tennis was less complicated, a player could score on the opponents serve but it was unlikely to happen in the most professional games.

It appeared that his team was about four points clear before Jim decided it was time to put his observations to action. His team had the serve and had gallantly launched the ball toward the opposition who had returned it with similar vigour. The ball bounced back and forward before it was aimed toward the spot that Jim was standing in. Behind him a taller player was poised ready to take the shot but Jim had decided this was his moment. With an energy that he wasn't aware he had he jumped up and smacked the ball with his fist.

He had seen this move played a few times and each time it had left the opposition with a torpedo of a ball to try and return. In anticipation of the surprise from his opponents Jim looked up in amazement as he felt his half closed fist hit the ball. His moment was quickly spoiled when he saw that his shot had hit the net and instead of an opposing player the net had returned the ball with the same force he had used. The ball hit him in the face before spiking in an upward motion for one of the other players on his team to safely fire toward the sand on the opposite side of the net.

In a moment of startled relief Jim watched the ball in slow motion as it left his fist and rebounded making a stinging contact with his face. He felt lucky that one of his team mates had seen the incident and had responded saving the point but that didn't stop him falling like a sack of potatoes to the floor. The silence that followed was almost deafening as his ears rung with the sounds that had been emulated by the balls revenge strike on his forehead.

Sasha had been quick to react and dash to his needs as he lay in a state of shock and amazement on the floor. She half covered his torso as she wiped his hair away examining the red mark left by the ball. Blinking back at her he heard her gently but hastily asking him if he was okay which he answered with a dazed nod of his head. Picking himself up he was escorted to the side to recover while the first half was comprehensively won by his team.

Sasha didn't wait for the half time celebrations of their team being ahead she ran straight over to check on Jim. Sitting next to him she examined the mark that had been made by the self-inflicted attack with the ball. Even though it still looked like quite an aggressive mark she hoped in her own mind that it wouldn't bruise. Having a partial ball shaped mark on his head wouldn't change her attraction to him but she knew it would leave a negative memory about their game which, after the first week's game, was something she didn't want.

Helping him to his feet she led him back to the playing field as the organiser signalled the game restarting. Around her the other players amicably welcomed Jim back to the pitch having taken advantage of the refreshments that had been offered in the short interval. Jim looked up at the net; he could see a distinct disadvantage for his team in the sun that was pointing directly at them. Around him some of the more experienced players had prepared for this and were now wearing sunglasses.

As the second half got underway Jim could see why the opposing team had been struggling against the sun. Luckily for him after his first attempt to hit the ball over the net his team mates were successfully managing to keep the ball away from him most of the time. Even though he saw this as a subtle way of saying that he was just making up numbers he actually found it comforting. Their ability to keep the ball away from him meant that on the occasions that he did hit the ball nothing was expected of him.

For most of the second half he had successfully pretended to be part of the team and enjoyed their on-going success much to their opposition's frustration. Jim had mentally worked out that the game was coming toward its final stages when the inevitable happened. He could see out of the corner of his eye that the organiser was preparing to blow the final whistle just as one of the players directly opposite him thumped the ball in his direction. His team mates had no chance of preventing him from hitting the ball in some fashion. In what felt like slow motion he lifted his hands above his head more out of defence than anything else. He felt the slap of the ball as it pounded against the palm of his hands and cowered under his arm.

From somewhere behind him one of his team mates appeared diving energetically to his rescue. For a brief moment Jim found himself staring at another man's genitals as they swung toward his face. Trying to avoid face to body contact he ducked into his own arm and heard a second thud as the ball was hit. Not wanting to look up for fear of what he might see he stayed in his self-made cocoon and was surprised when he found himself being lifted into the air.

Being thrown up and down by his team mates like a rag doll that no one wanted to let go of he peered round to try and see what the jubilation was all about. Avoiding the crowd around him Sasha was patiently waiting for him to be placed back on the ground. Across the other side of the net a thoroughly disgruntled team stood watching in disbelief. In front of them on the floor was the ball that had not been picked up since it landed. Without trying Jim had orchestrated the final manoeuvre of the game and set up the point that signalled victory for his team.

As the crowd settled down Sasha walked up to him casually before pulling him into her. It didn't matter to her how he had managed to create the final point of the game; no matter how he had done it the fact was that he had done it. He felt her warmth against his body as the rest of the team casually filed off the beach patting him on the back.

"What do you want to do after breakfast, Jim?"

They had been left alone on the beach, the hype surrounding the game had settled down and the players and spectators had all gone off on their own agendas. Jim had an idea for what he wanted to do but he knew Sasha wouldn't like it even before he mentioned it.

It was logical to him that they couldn't really take pictures or have pictures taken on the complex. Even if they got dressed themselves there was no guarantee that they would be the only people in the picture. The village was too far away and seemed pointless just for the sake of taking a few pictures for the memories. The easiest solution was the textile beach that he had found solace on until Greg had found him and returned him to Sasha.

He knew instinctively that the minute he mentioned leaving the complex it wouldn't go down well with Sasha. Asking her if she minded him taking some pictures of the two of them without mentioning the beach would sound even worse. During his time at the complex he had only seen one person with a camera and he felt sure that was for a very good reason. In the safe deposit box at the reception he knew he had a phone that would be comfortably suitable for taking the photographs and if Sasha wanted any of them he could email them from his phone too.

Carefully he approached the subject with her explaining that he wanted his friends to know who she was and that he wasn't making her up. He could see her concerns in her eyes and knew she was going to suggest they took pictures in the evening but he wanted daytime pictures and the beach was the perfect location. She almost seemed relieved when he told her that he wanted to do them off the complex and added that afterward they could just relax by the pool or do something she wanted.

He watched her patiently as she considered his request and processed all the information he had given her to back up his suggestion. In many ways she felt that it was a lovely idea and she could tell he had given thought and consideration to all aspects of it. She hadn't really given pictures much thought, her friends were used to her not showing them pictures of her holiday and eventually they had stopped asking.

Gently she pushed herself out of the embrace they were still in; the innocent vulnerability on his face reminded her of why she had fallen for him. If they had met on a textile holiday his request would have seemed quite normal but then again she hadn't been on a textile holiday in years. She calculated in her head that if they dealt with the photos straight after breakfast they would still get most of the day on the complex.

An hour off the complex wearing a bikini wasn't much to ask and in a way it showed her that he was proud of what they were and wanted his friends to know it. In a lot of ways it would be nice to introduce Jim to the few selected people that she considered trustworthy. She didn't have many real friends at home but that was her own personal choice not others pushing her away. No one would believe her about him if she didn't show them something and there was no way she was going to show them the painting pictures. Nodding softly she agreed to his request and watched the relief fill his body before leading him to the restaurant for breakfast.

Chapter Twenty-Six

A hunting distraction

Waking up on what she knew was her last full day on the complex Sasha was hoping that there would be some kind of easy distraction. She had avoided the subject of going home and was glad that Jim hadn't bought it up. At some point during the day she would have to mention it but it could wait until much later.

Being careful not to disturb him, she made her way out to the lounge area of the apartment, leaving him to sleep. On the small table next to the couch, the phone he had used as a camera sat idle. She picked it up and sat down peering over the back of the couch to check for any movement from the bedroom. The door remained half closed and beyond that she felt sure she heard the murmur of Jim as he turned in his sleep.

It was still early morning, there was no reason for either of them to be up yet but she had wanted a glass of water. Initially her intention had been to get the glass and return to the bed but the phone had given her a distraction. She knew it wasn't right to do what she was tempted to do but having the phone in her hand was pushing her curiosity to the limit. The only thing holding her back was the thought that hidden in this little gadget could be secrets that she didn't want to see. This was the key to an insight into his life beyond the complex; he hadn't held it from her but he also hadn't permitted her to look at it.

She stared at the blank screen and pressed one of the buttons almost hoping that it had a lock to prevent her accessing it any further. The screen sprung to life displaying a generic image and invitation to swipe the screen to unlock it. In many ways this was a good sign because it meant he wasn't trying to make his phone inaccessible but it also meant that if it was lost anyone could access his files. She made a note to try and subtly ask him about it with the view to encouraging him to lock it but, then again, maybe it was better that he didn't.

She half closed her eyes as she swiped her finger across the screen but found herself opening them again quickly. Staring back at her was a screen offering her access to every part of his phone, all his personal files, his text history, his pictures and anything else that might be hiding. Her heart jumped as she found herself peering at his texts, nothing special, nothing exciting only a few arrangements that had been made between him and friends for gaming sessions and a few that had light banter about teachers at school.

Taking a deep breath she opened the pictures folder, she had heard of friends that had done this before and it hadn't always ended up with good news. Staring back at her were the pictures they had spent an hour or more taking on the beach the previous day. She remembered the kind German that had offered to take some pictures of them together. Somehow these pictures were more special to her than the ones of them having been painted. Even though they didn't truly reflect the holiday that had met on these were the ones that could be shown to others.

He had offered to send her them by email which she had accepted for more than one reason. Even though she hadn't given him her email address she had every intention of doing so before she went home. This was her first confirmation that he intended to keep contact with her after they left the complex. Over time she felt confident that this would lead to other contact methods but email was a good start. Casually flicking through the images she found herself entering a world she didn't know – the world of Jims home life.

Just like his text messages there was nothing exciting coming up on the screen that would make her suspect or question him. She stopped as she came up to a picture of a woman holding a young child by the hand. The person with this woman was not Jim and the child was clearly too old to be his and contradicted with him saying he had never had a girlfriend. She looked closer at the picture, there were vague similarities between Jim's face and this girls face – maybe it was his sister. As she examined the picture she heard movement from the bedroom, he was awake.

Quickly she closed the picture folder and placed the phone back on the table before jogging through to the kitchen. The brief insight into his home life had left her with questions she couldn't answer as they related to things he hadn't told her about yet. Grabbing the glass of water she had promised herself she walked casually out toward the lounge. Standing with a tired expression on his face in the doorway to the bedroom was Jim looking over to her. Without breaking her stride she walked up to him and kissed him softly on the cheek.

"Morning," she whispered. "Just needed a glass of water. Are ye coming back to bed or am I going alone?"

He needed no further invitation.

It took him less than thirty seconds from the moment they crawled back under the covers to fall back into what seemed to be a deep sleep. She wondered for a few moments if he had actually been awake when she saw him at the doorway, maybe he had actually been walking in his sleep. His arm was draped across her somewhere between her breast and her stomach and his head was hidden deep in the pillow already humming itself toward a snore. In contrast she found herself awake but resting as she pondered over the forbidden fruits she had seen on his phone.

His lack of anything incriminating was in a way a compliment to everything he had told her but it lacked excitement. She was pleased in many ways that there were no images or texts that could be taken the wrong way because, even though she had not been told she could look, she knew she would have suspected any unexpected material. Having the phone within relatively easy reach gave her thoughts of ways she could discretely label him as hers.

He already had pictures of the pair of them together both on his phone and in a frame but she wanted to do something special for him. So far she had crossed boundaries she had never considered crossing before arriving on holiday but she felt good around him. Their first night together hadn't been magical but it had been a first for her and, if she trusted his words, which she did, it had been a first for him too. Before her holiday was over she wanted to ensure it wasn't just a one off experience as she didn't know when or if she would see him again but she wanted to make sure she left him with as much motivation as possible to see her again.

Unlike many people of her parents' generation her parents had accepted that sooner or later she was going to become sexually active. They had addressed the matter head on which in a way she had expected being that they had bought her to a naturist complex at such a young age. They had no way of hiding men from her and didn't try to but they also wanted her to keep her innocence as long as she could. She knew in her heart that they would frown on her for what she had allowed to happen between Jim and herself but she hoped if they found out they would accept it.

People she went to school with had told her how easy it was to use her body to manipulate men but she had started to resent them for it. She didn't see her body as a tool to use against men especially if the man they were with was one they wanted to be with. Jim was a man that she had chosen and wanted to be with, and she had even, in some ways, forced herself upon him. The biggest difference was that once she got on the plane home she didn't know when they would meet again.

Her friends saw their boyfriends every week and she had no doubt as to what they got up to even though the subject was never really discussed. She had less than two days left and that meant if she was going to experience intimacy with him she had to make sure it was soon without seeming too forward. She had no doubt in her mind that if she threw herself at him he would willingly accept but it had to be special not just animalistic.

Keeping all her thoughts on their future together at bay she focussed on her little plan. So far in their short time together he had treated her to as much as he could. Their trip to the turtles, the necklace and buying their photos were just a few ways that he had shown her dedication but now she could leave him a present. She knew there were risks in her plan and it betrayed everything she knew about naturism but she was willing to take the risk. Before the phone was put out of sight she was going to use it to give him some pictures for his eyes only, all she had to do was ensure that he didn't take it with him when they left the apartment for breakfast.

****

Over an hour passed and Sasha found herself still resting but not sleeping as she made it known to Jim that she was getting up. Unlike her previous discrete slipping out of the bed to get a glass of water this time she was much more obvious about her actions. Jim woke quite quickly and kissed her tenderly as she rolled out of bed and into the bathroom.

These next few moments were pivotal to her plan, if she didn't monitor everything he would pick up the phone and her idea would be ruined. There was nothing wrong with him taking the camera back to the reception but now she had an idea in place she wanted to implement it.

Spending minimal time in the bathroom she was quick to rush back to the bedroom allowing him to use the facilities. Now was in affect her perfect opportunity but if she started fiddling with his phone while he was so close it would raise suspicion and she wanted this to be a surprise. She would find an excuse later to return to the apartment, for now she had to get him out the door without his phone.

Keeping her tactics to herself she walked him around the couch the long way offering to make him tea before they left. He didn't seem to notice she had pulled him away from the shortest route out of the apartment. Her plan worked perfectly, instead of grabbing his phone he declined the tea suggesting they got it when they got to the restaurant.

Sasha smiled discretely on the way to the restaurant; she had been wondering how to distract Jim for long enough to go back to the apartment alone and the opportunity had presented itself to her. On the notice board inside the main building a sign advertising an organised activity offered the perfect opportunity. Admittedly it wasn't an ideal activity but it was one that she could use to her advantage.

The complex was organising a scavenger hunt for items that was due to start at ten a.m. She had seen activities like this advertised before and although there was usually no prize worth winning it was generally well attended. The winner would be given a voucher of some kind that could only be used in the onsite gift shops. In many ways this was both a clever and not so clever idea because it meant that any money that was spent would be spent on the complex. The only drawback she could see was that unless the people on the site wanted to go textile they were only going to spend money on the complex anyway.

She suggested the activity to Jim over a light breakfast and followed up her morning suggestion with a relaxing afternoon by the outdoor pool. During their entire time on the complex they had only used one pool so far and even then it had only really been the Jacuzzi. The reception offered a small selection of books that could be borrowed with no commitment to returning them.

These books were available to travellers that wanted something to read while soaking in the sun and although there was no reason to return them the collection seemed to grow rather than shrink. It was as if there was an unwritten rule that if you had too much luggage or really didn't like a book you could bring it with you and leave it at the complex. Most of the books were titles that no one would read more than once but they made a pleasant distraction from the pool for non-swimmers. She mentioned these books to Jim who seemed to take it as a rule that one of these books was compulsory and dutifully went to the reception in between breakfast and the hunt.

"I'll take them to the apartment for now," he offered helpfully.

Trying to hide a panicked expression Sasha successfully managed to convince him to let her do it. Her story of having something she needed to sort out was enough to prevent him asking any further questions.

Arriving back at his apartment she looked down at the small table noting the phone that was still where she had left it. Now was not the time to use it but she felt like she should move it just in case he returned unexpectedly. She was so close to completing her self-assigned task that she didn't want anything stopping her.

Quickly she grabbed it placing the books in the spot it had taken up before running back to her apartment with it. All she could do now is hope that he didn't return to his apartment or if he did that he didn't notice it was missing. By the time he returned for the books she could have it back in his apartment and nobody except her would know any different. A sigh of relief flowed out of her body as she walked casually back to the table where she had left Jim patiently waiting for her.

Immune to her plan Jim looked up as the door into the building opened and saw Sasha returning empty handed. Her suggestion of a scavenger hunt still confused him a little bit but it sounded like it could be a fun activity. The last time he had done anything like that had been years ago on a weekend away when Dad had decided to entertain his sister and him by making them compete against each other. Unknown to dad he didn't need a reason to compete with his sister he was already established in the rules of sibling rivalry. She had the upper hand of being older and being able to get away with things but he had a competitive streak.

They had been kept occupied for about an hour before being summoned back to Dad to compare their lists of items achieved. It came as no surprise to him that his sister claimed to have an item accounting for every request on the list. He had missed out on a couple of the more obscure items due to either not knowing what they were or not knowing where to find them. As she placed her items one by one she referenced them to the list with a few protests from Jim as to their relevance most of which were acknowledged by Dad but dismissed. A couple of times he had won his protest but that still wasn't enough to win the event which ended with them having a discrete mind battle afterward that the rents were blissfully unaware of.

Slowly more and more people arrived for the event either as individuals or in couples. Jim impressed himself by his ability to recognise a few of them even if he couldn't actually name them. A number of the competitors had been seen at either the chess tournament between Sasha and himself or the painting event. It was unusual seeing the painted people now without their paint but he found it easier not to look at their uncovered flesh.

One by one the teams were given bags and a list of items to retrieve and return to the atrium by lunch time. In many ways Jim was relieved that such a long time frame had been put on the hunt but he knew that the prize which he wasn't worried about winning would go to the first team or the one that retrieved the most of the thirty items that were in front of him. In his mind he had decided that if Sasha had wanted to do this she must have her reasons for it and therefore he had to try his best.

Slowly they left the building in a small crowd that were one by one trying to work out where to look for the items. In what seemed like a moments inspiration Sasha took hold of him by the arm and suggested they take advantage of being a couple and split the list between them for half an hour to get double the work done. Her plan was ingenious, he was almost sure no one else would think like that and she was right it would get the work done quicker. Selecting ten items each they agreed a meeting point and time and ran off in two directions.

Sasha was pleased with herself, she had tactically given herself a list of items she could find very easily and very quickly and sent him after items that would keep him away from the apartments. Running down the path she glanced round to ensure he was nowhere near before slipping into her apartment and out of sight. She had never done what she had in mind before but she felt like she wanted to give Jim something special. If her plan worked out right she could tell him about it before leaving the complex and give him something to look forward to.

Not only was her plan beyond anything she had ever done before it also went against all the rules of a naturist holiday. She had heard of friends that had given their partners special pictures or had allowed them to take private pictures and videos. If a person used a camera on the complex they would be looked at unfavourably unless it was only their friends or family around them. There weren't many places where privacy could be guaranteed so cameras were rarely seen.

She looked at the phone as she sat down on the couch, flicking the screen lock so she could work out how to use the camera. Poking at the settings she found what she was looking for, a timer switch, using this she could take the pictures she wanted, tasteful but a little cheeky, just for him. She stumbled on an option for video and had another idea that she decided on the spot she was going to do. It was bizarre but she loved it and she knew in her mind that Jim would enjoy it too.

Not only was she going to give him some pictures she was going to do a little strip routine for him too. Having used up half her time making sure her little phone surprise was as good as she could make it for Jim, she carefully returned the phone to his apartment, placing it on top of their books before scrambling round for the items she needed. Waiting patiently for her at their meeting place she could see Jim with a bag that was now bulging with items. Carefully she clutched the things she had against her body making sure not to drop any of them as she made her way to the table.

She sat opposite him and poured her items out of the cradle between her arms on to the table gesturing to him to do the same. Her mind filled with excitement over the cleverness of her little present for him but she forced herself not to show him any suspicious signs or tell him what she had done. In a way it would be nice to see his reaction to her carefully compiled folder of pictures and one very badly danced video but it had to be a surprise.

She found that she now had a new respect for the people that danced and stripped for a living. Dancing was hard enough but when removal of clothes was added it became an art form. She had never really thought about their job before but now she had done it in secret she could see how difficult it was to remove items while not tripping over yourself. At least now she knew why when she had sat through someone doing such a dance in a film they had kept their shoes on. Her first attempt at the video had been foiled by a pair of beach shoes that lacked dignity in their removal, which had been deleted in favour of a routine without the shoes on.

Marking off each item that they had collected between them on the list Sasha admired Jim's inventiveness with some of the more obscure items but wondered if the organiser would agree with his selection. She made a note to try and find alternatives for a few of his items as a backup just in case. Finishing a coffee that he had ordered for them in anticipation of her arrival they wondered off together to complete the tasks.

It took less than an hour for them to return to the main building laden with a bag full of oddities that completed the list of requests that had been handed to them. Sitting at one of the tables talking to one of the house keeping staff they could see the man that had given them the morning task. It seemed a shame to distract him when he was clearly trying his best to get a date with her. It wasn't clear how well he was doing as the girl he was amicably trying to impress was still casually leaning on the mop she had been using as she tried to show him that she was interested in whatever he was saying.

For a few seconds Sasha pulled back on Jims arm to slow their pace of arrival down. There was no one else around them that was carrying a bag and, unless someone fell over them to beat them to the table, they were either the first ones back or they weren't and they couldn't establish that until they got to him. Even if they weren't first back, there was a chance they were first back with a full complement of items and extras just in case.

It didn't take long for the mystery woman to nod in their direction advising their organiser of a returning group. They couldn't tell if the look the maid gave them as she scuttled past was relief or just a friendly smile but without trying to get his attention they had now been announced to him.

One by one he pulled the items out of the bag ticking off the ones he recognised and accepting most of the ones that had been created after a little protesting. They were up to twenty-eight out of thirty when the first signs of reluctance crossed the organiser's face. He picked up Jim's suggestion for something that floats, placing it in a cup of water and watching it sink.

Digging her hand into the bag producing her suggestion to fulfil the requirement Sasha handed it to the man. Even though Jim's item was perfectly capable of floating if it had enough water, instinct told her there would be a test to prove the buoyancy. She watched disgraced by herself when her item submerged and sat like a submarine not sinking but also not fully floating.

Thinking quickly Jim rushed off into the bar area and started pulling at the leg of one of the chairs. There was no way he was going to let Sasha down when they were so close to completing the list. He darted from one chair to the next pulling on each of the legs until finally the rubber foot came off one of them and fell into his hand.

Returning like a victorious hunter he presented the foot to the organiser who looked at him with a bewildered expression. Taking the item, he placed it into the glass of water joining the two failed attempts. Jim held his breath as the item bobbed up and down in the water but remained on top and got ticked off as a floating object.

The relief between Sasha and him was noticeable as the last item got ticked off without any questions being asked. Jim was sure the organizer had decided it was safer not to ask them to prove any more of their choices. He smiled at them both vaguely still trying not to show his amazement as he handed them the winning vouchers.

Chapter Twenty-Seven

The unavoidable chore

Sasha had got up intentionally early; she wanted to get the unavoidable chore of packing done as discretely as possible. Even though she knew that there was no way of hiding the fact she was going home she didn't want to push it in Jims face. Somehow she had still not managed to tell him that their pleasant afternoon by the pool together had bought her last full day on the complex to an end.

Today she was going to go all out to make sure Jim and she spent the last few hours together as memorable ones. There was nothing worse than saying goodbye and she didn't want to prolong the event. Her plan was outrageous but if it worked out she knew they would have fun together.

Never before had she even considered room service but this morning she wanted Jim all to herself and that was the best way to do it. Their flight was a late afternoon one but she was used to that, flights back home had always been late in the day.

There were many advantages to leaving the island so late, the main one was that it made the holiday feel like it was longer. There was nothing worse than having to rush out of the door for an early flight and not being able to enjoy the final few moments of a holiday. The main disadvantages were that even though you had a good relaxing last day you knew the people that you were leaving behind were going to have yet another night of fun and you had miles of travelling to look forward to.

Then there was the getting off the plane when you got home, that was never a great experience. That bit didn't seem to matter what time of day it was the temperature always felt like it was sub-zero in contrast with the climate you had left behind. Arriving home in the early hours of the morning made it worse because no matter what the time of year any remnants of warmth were a distant memory from the previous day and not yet ready for the new one.

Normally on her last day she would amble around the complex taking in the heat and filling her head with a few last memories of the complex. This overview gave her enough inspiration to hold her urges to return at bay until the following spring when she was almost sure the family holiday would be booking again. Once the booking was made it was just a case of waiting and counting down the weeks and days until they travelled.

She knew in her heart that there was a chance that her family might choose to go somewhere else and she had tried to influence them to try a different complex before.

Thankfully her parents seemed to like the atmosphere and safety that surrounded the place and she was fairly sure they had made acquaintances that they would want to meet again. Her biggest problem which was still a couple of years away was that eventually her parents would want to stop paying for her to come along. When that day happened she would have to make a decision as to whether to pay for herself or go elsewhere but she had plenty of time ahead of herself to worry about that.

For now, she had to focus on her plans for the morning with Jim and then they could wonder about for the afternoon. She sat casually flicking through the room service menu; a bland and boring selection stared back at her. It was no good; she was going to have to adapt her plans to include a trip to the restaurant. Quickly she finished packing her case leaving out a selection of clothes that she resented but knew she had to wear before the day was done and stuffed some warmer items into her hand luggage bag. Satisfied with her work she returned to the bed slipping in next to Jim as he mumbled almost acknowledging her return. In some ways the restaurant was a better place to tell him her sad news anyway.

Cuddling up next to him she ran her hands down his chest, his skin felt warmer than hers having never left the bed. She pressed closer to him pushing her body into his back and wrapping her arm across his stomach and stroking her way down toward his groin. She felt his hand cover itself over hers distracting her as he pulled it gently upward back to his chest. It surprised her at first that he was taking control of her motions without even muttering a word to her but as she felt him softly kissing her hand she realised he was awake.

Gently he guided her hand back to his stomach letting it go as he fumbled behind himself placing his hand awkwardly on her buttock. He squeezed it gently hearing her whimper lightly at his touch as her hand resumed its journey down his body. It didn't take long before she found what she had been expecting, her touch had aroused him just as much as his was arousing her. She hadn't fully intended to be in this position until much later in the morning, there was nothing prepared for such activity.

Stroking him she kissed the back of his neck as he continued to mould her buttocks with his hand. She felt naughty and good all at the same time, conscious that what she was doing could get out of control but wanting to keep going. He turned to face her kissing her lightly as she passed his manhood like a baton from one hand to the next. His hand slid round her body and started caressing the soft skin between her thighs. With animalistic urges she pressed herself against his hand as her strokes quickened.

She felt his body tensing as she pushed herself against his finger strokes, kissing him passionately. Almost as if he knew the rules, she was pleased that he didn't try to push himself on to her. This was the second time she had instigated such passionate and intimate activity and it thrilled her that he let her take the initiative. Gripping him tightly, she saw his body become tense and then, with an uncontrollable groan, go limp as his sticky present deposited itself across their bodies.

"Morning, shower and breakfast, I think." She smiled and kissed him, leading him to the bathroom.

****

Jim had been half way through what appeared to be a boiled egg when Sasha casually mentioned that she flew home later that day. He had found that despite the enjoyable way that he had been woken up his attention was on how come the eggs abroad always seemed to have whiter shells than the ones he saw at home. There had been no introduction to the subject, no lead up to her announcement just a casual but solemn statement.

In many ways he had been waiting for it to happen, nobodies holiday lasted forever and he had been fairly sure that she had arrived at the complex before he had. It surprised him that they had got as far as their last day without either of them mentioning the end of their respective holidays. Then again the more he reviewed her comment the more he found that he wasn't just surprised by it but was also grateful that they had managed to spend so long together.

The worst thing about meeting people on holiday was the unpredictability behind their time schedules. Jim had been careful on previous holidays to make sure that anyone that made acquaintance with him didn't get too familiar with him that way it was easier to deal with them going home. Sasha had been a first for him on more ways than she could know and he was glad that she had been many of those firsts.

She was the first girl he had called his girlfriend which also meant she was the first person he had got close to on holiday. And now she was the first one he knew he was going to miss when she wasn't there. Much more than all of that she was the first one that he wanted to make sure he kept contact with and so far although they had talked about it nothing had been done about it.

Suddenly the egg that he had spent time choosing from a wide range of eggs that were labelled for how long they had been boiled seemed less appealing. He looked across at her noticing her awkward smile as she made her way through the plate of pastries she had selected. Her nonchalant expression didn't give away any idea of how she felt about the situation. She had been so passionate toward him during their time so it seemed safe to assume she wanted to keep contact with him after they were both back home.

Sasha left Jim dipping a lone slice of toast into the egg that had now gone cold on his plate. She felt sure that her announcement had caught him off guard and, although he had surely expected it, it had still shocked him. She had tried to make light conversation while she finished her breakfast and acknowledged his efforts to respond to her but could see he had been hit hard. Like an injured animal, he had tried to make out that he was okay but it was clear in his eyes that he wasn't.

She told him that she would meet him back at his apartment in half an hour to give him time to finish his breakfast. Walking down the path toward her apartment she found herself consciously taking in the warm morning air on her skin, this was the last time she could walk around nude until their next holiday. The last time she would feel the Mediterranean heat on her body and feel its warmth embracing her for a year. This was the last time she would feel free from the demands of life to cover up to be deemed as normal. Every year she would take this walk after breakfast and embrace all that she enjoyed about naturism one last time.

Back in her own apartment she looked around peering in cupboards she never used and drawers that she had already emptied. One final glance in the bathroom to ensure that everything that belonged to her was now in her small suitcase. One last look through the wardrobe to make sure nothing had dropped off the hangers. On her bed were her two bags, one for checking in and the other holding the few items she was going to need during the day.

This second bag was going to get lighter as the day went on but for now it held the items of clothing she was going to have to wear before leaving the complex. She had also remembered to add extra layers to prevent the cold air from sending a chill through her body when she landed. Her passport and flight tickets were safe with her parents and the few items she had to entertain herself for the flight were safe in her bag.

Picking up her two cases she turned and made her way out of her apartment for the last time. Making her way to her parents apartment seemed like a very lonely walk but once it was done she had the rest of the day to herself. She peered through the window and could see her father waiting patiently on the couch for her to arrive. He opened the door and took her cases off her smiling at her to acknowledge that she had done as she had been asked. Her check out was now completed they wouldn't expect to see her again until later that afternoon.

"Would ye bring Jim with ye when ye meet us later?" The question had seemed strange but she didn't want to spend time asking why and nodded dutifully in response.

Sitting patiently, waiting for Sasha outside his apartment, Jim was in a way surprised to see her still nude. He had been ready for her to appear in some form of clothing and was prepared to finally spend a day dressed. Clearly she had preparations in place and he wasn't going to question it because that would mean talking about her leaving again. Mentally he had worked out what he needed to do was to get contact details for her before the day dragged on too far. It made sense to him that all the little bits should be arranged as quickly as possible before they enjoyed their last few hours together.

Sasha stood in front of him blocking the sun from view as she reached down to take his hands. Assisting her pulling motion he stood up facing her allowing her to pull his arms until they were wrapped round her body. Now the formalities were out of the way and she had the rest of the day to herself it was time to put the rest of her plan into action.

"Will ye let us in?" She whispered softly in his ear as she pushed him against the door, kissing his neck.

Something about it being their last day together was making her want him more and more. She felt rebellious and ravenous all at the same time and was glad that she had anticipated it in advance. Allowing him to turn round she pressed herself against his back as he fumbled with the key card. She nearly tripped as he pushed the door open trying to get him into the apartment and pushing him on to the couch.

Since first sharing herself with him she had felt so much passion toward him that she found it hard to restrain herself. Now with only a short time before there was no knowing when they would be together again she didn't want her passions to go unfulfilled.

Almost leaping on to his knees, she pushed her forehead against his as she slipped her hand down the side of the couch cushion. On one of her early morning ventures into the darkness of the apartment she had tactfully slipped the remaining foil packets from her first seduction of him into a safe place. She knew that if she left them anywhere too obvious they would get found by either him or the housekeeper and she didn't want that to happen. She wanted the element of surprise as to when or if she would want him in such an intimate way again to remain in place.

Pulling them out of their hiding place she felt her breath getting heavier and deeper as she placed them on his stomach and leaned in to kiss him deeply.

"Do ye think we can use them both before lunch, honey?" She smiled a devilish grin as the words slipped out of her mouth.

****

As lunchtime crept up Jim reflected on their morning together and decided that they had been extremely successful in fulfilling Sasha's cheeky request. For the second time that day he found himself laying on the bed but this time it was his own bed.

Sasha was lying next to him with a dreamy expression on her face, including a grin that seemed to be permanently attached.

Their biggest distraction had come when the house keeper had let herself into the apartment. They had been too busy teasing each other to notice her knocking at the door and had been in the heights of passion when she walked into the bedroom. The look of shock on her face was similar to the look Jim had given Sasha on his first day on the complex and in many ways he was glad it wasn't him giving the same look again. It hadn't taken long for the house keeper to make her apology in the form of a shy courtesy and disappear.

Stroking her hair gently he watched as Sasha's head tilted to look up at him with sleepy eyes. If they had just spent a day completing the most strenuous circuit training he was sure she would look less tired. The biggest difference was that their bodies didn't ache in the same way they would from lifting weights and running on treadmills. Slowly she sat up propping herself on one elbow and sliding her hand playfully up and down his skin.

She lifted one of her legs and stroked his calf with her foot as she kissed her way across his shoulder and on to his neck. This must be what it felt like to be completely satisfied by a man and know that everything she had done felt right with him she decided. She had heard people whisper about such wild activities with a partner but never had the inclination to try it but now she was pleased she had. Conscious of how little time she had left to enjoy the complex she climbed over him and gestured for him to join her on a trip into the outside world.

Pulling his arms round her, she stood, resting his head against her tummy and looking out through the window. Other guests would be getting on with their daily lives, enjoying their holidays and were blissfully unaware of the morning they had shared. In many ways their ignorance was a blessing as it wasn't the sort of thing that was spoken about but she wanted the world to know how happy and sad she was at the same time.

Leading him out of the door she walked with him up to the main building for a light lunch. As they ate she explained to him what she wanted to do with the remaining few hours. He listened intently trying to show interest in her plans but unable to express himself with any excitement. If it hadn't been her last day he would have recommended they return to the apartment and continued where they had left off. His body wouldn't be able to perform at the same pace they had done but it would be much more fun trying than her suggested itinerary.

It sounded to him like what she had in mind was some kind of high speed review of her holiday. She wanted to visit places that they had been before and do shorted versions of activities they had done at some of them. In a way he could understand her intentions because it gave things she had enjoyed a second chance but it sounded like a lot of energy in just a short time.

He knew that she had enjoyed their trip to see the turtles but was in a way pleased when she didn't suggest they tried to get out to the bay again. Body painting was also out of the question unless she had a secret stash of paint hidden somewhere. He was also relieved when she didn't mention volleyball or tennis again, he knew she had liked the volleyball but that was a team event. She did however want to revisit the mini golf course, not to play a game but just to wonder around the course and watch anyone else that was playing. Agreeing to entertain her idea he followed her back to the min golf as the first stop on their whistle stop tour of the complex.

It felt a little bit strange being in the area that was designated for mini golf without the equipment to play it but Jim was glad there were only two people playing. They watched from a distance as they carefully navigated their way round the first two holes before ambling past them and looking at the other holes. Sasha knelt down at the treasure chest and traced her finger around the glass that hid the maze from temptation of grabbing the ball.

Standing behind her Jim watched as she rubbed her finger tip over the glass and admired the work that had gone into the design. Standing back up, she walked over to the 'Ferryman to Hades' hole and watched it as the basic barge ushered an imaginary ball up and down the river. She gripped on to Jims hand as she gazed almost hypnotically at the little wooden barge and the artwork that had gone into designing the impression of hades.

From there she gazed over at Zeus, smiling at the large head that was waiting to swallow the oncoming golf balls. Part of her wanted to offer to play that last hole for the two people playing but instead of putting the ball she felt the urge to keep one as a souvenir. The plan was flawless, no one would ever know if she did it but then again she wouldn't have any use for such an object back at home so it was pointless. Quickly she walked back through the course pausing at the Parthenon for a few moments before leaving.

"Will ye take me there one day?" she smiled at Jim.

Suddenly in a rush of inspiration he realised they hadn't exchanged contact details. He knew that neither of them had a pen and paper on them so it wasn't possible unless he could get back to the apartment or up to reception. The problem plagued his mind with no logical answer but an urgent need to do it before she went which was only hours away.

The surprise to him was that she hadn't mentioned it either, maybe she had forgotten too or maybe she had decided not to bother keeping contact anymore. He found himself in a very awkward dilemma; he wanted to make sure they could keep in contact more than anything else. She had just hinted at them meeting again to see the Parthenon but maybe that was just a joke or maybe it was a dig at him.

"I'll need your contact details." He blurted the words out with a sense of urgency and without thinking.

Sasha's face turned pale as she realised that, in her rush to fulfil her carnal desires, she had overlooked such a simple thing. She wasn't sure what had spurred Jim to mention it but he was right they had no way of staying in contact after the holiday. Quickly she instructed him to meet her at the beach that they had first gone to as she ran back to the main building.

It wasn't like her to make such an oversight, but then again she had never been in such a position before. Anyone back at home that she met and wanted to meet again would be easily found just by asking. She had never met someone on holiday that she had particularly wanted to keep contact with except Greg and Alice and that was years ago. The afternoon was late enough and she knew there would be a shop or a bar man available that could complete her need for paper and a pen. She had hoped to return to the green with the chess board before going home but that wasn't as important as a last hour with Jim on the beach.

Scrambling round between shops and staff she achieved the items she needed with plenty of time. A sigh of relief flowed through her body when she realised how quickly she had rescued the situation. She wondered to herself for a moment as to whether she would have got as far as the plane steps without having given him her details. In her heart she felt that it would not be possible for one of them to realise it before it was too late. Apart from anything else her parents had asked for him to join them before they left, surely they would suggest it if no one else did.

Walking calmly to the beach she gripped the items in her hand as she passed the bushes hiding the golf course. She thought she could almost hear someone putting a ball into the mouth of Zeus as she passed. Patiently waiting for her on the beach looking out to the sea she could see Jim in almost the same place he had been on their first visit.

Adopting a place next to him she made herself comfortable presenting the required items to him. He looked at them at first noting that they were blank and accepted that she was requesting his details. This was now a game of trust and not a game he had played very often as he had seldom been interested enough in the people he met on holiday to want to contact or see them again. Carefully he folded the paper in two and tore it along the edge he had created handing one half to Sasha.

She gripped her small square of paper watching as he wrote his details awkwardly on a rock that he used as a table. She peered across his shoulder making note mentally of what he was writing out for her. Email address, Phone and home address, he was very efficient which impressed her. The only detail he had let slip was that his phone number didn't have the international code but she could work that out.

Taking the pen she carefully wrote out the same details for him making sure her writing was clear. Thankful that the problem that they had encountered had been resolved quickly she passed her paper to him and took his in return. This was one of the times when pockets or bags were a useful entity but she could hold on to the paper for the time she had left. Laying down to take in the afternoon sun she gazed casually over at him and smiled.

"My parents want you to join us in the main building before we go. I said you would be there." She said the words calmly as she gripped his hand.

Nodding at her, he smiled, accepting the offer.

Chapter Twenty-Eight

The long way home

In the five years she had been coming to the complex Sasha had never experienced a feeling like she was as she walked up to the main building with Jim. Every year she had friends or acquaintances, just like Greg and Alice had become, that she met and said goodbye to but this was different. She had never considered getting as close to a person on holiday as she had with Jim. Sometimes she had wondered if she would ever want to have a boyfriend as nobody at home appealed to her in that way.

Within the course of two weeks Jim had won a place in her heart that she had held as vacant for years. Relationships had never been something she wanted to rush but now she found herself in a place where she was in one but about to say goodbye to the person she was in it with. If she told anyone at home how far she had gone with him in such a short time they would scorn her but it had felt right and she knew she didn't regret any of it.

She gripped his hand tightly but conscious not to squeeze too hard as they made their way to the door. The pit of her stomach felt heavy as she controlled their pace to make sure it was slow enough to enjoy their last few moments but not so slow that her parents came looking for her. Beyond the door in the atrium she knew they would be sat waiting for her to arrive. This was a set piece that happened every year with the only difference being the time that it happened.

Across on one of the couches she spotted them and waved over to acknowledge that she was on her way. They always met her in plenty of time so they weren't rushing for their lift to the airport and this year was no different. The biggest differences this year were that firstly she had bought someone along with her and secondly her travelling clothes were in her bag not on her body. The last few meters over to their couch felt like the last walk of a convicted murderer toward the electric chair.

Her father stood to greet them gesturing to Sasha to join the family in an informal hug. He didn't question her lack of clothes, he knew she would have a contingency plan in place – she always did. Placing a hand across her shoulders he pulled her into the embrace before releasing her so she could grab her hand luggage bag. One by one she pulled the items out of her bag and started the process of preparing for the journey to the airport.

Jim watched the process choosing not to get involved as she reunited with her family. Suddenly, he felt like he was vulnerable as he watched Sasha dressing in preparation for leaving. He was now the only one in their little group that was embracing the naturist way of life. No one said anything about it but he found he was covering his manhood discretely in response to his new found self-awareness. Without flinching Sasha's father walked over toward him leaving his seat free for Sasha

"Would ye like to see Sasha off at the airport?" Jim felt a warm hand against his shoulder as the calm friendly voice put the suggestion to him.

He hadn't considered the idea of going with them to the airport before but it would be nice to see her off. Her father added assurance that they would get him back to the complex if he choose to go. Peering over to the couch he could see Sasha was calmly exchanging small talk with her mother. Suddenly she looked different to the way she had looked for the last twelve days. The excitement that had been in her eyes was now replaced by the reality that it was nearly all over.

He could see in her face that she was trying to hold back a sadness that reflected the feelings he was suppressing. The girl he had met seemed just a shell as she maintained a brave but distant smile. He wanted to hold her close and tell her it was all going to be alright but now didn't seem the time to do it. Nodding in acceptance of the kind offer he made his excuses as he ran out of the building and down to his apartment.

In one kind gesture he had been given an extra life, a chance to extend his time with her and he was going to take it. As he forced his way into his apartment he realised that he didn't actually care if they weren't going to get him back to the complex. Somehow he would find a way back but that wasn't as important as making the most of his time with Sasha.

Quickly he flicked through the items in his wardrobe selecting items that weren't too formal but looked smart. Pulling his clothes on he couldn't help but realize how much more restricting clothes were than the naturist lifestyle that Sasha had introduced him to. He made note of this change in his opinion and how much he had changed in such a short time. He knew that, without Sasha's influence, he would probably have spent his holiday hiding away somewhere, possibly in his apartment.

He ran back to the main building conscious that he had people waiting for him and he had no control over what they had to do. He didn't know their agenda all he knew was that sometime soon they would be leaving the complex. Pushing the door open he slid past a couple that were making their way back out into the afternoon sun. He could feel his heart racing in anticipation of not knowing if Sasha and her family were still there or not. He played out every scenario he could imagine and felt sure Sasha would find him before she left and was relieved to see them still where he had left them.

In a manoeuvre that was reminiscent of the way she had greeted him after he had disappeared due to their misunderstanding Sasha raced over to him. He braced himself ready for her but still felt himself fall backwards as she lunged herself at him. He could feel her chin pressed against his shoulder and the dead weight of her arms around his neck. Grabbing her trying to reassure her that he was back and wasn't going anywhere he felt a tear slip between her cheek and his.

She pulled her head away from him and looked at him through puffy eyes before running to the bathroom. Jim stood vacantly looking over at her parents who seemed pleased that he had such an effect on their daughter. He felt like they knew what had happened between them and had accepted that he was now almost like part of the family. After an awkward silence Sasha returned to them recomposed and supporting the same vague smile she had shown when she had first seen her parents.

Although she wasn't prepared for showing such emotion Sasha felt like she was handling things fairly well. Her parents had explained that they had invited Jim along to the airport and that had changed the game for her. She had prepared herself for a brief but emotional goodbye with him but now she had a chance to actually make it more meaningful. Once they arrived at the airport and were checked in she felt sure her parents would let her have some time with him to say a proper goodbye.

In a way their invitation to the airport was like an acceptance of him being part of her life. They seemed pleased with her choice and impressed with how pleasant he was and how happy she was around him. If they knew how far things had progressed with him they may have taken a much dimmer view of him but she wasn't going to tell them. What had happened between them behind closed doors was going to stay between them.

Dragging one chair over to the couch she directed Jim to sit down and placed herself across his knees. She had no reason to hide how close she felt to him and how much she trusted him. Jim looked over at her mother and father unsure how they would feel about their daughters seating arrangement but was relieved when they said nothing. Placing a hand round her waist he felt her hand gripping his arm like it was a safety strap on a rollercoaster.

They sat for half an hour exchanging memories of their holiday between each other. At first Jim was worried that Sasha might mention their ill-fated first volleyball game but she was focussed on happier memories. Her mother asked him about them staying in contact and seemed pleased and in many ways relived when they confirmed arrangements were in place.

Jim was just finding himself getting comfortable when Sasha's father nodded discretely over at them as a silent signal. No one else would understand the signal except those that were involved in the events that were due to happen. In some ways it was like some sort of code that only the privileged would know the meaning of and although Jim wasn't officially part of the elite group he knew what it meant.

His father had used similar gestures toward him and his mother at various points in his life. That single nod had a variety of meanings but in this case it was the signal that it was time to leave. Finishing the last of the cup of tea that she had been picking at Sasha rubbed her fingers along Jims arm. It was clear to him that she didn't want to be doing what she was about to do but she didn't have any choice.

She stood and pulled him to his feet holding him close behind her while her parents juggled with the array of cases that surrounded them. Jim wanted to offer assistance but it wasn't his place to help; his place was to silently assure Sasha that everything was going to be okay. Even though this was the first time he had been in such a position before he had seen similar situations to this many times. His gesture to help would be either ignored or politely refused but if Sasha offered she would be an acceptable candidate.

After a few seconds she gave in to the silent plea form her parents and grabbed her bags pulling herself back to the security of Jims arms as quickly as she could. Now Jim had the opportunity to help and he quickly offered to take one of her bags from her. Her mother smiled over at him acknowledging the gesture and adding mental notes to how kind he was. In one single movement that to him was instinct he had increased his rating within her family whether he knew he had or not.

Walking with them up to the reception he stood patiently with Sasha as her father walked in to deal with the final few formalities. Patiently awaiting them was a taxi that was similar to the one that Sasha and Jim had used for their trip to turtle bay. The driver who was keen to help with their bags picked them one by one from the ground by their feet and loaded them into the car.

As they got into the car Jim started to wonder how they were going to arrange for him to return to the complex. At this critical stage in their holiday it wasn't the time to be asking questions, all he could do was hope that her father was true to his word. Even if he did make the arrangements there was no way he could confirm they had been carried out, everything from here on in relied on trust.

There was a part of him that wanted to be getting on the plane with them but he knew that wasn't possible or practical. The rents would never understand or accept that he had suddenly decided to move to Ireland. Even if they did accept it he would have nowhere to live, he couldn't exactly throw himself at Sasha's family to put him up. Even though they seemed to be happy about his role in Sasha's life it would be a bit much to say to them by the way I am moving in with your daughter.

Adding to it all – even if both his and her parents accepted the arrangements there was his passport and clothes which were stranded back at the complex. He decided it was best not to mention his impromptu trip to the airport, there were some things the rents didn't need to know and this was one of them. He would be back before they knew it and then all he had to do was prepare himself for a night and day with them or avoiding them. At the moment there were other things to focus on – he could deal with that when he had arrived back at the complex.

Jim had tactically placed himself in between Sasha and her mother for the journey deciding that there he could stay close to her and also be in sight of both her parents. As much as he begrudged being in the spotlight it seemed the safest option. Tactical seating was something that he had used a few times before but usually to keep people separated. This time it was so he could keep Sasha close for the remainder of their time together.

Her father kept glancing through the mirror in the sun visor he wasn't as much watching them it was more a friendly 'I don't want to do this journey either' glance. There was nothing nice about the homeward journey of a holiday and it was definitely less comfortable when the only people making the journey were those you had bought with you on the holiday. Sasha kept a soft grip on Jim's hand balancing their arms in a non-committal location not quite on her knee and not quite on his. Her mother was happy to avoid eye contact by spending the journey looking out of the window.

They passed by a few little villages and towns until eventually the driver pulled into the airport. Jim had never seen the airport from this angle before, on the outbound journey he had been too busy trying to work out where they were going to take much notice of it. The building wasn't too elaborate, a grey exterior that could pass for an office block in a town environment. He had seen a number of foreign airports and this one seemed a better laid out one than many of them.

They pulled up at a taxi rank outside a set of glass doors that lead into the departures area. Sasha's father leaned over to the driver and in very slow English tried to negotiate a return to the complex for Jim. The Irish brogue made it hard for the driver to understand but eventually he seemed to get the message and agree a figure. Nodding in acceptance her dad told the driver to wait for about thirty minutes and tucked an additional note into his hand. Pleased with the gesture the driver nodded and smiled in a manner that seemed almost creepy but Jim knew it was meant to be reassuring.

In a flashback, Jim suddenly found he had visions of a journey back to the complex, trying to explain to the driver that he was English, not American. The biggest difference between the last time he had been mistaken was that this time he was stuck with the man for however long it took them to return to the complex. Building a mental battle plan Jim decided it was best to keep the man friendly as he was the only choice that was available for his return journey.

Jim glanced back as they pushed their way through the doors and noted that the driver was already leaning against the front of his car and had produced a cigarette.

This was the stance of a man that was prepared to wait which was the first assurance that the arrangement was going to be carried through.

The cool breeze of the air-conditioning hit them as they walked into the terminal building causing a visible shiver. Sasha's father gathered the bags and giving another silent gesture to her mother ushered her over to the check in leaving Sasha and Jim alone. Lost for words Jim looked at Sasha and smiled at her as she gazed into his eyes holding back the sadness that was building up inside.

In a moment of inspiration she quickly asked him to wait where he was and dashed over to her parents. Jim watched her as she spoke with them pulling gently on her mother's arm as she talked. Several gestures and a couple of glances back at Jim passed between them before Sasha threw her arms round her mother's neck. Whatever she had gone over to them enquiring about had clearly been approved as she ran back to him.

She grabbed Jims hands with the look of a person that had just won first prize in a competition no one else seemed to know about. Bouncing slightly she announced that she was taking him to the café so they could spend a little time together before they went home.

Jim peered round over his shoulder noting that the driver that had been assigned the task of returning him to the complex was now busy talking to other drivers. The airport seemed to act like a sort of communal meeting place for people in this job. Anyone that had parked here was nearly guaranteed a job or had already been pre booked to complete one. The problem Jim had was although his driver had been pre booked he had also been pre-paid so there was nothing except good faith keeping him here.

Despite the concerns passing through his conscious mind he followed Sasha as she rushed him away to a small café. Just like most airport eating establishments it had no real atmosphere about it but he hadn't expected much. There was no real point in making too much effort to make people feel welcome when they were either leaving home or on their way back home.

She carefully made her way through the military style rows of tables and chairs until she found a corner that was out of sight from most of the airport. Tactfully she had asked her parents to make themselves busy and arranged to meet them in an alternative location once she had said goodbye to Jim. Her mother had been the most understanding and had made the recommendation of the café as a good spot. Her father had responded by forcing a ten euro note into her hands mentioning that it was probable that Jim wouldn't have money on him.

Even though they had only met him a couple of times and both times he had appeared to be as close to a perfect gentleman as was possible there was no reason for him to carry cash. One of the problems with their chosen holiday destination was the fact that money was rarely needed.

Making her way to a counter that was thankfully not crowded Sasha ordered a couple of drinks and carried them carefully over to the table. She sat down opposite Jim and folded the coins into the note she was impressed to have received in her change. Placing it on the table, she reached down to her bag, pulling it up on to her knees and looking over at him.

It didn't matter where she went there were certain items that she took with her everywhere. Most of them were trinkets that to most people would have little or no meaning but to her they were memories. Each one held some significance to her in one way or another and she didn't want to risk losing them. Going on holiday had been no different except that because she was going to be enjoying the sun she had put the items in her bag to prevent sun lines. In many ways it would seem both foolish and forgetful to go to the trouble of visiting a resort where clothing was optional just to end up going home with tan lines from jewellery.

Untangling the items and laying them neatly on the table next to her coffee she found the item she was looking for. The necklace she had received from Jim was now her pride of place and quickly found its way back to its rightful location around her neck. Next to it was a small ring that had at one stage fitted her finger but was now too tight to wear. She had won it as a prize on a fun fair on one of her family holidays in Ireland and although it didn't have much significance to her it soon would.

Picking it up she slid it over to Jim who looked down at it and then up at her as she slid her hand away. Slowly she explained to him the tradition behind the ring that was known as a Claddagh and how it held significance depending on which finger it was placed on. She added hurriedly that she knew it was far too small for him to wear on his hand but she wanted him to have it as a gift from her.

Carefully he picked it up running his finger round it until the crafted design that was meant to sit on top of his hand faced him. A carefully crafted pair of hands reached out as if they were trying to reach for each other but a heart was preventing them meeting. Their fingertips gripped to the heart which had a crown sitting on top of it completing the design. He listened as Sasha described the ring to him and wondered which finger she would have wanted him to put it on if it had fitted.

"Thank you, it's lovely." He smiled at her, grabbing her hands from across the table.

The ring sat in front of him as they looked over at each other unsure of what to say but both waiting for the other to talk. Their silence was broken by her mother walking into the café and looking round for them before waving over to confirm she had found them. Sasha released her grip on Jim's hand briefly waving back to prevent them being interrupted any further.

Standing up she watched as Jim slipped the little ring into his pocket before gripping his hands again. The realisation that this really was the last time she was going to see him for what could be a long time hit her like a train. A lump caught itself in her throat as she looked at him unable to stop a small tear from pushing its way down her cheek.

"I'll see you again soon, I promise," he said in a soft voice, trying not to respond with a similar tear himself.

She smiled at him trying to push out the beginning of a cheerful giggle that refused to make itself known. A promise was the best she could ask for even though she wanted so much more from him. It was impossible to know what was going to happen next and all she could do was trust in his word. She knew that, although he was in the same situation, she was she had no alternative but to believe him.

"You better or I will come to find ya." She sobbed a little as she tried to be playful with her reply but her emotions failed her.

Releasing her hands Jim pulled her close for the last time this holiday and held her tight as his mind ran through all their memories together. His hands didn't seem to know what to do as they changed between rubbing her back and patting her back in reassurance. Gently she pulled away a bit making sure to keep his grip round her as tight as she could while looking round the restaurant. It was more a formality than anything else making her check who was around, in reality she didn't care.

Pulling herself in slowly she pushed her lips against his for a long and deep kiss as she placed her hands on his shoulders. She gripped tightly to him, forcing herself against him as she put all her emotion into her public display of affection. All around she could hear people chattering and was blissfully immune to what they were saying. The only thing that mattered was this moment, making it last as long as it could and making it count.

She pulled away from him briefly, catching her breath as she felt her eyes puffing up with emotion. Pausing, she looked at him deeply, leaning for a second more passionate – but briefer – kiss.

"Contact me the second you're home," she panted as she picked up her bag before leaning in for a third and final kiss.

Jim walked with her to the edge of the café and watched as she disappeared through the doors into the departures area. He felt sure he saw her look back several times as she disappeared from sight and almost wanted her to return but knew she couldn't. Clearing his throat and wiping the tear from his eye he jabbed his hand in his pocket making sure he could still feel the ring before running to get his taxi.

Chapter Twenty-nine

And then there was one

Even though Jim had never officially had a relationship, he had plenty of experience of counselling people at different stages of one. Being separated from the person you were with was sometimes a necessary evil and for Sasha and him it was going to become an integral part of their future. Both of them had avoided discussing where things were going to go after the holiday was over, for Jim that was because he never liked discussing the end of a holiday and he felt it was a similar reason for Sasha.

Their reluctance to approach the subject had left them in a situation where on Sasha's last day all they had was contact details and promises. It had been easy to tell that there was sincerity in the words and gestures that Sasha had made toward him as they said their last goodbyes at the airport and he had meant every word as well.

Waking up alone for the first time in over a week bought the reality of the situation crashing home for him. Next to him on his bed he had tried to preserve the spot that Sasha had occupied making an effort not to cross over the imaginary line as he slept. He had no way of knowing for sure that he had kept to his side of the bed but rather than question it he convinced himself he had stayed true to his intentions.

Staring up at the ceiling he found himself wondering what she was doing back at home and imagining what her home was like. He had never been to Ireland but if things went well with their promise of regular contact it looked like he might be going there soon.

Next to him, on the bedside table, was the ring that Sasha had presented him with before departing. Leaning over nonchalantly, he picked it up, twisting it against the tips of his fingers to confirm that it really wouldn't fit any of them. Even if it had fitted, he still didn't know which finger he was meant to put it on. Sasha's story had been precise and descriptive, and it had told him that the right hand was the correct place, but there were too many rules. Pondering for a few moments, he decided that he would wear it as a necklace and maybe they could buy a matching pair when he met her next.

Picking up the folded piece of paper that the ring had been weighing down to the table top he opened it. At the top of the page in the neatest writing he had seen were the careful details of her home address. The lack of a post code had at first concerned him but Sasha had explained that the town was too small for such formalities.

Below that, underneath the neat crease that had been carefully put there by Sasha, was her phone number. She had written the same number out three times once without the dialling code for Ireland, once with brackets defining the code and once with an explanation of how to dial her number with the dialling code. Her careful description of how to use the simple string of digits was in many ways a credit to her determination to ensure Jim had it right.

Toward the bottom of the page was her email address, she had highlighted to him that this was probably the easiest way to contact her. Underneath the email address she had written a series of words that she had instructed Jim to translate for her on his first email. He had looked at the words at first trying to work out how to phonetically say them just to be corrected on his pronunciation. This little phrase had been a clever plot to encourage him to contact her but he didn't need motivation, all he needed was internet access.

Friends had told him that there were hidden rules behind making contact after a first date. He knew that in theory he had been on several dates with Sasha but this was the first time contact was necessary. One person, one of the few that seemed to make logical sense when they were talking to him, no matter what the situation, advised him that there was a forty-eight hour rule.

From what he understood this rule stated that contact too soon or too late after a first date held different implications as to how the date had gone. If a text or in his case an email was sent too quickly he would seem over eager but he couldn't see how it was a bad thing to seem over eager. Waiting longer than two days was apparently a sign of not being interested enough to make an effort but waiting exactly two days was fine.

This rule caused him many problems, the first one was that he wasn't entirely sure how many dates Sasha and he had been on. They had seen each other every day and on some occasions more than once a day so was each occasion a new date or was their time together one continuous date. If they had been on many dates it didn't really matter how soon he contacted her as they had been seen by all around them as a couple.

Questioning his dilemma for a few moments he decided they had been together too much to consider themselves as only having had one date. If every time they met was only one date and their meetings lasted for days or weeks they would be seen to be having the longest dates in history.

Accepting his decision that they were a well-established couple he found himself wondering why he had even questioned it. If they hadn't been a proper couple there was no way they would have shared a bed as many times as they had. Maybe he was delirious or maybe it was just that he was missing her being around that was making him over think. Whatever the answer was all he knew for certain was that he didn't know if the complex even had public internet access.

On previous holidays depending on the flight time he would have either spent the remainder of his first day or his first morning orientating himself around the facilities he was most likely to use during his stay. Some of these were easy to find as everyone would sooner or later be using them, facilities like the restaurant and the swimming pool. Other facilities were more of a personal preference due to the need to find other teenagers like the games room. As an extension of the games room he had always found the public internet computers somewhere nearby.

With the happy event of meeting Sasha he hadn't followed any of the usual rituals of a holiday and now he found himself nearing the end of his holiday with no knowledge of where the games room was. Becoming part of Sasha's life and her holiday had been without doubt the best thing he could ever imagine happening to him but now he found himself with only a whisper of his holiday left and nowhere to spend it to avoid the rents.

Folding the piece of paper neatly he pushed himself out of bed gripping the ring tightly in one hand and her contact details in the other. These two items were the most important things he had to remember to take home with him. Carefully he pushed them into the zip pocket on the front of his case and looked at himself in the mirror.

Staring back at him was the same boy that he had looked at on his first evening before going to dinner with Sasha. The pasty white skin that had been staring back at him now had a healthy bronzed complexion. As an added bonus the usual tan lines that would plague him for weeks after going home were non-existent. The rents had already seen him once on his holiday but that time he had Sasha with him to distract him away from them. This time he was actually considering offering to spend time with them knowing firstly that they wouldn't be dressed and this time he was on his own. He shuddered at the idea of a full day in their company but accepted it as a small sacrifice for what had up to now been the best holiday of his life.

He gazed over at the wardrobe, sitting behind the basic wooden door was a large range of clothing that he had bought with him and barely used during his holiday. In the drawers below the mirror were the rest of his holiday items, the clothes that didn't warrant being hung up. There was nothing stopping him putting something on for his potential day with the rents. He stood looking vacantly into the mirror; Sasha wouldn't do it so he wasn't going to let her down by doing it either.

Breathing deeply he mentally prepared himself for the day he was going to have ahead of him. He walked out of the bedroom trying hard to convince himself that he wasn't going mad. If anyone had told him on day one of his holiday that he would be voluntarily offering to spend time with the rents before he went home he would have laughed at them.

He stood outside his parent's apartment for a few moments while he prepared himself for what he may encounter. Once he made his presence known it would be a matter of minutes before he was face to face with one or both of the rents nude. There was of course the possibility that they had already gone for breakfast which would buy him some time but he felt like he needed familiar company to keep his mind occupied.

Even though deep down he knew that what he was doing was in effect using them as a decoy from being alone but he felt sure they wouldn't mind. He rehearsed answers for their questions knowing that one of them would ask where Sasha was and he would have to find some tactical answer. If he simply told them she had gone home it would be glaringly obvious that he was only with them because there was no one else. His best option was to tell them she had gone home but add to it a reference to her recommending he spend some time with them.

Technically that would be a lie but she had asked him about the rents a few times during their time together and seemed surprised when he was vague with his replies. Even though she had discretely chosen not to comment on the distant relationship he had with them it was clear that she was much closer to her parents than he was to his. In a way her silent disapproval had encouraged him to spend time with them and her going home had given him the opportunity to do it.

He pictured her reaction when she read about him actually making an attempt to bond a closer relationship with them. In his mind he could see her smiling softly as she read about the day that he was about to try and convince the rents he wanted to have with them. He took a deep breath and walked up to the apartment raising his hand to knock but was beaten to it by the door opening.

Standing in front of him making their way out of the apartment toward the main building were both of his parents at the same time. All his preparation had told him he would be greeted by one of them and the other would follow a few moments later. Instead he was faced with a wall of parental flesh greeting him cheerily at the door.

"Jim, are you joining us for breakfast?" His mother beamed as she saw him standing poised to knock at the door.

He braced himself pulling away from a gesture that was inviting a hug as he smiled awkwardly at them. What had been seen could not be unseen and now even though he had seen them twice before on the holiday he had managed to tactically avoid a full body view of them. Now he had the image of the rents naked embedded on his mind and there was nothing that was going to remove that image from his brain. In a few years possibly Sasha would be able to calm him down enough for him to laugh about the occasion but for now therapy seemed the only way he was going to cope.

Nodding with a forced smile he gestured for them to walk ahead of him and was pleased when they accepted his motioned offer. Following them to the building made it easier to compose himself for the rest of the day. From his position all he had to put up with was a view of their backs and before eating that was enough.

Walking with them into the restaurant he made a conscious decision to choose his food from any buffet they were not going to. The few moments of solitude gave him time to recompose himself before suggesting to them that a day together might be nice. If he was clever maybe they would ask him to recommend an activity and he could suggest walking into the village.

After his last adventure into Vasillikos he knew that there was very little to see once getting there but he felt sure that the rents wouldn't have made the trip. In all the years they had gone on family holidays the only time they had left the hotel or complex they were staying at was by coach on a planned excursion. It was more likely that they would want to spend their last day relaxing by the pool or on the beach.

Small talk was never easy with the rents; he had avoided it on every opportunity back at home. The basic facts had always been the main goal of any conversation with them. It had usually started with how his day was but that conversation line had been frequently shut down with a simple response of OK. Sometimes they had gone on to ask what he had done at school which had a second standard answer of nothing much. At first Dad had questioned him with comments how it was impossible to do nothing much when at school.

Deep down Jim had known his father was correct but he didn't see much point in telling them about the lessons. He barely remembered what had been taught in most of them and by the end of his school life had been surprised by how much he had recalled for the exams. After a year of being told that nothing much had happened at school his dad had given up asking him and pretended to be busy reading while his mother amicably persisted with the daily routine of questioning.

Placing himself strategically at the table so he was exposed to as little flesh as possible while they ate he waited for the first question. This was the moment he had prepared for as they walked silently toward the main building. In a way he had been relieved for the silence as he didn't know what to say to the rents and he didn't particularly want to stop walking to have a conversation with them. If they were agreeable to a day as a family which so far they seemed to be it would be difficult enough without intermittent stops en route to a location to ask questions.

His dad was the first one to speak as he delicately nibbled at a badly made sandwich of ham and cheese. It wasn't much of a surprise when the first topic was how things were going with Sasha. Jim recognised this as an indirect way of asking where she was and why he was with them not with her. By asking how things were going it left the discussion open to the possibility that Sasha and him had argued and consequently were not talking.

He glanced at his mother, who seemed to be prepared for any answer, followed by relief when he advised them that she had gone home. It was clear that she knew that if there had been a break up it would put a dampener on the holiday and that was not needed on the last day. Quickly Jim added that she had encouraged him to spend more time with his family and this seemed a good time to do it. A look of pleasant surprise covered his father's face which in many ways was better than suspicion as to the truth behind the comment.

Taking advantage of this sudden urge to spend time with the family Jim's dad asked if there was anything in particular he wanted to do. A million thoughts filled Jim's mind as he contemplated the best way to address such an opportunity. Part of his mind wanted to suggest going for a walk off the complex toward the village but he felt sure that would come with objections such as having packed everything except their going home stuff.

Jim had seen this manoeuvre before and knew that even though it seemed like a friendly and open question it actually wasn't. Asking him what he wanted to do was a tactful way of trying to see if he was going to suggest something that didn't suit their unwritten itinerary. If he suggested something that didn't suit them this gave the rents the opportunity to offer to spend time together later and let him do whatever he wanted.

The only lifeline he could pull was suggesting an activity that involved more than one person but even then there were get out clauses. If he suggested a game of tennis they could suggest him finding someone his own age to play it with, maybe they would like the mini golf but there was no guarantee. There was only one way of responding that ensured he wasn't left to his own devices for the day.

"Anything you want will be fine, I just want to spend time as a family." He cringed inside as the words left his mouth but watched a long smile appear on his mother's face.

He categorised his response under the heading of tactically cute because it pushed the choice back to the rents but anyone else that heard it would cringe on the outside just like he had on the inside. The rents seemed to approve of his reply and took the opportunity to suggest starting the day by the poolside.

Jim nodded as he stood up excusing himself from the table before making his way out of the restaurant. Quickly he disappeared into the bathroom deciding it was the closest place he could get solace after his sickly display of interest that had given him the passport to company for the day. He splashed his face with water and stared into the mirror as the droplets fell from his skin. Waiting outside were the two people he had vowed to avoid for the fortnight he was away and now he was making an effort to be with them.

Composing himself he walked out of the bathroom and saw the rents sat patiently waiting for him. His father was the first to react by gesturing to him to join them at the coffee table. Whether they knew it or not they had chosen the same table that he had shared with Sasha on the night they met. Casually he walked over conscious that for the few moments it took to arrive and sit down he was on full view to both his parents.

Carefully he sat down and exchanged trivial stories about their holiday and the different things they had done. For a few moments he contemplated telling them about the trip he had taken with Sasha to see the turtles. On one hand they would probably approve of it as a kind and considerate place to take her but on the other hand it would encourage questions about his judgement on booking such an excursion alone. Avoiding the subject was definitely the best option if he wanted to avoid any potential awkwardness.

Patiently he sat glancing round the atrium while they sipped cordially at the coffee they had ordered. The waiter on duty looked like he remembered Jim but he wasn't sure which occasion it was from. He had been in this same atrium several times with Sasha under several different circumstances. Worst case scenario was that this waiter had possibly served him alcohol but he seemed to know not to ask Jim if he wanted anything to drink in his present company. Contemplating the day he had ahead it would have been nice to have something stronger than coffee.

After a few tense moments his mother stood and led them out of the building toward the pool. The waiter smiled at Jim as if to tell him whatever secret the man knew was safe with him for now. Jim acknowledged the smile with a casual nod and half a smile back which seemed to please the man.

On the last occasion that Jim had been at the pool he had been with Sasha and they had been armed with a book each. Not much reading had been done but most of the people around the pool seemed to have something in their hand to read or a board or card game to play while they enjoyed the sun. The only thing none of them seemed to have come to the outdoor pool prepared to do was swimming which seemed to be the most logical activity.

Choosing his seating carefully Jim made himself comfortable on a lounger that was in between his parents. This was a tactical decision because he had to make sure he could hear both of them without them having to get up.

The morning passed with what seemed to Jim to be great ease, somehow he had managed to get through a morning with the rents without a major debate starting.

Lunch had been a very casual affair and quite soon after eating the rents announced that they were going back to their room for a siesta. Jim peered at them as they made their announcement pondering on the idea of a mid-afternoon sleep that was a Spanish idea being carried out in a Grecian country.

Acknowledging their announcement cordially he watched them disappear and breathed a sigh of relief. Even though he was now in the position he had been trying to avoid of being alone it was in some ways nice to have time to himself. Quickly he moved away from the pool to prevent being encouraged by some random person to join in a game in the pool that he had no interest in.

Stopping at his apartment to get a towel he glanced over at his case and remembered the paper he had tucked inside the front pocket. Maybe now was a good time to explore or find out if there was somewhere he could use the internet. Pulling the piece of paper out of the pocket he read over the email address several times. It wasn't hard to remember but he wanted to make sure the numbers she had after her name were in his head before putting it back in his case.

Pockets were one of the things he had missed since adopting the naturist lifestyle. Little things like that piece of paper were impractical to carry around and as an unseasoned naturist he hadn't prepared for having nowhere to put things when he was out.

Looking out across the complex he glanced over at the rents apartment and smiled vaguely. All in all their morning together had worked out better than he had expected it to. As usual Sasha had been right about getting to know his parents; it wasn't as bad as he had thought it would be. He wasn't going to tell her just yet that he had intentionally spent time with them but at least now he had he could tell her in his own time.

Down beyond the pool was the beach that Sasha had taken him to and shown him as a secluded but sunny spot. That was going to be his home for the afternoon, after that he had already arranged dinner with the rents and in some ways he was looking forward to it.

Before he did anything else there was something else that in his mind was more important. Beyond the main building was the reception and that was the most practical place to answer his question. He made a note to himself that while he was there he could pick a book up to pass his time on the beach. But before he did anything else he had to find out if there was anywhere he could send a message to Sasha.

Chapter Thirty

Returning to Reality

Getting used to life back at home had never been easy for Sasha since the first year they had visited the complex. Just like anyone that had the luxury of spending their summer holiday abroad, the weather was the most notable difference. Even on a good day (which seemed to be rare), the heat didn't seem to reach anywhere near the same heights that she had enjoyed in Greece.

In an almost silent admission that they were missing the complex too, her parents made the tactical decision not to comment on dress codes too quickly after they got home. No one mentioned it but they all seemed to be in agreement that society's rules were at least a little bit outdated.

She remembered the first year she had visited the complex and how her parents had almost encouraged her to hold on to the lifestyle when she had got home. By the age of thirteen, they seemed less interested in whether she extended her naturist time or not. Gradually, over the course of a few days, things seemed to get back to normal and clothes became the rule instead of the exception. Usually, she accepted that.

Dad was always the first to fall back into line but Sasha had never been sure if that had been because he had to or because he wanted to. Several times she had pondered over how his boss would react if he went to work naked. That was if he managed to successfully get from home to work without anyone commenting on it or him being arrested.

After arriving back in the early hours of the morning, most of her first day back had been spent relaxing. She had gone to bed early in order to encourage her body back into a normal sleep pattern and found herself waking at what she classed as a civilised time. Casually she glanced over at the light green LED display on her alarm clock as she lay resting in bed.

Out of all the things she had in her bedroom, this was one of the things she had missed the most. The outdated clocks in the bedrooms of the apartments had seemed like a novelty at first but, after five years, she found them awkward to read. Logically she knew that, if she wanted to, she could pack her clock and take her more up-to-date lifestyle with her but it seemed pointless. Besides anything else, having it sitting at home waiting for her was almost like having a welcoming committee that she knew wouldn't let her down.

Gazing up at the ceiling, she reflected back to her time on the island and the boyfriend that she had left standing at the airport. She wondered what he had done with his last day and made a plan of what she would have done if it had been her left there.

The feelings that had grown between them over their fortnight were unlike anything she had experienced before. The pain in her stomach had sat there like a lead brick all the way home and was only now beginning to pass through her system. She wondered if he had reverted back to being a textile in her absence or if he had kept up the naturist lifestyle. It had taken her nearly a week to convince him that naturism wasn't as strange as he seemed sure it was when they had first met.

If it had been her that was forced to stay behind, she pondered over whether she would do the same as she had when she thought she had lost him. During that time, a period of her holiday she wanted to forget, she had chosen to wear a bikini and she couldn't remember why. Everybody on the complex knew her and knew that the only time she usually dressed was for the evenings. If she made a habit of dressing during the day, she felt like it would make people notice her more and she wouldn't want that.

Jim was different; these people didn't know him and had probably silently noticed that he had spent nearly half his stay dressed. If he returned to wearing clothes, they wouldn't take much notice of it, marking it down as someone who tried the lifestyle but didn't like it.

Quickly she moved her thoughts to what he might have done with his last day now that she was gone. There was a chance that he would try socialising with others but she decided it wasn't likely. The only people he had spoken to that weren't related to either of them while he was away had been Greg and Alice. They had been back home for a week and, even if they had still been there, she felt like he wouldn't make an effort to find them.

In the cold morning light she could feel the chain with a decorative letter "S" pressing against her skin. This had been his first gift to her and, even though it had arrived in her possession in the most awkward way possible, she knew that it was significant. The thought that he had clearly put into buying it had told her what she had thought was true; it had shown his sensitive side. She tickled her finger over it silently, acknowledging that she had no doubt that she had made the right decision to be his girlfriend.

Turning her head, she spotted the small folded piece of paper that he had presented to her in the dying hours of her holiday. His handwriting seemed hurried and shaky but the details on it were clear and precise. She remembered distinctly the moment they had exchanged their contact details and how he had added the international code to his number quickly after she reminded him that she lived in a different country to him.

Pushing her feet out of the bed, she shivered slightly as a cool tingle ran through her body. Casually, she grabbed the slip of paper and scuffed her way over to the wardrobe, pondering the idea of dressing. Deep down, she knew that her parents wouldn't make any comment if she appeared downstairs as she was but it seemed unnecessary.

Peering beyond her usual array of clothes, her eyes stopped when they spotted a robe that had been bought for her at the age of thirteen. Her father had noticed her looking at it as they went shopping and had decided to get it for her as a present on her confirmation.

Nobody had predicted it but, within a year of it being bought, she had finally had the long-awaited growth spurt that had seemed like it was never going to happen. As a result of it, the hem of the robe had moved from its original and acceptable location of mid-way down her thigh. Its new resting place was just below her buttock, making the robe more revealing than anyone had intended it to be.

By the age of fifteen, the change in her height had been complimented by other parts of her body changing in proportion. Her waist was still happy to remain hidden behind its silky material but her breasts seemed not to be as happy to comply anymore. Eventually, her mother made a discrete recommendation that it was time to replace the robe with a new one.

Pulling it off the hangar for the first time in over a year, she cringed as a rattle echoed through her room, announcing that she was awake. Holding it against herself, she glanced in the mirror before pulling it over her arm and watching the cuff rise up towards her elbow. Carefully, she pulled it across her shoulders, almost expecting the material to give up and tear as she slipped her other arm in.

Wrapping it around herself, she felt a smile form on her face when she noticed that the sides still overlapped each other. Tying it with the cord in a loose knot, she brushed it as she looked at herself in the mirror.

There was no doubt that her parents were right about it being far too small for day-to-day use. The extra year of growth made even the shallowest of breaths a risk of the gown falling open. If she doubled the knot, it would do for breakfast and she could change again afterward if the need arose.

As she tiptoed her way downstairs, she reflected on how strange it had felt having a bed to herself. Tiredness had prevented her from noticing it when she had arrived home but, now she had fully rested, she knew it felt like there was a void in her life. It was clear from the way her father had invited Jim to the airport that they had accepted him as being part of her life but they didn't know how far things had gone between them.

All the way home, she had wondered if it had really been her father's idea to let him join them in their return to the airport. Normally it was her mother that made the suggestion and her father that implemented it. Despite their openness, she felt sure that, when Jim visited, they wouldn't allow him to share her room at home.

Over in the corner of the front room, she could see the desk with the home computer sitting patiently, waiting to be used. Deep down, she wanted to check her emails in anticipation but she felt like it was too soon to hear from him.

The internet would also give her access to social networking, which she loathed, but knew that it was part of modern society. Friends had set her up with accounts that she didn't use but she kept her email up-to-date with their latest news. One click and she could tell everyone that she was no longer single but where was the fun in that? She only had a few close friends and she knew they would prefer to hear the news directly from her.

Online announcements had their advantages as they would hopefully stop the local lads from pursuing her. The only problem was that most of the boys' parents knew her parents and she didn't want to cause any stress. The new school year was only a short time away and that would give her plenty of opportunities to tell people about Jim without her parents having to answer for her.

Pondering over her options, she decided it was less hassle if she kept up her vigil of not using social networking. For now, she wanted to keep Jim's presence to herself, even if it was only to stop people asking where he was. Placing her hand in the pocket of the robe that was struggling to stay tied around herself, she walked over to the desk. Even if she didn't announce her happiness to the world, she wanted to let him know that she was home before the day was done. Carefully, she slipped the note under the keyboard in preparation to contact Jim after she had fed her grumbling stomach.

The kitchen floor felt cold but refreshing against her feet as she wandered between one unit and the next. Armed with bread, butter and a knife, she prepared a sparse sandwich for herself as she mentally composed her first email to him. There was so much she wanted to tell him but she didn't want her message to seem like it was an essay.

Using phrases like telling him that she missed him seemed a little over the top considering they had seen each other less than two days previous. She knew deep inside that her heart was telling her that she did miss him being around but she didn't want to scare him off. Her friends had told her about how boys reacted to such words and normally it seemed like they signalled the beginning of the end for their relationships. Clutching the badly made sandwich in her hand, she stared at it discerningly as she wandered back into the front room. Having something as meagre as a butter sandwich seemed like little consolation after the range of pastries she had been able to feast on at the complex; then again, she wasn't really all that hungry.

Sitting carefully on the couch, she glanced at the staircase as she heard a floorboard creaking upstairs. She knew the noise would be her mother as she had heard her father leave the house before she woke up. Peering down her body, she pulled her scant robe, trying to hide her breasts for the third time since she had made what was clearly an inappropriate choice of clothes.

In a way, it was nice to be able to get away with wearing so little around her parents. There was nothing that was hidden that they hadn't seen before and she felt sure her mother wouldn't make a fuss if she decided to discard it. For now, she wanted to make the effort to at least appear like she wanted to be dressed.

Focussing back on the stairs, she watched as her mother's leg made its way into view at the top of the stairs. In a way, it was a relief to her that she was alone at home with her mother; things always seemed easier when it was just the two of them. Even though she knew that there was a generation difference between them, it was almost like having an older sister.

A vague smile appeared on Mary's face as she stepped down on to the warm carpet of the front room. With a casual flip of her hand, she acknowledged that her daughter had beaten her downstairs for the second day in a row as she made her way into the kitchen.

Sasha remained motionless, munching on her bread as she listened to the kettle boil. It didn't matter what day it was, she knew that her parents relied on coffee as their motivation to wake fully. If it had been the weekend, she knew that the next move would be taking a mug up to her father as he was sure to be in bed still. For now, it was only the two of them and Sasha seldom drank coffee in the morning unless she was on holiday. Craning her neck, she glanced over her shoulder as the kettle rumbled to completion and smiled at her mother as she walked back into the room.

Without speaking, Mary made her way into the single chair that faced at an angle to the couch. In discrete moments, she had discussed the holiday with Diarmuid and they had both agreed that certain things needed to be cleared up before too long. Taking a deep breath, she managed to maintain a casual and friendly appearance as she took her first sip of coffee. Peering over at Sasha, she could tell that her daughter knew there was something on her mind as she relaxed back into her chair.

"So, tell me all about Jim." Mary's voice was calm and almost playful as she questioned her daughter.

She knew even before asking the question that, during their holiday, both Diarmuid and she had been introduced to him or more than one occasion. Over all, he seemed like a pleasant boy and they had agreed that it was good that Sasha had found someone her own age at last. The thing that was bugging them was that he had been introduced to them as her boyfriend.

Sasha had never used such a term to introduce anyone in the past, whether they had been at home or away. It was clear that this boy had meant a lot to Sasha while they were on holiday and they both knew that she had exchanged contact details with him.

From the time Sasha had turned fourteen, they had known eventually boys were going to become a factor in her life and they had accepted the consequences that would come with it. Boys at home had tried to catch her attention and Mary knew that one by one Sasha had somehow managed to avoid most of them.

It had been clear from the moment they moved into the departure lounge that Sasha was upset but she was trying to hide it. Mary had discretely pointed out to her husband that this was the first time they had seen Sasha in such a position. The emblem around her neck had been her centre of attention throughout the flight and somehow it seemed to be pacifying her.

The late time of the flight had meant they had arrived home too tired to discuss anything but that hadn't stopped Diarmuid's head from filling with questions. Deep down, Mary had hoped that, even though Sasha was staying in contact with Jim, anything else would eventually fizzle out. One by one, she listened to Diarmuid as he made his points clear and accepted that something had to be said and it was best for her to say it.

Feeling nervous as she waited for the reply, she kept a calm expression as she thought ahead. Depending on the reply, they would have to make allowances for Sasha to want to meet with him again. The most practical way would be for them to meet at the complex if they returned the following year.

If she took Sasha's reference to him as a boyfriend as being genuine, she felt sure that waiting a year was not something that Sasha would accept. If Jim was destined to be visiting, they would need to find somewhere for him to stay but that was a bridge they could cross if it happened.

Deep down, she wanted to ask Sasha a direct question about how far she had taken things with Jim. She knew that her daughter was more aware of sexuality than most girls of her age and it had been Diarmuid and her that had put Sasha in the position that had made her aware. Naturism had never been considered a bad move for them and, in a way, they preferred the idea of her learning about boys on the complex. Other girls would have found other ways to find out about boys; at least their way had been in an environment that wasn't intimidating.

Asking her direct questions wasn't the most practical solution, even though the questions were burning inside her. If it was her who had been the teenage daughter and her mother had asked her such intimate questions, she knew exactly what she would have done. Avoiding the answer or lying was the only safe way out of such a scenario and she didn't want to think of Sasha ever needing to do that.

Sasha felt her shoulders relax as she took in the question that her mother had presented to her. It seemed almost like a trivial question because she had already introduced him to both her parents. Deep down, she knew there was more to what had been said then the words that had been spoken.

With what seemed to be almost a reflex action, she placed her hand against her chest, gripping the chain. Feeling her face flush with redness, she glanced over at her mother who was silently acknowledging the gesture. By completing an action that to her was natural, she felt like she had already responded to the question even though no words had been used.

Her parents had seen the chain and surely knew it wasn't something she had owned before the holiday. Maybe they thought she had bought it for herself but surely they knew she wasn't the sort of person to do that. This chain was one of only a few things she had that connected Jim to her; surely her parents had concluded that it must have come from him.

"As you know, we have exchanged contact details. We are hoping to meet again soon." She felt a lump in her throat as she spoke, acknowledging that Jim was now too far away to see every day.

Mary looked calmly over at her daughter, realising that she was not going to get any more information without asking awkward questions. The response had been mature and well thought out, which was a credit to Sasha. Silently acknowledging the clever response, she smiled, accepting that there were some things it was better for a mother not to know.

It was clear that, as far as Sasha was concerned, Jim was now a part of her life and he was going to be for the foreseeable future. In a way, she wanted to prepare Sasha for the possibility of Jim not replying to her messages but she didn't want to be the one to burst a bubble that might not need bursting. The only thing she could do was update Diarmuid and prepare for the unexpected, just in case it happened.

Nodding, she stood up, clutching the warm mug as she stepped over towards the couch. Sasha watched her mother carefully, unsure of what she was going to do and felt her body tingle as Mary placed a hand lovingly on her thigh, squeezing it gently before moving away.

Somehow, without her noticing it, her daughter had matured beyond her years over the course of their holiday. It was hard to accept but she could see that they had taken her away as a carefree teenager and she had returned as a young woman.

Relieved, Sasha watched her mother disappear upstairs with her coffee, seemingly content with her mini inquisition. Relaxing back into the couch, she glanced around, spotting the computer again and wondering if she should send the message that she was still mentally composing. The longer she stayed at home, the more chance there was of her mother returning with more questions. Sasha knew there was a possibility that she had disappeared to discretely update her father and didn't want to give her the chance to return with the next instalment.

Not wanting to waste any more time, she scampered upstairs and back into her bedroom. Quickly, she untied the knot that had somehow managed to hide her body while her mother had quizzed her. Breathing deeply, she dropped the robe on to her bed and opened the wardrobe to find clothes that would be suitable for going out in.

Pawing through her clothes, she decided that she wasn't in the mood to actually be anywhere that she might see anyone she knew. A trip down the alleyway near her home was much safer as it would take her away from her parents and reduce the chance of anyone bumping into her.

Slipping on a pair of jeans and a T-shirt, she looked over at her desk and picked up a few of the magazines that she had placed there. She wasn't sure if it was impulse buying habit but, every week, she ended up buying one of these magazines from the local shops. She classed them in the heading of typical teenage magazines as she regularly saw other girls her age selecting the same ones. Slipping a few of them into a light cloth bag, she made her way back downstairs and out of the front door.

Just a few doors away from her house, she knew there was an alleyway that took its users away from the street and led towards a large green. On the few occasions she had wandered down it, she had always managed to find a quiet place on the grass to be alone with her thoughts.

She stopped at a point in the path where she spotted a second narrower path leading off in a slightly different direction. Contemplating the option, she accepted that, sooner or later, there was a chance it ended up at the same green but for now it was somewhere new to explore. Feeling a bit adventurous, she glanced at the normal path before heading down the new narrower one.

She wandered carefully along the mudded path, pushing branches out of the way that had clearly not seen the same amount of human traffic as the path she was used to. Stopping to allow her eyes to focus, she spotted what looked like the outside of a cottage and made her way to it.

In years gone by, she felt sure that this property would have been part of an estate that might have been part of the road she lived on. Now it stood on its own, the cruel victim to years of neglect and bad weather that had ripped away its roof and left holes that would have formerly held windows. In its present form, she knew it would offer very little protection from anything but it still seemed to maintain some of its charm.

With curiosity building up inside, she made her way up to it and peered through the vacant doorway. She could imagine a smart stone, or maybe wooden, floor filling the space that had now been taken over by mud. From the inside, it looked like the walls were held together by moss but she felt sure there was something else keeping them in place. Taking careful steps, she made her way through to the back of the abandoned building.

Staring up through a clearing in the trees, she could see that the sun was trying to make itself known to what would formerly have been the back garden. Carefully placing her hand on the wall where the back door used to stand, she glanced around and spotted an old plastic chair. Small puddles of water from rainy days filled the indented grooves that ran parallel to each other up and down the chair's seat.

For a while, she found herself wondering why it was there or who might have left it there. If someone had found this place before her, there was a chance they would return some day but hopefully not today. For now, this chair was in the perfect place for her to hide away from the questioning voice of her mother.

Pulling her magazine collection out of its bag, she placed the bag carefully over the wet seat and sat down, pushing her shoes off to stretch her toes. Relaxing back into the chair, she felt water from the plastic seat back seep through her shirt and onto her skin.

Quickly, she leaned forward, cursing herself for not realising that, if the seat was wet, the back would be too. Squirming slightly, she stood and glanced though the glassless window to check that no one was there before peeling her T-shirt off.

At first, it felt unusual standing in jeans and a bra but the sun against her back made it feel like it was okay. She peered down at herself, making the observation that, if she took her jeans off too, it would be like she was wearing a bikini. Glancing up at the sun, she knew how rare it was to have weather that would allow such a dress code. Peering at the chair, she noticed that the water was already seeping through the thin bag she had used to protect her clothes.

Logically, she knew the answer was to find somewhere else to sit but this cottage felt perfect. Huffing at her indecisiveness, she pushed her jeans down her legs, folding them neatly with her top and placing them on her shoes. A bikini felt acceptable and she knew there was very little chance of anyone finding her anyway.

Settling back into the chair, she shivered slightly as the water that had forced her to remove her top squelched against her back. Gazing up at the sun, she reminisced on days spent relaxing in Greece, wearing less than she was, and she smiled to herself.

Checking over her shoulder as if she expected to see someone standing at the back doorway, she reached for the clip on her bra.

"Sure no one's gonna see me anyway," she muttered as she flicked the straps off her shoulder and placed the discarded item on her knees.

Glancing down at the discarded bra, she realised that this was the first time she had been topless in Ireland. Most people would possibly try this in the comfort of their back garden but here she was in the back of a cottage. She paused for a moment, realising how nice it felt and noticing that the inhibitions she thought she should have were not there.

Standing, she covered her breasts as she placed her bra with the other items she had taken off and looked through the cottage. As had been expected, there was no one there and she knew in her heart there probably wouldn't be anyone there for the rest of the day at least. She glimpsed down her body that was still showing the tan she had picked up from her holiday.

"Seems stupid not to finish the job," she mumbled as she pushed her panties to the floor.

The excitement she gained from her first naturist experience in Ireland was one she wanted to share with someone but knew she couldn't. Bending down, she picked up the final article of clothing as she made her way back to the chair. Now she felt like she could enjoy the sun and, even though no one knew she was doing it, she could do it the way nature intended.

For hours she sat flicking through the magazines, reading over some articles to prolong her stay. Every so often, she stood and made her way over to the window, checking for anyone approaching. Each time, the thrill of knowing she was nude and out in public filled her body with a warmth that she couldn't describe.

By the middle of the afternoon, the sun had hidden behind one of the trees that was towering over her secluded garden. She shivered slightly as she felt the mild breeze passing over her skin and placed her third magazine down. For a few moments, she sat taking in the reality of what she had done and knew she had enjoyed every moment from the time she had removed the first item of clothing. Picking them up one by one, she quickly dressed before making her way back towards home.

The smell of baking filled the front room as she walked in and announced her return home. Her mother was in the kitchen, preparing dinner for when Dad came home, and she shouted out to her with a merry chirp. If her mother was to ever find out what she had done, she knew there would be severe reprimanding on its way but there was no way she could find out.

Brushing past the back of the couch, she sat down at the computer, knowing that, once Dad was home, she might not get the opportunity again. She hadn't checked her emails since returning from her holiday but that was because she had expected a pile of junk messages from companies she didn't care about. Now she wanted to compose the message she had been thinking about all day and was ready to contact Jim.

Quickly, she typed in the password and prepared herself for an extended session of email housekeeping before writing her much anticipated email. One by one, she clicked her way down the list, highlighting the ones she didn't need, ready for their removal. Her heart skipped as she reached an email address she thought she recognised. Quickly, she pulled the paper she had hidden away from its place and matched each letter on the screen to the ones that had been written.

With uncontrollable joy, she felt a smile beam across her face as she realised the email was from Jim.

Chapter Thirty-One

The end of the beginning

Like a sentry guard Jim's repacked suitcase stood motionless behind the couch in the front room of his apartment. Packing to go home was one of the worst parts of a holiday for him because it signalled that the end was near. Every year since he had been issued with his own case he had organized it with a separation of towels between clothes that needed washing and those that could be used again.

Normally the items not needing washing were limited to a few pairs of shorts, T-shirts and any clothing items he might have bought on holiday. Even though this method of separating the dirty items from the less dirty items had been requested by his mother normally everything ended up being washed. He had questioned her once about whether there was any point in the separation just to be reprimanded for speaking out of turn. Since it had seemed to him to be a simple and logical question he had decided it was just easier to go along with their request.

This year there had been a notable difference in the amount of barely worn items versus those that needed washing. The majority of items that he classed as needing washing belonged to his range of going out with friends items whereas the not needing washing items were the shorts and t-shirts he had packed for day to day wearing.

He smiled looking at the two piles of clothes before placing them carefully into his case. Naturism had shown him another advantage that he could take with him on holiday. He pondered on the idea of making his new found interest in naturism a theme for future holidays. Once he left home the washing after the holiday would be his job unless he moved in with someone like his sister had so maybe naturism was the way forward.

Next to him on the couch was a small pile of clothes that he had chosen for the journey home. Sasha had inspired him with her silent protest against clothes right up to the few moments before she had left the complex. He wondered how she was getting on with life back at home in Ireland and if she had received his email.

Once the rents had gone for their afternoon siesta it had given him a good opportunity to try and find a computer. After a short time on the secluded part of the beach he had earmarked as being Sasha and his he had wondered over to the main building. He had wondered around gazing into the shops that lined the atrium spending a long time outside the one that he had bought Sasha her necklace in before turning to the waiter and asking about any computers that could be used by the public.

The waiter he had chosen seemed to understand what he was looking for and pointed him toward the door that led to the indoor pool. Resisting the urge to ask if the computer had internet access he thanked the man and walked toward the doorway. Stopping outside it he recalled the last time he had gone down the corridor remembering the shock of seeing the rents and the much more positive time he had spent with Sasha afterwards. He could vaguely remember the entire corridor and couldn't recall anywhere that had looked like a computer room.

Disregarding the questions in his mind he had walked through the door anyway and started following the path toward the swimming pool entrance. The glass window overlooking the pool filled the entirety of one wall reducing the options even further. Just before the door leading into the Sauna where he had encountered the rents naked for the first time he saw a second door. He hadn't taken much notice of this door before because it didn't seem to lead anywhere but maybe this was the door the waiter had been referring to.

Pushing it he found himself in a second corridor that wasn't as well maintained as the one he had left. Framed pictures on the walls were the only thing that told him this was probably a public corridor not a staff only area. He walked along it until he saw a door with a picture of two table tennis bats crossing; this must be the games room that he hadn't found.

Pausing outside the room for a moment he realised that this room was possibly where he would find other teenagers. On any other holiday he wouldn't have any problem with entering this room and would most probably had spent most of his evenings in there already. Meeting Sasha had changed all that and bought him away from the repetitive behaviour. He listened for a few moments and was almost relieved when he couldn't hear any noise behind the door.

Suddenly for a few moments he had become conscious of the fact he was naked and had wondered if anyone behind the door would be too. Games rooms never followed the usual rules of a hotel because the people in them were trying to rebel against their families. He could be walking in to a room where he was the only one with no clothes on. He took a breath and pushed the door open walking in to what he realised very quickly was an empty room.

In a way the seclusion was nice because it meant he wouldn't feel out of place for following the dress code of the complex. It also meant he wasn't going to get into conversation with anyone else of his age and, with less than twenty-four hours of his holiday left, he didn't actually want to. Even if he hadn't met Sasha getting to know someone at such a late stage of a holiday seemed pointless. He had been the short term friend on previous holidays and it was never a nice thing.

Walking past the dated game machines, pool table that had been barely used and a table tennis table that was propped up he saw a small alcove that housed a computer. The screen looked like one he had seen in books but never seen in reality, its white outer case seemed heavy and badly designed. The keyboard had keys in places that he didn't recognise but he was conscious that this might be the European standard. The chair looked uncomfortable and unwelcoming but it was the only option available in the room.

Cautiously he sat down, selected an internet browser that he was familiar with and logged on to his email. A stream of unwanted and unanswered emails presented themselves to him as he repositioned himself in the chair. The cold plastic felt awkward against his back encouraging him to deal with the email he had searched this room for and get out quickly. Opening a new message, he typed in the email address he had memorised from Sasha's contact details and composed a brief but cordial message to her before sending it. Squirming awkwardly against the plastic seat he logged out and made his way back to the outside world and the warmth of the sun.

Now as he sat reviewing his email he realised he hadn't waited to see if the email had been sent or not. There was a possibility he had sent it to the wrong address or maybe Sasha had given him the wrong address. He didn't want to think about his email not arriving and chose to block the thought from his mind until he got home.

Grabbing the pile of items he had selected for travelling in he placed them in a ruck sack he always took on holiday with him. He had bought this rucksack years ago as part of a survival package he had seen in a shop that he had decided he needed to have. In its folded form it looked like a pencil case but once the zip was undone the bag itself burst out of the little pocket creating a bag that was big enough for a few essential items. On this occasion the essential items were the clothes he didn't need to wear until after lunch, the ring Sasha had given him and the paper with her contact details on.

Even though her contact details were not necessarily an essential item for his morning he felt better having them near him. He had decided the most practical thing to do with the ring was to find some way of wearing it. He had already tried it on each of his fingers and it was too small to fit comfortably even on his smallest finger. The best option was to buy a chain to put it on and wear it as a token around his neck.

He knew that if he was at home he would quite easily find a chain that he could slip the small ring on to but that wouldn't seem fair to Sasha. This was a gift she had chosen to give him and it deserved its own chain not one that had been bought for a different purpose. Tucking it carefully in one of the zipped pockets of the bag he grabbed his case and dragged it to the rents apartment.

For the second time in two days he found himself outside their door naked but this time he didn't fear what he was going to see. After spending time with them he had almost become immune to the fact they had no clothes on and was unafraid of them seeing him without any. Knocking on the door he was greeted by his father who smiled at him and efficiently pulled the case inside before arranging to meet with him for lunch. Even though he knew the shop he had bought Sasha's necklace in would have something to suit his needs he decided to look around a few of the other stores so he wasn't showing favouritism. He was fairly sure the store owners didn't go around bragging about how much they had taken but he wanted to be sure he was giving the others a chance to take some of his money too.

Wondering into the first store that he had decided might be a candidate for his purchase he found himself looking at tied necklaces with rounded stones attached to them. These little trinkets were nice as souvenirs but the shoelace style string was not what he wanted. A second store seemed to only have light chains that he could imagine breaking under the slightest of weights.

Bypassing the store he had bought from already he walked into a shop that seemed to sell a little bit of everything. In one corner was a range of soaps and fragranced items and next to them a range of postcards. Opposite that corner a range of books about the island sat next to some intricately made ornamental pieces. Nearer the front of the store were larger items that he couldn't imagine being easy to get home in a case and in another area was a range of watches similar to the one that Dad had bought specifically for their holiday.

Passing the watches he saw a range of chains that looked almost perfect for the item he wanted to hang off them. The shortest at one end of the neat row looked barely long enough to go around a wrist where at the other end the chain looked sufficiently long enough for the largest of necks and heavy enough to cause the average person severe neck problems.

Above the display Jim saw a label showing a from price, the worst type of pricing ever. This gave the shop keeper the licence to charge whatever he saw suitable for the item. Even if he had chosen the shortest and lightest of the chains on display, Jim felt sure the price wouldn't be the same as the one advertised. If anyone questioned it the keeper simply had to say was that the price advertised was a smaller or lighter chain that was conveniently not in stock.

Choosing a more tactical solution Jim beckoned the keeper over and asked about the price of the biggest of the chains. The keeper looked at Jim almost amused by the idea of such a small framed person wanting such a large chain. Politely he offered to take the chain out so it could be tried on and didn't seem surprised when the offer was declined.

He pulled a scrappy piece of paper out and wrote a figure down, crossing it out before writing a slightly lower figure down and pointing at it. Jim smiled and gestured as if he was contemplating the price while browsing over the other chains. From a carefully selected location the keeper watched and tried to gauge the interest Jim had in the chain.

Desperation seemed to creep in as the keeper started using signs to try and confirm if the chain was for him or someone else. Seeing the interest he was getting encouraged Jim to try and converse with the keeper by advising him it was for him and showing the keeper the ring. Slowly the keeper glanced between Jim, the ring and the chain and came to the realisation that this was not the time to sell the big chain. Thinking quickly he pointed to a different chain seemingly accepting that if he was going to get a sale he had to try to make a more realistic recommendation.

Jim could see a subtle irony in the fact that the chain the keeper was now pointing to was only two places nearer the most expensive chain than the one he had already mentally picked out. Smiling at the keeper he asked to see both selections as well as the largest chain so he could get a comparison. The keeper seemed to relax at the reply and quickly opened the wall display carefully taking the three options out and laying them on the table.

One by one, Jim picked them up as if he was examining the length of them and the weight nodding at each one before replacing it on the counter. Sweeping his hand over the range that was displayed for him he looked at the keeper and questioned the prices. He had never done any bartering before but he had seen it done and felt like he was in a good position to get a good price because even the largest chain was within his budget.

One by one, the keeper placed prices above each of the chains, glancing at Jim before crossing out the original price and placing a revised price below it. Once he had labelled each item he stood back patiently awaiting a response from his customer. Jim picked up his original choice and the one next to it reconsidering the two options. He glanced at the prices and noted there was very little difference in the cost of either chain, the one the keeper had recommended however was stronger and heavier. Turning to the man he handed over the keeper's recommendation and replaced his one on the counter nodding his agreement to buy.

Smiling vaguely at the shop keeper he walked out with the chain in his hand threading the ring through it as he walked. Sitting on one of the couches he carefully put the chain around his neck and flinched as the cold metal of the ring touched his chest. Somehow wearing the token Sasha had given him made him feel more complete and more committed to her.

Standing up he glanced over at the clock on the wall, it was still only mid-morning and he wasn't meeting the rents until lunch time. Casually he walked out of the building bouncing his steps slightly so the chain bobbed against his skin. He looked out across the complex taking in the view as he decided what to do with his last few hours. To his left was the route down to the beach but he had been there the previous afternoon and it wasn't as much fun without Sasha.

Walking down toward the pool he placed his rucksack next to one of the few vacant sunbeds. Surrounding him were several people who he knew were immune to the fact that he was going home. For two weeks it had been him in that position and now it was his turn to be counting the hours until he was getting on a plane. Lying back against the hard plastic he shielded his eyes from the sun and reviewed his holiday.

On her last day Sasha had made an effort to go to as many of the places she had seen during her stay as she could before going home. As he had been with her throughout her stay his list of places was the same as hers and the only ones that they hadn't returned to were off the complex.

It seemed wasteful to dwindle away his time by the pool alone but everything he had done had been with her or with the rents. She was now at home and they would be busy preparing to leave which was an activity he didn't want to get involved in.

He found himself reflecting on the day he had been dreading with the rents and surprised himself with his memories of it. After his initial apprehension and the awkward questions that he had anticipated over breakfast he had actually started to get on with them. The nudity had not been as awkward as he had expected it to be and they had started asking him questions about his holiday that he considered adult questions.

Maybe the holiday had changed things for him more than he had thought it would at first. Maybe it was time to test Sasha's comment about actually getting on with the rents. He had seen how surprised she was when he only vaguely knew them and had been relieved when she didn't make too much of his lack of knowledge. Maybe it was time he did something about it, if not for himself for Sasha as well. He knew it wasn't right to use her as a reason to fill the void he had created between him and his parents but maybe he could use her as the motivation to fill the void.

As lunch time approached Jim picked up his ruck sack and took last look around the complex. He grabbed at the chain taking a deep breath as he clutched it close to his chest. He knew that up in the main building his parents would be probably sat already waiting for him.

They had briefly told him the plan when he dropped his case off to them but he had been in too much of a rush to finalize details with them. All he knew was that they were meeting him for lunch and shortly after that they would be leaving the complex. Under normal circumstances that would be as much information as he needed but here it was different.

Before he could meet them he had to work out in his own head what the most likely dress code was going to be for the meal. On previous holidays he would have been dressed and ready to leave from the moment he dropped his case off but here he wasn't either dressed or ready to go. Despite his early objections to the holiday the complex had started to grow on him and now it was the only place that he currently had that he shared with Sasha.

In time he felt sure that if the plans they had discussed came to fruition there would be other locations but for now this was the only one they had. He was used to not wanting to leave a holiday but usually it was the weather he was reluctant to leave behind. This place held memories for him that he could not and did not want to replace.

Unzipping the rucksack he peered in at the items he had selected for his home journey. A pair of light pants, a T-shirt and a jumper in preparation for when they landed in the much cooler weather of home. Bundled into the shoes that he had left separate from the bag was a pair of socks that again were surplus to requirements until they landed. Pulling the pants free he shook them out and held them to his waist, all around him care free naked people were enjoying the sun and he was about to cover himself for the first time during daylight hours on this resort in over a week.

Hopping slightly he pulled them on and stuffed the shoes and socks into the space they had left vacant in his bag. Wearing pants without shoes seemed strange at first but he had concluded that the rents were probably already dressed and even if they weren't they would be soon. By wearing just one item he was adhering as closely as he dared to the dress code of the complex while showing some effort to be ready for going home.

Pulling the rucksack on to one shoulder he smiled as he looked one last time over toward his apartment. The door looked like it was open and a trolley was parked outside presumably owned by the maid. Already they were preparing it for the next person to use it which, in many ways, he understood but he felt upset too that this really did seal the end of his holiday.

Walking slowly up the path he smiled cordially at two strangers that passed him as he arrived at the main door. Walking in to the atrium he could see the rents sitting calmly waiting for him at a couch near the restaurant. His mother was dressed in a light blue dress that reminded him vaguely of the one Sasha had worn on their first night together. His father was fully dressed in a pale shirt that complimented his mother's dress and a pair of jeans.

Both of them looked different people to the ones that he had come on this holiday with. He questioned himself as to why it was and put it down to the more refreshing tone they had taken with him. In front of them were the cases that had been bought with them and a plastic bag of goods that they had prepared as their hand luggage. Smiling softly he joined them at their table just in time for the waiter that he recognised as the same one that had directed him to the computer appeared.

Taking charge of the situation his father ordered two drinks before turning to Jim and asking what he wanted. For a moment Jim wondered if he would get away with ordering an alcoholic drink. His father might allow it but with a four hour flight home it possibly wasn't worth the risk. He added a soft drink to the order and wasn't surprised when his father nodded in acceptance. For a split second he found himself hoping that his father was going to encourage him to get something stronger but that hope quickly faded. Choosing one of the smaller chairs he sat silently waiting, unsure what to say but filled with questions all at the same time.

In many ways it seemed unusual being in the minority of dressed people in the restaurant. The only other people that were notably dressed were the staff but Jim wondered how many of them would prefer to be nude. Maybe if he returned to the complex he could try to ask some of them but it seemed logical that only a person comfortable with nudity would work on such a complex.

Even though there was no rush intended during the meal Jim finished eating quickly and suggested returning to the atrium. He wondered if the driver coming to collect them would be the same one that had taken Sasha to the airport. If it was hopefully the driver wouldn't make it too obvious they had met before. Suddenly the thought that the driver that had taken him to turtle bay could be their lift to the airport hit him. The chances of it being this one were minimal but it was still an outside possibility.

He could just imagine the uncomfortable silence as the driver recognised him and referred to him as American. As it was their journey back to the airport there was a chance that his parents wouldn't notice it but if they did he would have to be prepared with an answer.

After a short time both his parents appeared at the restaurant doors struggling with the range of cases and bags. Jim hopped out of his chair and jogged over to them offering to take his case. His mother seemed pleasantly surprised with his reaction and was grateful to let him relieve them of the additional bags. Pointing out the time his father discretely hinted to Jim that it was time to get dressed properly.

Jim stopped in his tracks, this really was it, this was the last time he was going to see the complex for the foreseeable future. With a slight but silent reluctance he finished off putting his clothing on until he looked respectable for being in public and gathered his now almost empty rucksack and case.

No more was said between him and his parents as they walked up the path bypassing the reception as they had already checked out. Waiting in front of them was a driver at the door of a black car, Jim was relieved to see a strangers face not one of the drivers he had already met. The man took their cases and packed them into the car before helping them to begin their journey back to the airport.

Epilogue

It seemed like everyone that knew him expected his interest in Sasha to fall away after a week or two. Jim found their shallow opinion to be an insult to him considering the amount of time he had put into nurturing their broken relationships. In an effort to amuse them he had laughed along with them as they mocked him.

Contrary to their assumptions Sasha and he had maintained a healthy level of contact over the weeks. Email, text and video calls had become good friends to them with weekends seeing a peak in their contact.

Nobody that knew him had truly believed him about her or how close they were. By the time he had returned to school his acquaintances that had formerly been considered friends had forgotten about him and were focussed on their own failing relationships.

Keeping a mature attitude Jim hadn't brought up the fact that his relationship was growing while theirs were failing. To him their issues were a pass time that continued to remind him how lucky he was with Sasha. He prided himself on his set answers that seemed to accommodate most people's problems.

It wasn't until the October break came round that the reality of his relationship sank in. Others were asking him to join them and he was proudly saying no as he had other arrangements. The look on their face seemed to be somewhere in between disbelief and shock.

He had kept his arrangements discrete by telling them he was off to visit relatives. Once the presence of an aunt or uncle was brought into the equation, nobody asked any further questions. For him, the reality was a far extreme from the polite lie he was letting people believe.

Standing at a luggage carousel in Shannon Airport he remembered why Sasha had recommended it. Dublin would have been much easier to get to for both of them but Shannon was smaller and easier to get round. She had developed some of his analytical traits during their time together.

He waited patiently as the carousel meandered round empty watching the other passengers stream past with only hand luggage. If only this had been a trip to Greece, now he knew the complex he was sure he could almost get away with just hand luggage there.

During many of their conversations, he had often joked with Sasha about how her skin was by far his favourite outfit. She had always responded with a well-timed but playful remark that had forced a change of subject.

For the next few days he knew he was going to be a guest to her family. Any playful intentions would need to remain strictly between themselves if he was going to maintain a good impression.

Since their holiday this was the first time they were going to have seen him and even though they were familiar with him the rules were different this time. No matter what happened they had invited him to stay or at least agreed to him staying with them for the mid-term break. Sasha had told him about it excitedly and he had accepted the invite with the same enthusiasm.

Eventually he saw his bag appear and even though it looked like a marooned soldier he felt obliged to wait for it. The rents had taught him not to chase after his luggage even if there was no one preventing him from getting to it. He had never understood their policy but a few minutes extra wouldn't hurt.

Pushing his way out into the arrivals hall he could see Sasha waiting patiently for him. She seemed to almost light up as she spotted him encouraging him to quicken his pace. With eagerness he pushed his way through the disorganised crowd that were all waiting for someone to arrive and threw himself into her arms.

"I guess you had to leave my favourite outfit at home," he whispered cheekily into her ear as he felt her body next to his.

Reluctantly pushing him out of the embrace she looked at him with a subtle but cheeky grin. She had been waiting for over half an hour for his arrival and had anticipated some kind of comment from him.

Keeping her intentions discrete she had made preparations for him while she waited for the announcement of his plane arriving. By her feet she had a bag that she knew he wouldn't suspect held anything unusual. Even though she hadn't known if, how or when she was going to be able to complete her plans she had anticipated it since getting on the bus.

Glancing around herself she undid the belt that was holding her knee length coat together. Holding it tightly she ensured that he was the only person that could see as she opened it revealing her nudity. His face went from cheeky grin to pale and shocked as he stared at her.

"No, Jim." She winked, wrapping her coat back around herself. "I'm wearing it."

Jim was left speechless.

To be continued…

Leatherhead Food International

NUTRITION THROUGH THE LIFE CYCLE

Edited by
Prakash Shetty

This edition first published 2002 by
Leatherhead Publishing
a division of
Leatherhead International Ltd
Randalls Road, Leatherhead, Surrey KT22 7RY, UK
URL: http://www.lfra.co.uk

and

Royal Society of Chemistry,
Thomas Graham House, Science Park, Milton Road, Cambridge CB4 0WF,
UK
URL: http://www.rsc.org
Registered Charity No. 207890

ISBN No: 1 904007 40 6

A catalogue record of this book is available from the British Library

Typeset by Leatherhead International Ltd.
Printed and bound in the UK by IBT Global, 1B Barking Business Centre, 25 Thames Road, Barking,
London IG11 OJP

CONTENTS

CONTRIBUTORS   vii
PREFACE   ix
FOREWORD   x

1.   NUTRITION THROUGH THE LIFE CYCLE   1
   1.1   Approaches to the Study of Human Nutrition   1
   1.2   Nutrition through the Life Cycle   3
   1.3   Nutrition over the Last Century in the United Kingdom   4
   1.4   Diet and Nutrition Related Problems in the United Kingdom   6
     1.4.1   Anaemia in childhood and adolescent years   6
     1.4.2   Obesity   7
     1.4.3   Cardiovascular diseases   7
     1.4.4   Non-insulin-dependent diabetes mellitus (NIDDM)   8
     1.4.5   Diet-related cancers   9
     1.4.6   Osteoporosis   10
   1.5   A Life Course Approach to Promoting Health through Better Nutrition   10
   1.6   References   13

2.   NUTRITION IN INFANCY   15
   2.1   Introduction   15
   2.2   Infant Feeding   15
   2.3   Breastfeeding   16
     2.3.1   Effects of breastfeeding on the mother   17
     2.3.2   Mother's milk   18
     2.3.3   Possible hazards of breastfeeding   23
   2.4   Formula Milks   24
     2.4.1   Special formulas   25
     2.4.2   Other breast milk substitutes   26
     2.4.3   The WHO Code   26
   2.5   Weaning Feeds   27
   2.6   Nutrition and Growth   29
     2.6.1   Growth reference charts   30
   2.7   Nutrition, Development and Disease   31
   2.8   Infant Nutrition and Chronic Disease in Adult Life   31
   2.9   Conclusions   32
   2.10   References

3.   NUTRITION OF SCHOOL CHILDREN AND ADOLESCENTS   37
   3.1   Introduction   37

3.2	Dietary Habits of Young People in Britain		38
	3.2.1	Types and quantities of food consumed	38
	3.2.2	Social Influences on food choice in young people	40
3.3	Energy Intake, Physical Activity and Childhood Obesity		41
3.4	Macronutrient Intake		44
3.5	Micronutrient Intake		47
	3.5.1	Current intake and status of vitamins and minerals amongst young people	47
	3.5.2	Implications of sub-optimal vitamin and mineral intakes during childhood	52
3.6	Teenage Pregnancy		53
3.7	Regional and Socio-economic Differences		54
3.8	Oral Health		56
3.9	What Should be Done to Improve the Health of our Children?		57
3.10	References		59
4.	**NUTRITION IN PREGNANCY AND LACTATION**		63
4.1	Introduction		63
4.2	Pre-pregnancy Nutrition		64
	4.2.1	Body weight	64
	4.2.2	Folic acid	66
	4.2.3	Alcohol	67
	4.2.4	Faddy diets	67
4.3	Nutrition during Pregnancy		67
	4.3.1	Body weight and weight gains	67
	4.3.2	Energy costs of pregnancy	69
	4.3.3	Food and nutrient intake	74
	4.3.4	Folic acid	75
	4.3.5	Iron	75
	4.3.6	Calcium	76
	4.3.7	Vitamin D	76
	4.3.8	Supplements	77
4.4	Foods to restrict or Avoid during Pregnancy		77
	4.4.1	Alcohol	77
	4.4.2	Vitamin A	78
	4.4.3	Foodborne diseases	78
	4.4.4	Caffeine	79
	4.4.5	Maternal avoidance of specific foods to prevent allergies in the infant	79
	4.4.6	Other nutritional issues during pregnancy	80
4.5	Teenage Pregnancy		81
4.6	Post-partum Nutrition and Nutritional Status		83
	4.6.1	Lactation	83
	4.6.2	Changes in body weight, and post-partum obesity	85
4.7	Conclusions		86
4.8	References		87
5.	**ADULT NUTRITION**		91
5.1	Introduction		91
5.2	Dietary Reference Values		91

	5.2.1	DRVs for energy	92
	5.2.2	DRVs for protein, fat and carbohydrates	93
	5.2.3	DRVs for vitamins	93
	5.2.4	DRVs for minerals	95
5.3		The National Diet and Nutrition Surveys of British Adults	98
	5.3.1	National patterns of dietary consumption based on the NDNS survey of UK adults	98
	5.3.2	Low energy intake reporters in the NDNS survey of UK adults	102
	5.3.3	Clusters of dietary patterns among UK adults	103
5.4		Diet and Chronic, Non-communicable Diseases in Adults	107
	5.4.1	Diet and cardiovascular diseases	108
	5.4.2	Non-insulin-dependent Diabetes Mellitus (NIDDM)	111
	5.4.3	Diet, lifestyles and obesity in adults	112
	5.4.4	Diet and osteoporosis in adults	113
	5.4.5	Diet and cancers	113
5.5		References	116
6.		NUTRITION OF THE AGEING AND ELDERLY	118
6.1		Introduction	118
6.2		Nutrient Requirements of the Elderly	119
	6.2.1	Energy	119
	6.2.2	Protein	120
	6.2.3	Vitamins	120
	6.2.4	Minerals	121
	6.2.5	Fluids and alcohol	121
6.3		Nutritional Status and Dietary Intakes of the Elderly	122
	6.3.1	Desirable and healthy body weights for the elderly	123
	6.3.2	Micronutrient intakes and deficiencies in the elderly	123
6.4		The National Diet and Nutrition Survey: People aged 65 Years and Over	125
	6.4.1	Results of survey	126
	6.4.2	Clusters of dietary patterns among UK elderly	131
	6.4.3	Conclusions	134
6.5		Special Nutritional Problems of the Elderly	134
	6.5.1	Osteoporosis	135
	6.5.2	Anaemia	135
	6.5.3	Lowered immuno-competence	135
6.6		Malnutrition in the Elderly	135
6.7		Improving the Diet and Nutrition of the Elderly	137
6.8		References	138
7.		NUTRITION AND POLICY	140
7.1		Introduction	140
7.2		Nutrition Policy: Aims and Challenges	141
	7.2.1	Aims of policy in food and nutrition	141
	7.2.2	Challenges in food and nutrition policy	142
7.3		How Does Nutrition Policy Work?	145
	7.3.1	Policy actors in nutrition	146
	7.3.2	Policy instruments in nutrition	146
	7.3.3	Inequalities in food and nutrition	148

	7.3.4	Giving out food	149
	7.3.5	Nutritional targets and recommendations	153
7.4	Nutrition Policy Initiatives on a Europe-wide Basis		157
	7.4.1	The International Conference on Nutrition (ICN)	158
	7.4.2	World Food Summit (WFS)	159
	7.4.3	WHO European Office Action Plan for Food and Nutrition Policy	159
	7.4.4	European Union French Presidency Initiative	160
7.5	Key Nutrition Initiatives in the United Kingdom		160
	7.5.1	Nutrition Forum	160
	7.5.2	Health sector	161
	7.5.3	Cross-sectoral initiatives	161
7.6	Conclusions		162
7.7	References		163

8.	NUTRITION AND HEALTH PROMOTION		170
8.1	Introduction		170
8.2	What is Health Promotion?		170
	8.2.1	Public health policy	171
	8.2.2	Community development	172
	8.2.3	Health behaviour interventions	173
8.3	Evaluation of Health Promotion Interventions		173
	8.3.1	Why randomised controlled trials? – the experimental design	174
	8.3.2	Problems for the randomised controlled trial in evaluating health promotion	174
	8.3.3	Stages of evaluation	175
	8.3.4	Ecological study design	176
8.4	Who Should be Delivering Nutritional Health Promotion?		176
8.5	Factors Influencing Food Choice		177
8.6	Effectiveness of Nutrition Interventions		177
	8.6.1	Education institutions	180
	8.6.2	Workplaces	182
	8.6.3	Food outlets	183
	8.6.4	General community settings, e.g. Health Action Zones	184
	8.6.5	Clinical settings: one-to-one interventions	185
8.7	Conclusions		186
8.8	References		187

| INDEX | | | 193 |

CONTRIBUTORS

Professor Prakash Shetty
Public Health Nutrition Unit
Department of Epidemiology & Population Health
London School of Hygiene & Tropical Medicine
Bedford Square
London

Currently Chief
Nutrition Planning, Assessment and Evaluation
Food and Nutrition Division
Food and Agriculture Organization
Viale delle Terme di Caracalla
00100 Rome
Italy

Professor Barbara Elaine Golden
Department of Child Health
University of Aberdeen
Foresterhill
Aberdeen
AB9 2ZD

Ms Sara Stanner
British Nutrition Foundation
High Holborn House
52-54 High Holborn
London
WC1V 6RQ

Dr Judy Buttriss
British Nutrition Foundation
High Holborn House
52-54 High Holborn
London
WC1V 6RQ

Dr Gail R. Goldberg
British Nutrition Foundation
High Holborn House
52-54 High Holborn
London
WC1V 6RQ

Dr Jane A. Pryer
Royal Free and University College Medical School London
Gower Street
London
WC1E 6BT

Professor Astrid Fletcher
Department of Epidemiology & Population Health
London School of Hygiene & Tropical Medicine
Keppel Street
London
WC1E 7HT

Dr Elizabeth Dowler
Department of Social Policy and Social Work
University of Warwick
Coventry
CV4 7AL

Dr Margaret Thorogood
Health Promotion Research Unit
London School of Hygiene and Tropical Medicine
49-51 Bedford Square
London
WC1B 3DP

Dr Carolyn Summerbell
School of Health and Social Care
University of Teesside
Middlesbrough
Tees Valley
TS1 3BA

Dr Gill Cowburn
BHF Health Promotion Research Group,
Department of Public Health
Institute of Health Sciences
Old Road
Headington
Oxford
OX3 7LF

PREFACE

Yet another book in human nutrition? We sincerely hope not just another book! This book approaches nutritional needs and problems from both the life cycle and life course perspective and from a population point of view. It also fills an important lacuna in focusing very specifically on issues relevant to the United Kingdom so that students and practitioners of public health nutrition in the UK have an important resource base. Typical of problems associated with any multi-author publication, this book has also had a long gestation period and few opportunities for discussion and harmonisation in presentation. Criticism and feedback from readers would help us to do a better job the next time round if in fact our perceived notion that there is a need and possibly a place for such a book is reinforced in the future.

To the various authors who have contributed to this book much credit is due. We thank our publishers, Leatherhead Publishing and in particular Liz Tracey, who was instrumental in initiating this enterprise, and to Victoria Emerton, who successfully followed through with this effort to its successful completion. We owe much to their efforts and above all to their patience. I would like to acknowledge the sabbatical period that the London School of Hygiene & Tropical Medicine provided me from October 2000 that enabled me to contribute to this venture and my profound thanks to the Dean, Professor Andy Haines, for his Foreword to this book.

Prakash Shetty

FOREWORD

Traditionally, researchers, policy makers and practitioners have tended to focus on the influence of diet and other determinants of health at different ages in isolation. Recently, however, evidence has been accumulating that diet, in common with other determinants, has effects on health throughout the life cycle. Thus our health at a given point in time is determined by the balance of actions and exposures up to that time, as well as our genetic composition. According to this evidence, the health of populations is likely to be affected in years to come by decisions taken today and furthermore diet may have varying effects at different points during an individual's life course.

This book demonstrates how the nutritional situation of the UK population has changed substantially over the last century or so. Despite many advances, major challenges remain, encompassing diverse problems such as anaemia in childhood and adolescence, increasing obesity in adults and children and high incidence rates of diet-related cancers. Despite declining death rates from cardiovascular diseases, major social class gradients persist to which dietary factors make an important contribution. The UK population is now ethnically much more diverse than it was 50 years ago and there are substantial differences in the incidence of cancers thought to be related to diet between ethnic groups as well as, for example, a higher incidence of non-insulin-dependent diabetes in South Asians in the UK.

One of the implications of the life course perspective on diet and disease is that successful attempts to promote healthy diets should have benefits for individuals and society which accumulate over many years. This has major implications for the cost-effectiveness of health promotion programmes and government policy. This book effectively summarises much of what is known about the relationship between diet and health at different points in the life course and how interventions can potentially reap long-term benefits. It will therefore be of wide interest to researchers, practitioners and policymakers.

This book attempts to address food and nutritional issues that fall within the broad remit of public health nutrition, emphasising those aspects of food and nutrition that relate directly to the health of the population. By specifically addressing issues relevant to the United Kingdom, I am confident it will help fill a lacuna in the needs of students and practitioners in public health nutrition in the British Isles and in Europe.

Professor Andy Haines
Dean

London School of Hygiene & Tropical Medicine
London

1. NUTRITION THROUGH THE LIFE CYCLE

Prakash Shetty

1.1   Approaches to the Study of Human Nutrition

Most texts on the subject of nutrition approach it from the viewpoint of the various nutrients present in food in our daily diet; provide information on the chemical structure of the nutrient, its important biological actions and their physiological role in the body; highlight the important sources of these nutrients in the foods that compose our daily diet; explain how the nutrients are made available to the body from the food ingested; and provide descriptions of the various pathological conditions that are associated with their deficiency or excess.

Another approach would be to characterise the stages of life through the cycle of life from conception to death, with the reproduction of the species, through this cycle (see Fig. 1.1). This approach provides a detailed account of the nutritional needs throughout the *life cycle* and highlights the special nutritional features of each of these stages. It also provides an opportunity to highlight the nutritional problems (related to both deficiency and excess) that characterise that particular phase in the life cycle and gives an opportunity to suggest ways and means to intervene during these phases taking into consideration the special problems that one needs to be aware of during this period in the individual's life. It also enables one to look at the promotion of good nutrition, taking care of identified vulnerabilities during each of these periods and thus helping to ensure the nutritional well-being and good health of the population as a whole.

The expectation is that the latter approach to the study of nutrition is more holistic and puts the individual at the various life stages of growth, development and the continuing ageing process at the centre rather than the nutrients in our daily diet. A subtle but important distinction that needs to be made when one

1

approaches the study of human nutrition through the life cycle is to recognise that health and nutritional problems that manifest at the various *life stages* are not wholly dependent on inadequate or poor nutrition during that phase, although several nutrients may affect the individual during these critical periods in growth and development. The appreciation that what has happened in the past may continue to affect the individual and will interact with events and nutritional stresses later in life provides a *life course* perspective to nutritional problems that manifest at the various life stages throughout the life cycle. The life cycle approach to nutrition enables one to discuss these important interactions in a more meaningful manner than a didactic and reductionist approach to the science of human nutrition.

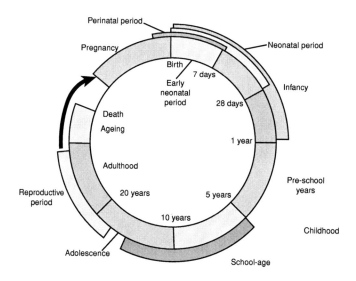

Fig. 1.1. Main stages of human life cycle

It would not be out of place to state that, just as one may consider the various life stages through one's life cycle, one has to acknowledge that the food industry that caters to us as consumers recognises us as several *life style* groups, which are specifically researched and targeted, such as for instance teenagers, young free and single, traditional families and retirees. On the other hand, organisations involved with promoting good nutrition and health may specifically target identified stages in the life cycle, such as pregnant mothers, babies, toddlers, school children, adolescents, adults (early, middle and late), elderly, etc.

1.2   Nutrition through the Life Cycle

The life cycle approach to nutrition provides an opportunity to look at the individual as she or he passes through the various life stages (the main stages of the life cycle are outlined in Fig. 1.1), as well as enabling the student to look at the entire population distributed at any given time throughout the various stages in the life cycle.

This approach has several advantages (1). It helps recognise age-specific vulnerability throughout the life cycle. Bartley *et al.* (2) summarise the various critical transitions and life events in human development, which occur side by side with the biological growth and development of the individual and may characterise periods of vulnerability of an individual in society (Fig. 1.2).

- Birth
- Transition from primary to secondary school
- School examinations
- Leaving parental home
- Establishing own residence
- Entry to labour market
- Transition to parenthood
- Job insecurity – job loss or change
- Onset of chronic illness
- Exit from labour market
- Loss of spouse and close friends

Fig. 1.2. Critical periods of transition in human development (2)

The life cycle approach helps us to understand that maximum benefits in one age group at a particular stage in the life cycle can best be derived from interventions made in an earlier stage or age group of individuals. For instance, it helps us to recognise that better nutrition and health during pregnancy will improve intra-uterine growth, improve birth outcomes and result in fewer

3

complications related to pregnancy outcome; or that improved physical growth and development in infancy translates into improved cognitive function and intellectual development during childhood and leads to better economic prospects both for the individual in adulthood and in turn for society; or that improved birth weights mean less risk of chronic disease and premature death in adulthood.

This approach also reinforces the view that interventions at several points across the life cycle are needed to sustain improvements in health and nutritional outcomes. For instance, one will find it easy to consider that, for good health outcomes, the importance of good nutrition begins in the diet and nutrition during pregnancy, and continues in exclusive breast feeding at birth and the timely and adequate provision of complementary feeds, and good nutrition and diets during childhood, adolescence and adulthood to ensure healthy ageing and a good quality of life in the last stage of one's life.

The life cycle approach also enables us to consider risks and benefits through the entire life cycle and across generations and thus provides an opportunity to understand the importance of the increasingly popular life course approach to health and nutritional well-being.

Thus, a life cycle approach can help us to assess risks at various life stages, recognise important environmental influences that may be inimical to good nutrition and health, and identify key interventions at the various stages in the life cycle to prevent or deal with these external factors. An understanding of the importance of the life cycle approach implies that we recognise that ensuring good nutrition and healthy lifestyles is a life-long function. An elderly individual is unlikely to benefit much from a change in diet and life style late in life; nor does the pursuit of good nutrition and healthy lifestyles come easy to someone who has not followed this course in the earlier phases of life.

1.3   Nutrition over the Last Century in the United Kingdom

Childhood malnutrition and nutritional deficiencies are now things of the past in the developed industrialised west – in the United Kingdom and the rest of Western Europe and in the USA. However, it may not be out of place to remind ourselves that at the end of the 19th and around the beginning of the 20th century, malnutrition was a serious problem in Victorian England. Over 1 in 10 children attending London schools were habitually going hungry, while between 40 and 60% of young men presenting for military service at the time of the Boer war were rejected on medical grounds, much of this attributable to malnutrition (3). It was reported that many from the labouring classes in Edinburgh did not have the income to obtain sufficient food and at the same time lacked the education to make correct food choices (4). These and other subsequent reports resulted in the mandated national policy for feeding needy children at school and, in 1907, in London alone, 27,000 children received school meals, with the numbers doubling 2 years later (5). Between the war years, a report published in 1936 by John Boyd Orr indicated that the poorest in the country (then numbering about 4.5 million) were on diets deficient in all vitamins and minerals, while the next poorest (about 9 million) had a diet adequate in macronutrients (protein, carbohydrates and fat) but deficient in all vitamins and minerals (6). Only 50% of the population who were surveyed had a diet adequate in all dietary nutrients. This situation existed in Great Britain in 1936 despite the fact that the per capita consumption of dairy products and fruits and vegetables had dramatically increased between the years 1909 and 1934. The recognition of the nutritional value of milk in improving body weights and heights of children resulted in 46% of the school children being provided with milk at school by the year 1945, while about 40% of the children were having school meals in the same year.

The nutritional situation of the population of the UK after World War II was a completely different story (7). Despite the rationing and shortage of food in the early post-war years, food supply began to increase, and, when rationing was withdrawn completely by the year 1954, meat consumption began to increase. In 1950, school lunches were provided for over half of all school children, which rose to 70% in 1966. The years of austerity of the early 1950s were replaced by rising incomes and increased consumption of meat and sugar, almost as though it was a reaction to the years of rationing of these commodities. Fruit and vegetable consumption began to decline from the 1970s and consumption patterns and the food culture began to alter along with other social, economic and technological changes that occurred over the next two decades or so.

Changes in the way in which society processed food, purchased and consumed it, and responded to changing tastes and conveniences obviously left their mark on the food and nutrition of the population as a whole over the same period of almost half a century after World War II. Meat, dairy products, bread and potatoes remain important constituents of the daily diet in the UK, while the consumption of fruits and vegetables continues to be relatively low compared with that in other parts of Europe. Since the 1970s, milk and egg consumption has dropped and so has the consumption of meat (beef, pork and lamb), while the popularity of white meat from poultry has increased. These and other dietary changes have reduced the amount of fat and sugar we consume in the daily diet as compared with the early post-war years. However, the consumption of fats and sugars in processed food is high. The purchase and consumption of processed foods are also reflected in a nearly 70% drop in the purchase of flour since the 1950s. A disturbing trend is the drop in the consumption of fresh vegetables over the same period, although the consumption of fresh fruits may be increasing and a particular feature of this may be that many of them are available all the year round.

The overall nutritional change resulting from these changes in our food choices over time is that energy intakes have decreased. The proportional contribution from fat to the total energy in the diet, which increased right up to the early 1980s, has now reversed and, on average, about 35% of food energy is from fat, with about 11% from saturated fat intakes (8). For a healthy diet, the UK population may need to further reduce consumption of fat and sugar, as well as salt in the diet – much of this from the consumption of processed food. The consumption of a varied and balanced diet rich in fruit, vegetables and starchy foods, with fewer foods high in fat or sugar, needs to be the goal for a healthy and nutritious diet.

1.4 Diet and Nutrition Related Problems in the United Kingdom

Given the brief historical outline of how dietary patterns and food consumption have changed over the last several decades in the UK, perhaps the question to ask is how does this translate into diet and nutrition related problems currently in the UK?

1.4.1 Anaemia in childhood and adolescent years

Iron deficiency and possibly anaemia have been recognised to be a problem in the UK, particularly among adolescents and young adults. In girls, with the onset of the menstruation, the already high demands for daily iron requirements associated with rapid growth are further exaggerated. Since much of haem iron – a main source of iron in the diet – is obtained from meat and other related products, the tendency among adolescent females to vegetarianism, particularly the avoidance of meat, also adds to the problem. Iron absorption is also relatively poor among those on a meat-free diet. Associations between iron deficiency and poor cognitive function are well known. Although in the UK iron deficiency is generally mild, the increasing evidence that borderline iron status in this age group can have adverse effects on cognitive function may have important implications in terms of learning ability and academic performance.

1.4.2   Obesity

Obesity is a major risk factor for cardiovascular disease, diabetes, hypertension and premature death, and is increasing amongst adults in the UK. Abdominal or android type obesity is recognised as a specific risk factor in relation to these chronic diseases. The prevalence of obesity increased gradually in most age groups in both sexes in the 1990s (9). The increase was greater in women than in men, and in those aged 45 years and over than in those aged 16-44 years. The prevalence of obesity in men was 17.3% and in women 21.2% in 1998. Several environmental factors, both diet- and lifestyle-related, contribute to increased obesity in communities. Social and environmental factors that either increase energy intake and/or reduce physical activity are critical. Changes both in the food consumed and in the patterns of eating behaviour may have contributed to increasing risk of obesity. Patterns of eating, particularly snacking between meals and frequent snacks, may be significant contributors. However, the overwhelming evidence seems to support the view that much of the energy imbalance that is responsible for the epidemic of obesity in modern societies such as the UK is largely the result of dramatic reductions in physical activity, both occupational and leisure time, when food availability is more than adequate and unrestricted.

1.4.3   Cardiovascular diseases

The commonest cardiovascular diseases that are diet-related are coronary heart disease (CHD) and hypertension. CHD emerged as a burgeoning public health problem in UK after World War II, and by the end of the 1950s, had become the single major cause of adult death. The risk of CHD in individuals is dominated by three major factors: (i) high serum total cholesterol, (ii) high blood pressure, and (iii) cigarette smoking (10). Obesity resulting from dietary and lifestyle changes is strongly related to changes in serum total cholesterol, high blood pressure and diabetes mellitus, which are risk factors for CHD. The increase in consumption of animal fat and the reduced intakes of fruits and vegetables noted earlier have contributed to the increase in CHD in the UK since the 1950s. The appropriate dietary recommendations would include lowering total fat intake to between 30 and 35% of total calories, restricting saturated fat intake to a maximum of 10% of total calories, and increasing intakes of fruits and vegetables. Translated into food components, this would mean reducing animal fat intake in particular and intake of hydrogenated and hardened vegetable oils, and increasing the consumption of cereals, vegetables and fruits.

Statistics from the Department of Health (11) indicate that CHD prevalence increases with age in both sexes, with men having a higher prevalence than women. In particular, the prevalence of angina (5.3% vs 3.9%) and heart attack (4.2% vs 1.8%) was higher in men than in women (respectively) in the survey. CHD continued to increase with age and showed a gradient according to social class and income in both sexes. For instance, the age-standardised prevalence was 5.2% in men in Social Class I and 11.3% in Social Class IV. There is also evidence to suggest that there are significant associations between greater sodium intake in the daily diet and high blood pressure. A diet rich in fruits, vegetables, and low-fat dairy foods and with reduced saturated and total fat can substantially lower blood pressure – a major risk factor for CHD. The White Paper 'Our Healthier Nation' (12) states that a good diet is important in protecting health and the target is to improve the diet of the population by educating and providing information about diet and health to groups at risk, and to ensure that there is adequate access to, and availability of a wide range of healthy foods. An increase in the intake of fruits and vegetables and a reduction in the consumption of fats and salt can have a beneficial influence on health.

1.4.4   Non-insulin-dependent diabetes mellitus (NIDDM)

NIDDM is a chronic metabolic disorder, which occurs in adulthood and is strongly associated with an increased risk of CHD. Obesity is a major risk factor for the occurrence of NIDDM and the risk in a community appears to be triggered by a number of environmental factors such as sedentary lifestyle and dietary factors. Ethnic minorities in the UK from South Asia (i.e. Indians, Pakistanis and Bangladeshis) have a higher incidence of NIDDM. The cause of NIDDM is unclear, but it seems to involve both an impaired pancreatic secretion of insulin and the development of tissue resistance to insulin. Overweight and obesity, particularly the central or truncal distribution of fat, accompanied by a high waist/hip ratio and a high waist circumference, seem to be invariably present with NIDDM. The most rational and promising approach to preventing NIDDM is to prevent obesity. Physical activity also helps improve glucose tolerance by weight reduction and also by its beneficial effects on insulin resistance. Diets high in plant foods are associated with a lower incidence, and vegetarians have a substantially lower risk than non-vegetarians of having NIDDM. The age-standardised death rates due to NIDDM in the UK are 10.2 and 11.3 per 100,000, respectively for men and women for the year 2000 (11).

1.4.5   Diet-related cancers

Although the relationships between specific dietary components and cancers are less well established than that between diet and cardiovascular disease, the overall impact of diet on cancer incidence appears to be significant. It is now widely accepted that one-third of human cancers could relate directly to some dietary component (13), and it is probable that diet plays an important role in influencing the permissive role of carcinogens on the development of many cancers (14). Thus up to 80% of all cancers may have a link with nutrition.

Colorectal cancer has a high incidence rate in the UK. Almost all the specific risk factors of colon and rectal cancer are of dietary origin (14). The most convincing evidence is that both increased intakes of vegetables and increased levels of physical activity reduce the risk of colon cancer. Obesity and total fat intake may possibly increase risk, while increased starch and fibre intake in the diet may possibly reduce risk. The age-standardised death rates due to colorectal cancer in the UK are 28.1 and 24.9 per 100,000, respectively, for men and women for the year 2000 (11).

Breast cancer is a common cause of death among women in the UK. The dietary factors that are possibly implicated in increased risk are obesity and alcohol intake while increased consumption of fruits and vegetables may possibly reduce risk. The age-standardised mortality due to breast cancer is 42.1 per 100,000 in the UK (11).

Dietary factors thus seem to be important in the causation of cancers, and dietary modifications may reduce cancer risk. However, at present, it is difficult to quantify the contribution of diet to total cancer incidence and mortality. Associations between diet and risk of cancers are not always conclusive, and the underlying mechanisms are poorly understood; however, the available current evidence can be used to initiate public health strategies to prevent cancer. Increased consumption of vegetables and fruits is associated consistently with reduced risk of cancer in most sites. Vegetables and fruits are exceptional sources of a large number of potentially anti-carcinogenic agents, including vitamin A and carotenoids, vitamins C and E, selenium, dietary fibre and a whole range of chemical compounds such as flavonoids, phenols and plant sterols. Much of their protective effect is unknown or poorly understood. The WHO and the more recent

World Cancer Research Fund (WCRF) report (14) recommend intakes of 400 g per day of fruit and vegetables (excluding potatoes) as a reasonable dietary goal. The recommendation to lower total fat intake to between 30 and 35% of total energy – a recommendation that is consistent with dietary recommendations to reduce cardiovascular risk – may also aid in the reduction of cancer risk.

1.4.6   Osteoporosis

The increase in numbers of elderly in the UK has seen an increase in health problems of the elderly, which affects their quality of life. Fracture of the hip is an important health problem, particularly among post-menopausal women. Fractures occur in the elderly following what appears to be a relatively trivial fall when there is osteoporosis and the density of the bone is reduced. Osteoporosis, a reduction in bone mass and density, leading to increased risk of fracture, back pain, weight loss, and curvature of the spine, results in about 60,000 hip fractures a year in the UK, 90% of which are in people over 50, and 80% of which are in women (15).

A range of factors influence the attainment of peak bone density during the life cycle, and may play a crucial role in the development of osteoporosis and the occurrence of fractures as age advances. Several factors determine the onset of osteoporosis, which include the lack of oestrogen in post-menopausal women, low body weights, and life style factors such as levels of physical activity, degree of mobility, smoking, and alcohol intake. Calcium intake is a likely dietary determinant, reflecting the recognition of its importance in contributing to the density of bone during growth and the need for attaining dense bones at the peak of adult life. High-protein and high-salt diets are known to increase bone loss, while calcium supplements, well above what may be considered physiological, in post-menopausal women may help to reduce the rate of bone loss and slow down the development of osteoporosis.

1.5   A Life Course Approach to Promoting Health through Better Nutrition

The health and nutritional well being that we enjoy at any moment in our life cycle is the sum of the living circumstances and actions undertaken during our entire lifetime preceding that moment. This conceptual approach presents new opportunities, as it implies that we may be able to influence how we grow from birth through childhood and adulthood into old age by adopting good diets, and by pursuing active and healthier life styles. However, it is also likely that some life course factors are not modifiable by the individual.

The life course begins when we are still in the womb; nutritional stress that we are exposed to in prenatal life may influence and programme our future health and nutrition. The evidence that adaptations that occur in prenatal life may influence the risk of cardiovascular disease, including coronary heart disease (CHD) and stroke, non-insulin-dependent diabetes mellitus (NIDDM) and obesity, is well accepted now. There is increasing support for the view that the effects of poor maternal nutrition on foetal development are not confined to a single generation. The two main determinants of an infant's birth weight appear to be both the mother's pre-pregnancy body weight and her own weight at birth. Thus the inter-generational effects of poor maternal nutrition may take several generations before nutrition in the womb is optimised.

The concept of foetal programming due to nutritional stress at a 'critical period' in life, however, does not undermine the importance of other risk factors operating throughout the 'life course', including risk factors during adolescence and in adulthood, such as smoking, excessive alcohol consumption, poor dietary habits and unhealthy, sedentary life styles. These environmental factors may complement and amplify the effects due to poor foetal nutrition. Thus pre- and peri-conceptional nutrition will interact with growth and development during infancy and childhood. Dietary practices and physical activity and lifestyles in childhood, adolescence and adulthood will in turn interact to determine the risk of chronic disease and premature death. They will also influence the attainment of optimal nutrition and a healthy life by their effects on bone and muscle function, and cognitive and immune function, thus contributing to the quality of life with ageing.

Even in the rich countries in Europe, poverty and inequalities exist to a variable extent, with perhaps the United Kingdom having a much bigger share of this problem. Poverty is linked to poor health and nutrition as the poor live in more harmful environments, have inadequate housing, and have poor access to adequate nutrition.

Several studies have demonstrated that lifetime social circumstances during childhood and adulthood, as well as cumulative experience during adult life, are strongly related to morbidity and mortality in adulthood (16). For some important causes of morbidity and mortality in adulthood, socially patterned exposures acting in early life appear to interact with, or accumulate with, later life exposures. Thus morbidity and mortality from respiratory disease in adulthood are related to housing conditions and infections acquired in childhood. Smoking and occupational exposures in later life then influence disease risk, in association with these earlier life factors (17). In the case of NIDDM, hypertension and CHD, low birth weight – which is strongly socially patterned and related to intergenerational experiences as well as maternal nutrition – interacts with obesity in later life, which is increasingly prevalent amongst people in unfavourable social circumstances to increase disease risk (18).

Poverty can influence health through a broad range of factors acting over the life course. This includes such determinants as low birth weight, short stature, obesity and lung function. There is increasing evidence of intergenerational influences on these attributes and the influence of nutrition (19). The extent to which health-related behaviours such as dietary patterns and smoking are constrained by structural factors related to poverty should be acknowledged when considering the underlying determinants of health inequalities (20).

Human health and development evolve throughout an individual's life and also influence the next several generations. Thus it would appear that the risk of non-communicable diseases (NCD) in adult life may be influenced by biological and social exposures in foetal life, infancy, childhood, adolescence and adulthood. The life course perspective enables us to consider the role of the various determinants and their interactions, especially at critical or sensitive periods, where they may be particularly powerful in influencing the risk of NCD.

Environmental factors related to our diet and life style choices are more important than heredity in determining future health. As we grow older, there are life course choices that we can make to increase the likelihood that we will remain healthy and independent in later life. The 1988 Surgeon General's Report on Nutrition and Health noted that two-thirds of all deaths in the US were due to diseases associated with poor diets and dietary habits (21). Thus, what we eat significantly affects our health, our quality of life, and our longevity. Good nutrition is essential in maintaining cognitive and physical functioning. It plays an essential role in the prevention of many chronic diseases, such as heart disease, cancer, stroke, diabetes, and osteoporosis. It has been estimated that unhealthy eating habits, in combination with physical inactivity, represent a risk behaviour that is responsible in the USA alone for at least 14% of preventable deaths per year (22), with only tobacco use causing more preventable deaths. Recent evidence indicates that good health may be extended and disability delayed by at least 7 years if we stop smoking, maintain a weight appropriate for our height, and remain physically active.

With the rapid changes in the demographic profiles of most industrialised societies, the number of individuals in Europe that are considered as aged and elderly is rising dramatically. European societies are in many respects ill prepared for the effects that these demographic trends will have on their societies (23). Adopting a life course approach to developing policies for nutrition and health recognises the complex interactions of genes and environment that have implications for people's health and nutritional well-being from the moment of their conception and then birth through infancy and childhood, adolescence, adulthood to ageing elderly status, until their death. A life course approach is more effective in reaching all groups of the population than only developing policies and programmes to deal with each problem as it occurs through chance, circumstance or choice at every stage in the life cycle. A life course approach ensures better health and nutritional outcomes for the entire population, both in the medium and long terms.

1.6   References

1.   Bustreo F. *Promoting the well-being of children: Applying the lifecycle framework and social risk management.* http://www1.worldbank.org/wbiep/fiscalpolicy. Accessed on 7 June 2002.

2.   Bartley M., Blane D., Montgomery S. Health and the life course: why safety nets matter. *British Medical Journal*, 1997, 314, 1194-6.

3.   Inter-Departmental Committee on Physical Deterioration. *Report of the Inter-Departmental Committee on Physical Deterioration.* 3 volumes. London. Wyman & Sons, 1904.

4.   Paton D.N,. Dunlop J.C., Inglis E.A. *A Study of the Diet of the Labouring Classes in Edinburgh, Carried Out under the Auspices of the Town Council of Edinburgh.* Edinburgh. Otto Schulze, 1901.

5.   Burnett J. The rise and decline of school meals in Britain, 1860-1990, in *The Origins and Development of Food Policies in Europe.* Edited by Burnett J., Oddy J. London. Leicester University Press, 1994.

6.   Boyd-Orr, J. *Food, Health and Income: Report on a Survey of the Adequacy of Diet in Relation to Income.* London. Macmillan, 1936.

7.   Food Standards Agency. *Fifty years of food* and *Fifty years of nutrition.* http://www.foodstandards.gov.uk/healthiereating. Accessed June 7 2002.

8.   Office of National Statistics. *National Food Survey, 2000.* http://www.statistics.gov.uk/ssd/surveys/national_food_survey.asp. Accessed June 7 2002.

9.   Department of Health. *Health Survey of England*. Office of National Statistics. 2000. http://www.statistics.gov.uk/statbase. Accessed June 7 2002.

10.   World Health Organization. *Diet, nutrition and the prevention of chronic diseases*. WHO Technical Report Series 797. Geneva. World Health Organization, 1990.

11.   Department of Health. *Health Survey for England 2000. Health of Older People*. London. The Stationery Office, 2002.

12.   Department of Health. *Saving lives: Our Healthier Nation*. White Paper. London. The Stationery Office. http://www.doh.gov.uk, 2002.

13.   Doll R., Peto R. *The causes of cancer*. Oxford. Oxford University Press, 1981.

14.   World Cancer Research Fund. *Food, nutrition and the prevention of cancer: a global perspective*. Washington DC. World Cancer Research Fund, 1997.

15.   Department of Health. *Fractures caused by osteoporosis*. http://www.doh.gov.uk/osteop.htm. Accessed June 7 2002.

16.   Davey-Smith G. Learning to live with complexity: ethnicity, socio-economic position, and health in Britain and the United States. *American Journal of Public Health*, 2000, 90, 1694-8.

17.   Mann S.L., Wadsworth M.E.J., Colley J.R.T. Accumulation of factors influencing respiratory illness in members of a national birth cohort and their offspring. *Journal of Epidemiology and Community Health,* 1992, 46, 286-92.

18.   Frankel S.J., Elwood P., Sweetnam P., Yarnell J., Davey-Smith G. Birthweight, body mass index in middle age and incident coronary heart disease. *Lancet*, 1996, 248, 1478-80.

19.   Gunnell D.J., Davey Smith G., Frankel S.J., Nanchahal K., Braddon F.E.M., Peters T.J. Childhood leg length and adult mortality: follow up of the Carnegie (Boyd Orr) survey of diet and health in pre-war Britain. *Journal of Epidemiology and Community Health,* 1998, 52, 142-52.

20.   Davey Smith G., Brunner E. Socio-economic differentials in health: the role of nutrition. *Proceedings of the Nutrition Society*, 1997, 56, 75-90.

21.   National Academy of Sciences. *Committee on Diet and Health. Implications for Reducing Chronic Disease Risk*. Washington DC. National Academy Press, 1989.

22.   McGinnis J.M., Foege W.H. Actual causes of death in the United States. *Journal of the American Medical Association*, 1993, 270, 2207-12.

23.   Krech R. Europe at a crossroads of health development. Discussion notes to the UN Economic Council of Europe. www\new\rkrece3.doc. Accessed 7 June 2002.

2. NUTRITION IN INFANCY

Barbara Golden

2.1   Introduction

Infancy encompasses the first year of life. At birth, the infant's nutritional status is determined by its prenatal experience. This chapter will concentrate mainly on infants of 'normal' pregnancies, born between 37 and 42 weeks' gestation and between 2.5 and 4.5 kg birthweight. Even within this normal range, however, differences in metabolism due to the prenatal environment appear to programme long-term morbidity and mortality (1).

2.2   Infant Feeding

At birth, the foetus has to change from receiving a continuous parenteral supply of oxygen, energy and nutrients delicately tuned to its needs to immediate establishment of breathing followed by milk feeding, which is totally dependent on a carer, normally its mother. The success of this major transition is vitally important. The infant relies, for at least the first few weeks, on just one liquid food, milk, for all its nutritional needs. These needs include all of the essential nutrients, to replace their inevitable loss and to grow new tissue; and energy, to replace its loss mainly as heat and to permit metabolic functions for maintenance, growth and development. The infant also needs to resist the continuous bombardment of the new, relatively hostile environment. This requires nutrients and energy to maintain its physical and chemical barriers and develop immunity.

In the first 4 months, the healthy infant doubles its weight. Over the first year, it triples its weight and doubles its surface area. Never again does it grow so quickly. At the same time, many of its functions mature and develop and the infant changes its shape and composition. For example, the intestinal mucosal epithelium matures rapidly during the first few weeks, increasing absorption of nutrients in line with needs while improving the barrier to foreign molecules. Kidney and liver functions also mature rapidly. The proportion of body fat increases, from about 16% at 3 months to about 30% at 8 months. All of these changes require a balanced, relatively large intake of easily absorbed essential nutrients and energy. This is provided by the infant's mother's milk. WHO recommends that, in general, exclusive breastfeeding should continue for the first 6 months of the infant's life, with introduction of complementary foods and continued breastfeeding thereafter (2). However, for a new mother, breastfeeding is a new experience, which has to be learnt. UNICEF launched its Baby Friendly Hospital Initiative in the 1980s in order to encourage exclusive breastfeeding and improve the support given to breastfeeding mothers. Breastfeeding rates, in much of Europe and the USA, had reached a nadir in the early to mid-1970s.

2.3   Breastfeeding

Within hours of birth, a healthy infant put on its mother's chest spontaneously roots, finds a nipple and starts to suckle. In many mammals, the initial milk, called colostrum, is necessary for survival. This is not the case in humans. However, both early suckling and colostrum play important roles in infant development, both physical and psychological.

Suckling induces a variety of hormonal responses in the infant and mother (3). In the mother, prolactin release stimulates milk production during early lactation while oxytocin release stimulates milk ejection, the 'let-down reflex', which brings milk to the point of delivery. Oxytocin also causes local skin vasodilatation, and thus warmth for the infant, as well as a pleasurable, sleepy sensation in the mother. In the infant, changes in somatostatin, gastrin and cholecystokinin release help stimulate the growth and development of the gastrointestinal tract, improve nutrient absorption and, increasingly, induce satiety. These effects are independent of the provision of maternal milk. When breastfeeding is the only source of food, the infant is in close contact with his mother for several hours a day. This helps ensure rapid 'bonding' between mother and infant. The infant learns to trust early, which fosters normal psychological development.

The endocrine changes in the mother are responsible for providing about 30 ml of colostrum per day for about 2 days after birth. After this, the major stimulus to milk production becomes the infant's suckling and resultant removal of milk. Thus, it is important not to delay or interrupt suckling. Suckling also stimulates the synthesis of lactose, which attracts water osmotically so that milk volume rises dramatically. By 10 to 15 days after birth, over 700 ml per day of 'mature' milk are being produced. The milk between colostrum and mature milk is termed 'transitional' milk. The more milk is removed, the greater the milk output. However, milk output is inversely proportional to its energy concentration so that energy intake by the infant varies less than expected. Thriving infants fed only breast milk by well-nourished mothers regulate their intake within a wide range. Most mothers never achieve their potential for milk production and are more than capable of feeding twins. Breastfeeding is not easily disturbed except by interference with its basic control mechanism – that is, suckling. However, when a mother lacks confidence in her ability to fully breastfeed, often as a result of poor support and/or poor technique, suckling may not be successful. This leads to inadequate output and a vicious spiral that, without appropriate intervention, tends to end in failure. This is common in regions where breastfeeding is no longer the norm. Other reasons for inadequate breastfeeding are: when the infant and mother are separated too much, when either of them is sedated or ill, when the infant is fed at all by other means, or when the mother is severely malnourished or in a highly stressful situation. Usually, however, in such circumstances, the best advice is to persist while trying to improve the circumstances. Supplemental suckling may be indicated if the infant is already malnourished. This involves providing a formula supplement through a fine tube while the infant is breastfeeding. One end of the tube is in the supplement, which is in a cup below the breast while the other end of the tube is placed alongside the mother's nipple so that the infant sucks the formula while suckling. This allows the infant to catch up in weight while frequent, appropriate suckling optimises breast milk production (4).

2.3.1 *Effects of breastfeeding on the mother*

Breastfeeding delays the return of ovulation and, therefore, conception. This is associated with increased basal circulating prolactin levels postpartum; these fall with time while fertility improves. This delay in ovulation may be exaggerated in poorly nourished mothers (3). Breastfeeding also reduces the risk of premenopausal breast cancer and probably also ovarian cancer. Compared with non-breastfeeding, it is associated with more rapid uterine involution and return to prepregnant weight. It is not detrimental to the mother's bone health (5).

However, lactation does cost the mother in energy and nutrients; it increases her requirements compared with non-lactating mothers.

2.3.2 Mother's milk

Maternal milk provides energy and essential nutrients and also a repertoire of antimicrobial agents and cells, hormones, enzymes, growth factors, binding proteins and many substances of indeterminate function. Table 2.I shows its approximate composition; but the ranges are wide as it varies from mother to mother, with the length of time postpartum, with the time of day and with the time into a feed.

2.3.2.1 Colostrum

This is particularly rich in secretory immunoglobulin A (sIgA), also serum immunoglobulins, lactoferrin and lysozyme, all with anti-infection properties (7). Albumin, cholesterol, phospholipid, vitamins A, E and K, sodium, zinc and selenium concentrations are also relatively high (8). Water, lactose and triglyceride concentrations are relatively low.

2.3.2.2 Mature milk

2.3.2.2.1 Fat

Over the first 2 weeks of breastfeeding, the triglyceride content of milk fat increases to over 98% while milk fat output doubles. Fat contributes around 54% of the total energy in mature milk. Just after birth, pancreatic lipase secretion and bile salt conjugation are inefficient; but lingual and gastric lipases are active and, also, breastmilk contains its own lipase, which is activated by bile salts in the infant's small intestine. The fat occurs as globules enclosed in membranes, which play important physical roles and help protect the fat from lipolysis and oxidation (9). Phospholipids, cholesterol, and some proteins and trace elements are also within the globules. Human milk fat comprises 42% saturated fatty acids. It is hydrolysed mainly to β-monoglycerides, which are easily absorbed.

18

TABLE 2.I
Selected constituents in mature human milk, unmodified cows' milk and a whey-dominant
infant formula

Constituent (per litre milk)	Human milk (7)	Cows' milk (6)	Formula[1]
Energy MJ	3.0	2.8	2.8
Protein (g)	9	31	15
Whey proteins (g)	6.4	5.8	9.0
α-lactalbumin (g)	2-3	1.1	1.6
β-lactalbumin (g)	0	3.6	4.1
Caseins (g)	2-3	27	6
Non-protein N (% total N)	18-30	5	10
Carbohydrate (g)	74	49	72
Fat (g)	42	38	36
(% Total energy)	54	53	49
linoleic acid % FA[2]	7.2	1.6	18.9
α-linolenic acid % FA	0.8	0.4	1.8
cholesterol (mg)	16	14	21
Major elements/ions (nmol)			
Sodium	7	25	7
Potassium	15	37	17
Calcium	9	30	12
Magnesium	1	5	3
Phosphate	5	31	11
Chloride	12	29	12
Trace elements (μmol)			
Iron	13	11	143
Zinc	48	63	92
Iodine	0.6	1.2	0.8
Vitamins			
A (RE[3] μg)	600	350	750
E (mg)	3.5	1.4	7.4
D (μg)	0.4	0.8	11.0
C (mg)	41	18	90
Thiamin (mg)	0.2	0.4	1.0
Riboflavin (mg)	0.3	1.7	1.5
Pyridoxine (mg)	0.1	0.6	0.6
Niacin (NE[4] mg)	7.2	8.2	9.0
Folic acid (μg)	52	55	80
Vit B_{12} (μg)	0.1	4.5	2.0

[1] SMA Gold (SMA Nutrition)   [3] 1 μg RE ≡ 1 μg retinol or 6 μg β-carotene equivalents
[2] FA = total fatty acids   [4] 1 mg NE ≡ 1 mg niacin or 60 mg tryptophan

The concentration and composition of fat and fat-soluble vitamins in mature milk are particularly variable (10). For example, their concentrations increase during a feed and also, usually, during the morning. They vary among different populations. Both fat content and fatty acid composition vary with the mother's fat intake. However, when she is starving herself, its composition varies with that of her adipose tissue, which is being catabolised. Human milk contains the essential fatty acids, linoleic (18:2ω-6) and α-linolenic (18:3ω-3) acids (Table 2.I) and also the derived long-chain polyunsaturated fatty acids (LCPs). LCPs form structural and functional components of membranes and are precursors of eicosanoids. Maternal milk, especially from mothers of preterm infants, contains higher concentrations of LCPs – in particular, docosahexaenoic acid (DHA, 22:6ω-3) – than either cows' milk or most infant formulae. For preterm infants at least, dietary DHA is essential for optimal membrane function in the nervous system and, hence, visual and cognitive development. For term infants, there is less evidence of essentiality. Whether they have the same dietary requirement or whether they are able to synthesise sufficient DHA from their dietary α-linolenic acid is not yet clear (11-13).

2.3.2.2.2   Protein

In mature milk, this comprises caseins and whey proteins in a 40/60 ratio. Of the whey proteins, over a third is α-lactalbumin. The caseins and α-lactalbumin supply the essential amino acids. Other important whey proteins are sIgA, lactoferrin and lysozyme, which protect against infection. As such, they are active throughout the intestine because they are poorly digested: a significant proportion emerges intact in the faeces. Secretory IgA antibodies are specific to the microorganisms to which both mother and infant are exposed (14). They bind bacterial antigens, preventing the bacteria from attaching to the intestinal (or respiratory) mucosa. They also neutralise toxins and viruses. Lactoferrin is a bacteriostatic glycoprotein: it binds free ferric iron (up to 2 atoms per molecule), withholding it from bacteria so that their growth is inhibited. Its other postulated roles include promotion of iron absorption and mitogenic or trophic activities in the intestinal mucosa (15). Studies of the role of breastfeeding in preventing or ameliorating infection in infants are fraught with the problem of confounding factors. Taking all these into account, it has been concluded that infants breastfed for over 3 months are protected against gastrointestinal and, to a lesser degree, respiratory infections for far longer than the period of breastfeeding (16).

Breastfeeding also seems to protect against manifestations of atopy. The mechanism is unclear (17). Again, there have been many studies in infants but their results have been conflicting (16). In a recent Finnish study, the manifestations of atopy, including 'food allergy', 'respiratory allergy' and eczema were all significantly reduced throughout childhood and adolescence in those who had been breastfed for over a month (18).

Many whey proteins act as enzymes, including lysozyme, which is bacteriostatic, and lipases, α-amylase, antiproteases and lactoperoxidase. Other minor whey proteins bind corticosteroids, thyroxin, folate, vitamin D and vitamin B_{12}. The caseins comprise β-casein with minor amounts of kappa-casein, linked together with inorganic ions, largely calcium and phosphate, to form small micelles. These result in a soft, flocculant coagulum in the infant's upper intestine; this aids casein digestion.

2.3.2.2.3   Non-protein nitrogen

Around a quarter of total nitrogen in mature milk is not in the form of protein. Of this non-protein nitrogen, half is urea and the rest a variety of diverse compounds. These include nitrogen-containing carbohydrates, mainly glucosamines but also, oligosaccharides incorporating N-acetyl neuraminic acid or the basic lacto-N-tetrose sequence, which is the 'bifidus factor'. This factor enhances colonisation of the breastfed intestine by *Lactobacillus bifidus*. Non-protein nitrogen also includes nucleotides, nucleic acids, polyamines, biologically active peptides such as epidermal, nerve and insulin-like growth factors, insulin itself, prolactin, thyroxin, thyroid-stimulating hormone and thyrotrophin-releasing hormone and calcitonin, choline and other amino alcohols, taurine and carnitine, creatinine, creatine, uric acid and ammonia (19). Urea may act as a nitrogen source for the compromised infant but, apparently, not to a significant extent in the normal infant. Various growth factors, nucleotides and polyamines appear to stimulate growth and maturation of the infant's intestine. The nitrogen-containing carbohydrates appear to influence the intestinal microflora. However, for the most part, the functions and significance of the non-protein nitrogen compounds are still unknown.

2.3.2.2.4   Carbohydrate

Lactose accounts for over 80% of the carbohydrate in mature human milk, about 38% of its total energy content. It is an infant-specific carbohydrate, as lactase activity in the intestinal mucosa is limited mainly to infancy except in Europeans, in whom it tends to persist. Unlike other milk constituents, lactose concentration varies little. Lactose, its hydrolysis product, galactose, and the 'bifidus factor' together promote colonisation by *Lactobacillus bifidus*. Unabsorbed lactose is converted to lactic acid by these intestinal microflora: the resulting low pH inhibits the growth of many pathogens and also increases the solubility and therefore absorption of calcium.

2.3.2.2.5   Essential elements

Some of the major and trace element levels in human milk are shown in Table 2.I. They are not affected significantly by the maternal diet. Calcium and phosphorus are associated with the caseins while the others are associated mainly with the whey proteins. For example, lactoferrin binds iron and manganese while albumin binds zinc and copper (20). The essential trace elements are also incorporated in proteins of the fat globule membranes. Selenium is found largely in selenomethionine and selenocysteine. The concentrations of these elements are low, probably lower than shown in Table 2.I but their bioavailabilities are very high (20). In this respect, it appears that iron bioavailability is increased by the presence of citrate, which renders it soluble, and by milk lactoferrin in conjunction with specific lactoferrin receptors in the infant's intestine. However, after about 6 months, maternal milk usually becomes an inadequate source of iron for the infant (21). Fluoride concentration is particularly low in human milk. If not essential, it is at least beneficial for dental health. In Germany, fluoride supplements are recommended from birth. In the UK, no recommendation has been made for breastfed infants.

2.3.2.2.6   Vitamins

The milk content of vitamins, particularly fat-soluble vitamins, is related to the vitamin intake and status of the mother (22). However, vitamin deficiencies are rarely reported in breastfed infants (8). Even where there is endemic thiamin deficiency, and milk concentrations are low, beri-beri is rarely reported. Human milk vitamin B_{12} content tends to be very low, but its bioavailability is high owing to a specific transfer factor in the milk. Rickets does occur, classically, in Middle Eastern breastfed infants. The main reason, however, is lack of exposure to sunlight (UV-B) for skin production of cholecalciferol, not dietary deficiency of vitamin D (8). In the UK, rickets is now uncommon in Caucasian infants but the risk remains high for those infants with dark skin who are kept indoors or covered up. In such cases, prevention is by vitamin D supplements given to the mother (23). It is also recommended that vitamin K supplements are given, usually by intramuscular injection, to all newborns. This is because, without this practice, haemorrhagic disease of the newborn (HDN), both classical and late-onset, occurs in a very few breastfed, but not formula-fed, infants. For susceptible infants, human milk is, indeed, an inadequate source of vitamin K. In fact, colostrum has about twice the vitamin K content of mature milk, so it is possible that some cases of HDN could be prevented by earlier feeding of colostrum, or by supplementing the lactating mother with vitamin K (8,24).

Other important components of human milk include water, cells and 'contaminants'. The water intake of an entirely breastfed infant is adequate even in very hot climates. The various cells include, in descending order of concentration, macrophages, lymphocytes and neutrophils. Together with sIgA, lactoferrin, lysozyme and other soluble immunoglobulins and enzymes, they protect the infant's immature intestinal mucosa against penetration by microorganisms; they also suppress the growth of some pathogens, kill others, allow *L. bifidus* to colonise the intestine and, thereby, make it inhospitable for pathogens, and stimulate epithelial maturation and enhance digestive enzyme production. Maternal milk also stimulates the development of the infant's own immunity (8). Thus, the protection against infection is substantial and long-lasting.

2.3.3   Possible hazards of breastfeeding

Breastfeeding can pose hazards that depend on the environment in which the mother-infant diad exists. They include the drugs, pesticides and other pollutants, hormones and viruses excreted into the milk. Breastfeeding is generally contraindicated when the mother is receiving cytotoxic drugs, but alcohol and many other commonplace substances imbibed by the mother, as well as acidic drugs, also appear in significant amounts in human milk. The concentration of lipid-soluble drugs depends on the milk fat content. Most chemical pollutants are lipid-soluble and pose a risk if, having accumulated in the mother's adipose tissue, they are released during lactation. This can be avoided if the mother continues to eat adequately so that her own fat is not being catabolised (22). In fact, there has been little clinical evidence of toxicity from pollutants in breastfed infants. On the other hand, maternal smoking may be detrimental to the breastfed infant as nicotine is excreted in the milk (25). However, this has to be weighed against the evidence that infants of smokers have more infections than those of non-smokers, and breastfeeding protects against infections. Oral contraceptives appear to suppress milk output, through the effect of their oestrogens on prolactin (22). There is also evidence of occasional transmission of a variety of viruses, including the human immunodeficiency virus (26). As a result, infected mothers in the UK are advised not to breastfeed (27). However, for poor communities in many parts of Africa, the risk of HIV infection from breastfeeding may still be less than the risks of other infections and undernutrition associated with inadequate, unhygienic bottle feeding (28). Several factors in maternal milk have been implicated in the genesis of breastmilk jaundice, an unconjugated hyperbilirubinaemia, which, although it occasionally lasts up to 2 months, is rarely pathological. It is familial, in that it tends to occur in breastfed siblings, but the cause is still not clear.

2.4   Formula Milks

Unmodified cows' milk is very different from human milk (Table 2.I). It is entirely unsuitable for young infants. Major reasons for this are its very high protein, sodium, calcium, phosphate and chloride concentrations, which are excess to needs and, therefore, present a huge solute load to the immature kidneys of a young infant. Cows' milk iron and copper concentrations are also too low. Processing eliminates these problems nowadays. Excess nutrients are diluted, deficient ones are added, the casein/whey ratio can be altered and indeed, these foreign proteins can be hydrolysed to their constituent amino acids and small peptides, thus reducing their antigenicity drastically. A variety of formula milks has emerged, whose composition is based on our present-day knowledge of the nutritional requirements for infants at different ages and stages of development. As our knowledge of requirements improves, so the composition of these formula milks is changing. However, there is still a long way to go, particularly in terms of formula composition for sick or very low birth weight infants. The provision of anti-infection properties is not yet envisaged.

For healthy term infants, some of the usual problems and advantages of formula feeds are outlined in Table 2.II. Chief among their advantages is that they are second best to maternal milk and successfully nourish infants unable to receive their mothers' milk. Specialised formula milks have also reduced morbidity and mortality in certain groups – for example, lactose-free milks for lactose-intolerant infants, and preterm milks for very low birth weight infants. Chief among the problems of formula milks is that they must be fed by bottle. The advantages of suckling are lost. Bottled feeds are far more likely to become contaminated by local pathogens, especially where hygiene is poor and the ambient temperature and humidity are high, which applies to much of the 'developing' world. Thus, they carry infection and do nothing to combat it. They are also expensive – costing far more than feeding the mother sufficient to permit normal lactation and her own health. Finally, increasing numbers of formula-fed infants are becoming milk-intolerant. The reasons are not clear. Hypersensitivity to bovine protein, probably ß-lactoglobulin, appears to play the major role.

TABLE 2.II
Comparison of breastfeeding and formula feeding

Breastfeeding	Formula feeding
1. Mother required	Mother not required
2. Low risk of contamination – by viruses including HIV, drugs, alcohol, fat-soluble toxins	High risk of contamination – by local pathogens, toxins, pollutants
3. Supply dependent on infant's need	Supply dependent on provider
4. Inexpensive – to feed mother	Expensive
5. Easily digested β-casein, α-lactalbumin	Less digestible α-casein, β-lactoglobulin
6. Easily absorbed β-monoglycerides	Less absorbable α-monoglycerides
7. Trace element bioavailability high	Trace element bioavailability low but formula is fortified
8. Low intake of vitamins D and K	Formula is fortified
9. Low intake of fluoride	Fluoride dependent on water content
10. Specific protection against infection	No protection against infection
11. Colonisation by *L. bifidus* $\rightarrow$ bowel pH low	Colonisation by *E. coli*, etc.
12. Accelerates maturation, e.g. gut, immunity	May have detrimental effects on immunity
13. Foreign antigens trace	Foreign antigens ++

2.4.1   Special formulas

Almost all infants can receive some of their mothers' milk and some is better than none in terms of nutrition provided and, in particular, protection against infection. Infants born very preterm have a much increased chance of survival and health if they can be fed adequately in spite of their immature intestinal function. Nowadays, parenteral and enteral specialised formulas are available in Europe either to supplement or substitute for maternal milk. Infants who develop intolerance of foreign proteins can be provided with formula in which the protein is hydrolysed to amino acids and small peptides, and infants with lactase deficiency, usually a temporary state following an episode of gastroenteritis, can be 'treated' with lactose free-formula. Infants with inborn errors of metabolism are catered for, with formulas containing, for example, low phenylalanine for phenylketonuria.

2.4.2   Other breast milk substitutes

Raw animal milks are unsuitable for human infants. Although recommended in some folklore, goat and sheep milk should not be fed to young infants as, like cows' milk, the resultant renal solute loads are too high and the mineral and vitamin concentrations are inappropriate (29). Soya 'milk' is very different from both cows' milk and human milk. It is deficient of methionine and carnitine and it contains phytates. These bind cations, especially calcium and zinc, but also iron and copper, reducing their bioavailabilities (30). Processed soya-based formulas have been promoted for infants being reared as vegetarians and for those intolerant of cows' milk based formula. As phytates are difficult to remove completely from soya milk, most formulas still contain some. Soya protein is antigenic, so, if an infant is cows' milk intolerant, he or she is likely also to become soya milk intolerant. The newer cows' milk formula milks containing hydrolysed protein should be recommended rather than soya formula in cases of protein hypersensitivity. One advantage of soya formulas is that they can be lactose-free and therefore useful for infants with lactase deficiency.

2.4.3   The WHO Code

In the early to mid-1970s, formula feeding had almost become the norm in many Western countries and, through commercial pressure, its use was increasing fast in the developing world, where it was, by and large, unaffordable and unsafe. It became an ethical issue, with global consequences; and it led to the creation of the WHO International Code of Marketing of Breastmilk Substitutes (31). Its aim was "to contribute to the provision of safe and adequate nutrition for infants, by the protection and promotion of breastfeeding and by ensuring the proper use of breast milk substitutes when these are necessary ..." Thus, the Code addressed advertising by infant formula manufacturers, and today's multinational corporations, in particular. Not all countries incorporated the Code fully into their national legislation but most of those that did not produced at least some relevant regulations.

In regions with high HIV prevalence, it is particularly important. The UNAIDS/WHO/UNICEF Policy document on mother-to-child transmission of HIV discusses the right to informed choice of feeding method for HIV+ve mothers and the right to provide safe and adequate feeds for their infant, but it pays little attention to the huge gulf between these rights and what is and what can happen (32). Also, with respect to the information available on whether breast or formula feeding is safer, there are, so far, few conclusive findings. We cannot yet advise with confidence – which is what many mothers wish.

2.5   Weaning Feeds

Weaning is the child's progressive transfer from his or her initial single-food milk diet to the family diet of a mixture of many foods. Queen Ann (1665-1714) is said to have lost 18 children in infancy from "spoonfeeding and wet nursing" (33). The weaning period is still one of nutritional vulnerability, even in Europe.

Recommendations as to when to start weaning have varied from 18 to 24 months in 1697, to 2 days in 1953. Today, only traditional societies start to wean late, up to 2 years, while most others start early, usually under 2 months. There is no doubt that infants can adapt to very early weaning but this hardly justifies its use. Newborns are equipped with a complex neurological capacity for suckling rather than drinking and an 'extrusion reflex' to prevent solids from being swallowed. They have little or no head control to aid swallowing. Their intestinal permeability is high and their kidneys are immature. By 6 months, these obstacles to weaning have largely resolved. Thriving infants need increasing intakes of energy and protein. From around 6 months of age, many but not all breastfed infants gain weight faster if supplemented with or changed to formula milk. Whether this is a benefit or not, in the short or long term, is unclear. Presuming that it is, then it appears that energy and protein intakes may become limited in some exclusively breastfed infants. Breastfed infants also tend to deplete their hepatic iron stores beyond 6 months, as demonstrated by a falling serum ferritin. This occurs earlier in infants fed cows' milk and later in those fed iron-supplemented formula milk (34). All in all, most breastfed infants can safely start to wean around 6 months of age.

In practice, infants, especially in poor homes in the developing world, often do not benefit from weaning for many weeks or months. This is because early weaning porridges replace milk but are usually less energy-, iron- and protein-dense than milk. Also, iron bioavailability from such porridges is very low. Another major problem is that contaminated weaning foods cause infection, which increases infants' dietary requirements but often reduces their appetite and therefore, intake.

Particularly in the developed world, weaning foods are sometimes pushed to the extent that the infant is overfed and becomes overweight. A weak positive association exists between obesity at a year and adult obesity; in one of many studies, twice as many fat infants as non-fat infants became fat adults (35).

Weaning foods are chosen by parents on the basis of their flexible consistency, their taste and acceptability. They should be more energy-dense than milk, preferably 30-40% fat, well balanced with respect to essential nutrients, and improve the status of those nutrients to which milk is making a progressively lower contribution. Common home-prepared weaning foods include milk-based custards, other cooked cereals and rootcrops, small amounts of egg and banana. In fact, meats, poultry, fish and legumes are better sources of protein, fat and bioavailable iron (33,36). High-fibre, highly acidic fruits or vegetables or highly seasoned food are not recommended. The ascorbic acid in orange juice improves the absorption of non-haem iron. For all infants, but particularly those in poor circumstances, breast or formula feeding should continue for at least the first few months of weaning. In Europe, commercial weaning foods are often used. Many of these are based on cereals (except wheat), precooked with milk or soya to improve nutrient quality and also supplemented with micronutrients such as iron and zinc. Guidelines are available for their manufacture (37). They tend to be less variable and closer to recommendations than home-prepared foods.

Each 'new' food should be offered in small quantities, carefully, to avoid choking, at intervals of several days. Solid foods should be crushed or, later, cut into small pieces. Cows' milk should not be offered as the main drink until their second year. This is because of its association with iron deficiency, even when not the only source of iron (38). Anaemia (haemoglobin < 110 g/l) is common in late infancy. In one study in London, 22% of children up to 2 years were anaemic (39). In Copenhagen, Michaelsen found 20% of otherwise healthy infants anaemic at 9 months (36). On the basis of serum ferritin and per cent transferrin saturation, these infants were not deemed iron-deficient but serum ferritin had fallen steadily and fairly dramatically from 2 months of age. It is possible that even mild iron deficiency slows mental and psychomotor development. Whether this is reversible is not known (40).

Occasionally, parents insist that their infant receives no animal-based foods. Strict veganism puts infants at great risk of energy, protein, calcium, iron, zinc, riboflavin and vitamins B_{12} and D deficiencies. Rickets, wasting, failure to thrive and poor psychomotor development have all been reported in breastfed infants of macrobiotic mothers, being weaned on to macrobiotic diets (41,42). A vegan mother should be advised to take a vitamin B_{12} supplement while breastfeeding, and also to give her child, up to 18 months, an iron and vitamin enriched soya protein isolate formula milk along with a legume-rich diet. Lacto-ovo-vegetarianism is much less risky for an infant but still tends to provide an energy-deficient weaning diet. In this case, a cows' milk based infant formula should be advised up to 18 months.

2.6   Nutrition and Growth

Growth in infants is a sensitive index of well-being, particularly nutritional well-being. Rate of weight change is the best estimate of short-term change as it is easier to measure weight accurately and precisely than length/height. A deviation in the rate of length/height change generally implies an insult or intervention that has occurred over a lengthy period; in most settings, length/height measurements over 6 months are required to show a real deviation. Recently, a more sensitive index of linear growth rate was devised. This is the rate of change in knee-heel length measured with an infant knemometer (43). This has proved valuable as a research tool to assess the factors affecting linear as opposed to ponderal growth over periods as short as 3 weeks.

Tissues and organs grow at different rates at different times from conception to death. Body proportions change during infancy. Relative to trunk growth, long bone growth is slow in early infancy and fast in the second year of life. Over the first year, body weight increases by 200% but body length and brain volume each increase by just 50%; body fat increases by over 50% in the first 6 months.

Rate of weight gain is never faster than in early infancy and it is largely influenced by nutritional quality (the composition and balance of essential nutrients and energy) and quantity. Initially, however, it is also affected by birth weight. In general, the heavier the infant at birth, the lower the rate of weight gain over the first few weeks. Genetic factors (mid-parental height being a proxy) also operate but only demonstrably so in well-nourished infants from about 6 months of age. Rate of weight gain is also perturbed by interventions and insults, such as drugs and disease, particularly infections. Infections slow growth, sometimes to the extent of weight loss, but this is normally followed by accelerated growth, ensuring complete catch-up. Failure to catch up as expected is usually the result of dietary inadequacy, either in quality or quantity. Appetite is a major factor controlling intake. Increased demand for particular nutrients and/or energy plays an important role when disease is present.

To assess whether an infant's rate of weight gain is adequate or not, more than one, ideally several, weight measurements must be taken over time. Both the weights and rates of weight gain are then compared with reference data obtained from 'healthy, well-nourished' population samples. These do not show normal, ideal or optimal data. They vary from population to population but far more in relation to socioeconomic status than ethnic group. Again, environment, especially nutrition, has the major effect on weight at any one time during infancy, and also rate of weight change.

2.6.1   Growth reference charts

Of the several sets of reference data obtained for infants in Europe, the UK Growth Charts are typical of national data while the Euro-growth data aim to represent 11 European countries (44,45). The UK Growth Charts for infants are based mainly on monthly cross-sectional measurements in healthy UK infants. The charts are distinguished by statistical transformations, which have resulted in the data being normalised so that the 50th centile represents the mean value and each pair of centile lines is separated by 0.67 standard deviations. This means that the centile lines shown are not the classical 3rd, 10th and 25th but rather the 0.4th, 2nd, 9th and 25th, and the 2nd centile is equivalent to −2 SDS, the cut-off between 'normal' and malnourished.

The European reference data were obtained longitudinally, monthly for the first 6 months, and 3-monthly up to a year. Dietary recall data, illnesses and demographic variables were also obtained. Thus, the data could be separated into those from breastfed and those from formula-fed infants. There were substantial differences in the data among the 22 sites. Overall, the infants were of above average socio-economic and education status. Seventy-four per cent were breastfed to some extent. Exclusively breastfed infants gained weight slightly faster in the first 2 months but more slowly thereafter. During their second year, there were no significant differences in weight attained. Thus, the final influence of breastfeeding on growth was small.

Both the UK Growth charts and the Euro-growth study have chosen to provide reference values for body mass index rather than weight-for-length/height to show the extent of under- or overweight. This is in contrast to the WHO reference data, which use North American infant data, collected in the 1970s, to construct charts to show how weight changes with length. The latter is simpler but flawed because the appropriate weight for length does, in fact, vary with age to a small extent. Unlike the UK data, which are relatively old, the Euro-growth longitudinal study is ongoing. It will contribute to the contemporaneous longitudinal WHO study of breastfed infants (46).

2.7 Nutrition, Development and Disease

Preterm infants who receive some breastmilk are at far less risk of necrotising enterocolitis than those who receive formula only. The possible reasons for this are numerous. The immature gut of the newborn is permeable to a variety of foreign molecules and microorganisms; it also malabsorbs. Breastmilk accelerates maturation, reducing permeability and improving transfer of nutrients into and losses from the intestine. At the same time, breastmilk passively immunises the intestinal tract and accelerates development of the infant's own immunity.

In the brain, although neuronal hyperplasia is maximal and almost completed before birth, glial hyperplasia is maximal in infancy. Both of these require particular nutrients, first via placental transfer, then in the infant's diet. From prospective, longitudinal studies by Lucas's group (47), brain development appeared to be superior in 7-year-old children who had been born preterm and breastfed rather than formula-fed. Consistent with this are the findings from a New Zealand study of 7- to 8-year-old children who had been very low birth weight, that the longer they were breastfed, the higher their verbal IQ (48). However, other studies have not shown this difference, even at an earlier age. Nonetheless, the recent studies of the effect of DHA supplements in formula-fed infants on their visual and cognitive functions provide one of the possible reasons for such positive findings.

2.8 Infant Nutrition and Chronic Disease in Adult Life

Several epidemiological associations have been demonstrated between infant growth, which, as described, is a sensitive outcome of infant feeding, and the risk of various chronic diseases, such as Type II diabetes mellitus and cardiovascular disease (49). There are further epidemiological associations reported between the type of early feeding, breast or formula milk, and Type I diabetes mellitus, auto-immune disease and atopic disease. None of the latter associations has been confirmed. However, it is reasonable to suppose that, since adult size is determined, often to a large extent, by nutrition in early life, so also may be other aspects of metabolism. It is likely that intra-uterine nutrition is of paramount importance and that early infant feeding is of secondary importance in this respect. However, it should also be remembered that, just as chronic or repeated infections have a large effect on growth in infancy and, hence, perhaps, the risk of later chronic disease, so also may other intra-uterine stresses, such as pre-eclampsia, have a large effect on both prenatal growth and later disease. The point is that the early environment can play a major role, and probably does, in the disease pattern throughout life. The mechanisms whereby deviations in metabolic behaviour originate are presently being studied and there is already evidence in animal experiments that simple nutritional interventions during pregnancy can determine metabolic behaviour in the offspring. It is also clear that diet in pregnancy is but one of several maternal factors affecting outcome. How much infant feeding, either quality or quantity, can affect what has already happened *in utero*, and hence the outcome in terms of chronic disease remains unknown.

Even a meta-analysis of studies of the relationship between infant diet and Type I diabetes mellitus was able only to conclude that there was a weak association between formula feeding and increased risk, but that this "may have methodologic explanations" (50).

2.9   Conclusions

The result of successful infant nutrition is a healthy child who has reached his or her genetic potential in both form (weight, height and body composition) and function (mental and physical development). Maternal milk appears to be ideal for this purpose up to 6 months, and it also supplies the important bonus of protection against infection. When breastfeeding ceases, then commercial cows' milk based formula provides a more nutritious drink than cows' milk, while more solid foods are gradually introduced during weaning to provide increasing requirements of energy and essential nutrients, particularly iron and protein.

2.10   References

1.   Jackson A.A. Nutrients, growth, and the development of programmed metabolic function. *Short and Long Term Effects of Breast Feeding on Child Health.* 2000, 478, 41-55.

2.   WHO Global Strategy for Infant and Young Child Feeding. 54th World Health Assembly. WHO, Geneva. May 2001.

3.   Uvnas-Moberg K., Winberg J. Role for sensory stimulation in energy economy of mother and infant with particular regard to the gastrointestinal endocrine system, in *Textbook of Gastroenterology and Nutrition in Infancy. 2nd Edn.* Edited by Lebenthal E. New York. Raven Press, 1989, 53-62.

4.   Golden B.E., Corbett M., McBurney R., Golden M.H. Malnutrition: trials and triumphs. *Transactions of the Royal Society of Tropical Medicine and Hygiene,* 2000, 94, 12-13.

5.   Kennedy K.I. Effects of breastfeeding on women's health. *International Journal of Gynaecology and Obstetrics*, 1994, 47 (Supplement), S11-S20.

6.   Holland B., Welch A.A., Unwin I.D., Buss D.H., Paul A.A., Southgate D.A.T. McCance and Widdowson's *The Composition of Foods, 5th Edn.* The Royal Society of Chemistry, Cambridge. 1991.

7.   Williams A.F. Lactation and infant feeding, in *Textbook of Paediatric Nutrition, 3rd Edn.* Edited by McLaren D.S, Burman D., Belton N.R., Williams A.F. Edinburgh. Churchill Livingstone, 1991, 21-45.

8.   Akre J. Infant feeding. The physiological basis. *Bulletin of the World Health Organisation.* 1991, Supplement to volume 67.

9.   Chan G.M. Human milk membranes: an important barrier and substance. *Journal of Pediatric Gastroenterology and Nutrition,* 1992, 5, 521-2.

10. Jensen R.G. Lipids in human milk – composition and fat-soluble vitamins, in *Textbook of Gastroenterology and Nutrition in Infancy, 2nd Edn.* Edited by Lebenthal E. New York. Raven Press, 1989, 157-208.

11. Makrides M., Neumann M.A., Simmer K., Gibson R.A. A critical appraisal of the role of dietary long-chain polyunsaturated fatty acids on neural indices of term infants: a randomised, controlled trial. *Pediatrics,* 2000, 105, 32-8.

12. Jorgensen M.H., Hernell O., Hughes E.L., Michaelsen K.F. Is there a relationship between docosahexaenoic acid concentration in mothers' milk and visual development in term infants? *Journal of Pediatric Gastroenterology and Nutrition,* 2001, 32, 293-6.

13. Decsi T., Koletzko B. Role of long-chain polyunsaturated fatty acids in early human neurodevelopment. *Nutritional Neuroscience*, 2000, 3, 293-306.

14. Hanson L.A., Carlsson B., Jalil F. *et al*. Antiviral and antibacterial factors in human milk, in *Biology of Human Milk*. Nestlé Nutrition Workshop Series, Volume 15, Edited by Hanson L.A. New York. Raven Press, 1988, 141-56.

15. Lönnerdal B., Iyer S. Lactoferrin: molecular structure and biological function. *Annual Reviews of Nutrition*, 1995, 15, 93-110.

16. Forsyth J.S. The relationship between breast-feeding and infant health and development. *Proceedings of the Nutrition Society*, 1995, 54, 407-18.

17. Hanson L.A., Hahn-Zoric M., Wiedermann U. *et al*. Early dietary influence on later immunocompetence. *Nutrition Reviews*, 1996, 54, S23-30.

18. Saarinen U.M, Kajosaari M. Breastfeeding as prophylaxis against atopic disease: prospective follow-up study until 17 years old. *Lancet*, 1995, 346, 1065-9.

19. Carlsson S.E. Human milk non-protein nitrogen: occurrence and possible functions, in *Advances in Pediatrics, Vol. 32*. Edited by Barnes I.A. Chicago. Year Book Medical 1985, 43-70.

20. Lönnerdal B. Concentrations, compartmentation and bioavailability of trace elements in human milk and infant formula, in *Trace Elements in Nutrition of Children – II*. Nestlé Nutrition Workshop Series. Volume 23. Edited by Chandra R.K. New York. Raven Press, 1991, 153-71.

21. Lönnerdal B., Hernell O. Iron, zinc, copper and selenium status of breast-fed infants and infants fed trace element fortified milk-based infant formula. *Acta Paediatrica*, 1994, 83, 367-73.

22. Hambraeus L. Human milk: nutritional aspects, in *Clinical Nutrition of the Young Child*. Edited by Brunser O., Carrazza F.R., Gracey M., Nichols B.L., Senterre J. New York. Raven Press, 1991, 289-301.

23. Department of Health and Social Security. *Report on Health and Social Subjects: 41. Dietary reference values for food energy and nutrients for the United Kingdom*. London. HMSO, 1991.

24. van Kries R., Shearer M., McCarthy P.T., Hang M., Harzer G., Göbel U. Vitamin K_1 content of maternal milk: influence of the stage of lactation, lipid composition and vitamin K_1 supplements given to the mothers. *Pediatric Research*, 1987, 22, 513-7.

25. Dahlstrom A., Lundell B., Curvall M., Thapper L. Nicotine and cotinine concentrations in the nursing mother and her infant. *Acta Paediatrica Scandinavica*, 1990, 79, 142-7.

26.   Oxtoby M.J. Human immunodeficiency virus and other viruses in human milk: placing the issues in broader perspective. *Pediatric Infectious Diseases Journal*, 1988, 7, 825-35.

27.   Department of Health. *HIV and Infant Feeding. Guidance from the UK Chief Medical Officers' Expert Advisory Group on AIDS.* 2001, <www.doh.gov.uk/eaga/hivinfant.pdf>

28.   Lederman S.A. Estimating infant mortality from human immunodeficiency virus and other causes in breast-feeding and bottle-feeding populations. *Pediatrics*, 1992, 89, 290-6.

29.   Taitz L.S., Armitage B.L. Goats' milk for infants and children. *British Medical Journal (Clinical Research Edition)*, 1984, 288, 428-9.

30.   Lönnerdal B. Dietary factors affecting trace element bioavailability from human milk, cow's milk and infant formulas. *Progress in Nutrition and Food Science*, 1985, 9, 35-62.

31.   WHO *International Code of Marketing of Breast-milk Substitutes.* Geneva. WHO, 1981.

32.   WHO/UNICEF/UNAIDS. *HIV and Infant Feeding.* Geneva. WHO, 1998.

33.   Hervada A.R, Newman D.R. Weaning: historical perspectives, practical recommendations and current controversies. *Current Problems in Pediatrics*, 1992, 22, 223-40.

34.   Wharton B.A. Weaning and early childhood, in *Textbook of Paediatric Nutrition, 3rd Edn.* Edited by McLaren D.S., Burman D., Belton N.R., Williams A.F. Edinburgh, Churchill Livingstone, 1991, 47-58.

35.   Rolland-Cachera M.F., Deheeger M., Guilloud-Bataille M., Avons P., Patois E., Sempe M. Tracking the development of adiposity from one month of age to adulthood. *Annals of Human Biology*, 1987, 14, 219-29.

36.   Michaelsen K.M. Nutrition and growth during infancy. The Copenhagen Cohort Study. *Acta Paediatrica*, 1997, 86, Supplement 420.

37.   ESPGAN Committee on Nutrition. Guidelines on infant nutrition II: Recommendations for the composition of follow-up formula and Beikost. *Acta Paediatrica Scandinavica*, 1981, 287(suppl), 1-36.

38.   Zlotkin S.H. Another look at cow milk in the second 6 months of life. *Journal of Pediatric Gastroenterology and Nutrition*, 1993, 16, 1-3.

39.   Mills A.F. Surveillance for anaemia: risk factors in patterns of milk intake. *Archives of Disease in Childhood*, 1990, 65, 428-31.

40. Fairweather-Tait S.J. Iron deficiency in infancy: easy to prevent – or is it? *European Journal of Clinical Nutrition*, 1992, 46 Supplement 4, S9-14.

41. Dagnelie P.C., van Staveren W.A., Vergote F.J. *et al.* Nutritional status of infants aged 4 to 18 months on macrobiotic diets and matched omnivorous control infants: a population-based mixed-longitudinal study. II. Growth and psychomotor development. *European Journal of Clinical Nutrition*, 1989, 43, 325-38.

42. Dagnelie P.C., Vergote F.J., van Staveren W.A., van den Berg H., Gingjan P.G., Hautvast J.G. High prevalence of rickets in infants on macrobiotic diets. *American Journal of Clinical Nutrition*, 1990, 51, 202-8.

43. Michaelsen K.F., Skov L., Badsberg J.H., Jørgensen M. Short-term measurement of linear growth in preterm infants: Validation of a hand-held knemometer. *Pediatric Research*, 1991, 30, 464-8.

44. Freeman J.V., Cole T.J., Chinn S., Jones P.R.M., White E.M., Preece M.A. Cross-sectional stature and weight reference curves for the UK, 1990. *Archives of Disease in Childhood*, 1995, 73, 17-24.

45. Haschke F., Van't Hof M. and the Eurogrowth Study Group. Eurogrowth Program for monitoring the growth of children. 2000, http://www.eurogrowth.org

46. Garza C., de Onis M. A new international growth reference for young children. *American Journal of Clinical Nutrition*, 1999, 70, 169S-172S.

47. Morley R., Lucas A. Influence of early diet on outcome in preterm infants. *Acta Paediatrica*, 1994, 83, 123-6.

48. Horwood L.J., Darlow B.A., Mogridge N. Breast milk feeding and cognitive ability at 7-8 years. *Archives of Disease in Childhood*, 2001, 84, F23-27.

49. Osmond C., Barker D.J.P. Fetal, infant, and childhood growth are predictors of coronary heart disease, diabetes, and hypertension in adult men and women. *Environmental Health Perspectives*, 2000, 108, 545-53.

50. Norris J.M., Scott F.W. A meta-analysis of infant diet and insulin dependent diabetes mellitus: Do biases play a role? *Epidemiology*, 1996, 7, 87-92.

3. NUTRITION OF SCHOOL CHILDREN AND ADOLESCENTS

Sara Stanner and Judy Buttriss

3.1   Introduction

It is well recognised that diet is of paramount importance for the well-being, growth and development of a child. In the longer term, food consumed in childhood, particularly adolescence, can set the pattern for future food preferences and eating behaviour in adult life. There is also substantial evidence to suggest that poor eating and physical activity habits in childhood can store up problems for later life, particularly in relation to obesity, heart disease, diabetes, osteoporosis and cancer.

Comprehensive national data on the eating patterns and nutrient intakes of young people in Britain have recently been published (1). *The National Diet and Nutrition Survey* (NDNS) *of young people aged 4-18 years* provides information on nutritional status and various lifestyle factors such as physical activity levels (1), and a separate report (2) provides data on oral health. Whilst poor growth and illness due to micronutrient deficiencies are now rare in the United Kingdom, the findings of this survey have identified several areas of concern about the nutritional consequences of imbalanced diets for the health of young people in Britain.

3.2 Dietary Habits of Young People in Britain

3.2.1 Types and quantities of food consumed

The NDNS report provides information about the proportion of young people consuming selected foods and drinks during the 7-day recording period (Table 3.I). The most commonly consumed foods, eaten by over 80% of the group, were white bread, savoury snacks, crisps, chips, boiled, mashed and jacket potatoes, biscuits and chocolate confectionery. Chicken and turkey dishes were the most commonly consumed types of meat, eaten by 70% of young people. Under half of boys and 59% of girls ate raw and salad vegetables (excluding tomatoes), around 40% ate cooked leafy green vegetables and about 60% other cooked vegetables. Apples and pears were the most commonly consumed fruits, eaten by over half the group, followed by bananas eaten by just under 40%. Carbonated soft drinks were the most popular drink; standard versions were consumed by three-quarters of young people and low-calorie versions by just under half.

TABLE 3.I
Percentage of consumers, by age and sex, of selected foods and drinks during the 7-day dietary record
© British Nutrition Foundation reproduced with kind permission from Smithers G., Gregory J.R., Bates C.J., Prentice A., Jackson L.V., Wenlock R. The National Diet and Nutrition Survey: young people aged 4-18 years. *British Nutrition Foundation Nutrition Bulletin*, 2000, 25 (2), 105-111

	Males (age in years)				Females (age in years)			
	4-6	7-10	11-14	15-18	4-6	7-10	11-14	15-18
White bread	91	98	94	96	93	92	89	90
Biscuits	93	91	84	70	89	88	79	66
Whole milk	78	59	40	47	70	51	38	41
Semi-skimmed milk	54	53	64	63	47	52	58	59
Beef & veal dishes	45	52	48	63	43	52	46	45
Chicken & turkey dishes	69	75	75	79	69	71	65	69
Raw & salad vegetables[1]	37	44	53	51	52	49	56	66
Leafy green vegetables	46	41	32	38	44	42	40	40
Chips	89	88	90	87	85	88	79	80
Apples and pears	70	59	48	39	66	61	47	44
Citrus fruit	26	29	21	19	29	33	23	20
Bananas	47	42	32	33	50	38	28	30
Carbonated soft drinks[2]	67	73	85	85	66	72	73	73
Coffee	6	7	14	39	6	11	14	32
Tea	29	40	48	61	33	43	49	56

[1] excluding raw carrots and tomatoes
[2] excluding low-calorie versions

The quantities of foods consumed generally increased with age, with the exception of whole milk, the consumption of which decreased with age. Boys ate larger amounts than girls of all foods by the age of 11 years and of some foods by the age of 7 years. One in five young people said that they took vitamin and mineral supplements.

It is generally recognised that the more varied the diet the more likely it is to provide the many vitamins and minerals needed for health. To assist in communicating this message, devices such as the 'Balance of Good Health' (see Fig. 3.1) are often used, which divide foods into categories, roughly based on the nutrients they provide. One of the largest categories, recommended to represent about a third of the diet, is fruit and vegetables. Current government advice is that we should aim for a minimum of five daily servings of fruit and vegetables (about 400 g per day for adults), incorporating a variety of different types. Young people in Britain are on average eating less than half the recommended five portions of fruit and vegetables per day and one in five ate no fruit at all during the week of the study. The proportion of young people who ate fruit fell markedly with age, reaching 30% in the oldest group. Overall, 4% ate no vegetables during the survey week. The low intake of these foods amongst young people is of concern as foods in this group are important sources of a range of vitamins and minerals, and also provide dietary fibre.

Fig. 3.1. The Balance of Good Health
Reproduced with kind permission from the Food Standards Agency

The Government has recognised a need to encourage young people to increase their fruit and vegetable intake, and is providing financial support for several schemes, including fruit tuck shops and breakfast clubs in schools around the country. The National Health Service Plan includes specific commitments to increase fruit and vegetables consumption amongst young children (3). Activities include the introduction of a National School Fruit Scheme, providing every child in nursery school with a piece of fruit each day, a five-a-day promotion programme, and collaboration with industry and producers to increase the provision of, and access to, fruit and vegetables.

3.2.2   Social influences on food choice in young people

In general, children have greater freedom in food selection than ever before, as reflected by food product sales targeting the variety of child-oriented foods available and children's own purchasing power. A wide and complex range of social and cultural forces shapes food preferences and eating patterns during childhood and adolescence. The relative importance of many of these factors, however, changes as children grow older, become increasingly independent and take more responsibility for controlling their own lifestyles. For example, as children move towards adolescence parental influence declines, as peer pressure and media-led fashions become increasingly important. Developing independence can lead to rebelliousness over what is eaten with the family and the rejection of foods considered to be 'healthy' by those in authority. Parental control over children's eating habits is further diminished by a 'grazing' style of eating, as communal meal times are sacrificed to the competing demands of other time commitments or meals eaten in front of the television.

The media have an important influence on young people's lifestyles, including their choice of food. In particular, millions of pounds are spent on food advertisements each year to enhance the appeal of products to young people. Advertisements targeted towards these age groups tend to promote snack foods, sweets and soft drinks. These foods are fine as part of a balanced diet (i.e in moderation), but, if eaten in excess, might result in the type of dietary pattern associated with an increased risk of obesity and dental caries in childhood; and cardiovascular disease, diabetes and cancers in adulthood (4). This uneven distribution of advertising expenditure has led to calls for a code of practice on the promotion of foods to children. Whilst research suggests that children tend to request food products that are more frequently advertised on television, the degree to which advertisements influence the type, rather than the brand, of food selected remains unclear.

Idealism over environmental issues may change attitudes to eating, particularly during adolescence. Vegetarianism is common amongst teenagers. For example, in the recent government survey, one in ten girls in the 15-18 year age group reported that they were vegetarian or vegan (1). This is not in itself a problem and can be a healthy way of eating. However, the unsupervised adoption of vegan diets can lead to problems amongst growing children and teenagers, who have increased requirements for several nutrients.

Another important social influence over eating habits amongst young people is the pressure placed upon girls to be 'slim'. Emotional factors and attitudes to appearance and body image are extremely important in this age group, particularly amongst girls. Sixteen per cent of girls aged 15-18 years in the NDNS reported that they were currently dieting to lose weight, compared with 3% of the corresponding group of boys. Hill and colleagues (5) have shown that, even amongst 9-year-olds, there are girls who are highly restrained eaters and who report frequent bouts of dieting. The avoidance of breakfast and taking up smoking are often strategies employed to assist in this mission. Teenagers on slimming diets are more likely to be short of essential vitamins and minerals than children on higher energy intakes. Self-imposed dieting during this period, particularly when the child is not overweight, is far more likely to precipitate anorexia nervosa than in an adult. Bulimia nervosa is another problem in this age group.

3.3   Energy Intake, Physical Activity and Childhood Obesity

The NDNS found that, in each age and sex group, the mean energy intake of the young people studied fell below the Estimated Average Requirement (EAR), defined as the amount estimated to meet the average requirements of a population group (Table 3.II). Energy intake was lowest in relation to the EAR for 15- to 18-year-old girls. However, young people in the survey were taller and heavier compared with those in earlier surveys of the same age groups (6), suggesting that, though low, these energy intakes are unlikely to be inadequate in the context of existing physical activity patterns.

With the exception of very young children (4- to 6-year-olds), young people in Britain are largely inactive as judged by the amount of time spent in moderate or vigorous activity (1). About 40% of boys and 60% of girls spent less than one hour per day in activities of at least moderate intensity and therefore failed to meet the former Health Education Authority's recommendations for young people. In the oldest age group, 15-18 years, the proportions who were inactive rose to 56% of boys and 69% of girls.

TABLE 3.II
Average energy intake by age and sex
© British Nutrition Foundation reproduced with kind permission from Smithers G., Gregory J.R., Bates C.J., Prentice A., Jackson L.V., Wenlock R. The National Diet and Nutrition Survey: young people aged 4-18 years. *British Nutrition Foundation Nutrition Bulletin*, 2000, 25 (2), 105-111

Age and sex	Mean energy intake (MJ (kcal) per day)	Average daily energy intake (% EAR[1])
Males		
4-6 years	6.39 (1520)	89
7-10 years	7.47 (1777)	91
11-14 years	8.28 (1968)	89
15-18 years	9.60 (2285)	83
Females		
4-6 years	5.87 (1397)	91
7-10 years	6.72 (1598)	92
11-14 years	7.03 (1672)	89
15-18 years	9.82 (1622)	77

[1] EAR: Estimated Average Requirement

The physical inactivity identified in the survey carries many implications, and, if this can be tackled, it promises to bring benefits both in the short term and in the longer term. The children who were more active generally ate more food and hence had a greater chance of meeting their needs for vitamins and minerals, although this would depend to some extent on the types of food choices made. They also had lower blood pressure. Physical activity among adolescents has been correlated with behavioural health benefits, such as increased self-esteem and lower levels of anxiety and stress. An example of this was provided by a study of 5,000 adolescents in the UK, which showed a significant association between participation in sport and recreational activity and emotional well-being (7). In the longer term, regular physical activity is an important aspect of developing and maintaining a strong skeleton, and carries benefits in terms of general health and well-being. Taking more physical activity is also a key strategy to the maintenance of a healthy body weight and is therefore associated with less risk of obesity.

Whilst there is a lack of agreement between studies over the definition of obesity in children, studies consistently report a high prevalence of childhood obesity in the UK, and rates appear to be increasing (8). Apart from the social and psychological problems experienced by overweight children, there are also long-term risks. There is some evidence to suggest that children's weight tends to 'track' into adult life. Children who are overweight in their early teens (unlike during infancy) are more likely to be overweight as adults (9) and adult obesity with childhood onset is frequently more severe. The probability that an overweight child will be obese in early adult life increases substantially as the obesity becomes more severe and as the child gets older (9). Must *et al.* (10) demonstrated this 'tracking' effect to be accompanied by an increase in cardiovascular risk factors and in death from coronary heart disease during adulthood. Other health consequences of adult obesity include increased risk of morbidity and mortality from hypertension, type II diabetes mellitus and some forms of cancer.

There is also some evidence that overweight adolescents, regardless of whether they remain obese as adults, are more likely to develop these chronic diseases (10). Also, compared with normal weight children, obese children have higher blood pressure and plasma insulin levels and more atherogenic lipid patterns (11,12); and longitudinal changes in relative weight are associated with changes in these risk factors. This clustering of risk factors has been linked to the acceleration of atherosclerotic lesions in the coronary arteries of young individuals (13) and emphasises the importance of prevention and treatment of obesity in early life.

It is, however, essential that any dietary modification does not prevent normal growth or development of the child. There is also a need to be careful about the emphasis placed on body weight in young people because of the risk of tipping the balance in favour of eating disorders (14). Strategies should, therefore, focus primarily on increasing physical activity, particularly among the older girls, in whom levels appear to be lowest.

Research is needed urgently into the factors that influence children's activity patterns. Work underway at Bristol University suggests that both normal weight and overweight children are much more active during school days than at weekends or during the school holidays. Travelling to school and school break times provide opportunities for opportunistic activities, which are less likely to occur at home (15). It is, therefore, essential to promote active school policies and to address the causes of inactivity in the home. Most importantly, children should participate in activities they enjoy and which can become part of their daily routine (e.g. walking, cycling).

3.4   Macronutrient Intake

Consistent with data from the National Food Survey (16), it would seem that there has been a reduction in energy intake and in fat intake, as a percentage of energy, with a corresponding increase in the proportion of energy derived from protein and from carbohydrate (Table 3.III).

TABLE 3.III
Comparison of fat intake and percentage energy from fat among
young people aged 10-15 years
© British Nutrition Foundation reproduced with kind permission from Smithers G.,
Gregory J.R., Bates C.J., Prentice A., Jackson L.V., Wenlock R. The National Diet and
Nutrition Survey: young people aged 4-18 years. *British Nutrition Foundation Nutrition
Bulletin*, 2000, 25 (2), 105-111

	Fat, g/day	% Energy from fat
1983, 10-11 year olds (6)		
Males	87.6	37.4
Females	78.9	37.9
1997, 10-11 year olds (1)		
Males	75.8	35.7
Females	67.2	36.0
1983, 14-15 year olds (6)		
Males	106.3	37.9
Females	82.2	38.7
1997, 14-15 year olds (1)		
Males	86.5	35.9
Females	65.9	36.1

Specific dietary reference values (DRVs) for fat and carbohydrate (expressed as population averages) and fibre do not exist for this age group. However, using adult guidelines as a benchmark, diets contained a reasonable amount of total fat (35.4% food energy in boys, 35.9% in girls; adult DRV is 35% of food energy) but were high in saturates (14.2% food energy in boys, 14.3% in girls; adult DRV 11% of food energy). The proportion of energy from saturates tended to fall with age. Overall, cereals and cereal products (mainly cakes, biscuits, buns and pastries) provided 22% of saturates intake; meat and meat products provided 19% in boys and 16% in girls; milk and milk products provided 23%; vegetables, potatoes and savoury snacks provided 14%; and fat spreads provided 8%.

Mean plasma total cholesterol was 4.0 mmol/litre for boys and 4.2 mmol/litre in girls. Overall, 8% of boys and 11% of girls had a concentration at or above 5.2 mmol/litre (the reference value indicating an elevated level). Correlations with dietary fat intake were weak.

The recommended population average intake for *cis* n-3 and n-6 polyunsaturated fatty acids as a percentage of total energy intake from food in adults is 6.5% (17); the boys had an average intake of n-6 fatty acids of 5.1% of food energy and the girls 5.3%. For n-3 fatty acids, the intake was 0.8% in both sexes. Vegetables, potatoes and savoury snacks provided over a third of n-3 intake (34% in boys and 38% in girls), mainly from roast and fried potatoes and chips. Cereals and cereal products contributed 18% of intake for boys and 16% for girls; and meat and meat products provided 17% in boys and 16% in girls. Overall, fish and fish dishes provided 5% of n-3 fatty acids in boys and 6% for girls, mainly in the form of coated and fried white fish. Consequently, this would not have included many of the very long chain n-3 fatty acids, intake of which has been specifically recommended in relation to heart disease (18), as these are found primarily in oil-rich fish. Oil-rich fish provided only 2% of n-3 fatty acid intake.

Total carbohydrate provided an average of 51.6% of food energy in boys and 51.1% in girls. There were no significant differences between age groups. The main sources did not differ much with age or gender: cereals and cereal products were the major source, contributing 45% of total carbohydrate intake for boys and 42% for girls, of which bread contributed 16%, and breakfast cereals 11% for boys and 8% for girls. Vegetables, potatoes and savoury snacks contributed 16% for boys and 18% for girls, of which 7% came from roast or fried potatoes and chips. Drinks contributed 11%, at least two-thirds of which was from soft drinks (not low-calorie). Sugars, preserves and confectionery also together contributed 11% of total carbohydrate intake, of which chocolate confectionery contributed about half.

Starch provided about 55% of total carbohydrate intake. Almost two-thirds of this (63% for boys and 60% for girls) came from cereals and cereal products, with bread contributing 28% and 27%, and breakfast cereals 15% and 11%, respectively, for boys and girls. The only other food group contributing more than 10% of intake was vegetables, including potatoes and savoury snacks, which contributed 27% for boys and 29% for girls. Fibre intake was low, 11.2 g for boys on average and 9.7 g for girls. The main sources were vegetables, potatoes and savoury snacks (about 40% of intake), and cereals and cereal products also provided about 40%.

In the NDNS report, information on intake of sugars is categorised as non-milk extrinsic sugars (NMES), intrinsic sugars and milk sugars. The report defines extrinsic sugars as 'those not contained within the cellular structure of the food, whether natural and unprocessed or refined'. The mean daily intake of NMES was 85 g among boys and 69 g among girls, representing about 72% of total sugars intake. Intake increased significantly with age in the boys, from a mean of 66 g for those aged 4-6 years to 97 g for those aged 15-18 years. No such differences with age existed among the girls. The dietary reference value for NMES is 11% of food energy, expressed as a population average intake. Intakes of NMES in boys averaged 16.7% of food energy and in girls 16.4% of food energy. Young people at the upper 2.5 percentile of the intake distribution were obtaining more than a quarter of their food energy from NMES. The main sources were drinks (e.g. squash and carbonated drinks) and the foods grouped as sugar, preserves and confectionery. The proportion provided by drinks increased with age – for example, from 27% of intake in boys aged 4-6 years to 42% in boys aged 15-18 years.

In summary, young people are getting a disproportionately large amount of their dietary energy from saturated fatty acids and sugars, and many have inadequate fibre intakes. As well as promoting obesity, diets that are high in fat, particularly saturates, show the same relationship with cardiovascular risk factors in children as demonstrated in adults. Even in children as young as 10 years (19), higher contributions of fat to total energy intake are associated with raised blood cholesterol levels, and intake of polyunsaturated fatty acids is inversely associated with serum triglyceride levels.

The high intake of NMES amongst children is also of importance because of the reported association between frequency of consumption of these types of sugar and risk of dental caries, particularly if dental hygiene is poor or fluoride not used (see section 3.8 on Oral Health).

The implications of low fibre intakes are less clear. While poor intakes of dietary fibre have been linked to diverticular disease and colon cancer in adults, the extent to which adult intakes are related to habits in childhood is unknown. Nevertheless, a low dietary fibre intake is likely to be associated with increased risk of constipation.

3.5 Micronutrient Intake

3.5.1 Current intake and status of vitamins and minerals amongst young people

Average intakes of all vitamins from the diet were well above the reference nutrient intakes (RNIs) except for vitamin A (Table 3.IV) (1). An RNI is the amount judged to be adequate or more than adequate for 97.5% of a given group of the population. Depending on the age or sex group, 6-20% of the children surveyed were below the LRNI (lower reference nutrient intake) for vitamin A. Intakes that are regularly below the LRNI are judged as likely to be inadequate as the LRNI is sufficient for only those in the population with the bottom 2.5% of requirements for a particular nutrient (20).

The youngest age group (4-6 years) fared best in terms of vitamin intakes. Amongst older children, a proportion had intakes of riboflavin below the LRNI: over 20% (22% and 21%, respectively) of 11- to 14-year-old and 15- to 18-year-old girls, and 6% each of boys in these two age groups. There was some evidence of impaired riboflavin status among those with low intakes. Three per cent of girls aged 11-14 years and 4% aged 15-18 years had folate intakes below the LRNI. Marginal status for folate (as assessed by red cell levels) was evident in 7% of boys and 9% of girls overall.

There is no RNI for vitamin D for children aged over 4 years as it has been assumed that children get sufficient sunshine exposure, by playing outside, to synthesise the vitamin D that they need in their skin. Mean intakes of vitamin D from food were low – 2.6 µg for boys and 2.1 µg for girls (the RNI for children under 4 is 10 µg/day). The largest contribution (over a third) was made by cereals and cereal products (breakfast cereals alone contributed a quarter). Fat spreads and meat each contributed a quarter of the total. Oily fish, a rich source of vitamin D, contributed less than 10%.

Vitamin D status was found to pose a problem for a significant proportion of the young people surveyed. In both boys and girls, plasma levels of 25-hydroxyvitamin D fell with age, and significant proportions of those in the older age groups had a poor vitamin D status (a level less than 25 nmol/litre): 11% of boys and girls aged 11-14 years; 16% of boys and 10% of girls aged 15-18 years. Overall, 13% of 11- to 18-year-olds had low vitamin D status (see Fig. 3.2). There was also a strong seasonal variation, with levels being highest in samples taken between July and September. For samples taken between April and June, one in four 15- to 18-year-old boys had a mean plasma 25-hydroxyvitamin D below 25 nmol/litre.

47

TABLE 3.IV

Average daily intake of vitamins from food sources[1] as a percentage of RNI[2] and percentage with intakes below the LRNI[3] for young people aged 4-18 years

© British Nutrition Foundation reproduced with kind permission from Smithers G., Gregory J.R., Bates C.J., Prentice A., Jackson L.V., Wenlock R. The National Diet and Nutrition Survey: young people aged 4-18 years. *British Nutrition Foundation Nutrition Bulletin*, 2000, 25 (2), 105-111

	Males (age in years)								Females (age in years)							
	4-6		7-10		11-14		15-18		4-6		7-10		11-14		15-18	
	% RNI	% < LRNI	% RNI	% < LRNI	% RNI	% < LRNI	% RNI	% < LRNI	% RNI	% < LRNI	% RNI	% < LRNI	% RNI	% < LRNI	% RNI	% < LRNI
Vitamin A	114	8	101	9	93	13	88	12	112	6	96	10	78	20	91	12
Thiamin	181	-	202	-	189	0	173	-	163	-	182	1	200	1	172	1
Riboflavin	194	-	162	1	144	6	148	6	175	-	137	1	120	22	118	21
Niacin	207	-	216	0	200	0	203	0	186	-	195	-	205	-	180	1
Vitamin B6	189	-	194	-	182	0	180	0	169	-	174	1	190	1	150	5
Vitamin B12	499	-	395	-	372	0	330	-	446	-	347	1	270	1	225	2
Folate	191	-	141	-	123	1	152	-	169	-	126	2	102	3	105	4
Vitamin C	223	-	243	-	218	-	208	-	217	0	245	-	202	1	185	0

[1] excluding dietary supplements
[2] average intake as percentage of RNI calculated for each young person; values for all young people in the group pooled to give the mean
[3] LRNI: lower reference nutrient intake

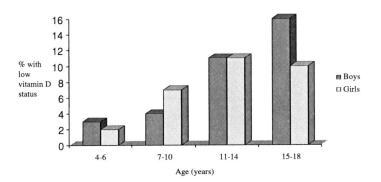

Fig. 3.2. Percentage of young people with low vitamin D status

In the youngest age group (4-6 years), intakes of most minerals were above the RNI and the proportions below the LRNI were small, except in the case of zinc (Table 3.V). However, for older age groups, intakes of a number of minerals were below the RNI: zinc for all age groups; magnesium and calcium for older boys and girls; iron, iodine and copper for older girls. A significant proportion had intakes below the LRNI for zinc, calcium, potassium, magnesium and iron.

For calcium, about 10% of older boys and about 20% of older girls had intakes below the LRNI. These data for calcium are comparable to those reported in the youngest age group (16- to 18-year-olds) in the survey of British adults (21,22), in which 27% of young women had calcium intakes below the LRNI. In the oldest age group, 15% of girls and 12% of boys reported not drinking milk, a major source of calcium in the British diet according to the National Food Survey (16), providing 40% of calcium intake.

For potassium, up to 15% of older boys, a fifth of 11- to 14-year-old girls and over a third of the oldest girls (15-18 years) had low intakes. Magnesium intakes were low (below the LRNI) in over half the older girls and a quarter of the older boys. The main sources were cereals, milk and meat. The main sources of iron in the survey were breakfast cereals (about a quarter), vegetables and potatoes (17%), meat (14%) and bread (13%). Iron intakes were low in up to half the older girls. Similarly, in the survey of British adults, 33% of women aged 16-18 years had intakes of iron below the LRNI, 39% had low magnesium intakes and 30% low potassium intakes (22).

49

TABLE 3.V

Average daily intake of minerals from food sources[1] as a percentage of RNI[2] and percentage with intakes below the LRNI[3] for young people aged 4-18 years

© British Nutrition Foundation reproduced with kind permission from Smithers G., Gregory J.R., Bates C.J., Prentice A., Jackson L.V., Wenlock R. The National Diet and Nutrition Survey: young people aged 4-18 years. *British Nutrition Foundation Nutrition Bulletin*, 2000, 25 (2), 105-111

	Males (age in years)								Females (age in years)							
	4-6		7-10		11-14		15-18		4-6		7-10		11-14		15-18	
	% RNI	% < LRNI	% RNI	% < LRNI	% RNI	% < LRNI	% RNI	% < LRNI	% RNI	% < LRNI	% RNI	% < LRNI	% RNI	% < LRNI	% RNI	% < LRNI
Iron	134	-	111	1	95	3	111	2	119	1	96	3	60	45	58	50
Calcium	157	3	135	2	80	12	88	9	146	2	119	5	80	24	82	19
Phosphorus	263	-	224	-	146	-	172	-	242	-	203	-	149	-	153	-
Magnesium	143	3	97	2	78	28	85	18	129	1	89	5	65	51	64	53
Sodium	296	-	200	-	168	0	204	-	265	-	180	-	142	0	143	0
Chloride	282	-	200	-	161	-	198	-	253	-	179	-	136	-	139	-
Potassium	177	-	107	-	77	10	81	15	161	-	101	1	68	19	62	38
Zinc	85	12	88	5	79	14	92	9	75	26	81	10	66	37	87	10
Copper[4]	117	n/a[4]	116	n/a	112	n/a	106	n/a	106	n/a	105	n/a	98	n/a	80	n/a
Iodine	156	2	140	1	124	3	139	1	143	2	119	3	92	13	96	10

[1] excluding dietary supplements
[2] average intake as percentage of RNI calculated for each young person; values for all young people in the group pooled to give the mean
[3] LRNI: lower reference nutrient
[4] no LRNIs have been set for copper

50

Consistent with the intake data for iron, 14% of the girls and 13% of the boys had low ferritin levels (a measure of iron status), suggesting low iron stores and an increased risk of anaemia. The proportion rose to 27% in the oldest group of girls (see Fig. 3.3).

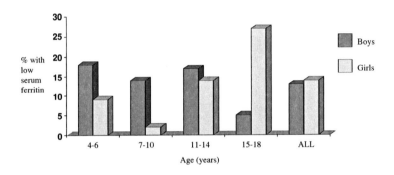

Fig. 3.3. Percentage of young people with low serum ferritin status

Five per cent of girls and 1% of boys reported being a vegetarian or vegan. Amongst girls, the proportion rose from 2% among 4- to 6-year-olds to 10% among girls aged 15-18 years. There was no variation with age amongst the boys. These young people were more likely to come from non-manual than from manual backgrounds. Almost two-thirds reported becoming vegetarian for moral or ethical reasons, and a third because they did not like the taste of meat. Parental vegetarianism or religious reasons were given far less often. Plasma iron and haemoglobin levels were significantly lower in vegetarians compared with meat-eaters but, perhaps surprisingly, there was no difference in vitamin B_{12} status. However, status of several other vitamins and of selenium was better and LDL-cholesterol levels were lower.

Intakes of sodium, excluding additions during cooking and at the table, were on average about twice the RNI level.

3.5.2 Implications of sub-optimal vitamin and mineral intakes during childhood

A conclusion of the NDNS report is that vitamin intake does not seem to be a problem for the majority of the young people. Furthermore, the quality of the diet with respect to vitamin content (i.e. amount expressed in terms of energy intake) seems to have improved generally, in spite of the overall reduction in energy intakes seen over recent decades. However, as was found in the recent survey of people over the age of 65 (23,24), there is evidence of apparently sub-optimal intakes of a number of minerals in young people.

Vitamin C intake is adequate amongst most young people. Whilst it is unclear whether there are any long-term protective effects of high intakes of antioxidant nutrients during childhood, studies in adults suggest that increased consumption of fruits and vegetables, which are rich sources of antioxidant vitamins, is protective against heart disease and cancer (25). At the moment, however, it is not known to what extent these adult diseases are related to tissue damage that may originate in childhood.

Perhaps one of the most surprising findings of the NDNS was the prevalence of poor vitamin D status, particularly in the older age groups, at which time growth is very rapid. Vitamin D is required for the efficient absorption of calcium, which in turn is required for bone development. Calcium requirements are particularly high during adolescence, when 40% of peak bone mass is acquired (26). Low calcium intake during these important years has been implicated in low bone mass in adulthood and increased risk of developing osteoporosis after the menopause. Physical inactivity is also detrimental to bone health, as participation in regular weight-bearing exercise provides the stimulus to the body to build and retain bone.

Iron deficiency was identified to be a common problem, especially amongst adolescent girls, when the onset of the menstrual cycle adds to high daily iron requirements associated with rapid growth. Vegetarianism, particularly the avoidance of meat, is common amongst adolescents. About 90% of dietary iron is present as non-haem iron; the remainder is as haem iron, the main source of which is red meat. Whilst haem iron is well absorbed, the extent to which non-haem iron is absorbed is highly variable and depends on the individual's iron status and on other components of the diet (e.g. vitamin C enhances absorption, as does meat, fish and poultry). On the other hand, bran, polyphenols, oxalates, phytates and tannins inhibit absorption. The absorption of haem iron is not strongly influenced by such factors. For these reasons, iron absorption is sometimes relatively poor among those on a meat-free diet.

In developing countries, where anaemia is generally more serious than in the UK, associations between iron deficiency and poor cognitive function are evident (27). In Britain, iron deficiency is generally mild. However, there is growing evidence that borderline iron status in this age group can have adverse effects on cognitive function (28). Lower haemoglobin levels and higher serum transferrin receptor values have been linked with lower intelligence quotients amongst adolescent girls (29). Any effect on cognitive function could have important implications in terms of learning ability and academic performance.

High sodium intake has been linked to higher blood pressure levels in children and adolescents. The recent government survey found systolic blood pressure to be significantly higher in boys and girls who added salt to their food at the table and in girls who had salt added to their food during cooking (1). Longitudinal studies have shown blood pressure in young adults to be related to blood pressure in older adulthood (30) and to predict mortality from cardiovascular disease (31). Thus, reducing sodium intake and establishing a taste for less salty foods in childhood may reduce adult hypertension. Blood pressure was also higher amongst young people who smoked or drank alcohol (1). The most inactive children also tended to have the highest blood pressure.

3.6 Teenage Pregnancy

The UK has one of the highest rates of teenage pregnancies in western Europe; 56,000 babies are born to girls aged 15-19 in England each year (32). Pregnancy during adolescence imposes additional physiological and emotional stresses, creating the potential for competition for available nutrients between the still-growing mother and the developing foetus. The increased risk of delivering a low birth weight infant (<2,500 g) associated with adolescent pregnancy is well known. For multiparous teenagers aged 16 years and under, risk is increased nearly twofold compared with multiparous women over 16 of the same ethnic group. Low birth weight is the leading cause of neonatal and infant mortality and is associated with childhood morbidity, problems in growth and cognition, and increased risk of chronic diseases such as diabetes, hypertension and heart disease in adult life (33). Iron is one of several nutrients recognised as being important during pregnancy, when anaemia is associated with increased risk of stillbirth, pre-term delivery and low birth weight (34) and an increased placental to birth weight ratio (35). Poor intakes of several B vitamins, including folate, as well as iodine and zinc, may also be of significance for young women who become pregnant in their teenage years. For example, poor folate status at the time of conception and during the first 3 months of pregnancy has been shown to be related to the risk of having a baby with a neural tube defect, e.g. spina bifida (36). As most teenage pregnancies are unplanned and many girls present relatively late for antenatal care, pre-conceptual and first trimester folic acid supplement intake is unlikely, particularly as teenage mothers are less likely to be aware of this health message.

3.7   Regional and Socio-economic Differences

The NDNS population was divided into four regions: Northern, Central/South West/Wales, Scotland and London/South East. Despite considerable differences in the types of food eaten, there was very little difference between the regions in mean energy intake or protein, carbohydrate or alcohol intake. There were no regional differences in total fat intake, but girls in Scotland and the Northern region derived significantly more energy from monounsaturated fatty acids than those from the other regions. There were very few regional differences in vitamin and mineral intakes or the related blood values. Girls in London and the South East had higher iron stores than elsewhere, girls in the North had the lowest plasma vitamin C levels, and boys in the Central /South West and Wales region had a higher plasma cholesterol than those in Scotland.

Intakes of most vitamins and minerals tended to be lower in Scotland and to a lesser extent in the north of England than elsewhere. Some of these differences persisted when adjusted for energy intake; for example, in Scotland, vitamin D, iron and manganese in boys, and thiamin, folate and pantothenic acid in girls. Those in Scotland and the North also tended to have a poorer biochemical status of vitamins such as vitamin C and folate than young people in the other three regions. The latter is likely to be linked with intakes of foods such as fruit and vegetables.

Among young people, differences in relation to parents' receipt of benefits and to household income level were more marked than the regional differences. No differences in energy intake were found overall, but among boys there were marked differences depending on whether or not their parents were in receipt of benefits (7.22 MJ vs 8.27 MJ per day). Mean intakes of protein, total carbohydrate, NMES and fibre were significantly lower for young people from households in the lower income groups and for those from households that were in receipt of benefits than for other young people. No socio-economic differences were found with regard to absolute fat intakes. However, when expressed as a percentage of energy, the diets of boys from a manual home background were richer in *cis* monounsaturated and polyunsaturated fatty acids than those from non-manual backgrounds. For girls, there were no significant differences in fatty acid intakes with income level.

Children in households in receipt of benefits were less likely than other children to eat a number of types of fruit and vegetables, including raw and salad vegetables, citrus fruit and fruit juice (see Fig. 3.4). Although there was a general pattern for children in manual class homes to have poorer mean daily intakes of vitamins than those in non-manual households, there were few statistically significant differences and the majority disappeared when account was taken of differences in energy intake. An exception to this was vitamin C, for which intakes remained markedly lower in both boys and girls of lower social class backgrounds, even after adjustment for energy intake.

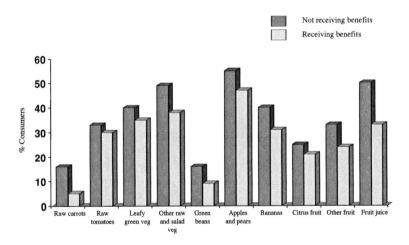

Fig. 3.4. Proportion of boys consuming selected fruit and vegetables during the NDNS survey week

As was found with energy intake, average daily intakes of all minerals (except haem iron) were significantly lower among boys, but not girls, in households receiving benefits compared with other households. Most of these differences were accounted for by differences in energy intake. The exceptions were calcium for boys, and calcium, phosphorus and iodine for girls.

The Government's concern about the need to reduce health inequalities (37) is, therefore, well founded. Strong socio-economic differences in health experiences exist in Britain and there is also evidence of dietary differences when income groups are compared. The need to improve the health of the worst off in society and to narrow the health gap has been clearly identified (38), and discussed in an independent review (39). Many government activities are currently focusing on low-income families; these include the work of the Social Exclusion Unit, which has looked at access to shops selling affordable fruit and vegetables; the National Health Service Plan, which is considering ways of increasing fruit and vegetable consumption among school children; and the cross-departmental working group looking at ways of building the findings of the survey into the activities of the Healthy Schools Programme. There is also ongoing work in Health Action Zones and through Sure Start, which aims to improve access to healthy food.

3.8   Oral Health

In the recent NDNS survey, evidence of dental caries (including active tooth decay and fillings) was present in 53% of 4- to 18-year-olds, 37% of 4- to 6-year-olds, 55% of 7- to 10-year-olds, 51% of 11- to 14-year-olds, and 67% of 15- to 18-year-olds (2). Levels were highest in Scotland (66%) and lowest for those in London and the South East regions (44%). Dental caries experience was significantly higher among young people from manual households, in families in receipt of benefits, or where the mother had no formal educational qualifications. These prevalence rates indicate that the decline in dental caries apparent in the national survey conducted in 1993 has continued. For example, in 5-year-olds in 1983 and 1993, the prevalence rates of active decay or fillings were 59% and 45%, respectively. For 9-year-olds, the respective values were 71% and 61% (40).

The survey found a general trend between the *frequency* of sugar consumption (foods and drinks) and dental caries experience for all age groups, but no significant association emerged between dental caries experience and the total *amount* of sugar-containing foods and drinks or sugar confectionery. There were no consistent trends between intake of non-milk extrinsic sugars and dental caries, and none of the differences were statistically significant, with one exception: 15- to 18-year-olds with the upper range of non-milk extrinsic sugars intake were more likely to have experienced caries than those in the lowest third – 70% compared with 52%.

There was evidence of erosion of the upper incisors or first molars in over half the children examined. Unlike dental caries, this condition is associated with consumption of acidic foods and drinks. Erosion was evident in the first molars of 46% of 4- to 6-year-olds and, for 12% of this age group, the erosion extended to the dentine or dental pulp. Erosion was slightly less likely in the permanent first molars of older children. For example, in 15- to 18-year-olds, the equivalent figures were 34% and 5%, respectively. Unhealthy gums were evident in 35% of 4- to 18-year-olds; increasing from 16% in 4- to 6-year-olds to 44% of 11- to 18-year-olds. Overall, 26% of 4- to 6-year-olds had dental plaque compared with 44% of 7- to 10-year-olds, 51% of 11- to 14-year-olds and 43% of 15- to 18-year-olds. In the oldest age group, boys were significantly more likely to have dental plaque than girls.

There was little variation in the consumption of soft drinks, chocolate or confectionery (the largest contributors to sugar consumption) with social class, despite the difference in dental caries experience, or with family structure. However, those in families in receipt of benefits were more likely to report consumption more than once a day of standard carbonated soft drinks – a difference that peaked in 11- to 14-year-olds. There was evidence of a positive association between higher than average consumption of non-low-calorie carbonated drinks and caries experience in the primary dentition, but this was not evident in the permanent dentition. Frequent consumption of tea or coffee sweetened with sugar was found to be positively associated with dental caries experience for both primary and permanent dentition, although not all differences were significant.

A higher proportion of young people who reported brushing their teeth less often than twice a day had caries experience compared with those who brushed at least twice a day; 62% compared with 48%. This group was also more likely to have unhealthy gums (44%) and dental plaque (52%), compared with 30% and 36%, respectively, for regular brushers.

3.9   What Should be Done to Improve the Health of our Children?

Clearly, in the context of government recommendations, the recent national report (1) has identified several areas of concern about the eating and physical activity habits of young people in this country. Although the reduction in the proportion of energy provided as fat demonstrated by the NDNS is good news, young people in Britain are still getting a disproportionately large amount of their dietary energy from saturated fatty acids and sugar; many are also consuming large amounts of salt (sodium) and far too few fruits and vegetables. Physical inactivity amongst children and adolescents is common. Accumulating evidence suggests that these habits are likely to have detrimental effects on health in both the short and long term.

The need to encourage greater consumption of fruit and vegetables is currently, quite rightly, attracting considerable attention. But it will be clear from the statistics presented earlier (and summarised in Table 3.V) that a number of minerals not present to any great extent in these foods, particularly in fruit, appear to be in short supply in the diets of a large number of young people. Consequently, as well as increasing their intake of fruit and vegetables, many young people could benefit by drinking more semi-skimmed milk (particularly the older girls, who drank very little milk), eating more foods containing bioavailable iron such as lean meat (again particularly the older girls), and eating more 'whole grain' cereals and cereal products. Such modifications would help to ensure that vitamin and mineral needs are met. The importance of breakfast needs to be emphasised, and more thought given to the choice of snacks, which are an important part of most young people's diets, such that nutrient density of the diet is improved with respect to the amounts of vitamins and minerals provided. However, it is important that dietary messages are put into the context of a healthy lifestyle, and that other issues such as smoking, sensible weight control and alcohol consumption are also addressed.

There is clear evidence from the survey to justify the Government's concern about the diets of children living in households where there is relative poverty. In particular, boys in households in receipt of benefits seem to have lower energy intakes and poorer quality diets.

Many individuals and organisations have tried and failed to get healthy eating and healthy living messages across to the public, and young people, particularly teenagers, are a notoriously difficult group to reach. Food manufacturers, retailers, caterers and food policy makers are key in that they can develop and make available products that support the messages and yet are attractive to young people. The media also represent a very influential player and can perform an important role in changing people's attitudes. It is crucial, however, that the information conveyed is balanced and scientifically accurate, and does not serve to encourage the wrong types of behaviour, such as an obsession with body weight. Health professionals also have an important part to play, particularly those who encounter groups of healthy young people in the community. Finally, increasing knowledge and skills regarding food choice and preparation via the school curriculum is likely to go a long way to empowering young people to make healthy choices.

It is crucial that all those who deliver public health messages give clear, evidence-based information. This can best be achieved by the setting of clear policies, by involving young people in the process and by all interested parties working together.

3.10   References

1.   Gregory J., Lowe S., Bates C.J., Prentice A., Jackson L.V., Smithers G., Wenlock R., Farron M. *National Diet and Nutrition Survey: Young People Aged 4 to 18 Years.* Volume 1: Findings. London, The Stationery Office. 2000.

2.   Walker A., Gregory J.R., Bradnock G., Nunn J., White D. *National Diet and Nutrition Survey: Young People Aged 4 to 18 Years.* Volume 2: Report of the Oral Health Survey. London, The Stationery Office. 2000.

3.   Department of Health. *National Health Service Plan.* The Stationery Office, London. 2000.

4.   Wilson N., Quigley R., Mansoor O. Food ads on TV: a health hazard for children? *Australia and New Zealand Journal of Public Health*, 1999, 23, 647-50.

5.   Hill A.J., Oliver S., Rogers P.J. Eating in the adult world: the rise of dieting in childhood and adolescence. *British Journal of Clinical Psychology*, 1992, 31, 95-105.

6.   Department of Health. Report on Health and Social Subjects 36. *The Diets of British Schoolchildren.* London, HMSO. 1989.

7.   Steptoe A., Butler N. Sports participation and emotional wellbeing in adolescents. *Lancet*, 1996, 347, 1789-92.

8.   Chinn S., Rona R.J. Trends in weight-for-height and triceps skinfold thickness for English and Scottish children, 1972-82 and 1982-1990. *Paediatric & Perinatal Epidemiology*, 1994, 8, 90-106.

9.   Whitaker R.D., Wright J.A., Pepe M.S., Seidel K.D., Dietz W.H. Predicting obesity in young adulthood from childhood and parental obesity. *New England Journal of Medicine*, 1997, 337, 869-73.

10.   Must A., Jacques P.F., Dallal E., Bajema C.J., Dietz W.H. Long-term morbidity and mortality of overweight adolescents. *New England Journal of Medicine*, 1992, 327, 1350-5.

11. Csabi G., Torok K., Jeges S., Molnar D. Presence of metabolic cardiovascular syndrome in obese children. *European Journal of Pediatrics*, 2000, 159, 91-4.

12. Freedman D.S., Dietz W.H., Srinivasan S.R., Berenson G.S. The relation of overweight to cardiovascular risk factors among children and adolescents: the Bogalusa Heart Study. *Pediatrics*, 1999, 103, 1175-82.

13. McGill H.C., McMahan C.A., Malcom G.T., Oalmann M.C., Strong J.P. Relation of glycohemoglobin and adiposity to atherosclerosis in youth. *Arteriosclerosis, Thrombosis and Vascular Biology*, 1995, 15, 431-40.

14. Patton G.C., Selzer R., Coffey C., Carlin J.B., Wolfe R. Onset of adolescent eating disorders: population based cohort study over 3 years. *British Medical Journal*, 1999, 318, 765-8.

15. Fox K.R., Riddoch C. Charting the physical activity patterns of contemporary children and adolescents. *Proceedings of the Nutrition Society*, 2000, 59, 497-504.

16. Ministry of Agriculture, Fisheries and Food (MAFF). *National Food Survey 1998*. London, The Stationery Office. 1999.

17. Department of Health. *Dietary Reference Values for Food Energy and Nutrients for the United Kingdom*. Report on Health and Social Subjects 41. HMSO, London. 1991.

18. Department of Health. *Nutritional Aspects of Cardiovascular Disease*. Report on Health and Social Subjects 46. HMSO, London. 1994.

19. Berenson G.S. *Cardiovascular Risk Factors in Childhood*. Oxford, Oxford University Press. 1994.

20. Buttriss J. Nutrient requirements and optimisation of intakes. *British Medical Bulletin*, 2000, 56 (1), 18-33.

21. Gregory J., Foster K., Tyler H., Wiseman M. *The Dietary and Nutritional Survey of British Adults*. London, HMSO. 1990.

22. Ministry of Agriculture, Fisheries and Food (MAFF). *The Dietary and Nutritional Survey of British Adults – Further Analysis*. London, HMSO. 1990.

23. Finch S., Doyle W., Lowe C., Bates C.J., Prentice A., Smithers G., Clarke P.C. *National Diet and Nutrition Survey: People Aged 65 Years and Older*. Volume 1: Report of the Diet and Nutrition Survey. London, The Stationery Office. 1998.

24. Buttriss J. Nutrition in older people – the public health message. *British Nutrition Foundation Nutrition Bulletin*, 1999, 24 (1), 48-57.

25. Block G., Patterson B., Subar A. Fruit, vegetables and cancer prevention: a review of the epidemiological evidence. *Nutrition and Cancer*, 1992, 18, 1-29.

26. Weaver C.M. The growing years and prevention of osteoporosis in later life. *Proceedings of the Nutrition Society*, 2000, 59, 303-6.

27 Pollitt E. *Malnutrition and Infection in the Classroom*. Paris. UNESCO. 1990.

28. Bruner A.B., Joffe A., Duggan A.K., Casella J.F. Randomised study of cognitive effects of iron supplementation in non-anaemic iron deficient adolescent girls. *Lancet*, 1996, 348, 992-6.

29. Nelson M. Childhood nutrition and poverty. *Proceedings of the Nutrition Society*, 2000, 59, 307-15.

30. Nelson M.J., Ragland D.R., Sume L.S. Longitudinal prediction of adult blood pressure from juvenile blood pressure levels. *American Journal of Epidemiology*, 1992, 136, 633-45.

31. McCarron P., Davey Smith G., Okasha M., McEwen J. Blood pressure in young adulthood and mortality from cardiovascular disease. *Lancet*, 2000, 355, 1430-1.

32. The Social Exclusion Unit. *Teenage Pregnancy*. London, The Stationery Office. 1999.

33. Barker D.J. Maternal nutrition, fetal nutrition and disease in later life. *Nutrition*, 1997, 13, 807-13.

34. Scholl T.O., Hediger M.L., Fischer R.L., Shearer J.W. Anemia vs iron deficiency: increased risk of preterm delivery in a prospective study. *American Journal of Clinical Nutrition*, 1992, 55, 985-8.

35. Godfrey K.M., Redman C.W., Barker D.J., Osmond C. The effect of maternal anaemia and iron deficiency on the ratio of fetal weight to placental weight. *British Journal of Obstetrics and Gynaecology*, 1991, 98, 886-91.

36. Department of Health. *Folic Acid and the Prevention of Disease*. Report on Health and Social Subjects 50. The Stationery Office, London. 2000.

37. Department of Health. *Saving Lives: Our Healthier Nation*. London, Department of Health. 1999.

38. Department of Health. *Our Healthier Nation: a Contract for Health*. London, The Stationery Office. 1998.

39. Acheson D. *Independent Inquiry into Inequalities in Health*. London. The Stationery Office. 1998.

40. O'Brien M. *Children's dental health in the United Kingdom* 1993. London. HMSO. 1994.

41. Smithers G., Gregory J.R., Bates C.J., Prentice A., Jackson L.V., Wenlock R. The National Diet and Nutrition Survey: young people aged 4-18 years. *British Nutrition Foundation Nutrition Bulletin*, 2000, 25 (2), 105-111.

4. NUTRITION IN PREGNANCY AND LACTATION

Gail Goldberg

4.1   Introduction

Maternal nutritional status and nutrient intake during pregnancy and lactation can have profound effects at all stages of life for both the mother and her infant. The better a pregnant woman's state of health and nutrition, the greater the likelihood of a successful outcome to her pregnancy for her and her baby. A woman's nutritional status (and that of her partner) can affect whether or not she conceives, has a major bearing on whether or not her pregnancy has a healthy course and outcome, and also to some extent determines her postpartum nutrient status (e.g. for lactation). In turn, these factors can affect both her short- and longer-term health. A mother's nutritional health is also of course very important for the health of the baby during pregnancy and early infancy. Furthermore, there is an increasing body of evidence to suggest that adverse *in utero* conditions, including the nutrient environment, may have consequences for the baby that might not become apparent until he/she reaches middle or old age.

A gross comparison of maternal health in developed and developing countries indicates major differences and issues of concern. For example, in the UK now, chronic undernutrition with respect to energy, macronutrients and micronutrients, and its consequences are relatively uncommon in women of childbearing age, while the situation remains very different in many developing countries. However, many nutritional matters associated with pregnancy and lactation are common to all women regardless of where they are in the world, because they are determined mainly by socio-economic and cultural factors, not directly by physiology. So, whilst the magnitude of a given problem (e.g. low-birthweight infants, iron-deficiency anaemia, teenage pregnancy) may be very different depending on where in the world a women lives, the basic issues are the same. This chapter summarises the main topics related to maternal nutrition in countries such as the UK. Prenatal care in the UK aims to provide advice and education about a healthy balanced diet, avoiding foodborne infection, smoking, alcohol intake, and taking peri-conceptual folic acid to reduce the risk of neural tube defects (NTDs) such as spina bifida. The health professionals that women see before, during and after pregnancy rarely include a dietitian unless there are pre-existing or recently diagnosed conditions such as diabetes, hypertension or thyroid disorders.

4.2   Pre-pregnancy Nutrition

4.2.1   Body weight

It is well recognised that, during periods of low food intake (famine being an extreme example), the fecundity of both males and females is reduced. This seems to be nature's way of preventing reproduction (i.e. conception) in uncertain nutritional circumstances. Women at both extremes of body weight, including those with a history of eating disorders, recent dieting experience and those who are highly trained athletes, often experience irregularities in menstrual cycles and have a tendency towards anovulatory cycles, and thus often take longer to conceive. There are also many women who habitually maintain a low body weight by restraining their food intake, and for such individuals the profound changes in body weight and shape that occur during pregnancy may be a particular concern. Weight gain and nutrient intake may be compromised, or conversely weight gains may be excessive as women lose their restraint (1-3).

The prevalence of overweight and obesity has almost trebled in the UK over the last 20 years, and is still increasing. Data from the 1998 Health Survey for England indicate that women aged 25-34 have an average BMI of 25.5, and 45% of this age group are overweight or obese (4). Dieting is not recommended during pregnancy, so overweight and obese women should attempt to lose excess weight before trying to conceive. Being overweight or obese or underweight prior to pregnancy is associated with a greater risk of complications (see Table 4.I). Because of the increasing prevalence of obesity in the UK and elsewhere, the rates and consequences of the complications listed in Table 4.I are also likely to increase. Furthermore, the problems are not confined to serious obesity; complications increase as pre-pregnant BMI increases (5) (see Fig. 4.1).

TABLE 4.I
Conditions that are more likely to occur as a result of being obese or underweight prior to and during pregnancy

Obesity

Fertility problems
Increased risk of gestational diabetes, pregnancy-induced hypertension and pre-eclampsia (38)
Increased risk of foetal macrosomia (38)
Increased risk of abnormal labour (38)
Increased risk of emergency Caesarean section (38)
Increased risk of congenital defects (39)
Decreased viability of pre-term infants (40)
Risk of subsequent disorders of glucose metabolism (33)
Risk of subsequent hypertensive and renal disorders (34)

Underweight

Fertility problems (41)
Increased risk of low birthweight (8,42)
Increased risk of infant morbidity and mortality (10)
Degenerative disease in adulthood

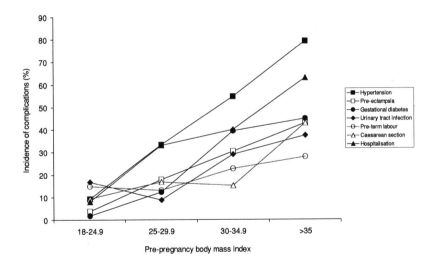

Fig. 4.1. Increased incidence of complications during pregnancy as pre-pregnancy BMI increases. Data taken from (5)

4.2.2   Folic acid

The importance of folic acid pre- and peri-conceptually – at a time before many women realise that they are pregnant, is now very well established. The definitive study was a randomised double-blind prevention trial, which established a specific role of folic acid in the prevention of NTD. This was conducted by the Medical Research Council in 33 centres in seven countries (6). Four groups of women at a high risk of having an NTD-affected pregnancy were studied. The groups were given either folic acid, seven other B vitamins, both folic acid and other B vitamins, or placebo. After more than 1,800 women had entered the trial, the results were sufficiently conclusive for the code to be broken and the trial stopped. Folic acid had a 72% protective effect; the other vitamins had no effect on the incidence on NTD-affected pregnancies.

The recent COMA report on folic acid and health (7) endorsed the prevailing advice that folic acid supplementation of the diets of women of childbearing age could reduce the risk of the occurrence or re-occurrence of NTD in their offspring. Current advice in the UK is that all women of childbearing age who may become pregnant or who are planning a pregnancy should take a 400 μg daily supplement of folic acid (the manufactured form of folate), in addition to their usual dietary intake (about 200 μg/day in women of childbearing age). For women who have already had an NTD-affected pregnancy, the advice is that they should take 5 mg folic acid per day.

Natural folates are less bioavailable than the synthetic form, folic acid – hence the emphasis on the latter. It is also difficult to achieve the extra folate intake needed through foods that are naturally good sources (e.g. green vegetables and oranges) alone (8). Therefore, fortified foods such as some breakfast cereals and bread (as well as folic acid supplements) are an increasingly important source. The folic acid campaign begun in 1995 by the Health Education Authority means that many women are now familiar with the need to increase folic acid prior to and during early pregnancy. However, many pregnancies are unplanned, and, because of the potential public health benefit of ensuring that all women of childbearing years have increased intakes of folate, the question of statutory fortification of flour in the UK is currently under consultation. A level of 240 μg per 100 g in food products as consumed has been estimated to reduce the risk of an NTD-affected pregnancy by 41% without resulting in unacceptably high intakes in any other group of the population (7).

4.2.3   Alcohol

Alcohol has been shown to adversely affect the ovum by influencing the rate of conception and viability of conception. The Department of Health advises that, to minimise the risk to the unborn child, women who are trying to become pregnant should not drink more than 1 or 2 units of alcohol once or twice a week, and should avoid heavy drinking sessions. It is of particular concern that, in general, alcohol intake in young women is increasing, and that the frequency of binge drinking in women is also on the increase in the UK. Thus many women may be drinking regularly and heavily before they are aware they are pregnant. It should also be noted that folate absorption and utilisation are compromised by alcohol.

4.2.4   Faddy diets

One of the worst times for a woman to start excluding nutrient-rich foods, such as milk or bread, from her diet is when she is planning to conceive. Inappropriate and unnecessary exclusion of foods could prevent her and the developing foetus from obtaining the nutrition they both need. So, for example, if food intolerance is suspected, self-diagnosis must be discouraged and the individual referred to an appropriate specialist or a State Registered Dietitian. The use of multivitamins and mega-doses of supplements should also be looked at with caution (see below).

4.3   Nutrition during Pregnancy

4.3.1   Body weight and weight gains

There are many interrelationships between pregnancy and body weight (Table 4.II). Gestational weight gain is a very important determinant of birthweight (9) and extremes of weight gain pose risks of various complications during and after pregnancy. In turn, weight gain is an important component of the overall energy costs and therefore the extra energy requirement of pregnancy.

A total gestational weight gain of 12.5 kg has been shown to be associated with least risk of complications during pregnancy (such as gestational diabetes, pregnancy-induced hypertension, complications during labour) and less risk of having low-birthweight infants, with their consequent problems of morbidity and mortality. However, this figure can only be a rough guide for an average woman.

One woman's weight gain may be 'all baby', whereas another will start to put on weight rapidly and progressively throughout gestation. Anecdotally, individual women report successive pregnancies as being very different. Data from groups of well-nourished women, of normal pre-pregnant BMI, with uncomplicated pregnancies resulting in normal-birthweight babies indicate that mean total gestational weight gains in Europe, North America and Australia are between 11 and 16 kg. The variability in gestational weight gain is very large, indicated by standard deviations that are typically 3-4 kg, and in those studies that have reported ranges, the greatest increments ranged from 18 to 33 kg. There are currently no official weight gain recommendations in the UK. In the USA, different recommendations apply according to pre-pregnancy BMI, ethnic background and age (10).

TABLE 4.II
Conditions that are more likely to occur as a result of extremes of weight gains during pregnancy

Excessive weight gain	Inadequate weight gain
Increased risk of gestational diabetes, pregnancy-induced hypertension and pre-eclampsia	Increased risk of low birthweight Increased risk of infant morbidity and mortality
Increased risk of foetal macrosomia	Effect of energy-sparing adaptations
Increased risk of abnormal labour	Degenerative disease in adulthood
Increased risk of emergency Caesarean section	
Risk of overweight or obesity post-partum	
Risk of Type 2 diabetes post-partum	

Low or inadequate gestational weight gains are a direct cause of low-birthweight (<2,500 g) infants who are small for gestational age, and this in turn leads to increased infant mortality and morbidity (11). In the UK, only about 7% of infants are low-birthweight (LBW), and the most usual cause is prematurity. This is in marked contrast to global figures, which show that worldwide about 16% of babies are LBW. Rates in individual countries may be as high as 50%. The vast majority of LBW infants are not premature but have intrauterine growth retardation, a major direct cause of which is nutritional, particularly low weight gains in the mother. LBW is a major factor in the deaths each year of 4 million infants worldwide in their first month of life, and in illnesses that affect many more (11).

68

4.3.2   Energy costs of pregnancy

The extra energy costs of human pregnancy, what they are, and how they are met affect both mother and infant during and after gestation and have important public health, clinical and dietetic implications. The additional energy costs of pregnancy result from the need to deposit energy in the form of new tissue (foetus, placenta, amniotic fluid), and hypertrophy of existing maternal tissues (e.g. breast, uterus); an increased energy requirement for tissue synthesis; increased oxygen consumption by maternal organs, and, particularly in later pregnancy, the energy needs of the products of conception; and extra maternal fat deposition. Because of the increased body mass, weight-bearing activities will also require more energy. The energy costs of pregnancy based on theoretical calculations and data from cross-sectional studies have been estimated to be about 335 MJ or 80,000 calories (equivalent to 1.2 MJ/day over 280 days) (12). A breakdown of the costs of a healthy term pregnancy is shown in Table 4.III.

TABLE 4.III
Theoretical metabolic energy costs of pregnancy for maternal weight gain of 12.5 kg, birthweight of 3.3 kg, maternal fat deposition of 3.5 kg

Requirements	MJ
Tissue deposited as foetus, placenta, amniotic fluid	45
Extra maternal tissues (uterus, mammary gland, blood)	
Maternal fat	140
Increased energy requirement for tissue synthesis	150
Increased oxygen consumption by maternal organs	
Energy needs of the products of conception	
Total	335

Women can meet these costs by adopting one or more strategies. They can increase their energy intake, become more efficient in their energy metabolism, utilise energy stored in body fat, and save energy by being more sedentary. It is notable that currently no recommendations include any allowance for the extra energy cost of weight-bearing activities due to increased body weight. Expert committees have issued conditional figures for energy intakes based on the assumption that changes in maternal behaviour result in a decrease in the energy expended on physical activity. Thus it is considered unnecessary to increase energy intake by as much as 335 MJ.

The current energy requirements for pregnancy and lactation used by the WHO (12) are currently under review (13). There are now a number of longitudinal studies that have measured the components of energy requirements, in both developing and developed countries. It has been recommended that, in line with all other groups of adults, the energy requirements of pregnant women be (partly) based on multiples of basal metabolic rate (i.e. physical activity levels) to take account of differences in physical activity. It has also been recommended that the requirements listed in Table 4.III for optimal outcomes should be defined separately (by fixed increments for each trimester) and be the same for all women. This would in effect remove the assumption that women will exhibit energy-sparing alterations in metabolism or that this is desirable.

Whilst a reduction in physical activity is a way of saving energy, in general the women most likely to be able to do this are affluent, already have labour-saving devices, do not have to work physically hard for a living, and may have help with childcare and running a home. In general, but not necessarily, such women are more likely to live in developed countries such as the UK, where already very sedentary lifestyles restrict the potential for reducing physical activity still further. However, it should not automatically be assumed that such women do become less active. Many do not change their lifestyles, so even doing the same things will cost more energy (because of increased body weight and tissue mass). Some women actually become more active because, for example, they go on maternity leave from a sedentary job and spend their time being more active. Significant reductions in physical activity are more plausible in women whose habitual levels are very high. However, in general, such women are more likely to live in developing countries where subsistence lifestyles oblige them to maintain high levels of energy expenditure.

Results from longitudinal studies conducted in developed countries show that the average energy costs of pregnancy are very similar to theoretical requirements and recommendations. However, the variability in the components of these total costs (metabolic rate, fat deposition, physical activity), and therefore in the overall costs is very variable (13). An indication of the individual variability of the components of the energy costs of pregnancy, and the total costs, and how these compare with estimated or assumed costs are shown in Figs 4.2, 4.3 and 4.4 using longitudinal data from studies conducted in England (14) and the USA (15). How a woman may change metabolically, physiologically or behaviourally cannot be predicted for any given pregnancy. These and other data demonstrate that, for individuals (in contrast to populations), the best way at present is to monitor weight gain and foetal growth. If these increases are considered to be appropriate, then it is likely that the woman's energy intake is sufficient for her given lifestyle. In turn, energy intake is often used as a proxy measure and an indication of the adequacy of the overall diet.

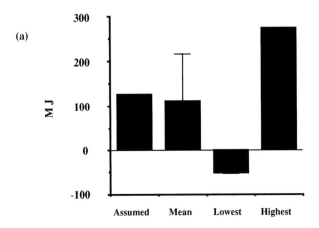

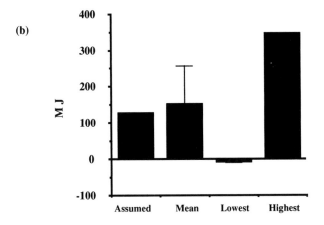

Fig. 4.2. Cumulative changes in BMR during pregnancy.
Data taken from (12,14,15)

(a)

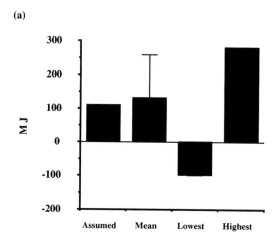

(b)

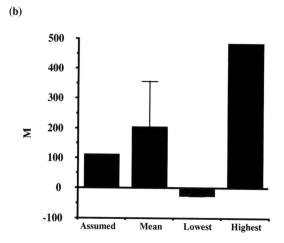

Fig. 4.3. Cumulative changes in maternal fat during pregnancy. Error bars are SD. Data taken from (11,13,14)

(a)

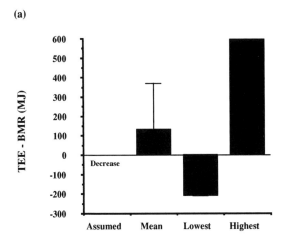

(b)

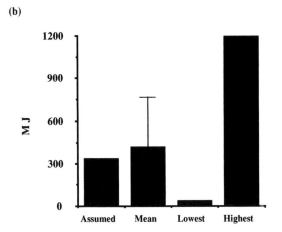

Fig. 4.4. Cumulative changes in energy expended on physical activity during pregnancy and total energy costs of pregnancy (sum of BMR, fat and physical activity +45 MJ for products of conception). Data taken from (14)

4.3.3   Food and nutrient intake

Whilst a pregnant women does not literally have to 'eat for two' with respect to quantity, she does have to consume a nutrient-rich diet. The developing foetus obtains all its nutrients from the mother via the placenta, so dietary intake has to be sufficient to meet not only maternal needs but also those of the products of conception (foetus and placenta). With a few exceptions, the guidelines for healthy eating are much the same for pregnant as for non-pregnant women. These include eating a wide variety of foods, including at least five portions of fruit and vegetables a day; plenty of starchy foods such as bread, pasta, rice, breakfast cereals and potatoes; milk and dairy milk products for calcium; lean meat and/or alternatives such as fish, chicken, eggs or pulses; and only small amounts of foods that are high in fat and in sugar.

There are no nationally collected datasets of dietary intakes of pregnant and lactating women in the UK. The data from Dietary and Nutritional Survey of British Adults (16) are now rather old, and data for the National Diet and Nutrition Survey (NDNS) of adults aged 18-64 are currently being collected. These should be very valuable in determining the dietary and nutritional status of women of childbearing age in the UK. However, the recent NDNS survey of young people aged 4-18 years (see chapter 3) gives some important insights into the diet and health status of teenage girls, and these are likely to be particularly relevant in teenage pregnancy.

Data obtained from food frequency questionnaires at 32 weeks' gestation from nearly 12,000 women participating in the Avon Longitudinal Study of Pregnancy and Childhood (ALSPAC) have indicated that, on the whole, nutrient intakes compared well with the Dietary and Nutrition Survey of British Adults. This suggested to the authors that the diets of pregnant women in the UK are likely to be adequate except for iron, potassium, magnesium and folate (17). Other studies, by Doyle and her colleagues, have highlighted important differences in nutrient intakes and pregnancy outcome between affluent and deprived women in the UK (18-20).

The COMA panels in the UK have set specific reference nutrient intakes for some nutrients for pregnant women. These are shown in Table 4.IV. For these and many other nutrients, it is assumed that intakes will automatically increase to required levels because of overall increases in food and energy intake. It is considered that extra calcium and iron intake is not required during pregnancy because it is assumed that changes in metabolism lead to more efficient utilisation and uptake from the diet. So, provided the woman's intake is in line with general recommendations, an increase in dietary supply is not considered necessary.

Table 4.IV
Specific Reference Nutrient Intakes (Rnis) for pregnancy where they exist (7,21,22)
(amounts are in addition to RNIs for non-pregnant women)

Nutrient	RNI	Comment
Energy*	+0.80 MJ/day	Last trimester only
Protein	+ 6 g/day	Throughout pregnancy
Thiamin	+0.1 mg/day	Last trimester only
Riboflavin	+0.3 mg/day	
Folate	+100 µg/day	+400 in first trimester
Vitamin C	+10 mg/day	
Vitamin A	+100 µg/day	
Vitamin D	10 µg/day	

* Estimated Average Requirement, not RNI

4.3.4   Folic acid

The importance of pre-conceptual folic acid has been discussed above. Current recommendations are that supplementation should continue throughout the first trimester. Even if folic acid has not been taken pre-conceptually, supplementation should start as soon as a women knows or suspects that she might be pregnant.

4.3.5   Iron

More iron is required during pregnancy to supply the growing foetus, the placenta and the increased number of maternal red blood cells. However, it is assumed that these extra demands (about a three-fold increase) can be met without the need to increase RNI because menstrual losses cease, maternal stores are mobilised and intestinal absorption is increased. However the COMA report recognises that, when iron stores are inappropriately low at the start of pregnancy, supplementation may be necessary. A large proportion (perhaps as many as 50%) of women of childbearing age have low iron stores, and this puts them at increased risk of anaemia should they become pregnant. It is clear from the national surveys of adults (aged 16-64) and of young people (aged 4-18, see chapter 3) that the iron intake and iron status of women of childbearing years in the UK are low because insufficient iron-rich foods are consumed by many women and young girls. Potentially, therefore, they are more likely to become iron-deficient/anaemic during pregnancy. In practice, many women are prescribed iron supplements at some stage during pregnancy, even though iron deficiency and anaemia are difficult to ascertain. Iron-deficiency anaemia affects 70% of women worldwide, and is responsible for about 20% of maternal deaths (estimated to be more than 500,000 per year in total) (11).

4.3.6   Calcium

Active transport mechanisms in the placenta enable levels of foetal plasma calcium to be maintained at higher levels than in the maternal circulation. The placenta can also synthesise $1,25(OH)_2$ vitamin D. These increases in the efficiency of absorption of dietary calcium allow a woman to meet the increased calcium requirements of pregnancy by adaptation without the need for a dietary increment. An exception to this would be teenage girls who become pregnant, as they are still developing their own skeleton. The RNI for calcium for teenage girls is 800 mg/day rather than 700 mg for older women. Worldwide obstructed labour due to stunting in childhood and adolescence is a major cause of maternal morbidity and mortality (11).

4.3.7   Vitamin D

There is no RNI for adults under 75 years of age in the UK. Most vitamin D is synthesised in the skin by a reaction with ultraviolet light. Some vitamin D is naturally available from food, e.g. oil-rich fish, eggs and meat, and it is added by law to margarine. It is also added voluntarily to low-fat spreads and breakfast cereals. The mother provides a store of vitamin D to her foetus during pregnancy. So, in order to meet the demand, pregnant women should be well provided with vitamin D themselves. The COMA report considered that the majority of pregnant women appeared to have no difficulty in maintaining their own vitamin D status satisfactorily as well as providing for their foetus. However a substantial minority are vulnerable to deficiency because of the season of the year, latitude of abode, skin pigmentation and dietary and other cultural habits. During pregnancy, as a prudent approach, it is recommended that all women should receive supplementary vitamin D to achieve an intake of 10 µg/day. This may be particularly important for women who receive little sunlight exposure and also for

76

vegetarians, and particularly vegans, who eat a much narrower range of vitamin D containing foods.

4.3.8   Supplements

With the exception of folate, iron, vitamin D and vitamin A , the advice with respect to supplements is the same as for non-pregnant women. A wide variety of food and drinks consumed as part of an overall healthy balanced diet should provide all the nutrients in sufficient amounts. If individuals consider that their diets are not as good as they should be, then multivitamin supplements are best because they are more likely to provide nutrients in balanced amounts, and hence avoid possible overdose and adverse interactions between nutrients. There are a number of specially formulated supplements for pre-pregnant and pregnant women. The use of supplements does present a paradox because, whilst women want to be in optimal health with respect to nutritional status, they are rightly cautious about taking any form of 'medication' during pregnancy. The advice of health professionals in this respect is therefore especially important. Overall, the majority of pregnant women in countries such as the UK are unlikely to be deficient in nutrients (except folate and iron) during pregnancy. However, there are vulnerable groups who require closer attention. These include teenage girls and women of lower socio-economic groups (18). The Welfare Food Scheme, which has been in existence in the UK for over 60 years, and which focuses on the needs of mothers and children, is currently under review by the Scientific Advisory Committee for Nutrition (formerly COMA).

4.4   Foods to Restrict or Avoid during Pregnancy

4.4.1   Alcohol

In the UK, current advice for non-pregnant women is that they should not consume more than 14-21 units of alcohol during the course of a week, or more than 2-3 units a day. Alcohol is teratogenic (causes birth defects), and high levels of intake, and especially binge drinking, are associated with birth defects, low birthweight, and, at very high intakes, foetal alcohol syndrome (23). Current evidence is not consistent in showing a clear-cut relationship between adverse effects in pregnancy and lower levels of maternal consumption (23). Part of the problem is the definition of moderate, light and excess intakes both between and within countries and populations. There is some evidence of a threshold of drinking below which adverse effects cannot be detected. The Department of Health advises that, to minimise the risk to the unborn child, women who are at any stage of pregnancy should not drink more than 1 or 2 units of alcohol once or twice a week, and should avoid heavy drinking sessions. It should also be noted that folate absorption and utilisation are compromised by alcohol. In practice, many women develop a spontaneous aversion to the taste and smell of alcoholic beverages in early pregnancy.

4.4.2   Vitamin A

High intakes of vitamin A can be teratogenic. Because vitamin A deficiency is not a problem in the UK, the Department of Health advises that pregnant women should avoid consuming foods that contain very high concentrations of vitamin A (such as liver and liver pâté) and supplements that contain vitamin A. The situation is very different in many parts of the world, where vitamin A deficiency is endemic. Hypovitaminosis A suppresses immune function, increases morbidity and mortality and increases mother-child transmission of HIV-1.

4.4.3   Foodborne diseases

The advice from the Department of Health has been for many years now that pregnant women should avoid eating dishes containing raw egg, and cheeses made from unpasteurised milk. This is because of the risk of salmonellosis and listeriosis, respectively – both conditions that can be particularly serious for pregnant women. Listeriosis is a rare flu-like illness caused by the bacterium *Listeria monocytogenes*. Listeriosis in pregnancy may cause miscarriage, still-birth or severe illness in the newborn baby. Consequently, pregnant women are advised to avoid those foods where high levels of the bacteria have occasionally been found, including all types of pâté, and soft and blue-veined varieties of cheese such as Brie, Camembert and Stilton.

Poultry and eggs are foods particularly associated with *Salmonella* bacteria. *Salmonella* poisoning is not likely to have a direct adverse effect on the baby. However, as a precaution, pregnant women should avoid eating raw eggs or food that contains eggs that are raw or partially cooked. Raw meat and chicken can also be a source of *Salmonella* bacteria. All meat, especially poultry, should be thoroughly cooked. It is also advised that pregnant women wash fruit and vegetables well, especially if they are to be eaten raw.

4.4.4   Caffeine

Consumption of caffeinated beverages has been associated with reduced fertility, defects in foetal development, and miscarriage (10). However, there are a number of difficulties in generally interpreting the data, particularly when caffeine consumption is confounded by alcohol intakes, smoking and substance abuse. The effect of caffeine-containing foods and drinks *per se* (i.e. coffee, tea, colas and chocolate) is thus very difficult to assess. The Committee on Toxicity of Chemicals in Food, Consumer Products and the Environment (COT) in the UK has very recently reviewed the evidence on the reproductive effects of caffeine. As a result The Food Standards Agency in the UK now recommends that caffeine intake is limited to 300 mg per day. As with alcohol, many pregnant women spontaneously go off tea and coffee.

4.4.5   Maternal avoidance of specific foods to prevent allergies in the infant

There have been suggestions that maternal avoidance (during pregnancy and lactation) of potentially allergenic foods could help to prevent allergy in infants. Infants whose parents have a history of allergic disease are more likely to go on to develop allergy themselves. It has been suggested that sensitisation to foreign proteins that cross the placenta (or reach the infant via breast milk) may occur in such babies. On the other hand, exposure to a range of potential allergens, during foetal life and infancy, enables the baby to develop normal tolerance to the many foreign proteins in the environment. Where there is a family history of atopic disease, maternal avoidance of specific foods, particularly during breast feeding, may be advised. In theory, sensitisation to a food protein may occur pre- or post-natally, although the evidence that pre-natal exposure leads to subsequent development of allergic disease is tenuous. Unless there is a strong family history of allergic disease, at present there is no convincing evidence that maternal food avoidance during pregnancy is protective against childhood allergy, even in high-risk infants. Furthermore, it has been suggested that such avoidance results in significantly reduced gestational weight gain and a tendency towards lower birthweights. Because of the potential risks to the baby associated with restrictive diets that may effectively limit supply of essential nutrients, it is recommended that avoidance of foods known to cause allergy (e.g. milk and milk products, or egg) should be practised under medical supervision and only where there is a major risk because of a strong family history (24).

Allergy to peanuts seems to be on the increase and is a cause for concern because allergy to peanut protein can cause anaphylaxis. A recent DEFRA review found inconclusive relationships between peanut consumption by pregnant (and breast feeding) women and the incidence of peanut allergy in their offspring. The report recommends that pregnant women who are atopic (or whose partner or any sibling of the unborn child has an atopic disease) may wish to avoid eating peanut and peanut products during pregnancy.

4.4.6   Other nutritional issues during pregnancy

Nausea and vomiting (especially in early pregnancy) affect about 70% of pregnant women, but only in a very few (2%) women is the condition severe enough (hyperemesis gravidarum) for medical intervention. The causes of nausea and vomiting are unknown. Other problems often faced by pregnant women include indigestion, heartburn and intestinal discomfort (especially in later pregnancy when the baby takes up more space and displaces or squashes internal organs). Individual women often learn by experience which foods to avoid or actively choose to prevent or alleviate these problems, which are often transient. Although many women often avoid preparing or cooking specific foods, they are still able to eat them. Thus there are unlikely to be major nutritional problems as a result, unless of course there is prolonged avoidance of foods that are a major source of important nutrients, such as calcium in dairy products, or iron in meat.

Many women also experience food cravings and food aversions – powerful urges to consume or avoid particular foods – during pregnancy. Again, their cause and purpose is unknown (3,25). They are unlikely to have an adverse effect, and so are not a cause for concern, provided that the overall diet consumed is nutritionally balanced. Dairy and sweet foods are most commonly reported as being craved and the most common aversions are to alcohol, caffeinated drinks and meats. Therefore, in general, most food cravings cause an increase in calcium and energy intake, whereas food aversions cause a decrease in intakes of alcohol, caffeine and animal protein.

4.5   Teenage Pregnancy

Adolescent pregnancy presents many nutritional concerns in both developed and developing countries. The world average is about 65 per 1,000 births, with rates in some sub-Saharan African countries of over 200 and in east/south Asia and Pacific, and Latin America of over 100. In England, the rate is about 25 per 1,000; each year more than 56,000 babies are born to teenage girls; 87,000 children have a teenage mother and 4% of adult men and 13% of adult women report having a child before the age of 20. Rates of teenage pregnancy in the UK are the highest in Europe, and are still on the increase, whilst rates have been falling in many other countries (26).

In countries such as the UK, teenage pregnancies are mostly unplanned and unwanted and are a cause and a consequence of social exclusion. Nutrition-related problems include restriction of weight gain (because of fear of discovery or body image concerns); late presentation for antenatal care (because of fear or ignorance); high rates of smoking and alcohol consumption; less likelihood of peri-conceptual folic acid; and concerns highlighted by the NDNS of young people (27).

In general, compared with women in their 20s and 30s, many studies conducted worldwide have shown that pregnant adolescents have lower gestational weight gains, more LBW infants, increased risk of pregnancy-induced hypertension, pre-term labour, iron-deficiency anaemia, complications during labour, and maternal mortality. However, many studies (conducted in developed countries) have not controlled for parity, pre-pregnant weight for height, length of gestation, ethnic origin, alcohol and tobacco intake. The effect of age *per se* as an independent determinant of intrauterine growth and duration of gestation is still controversial. The negative outcomes are reported to be more directly related to ethnicity, martial status, education level, pre-natal care, and alcohol and tobacco intake than to age.

There are, however, concerns about the potential competition for nutrients and whether teenage girls continue to grow during pregnancy. This is because the increased nutritional requirements for the adolescent growth spurt occur simultaneously with the additional nutritional requirements of pregnancy. There is potential competition for available nutrients between the still-growing mother and the developing foetus and placenta. For the same weight gain, teenage mothers have lower-birthweight infants, so, to derive a greater benefit, gestational weight gains need to be higher. This is taken into account in the recommendations for gestational weight gain used in the USA (10).

81

Several studies indicate no significant differences in foetal growth in adolescents once differences in gestational weight gain, pre-pregnant weight and other confounders have been controlled for. The research findings are not unanimous, but they undermine the notion of a competition between the adolescent's own requirements for growth and those of her foetus (10).

Studies of growing and non-growing pregnant teenagers and mature controls have found that growing girls continued to accrue fat and had higher weight gains, but had significantly lower-birthweight babies. Non-growing and mature subjects lost fat in late pregnancy, suggesting that fat stores are not mobilised to enhance foetal growth, but to support maternal growth. With respect to higher rates of LBW infants, lower gestational weight gains, pregnancy-induced hypertension (PIH), anaemia and pre-term labour are all risk factors. Results from cord blood and Doppler ultrasound studies suggest that there is a reduced flow of nutrients to the foetus because of immature placental development (28,29).

Folate intake is a particular concern with respect to teenage pregnancy. In general, those least likely to take folic acid supplements are most likely to have an unplanned pregnancy; 75% of teenage pregnancies are unplanned. Despite the HEA campaign in the UK, it has been found that only 8-15% of 16- to 19-year-olds were aware of the importance of peri-conceptual folic acid. Added to this is the problem that first trimester supplementation is less likely because girls often present late for antenatal care and advice.

Nutrient intake in adolescents in the UK is discussed in detail in chapter 3. The NDNS highlighted problems and concerns of some nutrients that are particularly important in pregnancy (see Tables 4.V and 4.VI).

TABLE 4.V
Per cent of teenage girls with nutrient intakes below the Lower Reference Nutrient Intake
(LRNI)*
(data taken from the NDNS of young people aged 4-18 (27))

Nutrient	% Girls aged 11-14 years	% Girls aged 15-18 years
Vitamin A	20	12
Riboflavin	22	21
Folate	3	4
Zinc	37	10
Iron	45	50
Calcium	24	19

* This value is considered to be adequate for only 2.5% of the population who have low requirements. Therefore, in a nationally representative survey, up to 3% of the sample may be expected to have values equal to this.

TABLE 4.VI
Per cent of teenage girls with poor nutrient status
(data taken from the NDNS of young people aged 4-18 (27))

Parameter	% Girls aged 11-14 years	% Girls aged 15-18 years
Haemoglobin (<12 g/dl)	4	9
Ferritin (<15 g/l)	14	27
Vitamin D (<25 nmol/l)	11	10
Red cell folate (<350 nmol/l)	11	14
(<425 nmol/l)	28	39
Serum folate (<6.3 nmol/l)	1	1
(<10 nmol/l)	6	14

4.6   Post-partum Nutrition and Nutritional Status

4.6.1   Lactation

On a daily basis, lactation is much more nutritionally demanding than pregnancy. However, lactation seems to be a more robust process with respect to nutritional status. Despite very different nutritional circumstances, comparison of data from developed and developing countries show a remarkable consistency in milk quantity and quality (30). This is in marked contrast to the nutritional influences on pregnancy (13,31).

The energy requirements for lactation are partly dependent upon whether fat is deposited during pregnancy. In addition to assumptions about physical activity, it is assumed that, if body fat is deposited, it is mobilised to support lactation. So women who do not deposit fat or who have to mobilise it during pregnancy begin lactation with reduced energy reserves. This should not pose a problem for those who are able to increase food intake or reduce physical activity.

The additional energy costs of lactation result from the energy requirement for milk synthesis, and because energy is exported as the macronutrients, protein, fat and carbohydrate. The daily energy costs of lactation have been estimated to be about 2.9 MJ or 700 calories (12). A breakdown of the energy costs is shown in Table 4.VII. Micronutrients are also exported in breast milk, and the Reference Nutrient Intakes for lactation reflect these daily losses (see Table 4.VIII).

TABLE 4.VII
Estimated daily energy costs of lactation

Requirement	MJ
Milk synthesis	0.5
Proximal constituents in milk	2.4
Total	2.9

Assumes *800 g milk/day; 1.2 g protein, 4.0 g fat, 7.0 g lactose per 100 g.

TABLE 4.VIII
Specific Reference Nutrient Intakes (RNIs) for lactation where they exist (21)
(amounts are in addition to RNI for non-pregnant women)

Nutrient	RNI	Comment
Energy*	+1.9-2.4 MJ/day	Depending on stage of lactation
Protein	+ 11 g/day	0-4 months
	+8 g/day	4+ months
Thiamin	+0.2 mg/day	
Riboflavin	+0.5 mg/day	
B12	+0.5 µg/day	
Folate	+60 µg/day	
Vitamin C	+30 mg/day	
Vitamin A	+350 µg/day	
Vitamin D	+10 µg/day	
Calcium	+550 mg/day	
Phosphorus	+440 mg/day	
Magnesium	+50 mg/day	
Zinc	+6 mg/day	0-4 months
	+2.5 mg/day	4+ months
Copper	+0.3 mg/day	
Selenium	+15 mg/day	

* Estimated Average Requirement, not RNI

4.6.2 Changes in body weight, and post-partum obesity

Whilst it is well established that body weight status affects the course and outcome of pregnancy, the role that pregnancy may play in the development of overweight and obesity is less clear. During pregnancy women usually deposit fat and this is thought to play a biological role in sustaining the foetus if necessary in the later stages of pregnancy and acts as an energy store to buffer the high energy demands of lactation. However, women who are able to deposit extra fat during pregnancy because of increased intake and/or decreased energy requirements for physical activity are likely to be able to support the costs of lactation by adopting these two strategies, and therefore have no need to break into the extra fat stores. Studies in affluent well-nourished women have shown that some actually increase weight and body fat during lactation (32,33). Clearly, this is a potential risk for post-partum obesity, but it also illustrates that clear messages need to be given with respect to breast feeding. This is very important for the baby, but a mother should not assume that all the extra weight will automatically disappear if she breastfeeds. This is particularly so in women who decide on this method of feeding because they believe it will cause them to lose weight after their baby is born.

It is now apparent that conditions that arise only during pregnancy may not, as previously assumed, be completely alleviated on delivery. For example, many women who have had gestational diabetes are left with residual sub-clinical abnormalities in glucose tolerance with a much increased risk of developing Type 2 diabetes in later life (34). There is also evidence that women who have had pre-eclampsia or pregnancy-induced hypertension may be at increased risk of later hypertensive and renal disorders (35). As discussed earlier, there is a large variability in weight and fat gain during pregnancy, and concern has been expressed about the impact of excessive gestational weight gains on the prevalence of obesity. Many studies have found a significant and positive correlation between gestational weight gain and post-partum weight retention; again the variability is very large. Mean weight changes one year post-partum relative to pre-pregnant weight range between -1 and +8 kg, with associated standard deviations of a similar magnitude.

Pregnancy *per se* is not the only cause of parity-associated weight gain. Women also gain weight post-partum, indicating that there are other factors involved. Breastfeeding has a limited effect on the pattern of post-partum weight retention or loss, and it is recommended that minimal emphasis be placed on lactation as a means of weight control. Studies of lactating women have shown that significant weight and fat losses do not necessarily occur, especially in well-nourished, affluent women who are able to increase energy intake and/or decrease physical activity (13). It has been suggested that some of the differences in post-partum weight changes observed between lactating and non-lactating women may be because the latter actively attempt to lose weight after pregnancy. Lactating women are often advised not to attempt to lose weight by diet or vigorous exercising to avoid compromising their health and the quantity and quality of their milk. However, in studies of well-nourished women whose babies were exclusively breastfed, neither exercise nor weight loss programmes adversely affected milk output or infant growth (36-8).

Behavioural and environmental factors have an important modulating role on post-partum weight change and can be significant determinants of weight gain during a reproductive cycle. Many studies have examined the factors that affect weight loss in the first year post-partum. In summary, no difference was found in weight changes associated with self-reported exercise levels. Women who returned soonest to work outside the home had the greatest weight loss at 6 months. This may have been due to increased physical activity and/or restricted access to food. Women who did not resume paid employment remained 2 kg above their pre-pregnant weight. Post-partum weight retention has also been found to be greater in women who increased their total energy intake during and after pregnancy, increased the frequency of snacking post-partum, had more irregular eating patterns, spent less time on physical activity, were older, or were single. At present, post-partum obesity is a problem in developed countries. However, these problems are likely to extend to some populations in developing countries as the prevalence of obesity increases.

Over the longer term, the effect of reproduction on body weight are much more difficult to determine. Studies have shown that the time between the index pregnancy and data collection is extremely variable; most data are obtained retrospectively; in many studies there is no control group. Furthermore, both weight and parity increase with age, and both parity and obesity are associated with socio-economic status and ethnicity.

4.7   Conclusions

Pregnancy and lactation are periods of heightened concern and interest about all aspects of health, not just nutrition, but also smoking, physical activity, alcohol intake and other aspects of lifestyle. It is not just the individual woman but the health and wellbeing of her baby that is at stake, and, at a population level, it is also the health of the next generation. Pre-pregnant and pregnant women and their partners and family are particularly receptive to advice, and changes made to diets and other aspects of lifestyle are more likely to be heeded by them than by other sub-sections of the population. Moreover, the changes are more likely to be long-term permanent alterations, benefiting not only the woman and her baby but other members of the family too. Pregnancy therefore represents a window of opportunity for taking up better dietary and other habits. Anderson has recently discussed in some depth the reasons why pregnancy may or may not be a good time for dietary change (3).

In general, in countries such as the UK, the majority of pregnancies have a healthy course and outcome. In some individuals and populations, extremes of pre-pregnant weight and/or gestational weight gains pose significant clinical problems for both the mother and the infant in the short and longer term. Socio-economic status also affects nutritional status and outcome of pregnancy. Pregnant teenagers may pose particular problems. For some women, elements of the reproductive cycle may be risk periods for becoming overweight or obese.

4.8   References

1.   Conway R. Dietary restraint and weight gain during pregnancy. *European Journal of Clinical Nutrition*, 1999, 53, 849-53.

2.   Clark M., Ogden J. The impact of pregnancy on eating behaviour and aspects of weight concern. *International Journal of Obesity*, 1999, 23, 18-24.

3.   Anderson A.S. Pregnancy as a time for dietary change? *Proceedings of the Nutrition Society*, 2001, 60, 497-504.

4.   Health Survey for England. www.doh.gov.uk/stats.

5.   Galtier-Dereure F., Montpeyroux F., Boulot P., Bringer J., Jaffiol C. Weight excess before pregnancy: complications and cost. *International Journal of Obesity*, 1995, 19, 443-8.

6.   MRC Vitamin Study Research Group. Prevention of neural tube defects: results of the Medical Research Council Vitamin Study. *Lancet*, 1991, 338, 131-7.

7.   Department of Health. *Folic Acid and the Prevention of Disease*. London. The Stationery Office, 2000.

8.   Cuskelly G.J., McNulty H., Scott J.M. Effect of increasing dietary folate on red-cell folate: implications for prevention of neural tube defects. *Lancet*, 1996, 347, 657-9.

NUTRITION THROUGH THE LIFE CYCLE

9.   Kramer M.S. Determinants of low birth weight: methodological assessment and meta-analysis. *Bulletin of the World Health Organisation*, 1987, 65, 663-737.

10. Institute of Medicine. Subcommittee on Nutritional Status and Weight Gain During Pregnancy. *Nutrition during Pregnancy. Part I Weight Gain. Part II Nutrient Supplements.* Washington DC. National Academy Press, 1990.

11. Goldberg G.R. Pregnancy and lactation: a global nutritional challenge. *Proceedings of the Nutrition Society*, 1997, 56 (1B), 319-33.

12. FAO/WHO/UNU. Report of a joint expert consultation. *Energy and Protein Requirements.* Technical Report Series 724. Geneva. WHO, 1985.

13. Prentice A.M., Spaaij C.J.K., Goldberg G.R., et al. Energy requirements of pregnant and lactating women. *European Journal of Clinical Nutrition*, 1996, 50 (suppl 1), S82-S111.

14. Goldberg G.R., Prentice A.M., Coward W.A., et al. Longitudinal assessment of energy expenditure in pregnancy by the doubly-labelled water method. *American Journal of Clinical Nutrition*, 1993, 57, 494-505.

15. Koop-Hoolihan L.E., Van Loan M.D., Wong W.W. *et al.* Longitudinal assessment of energy balance in well-nourished pregnant women. *American Journal of Clinical Nutrition*, 1999, 69, 697-704.

16. Gregory J., Foster K., Tyler H., Wiseman M. *The Dietary and Nutritional Survey of British Adults.* London. HMSO, 1990.

17. Rogers I., Emmett P. Diet during pregnancy in a population of pregnant women in south-west England. *European Journal of Clinical Nutrition*, 1998, 52, 246-50.

18. Doyle W., Crawford M.A., Laurance B.M., Drury P. Dietary survey during pregnancy in a low socio-economic group. *Human Nutrition:Applied Nutrition*, 1982, 36A, 95-106.

19. Wynn S., Wynn A., Doyle W., Crawford M. The association of maternal social class with maternal diet and the dimensions of babies in a population of London women. *Nutrition and Health*, 1994, 9, 303-15.

20. Doyle W., Srivastava A., Crawford M., Bhatti R., Brooke Z., Costeloe K. Inter-pregnancy folate and iron status of women in an inner-city population. *British Journal of Nutrition*, 2001, 86, 81-7.

21. Department of Health. *Dietary Reference Values for Food Energy and Nutrients for the United Kingdom.* London. HMSO, 1991.

22. Department of Health. *Nutrition and Bone Health: with Particular Reference to Calcium and Vitamin D.* London. The Stationery Office, 1998.

88

23. Goldberg G.R. Environmental factors influencing birthweight: Alcohol consumption and pregnancy outcome, in *The Cambridge Encyclopaedia of Human Growth and Development*. Edited by Ulijaszek S.J., Johnston F.E., Preece M.A. Cambridge. Cambridge University Press, 1998, 310-11.

24. Buttriss J. (Ed.) Adverse reactions to foods, in *The Report of the British Nutrition Foundation Task Force*. Oxford. Blackwell Science, 2001.

25. Schenker S. Gruesome gourmets. *Nutrition Bulletin*, 2001, 26, 11-12.

26. The Social Exclusion Unit. *Teenage Pregnancy*. London. The Stationery Office, 1999.

27. Gregory J., Lowe S., Bates C.J., *et al. National Diet and Nutrition Survey: Young People Aged 4 to 18 years. Volume 1: Report of the Diet and Nutrition Survey.* London. The Stationery Office, 2000.

28. Scholl T., Stein T., Smith W. Leptin and maternal growth during adolescent pregnancy. *American Journal of Clinical Nutrition*, 2000, 72, 1542-7.

29. Scholl T., Hediger M., Schall J., Khoo C., Fischer R. Maternal growth during pregnancy and the competition for nutrients. *American Journal of Clinical Nutrition*, 1994, 60, 183-8.

30. Prentice A.M., Paul A., Prentice A., Black A.E., Cole T.J., Whitehead R.G. Cross-cultural differences in lactational performance, in *Human Lactation 2*. Edited by Hamosh M., Goldman A.S. Plenum Publishing Corp., 1986, 13-44.

31. Poppitt S.D., Prentice A.M., Goldberg G.R., Whitehead R.G. Energy-sparing strategies to protect human fetal growth. *American Journal of Obstetrics and Gynaecology*, 1994, 171, 118-25.

32. Forsum E., Sadurskis A., Wager J. Estimation of body fat in healthy Swedish women during pregnancy and lactation. *American Journal of Clinical Nutrition*, 1989, 50, 465-73.

33. Goldberg G.R., Prentice A.M., Coward W.A., et al. Longitudinal assessment of the components of energy balance in well-nourished lactating women. *American Journal of Clinical Nutrition*, 1991, 54, 788-98.

34. Dornhorst A., Bailey P.C., Anyaoku V., Elkeles R.S., Johnston D.G., Beard R.W. Abnormalities of glucose tolerance following gestational diabetes. *Quarterly Journal of Medicine*, 1990, 284, 1219-28.

35. Nisell H., Lintu H., Lunell N.O., Mollerstrom G., Pettersson E. Blood pressure and renal function seven years after pregnancy complicated by hypertension. *British Journal of Obstetrics and Gynaecology*, 1996, 102, 876-81.

89

36. Lovelady C., Garner K., Moreno K., Williams J. The effect of weight loss in overweight lactating women on the growth of their infants. *New England Journal of Medicine*, 2000, 342, 499-53.

37. Dewey K.G., Lovelady C.A., Nommsen-Rivers L.A., McCrory M.A., Lonnerdal B. A randomised study of aerobic exercise by lactating women on breast-milk volume and composition. *New England Journal of Medicine*, 1994, 330, 449-53.

38. Lovelady C.A., Lonnerdal B., Dewey K.G. Lactation performance of exercising women. *American Journal of Clinical Nutrition*, 1990, 52, 103-9.

39. Gross T., Sokol R.J., King K.C. Obesity in pregnancy: Risks and outcomes. *Obstetrics and Gynaecology*, 1980, 56, 446-50.

40. Prentice A.M., Goldberg G.R. Maternal obesity increases congenital malformations. *Nutrition Reviews*, 1996, 54, 146-52.

41. Lucas A., Morley R., Cole T.J., et al. Maternal fatness and the viability of preterm infants. *British Medical Journal*, 1988, 296, 1495-7.

42. van-der-Spuy Z.M., Steer P.J., McCusker M., Steele S.J., Jacobs H.S. Outcome of pregnancy in underweight women after spontaneous and induced ovulation. *British Medical Journal*, 1988, 296, 962-5.

43. Edwards L.E., Alton I.R., Barrada M.I., Hakanson E.Y. Pregnancy in the underweight woman. Course outcome and growth paterns of the infant. *American Journal of Obstetrics and Gynaecology*, 1979, 135, 297-302.

5. ADULT NUTRITION

Jane Pryer and Prakash Shetty

5.1   Introduction

This chapter outlines three important issues related to adult nutrition in the United Kingdom. It begins by establishing the basis of as well as the recommendations for the requirements of macronutrients (energy, protein, carbohydrates, fats) and micronutrients (vitamins, minerals and trace elements) of adults in the UK. It then provides an outline of what adults in the UK consume as food and as nutrients in their daily habitual diets based on the last National Diet and Nutrition Survey (NDNS) conducted in representative samples of British adults in the 1990s. The last section of this chapter deals with the topic of changes in diet and related lifestyles that increase the risk of chronic non-communicable or degenerative diseases that occur in adulthood in this population. Their links to health promotion and food and nutrition policies will be made recognising that these are dealt with in much greater depth and detail in the later chapters.

5.2   Dietary Reference Values

The UK adopted the concept of referring to dietary and nutrient requirement recommendations as Dietary Reference Values (DRVs) rather than as Recommended Dietary Intakes (RDIs) or as Recommended Dietary Allowances (RDAs) (1). It has long been assumed that the distribution of requirements for nutrients in the diet in a group of individuals for any nutrient is a normal distribution. This provides a notional mean requirement or Estimated Average Requirement (EAR) with the inter-individual variability in requirements illustrated by the distribution. The Reference Nutrient Intake (RNI) has been defined as two notional standards (2sd) above the EAR. A further value, two standard deviations below the mean is the Lower Reference Nutrient Intake (LNRI). Intakes above the RNI will almost certainly be adequate for almost all of the population. The LRNI represents the lowest intakes, which will meet the needs of some individuals in the group, but intakes below this level are certainly inadequate for most individuals in a population. These apply to all nutrients, both macro and micro, except energy, which is expressed as the EAR for reasons which will be discussed later. A summary of the recommendations made by the Department of Health's Expert Panel (1) are summarised in Table 5.I.

TABLE 5.I
Estimated average requirements for energy, and recommended nutrient intakes for protein, and dietary reference values for fats and carbohydrates as a per cent of total energy and (per cent of food energy) for adults aged 19-50 years

Estimated average requirement for energy	MJ/d (kcal/day)
Male	10.60 (2,550)
Female	8.10 (1,940)

Recommended protein intake	g/day
Male	55.5
Female	45.0

Dietary Reference Values for fats and carbohydrates for adults*	per cent of total energy (per cent food energy)
Saturated fatty acids	10 (11)
Cis monounsaturated fatty acids	12 (13)
Trans fatty acids	2 (2)
Total fatty acids	30 (32.5)
Total fat	33 (35)
Non-milk extrinsic sugars and starch	10 (11)
Total carbohydrate	47 (50)
Non-starch polysaccharides (g/day)	18

Source: Department of Health (1)

5.2.1   DRVs for energy

Recommendations for energy have always been set for the average of energy requirements (AER) for any population group since both excess of energy and deficits in AER increase the risk of over- or under-nutrition in a proportion of the population. The Panel for Dietary Reference Values has therefore calculated EARs for energy, but not LRNIs or RNIs. The DRVs for energy were set on the basis of current estimates of energy expenditure while being aware of evidence that overweight and obesity are increasing in the British adult population.

5.2.2   *DRVs for protein, fat and carbohydrates*

There have been two approaches for setting adult protein requirements. The first, based on observations made in free living healthy populations, has relied on the apparent adequacy of those intakes, and the estimated requirements have been expressed as g/day or as a percentage of the dietary energy. The second approach is based on nitrogen balance studies and derives daily protein requirements with additions for specific physiological situations such as growth and pregnancy – an approach adopted by the FAO/WHO/UNU Expert Consultation (1985), and has formed the basis of the recommendations for UK DRVs shown in Table 5.I. In Table 5.I, the average percentage contribution of macronutrients to total energy does not total 100% because figures for protein and alcohol have been excluded. Protein intakes average 15% of total energy, which is above the RNI. It has been recognised that many individuals will derive some energy from alcohol, and this has been assumed to average 5% of current intake. However, some groups of individuals may not drink alcohol and for this reason nutrient intakes are represented as a percentage of energy or food energy (without alcohol).

5.2.3   *DRVs for vitamins*

DRVs for vitamins for adults aged 19-50 years are summarised in Table 5.II.

5.2.3.1   *Requirements of B group vitamins*

Many different approaches have been used to arrive at requirements and RNIs of B vitamins, which are water-soluble. Estimations of thiamin requirements have been based upon a variety of biochemical methods. However, the findings that urinary thiamin output falls below 15 µg/day in patients with beri beri provides the reference point against which other methods are compared. The Erythrocyte Glutathione Reductase Activity Coefficient (EGRAC) test has been used to assess riboflavin requirement and measures the saturation and long-term riboflavin status, and has the advantage of being both stable and extremely sensitive.

EGRAC values below 1.3 represent more or less complete saturation of the tissues with riboflavin, and the results obtained by this method were used to arrive at the DRVs for riboflavin. There is no wholly satisfactory laboratory assessment of niacin status. The determination of the urinary excretion of N-methyl nicotinamide (NMN) and its onward metabolite methyl pyridone carboxamine (MPCX) offers the best option and has been used to derive RNI for niacin. Useful estimates of vitamin B_6 requirements come from studies of changes in tryptophan and methionine metabolism, and blood vitamin B_6 levels during depletion and repletion of adults maintained on controlled diets. B_6 deficiency develops faster on relatively high protein intakes than on lower intakes and this needs to be factored in since, during repletion of deficient subjects, tryptophan and methionine metabolism and blood vitamin B_6 are normalised at low rather than at high levels of protein intakes. This has considerable relevance in populations in the developed world on relatively high protein intakes. Experimental depletion studies have not been undertaken to produce vitamin B_{12} deficiency in humans, or to measure the daily requirement directly since this would take too long and be considered hazardous. The usually accepted criterion for vitamin B_{12} inadequacy is a serum level below 130 pg/ml or about 100 pmol/litre. Biochemical evidence of folate status can be obtained from a variety of indicators. The lower limit of normal serum folate concentration is usually accepted as 3 ng/ml. Tissue levels are better indicated by concentration of folate in red cells, which is buffered against short-term changes. Red cell levels below 100 ng/ml are considered to be severely deficient, while levels between 100 and 150 ng/ml indicate marginal status. Liver levels greater than 3 $\mu g/g$ indicate adequate reserves.

5.2.3.2   *Requirements of vitamin C*

RNIs for vitamin C for adults are provided in Table 5.II. In normal adults, about 2.7% of the exchangeable body pool of vitamin C as ascorbic acid is degraded each day. This is independent of body pool size, so that at zero intake there is a first-order rate of loss from the tissues. When the body pool falls to 300 mg or less there is evidence of impaired function of most organs and tissues, and the lower limit of 15 $\mu g/10$ cells is frequently accepted as an indicator of deficiency. Plasma vitamin C levels are more sensitive to recent intake, with values less than 11 $\mu mol/litre$ indicating biochemical depletion.

TABLE 5.II
Reference Nutrition Intakes for vitamins for adults aged 19-50 years

Reference Nutrient Intakes for vitamins	Male	Female
Thiamin (mg/day)	1.0	0.8
Riboflavin (mg/day)	1.3	1.1
Niacin (nicotinic acid equivalent) (mg/day)	17	12
Vitamin B_6 (mg/day)	1.4	1.2
Vitamin B_{12} (μg/day)	1.5	1.5
Folate (μg/day)	200	200
Vitamin C (mg/day)	40	40
Vitamin A (μg/day)	40	40

Source: Department of Health (1)

5.2.3.3   Requirements of vitamin A

Most assessments of vitamin A requirements of adults have been based upon repletion studies in vitamin A depleted volunteers. An alternative approach based upon the pool size was adopted in the recent FAO/WHO recommendations and has been chosen by the UK DRV report (1). Adequate vitamin A status can be defined in terms of an adequate body pool based on the amount of vitamin A in the liver, which contains the great majority of vitamin A in the body. A liver concentration of 20 μg retinol was used as the basis for the FAO/WHO recommendations. This concentration should maintain an adult on a diet containing no vitamin A free from deficiency signs for a period of several months.

5.2.4   DRVs for minerals

DRVs for minerals and trace elements recommended by the UK Department of Health Report (1) are summarised in Table 5.III.

5.2.4.1   Requirements for calcium, phosphorus and magnesium

For calcium, in spite of the clear biological essentiality of the element, the very diversity of its functions made it difficult to define the appropriate end point to use for assessing the adequacy either of the dietary supply or of its delivery to the relevant tissues. The Department of Health Report (1) recommended a number of possible parameters, including plasma calcium or the maintenance of positive balance to preserve the skeleton. In the factorial approach, theoretical calculations can be made of the needs for calcium for growth and maintenance. As the development of osteoporosis is seen by some as an outcome measure of calcium deficiency, its occurrence might also be considered a possible end point. The Report found no single approach as being satisfactory and opted for the factorial approach. Phosphorus requirements are conventionally set as equal to calcium in mass terms (1 mol P=1 mol Ca) since these elements are present in the body in nearly equimolar amounts. Hence, as a matter of prudence, the RNI for P was set equal to the calcium RNI in mmol. Available data suggest that Mg balance is achieved in adults on about 50 mg. The efficiency of absorption increases from 15% on high Mg diets to about 75% on Mg-restricted diets. In normal adults, positive balance could be maintained on 3 mg/day over a 6- to 9-day experimental study, and an intake of 3.4 mg/kg/day would be adequate for all.

TABLE 5.III
Reference Nutrient Intakes for minerals (SI units) for adults aged 19-50 years

Reference Nutrient Intakes for minerals	Male	Female
Calcium (mg/day)	700	700
Phosphorus (mg/day)	550	550
Magnesium (mg/day)	300	270
Sodium (mg/day)	1,600	1,600
Potassium (mg/day)	3,500	3,500
Chloride (mg/day)	2,500	2,500
Iron (mg/day)	11.3	14.8
Zinc (mg/day)	9.5	7.0
Copper (mg/day)	1.2	1.2
Selenium (µg/day)	75	60
Iodine (µg/day)	140	140

Source: Department of Health (1)

5.2.4.2 Requirements for sodium, potassium and chloride

Healthy adults maintain balance on intakes of sodium as low as 3-20 mmol/day and some healthy populations have daily intakes of less than 40 mmol. The Report cautioned against any trend towards higher sodium intakes, and suggested that current intakes were needlessly high, and decided to set DRVs on the basis of the balance of risks and benefits (e.g. increased risk of hypertension or heart

ADULT NUTRITION

disease). There are difficulties in determining precisely the requirements for potassium, but they can be gauged from the amount accumulated with growth and from reported urinary and faecal excretion, although the latter may represent homeostatic excretion of excessive intakes and losses incurred in maintaining sodium homeostasis. Additional allowance needs to be made for amounts lost via the skin and by urinary excretion. It has been argued that chloride and sodium interact in inducing hypertension in man. Since the dietary intake and systemic metabolism of chloride match closely and are interdependent with those of sodium, it was concluded that, in the absence of more definitive information, recommended intakes of chloride from the diet should be equal to sodium intakes in molar terms, and DRVs for chloride should therefore correspond to those of sodium.

5.2.4.3   Requirements for iron

Iron homeostasis is regulated by both uptake and transfer at the intestinal mucosa and there are no major excretory pathways for endogenous iron. Daily losses of endogenous iron include desquamated gastrointestinal cells, in bile and in urine. Losses from the skin and sweat are small. Blood loss depletes the body of iron. Basic losses appear to have a coefficient of variation of about 15% among normal adults.

5.2.4.4   Requirements for iodine

A urinary iodine excretion of less than 50 µg/g creatinine is usually associated with a high incidence of goitre in a population. There are no data on requirements for iodine and hence the EAR for iodine was not calculated. Nevertheless, in adults, an intake of 70 µg/day appears to be the minimum necessary to avoid signs of goitre in a population.

5.2.4.5   Requirement for zinc, copper and selenium

The assessment of zinc in adults has been based on determining basal losses during metabolic studies of deprivation and from the turnover time of radiolabelled endogenous zinc pools. In order to avoid disturbed metabolism of other nutrients, the systemic needs are 2-3 mg/day. Assuming a normal distribution, RNIs are 9.5 mg for men and 7.0 mg for women; the LRNIs are

5.5 mg for men and 4.0 mg for women. There are limited data on human copper requirements, and hence it is not possible to derive EARs or LRNIs with sufficient confidence. However, sufficient data from biochemical changes in adults associated with varying copper intakes were available on which the UK Report based its RNIs for copper. Blood selenium levels in the UK are just above the value of 100 ng/ml at which glutathione peroxidase (GHSPx) activity reaches a plateau, suggesting that current levels of selenium in diets are adequate. No adverse consequences arise from somewhat lower blood levels of selenium. However, since intakes that permit functional saturation appear to be the norm in the UK, the RNI has been established at a level to maintain this, at 1 µg (13 nmol/kg).

5.3   The National Diet and Nutrition Surveys of British Adults

The National Diet and Nutrition Surveys (NDNS) are carried out periodically in the UK and cover different segments of the population. The NDNS survey of British adults was carried out between October 1986 and August 1987. The aim was to recruit a nationally representative sample of adults aged 16-64 years living in private households, and to obtain detailed information on current dietary behaviour and nutritional status of the adults in these households. The sample for the NDNS of adults was recruited using a multistage random probability design. A total of 2,197 people completed a full 7-day dietary survey, and took part in an interview, which included household, social and lifestyle questions as well as questions on use of dietary supplements. A 24-hour urine collection was made by 77% of people who co-operated with some aspect of the survey, and 76% of respondents aged 18-64 years gave a specimen of blood.

5.3.1   National patterns of dietary consumption based on the NDNS survey of UK adults

5.3.1.1   Foods

A wide range of foods was consumed by UK adults. Broad categories of foods included whole milk, cheese, eggs and egg dishes, beef and veal dishes, bacon and ham, white bread, biscuits, potatoes, potato chips, coffee and tea. There were differences between men and women in both the types and quantities of food consumed. Men generally consumed larger quantities of food. A larger proportion of women than men consumed wholemeal bread, reduced-fat milks, salads and vegetables, fresh fruit and confectionery. Conversely, men were more likely than women to have eaten fried white fish, sausages meat pies and chips. Older informants were more likely than younger informants to have eaten potatoes, milk puddings, butter and preserves and fresh fruit and vegetables. Younger adults more commonly ate savoury snacks and take-away items, such as meat pies, burgers and kebabs than those aged 35 years or more (2).

5.3.1.2   Energy intakes and body mass index (BMI)

The average daily energy intake was 2,450 kcal (10.3MJ) and 1,680 kcals (7.05 MJ) for men and women, respectively. The relatively low ratios of recorded energy to calculated basal metabolic rate (BMR) was indicated by 27% of men and 40% of women who reported energy intakes, less than 1.2 times BMR. These recorded intakes are unlikely to have represented habitual intakes. Body mass index (BMI) was 24.9 in men and 24.6 in women, and tended to be higher in older groups. Obesity (i.e. a BMI of 30 or more) was recorded in 12% of women as compared with 8% reported in 1980. This increase over time was less marked in men (2).

5.3.1.3   Fat intakes

Average daily fat intake was 102.3 g for men and 73.5 g for women. This represented 37.6% of total energy for men and 39.2% for women. Only 12% of men and 15% of women had fat intakes that met the recommended target of 35% or less of food energy from fat. Men consumed on average 42 g of saturated fat and 5.6 g of *trans* fatty acids, compared with 31.1 g and 4.0 g for women. Saturated fatty acids contributed 16.5% and 17% of food energy in men and women, respectively. Only 11% of men and 12% of women derived less than the recommended target of 10% of food energy. The average ratio of polyunsaturated to saturated fatty acids (P:S) was similar for men and women (0.40 and 0.38, respectively) (2).

5.3.1.4   Blood lipids

Blood samples were analysed for total and high-density lipoprotein (HDL) cholesterol. Low-density lipoprotein (LDL) cholesterol was not measured directly but was estimated indirectly as total minus HDL cholesterol. The average serum total cholesterol concentration was 5.8 mmol/litre in men and was higher in older age groups. Overall, 32% of men had serum cholesterol less than 5.2 mmol/litre and that proportion fell with age so that 13% of men aged 50 to 64 years had serum cholesterol below this level. Conversely, 6% of men had serum cholesterol of 7.8 mmol/litre or greater, which rose to 10% in those aged 50 to 64 years. In women, average serum cholesterol was also 5.8 mmol/litre but the rise was marked over 50 years of age. Only 36% of women, and 10% of those aged 50-64 years had serum cholesterol lower than 5.2 mmol/litre. Overall, 8% of women had serum cholesterol of 7.8 mmol/litre or more, but in those aged 50-64 years this proportion rose to 21%. Apart from age, the main predictor of serum cholesterol was body mass index (BMI). Serum cholesterol increased with BMI, but the relationship with other variables was less marked. The proportion of food energy intake derived from saturated fatty acids, and dietary cholesterol intake but not total fat intake were associated with total serum cholesterol. In contrast, the proportion of food energy derived from total fat showed an association with HDL cholesterol. The average HDL cholesterol concentration was 1.2 mmol/litre in men and 1.4 mmol/litre in women. Although not consistently associated with age, HDL cholesterol tended to be lower in those of both sexes who smoked or had a higher BMI, and rose with the amount of alcohol consumed (2).

5.3.1.5   *Protein, carbohydrate and dietary fibre*

On average, the daily intake of protein was 84.7 g for men and 62.0 g for women, which provided 15.2% of total energy for women and 14.1% for men – well in excess of the RDA of 10%. On average, men consumed 272 g and women 193 g of carbohydrate, which represented 44.7% and 44.2% of food energy, respectively. Total sugars provided 42% of carbohydrate for men and 45% for women. The average intake of dietary fibre was 24.9 g (10.3 g per 1,000 kcal) for men and 18.6 g (11.2 g per 1,000 kcal) for women.

5.3.1.6   *Vitamin and mineral intakes*

Intakes of a wide range of vitamins, minerals and trace elements were calculated from the food consumption data. These were compared with the UK RDAs where they existed. Average intakes of vitamins from food (excluding food supplements) were well above the RDA levels, as were the minerals. A wide range of dietary supplements was used by the representative UK adult population. The most common categories were multivitamins, cod and halibut liver oils, vitamin C and B complex. Informants who took these had a higher intake of vitamins and minerals.

5.3.1.7   Blood pressure

Of those on no medication, the average blood pressure was 125/77 mm Hg among men and 118/73 mm Hg among women, and tended to rise with age in both sexes. Overall, 3% of untreated men had a systolic blood pressure of 160 mm Hg or more, although this proportion was 6% in those aged 50-64 years. Six per cent of all men and 9% of those aged 50-64 years had diastolic blood pressure of 95 mm Hg or more. Systolic pressure of 160 mm Hg or more was confined to those aged 50 to 64 years. Six per cent of men and 8% of women were in that category. Overall, 3% of women had diastolic blood pressure of 95 mm Hg, and the proportion rose with age to 6% in those aged 50-64 years. In men, but not in women, both systolic and diastolic blood pressure rose consistently with increasing alcohol consumption. Higher BMI was consistently associated with higher blood pressure in both sexes.

5.3.1.8   Residence

The average recorded energy intake was lower for those living in Scotland (2,240 kcal/day) compared with 2,450 kcal/day for all men. On average, Scottish men and women were shorter and had lower BMIs than those in other parts of the country. Men in Scotland and in the northern regions consumed more alcohol on average, and derived a greater proportion of energy from alcohol than men in other regions. Although men in Scotland consumed less fat and both saturated and polyunsaturated fatty acids than men in other regions, these differences were not apparent when expressed as a percentage of food energy. Although men in Scotland had lower intakes for a number of vitamins and minerals, these differences were not apparent when expressed per 1,000 kcal of energy intake. Plasma carotene tended to be higher in London and the south-east for both men and women. In Scotland, urinary sodium excretion was higher, and urinary potassium excretion in both men and women was lower than in other regions. There were no significant differences in blood pressure, total serum cholesterol or HDL cholesterol concentration by region.

5.3.1.9   Socio-economic characteristics

Recorded energy intakes were lower for unemployed men than for other men, and also lower for men and women in households receiving benefits. For women there was a trend towards lower average energy intakes in lower social classes. Women from social classes IV and V had the highest BMI, but there was no consistent trend with social class for men. Men and women in social classes IV and V were found to be shorter by 1.8 cm and 2.8 cm, respectively, than those from social classes II and I. Among men and women, intakes for fibre and sugars tended to be higher among those in social classes I and II than those in social classes IV and V. Unemployed men and those living in households receiving benefits had lower intakes for fat and fat as a percentage of food energy. The intakes of polyunsaturated fatty acids were higher in social classes I and II and the P:S ratio tended to be lower for the lower social classes. Unemployed men and women had lower intakes of many vitamins and minerals. In women, consumption of most vitamins and minerals tended to decline with social class. With the exception of iron, average intakes by all social classes met the DRVs.

5.3.2   Low energy intake reporters in the NDNS survey of UK adults

The 7-day weighed dietary intake method has been traditionally viewed as a "gold standard" among dietary assessment methods. Until recently, most studies that have used this method have made the tacit assumption that either this is a valid measure of "habitual" food intake or that bias, if present, operates equally across participants and thus within-study comparisons remain valid. However, validation studies of the weighed intake method, with either doubly labelled water as a marker for energy intake or urinary nitrogen as a marker for nitrogen intake, indicate that under-reporting bias is evident, especially at the lower end of the reported energy intake distribution (3,4). In population surveys, little is known about whether (and how many) people change their diets when surveyed, or under-report habitual intake, whether change or under-reporting is food and nutrient neutral, or whether there is a higher degree of change or under-reporting for specific foods and nutrients. When an average reported energy intake over a 7-day period is less than 1.2 times the estimated BMR, such intake is considered to be incompatible with long-term maintenance of energy balance and the individual is considered to be a Low Energy Reporter (LER).

Five hundred and nine women (46%) and 315 men (29%) of the NDNS adult sample reported a dietary energy intake less than 1.2 times their estimated BMR

(5). Compared with non-LERs, LERs had higher ratios of urinary urea nitrogen to dietary nitrogen and urinary potassium to dietary potassium, indicating that, as a group, LERs were under-reporting at least for protein and potassium intakes. Overall, LERs were over-represented among manual social classes, and in men among those in receipt of benefits. For both men and women, LERs were concentrated among smokers and self-reported non-alcoholics, and in men they tended to be concentrated among Black, Asian and unmarried subjects. The LERs were on average heavier and had a higher BMI than non-LERs.

There was also an indication of differential reporting of foods by LERs. Women and men LERs reported significantly lower intakes of many food groups, including lower contributions from biscuits/pastries/puddings and sugar/ confectionery – food with a "naughty but nice" image. LERs of both sexes reported significantly lower intakes of all nutrients; however, when adjusted for energy, LERs reported significantly lower densities of sugar and carbohydrate, but not total fat, and significantly higher densities of protein, starch, monounsaturated fat, n-3 polyunsaturated fat and cholesterol, and, among women, fibre. Similarly, differential reporting of micronutrients between LERs and non-LERs was evident, with LERs reporting significantly higher densities of around half of the micronutrients examined. A Danish study found differential reporting of protein and energy to be associated with obesity. With increasing obesity there appears to be a greater under-reporting of energy compared with under-reporting of protein, suggesting selective under-reporting of foods by obese people (6).

Dietary under-reporting will affect estimates of the overall mean and range of intakes within a population. Under-reporting may be concentrated within specific subgroups and may not be food and nutrient neutral; differential reporting would be likely to affect not only estimates of absolute values of intake, but also the relative ranking of individuals within a population in terms of their food and nutrient intakes. This could have serious implications for the design and interpretation of epidemiological studies of diet and disease (5).

5.3.3 Clusters of dietary patterns among UK adults

In recent years there has been increasing interest in the identification of dietary patterns as consumed by populations. It has been suggested that such analyses could shed light on the complex relationship between diet and chronic disease (7,8). From a public health perspective, identification of groups within a population that follow similar patterns of diet would be of value to policy makers for translating national dietary goals into practical dietary recommendations for the public, for monitoring population trends towards nutritionally "healthier" diets, for identification and surveillance of those at nutritional risk, and for tailoring and targeting public health nutritional interventions.

Previous approaches to an analysis of dietary patterns have utilised frequency of food use to develop food variety scores or a qualitative food use profile of a population. More recently, multivariate statistical techniques have been used to examine the combination of foods consumed by populations, relating these either to population characteristics or to morbidity. Several studies have used factor analysis to classify dietary patterns according to the frequency of reported food consumption or reported food intake. However, the factors identified by this technique do not refer to identifiable groups of individuals within a population, and hence do not give an indication of the prevalence of a particular type of diet. Cluster analysis, on the other hand, aims to identify relatively homogeneous groups within the population based upon selected attributes of the diet.

Such cluster analysis of the NDNS data revealed that 93% of men and 86% of women fell into one of four distinct diet groups. Among men, the most prevalent diet group was "beer and convenience food" (34% of the male population), with high intakes of beer/cider, and full-fat margarines, and moderately high intakes of prepared meat, meat products, chips and white bread. Low intakes were recorded for whole-grain cereals, fruits and nuts; and zero intake for polyunsaturated fats, low-fat dairy products, fish/shellfish, fruit juice, wines/liqueurs and spirits. Second was "traditional British diet" (18%), with high intakes for white bread/refined cereals, butter and full-fat margarines, tea and sugar and confectionery. There were moderately high intakes for cakes/pastries, puddings, high-fat dairy products and meat ham/bacon, potatoes and vegetables. Low intakes included those of whole grain cereals and pasta/rice, and zero intakes for low-fat dairy products, polyunsaturated spreads, pasta/rice fish/shellfish, fruit juices, wines/spirits and liqueurs. The third group was "healthier but sweet diet" (17.5%), with high intakes of wholegrain cereals, fish/shellfish, fruits and nuts and cakes and pastries. Moderately high intakes included high-fat dairy products and coffee, low-fat spreads, polyunsaturated fats, and wines/spirits and liqueurs. Zero intakes included fruit juices and full-fat margarines. The fourth diet cluster was the "healthier diet" (17%); high intakes included those of wholegrain cereals, fish/shellfish, and fruit and nuts. Moderately high intakes included pasta/rice and coffee, and median intakes were wines/spirits/liqueurs, low-fat dairy products, polyunsaturated fats spreads, and fruit juices. Among women, the most prevalent diet group was "traditional British diet" (32%), high in white bread/refined cereals, butter and high-fat dairy products, and moderately high in prepared meat products, tea, chips/roast potatoes, cakes/pastries and preserves/confectionery, and low in alcoholic drinks, fruit juices, fish/shellfish and low-fat dairy products. Zero intakes included polyunsaturated fat spreads, low-fat spreads, and moderately low intakes included vegetables, fruit and wholegrain cereals/breads. The second diet was "healthy cosmopolitan diet" (25%); high intakes included wholegrain cereals, low-fat dairy products, fish/shellfish, fruit and nuts, and wines/spirits and liqueurs. Moderately high intakes included polyunsaturated fat, fruit juice, vegetables, salads, poultry, prepared meat products, pasta/rice and coffee. Low intakes were refined cereals and chips, and zero intakes were beer/cider and other margarines. The third diet was a "convenience food diet" (21%); reported intakes for high and moderately high included tea, pasta/rice, white bread/refined cereals, prepared meat products, chips/roast potatoes, sugar/confectionery and soft drinks, while median intakes were full-fat margarines, and low intakes included low-fat dairy products, wholegrain cereals, fruits, nuts, fruit juices, liqueurs/wines/spirits. Zero intakes were polyunsaturated fat, low-fat spreads and fish/shellfish. The fourth diet was the "healthier but sweet diet" (15%); high intakes were wholegrain cereals, low-fat dairy products, fish/shellfish, fruits and nuts. Moderately high intakes were for polyunsaturated fats, vegetables, salads, ham/bacon, cakes/puddings, biscuits and tea. Moderately low intakes were of white bread/refined cereals, high-fat dairy products, chips/roast potatoes, and soft drinks. Zero intakes were full-fat margarines and beer/cider (9).

Energy intake was highest in the male and the female "traditional" diet and lowest in the male "healthier" diet, and among females in the "convenience" diet. The percentage of LERs was highest in the male "beer/convenience" diet and lowest in the male "mixed sweet" diet. Among women, the percentage of LERs was much higher, with the highest in the "convenience" diet and the lowest in the "traditional" and "healthier/sweet diet". The percentage of slimmers was low among the males, but, in females, those with the highest proportions of slimmers were in the "healthier/cosmopolitan" cluster.

The healthy diets had the lowest mean total fats, saturated fat and *trans* fat, carbohydrate and starch. Conversely, the "convenience" diets had the highest mean densities for total fat and starch and the lowest densities for fibre. In the "mixed and sweet diets" and "healthy but sweet" diets, the highest mean sugar densities were in the "mixed but sweet" and the "healthy sweet" diets, which had the highest polyunsaturated fat density. The "traditional" diets had the lowest mean micronutrient densities, while the "healthier" diet clusters had the highest mean micronutrient densities.

Compared with the population averages, the "convenience" diets and "traditional" diets were characterised by higher proportions from the manual social classes and/or those in receipt of State benefits. Higher proportions from both diet clusters smoked and among women fewer took micronutrient supplements. The "convenience" diet clusters were on average younger and had higher proportions of single people from ethnic minorities. Higher proportions from the male "convenience" diets came from the north and Scotland, whereas higher proportions of the female "convenience" diets came from London and the south-east. In contrast, higher proportions of the "healthier" diet clusters and "mixed but sweet" diet and the "healthy sweet" diets were from the non-manual social classes, and were non-smokers. Compared with the population average, higher proportions of male "healthier" eaters were from central/ south-west areas and Wales. And the "healthy but sweet" male diet cluster came from London and the south-east. Among women, higher proportions of "healthy eaters" were from London and the south-east (9).

This type of cluster analysis to identify groups within the British population who report similar patterns of diets is potentially of great relevance to public health nutrition policy as people eat foods not individual nutrients. There are a number of reasons why epidemiologists may wish to characterise specific food patterns rather than focus on nutrients. Firstly, foods are not fully represented by their nutrient composition. Secondly, it is not possible to characterise the health effects associated with a given food solely on the basis of its nutrient content; this is because different components of a particular meal may compete with, antagonise, or alter the bioavailability of any single nutrient contained in that meal. Thirdly, it can be difficult to disentangle the effects of various nutrients on health outcomes owing to problems of multicollinearity. Finally, analyses based on foods are more directly related to dietary recommendations, and it becomes more feasible to identify practices that need to be modified in order to improve health outcomes. Diet groups derived from cluster analysis might well predict important diet-related chronic disease outcomes, such as cancer, heart disease, or hypertension.

Lifestyle variables such as smoking and poor diet can independently affect health status, and a combination of lifestyle practices may introduce a health risk that is greater than would be expected from the sum of individual risk factors (10). Important differences in socio-demographic and behavioural characteristics occur across the diet clusters. For example, a high prevalence of smoking and manual social class was characteristic of the "beer and convenience/convenience diet" and "traditional diet" groups in men and women. On the basis of such analysis, the mix of risk factors that confer a high risk of cardiovascular disease or cancer in associated diet clusters can be predicted and is likely to contribute to effective and targeted intervention strategies.

Clusters differ in multi-dimensional ways and the determinants of food habits and lifestyles are also likely to vary. Factors such as convenience, cost, peer-group pressure and occupation may be relevant to food choices and lifestyle. Understanding this may help targeting risk groups with appropriate health promotion strategies.

5.4   Diet and Chronic, Non-communicable Diseases in Adults

The risk factors for chronic non-communicable diseases (NCDs) are grouped in three main categories: (i) non-modifiable risk factors, which include age, gender and the genetic make up of the individual; (ii) behavioural or life style risk factors, such as tobacco use, diet, alcohol intake, and physical inactivity; and (iii) societal risk factors, which include a very complex mixture of interacting socio-economic, cultural and environmental parameters. Other related morbidities, such as obesity, hypertension and diabetes should be considered not only as endpoint diseases, but also as intermediate risk factors for other NCDs such as coronary heart disease, (CHD), stroke and several cancers.

The evidence relating diet to NCDs, such as cardiovascular disease (CVD), non-insulin-dependent diabetes mellitus (NIDDM) and some cancers comes from population-based epidemiological investigations. Descriptive population-based epidemiological investigations yield valuable data, which lead to important hypotheses, but they cannot be used alone to establish the causal links between diet and disease. The most consistent correlation between diet and chronic diseases have emerged from comparisons of populations or segments of the population with substantially different dietary habits. Analytical epidemiological studies, such as cohort studies and case control studies, that compare information from groups of individuals within a population usually provide more accurate estimates of such associations. It is important to recognise, when examining population-based epidemiological data relating diet to disease, that every population consists of individuals, who vary in their susceptibility to each disease. Part of this difference in susceptibility is genetic. As the diet within a population changes in the direction that measures the risk of the specific disease, an increasing proportion of individuals, particularly those most susceptible to the risk, develop the disease. As a result of this inter-individual variability in the interaction of diet with an individual's genetic make-up and therefore the individual's susceptibility to disease, some diet-disease relationships are difficult to identify within a single population.

5.4.1   Diet and cardiovascular diseases

The most common cardiovascular diseases that are diet-related are coronary heart disease and hypertension.

5.4.1.1   Coronary heart disease (CHD)

CHD emerged as a serious public health problem in the UK, mainland Europe and North America after World War II and, by the end of the 1950s, had become the single major cause of adult death. The five-fold difference in CHD rates among the various developed countries and the intra-population variations in rates, by socio-economic class, ethnicity and geographical location, as well as the marked changes in CHD rates in migrant populations that moved across a geographical gradient in CHD risk, provided evidence of the environmental nature of the causative factor, i.e. a change in diet and lifestyle.

The relationship between dietary factors and CHD was supported by the results of the Seven Country Study (11). Saturated fat intake varied between 3% of total energy in Japan and 22% in eastern Finland, while the annual incidence of CHD among 40- to 59-year-old men initially free of CHD was 15 per 100,000 in Japan and 198 per 100,000 in Finland. Measurement of food consumption by the people in the seven countries and its correlation to 10-year incidence rate of CHD deaths provided support for this causal association, and the strongest correlation was noted between CHD and percentage of energy derived from saturated fat, while total fat intake was not significantly correlated. In the Seven Country Study, serum total cholesterol values were 165 mg/dl in Japan and 270 mg/dl in Finland, and suggested that the variation in serum total cholesterol levels between populations could be largely explained by differences in saturated fat intake. On a population basis, the risk of CHD seemed to rise progressively within the same population, with increases in plasma total cholesterol. The study showed a strong positive relationship between saturated fat intake and total cholesterol level; populations with an average saturated fat intake between 3% and 10% of the energy intake were characterised by serum total cholesterol levels below 200 mg/dl and by low mortality rates from CHD. As saturated fat intakes increased to greater than 10% of energy intake, a marked and progressive increase in CHD mortality was noticed.

Several prospective studies have shown an inverse relationship between high-density lipoprotein cholesterol (HDL) and CHD incidence. The recognition of the protective association of HDL has led to the ratio of total to HDL cholesterol emerging as a strong predictor of CHD risk. However, HDL cholesterol levels are influenced by several non-dietary factors, and HDL levels do not contribute to explain differences in CHD mortality between populations. The role of different unsaturated fatty acids, such as mono-unsaturated (MUFAs) and n-3 and n-6 polyunsaturated fatty acids (PUFAs) and their role in the prevention of CHD are unclear. Populations that have high intakes of MUFAs from olive oil or have diets rich in n-3 polyunsaturates of marine origin also have low CHD rates. There is emerging evidence that some isomers of fatty acids, such as *trans* fatty acids may contribute to increasing the incidence of CHD by increasing low-density lipoprotein (LDL) cholesterol levels.

Other dietary components, e.g. dietary fibre or complex carbohydrates, in the diet seem to influence serum cholesterol levels and the incidence of CHD through complex mechanisms, many of them indirect. Population sub-groups consuming diets rich in plant foods with a high content of complex carbohydrates have lower rates of CHD; vegetarians have a 30% lower rate of CHD mortality than non-vegetarians and their serum cholesterol levels are significantly lower than those of lacto-ovo-vegetarians and non-vegetarians. Alcohol consumption also reduces the incidence of CHD. A number of studies suggest that light-to-moderate drinkers have a slightly lower risk of CHD than abstainers. However, the relationship between alcohol intake and CHD is complicated by changes in blood pressure and also the nature of the alcoholic drink. The presence of phenolic compounds in red wine may contribute to the benefits of drinking red wine as compared with alcohol consumption *per se* in reducing the incidence of CHD. The relationship between folate and CHD has been made through its effect on plasma homocysteine, now considered as an independent risk factor. However more recent evidence seems to question this assumption, since prospective studies failed to find an association independent of other risk factors. It has been suggested that elevation of plasma homocysteine is a consequence rather than a cause of atherosclerosis and risk of CHD.

Among the range of risk factors, the risk of CHD in adults is dominated by three major factors: (i) high serum total cholesterol, (ii) high blood pressure, and (iii) cigarette smoking, and there is considerable synergism between these risk factors (12). Body weight changes induced by dietary and lifestyle changes, such as in levels of physical activity, are strongly related to changes in serum total cholesterol, blood pressure and obesity. Obesity in turn is strongly related to NIDDM, and both are risk factors for CHD. Prevention of CHD is best assured by a prudent diet. Current recommendations include lowering total fat intake, restricting saturated fat intake to 10% of total energy, and increasing intakes of complex carbohydrates and dietary fibre by increasing intakes of cereals and fruits and vegetables.

5.4.1.2   Hypertension and stroke

The risk of CHD and stroke increases progressively throughout the observed range of blood pressure based on nine major studies conducted in a number of different countries (13). From the combined data, it appears that there is a five-fold difference in CHD and a ten-fold risk of stroke over a range of diastolic blood pressure of only 40 mm Hg. Obesity and alcohol intake are related to hypertension since weight reduction and restricting alcohol intake can lower blood pressures. The dietary factors that are implicated (in addition to alcohol and caffeine intakes) are excessive sodium and saturated fat intake and low potassium and calcium intake. The role of dietary sodium in hypertension has been a subject of considerable debate. The Intersalt Study (14) compared standardised blood pressure measurements with 24-hour urinary sodium excretion in 10,000 individuals aged 20-59 years in 32 countries and showed that populations with very low sodium excretion (implying low sodium intakes) had low median blood pressures, a low prevalence of hypertension and no increase in blood pressure with age. Although sodium intake was related to blood pressure levels and also influenced the extent to which blood pressures increased with age, the overall association between sodium, median blood pressure and the prevalence of hypertension was less than significant. The results of intervention trials of sodium restriction also tend to support this relationship. Aggregation of the results of 68 cross-over trials and 10 random control trials of dietary salt reduction have shown that moderate dietary salt reduction over a period of a few weeks lowers systolic and diastolic blood pressure in those individuals with high blood pressure (15). The more recent DASH (Dietary Approaches to Stop Hypertension) trial (16) showed that reduction in sodium intake resulted in significant lowering of both systolic and diastolic blood pressures. The other dietary component that has been investigated by the Intersalt Study (14) has been potassium. Urinary potassium excretion, an assumed indicator of intake, was negatively related to blood pressure, as was the urinary sodium/potassium concentration ratio. It has also been observed that potassium supplementation reduces blood pressure in both normotensive and hypertensive subjects (17). Some, but not all, cross-sectional and intervention studies suggest a beneficial effect of calcium intake on blood pressure. Epidemiological studies also consistently suggest lower blood pressures among vegetarians than among non-vegetarians, independent of age and body weight. These studies may also support the role of other dietary components; i.e. vegetarian diets rich in complex carbohydrates are also rich in potassium and other minerals. Nutritional intervention is thus likely to reduce the occurrence of hypertension and the consequent complications of stroke and CHD among adults.

5.4.2   Non-insulin-dependent diabetes mellitus (NIDDM)

NIDDM is a metabolic disorder occurring in adulthood, and is strongly associated with an increased risk of CHD. Obesity is a major risk factor for the occurrence of NIDDM, the risk being related both to the duration and to the degree of obesity. The occurrence of NIDDM in a community appears to be triggered by a number of environmental factors, such as sedentary lifestyle, dietary factors, stress, urbanisation and socio-economic factors. Certain ethnic groups in the UK, e.g. Indians, Pakistanis and Bangladeshis, have a higher incidence of NIDDM and hence risk of CHD. The cause of NIDDM is unclear, but it seems to involve both an impaired pancreatic secretion of insulin and the development of tissue resistance to insulin. Overweight and obesity, particularly the central or truncal distribution of fat accompanied by a high waist/hip ratio and a high waist circumference, seems to be invariably present with NIDDM. Hence, the most rational and promising approach to preventing NIDDM is to prevent obesity. Weight control is hence of fundamental importance in a population strategy for the primary prevention of this disorder, but is also essential to tackle high-risk individuals in this group. Physical activity also helps improve glucose tolerance by weight reduction and also by its beneficial effects on insulin resistance. Diets high in plant foods are associated with a lower incidence of NIDDM, and vegetarians have a substantially lower risk than others of NIDDM. The factor of prime importance is to achieve and maintain a desirable body weight and, if possible, prevent weight gain in the first place.

5.4.3   Diet, lifestyles and obesity in adults

Obesity is one of the most important public health problems in adults in the UK, and the prevalence of obesity is increasing year by year. Overweight and obesity are normally assumed to indicate an excess of body fat. Recent recommendations of the WHO (18) include the suggestion that a body mass index (BMI) of between 18.5 and 24.9 in adults is appropriate weight for height. A BMI between 25 and 29.9 is indicative of overweight and possibly a pre-obese state, while obesity is diagnosed at a BMI >30.0. The main health risk of obesity is premature death due to CVD and other NCDs. In the presence of other risk factors (both dietary and non-dietary), obesity increases the risk of CHD, hypertension and stroke. In women, obesity seems to be one of the best predictors of CVD. Longitudinal studies have demonstrated that weight gain in adults, in both sexes, is significantly related to increases in CVD risk factors. Weight gain was strongly associated with increased blood pressure, elevated plasma cholesterol and triglycerides and hyperglycaemia (fasting and post-prandial). The distribution of fat in the body in obesity may also contribute to increased risk; with high waist-hip ratios (i.e. fat predominantly in abdomen and not subcutaneous) increasing the risk of CHD and NIDDM. The co-existence of NIDDM among the obese is also an important contributor to morbidity and mortality in obese individuals. Obesity also carries increased risk of gall bladder stones, and breast and uterine cancer in females and possibly of prostate and renal cancer in males. Body weight increase (with increased BMI) is also associated with increasing mortality, both in smokers and in non-smokers.

Several environmental factors, both dietary and lifestyle-related, contribute to increasing obesity in communities. Social and environmental factors that increase energy intake and/or reduce physical activity are important in adults as contributors to the development of obesity. Changes in the food consumed and in the patterns of eating behaviour may contribute to increased intakes of energy well beyond one's requirements. Patterns of eating, particularly snacking between meals and frequent snacks, may contribute to increased intakes. However, overwhelming evidence seems to support the view that much of the energy imbalance that is responsible for the epidemic of obesity in modern societies such as the UK is largely the result of dramatic reductions in physical activity levels (both occupational and leisure time) when food availability is more than adequate.

Preventive measures to deal with the increasing prevalence of obesity among adults in the UK have to start very early. Primary preventions may have to be aimed at schoolchildren. This includes nutrition education of children and parents and dealing with problems of school meals, snacking, levels of physical activity and other issues. Public health initiatives should include attempts to tackle all social and environmental issues that may contribute to the increasing energy and fat intakes and the reducing physical activity levels. Since the issues are too complex, attempts have to be made to address issues related to transportation policies, work site facilities for exercise, and several other factors that contribute to this complex problem.

5.4.4   Diet and osteoporosis in adults

Bone density increases in childhood and adolescence and reaches a peak at about 20 years of age. Bone density falls from menopause in women and from about the age of 55 years in men. The variation in bone density between individuals is large and of the order of $\pm 20\%$. Since bone density declines with increasing age, those that attain high levels of peak bone mass at the end of adolescence and retain higher levels of bone density during adulthood become osteoporotic with advancing age much more slowly than those with lower bone densities to start with. Hence, the range of factors that influence the attainment of peak bone density may play a crucial role in the development of osteoporosis and the occurrence of fractures as age advances.

Several factors determine the onset of osteoporosis, which include the lack of oestrogen in postmenopausal women, degree of mobility, smoking, and alcohol intake. Calcium intake is a likely dietary determinant that may contribute to the onset and degree of osteoporosis. The traditional emphasis on calcium intakes possibly reflects the recognition of its importance in contributing to the density of bone during growth and the need for attaining dense bones at the peak of adult life. High-protein and high-salt diets are known to increase bone loss, while calcium supplements, well above what may be considered physiological, in postmenopausal women may help to reduce the rate of bone loss and slow down the development of osteoporosis.

5.4.5   Diet and cancers

Although the relationships between specific dietary components and cancers are less well established than that between diet and CVD, the overall impact of diet on cancer incidence appears to be significant. It is now widely accepted that one-third of human cancers could relate directly to some dietary component (19) and it is probable that diet plays an important role in influencing the permissive role of carcinogens on the development of many cancers. Thus, up to 80% of all cancers may have a link with nutrition.

5.4.5.1   Colon cancer

This is the third most common form of cancer and the incidence rates are high in UK adults. Almost all the specific risk factors of colon cancer are of dietary origin. Diets low in dietary fibre or complex carbohydrates and high in animal fat and animal protein increase the risk of colon cancer. The epidemiological data relating dietary fibre intakes to colorectal cancer are largely equivocal, despite the demonstration by several studies of the existence of an inverse relationship between the intake of foods that are rich in dietary fibre and colon cancer risk. The large majority of studies in humans has found no protective effect of fibre from cereals but has found a protective effect of fibre from vegetables and possibly fruits (20). Diets rich in fibre are also rich sources of nutrients such as antioxidant vitamins and minerals with potential cancer inhibiting properties. Vegetarian diets seem to provide a protective effect from the risk of colon cancer.

Epidemiological studies consistently show that fat intake is positively related to colorectal cancer risk. Energy intakes also seem to be consistently higher in cases with colorectal cancer than in comparison groups and many studies have hitherto failed to show an energy-independent effect of fat intake. More recently Willett *et al.* (20) have shown, after adjusting for total energy intake, that the consumption of animal fat was associated with increased colon cancer risk. They also demonstrated that the trend in risk was highly significant when the relative risk of different quintiles of fat intake was related to the risk of large bowel cancer. The risk was not, however, associated with vegetable fat but with the consumption of saturated animal fat.

In summary, dietary factors seem to be important determinants of colon cancer risk. An effect of saturated fat intake appears to exist independently of energy intake. Meat intake may increase risk – an effect that may not be independent of saturated fat intake, although it is likely that the manner of cooking meat may be mutagenic. Dietary fibre from vegetable sources may also be protective and reduce risk, while the possible protection from the consumption of cereal fibres seems to be uncertain.

5.4.5.2   Breast cancer

This is a common cause of death among women in the UK. Correlation studies have provided evidence of a direct association between breast cancer mortality and the intake of energy and dietary fat, and specific sources of dietary fat such as milk and meat. Cross-cultural ecological studies have provided evidence of the association of fat intake with breast cancer risk. However, neither case-control studies nor prospective studies reported to date provide unequivocal support for the association between fat intake and risk of breast cancer in postmenopausal women. The most recent analysis has found no association between fat intake and intake of dietary fibre and breast cancer risk in either pre- or postmenopausal women (21). Other dietary factors that may be implicated are vegetable consumption, which may be protective, while a modest increase in risk has been consistently seen with increased alcohol intake in women.

5.4.5.3   Role of diet in cancers

The available evidence suggests that high intake of total fat in the diet, more specifically the intake of saturated fats of animal origin, may be associated with an increased risk of cancers of the colon and breast. Diets high in plant foods, especially green and yellow vegetables and fruits, are strongly associated with a lower incidence of a wide range of cancers. Such diets tend to be low in saturated fat, high in complex carbohydrate and fibre and rich in several antioxidant vitamins, including vitamin A and beta-carotene. Sustained and consistent intake of alcohol is also associated with cancers, in particular those of the upper alimentary tract. Dietary factors thus seem to be important in the causation of cancers at many sites, and dietary modifications may reduce cancer risk. At present, it is difficult to quantify the contribution of diet to total cancer incidence and mortality. However, a good preventive measure is to increase the consumption of fruits and vegetables. Innumerable studies have helped conclude that the consumption of higher levels of vegetables and fruits is associated consistently with reduced risk of cancer in most sites. Vegetables and fruits are exceptional sources of a large number of potentially anti-carcinogenic agents, including vitamin A and carotenoids, vitamins C and E, selenium, dietary fibre and a whole range of chemical compounds such as flavonoids, phenols and plant sterols. Much of their protective effect is unknown or poorly understood. The WHO and the more recent World Cancer Research Fund (WCRF) report (22) recommend intakes of 400 g per day of fruit and vegetables (excluding potatoes) as a reasonable dietary goal to aim for to reduce the risk of cancers in adults.

In summary, a prudent diet, which is limited in total fats and is low in saturated and *trans* fatty acids, and has an acceptable level and balanced mix of PUFAs from fish and appropriate plant sources, and provides a high MUFA content and with adequate amount of carbohydrates mainly from cereal sources would help prevent many of the diet-related NCDs. Consumption of a wide variety of fruits and vegetables in sufficient quantities daily is also essential. Restriction of salt and alcohol intake is also essential. The importance of preventing physical inactivity cannot be emphasised too strongly.

5.5   References

1.   Department of Health. *Dietary Reference Values for Food Energy and Nutrients for the United Kingdom.* Report on Health and Social Subjects No. 41. Report of the Panel on Dietary Reference Values of the Committee on Medical Aspects on Food Policy. London. HMSO, 1991.

2.   Gregory J., Foster K., Tyler H., Wiseman M. *The Dietary and Nutritional Survey of Adults.* London. HMSO, 1990.

3.   Black A.E., Prentice A.M., Goldberg G.R. *et al.* Measurement of total energy expenditure provide insights into validity of dietary measurements of energy intake. *Journal of the Dietetic Association,* 1993, 93, 572-79.

4.   Livingstone M.B.E., Prentice A.M., Strain J.J. *et al.* Accuracy of weighed dietary records in studies of diet and health. *British Medical Journal,* 1990 (300), 708-12.

5.   Pryer J.A., Vrijheid M., Nichols R., Kiggins M., Elliott P. Who are the "low energy reporters", in The Dietary and Nutritional Survey of British Adults. *International Journal of Epidemiology,* 1997, 25 (1), 146-54.

6.   Hietmann B., Lissner L. Dietary underreporting by obese individuals – is it specific or non-specific? *British Medical Journal,*1986, 292, 983-87.

7.   Schwerin H.S., Stanton J.L., Smith J.L., Riley A.M., Brett B.E. Food, eating habits and health: a further examination of relationships between food eating patterns and nutritional health. *American Journal of Clinical Nutrition,* 1982, 35, 1319-25.

8.   Randall E., Marshall J.R., Grahman S., Brasure J. Patterns of food use and their associations with nutrient intakes. *American Journal of Clinical Nutrition,* 1990, 52, 739-45.

9.   Pryer J.A., Nichols R., Elliott P., Thakrar B., Brunner E., Marmot M. Dietary patterns among a national random sample of British adults. *Journal of Epidemiology and Community Health*, 2001, 55, 29-37.

10.   Marmot M., Elliott P. (Editors) *Coronary Heart Disease Epidemiology. From Aetiology to Public Health.* Oxford. Oxford University Press, 1992.

11.   Keys A. *Seven Countries: A Multivariate Analysis of Death and Coronary Heart Disease.* Cambridge, Massachusetts. Howard University Press, 1980.

12.   WHO Expert Committee. *Prevention of Coronary Heart Disease.* Technical Report Series. Geneva. World Health Organization, 1982.

13.   MacMohan S., Peto R., Cutler J. *et al.* Blood pressure, stroke and coronary heart disease. *Lancet*, 1990, 335, 65-774.

14.   Intersalt Cooperative Research Group. Intersalt: an international study of electrolyte excretion and blood pressure. *British Medical Journal*, 1988, 298, 920-4.

15.   Law M.R., Frost C.D., Wald N.J. By how much does dietary salt reduction lower blood pressure? *British Medical Journal*, 1991, 302, 811-24.

16.   Sacks F.M., Svetkey L.P., Vollmer W.M. *et al.* Effects on blood pressure of reduced dietary sodium and dietary approaches to stop hypertension (DASH) diet. *New England Journal of Medicine*, 2001, 344, 3-10.

17.   Cappucio F.P., MacGregor G.A. Does potassium supplementation lower blood pressure? A meta-analysis of published trials. *Journal of Hypertension*, 1991, 9, 465-73.

18.   World Health Organization. *Obesity: Preventing and Managing the Global Epidemic.* Report of an Expert Consultation. Technical Report Series, 894. Geneva, 2000.

19.   Doll R., Peto R. *The Causes of Cancer.* Oxford University Press, Oxford, 1981.

20.   Willet W.C., Stampfer M.J., Colditz G.A., Rosner B.A., Speitzer F.E. Relation of meat, fat and fibre intake to the risk of colon cancer in a prospective study among women. *New England Journal of Medicine*, 1990, 323, 1664-72.

21.   Willet W.C., Hunter D.J., Stampfer M.J. *et al.* Dietary fat and fibre in relation to role of breast cancer. *Journal of American Medical Association*, 1992, 268, 2037-44.

22.   World Cancer Research Fund. *Food, Nutrition and the Prevention of Cancer: a Global Perspective.* Washington DC. American Institute for Cancer Research, 1997.

6. NUTRITION OF THE AGEING AND ELDERLY

Prakash Shetty, Jane Pryer and Astrid Fletcher

6.1   Introduction

The elderly are an increasingly important demographic constituent of the population and for a number of reasons are vulnerable to poor nutritional health. The aged and the elderly are not a homogeneous group. They comprise individuals still actively pursuing careers or enjoying a healthy retirement or even caring for frail and dependent relatives. They may also be frail and dependent themselves. The elderly are categorised as the 'young old' aged 60–69 years, 'old old' aged 70–79 years and the 'oldest old' who are 80 plus years. In the UK, it was estimated in 1997 that 14.4 million individuals were over 65 years while 3.56 million were over 80 years. In general, in industrialised countries such as the UK, the proportion of the oldest is growing more rapidly than that of any other age group. Their numbers are expected to increase by the year 2025 to 26.8% of the population from the current 16.3% in these developed societies.

The elderly are to be considered a special group for a number of important reasons, which include their physical and mental frailty, widespread prejudice and ageism. Unrecognised health problems, including nutritional problems, are common among the elderly. They are also commonly victims of multiple pathologies and rarely have a single health problem. They have loss of adaptability and the increasing costs of care contribute to prejudicial views of their ability to benefit from health care investments. This chapter will outline the nutrient requirements of the elderly, present data on the current dietary and nutritional situation of the elderly in the United Kingdom and provide an outline of the nutritional and related health problems of this vulnerable age group within our population.

6.2   Nutrient Requirements of the Elderly

Decline in organ function and changes in body mass and body composition as well as declines in physical activity levels that occur with ageing are bound to influence the nutrient needs of the elderly individual. Most recommended allowances for nutrients for the elderly, apart from energy, are not broken down separately by decade since data that permit such disaggregated recommendations are lacking.

6.2.1   Energy

It is well documented that the energy needs of the elderly decrease with age. This is attributed both to a reduction in physical activity levels (which accounts for almost two-thirds of the reduction) and to a decrease in basal metabolism. The reduction in physical activity is due to lack of occupational activities on retirement and a reduced load of optional household activities. Disabilities associated with ageing may also contribute to a reduction in energy expended on physical activities. However, there is evidence of an increase in the energy cost of activity due to reduced efficiency of movements. Table 6.I provides estimates of the average energy requirements of men and women aged over 60 years for the UK (1). The general consensus of the UK Expert Committee was that a physical activity level (PAL) of 1.5 times basal metabolic rate (BMR) be considered appropriate for those aged 60+ years irrespective of sex or of whether they were housebound, or institutionalised or living at home.

TABLE 6.I
Estimated energy requirements for elderly (60+ years) men and women

	Weight (kg)	Energy requirement MJ per day	Calories per day
Men:			
60-64 years	74.0	9.93	2380
65-74 years	71.0	9.71	2330
75+ years	69.0	8.77	2100
Women:			
60-64 years	63.5	7.99	1900
65-74 years	63.0	7.96	1900
75+ years	60.0	7.61	1810

Source: Department of Health (1)

119

6.2.2   Protein

Little information on the protein needs of the elderly as different from that of adults is currently available. However, studies support the conclusion that the protein needs of the elderly are not lower than those of younger adults and that they may in fact require more dietary protein per kg body weight to maintain nitrogen balance at their customary levels of energy intake, which is lower than that of young adults. The current recommendation would be 0.8 g high-quality protein per kg of body weight. On the whole, it would be advisable to have a daily intake of 1.0 g per kg body weight in the elderly.

6.2.3   Vitamins

Low or inadequate energy intakes and the physiological changes in the gut with ageing, which may decrease the absorption of vitamins, may influence the recommended allowances for vitamins for the elderly.

It would be reasonable to assume that the requirements for the B group vitamins – thiamin (1.0-1.2 mg), riboflavin (1.2-1.4 mg), folate (180-200 µg) and for ascorbate (vitamin C: 60 mg) may be adequate at the levels recommended for adults (the values in parenthesis are those recommended for US adults). The adult recommendations for vitamin D (5 µg), vitamins B_6 (1.6-2.0 mg) and B_{12} (2.0 µg) may be too low for the elderly. Lack of exposure to sunlight, reduced vitamin D synthesis in the ageing skin, and impaired renal conversion to active vitamin D are the reasons why requirements for vitamin D may be higher in the elderly. This is compounded by the observation that the elderly generally consume less vitamin D rich foods, such as seafood and fortified milk products. On the other hand, the recommended intake for vitamin A for young adults (800-1,000 µg of retinol equivalent) may be too high for the elderly. The reasons attributed are the possibility of a higher absorption in the elderly due to changes in the luminal epithelium as well as a decreased uptake by the liver. Whether requirements of other vitamins are different from those of young adults is not clear, largely because there are insufficient or conflicting data in the literature. Table 6.II summarises the recommendations made for the elderly for vitamins by the UK Department of Health report of 1991.

TABLE 6.II
Reference Nutrition Intakes for vitamins for adults aged 50+ years

Reference Nutrient Intakes for vitamins	Male	Female
Thiamin (mg/day)	0.9	0.8
Riboflavin (mg/day)	1.3	1.1
Niacin (nicotinic acid equivalent) (mg/day)	16	12
Vitamin B_6 (mg/day)	1.4	1.2
Vitamin B_{12} (µg/day)	1.5	1.5
Folate (µg/day)	200	200
Vitamin C (mg/day)	40	40
Vitamin A (µg/day)	600	600

Source: Department of Health (1)

6.2.4   Minerals

As with vitamins, direct studies that may throw light on the requirements of minerals in the elderly are relatively few, and hence the ability of national and international committees to makes separate recommendations for the elderly is restricted. However, most countries recommend a decreased intake of iron, calcium and iodine. The reduced requirement for iron is the only one well documented, particularly for women, since the onset of menopause results in substantial decreases of iron requirements, i.e. a reduction of 1.5 or 1.8 mg per day from the adult recommendations of 10 mg per day. Table 6.III summarises the recommendations made for reference nutrient intakes (RNIs) of minerals for the elderly by the UK Department of Health report of 1991 (1).

6.2.5   Fluids and alcohol

Since the water content of the body is reduced and possibly the ability of the kidney to concentrate urine decreases with age, an increased water intake is recommended to excrete the waste products form the body. Proper fluid intake becomes even more important if the elderly are on medication or have impaired renal function because of disease. The elderly need to be advised about alcohol use since the lower levels of body water tend to raise blood alcohol levels more readily than in young adults. In addition, it is important to caution the elderly about the interaction of some drugs, such as barbiturates, which may have an adverse reaction with alcohol.

TABLE 6.III
Reference Nutrient Intakes for minerals (SI units) for adults aged 50+ years

Reference Nutrient Intakes for minerals	Male	Female
Calcium (mg/day)	700	700
Phosphorus (mg/day)	550	550
Magnesium (mg/day)	300	270
Sodium (mg/day)	1,600	1,600
Potassium (mg/day)	3,500	3,500
Chloride (mg/day)	2,500	2,500
Iron (mg/day)	8.7	8.7
Zinc (mg/day)	9.5	7.0
Copper (mg/day)	1.2	1.2
Selenium (µg/day)	75	60
Iodine (µg/day)	140	140

Source: Department of Health (1)

6.3   Nutritional Status and Dietary Intakes of the Elderly

The elderly need a good diet, like the general adult population, to enable them to meet their nutrient needs. Elderly people are less physically active and may hence need lower energy intakes. They may also have a lowered appetite, which may be aggravated by other illnesses that they are more prone to with ageing. Very often they may be on medication that affects their appetite or desire for food further. Older people who have lost their teeth or have other oral or gum problems may find it difficult to chew their food and may need softer foods. On a normal family diet, they may eat little and become malnourished. They may therefore eat less food and as a result get lower levels of micronutrients, although their requirements for micronutrients are unchanged while their requirements for total energy are lowered. Consequently, micronutrient deficiencies are common in the elderly. In traditional societies, the elderly continue to be cared for at home (although this is rapidly changing), while in other more affluent societies the elderly are often institutionalised. The atmosphere in these situations may not always be suitable to the needs of the elderly and may precipitate emotional and psychological problems that would in turn influence their feeding behaviour. Chronic illnesses and diminishing vision and hearing and increasing disability will also constrain the ability of the elderly to purchase, cook and provide for nutritious diets even when they live at home by themselves.

6.3.1 *Desirable and healthy body weights for the elderly*

There is no universal agreement with regard to what is a desirable body weight for the elderly male or female. Height decreases with age – probably about 3 cm in men and 5 cm in women. Body weight, on the other hand, peaks in men between the ages of 35 and 65 years but may continue to increase in women. This means that the body mass index [BMI = weight (in kg)/height squared (in metres)] will continue to increase with age. The relationship between BMI and morbidity/mortality from chronic diseases in the elderly are not as clear as one expects from adults. There is some evidence that mild or moderate overweight among the elderly is not such a potent risk factor even after correcting for smoking (2). There is much that needs to be understood in this area.

6.3.2 *Micronutrient intakes and deficiencies in the elderly*

Decreased intake of food, whatever the contributing cause, together with a lowered energy intake and requirement coupled with a generally unaltered requirement for vitamins and minerals, increases the risk of micronutrient deficiencies in the elderly.

The recognised micronutrient deficiencies in the elderly are outlined in Table 6.IV.

TABLE 6.IV
Vitamin deficiency syndromes in the elderly

Deficiency	Syndrome or clinical manifestations
Vitamin A	Failure of dark adaptation
Vitamin D	Osteomalacia
Vitamin K	Haemorrhagic states
Thiamin	Beri-beri, Wernikes-Korsakoff's syndrome
Riboflavin	Angular stomatitis, glossitis, dermatitis
Vitamin B_6	Dermatitis, peripheral neuritis, depression, anaemia
Folic acid	Anaemia, organic brain syndrome
Vitamin B_{12}	Anaemia, glossitis, anorexia, peripheral neuropathy
Vitamin C	Non-specific (confusional state, lassitude, fatigue), scurvy
Calcium	Osteoporosis
Iron	Anaemia

Adapted from Roe (3)

Clinically evident micronutrient deficiencies are seen among the more vulnerable elderly, who include the socio-economically deprived, those with limited educational background, the isolated, the institutionalised, those with mental and physical handicaps, those who abuse alcohol and others who use medication that may manifest drug-nutrient interactions.

6.3.2.1   B Group vitamins

Although thiamin requirements are not altered in the elderly, thiamin deficiency in the elderly, when seen, is largely the result of alcoholism possibly accompanied by lowered thiamin intake. Requirements of riboflavin, niacin and folate are not different from those of young adults. Although atrophic gastritis with ageing causes malabsorption of folic acid, this is more than offset by the folate synthesised by bacteria in the large bowel and which is absorbed. The requirements for B_{12} are not likely to be different and the evidence from studies suggests that the levels of B_{12} in the elderly are low. This implies that there may be decreased absorption of the vitamin, particularly in the presence of atrophic gastritis.

6.3.2.2   Vitamin C

The requirements for vitamin C are not different from those of young adults in the case of the elderly and there is nothing to suggest that the absorption of ascorbic acid is affected in any way with age. However, factors such as smoking, medications and emotional and environmental stress all adversely affect vitamin C status in the elderly.

6.3.2.3   Fat-soluble vitamins (A, D, E & K)

Although the need for vitamin A may be reduced in the elderly, it would be prudent to assume that maintaining adequate levels similar to those of young adults is highly desirable. For a number of reasons outlined earlier, the elderly are prone to vitamin D deficiencies and hence supplementation is recommended, particularly for those who are homebound or in nursing homes. There is no evidence of increased need for vitamins E and K and no evidence of deficiencies in the elderly.

6.3.2.4   Minerals

The level of calcium intake throughout one's lifetime is a factor contributing to the risk of osteoporosis in the elderly – particularly in post-menopausal women. Calcium absorption decreases with age, and achlorhydria seen in some elderly can make this worse. Poor vitamin D status and reduced physical activity are other factors that may increase the risk of osteoporosis.

Iron deficiency is commonly seen in the elderly and is due to inadequate iron intake, reduced iron absorption in the presence of achlorhydria or atrophic gastritis and blood loss due to chronic disease.

6.3.2.5   Vitamin supplements

The consumption of vitamin supplements is widespread among the elderly in developed countries; women are more likely to use supplements than men (53% vs 38%). The fact that the mechanisms to clear and eliminate these nutrients is impaired with age should be a matter of concern when taking supplements, particularly when setting upper limits of intakes. There is a growing interest in the issue of supplements in preventing the occurrence of chronic diseases, slowing the ageing process and particularly functions such as vision and reducing the risk of cataracts in the elderly.

6.4   The National Diet and Nutrition Survey: People aged 65 Years and Over

The National Diet and Nutrition Survey (NDNS) provides a valuable database of the real situation with regard to the nutritional status and dietary patterns of the elderly in the UK. Two nationally representative samples were drawn from adults aged 65 years and over from (i) free-living individuals, and (ii) individuals living in institutions, and was designed to consist of roughly equal numbers of men and women in the 65-74 and 75-84 age groups and of women aged 85 years and over. A smaller number of men aged 85 years or more were sampled, as a proportion of men in this age group in the population is relatively low. Selected residential and nursing homes drew the sample of elderly people in institutions.

The survey design included an interview to provide general information about dietary habits and background information about health status, medication and socio-economic characteristics; a weighed dietary record of food and drink consumed over four consecutive days; a 7-day record of bowel movements; an interviewer-administered "memory questionnaire" to test cognitive function; a "depressive questionnaire"; physical measurements of height, weight, demi-span, mid-upper arm circumference, waist and hip circumference, blood pressure and hand grip strength; request for samples of blood and urine; and an interview to provide information on oral health, followed by a dental examination. In the free-living sample, the participants completed the dietary record with help from the interviewer, while in institutions it was completed by the interviewer and care staff. The fieldwork was carried out over 12 months to take account of possible seasonal variations in eating habits. The interview, which was the first stage of the survey protocol, was completed by 75% and 94%, respectively, of the eligible samples of free-living people and people in institutions. Records of weighed dietary intake were obtained from 1,275 free-living people and 412 people in institutions. Physical measurements were obtained for 71% of the free-living sample, and 85% of people in institutions. A blood sample was obtained for 60% and 68%, respectively, of the free-living sample and the institutionalised sample.

6.4.1 Results of survey

6.4.1.1 Foods and drinks consumed by the NDNS elderly

In the free-living group, the food and drink consumed during the 4-day period were tea (95%) boiled, mashed or baked potato (87%), white bread (74%) and biscuits (71%). Whole-grain cereals and high-fibre cereals were eaten by 50%, while other breakfast cereals were eaten by 28%. Whole milk was consumed by 58%, compared with 45% for semi-skimmed milk, and 11% for skimmed milk. Sixty-two per cent ate cheese. Of fats used for spreading, butter was consumed by 43%, while 23% used polyunsaturated reduced-fat spreads, 13% used other reduced-fat spreads, and 10% used soft margarine. The most commonly consumed meats were bacon and ham (64%) followed by beef, veal and dishes (49%), chicken, turkey and dishes (43%), pork (23%), and lamb (21%). Coated or fried fish was consumed by 36%, oily fish by 32% and other white fish dishes by 21%. Raw tomatoes were eaten by 52% and salad and other raw vegetables by 47%. Cooked leafy green vegetables were eaten by 51%, cooked carrots by 39%, and other cooked vegetables by 66%. Forty-four per cent ate chips. Of fresh fruit, apples and pears were consumed by 48%, bananas by 44%,and citrus fruits by 27%. Table sugar was consumed by 55%, preserves such as jams and marmalade by 51%, and chocolate and confectionery by 22%. Coffee was consumed by 60%,

126

non-diet soft drinks by 28%, fruit juice by 26%, beers and lagers by 19%, wine by 16% and spirits by 14%.

In institutions, the most common foods consumed were boiled, mashed or baked potatoes (98%), tea (96%), buns, cakes and pastries and cereal-based milk puddings (89%), other cooked vegetables (84%), white bread (82%), biscuits (77%), leafy green vegetables (77%), peas (74%), table sugar (76%), cooked carrots (72%), and other cereal-based puddings (72%). Fifty-two per cent drank whole milk, 49% drank semi-skimmed milk, and 3% drank skimmed milk; 49% ate cheese. Of fats used for spreading, butter was consumed by 44%, polyunsaturated-reduced spreads by 22%, other reduced spreads by 23% and soft margarines by 15%. The most commonly eaten meats were beef and veal and dishes made from them, followed by bacon and ham, chicken and turkey, lamb, and pork. Among fish, coated or fried fish was consumed by 56%, oily fish by 34% and other white fish and fish dishes by 18%. Seventy-seven per cent ate green leafy vegetables, 42% ate raw tomatoes, and 36% ate salad and other raw vegetables. Of fresh fruit, bananas were consumed by 35%, apples and pears by 25% and citrus fruits by 12%. Table sugar was used by 76% and preserves by 69%. Non-diet soft drinks were consumed by 49% and coffee by 40% (4).

6.4.1.2   *Energy and protein intake*

The mean daily energy intake for free-living men was 8.02 MJ (1909 kcal), and 5.98 MJ (1422 kcal) for free-living women. For those institutionalised, the daily energy intake for men was 8.14 MJ (1935 kcal), and 6.94 MJ (1650) kcal for women.

The daily protein intake for free-living men was 71.5 g for men and 56.0 g for women. The average intake was 134% of the RNI for free-living men and 120% of the RNI for women. In the institution group, the average daily protein intake for men was 66.5 g, and 56.7 g for women, which was 125% of the RNI for men and 122% of the RNI for women.

6.4.1.3   *Carbohydrate and dietary fat intake*

The average daily intake of total carbohydrates was 232 g for free-living men and 175 g for women. In the institution group, the average daily intake of total carbohydrate was 256 g for men and 222 g for women. In the free-living sample, the average daily total fat intake was 74.7 g for men and 58.0 g for women, which contributed 35.7% and 36.1% of food energy, respectively. In the institution group, the average daily total fat intake was 76.9 g for men and 65.5 g for women, which contributed 35.1% and 34.8% of food energy, respectively. These contributions to food energy matched the population average dietary reference value (DRV) of no more than 35% energy derived from fat recommended by most committees, including COMA. Saturated fatty acids contributed an average of 14.6% and 15.3% of food energy for men and women in the free-living group, respectively, and 15.2% for men and 15.4% for women in the institution group. These contributions to food energy exceeded the population average DRV of no more than 11% recommended by COMA. *Cis* monounsaturated fatty acids provided 11% of food energy in the free-living group and 10.5% for the institution group, below the population average DRV of 13% recommended by COMA. *Cis* n-6 polyunsaturated fatty acids contributed 4.9% of food energy in the free-living group, and 4.1% in the institution group. *Cis* n-3 polyunsaturated fatty acids contributed less than 1% of food energy. The total *cis* polyunsaturated fatty acids contributions to food energy in both groups were slightly below the population average DRV of 6.5% recommended by COMA (4).

6.4.1.4   *Vitamin and mineral intakes*

Intakes of all vitamins were above the RNI for free-living and institutional groups, apart from that of vitamin D. Ninety-seven per cent of the free-living group and 99% of the institutional group had intakes of vitamin D below the RNI. Calcium, phosphorus, manganese, iodine, chloride and sodium and copper were above the RNI for both sexes in the free-living and in the institutional group. Iron, potassium and zinc were below the RNI.

6.4.1.5   *Nutritional status*

The mean heights of free-living men and women were 169.8 cm and 150.0 cm, respectively. Men living in institutions were shorter than the free-living group, at 164.5 cm; however, women had the same mean height as their free-living counterparts. In the free-living group, the mean weight of men was 76.5 kg and that of women was 64.9 kg. In the institution group, men weighed 66.1 kg on average, compared with 56.5 kg for women. The mean BMI was 26.5 for men and 26.8 for women in the free-living sample, and 25.0 for men and 24.9 for women in the institution group. About two-thirds of free-living participants were classified as overweight (BMI over 25), and 46% of institution group were overweight. Waist-hip circumference was used as a measure of the distribution of body fat. Fat deposited around the abdominal region is associated with increased risk of disease, for example heart disease. The mean waist-hip ratio for men was 0.93 and 0.83 for women in the free-living group, and 0.93 for men and 0.86 for women in the institution group (4).

6.4.1.6   Blood pressure

Systolic and diastolic blood pressure was measured and participants who were taking drugs that lowered blood pressure were not excluded from the results. Mean systolic pressure was 149 mmHg for men and 155 mmHg for women and the mean diastolic pressure was 80 mmHg for men and 78 mmHg for women in the free-living group. For those in the institution group, mean systolic pressure was 136 mmHg for men and 147 mmHg for women; the mean diastolic pressure was 71 mmHg for men and 73 mmHg for women (4).

6.4.1.7   Regional differences

The nationally representative sample of free-living participants was classified into three regions: Scotland and the North; Central, South West and Wales; London and the South East. A number of differences were observed between the North and South regions, with results from Central, South West and Wales region tending to fall between those of the other two groups. Free-living participants from Scotland and the North were less likely to consume fruit than in other regions, but were more likely to consume beef, veal and dishes made from them, meat pies and pasties, and soup. They were more likely to consume potato chips, while participants in London and the South East were more likely to consume fried or roast potatoes, and were more likely to consume leafy vegetables, semi-skimmed milk and coffee than those in Scotland and the North. There were no significant differences by region in energy intake. Average intake of total sugars was lowest in Scotland and in the North, and highest in the Central, South West and Wales regions. Participants from Scotland and the North had the lowest intake for NSP. There were no differences in average intake of total fat or fatty acids between regions. Average intakes of vitamins were higher in London and the South East than in Scotland and the North. Participants in Scotland and the

North had higher intakes of sodium and chloride per unit of energy and lower intakes for potassium and calcium per unit of energy (4).

6.4.1.8   Socio-economic factors

Free-living participants were classified into two social class groups based on the current or former occupation of the household head, (manual or non-manual) and two groups according to whether they received benefits (excluding pension) and into four groups by income. There were differences in food consumption between manual and non-manual groups. Participants who were in the non-manual group were more likely to consume the following foods and drinks: bread other than white, biscuits, wholegrain or high-fibre breakfast cereals, cream, yoghurt, oily fish salad, raw tomatoes and other raw vegetables, cooked vegetables, fruit, fruit juice, coffee, wine and spirits. Those in the manual group were more likely to consume white bread and soft margarines than those in the non-manual group. Average energy intakes were lower among participants who were in the manual social class group, those who were receiving benefits and those in the lowest income group. These groups had the lowest average intakes of protein, total carbohydrate, total sugars and non-starch polysaccharide (NSP). In regard to vitamins and minerals, men and women in the manual social class group had lower intakes per unit of energy intake of vitamin C, biotin, iron, calcium, phosphorus, magnesium, potassium and manganese but higher intakes of sodium. Men in the lowest income group had lower intakes per unit of energy of vitamin C, vitamin A, retinol, riboflavin, pantothenic acid, phosphorus and potassium than those in other income groups, while women in this group had lower intakes per unit of energy for vitamin C, biotin, magnesium potassium and manganese (4).

6.4.1.9   Household composition

Average daily energy intakes were lower for both men and women who lived alone compared with those who lived with others. For men but not women, this difference in energy intake was reflected in lower intakes among those who lived alone for protein, total carbohydrate, starch and NSP, and also for calcium, and lower plasma C concentration than in those who lived with others (4).

6.4.2   Clusters of dietary patterns among UK elderly

There has been increasing interest in the identification of patterns of diet consumed by the elderly since it is the combination of foods that groups of individuals eat that constitutes the overall diet rather than the presence or absence of specific food items. It is these patterns and clusters that are of importance to nutritional and health status of the individual within the group and is also amenable to change by interventions. The NDNS survey was subjected to a multivariate statistical technique of cluster analysis to identify groups within this population who reported similar patterns of diet. Analyses were conducted for men and women separately. Twenty-seven food/drink groups were used in the analysis. Continuous food and beverage group values (all estimated in g per week) were standardised by converting to the standard normal deviate. This was to ensure that clusters were not influenced by food categories with high specific gravity, such as beverages. Statistical comparisons were made across the clusters in terms of reported food group consumption, and the intakes of macronutrients and micronutrients (5).

Among men, three large clusters were identified, making up 86% of the male sample, and three small clusters accounting for the rest (14%). Among women, three large clusters were identified, making up 83% of the female sample, and three small clusters accounted for the remaining 17%.

6.4.2.1   Male dietary clusters

The most prevalent male dietary group or cluster (48% of the male sample) reported median food/drinks groups in the 'high' category such as whole milk and cream and low-fat spreads. This cluster also had a 'moderate-high' consumption of refined cereals, including white bread, biscuits, cakes and pastries, eggs, bacon and ham, beef, veal, lamb, pork, liver and meat products, fish, potatoes, vegetables, sugar and tea/coffee. They also had a 'moderate-low' consumption of brown bread, cheese, and fruit, sauces and pickles. This dietary pattern is interesting in that it had elements of the traditional diet, and also had elements of a healthy diet. This pattern was designated a "mixed diet".

The second dietary cluster among males (i.e. 21% of the male sample) reported food/drinks groups in the 'high' category for brown bread, low-fat spreads, fruit and alcohol, and in the 'moderate-high' category for biscuits, cakes, pastries, cheese, liver and meat products, fish, potatoes, vegetables, tea/coffee, sauces and pickles. This cluster also demonstrated 'moderate-low' for whole milk and cream,

131

eggs, bacon and ham, beef, veal, pork, sugar and preserves, with 'low' consumption of food items such as refined cereals, including white bread, rice and pasta, yoghurt and ice cream, butter, margarine, chicken and turkey, fruit juice, soft drinks, soup and pickles. This dietary pattern could be considered a "healthy diet". However, this diet was also high in alcohol, which has generally not hitherto been considered an attribute of a "healthy" diet.

The next cluster of males had median intakes in the 'high' category, including those of whole milk and cream, cheese, and alcohol; and in the 'moderate-high category' for refined cereals, including white bread, biscuits, cakes and pastries, eggs, meat products, fish, fruit, tea/coffee, and potatoes, vegetables and fruit. This third male cluster also showed a 'moderate-low' category for brown bread, butter, margarine, bacon and ham, beef, veal, pork, sugar and preserves and sauces and pickles as well as a 'low' category for food items such as pasta and rice, low-fat milk, yoghurt and ice cream, chicken and turkey, fruit juice, soft drinks, and soups and pickles. This dietary pattern may be considered a "traditional diet high in alcohol".

6.4.2.2   Female dietary clusters

The most prevalent female dietary group was a cluster of 33% of the female sample with reported food/drink groups in the 'high' category, including biscuits, cakes, pastries, whole milk and cream, sugar and preserves; and a 'moderate-high' for brown bread, eggs, meat products, potatoes, vegetables, and fruit. This female group also demonstrated a 'moderate-low' response for white bread, cheese, bacon/ham, beef, veal, pork, fish, tea/coffee, and sauces and pickles and a 'low' for butter. This diet was a "sweet, traditional diet". The second female dietary cluster (32% of female sample) reported median food/drink groups in the 'high' categories, including brown bread and whole grain cereals, low fat milk, yoghurt, cheese, low fat spread, chicken and turkey, fruit. This cluster had a 'moderate-high' for beef, veal, pork, fish, potatoes, vegetables, sauces and pickles; and a 'moderate-low' for white bread, biscuits, cakes, pastries, eggs, bacon/ham, meat products, meat products, sugar and preserves, and tea/coffee. This cluster also showed a 'low' for whole milk and cream. This diet could be considered a 'healthy' diet. The last female cluster reported food/drink groups in the 'high' category for white bread, and low-fat milk; and 'moderate-high' for low-fat spread, bacon/ham, beef, veal, pork, chicken, meat products, fish, sugars and preserves, tea/coffee, and potatoes. They also had a 'moderate-low' response for brown bread, biscuits, cakes, pastries, vegetables, fruit, sauces and pickles;

and a 'low' for whole milk and cream. This diet is interesting as it has elements from a healthy diet: low-fat milk and spread, brown bread, low in biscuits, cakes and pastries, high in white meats and fish – along with elements from a traditional diet, i.e. white bread, potatoes, red meat, and meat products, and low vegetables and fruit, and high sugars and preserves. This dietary pattern could be considered a 'mixed diet'.

6.4.2.3   Macronutrient densities

Of the clusters, the 'healthy' diet clusters had the lowest mean densities for total fats, saturated fats, and *trans* fatty acids and highest for carbohydrate, starch, n-6 polyunsaturated fatty acids, and fibre. Conversely, the 'traditional' diet cluster had the highest mean densities for total fats and saturated fats, and had the lowest mean density for fibre. The diet clusters with elements of a 'traditional and healthy' diet, compared with the 'traditional' diet, had higher mean densities for carbohydrate, protein, n-6 polyunsaturated fatty acids, n-3 polyunsaturated fatty acids, polyunsaturated fatty acids and starch, and lower mean densities for total fats and saturated fat. The male traditional diet high in alcohol, compared with the traditional diet, had lower mean densities of carbohydrates, *trans* fatty acids, n-6 unsaturated fatty acids, n-3 unsaturated fatty acids total sugars and starch, and higher mean densities of alcohol, total fatty acids and saturated fats.

6.4.2.4   Micronutrient densities

The 'healthy' diet clusters had the highest mean densities for 18 of 20 minerals and vitamins. The traditional diets had the lowest mean micronutrient densities for 16 of 20 micronutrients. The others had the lowest mean micronutrient densities for 15 of 20 micronutrients. Interestingly, those clusters with elements from both a traditional diet and a healthy diet had mean micronutrient densities higher than the traditional diet for 12-14 of 20 micronutrient densities. Lastly, the 'traditional' diet high in alcohol, compared with the 'traditional' had mean densities of micronutrients lower for seven nutrients, including phosphorus, copper, vitamin D, vitamin E, vitamin C, thiamin and pantothenic acid, and higher for nine nutrients, including calcium, potassium, magnesium, iodine, vitamin A, niacin, vitamin B_{12}, folate, and biotin.

6.4.2.5   Socio-demographic and behavioural profiles

Elderly males and females in the 'traditional diet' and the 'mixed diet' groups were more likely to be smokers and to come from manual social classes. They were more likely to be in receipt of state benefits and to be on lower incomes than those in the 'healthy diet' groups. Among men, those adopting the 'healthy diet' had in general more years of education than those in the 'traditional diet' and 'mixed diet' groups, but this was not so amongst women. Women in the 'healthy' and 'mixed diet' groups were more likely to report having consciously changed their diet in the past. There was an age effect in both men and women, with higher proportions of young elderly in the 'healthy' diet group, and the more elderly individuals in the 'traditional' and 'mixed diet' groups.

6.4.3   Conclusions

Cluster analysis of the elderly NDNS survey has enabled the identification of six large groups among UK men and women aged 65 years and over, who differed not only in terms of reported dietary intakes but also with respect to their nutritional status, social status and behavioural profile. Further research is needed on mortality and morbidity by clusters. Nevertheless, these results should be of relevance to the development, monitoring and targeting of public health nutrition policy in the UK. In particular, they could be used to develop a tailored health promotion programme based on diet clusters, by positively reinforcing the healthy diet, pointing out deficiencies in the mixed diet and targeting the traditional diet for improvements.

6.5   Special Nutritional Problems of the Elderly

There are several health problems that are related to diet and nutrition that the elderly are particularly vulnerable to. These are in addition to the chronic degenerative diseases all adults are increasingly at risk of as age advances, such as cardiovascular disease and cancer. Only some of the important ones are dealt with briefly here.

6.5.1   Osteoporosis

Primary osteoporosis affects elderly post-menopausal women in particular. It may appear before the age of 70 or thereafter and is often subdivided into simple and accelerated forms. The principal risk factors include race, in addition to gender, and include a range of environmental risk factors such as sedentary lifestyles, smoking, alcohol abuse, high-protein diets, high-fibre and high-phytate diets, as well as medication such as aluminium hydroxide gels and lithium use. In the elderly, osteoporosis increases risk of fractures and the risk factors to be considered in the environment include those that increase risk of falls, such as waxed floors, throw rugs, poor lighting and hypotensive medication.

6.5.2   Anaemia

The prevalence of nutritional anaemias in the elderly generally reflects that in the adult population, since their requirement for iron is lower. However, the environmental and other factors that result in poor dietary intakes, medication for a number of health problems and contributions from other complicating diseases may increase the risk of iron, folate and B_{12} deficiencies in the elderly, increasing risk of anaemia in this group.

6.5.3   Lowered immuno-competence

The elderly experience a higher frequency of illness than younger adults. The presence of nutritional deficiencies and the body composition changes that occur with ageing may lower the immune competence of the elderly and contribute to increased morbidity.

6.6   Malnutrition in the Elderly

A range of biological/medical, social and environmental factors interact to predispose the elderly to malnutrition/undernutrition. Table 6.V outlines the primary and secondary causes of malnutrition in the elderly recognised by Exton-Smith (6). Table 6.VI identifies the social and medical causes of undernutrition in the elderly.

TABLE 6.V
Primary and secondary causes of malnutrition in the elderly

Primary	Secondary
Ignorance	Impaired appetite
Social isolation	Masticatory inefficiency
Physical disability	Malabsorption
Mental disturbance	Alcoholism
Iatrogenic disorder	Drugs
Poverty	Increased requirements

The DHSS Report on the elderly (7) associated the incidence of undernutrition in the elderly and drew the distinction between social and environmental causes as opposed to physical/mental disorders.

TABLE 6.VI
Social and medical causes of undernutrition in the elderly

Social	Medical
Living alone	Chronic bronchitis
House-bound	Emphysema
No regular cooked meals	Gastrectomy
Supplementary benefits (poverty)	Poor dentition
Social class IV & V	Difficulty in drinking
Low mental-test score	Smoking
Depression	Alcoholism

Many of these factors are inter-related and, according to Exton-Smith (6), elderly individuals with four or more factors present are at increased risk of malnutrition. Lists such as these are useful to establish priorities for action at national or regional levels.

Davies (8) has identified ten main risks for non-institutionalised elderly in the UK that increase their nutritional vulnerability. They are:

i)   Fewer than eight main meals (hot or cold) per week.

ii) Very little milk consumption.

iii) Virtual absence of fruits and vegetables in the diet.

iv) Waste of food, even when delivered hot and ready to eat.

v) Long periods in the day without food or beverage.

vi) Depression or loneliness.

vii) Unexpected weight changes (more significant than under- or overweight).

viii) Shopping difficulties.

ix) Poverty.

x) Disabilities, including alcoholism.

It is important to recognise that each risk factor is only a potential danger sign and has to be considered in relation to others.

For those already at risk of, or suffering from nutrition-related disease among the elderly, the recommendations for action to prevent malnutrition are specifically (9):

- Meals programmes and simple nutrition education to address the requirements of the nutrition-related disease

- Implementation by the medical profession of measures to prevent ill effects from over-medication and drug-nutrient interaction.

- Recognition of the short- and long-term nutritional effect of surgical interventions, hospitalisation or medical treatment.

6.7 Improving the Diet and Nutrition of the Elderly

It is quite evident from what has been outlined earlier that the diet of the elderly needs special attention. The following recommendations may be appropriate:

- The elderly need to be encouraged to eat adequate amounts of food that will meet their energy, protein and micronutrient needs. The recognition that energy needs decrease with age and the reduced food intake may in turn influence the consumption of micronutrients needs to be borne in mind. Special attention needs to be given to situations that may impair adequate consumption of food owing to poor appetite, inability to masticate and swallow easily, and also side-effects from drugs.

- Increasing the consumption of fruits and vegetables (at least five portions a day) needs to be encouraged.

- Limiting the intakes of fat, particularly saturated fat to recommended levels, i.e. 30-35% of total energy, may be a useful goal even in the elderly.

- Consumption of milk and milk products needs to be encouraged.

- Adequate intake of dietary fibre and starch in the diet is essential to help bowel movements.

- Adequate fluid intake needs to be encouraged.

- Physical activity should be promoted. This will increase energy requirements and help meet micronutrient requirements, reduce the onset of early disability and postpone osteoporosis in the elderly.

- The consumption of alcohol needs to be regulated.

- The elderly on medication need to be cautioned about drug-nutrient interactions and the dangers of concurrent abuse of alcohol.

- Encouraging the elderly to be outdoors whenever possible and providing for better social interactions with others and maintenance of good emotional health will help older individuals to have good dietary intakes and maintain better nutritional status as age increases.

6.8   References

1.   Department of Health. *Dietary Reference Values for Food Energy and Nutrients for the UK*. London. HMSO, 1991.

2.   Andres R. Obesity in longevity in the aged, in *Ageing, Cancer and Cell Membranes*. New York. Thieme-Stratton, 1980.

3.   Roe D.A. *Geriatric Nutrition*. New Jersey. Prentice-Hall, 1983.

4.   Finch S., Doyle W., Lowe C., Bates C.J., Prentice A., Smithers G., Clarke P.C. *National Diet and Nutrition Survey: People Aged 65 Years and Over. Volume 1: Report of the Diet and Nutrition Survey*. London. Stationery Office, 1998.

5.   Pryer J.A., Cook A., Shetty P. Identification of groups who report similar patterns of diet among a representative national sample of British adults aged 65 years of age or more. *Public Health Nutrition*, 2001, 4, 787-95.

6.   Exton-Smith A.N. Nutrition of the elderly. *British Journal of Hospital Medicine*, 1971, 5, 639-45.

7.   DHSS. Committee on the Medical Aspects of Food Policy. *Nutrition and Health in Old Age*. Reports on Health and Social Subjects, No. 16, HM Stationery Office, London.

8.   Davies L. *Three Score Years...and Then?* London. Heinemann, 1981.

9.   Davies L. Risk factors for malnutrition, in *Nutrition in the Elderly*. Published on behalf of WHO. Oxford. OUP, 1989.

7. NUTRITION AND POLICY

Elizabeth Dowler

7.1   Introduction

Policy is about who gets what, when, where and how, and who controls these processes (1). Policy for nutrition should be about enabling people to eat a diet that satisfies them and leads to a healthy life. This seems a reasonable outcome for policy activities, and much of the current writing on nutrition policy is about such issues. But policy is as much about processes (how things happen) and power (who makes them happen and why) as it is about content (what happens – policy activities). Food and nutrition are so fundamental for life and well being that it is remarkable how little research has been done on policy practice in the UK. There is a growing literature on responses to anxieties about food safety; the ways in which government, producers, the industry, the voluntary sector and consumers have reacted to crises such as bovine spongiform encephalopathy (BSE) and new variant Creutzfeldt Jakob Disease (vCJD). But there has been little published research on how policy is formulated and implemented in relation to the nutritional well being of, for instance, children, mothers, or those in institutions such as hospitals and schools.

Food in general is usually seen as the responsibility of the agricultural sector, the 'food industry' (companies that manage production, trade, distribution, storage, processing and retail), and the trade sector. Nutrition, on the other hand, can be the responsibility of many different institutions and departments in government, non-governmental organisations and international agencies. Nutrition itself is a relatively non-contentious issue (no-one is against good nutrition or in favour of malnutrition), but it has often been a weak area in policy terms. There is no powerful lobby to argue for the nutritional well being of vulnerable people of whatever age, although there are said to be plenty to protect the interests of those who grow, trade, process and distribute food, nationally and on a global scale.

This chapter examines policy practice in relation to nutrition, focusing on the UK, but drawing on present European initiatives and relevant experiences. It begins by trying to draw boundaries around nutrition and food policy and the challenges faced by those constructing and implementing them.

7.2   Nutrition Policy: Aims and Challenges

Food and nutrition policies tend to overlap in both definition and practice because they are on a spectrum of aims, activities and outcomes (2). It is often difficult to distinguish clearly and consistently where one ends and the other begins. Perhaps the only times such distinctions really matter are when territorial negotiations are carried out by institutions of the state: which department should have responsibility (and the budget) for which set of activities; which department should advise the general public, or specific groups within it, on what is safe and good to eat; who should people trust to tell them the truth about their food?

7.2.1   Aims of policy in food and nutrition

The fundamental aims of policy in food and nutrition should be to ensure

- that food is produced or traded in ways that are sustainable, moral and equitable;

- that all people can obtain sufficient food that is appropriate for health, safe, reliable, reasonably priced, and of good quality, whenever they need it;

- that all people can acquire and share food in ways that do not demean them or their culture.

These aims should not undermine national goals for food and agricultural policies, which are usually to maintain national food supply, through domestic production or imports and storage, and sometimes to maintain an economically sound farming sector as well as a healthy food industry, which is usually in the private sector. The challenge for public health policy is to examine the extent to which such goals can be reconciled with the wider policy aims outlined above, while taking into account the requirement of universal access to sufficient and safe food, necessary and acceptable for a healthy life, produced and distributed by environmentally sound and safe means (3,4).

Nutrition policies, which tend to focus on objectives concerned with provision and consumption of nutritionally satisfactory diets, seem initially to be more concerned with the individual and their health outcomes. Indeed, much of this book addresses the nutritional conditions and needs of people in various ages and stages of life, and ways of improving them, along with the individual health and other costs of failing to do so. Nutrition practice in countries such as the United Kingdom has often bypassed the wider structural issues of access, availability and entitlement, and the cultural and social aspects of how people obtain their food and why they choose the foods that they do (5,6). Rather, the concern has been with defining an appropriate diet (through recommended dietary intakes or nutrient reference values, or food-based dietary guidelines) and giving people information to enable them to 'make informed food choice'. It is only recently that these wider issues have come onto the policy scene. Examples are discussed below.

There are in fact only a few countries that have an explicit national nutrition policy *per se*. Few governments have a strong commitment to effect lasting changes in the nutritional well being of their populations; as in the food safety arena, governments tend to react to crises and pressures, whether internally generated from consumers or producers, or externally from international agencies such as the EU or the UN. Where governments do adopt an explicit nutrition policy, as some European countries have, for instance, over the last two decades, the institutional and legislative framework for activities has usually been established only slowly. Equally, most food and agricultural policies seldom explicitly address nutritional objectives in practice even though the maintenance of a healthy national diet may be a stated goal. Norway and the North Karelia province in Finland are much cited examples of exceptions (7,8).

7.2.2   Challenges in food and nutrition policy

The complexities of and risks within the modern food system pose challenges to us all, not least in regard to whether it is imposing environmental or public health costs that are higher than most citizens realise or are prepared to bear (9,10). On one hand, the majority of consumers now have a choice from the greatest range of safe foodstuffs in history. In global terms, the world can feed populations of previously unthinkable size through application of technology, and the system can provide food tailored to meet defined public health needs (11). On the other hand, some argue that the systems for producing, storing and distributing food are unsustainable, irrevocably expensive of world resources, and deeply divisive. A few corporations own the means of food production for, and control the livelihoods of, vast numbers of people who have no say in the process or the outcome (12). Old and new technological changes are driven as much by shareholder profit as by human needs (13,14). Individual countries' national policy agendas do not often address these international issues.

Another potential policy conflict is how the representation of interests of public health and consumer protection versus the interests of agriculture and the food industry is structured and managed. These issues have come to the foreground in the last decades, partly because of the BSE/vCJD crises, first in the UK and now across Europe, and partly because of the new biotechnology developments. One way of dealing with it is for governments to create new institutions charged with regulation of food practice. In Europe, a White Paper on Food Safety was introduced in January 2000, which announced the process for a new General Food Law, and 84 specific proposals (at least one of which was on nutrition), and set up the promised new European Food Authority (15,16). Its structure and management are as yet unclear, as is how strong a role nutrition and public health concerns will play, beyond the responsibility for ensuring that food is uncontaminated. Similar challenges were faced in the UK when the national Food Standards Agency and regional offices were set up in 2000. How independent of government and the food industry/producers would it/they be; who would be on the Board and work within them; where would nutrition and public health concerns fit? Some of these concerns have been addressed by the open system of appointments to the Board, the open Board meetings and the choice of members of the Consumer Panel, as well as the provision of feedback opportunities to members of the public (17-19)[1].

Thirdly, nutrition and food as elements of public health are constantly sidelined in European and, to some extent, national discussions about food, in favour of intense concerns about food safety. Food safety is usually interpreted as food that is 'uncontaminated' by pathogens, chemical residues, or (latterly) genetically modified elements. This focus is not necessarily justified in terms of either actual consumer anxieties or potential health gain. The general public

---

[1] See FSA Web site (http://www.foodstandards.gov.uk) for details of its current structure and workings.

clearly does worry about whether food is safe to eat; respondents say so when consulted in surveys and opinion polls and seem to change their purchasing patterns (briefly?) when issues hit the headlines. Yet, if people are interviewed in depth about food choices, they express rather different concerns: most refer to convenience, price, value and quality of food as important when shopping, rather than anxieties about safety (20). The nutritional quality of food, and its contribution to public health, far outweigh the safety aspects of food in terms of costs to the Exchequer or the individual. Preliminary analyses from the Swedish Institute of Public Health, estimated in terms of disability-adjusted life years (DALYS), suggest that costs due to diet and a sedentary lifestyle exceed those of tobacco use in EU Member States[2] (21). In Britain alone, the British Heart Foundation estimates that coronary heart disease, for instance, costs the UK economy up to GBP10bn a year; since current estimates are that nearly a third of deaths from CHD are probably diet-related, food-related ill health poses a considerable burden on the country as well as on individuals (22). Recent analyses of the rather limited number of comprehensive studies available, by the International Centre for Health and Society in London University, suggest that estimated costs per life year gained from population-based health promotion strategies around eating were comparable to or lower than those for anti-smoking strategies (GBP140-560 versus GBP300-790) and considerably more cost-effective than cholesterol-lowering drug strategies or screening and primary care advice (GBP6,200-11,300 and GBP900 minimum, respectively) (23). We have to wonder whether the huge apparatus of regulation, institutions and inspection in relation to food safety currently being implemented throughout Europe, as well as Britain, is more a reflection of the health needs of the food industry than of those of the consuming public.

Lastly, an important challenge in nutrition policy is that policy activities should apply to all consumers, not only those with sufficient voice and money to be heard and have their needs and wants met. There is growing evidence that inequalities in health outcomes can in part be attributed to nutritional inequalities (24,25). These issues are also discussed in the chapter on Health Promotion; they are critical to the current formulation and implementation of policy. Policy may in general be based on the premise of informed choice, but, until recently, the UK state did not examine whether or not people could in fact exercise choice –

---

[2] Total of DALYs related to poor nutrition and physical activity is estimated at 9.6%, of which 4.5% are due to nutrition, 3.7% to obesity and 1.4% to physical activity. This compares with 9% due to smoking (National Institute of Public Health, 1997).

whether the places they live in have sufficient shops, offering an appropriate range of commodities at affordable prices; whether people have sufficient money when other needs have been met to buy enough food; whether those who live in deprivation or near destitution have the confidence and/or skills to buy and prepare/cook foods recommended as healthy. The evidence is that structural and social issues, such as the amount of time and money people can devote to the pursuit of good food and active living, the cost and accessibility of each of them, the physical area where households are located, and the general social circumstances of the lives of those classified as deprived by whatever indicators, constrain and govern choice to a considerable extent (26,27). Furthermore, for those who have little money and power, choosing and enjoying a diet conducive to health may be difficult when their main focus is survival, both of the household unit and in terms of daily living (28).

7.3   How Does Nutrition Policy Work?

There is no space here to discuss theories of the policy process, even as applied to nutrition (29-31). Policy practice is usually described as a matter of agenda setting, problem definition, prioritising responses, implementing them and evaluating impact. These, in turn, are said to feed back into refining problem definition, choices of intervention and so forth. This iterative cycle does reflect a reality at some level. Yet, as we have seen, nutritional issues often do not get onto the key policy agendas very easily, if at all, even though many people regard them as an important component of public health. In the UK, the New Labour Government is keen to implement evidence-based policy, so the Department of Health and the Food Standards Agency are both interested in research into 'what works' in changing people's diets. The previous Health Education Authority, and now the Health Development Agency, commissioned effectiveness reviews, which are available on their effectiveness research Web site (32,33). The extent to which policy in nutrition is actually driven by such processes, in terms of priority setting and intervention selection, is not yet clear. The effectiveness reviews often comment how few well-conducted, reliable studies have been carried out on nutrition interventions, particularly those concerned with inequalities in food access or intake. Some that have been are described in chapter 8. It is also notable that the criteria used to judge effectiveness are usually those defined by policy makers and health professionals, such as improved nutrient intakes, or blood levels, because these indicators are judged to have a quantitative relationship with desired health outcomes, such as lowered rates of cardiovascular disease or cancer. The general public, on the other hand, while not averse to, say, improved iron, vitamin C or calcium levels, may also want to know that the food they or their children are eating is tasty, enjoyable and acceptable (in social and cultural terms) as well as conducive to good health in the short or long term. These factors are harder to assess reliably in the evaluation of interventions (34).

7.3.1 Policy actors in nutrition

Policy actors in nutrition, that is, those with an interest in agenda setting, implementing intervention and/or changing outcomes, include the following:

- government policy makers and the executive at national and local levels (including health, agriculture, environment and education departments);
- consumers and those who represent them;
- producers, manufacturers and retailers, who largely operate in the private sector;
- scientific and medical communities, in academic and other public or private institutions;
- non-governmental organisations, such as consumer and trade organisations, and health-related charities;
- international agencies, such as the United Nations World Health Organization, Food and Agriculture Organization and UNICEF;
- the media (primarily TV, radio and newspapers) for informing consumers, giving them voice, or as part of campaigning and promotion efforts by any or all of the above.

These actors will have different policy goals and instruments for bringing about change, which sometimes are in conflict.

7.3.2 Policy instruments in nutrition

There are a number of ways in which policy makers can maintain or change what people eat in a free market economy. These instruments are mostly rather blunt and indirect in action; governments cannot force people to eat what they do not want to eat – they can only encourage and enable. Nonetheless, there is considerable scope for intervention by policy makers at national and local levels, to influence household and individuals' nutritional well being. Broadly speaking, these include:

- giving out food (as in rations, vouchers, or institutional provision through schools, care homes, workplaces, hospitals, prisons);

- changing food prices (through subsidy or taxation; these can also affect food provided in institutions, in terms of their cost or what commodities are available);

- giving information, both to consumers on what to eat (through dietary guidelines), and on food (by labelling commodities with lists of ingredients or nutrient contents);

- encouraging consumers to purchase/eat – or not to purchase/eat – particular commodities (by exhortation, reward systems, permitting or restricting advertising);

- legislation or guidelines: on standards or procedures of practice or expected outcomes;

- improving availability of certain, desirable commodities in the market (e.g. more fresh fruit, more low-fat or low-salt products), which in turn requires policy activities directed towards the agricultural, production or retail side;

- ensuring that consumers have enough money to buy appropriate food;

- ensuring that consumers have enough confidence to buy and prepare appropriate food (which might mean encouraging cooking skills, or giving opportunities to taste different foods, or confidence to handle advertising or product promotion).

Some of these policy actors and policy instruments are described and discussed in other chapters in this book. Here, we look first at critical issues in addressing inequalities, and activities that involve giving out food. Then dietary reference values and guidelines are discussed, and their role in addressing nutritional improvement. Finally, key initiatives that are being promoted on a European basis are outlined, along with major activities in the UK.

7.3.3   Inequalities in food and nutrition

To some extent, recent policy attention has been paid to structural issues that prevent people from obtaining the food they need: accessibility, affordability and practicality. For instance, some policy initiatives promote development and support for community-based activities to improve local food access, through Health Action Zones, Education Action Zones and New Deal, by encouraging the setting up of volunteer-run food co-operatives or community cafes (35). Other locally based initiatives try to address issues of confidence and skills, with 'cook-and-eat' classes. These local activities achieve some successes, usually with small numbers, primarily when they are rooted in locally defined needs, engage and/or are owned by the community, and can secure sustainable funding rather than continually relying on start-up funds (36). The Department of Health is encouraging the targeting of its 'Five a Day' initiative (which promotes consumption of fruit and vegetables across the population) to low-income communities, and is supporting the distribution of free fruit to infants through schools on a daily basis, initially in Health Action Zone areas, but eventually to all Government Office Regions, to improve familiarity and access (37). Breakfast Clubs and Sure Start initiatives also focus activity and attention on the needs of low-income children (38).

There is as yet little focused attention on two of the main policy arenas for imaginative change: that many people do not have sufficient money for food, and the need to develop and maintain viable local retailing in deprived neighbourhoods (39). Recent changes to the tax and benefit regime in the UK have left low-income families with young dependent children better off than previously, but those with older children, unemployed adults, and those working for wages at the minimum wage, still have incomes well below that needed to purchase a healthy diet (40-42). Households that are indebted (to private sector utilities, loan companies, or who are repaying Social Fund loans or mature student access loans) often cut back on food expenditure to attempt to meet repayment demands (43,44). As yet, there are few policy initiatives that take explicit account of food costs in dealing with low income or indebtedness. These issues are discussed in detail elsewhere (45).

On the viable local retailing front, many deprived areas have seen the demise of specialist food shops and withdrawal of the major supermarkets and banks. Many who live on low incomes now live in places with few or no shops, and where the shops that do manage to survive, of necessity, have to charge higher prices than the major supermarkets for basic foodstuffs and household goods.

They also carry limited ranges and limited fresh produce (46-48). Some local authorities and health authorities have appointed food policy officers to work across the board at local levels. A few of these are developing collaborative work with planning departments and local trade associations as well as health, to support and maintain viable small retail businesses, so that they can provide a good range of foods appropriate for health at reasonable prices – something many small, local retailers currently struggle to do. The Food Standards Agency is looking for ways to provide central support for these local activities, in conjunction with the Local Government Association. Earlier work by the Cabinet Office Social Exclusion Unit (SEU) is relevant here: during the first Labour Government, the SEU set up a number of cross-cutting Policy Action Teams (PATs) to examine aspects of deprivation and exclusion. PAT 13 was responsible for reviewing the problems of access to shops and services. Their report, published by the Department of Health, outlined very clearly both the problems faced by small local retailers, and potential ways forward, including the setting up of local food retailing task forces (49). To date, there has been little action by central or local government in response.

7.3.4   Giving out food

Where people have neither the money nor the opportunity to express choice (for instance, those in destitution or in prison, or with severe disability), subsidies, rations or food transfers are necessary. Direct food transfers to those in need can be through statutory measures, where the state can specify what is to be provided, by whom, how much and by what mechanisms. In the UK, there is no direct food transfer from the state for those who are destitute because they are able to claim the basic social assistance benefit (income support), which is seen by government as sufficient to enable people to purchase minimal food needs, although in practice it is often insufficient (50). There are some benefits 'in kind' for income support claimants, only a few of which relate to food, and to which only claimants in certain restricted categories are entitled. These food elements of state benefits are discussed further below, under the Welfare Food Scheme and school meals. Those who cannot meet their nutritional (or social) needs from income support – and the majority cannot for more than a few months – are forced either to go without food or to obtain it from the private or voluntary sector through food redistribution networks such as Day Centres and community cafés, where food is free or heavily subsidised. These networks are based on the surpluses generated within the food system[3] (51,52). The state's role here can be one of encouraging (or discouraging) such action, through taxation rules that affect the retail private sector, or by supporting or enabling charitable institutions to access and distribute free or cheap food. Such is the case in the United States and Canada, where systems based on food banks and community distribution are widely used, with state support, to address food inequalities. They are fast developing within the UK and other parts of Europe, where numbers living below the poverty line are growing, because of low wages, unemployment and/or the failure of state social assistance schemes. There are also increasing numbers who are homeless (whether rough sleepers or marginally housed), many of whom seem only to be able to obtain food by begging on the street, or by using the same charitable feeding centres sourced from food banks (53). In recent years, a number of academics and advocacy groups have challenged the policy community – and society generally – on the social and political acceptability of the increasing role and influence of food banks and community food distribution schemes, which both institutionalise the usage of surplus foods to feed poor and needy people, and potentially contribute to marginalising problems of hunger in welfare societies (54,55).

Many people in the UK assume that most of the clients of such redistributive networks are 'homeless rough sleepers', rather than the low-waged, insecurely employed or unemployed that the majority often are. More challenging to society and, some claim, to systems of social assistance in Europe at present are refugees and/or asylum seekers, whose numbers have risen in response to political and economic instabilities in many parts of the world. Their conditions and circumstances vary considerably from country to country, and are not covered here (56). However, in relation to food, in the UK, asylum seekers have been subject to strict state regulation on food access; they receive a lower rate of income support than other claimants, and are instead given vouchers, which can be exchanged for foodstuffs (only) at designated stores. Evidence is accumulating that families living under these restrictive conditions are unable to obtain all the food they need (57). In February 2002, the Home Secretary announced an end to the voucher system from April 2002, but the intention seems to be that this will apply to future, new asylum seekers, rather than existing families, who continue having to use food vouchers.

---

[3] Crisis Fairshare is one of the best known in the UK.

There is a limited food element to the 'in kind' entitlement for income support and Job Seekers' Allowance claimants in the UK Welfare Food Scheme. Those responsible for children aged under 5 years, or women who are pregnant or breastfeeding, can get a token or voucher, which can be exchanged for one free pint of whole or semi-skimmed milk per day (or 4 litres a week) at an appropriate shop, and a Department of Health vitamin supplement from clinics. Non-breastfed children under 1 year can have 900 g infant formula free per week and a vitamin supplement. Some parents who claim Working Family Tax Credit, and who have non-breastfed children, can also purchase 900-g infant formula per week at reduced rates under the Scheme. In addition, children under 5 years attending Scheme-registered day care facilities can receive a third of a pint of milk a day.

The Welfare Food Scheme has been under review for some years, and, in November 1999, the Review Group accepted a Draft Report with the following comments and recommendations (58):

- The Scheme offers significant economic and nutritional benefits to low-income households, and is potentially very important in improving the health of vulnerable mothers and young children.

- Uptake of vitamin supplements, regarded as a simple, cost-effective intervention, is very low; improved systems of provision are needed.

- Uptake of milk is very high. Most mothers use tokens to obtain infant formula, reflecting very low breastfeeding rates among low income households. About 50% children in day care attend facilities registered with the Scheme, some of whom may receive excessive milk if they also receive Scheme milk at home. Reduction in currently excess volume of formula for those over 6 months in favour of provisions to promote timely complementary feeding would be appropriate. Extension of formula provision to older children would reduce the prevalence of iron deficiency.

- Potential amendments include choices other than milk, and improved composition of vitamin supplements to pregnant women; breastfeeding incentives; reduction in liquid cows' milk to children under one year.

- Free vitamin supplements should be extended to children from minority ethnic groups.

- The Disability Living Allowance should take account of the special needs of children in low-income families that are not currently met by a daily pint of cows' milk.

There has been a long process of consultation about the changes needed, but implementation is still awaiting ministerial decision.

Another instance of food provision in which the state may play a significant role is food given, either free or at subsidised prices, to those who are in institutions of one sort or another, such as in hospital, or in school, and those living supported in the community through social care. There is considerable variation from one country to another in what food is provided and how, depending on who is managing and funding the system. In the UK, food provision through schools and hospitals has not been managed or carried out by national bodies for some years. Until recently, local health and education authorities, or the private sector, provided such food as they saw fit. What was provided, and how, varied in different parts of the country, and from one school to another. Now, guidelines for provision of food, in terms of quality, what is available, and how it is presented, have been revised and new nutritional standards versions promoted by the Department of Health and Department for Education and Skills. These are discussed in chapter 3.

However, one critical area where social and nutrition policy overlap is the targeted food element of state welfare by the provision of free school meals to children of social assistance claimants. In the UK, this provision is now restricted to school-aged dependants of income support claimants, and to provision during school terms only. There are no regulations governing what is in the free school meal, other than the general nutritional standards recently established. In fact, nearly one in three children rely on the school meal as a main meal of the day, particularly those who are from the poorest households; for these children the nutritional quality is particularly important. The enforcement of nutritional standards can only be achieved at a reasonable minimal cost allowance, which for many schools is higher than they currently allow (59). Minimum cost standards should apply to the free school meal, which then forms the basis for the rest of the meal delivery, including packed lunch quality. In practice, in many schools in the UK, the free meal ticket does not currently cover the cost of sufficient food to fill the child up, healthily, or to include a drink (60). Maintaining the quality of free school meals at designated cost is critical not only to ensure that children who particularly need it are likely to get the essential nutritional boost, but also to avoid alienating children from eating school meals at all, free or otherwise. There are considerable anxieties at present about the low take-up of school meals, and free school meals in particular; stigma and the poor quality of food provided are key contributory elements (61).

7.3.5   *Nutritional targets and recommendations*

One key policy activity, and an outcome of nutrition problem definition and agenda setting, is often the construction of nutritional targets and recommendations – that is, statements about the kinds of diet (foods or nutrients) people should eat. Nutrient requirements or reference standards are usually known as Dietary Reference Values (DRVs). They are the levels of intake of nutrients or food constituents (such as fibre/non-starch polysaccharide) that, on the basis of scientific knowledge, are judged sufficient to meet the needs of most healthy people for that dietary component. For some nutrients, enough data are available on the risks to health of high intakes to establish upper 'safe' levels (62). They are usually specified for different age and gender groups, and for pregnancy and lactation, and are updated at regular intervals as more information becomes available. Various terms are usually used:

- an estimated average requirement (in UK, this is used for energy)

- a reference nutrient intake (RNI) (which is the mean requirement plus 2 standard deviations)

- a lower reference nutrient intake (mean requirement minus 2 standard deviations)

- an upper limit of safety.

Reference levels are probability statements; using them we can estimate the likelihood that a group of people is eating enough (or too much) of a nutrient. The further from the RNI a group's mean nutrient intake is, the more likely it is that some members of that group are eating insufficient amount of the nutrient to avoid risk to their health. They cannot be used to say 'Z% of the population is malnourished because their intakes of nutrient X are below the RNI', but to estimate the likelihood that health is at risk from a low (or high) intake. Intakes at or above the RNI carry a very low risk of deficiency. Reference levels can be used:

- to evaluate the dietary intake of population subgroups

- to plan food supplies for large groups (e.g. in catering for people in institutions)

- to guide or interpret nutrient labelling of food products and dietary supplements (e.g. 'one portion will supply Y% of RDA')

- as a basis for provision of general nutrition information and guidance.

They should not be used to judge whether or not an individual's diet is inadequate.

Reference Values are usually set by government committees of experts, and can vary over time and between places. (For instance, the French requirement for calcium, and the American requirement for vitamin C are slightly different from the UK requirements for those nutrients.) This is not because the committees are wrong, but because different weightings are given to different kinds of evidence (clinical, epidemiological, animal models) and different degrees of risk are deemed acceptable. Also, of course, the knowledge base changes over time. One of the problems in the past has been that more research was done on men than on women or children at different ages, so that results have had to be extrapolated to those groups, and the assumptions made in doing so can change.

One policy usage for Reference Values is in producing dietary guidelines – that is, policy statements about what people should, or should not, eat to ensure their future health, or that of their offspring if they are women who are pregnant or likely to become so. Dietary guidelines have now been developed by international agencies such as WHO and FAO, and by a number of individual countries. They are different from statements about requirements for individual nutrients in that they are more advisory than authoritative. Guidelines often specify foods, or combinations of foods (rather than nutrients) that people could eat to contribute to or maintain their health and they are broad targets for people to aim at, rather than statements of daily needs. Producing food-based guidelines is quite a skill, needing knowledge of food patterns and culture as well as quantities currently eaten and feasibility of change. Some guidelines use phrases such as 'eat plenty of', 'eat less of/only a little'; others recommend actual quantities of different foods to be eaten. One well-known example is the WHO recommendation that everyone should eat at least 400-g fruit and vegetables a day. Sometimes, a numeric quantity such as this has been further interpreted by national committees in more practical terms, to be useful to professionals and the general public. In the UK, for instance, 400 g has been interpreted as 'five portions of fruit and vegetables a day' (63). Some people find this a useful personal and (if relevant) professional guideline; others remain confused about, for instance, what constitutes a portion, or whether fruit juice or potatoes count (yes and no, respectively). This confusion shows how difficult it is to produce a seemingly simple guideline that can be interpreted by everyone. The latest UK version, The Balance of Good Health, has been republished by the Food Standards Agency, having first been produced by the Health Education Authority[4] (64) (see Fig. 3.1, Chapter 3). Whether such guidelines can actually be put into practice, of course, depends on availability and accessibility (including cost), quite apart from matters of taste and preference.

Originally, DRVs and guidelines were primarily focused on avoiding ill health through nutrient deficiency, but, in the last decade or so, recommendations have also been constructed to help prevent non-infectious or chronic diseases (initially heart disease and hypertension, but now also obesity, osteoporosis, diabetes, and cancer). The EU recently commissioned a large group of scientists and other experts to *'contribute towards a co-ordinated EU and member state health promotion program on nutrition, diet and healthy lifestyles by establishing a network, strategy and action plan for development of European dietary guidelines, which [in turn] provide the framework for development of national food-based dietary guidelines'* (65). The process was a lengthy but comprehensive one, taking 2 years to produce the report and framework for development of guidelines. The Core Report was published in April 2001 in two Special Issues of *Public Health Nutrition*, covering, firstly, reports from four Working Parties, convened to examine the evidence, the framework, the strategies and the policy potential, and secondly, scientific papers commissioned to give in-depth coverage of specific and general topics. The most commonly applicable food-based dietary guidelines for the EU as a whole are:

- an increase in fruit and vegetable consumption
- increased prevalence and duration of breastfeeding
- promotion of increased physical activity.

Some elements of the implications for structures and instruments to bring about the desired changes are also discussed in the papers.

---

[4] The Health Education Authority no longer exists. The Health Development Agency has taken over some of its functions, and HEA publications can sometimes be obtained from the HDA. Unlike the HEA, the HDA has no remit for direct public education.

Dietary guidelines can thus be seen as a neat summary of useful advice for many different professionals – health care, public health, education, retailers, advertisers, journalists and, of course, government. In practice, they carry implications for the agricultural, food and retail sectors, which are not often addressed in nutrition policy circles. For instance, if the British population took up the current recommended increases in fruit and vegetable consumption, would the UK be able to produce or import sufficient commodities? What would be the implications of increased water and fertiliser usage where fruit or vegetable production was markedly increased? So far, there has been only limited research on these issues. The food industry is very quick to respond to scientific news, and to use dietary guidelines both to develop new products and to promote their purchase through advertising that the products help people meet them. This may be excellent news for consumers. Sometimes, however, things are not so straightforward; one result has been the increasing development of totally new food products (sometimes defined as 'functional foods'[5]), which may be more expensive than the products they are designed to supplant, and which some argue are part of a trend to medicalise food (66,67). Secondly, products that, by and large, health professionals do not recommend for regular consumption (such as fizzy, sweetened drinks), can be fortified with nutrients not normally found in them, and promoted on the basis that they now contain nutrients recommended for health and which help to meet current dietary guidelines.

There are two additional challenges in using dietary guidelines as policy instruments to bring about improvements in diet. The first is the notion that scientific consensus exists about the relationship between nutrient(s), foods, and health outcomes, which derives from a positivist model of science: that 'facts' guide knowledge and drive policy, with the scientists' role simply as one of sifting, evaluating and summarising key, reliable information and facts. However, the 'facts' and weight given to them depend on which scientists are present, and whose research is funded, published, or cited (68). None of these processes is as objective or value-free as might be supposed (69). In practice, scientific consensus on requirement figures, and the guidelines based on them, is often the outcome of processes of compromise and negotiation. Policy practice is not necessarily rational, but a reflection of partisan, partial views, and is more likely to maintain the status quo than introduce the radical.

---

[5] Some people use this term for all foods with technological intervention, i.e. they include products such as fortified breakfast cereals in 'functional foods'; others use the term only to refer to new products such as 'Yakult' or 'Benecol'.

The second challenge is that guidelines work on the premise that people will choose food because they know it is good for their health, and are able to implement rational choice. In practice, people choose foods for a wide variety of reasons, of which immediate or long-term health gain may play a part, – but only a part, and for some people, a rather limited one. Furthermore, food choice is less of an individual matter and more one governed by social and economic factors outside individuals' control than is implied by usage of many food-based dietary guidelines. Apart from the cultural and economic aspects, in many countries the food processing and retailing industries, at both national and international levels, are so complex that individuals may find it difficult to exercise real choice over the nutrients or foods they are consuming. Therefore, simply providing information aimed at consumers as individuals, with encouragement or exhortation to behave in certain ways (which is how guidelines tend to be used by health professionals) in practice often has less than hoped-for effects on dietary behaviour or health outcomes, other than in the short term[6].

In particular, people living in poverty, on low incomes, or in areas of collective deprivation, are much less likely or able to put recommendations and guidelines into practice. This is partly because the kinds of food recommended for health are often more expensive than those regarded as detrimental (often the latter are cheaper for the food processing and retail industries to mass produce and distribute) (70,71). Partly it is because people on low incomes may live where foods recommended for health, particularly fruit and vegetables, are more difficult to obtain (72). Poorer people may worry about their health, but in practice face more pressing, immediate problems, which take up all their time, energy and money to solve. People in such circumstances have less sense of control over their lives – which probably reflects the reality – and less opportunity to implement choice in everyday life, including over which foods to choose and buy (73).

7.4 Nutrition Policy Initiatives on a Europe-wide Basis

During the last decade, there have been several challenges to European governments to take nutritional issues seriously in policy terms. For instance, all European Member States have signed at least two sets of international agreements

---

[6] The Department of Health has a current policy commitment to working with the food industry to reduce levels of salt and sugar in processed foods.

that committed them to developing national plans to address nutrition and food security. WHO European Office, and the European Union have also produced important policy action documents on nutrition, which Member States have endorsed – including the UK.

7.4.1   The International Conference on Nutrition (ICN)

In 1992, a joint FAO/WHO International Conference on Nutrition was held in December, at which all Members States (including the UK) agreed to develop National Nutrition Plans of Action. These plans were to include the following 'action-oriented strategies', many of which are still pertinent to national nutrition plans in the UK:

- incorporating nutritional objectives, considerations and components into development policies and programmes

- improving household food security

- protecting consumers through improved food quality and safety

- promoting breastfeeding

- caring for the socio-economically deprived and nutritionally vulnerable

- preventing and controlling specific micronutrient deficiencies

- promoting appropriate diets and healthy lifestyles

- assessing, analysing and monitoring nutrition situations

- preventing and managing infectious disease (which interact with poor nutrition).

Some of these strategies are in place in the UK (promoting breastfeeding and appropriate diets as part of healthy lifestyles, nutritional surveillance, protecting food safety and quality); but there is still some way to go in incorporating nutritional or food considerations into urban or regional development plans, or in protecting household food security, or in caring for the nutrition of those who are socio-economically vulnerable.

The WHO European office reviewed national progress towards Nutrition Action Plans in 1998 (74,75). It highlighted key elements to securing effective implementation:

158

- political commitment (that is, a committed budget, and/or a food and nutrition policy as part of a national development policy);
- a focused approach, with targeted priorities and timescales;
- an institutional infrastructure for nutrition (for example, a national institute).

These are certainly the features of, for instance, the success stories of Norway and Finland.

7.4.2   World Food Summit (WFS)

A second international commitment to food and nutrition was made at the FAO World Food Summit in 1996, when countries affirmed the right of everyone to have access to safe and nutritious food, and asserted that poverty was a major cause of food insecurity throughout the world. There was a Five-Year Follow-up to the World Food Summit in June 2002: although most attention was on the likely international failure to reduce the number suffering chronic hunger by 50% by the year 2015, the UK Government, among many in the rich north, could also be held to account for those still facing food insecurity at home.

7.4.3   WHO European Office Action Plan for Food and Nutrition Policy

The WHO European Office has given prominence to nutrition as a critical component of public health, with particular emphasis on the nutritional and food security needs of low-income groups in Europe as a means of reducing premature mortality rates throughout the region. An Action Plan for Food and Nutrition Policy was endorsed by members of the relevant 51 states in September 2000 (76). The Action Plan stresses the complementarity of different sectors in formulating and implementing policies aimed at improving:

- food safety (which is where most of the current policy emphasis is occurring)
- nutrition for low-income groups throughout the life-cycle
- a sustainable, equitable food supply.

The Action Plan also highlights the need to assess the public health impact of an increasingly globalised economy, and that this must include both the food economy and the nutritional consequences of globalisation (77).

7.4.4   European Union French Presidency Initiative

In 2000, the French assumed presidency of the European Union (EU) and produced a report both on the importance of food and nutrition as major determinants of health, and on the economic and social costs of ignoring them. The Report and Resolution for European Action were accepted by the Council of Ministers on 14 December 2000 (78). It endorses the principle of subsidiarity: that EU Member States are primarily responsible for developing and carrying out nutrition and food policies; the EU policy role is one of giving added value. Dietary diversity and cultural identity are to be respected, as is the possibility of free and informed choice for all the population. A strong scientific basis for policies is encouraged, as is the need for policies that respect social justice, with priority given to influencing access to a nutritious diet for disadvantaged groups. Food poverty is not yet as important in many other European countries as in the UK, but its relevance is rising as social conditions worsen, and social protection measures fail to keep pace.

7.5   Key Nutrition Initiatives in the United Kingdom

7.5.1   Nutrition Forum

In early 2002, the Food Standards Agency convened its new Nutrition Forum as a means of bringing together key stakeholders in nutrition on a regular basis, to exchange views and information, and to facilitate communication (79). The Forum members come from:

- Government departments (national and local)
- health institutions (NHS and professional bodies)
- consumers and voluntary organisations
- food industry (retailers, growers, manufacturers).

The Terms of Reference and Code of Practice were published on the FSA Web site in early 2002, with the commitment to openness in the business of the Forum and conduct of members, so that transparency and availability of information are widely promoted. It will be important to monitor any changes, particularly any improvements, in nutrition policy formulation and practice as a result of this new institution and manner of working.

7.5.2   Health sector

There have been important shifts in policy practice under New Labour in that nutritional issues have been addressed through general policy documents, rather than relegated to specific initiatives labelled as 'nutrition'. For instance, the White Paper on public health – *Saving Lives: Our Healthier Nation: a contract for health* – signalled changing government and health authority priorities in that poverty and deprivation were acknowledged as prime causes of ill health and mortality, and the improvement of the health of the worst off in society was established as a principal aim (80). The policy document drew on a summary of research in inequalities in health, known as the Acheson Inquiry (81). Access to food was listed as one of the key factors contributing to health inequalities, along with the lack of opportunity that people on low incomes have to put their knowledge about what is good for health into practice. However, in practice, the policy proposals were not for structural changes (in retail provision, or levels of income) but for promotion of community food projects. These were seen as integral to the new agenda of private:government:community partnerships, and area-based regenerative activities, as means to improving public health.

Secondly, the NHS Plan particularly mentioned the need to increase fruit and vegetable consumption, through improving the availability and affordability at local levels (82). Among commitments to action by 2004 are:

- reform of welfare foods programme and increased support for breastfeeding and parenting
- the National School Fruit Scheme, where every child in nursery and aged 4-6 in infant schools will be entitled to a free piece of fruit each school day (following pilots)
- a 'five-a-day' programme to increase fruit and vegetable consumption
- work with the retail industry and producers to increase provision and access through local initiatives and co-operatives.

7.5.3   Cross-sectoral initiatives

In addition to these programmes, there is encouragement for new initiatives that cut across departmental or professional boundaries (although in practice one or other department usually takes the lead). Local partnerships have to be set up, to tender for funding to support locally designed initiatives that meet broad policy goals. Many of these have involved food initiatives. For example, Health or Education Action Zone status, won by competitive tender, often features food co-operatives, community cafés or school breakfast clubs in the bids and proposed activities. Sure Start programmes, another area-based cross-government initiative to improve services for young children under 4 and their families in areas of disadvantage, often include community-based food and nutrition initiatives. The challenge for such community-led activities is that, although they can achieve short-term goals, they are heavily dependent on volunteer labour, and short-term start-up funding. Follow-on funding and full community engagement is often hard to generate and maintain, although there are some success stories (83). Other policy initiatives, such as school breakfast clubs, and the health promoting school, are discussed in chapter 3.

7.6   Conclusions

This chapter has reviewed some elements of policy in nutrition, particularly how issues are addressed within the different agendas of various potential policy actors with an interest in food. We have explored some contemporary challenges to the general public and to government, national and local, in constructing a system of food and nutrition whereby the production, distribution, retail and consumption of food can be organised and managed in ways that are reasonably transparent and meet the needs of all for a healthy diet. We have concentrated on the issue of inequalities, on the policy response of food provision by various means, and on the process of constructing and using dietary guidelines, as a means of illustrating some of the more general principles of policy practice. Dietary guidelines, whose construction and use are traditionally key policy activities, are often used as the basis of health promotion, but, as is discussed elsewhere in the book, such practices are effective only when part of a sustained and widespread campaign, and when they build on perspectives or activities that make sense to people. Indeed, people need to be empowered and informed rather than told what to do; people mistrust governments and/or scientific or nutritional experts' advice, particularly as regards 'healthy food', which is often regarded as unpleasant, boring and undesirable. Perhaps this is another policy hurdle – to overcome such a misperception.

In practice, governments also face the real challenges of sustaining political commitment to improvement of nutritional conditions and household food security for all members of society, along with mobilising and maintaining public support for government expenditure on nutritional problems. In the UK, the next few years present a critical opportunity for such activity, with public desire for healthy food production and access growing, in the wake of BSE and foot-and-mouth, and when the 'body beautiful' is much admired. Public disquiet over many aspects of the food system led to a Policy Commission on the Future of Food and Farming, set up to advise the Government, for England, '*how a sustainable, competitive and diverse farming and food sector can be created, which contributes to a thriving and sustainable rural economy, advances environmental, economic, health and animal welfare goals, and consistent with the Government's aims for CAP reform, enlargement of the EU and increased trade liberalisation*' (84). A joint response by a number of public health bodies, food policy academics and nutritionists makes the critical point that health should be the central concern of the nation's farming and food system. It examines the health and health inequality impacts of current farming and food policy and makes a number of proposals for change. It argues the need for a modern, reformed Farming and Food Policy, which takes account of the health of the population and the government's support for tackling health inequalities and introducing the principle of sustainable development (85).

A new Department for Environment, Food and Rural Affairs was created in 2001, to address sustainable development "*which means a better quality of life for everyone, now and for generations to come*", and in which the food economy has a critical role to play (86). This is a stimulating addition to the newly structured independent Food Standards Agency in 2000, and broader focus on food and nutrition in both the Department of Health and Department of Education and Skills, within their different remits, means that potentially exciting opportunities lie ahead to regenerate new nutrition and food policy to the benefit of all.

7.7   References

1.   Tansey G., Worsley T. *The Food System: a Guide*. London. Earthscan Publications Ltd, 1995.

2.   Draper A., Dowler E. Nutrition Policy in Developed Countries, in *Encyclopedia of Nutrition*. London. Academic Press, 1998.

3.   Lang T. The public health impact of globalization of food trade. ch 9, in *Diet, Nutrition and Chronic Disease: Lessons from Contrasting Worlds*. Edited by Shetty P.S., McPherson K. Chichester. John Wiley & Sons, 1997, 173-87.

4. Waltner Troes, D., Lang T. A new conceptual base for food and agriculture: the emerging model of links between agriculture, food, health, environment and society. *Global Change and Human Health*, 2000, 1, 2, 116-30.

5. Drèze J., Sen A. *Hunger and Public Action*. Oxford. Clarendon Press, 1989.

6. Dobson B.D. in *Poverty and Food in Welfare Societies*. Edited by Köhler B., Feichtinger E., Barlösius E., Dowler E. Berlin. Sigma Edition, 1997, 33-46.

7. Norum K.P. Some aspects of Norwegian nutrition and food policy. ch 10, in *Diet, Nutrition and Chronic Disease: Lessons from Contrasting Worlds*. Edited by Shetty P.S., McPherson P. Chichester. John Wiley & Sons, 1997, 195-205.

8. Puksa P., Tuomilehto J., Nissinen A., Vartiainen E. (Eds) *The North Karelia Project: 20 Year Results and Experiences*. Helsinki. National Public Health Institute, 1995.

9. Lang T. The public health impact of globalization of food trade. ch 9, in *Diet, Nutrition and Chronic Disease: Lessons from Contrasting Worlds*. Edited by Shetty P.S., McPherson K. Chichester. John Wiley & Sons, 1997, 173-87.

10. Marsden T, Flynn A., Harrison M. *Consuming Interests: the Social Provision of Foods*. London. UCL Press, 2000.

11. Heasman M., Mellentin J. *The Functional Foods Revolution: Healthy People, Healthy Profits?* London. Earthscan, 2001.

12. Tansey G., Worsley T. *The Food System: a Guide*. London. Earthscan Publications Ltd, 1995.

13. Madeley J. *Hungry for Trade: How the Poor Pay for Free Trade*. London. Zed Books, 2000.

14. McMichael P.M. The impact of globalization, free trade and technology on food and nutrition in the new millennium. *Proceedings of the Nutrition Society*, 2001, 60, 215-20.

15. Lang T., Barling D., Caraher M. Food, social policy and the environment: towards a new model. *Social Policy and Administration*, 2001, 35, 5, 538-58.

16. Trichopoulou A., Millstone E., Lang T., Eames M., Barling D., Naska A., van Zwanenberg P. *European Policy on Food Safety*, Report to Science & Technology Options Assessment (STOA). Luxembourg. European Parliament, 2000.

17. James W.P.T. *Food Standards Agency Report – An Interim Proposal*. (no publisher given but obtainable from the Cabinet Office Press Office, Great George Street, London SW1, or the FSA Web site archive: http://www.food.gov.uk/maff/archive/food/james/cont.htm), 1997.

18. MAFF. *The Food Standards Agency: A Force for Change*. Cm 3830, London. The Stationery Office.

19. McKee M., Lang T., Roberts J. Deregulating health: policy lessons from the BSE affair. *Journal of the Royal Society of Medicine*, 1998, 89, 424-6.

20. Cragg A., Gilbert R. *Public Attitudes to Food Safety Report to the Food Standards Agency*, London. Cragg Ross Dawson Ltd (from the Food Standards Agency Web site: http://www.food.gov.uk/research/qualitative.htm, April 2001), 2000.

21. National Institute of Public Health. *Determinants of the Burden of Disease in the European Union*. Stockholm. National Institute of Public Health, 1997, cited in, World Health Organisation *The Impact of Food and Nutrition on Public Health: Case for a Food & Nutrition Policy and Action Plan for the European Region of WHO 2000-2005*. Food and Nutrition Policy Unit, Regional Office for Europe. Copenhagen. WHO, 2000.

22. Petersen S., Rainier M., Press V. *Coronary heart disease statistics*. London. British Heart Foundation, 2001.

23. Brunner E., Cohen D., Toon L. Cost effectiveness of cardiovascular disease prevention strategies; a perspective on EU food based dietary guidelines. *Public Health Nutrition*, 2001, 4, 2 (B), 711-5.

24. James W.P.T., Nelson M., Ralph A., Leather S. The contribution of nutrition to inequalities in health. *British Medical Journal*, 1997, 314, 1545-9.

25. Davey Smith G., Brunner E. Socio-economic differentials in health: the role of nutrition. *Proceedings of the Nutrition Society*, 1997, 56, 75-90.

26. Dowler E. Inequalities in diet and physical activity in Europe. *Public Health Nutrition*, 2001, 4, (2B), 701-709

27. Dowler E., Turner S. with Dobson B. *Poverty bites: food, health and poor families*. London. Child Poverty Action Group, 2001.

28. Leather S. *The making of modern malnutrition: an overview of food poverty in the UK*. London. The Caroline Walker Trust, 1996.

29. Hill M. *The Policy Process in the Modern State*. 3rd edition. London. Prentice Hall, 1997.

30. Tansey G., Worsley T. *The Food System: a Guide*. London. Earthscan Publications Ltd, 1995.

31. Walt G. *Health Policy: an Introduction to Process and Power*. London. Zed Books, and Johannesburg, Witwatersrand University Press, 1994.

32. Roe L. Hunt P., Bradshaw H., Rainier M. *Health Promotion Interventions to Promote Healthy Eating in the General Population: a Review.* London. Health Education Authority. Series of effectiveness reviews on healthy eating promotion in different age groups, Summary Bulletins 1998, 1997.

33. see http://www.hda-online.org.uk/evidence/eb2000/corehtml/intro.htm.

34. McGlone P., Dobson B., Dowler E., Nelson M. *Food projects and how they work.* York. York Publishing for Joseph Rowntree Foundation, 1999.

35. Department of Health. *Saving Lives: Our Healthier Nation.* White Paper July 1999. Cm 4386 London. The Stationery Office, 1999.

36. McGlone P., Dobson B., Dowler E., Nelson M. *Food projects and how they work.* York. York Publishing for Joseph Rowntree Foundation, 1999.

37. Department of Health. *The National School Fruit Scheme.* London. Department of Health. obtainable from http://www.doh.gov.uk/schoolfruitscheme/, 2000.

38. Donovan N., Street C. (Eds). *Fit for school: how breakfast clubs meet health, education and childcare needs.* London: New Policy Institute with the Kids' Clubs Network, 1999.

39. Dowler E., Turner S. with Dobson B. *Poverty bites: food, health and poor families.* London. Child Poverty Action Group, 2001.

40. Barnes M., Fimister G. Children's benefits and credits: is an integrated child credit the answer? in, G Fimister (Ed.) *An end in sight? Tackling child poverty in the UK.* London. CPAG, 2001, 28-42.

41. Morris J., Donkin A., Wonderling D., Wilkinson P. Dowler E. A minimum income for healthy living. *European Journal of Epidemiology and Community Health*, 2000, 54, 885-9.

42. Parker H. with Nelson M., Oldfield N., Dallison J., Hutton S., Paterakis S., Sutherland H., Thirlwart M. *Low Cost but Acceptable: a minimum income standard for the UK.* Bristol: the Policy Press and Zacchaeus Trust for the Family Budget Unit, 1998.

43. Kempson E., Bryson A., Rowlingson, K. *Hard Times: How poor families make ends meet.* London. Policy Studies Institute, 1994.

44. Dowler E. Budgeting for food on a low income: the case of lone parents. *Food Policy*, 1998, 22, 5, 405-17.

45. Dowler E., Turner S. with Dobson B. *Poverty bites: food, health and poor families.* London. Child Poverty Action Group, 2001.

46. Piachaud D., Webb J. *The price of food: missing out on mass consumption.* Suntory and Toyota International Centre for Economics and Related Disciplines, London. London School of Economics, 1996.

47. Caraher M., Dixon P., Lang T., Carr-Hill R. Access to healthy foods: part 1. Barriers to accessing healthy foods: differentials by gender, social class, income and mode of transport. *Health Education Journal*, 1998, 57, 191-201.

48. Harrison M., Hitchman C., Christie I., Lang T. *Inconvenience Foods.* London. Demos, 2002 forthcoming.

49. Department of Health. *Improving shopping access for people living in deprived neighbourhoods.* A Paper for Discussion, Policy Action Team: 13, National Strategy for Neighbourhood Renewal. London. Department of Health, 1999.

50. Parker H. with Nelson M., Oldfield N., Dallison J., Hutton S., Paterakis S., Sutherland H. & Thirlwart M. *Low Cost but Acceptable: a minimum income standard for the UK.* Bristol: the Policy Press and Zacchaeus Trust for the Family Budget Unit, 1998.

51. Craig G., Dowler E. "Let them eat cake!" Poverty, hunger and the UK state. ch. 5, in *First World Hunger: Food Security and Welfare Politics.* Edited by Riches G. Basingstoke. Macmillan Press, 108-33.

52. Evans N.S., Dowler E.A. Food, health and eating among single homeless and marginalized people in London. *Journal of Human Nutrition and Dietetics*, 1999, 12, 179-99.

53. Dowler E., Dobson B. Nutrition and poverty in Europe: an overview. *Proceedings of the Nutrition Society*, 1997, 56, 1, 51-62.

54. Riches, G. Hunger, food security and welfare politics. *Proceedings of the Nutrition Society*, 1997, 56, 1a, 63-74.

55. Hawkes C., Webster J. *Too Much and Too Little? Debates on surplus food distribution.* London. Sustain, the alliance for food and farming, 2000.

56. Köhler B., Feichtinger E., Barlösius E., Dowler, E. (Eds). *Poverty and Food in Welfare Societies.* Berlin. Sigma Edition, 1997.

57. Sellen D., Tedstone A., Frize J. *Young Refugee Children's Diets and Family Coping Strategies in relation to Food. A feasibility study in East London.* Final Report, London School of Hygiene & Tropical Medicine. (obtainable from: alison.tedstone@foodstandards.gsi.gov.uk).

58. McLeish J. *Report of the Welfare Foods Consultative Conference.* London. Maternity Alliance, 2000.

59. McMahon W., Marsh T. *Filling the gap: free school meals, nutrition and poverty.* London. Child Poverty Action Group, 1999.

60. Storey P., Chamberlin R. *Improving the take up of free school meals.* Research Report 270, London. DfEE, 2001.

61. Storey P., Chamberlin R. *Improving the take up of free school meals.* Research Report 270, London. DfEE, 2001.

62. Department of Health. *Dietary Reference Values for Food Energy and Nutrients for the United Kingdom.* Report of the Panel on Dietary Reference Values of the Committee on Medical Aspects of Food Policy, Department of Health. Report on Health and Social Subjects no 41. London. HM Stationery Office, 1991.

63. Williams C. Clarifying healthy eating advice. *British Medical Journal*, 1995, 310, 1453-5.

64. Food Standards Agency. *The Balance of Good Health.* Obtainable from the FSA on (tel) 0845 6060667; (e-mail) foodstandards@ecologistics.co.uk; FSA, PO Box 369, Hayes, Middlesex, UB3 1UT, 2001.

65. Kafatos A., Codrington C. Nutrition & Diet for Healthy Lifestyles in Europe: the Eurodiet Project. Editors preface in *Public Health Nutrition* Special Issue: Eurodiet Reports and Proceedings, 4, 2(A), 2001.

66. Lawrence M., Germov J. Future Food: the Politics of Functional Foods and Health Claims, in *A Sociology of Food and Nutrition: the Social Appetite.* Edited by Germov J., Williams L. Victoria. Oxford University Press, 1999.

67. Heasman M., Mellentin J. *The Functional Foods Revolution: Healthy People, Healthy Profits?* London. Earthscan, 2001.

68. Dallison J. *RDAs and DRVs: Scientific Constants or Social Constructs? The Case of Vitamin C.* Unpublished PhD Thesis, University of Sussex, 1996.

69. Smith D. The Social Construction of Dietary Standards: The British Medical Association – Ministry of Health Advisory Committee on Nutrition Report of 1934. ch13, in *Eating Agendas: Food and Nutrition as Social Problems.* Edited by Maurer D. Sobal J. New York. Aldine de Gruyter, 1995, 279-303.

70. Davey L. Healthier diets cost more than ever! Food Magazine, 2001, 55, 17.

71. Piachaud D., Webb J. *The price of food: missing out on mass consumption.* STICERD, London. London School of Economics, 2001.

72. Dowler E., Blair A., Donkin A., Grundy C., Rex, D. *Mapping access to healthy food in Sandwell.* Report to the Health Action Zone. Sandwell. Sandwell Health Authority, 2001.

73. Dobson B., Beardsworth A., Keil T., Walker R. Diet, *Choice and Poverty: social, cultural and nutritional aspects of food consumption among low income families.* London. Family Policy Studies Centre, 1994.

74. WHO Regional Office for Europe. A comparative analysis of the situation regarding nutrition policies and plans of action in WHO European Member States made on the basis of country reports submitted at a consultation held in Warsaw, Poland, 2-4 September 1996, Copenhagen. WHO Regional Office for Europe. 1988.

75. Robertson A., Mutru T. WHO Perspective on the Nutrition Situation in Europe, in *Public Health and Nutrition: the Challenge*, Edited by Köhler B., Feichtinger E., Winkler G., E. Dowler, 1999, 27-43. Sigma Edition: Berlin.

76. Robertson A. WHO tackles food inequalities: Europe's first comprehensive Food and Nutrition Action Plan debate, Malta. *Public Health Nutrition*, 2000, 3, 1, 99-101.

77. World Health Organization. *The Impact of Food and Nutrition on Public Health. Case for a Food and Nutrition Policy and Action Plan for the WHO European Region 2000-2005.* Food and Nutrition Policy Unit, Copenhagen. WHO Regional Office for Europe, 2000.

78. Council of the European Communities. *Health and Human Nutrition: Elements for European Action.* French Presidency of the European Union Working Paper and Resolution. see Société Française de Santé Publique http://www.sfsp-publichealth.org/europe.html, 2000, 54-76.

79. Food Standards Agency Web site: www.food.gov.uk/science/sciencetopics/nutritionforum.

80. Department of Health. *Saving Lives: Our Healthier Nation.* White Paper July 1999. Cm 4386 London. The Stationery Office, 1999.

81. Acheson D. *Independent inquiry into inequalities in health.* London. Department of Health, 1998.

82. Department of Health. *The NHS Plan.* Cmd Paper no 4818. London. The Stationery Office, 2000.

83. McGlone P., Dobson B., Dowler E., Nelson M. *Food projects and how they work.* York. York Publishing for Joseph Rowntree Foundation, 1999.

84. DEFRA Web site: http://www.defra.gov.uk.

85. Lang T., Rainier G. (Eds) *Why Health is the Key to the Future of Food and Farming.* Joint Submission to the Policy Commission on the Future of Farming and Food. available on: http://www.ukpha.org.uk/health_key.pdf, 2001.

86. DEFRA Web site: http://www.defra.gov.uk/corporate/aims/index.htm.

8. NUTRITION AND HEALTH PROMOTION

Margaret Thorogood, Carolyn Summerbell and Gill Cowburn

8.1   Introduction

The preceding chapters have demonstrated very clearly the important role of nutrition in determining the health of people. It follows, therefore, that there is a great deal of scope to improve health through changes in diet and nutrition. In general, the diet eaten in the UK contains too much saturated fat and does not include enough fruit and vegetables. There is also too much salt in the diet, which results in high blood pressure levels. The health of British people could be greatly improved by some moderate changes in their diet. However, changing diet is difficult at a community level, and very difficult indeed for an individual who tries to change diet in ways that do not conform to the dietary norms of their community. The theory and methods of health promotion have much to contribute in demonstrating effective ways of supporting health-enhancing changes in diet.

8.2   What is Health Promotion?

Health promotion is about changing factors in ways that will lead to improvements in either physical or mental health. Those factors could be environmental, social, economic or psychological, and it can be seen that the area covered is broad. Health promotion is a relatively new concept, which has grown over the last few decades. A seminal moment in health promotion was the publication of the WHO Ottawa Charter, which defined health promotion as 'the process of enabling people to increase control over and to improve their health' and defined health as 'a resource for everyday life, not the objective of living' (1).

This enshrines important concepts. Health promotion is about giving people the power to lead the lives they want to lead. The aim of health promotion in nutrition is not to make everybody eat the diet that nutritional experts currently consider ideal, but to give everyone the knowledge, access and ability to choose the diet that will best achieve their health objectives. Health promotion aims to ensure that people are not restricted in controlling and improving their health by their environment or material circumstances.

As a new discipline, health promotion has borrowed extensively, and productively, from a wide range of other relevant disciplines, including sociology, anthropology, psychology, economics and epidemiology, amongst others. With such ambitious aims, health promotion also embraces a wide range of approaches from the global to the individual. These approaches include healthy public policy, community development and preventive medicine, including activities such as screening and immunisation as well as one-to-one health behaviour change interventions (2,3).

It can be difficult to define the boundaries of health promotion, that is, to say what is and what is not health promotion. This is partly because the philosophy underlying health promotion recognises the importance of the social determinants of health, the importance of increasing individual and community control over those determinants, and that these can and should inform the actions of all health professionals, whether a consultant surgeon or a community dietitian.

8.2.1 Public health policy

What a population eats is determined very largely by economic and agricultural policy (4). With the globalisation of the food industry, and the emergence of large international food industry corporations, global economic policy has become increasingly important in determining the availability of food and the price and quality of that food. An example of this can be seen in the Trade War that broke out between Europe and the US because Europe wanted to ban the import and sale of hormone-treated beef. Issues of public health became subservient to the economic threats that the USA was making towards the Scottish cashmere industry. (5).

Changes in the international trading situation are important for health promotion when they impact on the relative accessibility of healthy food. A striking example of this can be seen in data from Poland. After the fall of the Soviet Union, general purchasing power fell, and the large subsidies for food of animal origin were withdrawn. There was a consequent shift towards vegetable fats. This was accompanied by increased consumption of citrus fruits and bananas as a result of new trade routes opening up. These changes in diet appeared to have a dramatic effect on public health. Death rates from circulatory diseases in middle-aged people (aged 35 to 60 years) fell by more than 20% in the 3 years from 1991 to 1994 (6).

Public policy can also impact more directly on health, for example by controlling the use of additives in food. It is now well accepted that the supplementation of women's diets with an extra 400 micrograms of folate and folic acid before conception and during the first 12 weeks of pregnancy will reduce the incidence of babies born with neural tube defects (7). Folic acid deficiency is also associated with high homocysteine levels (8), which are in turn associated with an increased risk of cardiovascular disease (9). In the US, the Government have acted on this evidence by requiring the fortification of bread flour with folic acid (10). In contrast, the UK Government has decided against compulsory fortification (11), and had opted instead for a campaign to raise awareness of the importance of folic acid supplementation, which relies on advice giving. This approach is problematic in that it depends on the relatively weak effects of a mass media health education campaign and on the assumption that all or most pregnancies are pre-planned.

8.2.2   *Community development*

The concept of community development as a health-promoting activity is based on the belief that community participation is in itself beneficial to health (12). In a community development approach there will be active engagement with a defined community over a period of time. The community could be defined either geographically (the residents of a small town, for example) or by other characteristics (for example, Bengali-speaking people). In such an approach, members of the community are involved in setting the priorities, and participate in the development of interventions to address those priorities. By participation, individuals will develop skills and competencies that can then be used in other areas of their lives, thus empowering them to take greater control over their lives (13). At the same time, the process of bringing together individuals to achieve commonly agreed goals would generate social capital, strengthening the social and mutually supportive networks within the community. Many food projects, such as the establishment of community cafés or food buying cooperatives, are based on the principles of community development.

8.2.3 Health behaviour interventions

The discipline of health promotion grew out of early attempts at health education, but has long since abandoned most of the crude techniques of didactic health education.

As one sociologist described the new thinking: "the ethos of the new health promotion philosophy strongly rejects anything that smacks of manipulation and authoritarianism" (14). While such techniques may (temporarily) increase knowledge, experience has shown that they are rarely, if ever, effective in changing behaviour (15,16). Any experienced dietitian would confirm that simply providing information about which foods are better for health has virtually no effect in changing someone's diet (although it might have an effect in changing what they report eating!). Moreover, simple advice giving, that is, telling people how they should change their behaviour to improve their health, has been shown to be not only ineffective, but often counter-productive in setting up a resistance to the need for change.

One-to-one health behaviour interventions, then, demand a great deal more skill from the health professional, and, even more importantly, a great deal more awareness that the other party in the interaction is also coming with their own strongly held beliefs, anxieties, and barriers to action (17,18). While this is true of any one-to-one interventions, it is particularly true for any intervention that involves food. Eating is not just a means of providing nutrients to stay alive; it is also the focus of social activities, and an important source of feelings of well-being. Whether it is a group of schoolchildren in MacDonald's, a family sitting down to Sunday lunch or colleagues sharing a table in the work canteen, the actual food consumed will take second place to the social interactions that are occurring at the same time (19,20). Changes to eating patterns in ways that will disrupt these social interactions are inevitably very difficult to achieve, however strongly an individual may feel the importance of protecting or improving their health.

8.3 Evaluation of Health Promotion Interventions

Evaluation has become increasingly important, not least because funding bodies are increasingly demanding 'rigorous evaluation' when grants are awarded. This is often seen as a demand for the findings of randomised controlled trials, but many of the activities of health promotion are not appropriately evaluated by the traditional randomised controlled trial.

8.3.1   Why randomised controlled trials? – the experimental design

The concept of testing the effectiveness of a nutritional intervention on humans by experimentation has a long history. One early example was the discovery of a cure for scurvy. In 1747, James Lind, a ship's surgeon, was looking for a cure for scurvy, which was then a major problem. He took 12 sailors with scurvy and assigned them, in pairs, six different medications, including vinegar, cider, sea water, 'elixir vitriol', a mixture including garlic and mustard seed amongst other things, and *'each two oranges and one lemon every day'*. The results were dramatic: *'the most sudden and good effects were perceived from the use of the oranges and lemon; one of those who had taken them being at the end of six days fit for duty'* (21, p22).

This early example of a nutritional trial contained many of the aspects that are still important today. The trial was 'controlled' in that there was a comparison between groups with different interventions. There was also an attempt to control possible confounding factors, in that sailors were treated in the same way, apart from the mixtures they were given. It is not clear from Lind's experiment whether the choice of treatment was allocated randomly.

8.3.1.1   Why is randomisation important in a randomised controlled trial?

If people are randomised into groups, it is likely that any confounding factors, whether measured or not, will be equally distributed between the groups (22). Confounding factors are variables that are linked both to the intervention (for example, type of diet) and to the observed outcome (for example, change in health). These factors, such as age or social class, can distort the relationship between an intervention and outcome, unless they are equally distributed between the groups.

8.3.2   Problems for the randomised controlled trial in evaluating health promotion

The randomised controlled trial has limited application in relation to health development strategies, particularly because of the requirement it imposes for tight standardisation of the intervention. Rigorous evaluation is important, but that does not mean that a randomised controlled trial is the best method in every circumstance (23). The interventions that are usually evaluated by randomised controlled trials.

Firstly, health promotion interventions are aimed at achieving behavioural change at either an individual or a societal level. This has repercussions for the design of trials, both in terms of who receives the intervention (it might be an individual, a whole community, or a whole nation) and in terms of the concepts of comparisons. It is difficult to devise a comparison intervention for a community development intervention, where the enthusiasm and commitment of members of the community are an important part of the intervention. There is also the risk that neighbouring communities, which are acting as control groups, will adopt the practices of the intervention community. Such contamination is hard to prevent or control and may, in fact, undermine one of the main aims of health promotion activity – encouraging a widespread uptake of new ideas.

Secondly, the recipients of health promotion interventions exist within a social context and will respond to health messages within that context. If the social context is ignored, an understanding of underlying mechanisms may be lost (17). Understanding the process by which an intervention operates may be as important as the final outcome.

Thirdly, one of the features of health promotion is that the interventions are intended to prevent future ill health rather than cure existing illnesses. This is equally true of community development interventions as of personalised health advice. The focus of health promotion on outcomes in the (often distant) future makes it difficult or practically impossible to design and run suitable randomised controlled trials.

8.3.3   Stages of evaluation

Evaluation is often described as taking place at three stages. These are the formative, process and outcome stages (24). In the formative stage, evaluation is used to help in the process of developing an intervention. At this stage, the questions addressed by evaluation will be those such as whether the intervention is appropriate, whether the message is clear, whether it is culturally appropriate, and whether the right target groups have been identified. At the end of an intervention, outcome evaluation will take place, but in between these two stages, important data will be obtained from process evaluation. Process evaluation will help to answer the all-important questions about why an intervention was successful or otherwise, as well as helping to identify unexpected and unintended outcomes, which could be either beneficial or adverse. While a lot of emphasis is placed on outcome evaluation, process evaluation can be just as illuminating, and, in some cases, even more illuminating.

Many different methods for evaluation can be used and different methods will be used at each stage. Roughly, formative evaluation calls for qualitative research methods, and outcome evaluation calls for quantitative research methods (although not necessarily randomised controlled trials). Process evaluation often uses a mixture of quantitative and qualitative methods – for example, counting the users of a new service, but also carrying out in-depth interviews with some users to understand better what their experience of the service is.

It is self-evident, but often forgotten or ignored, that the outcome of health promotion activity should be evaluated against its declared aims and objectives (25), not against the arbitrarily defined objectives of the evaluator. It is important, therefore, that aims and objectives are discussed with a range of stakeholders, agreed, and clearly stated beforehand.

8.3.4   *Ecological study design*

There is a strong case for using the ecological study design to estimate the effect of an intervention on the health of populations while controlling for confounders. Viewing health promotion as an environmental influence on health allows the measurement of different outcomes on a common scale through various methods of rating or ranking (25). These ideas are now being explored and new developments in the evaluation of health promotion can be expected.

8.4   Who Should be Delivering Nutritional Health Promotion?

It can be seen that both the scope and the approach of health promotion are wide-ranging. It is equally the case that the channels of delivery are inclusive rather than exclusive. The skills required range from media advocacy, lobbying and facilitating community meetings (26) to negotiation of an individual's plan for making changes to his or her diet (27,28). No single person and no single profession can encompass all these skills. While dietitians have an important role to play, the skills of doctors, nurses, teachers, community development workers, local lay volunteers and many others will also be needed. Many professionals working in this arena may feel that they require additional training to develop new skills in order to feel confident to engage in health promotion activities.

8.5 Factors Influencing Food Choice

Although we talk about the role of nutrients in health, it is worth remembering that people eat foods, not nutrients. Any successful health promotion intervention must not only pay attention to the foods that are sources of important nutrients but also focus on why and how people choose to eat the foods they do (29).

Whether particular foods are readily available plays an important role in influencing what is eaten. Availability of food is affected at a global level by global trade agreements, as well as by the physical and economic constraints of shipping perishable goods over long distances. These problems can have a profound effect on food supplies in poorer countries, but the effects are less in wealthy countries. In the UK, food is plentiful in the shops and food from all parts of the world is available, providing, for example, year round supplies of different fruits and vegetables. Despite an apparently wide choice of food, many individuals have a limited degree of control over the foods they eat (30). The social function food plays in society can constrain food choice for individuals who feel pressurised to conform to cultural, family and peer norms. Many people, especially women, strive to control their body weight (31) through restrained eating practices in cultures where the importance of body thinness is over-emphasised. The increasing prevalence of overweight and obesity in the UK (32) has taken place against a backdrop of 'blaming' those people (33) who are unable or unwilling to adopt healthier eating habits. People living on restricted incomes may face even greater limitations to their food choice. Households with the least income use a larger proportion of their disposable income on food compared with those with greater income (34). In spite of efficient budgeting skills, they spend more money on unhealthy foods that provide cheaper energy than healthier foods such as fruit and vegetables (35,36). For people without access to a car, the physical inaccessibility of large cheap retail outlets may mean paying higher prices in smaller local shops. In some cases, smaller shops may not stock healthier foods. Diets of families may lack variety owing to the expense of supplying choice and the potential for food waste (37).

8.6 Effectiveness of Nutrition Interventions

Although it is difficult to evaluate health promotion activities, there is a need for evidence-based practice and so it is important to know what types of intervention are effective. There have been a number of studies that have looked at this question, in relation to promoting healthier eating behaviour. Narrative and systematic reviews of interventions offer some insights into the characteristics of the successful ones.

Roe *et al.* (38) carried out a systematic review of health promotion interventions to promote healthy eating in the general population. Healthy eating was defined as a diet reduced in fat and increased in starchy foods, fruit and vegetables. They included mostly randomised controlled trial evidence from literature published up until early 1996, and concluded that well-designed and well-implemented healthy eating interventions in a variety of settings and populations were effective in changing behaviour. Benefits were shown by modest changes in several outcomes – reductions in blood cholesterol, reductions in dietary fat as measured by validated methods and an increase in purchases of healthy food items. The reviewers found very limited data relating to interventions aimed at people on a lower income or from minority ethnic populations. Very little of the information related to interventions carried out in the UK. They noted that little is known about the cost-effectiveness of healthy eating interventions in the general population, and calls have been made for activity to encourage the development of good-quality cost benefit analyses (39).

A number of important characteristics of effective healthy eating interventions were identified:

In schools, workplaces, primary care and the community:

- the content focused on diet only, or diet and physical activity, rather than multiple risk factors
- an intervention model based on behavioural theories and goals, rather than simply information provision
- intervention methods that emphasised personal contact with individuals or in small groups, using active involvement and specific behaviour change strategies
- some degree of personalisation of the intervention
- the provision of feedback on individual changes in behaviour and risk factors
- multiple contacts over a substantial time period
- support provided for individual dietary change by involving family members, colleagues and others and by promoting changes in the local environment.

In supermarket and catering outlets:

- identification of healthier choices, accompanied by explanatory leaflets, and local promotions; these signs had an effect for at least as long as they were in place
- covert manipulation of food composition of catered meals, which changed the nutrient content of specific meals, although the effect on total diet was not usually measured
- changes in the availability of healthier food choices, and the accessibility of less healthy choices resulted in short term changes in food choice whilst the intervention was in place.

A review of the effectiveness of healthy eating interventions concluded that 'the most effective interventions

(i)   adopt an integrated, multidisciplinary and comprehensive approach
(ii) involve a complementary range of actions and
(iii) work at an individual, community, social, environmental and policy level' (40).

Although there appears to be a general acceptance that interventions should be targeted to the unique needs of specific population groups, little has been published about how best to achieve this or whether it increases the impact of interventions (41).

A range of settings for healthy eating interventions can be considered. These are:

- **educational institutions** (including pre-school nurseries, school and adult education)
- **workplaces**
- **food outlets**, including commercial manufacturers, retailers and caterers and not-for-profit retailers such as food co-operatives or community shops and caterers such as community cafés
- **general community settings** using new or existing social structures (for example, Health Action Zones, social clubs for older people, youth clubs, tenants groups, shelters for the homeless, residential homes, religious centres, etc.)
- **one-to-one interventions**

8.6.1   Education institutions

Schools provide a potentially useful setting for nutrition-related health promotion activities as there is access to a captive audience, which often takes at least one meal a day in school (42). Moreover, school children are already interested in food, which provides a good basis for any kind of intervention about eating. A variety of school-based approaches to promote healthy eating have been developed. Interventions range from educational approaches via the classroom curriculum to 'healthy' school approaches, which move beyond the taught curriculum and also consider the whole school environment, ethos and social context.

Tedstone (43) completed a systematic review to examine the effectiveness of interventions to promote healthy eating in pre-school children aged 1 to 5 years. She concluded that, although insufficient evidence was available at that time to predict the format of successful healthy eating interventions in this age group, promising approaches might involve integrating nutrition into pre-school curricula and involving parents as nutrition educators.

A meta-analysis of the influence of 'heart-healthy' behaviours following a school-based intervention supports the effects of school-based cardiovascular health promotion programmes that include eating behaviours as a component of the intervention. McArthur (42) found that there was no difference in effect on outcomes according to the age group of participants and suggested that school-based interventions were effective among a variety of ethnic and socio-economic population groups. School-based healthy eating interventions should integrate long-term behaviour-oriented programmes into the curriculum and support dietary change by modifications in the school environment, including the school meals service.

In their review of the effectiveness of health promotion in schools, Lister-Sharp *et al.* (44) concluded that:

- healthy eating interventions in schools have employed a more restricted range of classroom approaches than programmes targeting other health-related topics such as substance misuse

- school-based healthy eating programmes that target school lunches can be relied upon to improve their content

- involving parents in school healthy eating programmes is important

- interventions that combined a classroom component with environmental change were able to achieve their goals, whereas programmes involving lunchtime activities were less successful
- longer and more frequent interventions were associated with an indication of greater benefit
- interventions that provide a choice are more likely to have a long-term impact on dietary intake.

The provision of at least one meal each school day is considered by many to be fundamentally important to the nutritional status of children living with families on a low income (45). In 2001, the reintroduction of legislation requiring school lunches to meet minimum nutritional standards will help to ensure the adequacy of free school meal provision in the future. Another part of the Government's strategy to help tackle health inequalities has included funding school breakfast clubs in areas of deprivation, and evaluations of this initiative are currently taking place. The National Health Service Plan (46) included a commitment to a National School Fruit Scheme by 2004. This scheme entitles every child in nursery and aged 4 to 6 in infant schools to a free piece of fruit each school day. Provisional evaluation of the pilot scheme appears positive. Other school-based initiatives currently being implemented include healthy tuck shops/vending schemes and after-school clubs.

A Sustain project (47), 'Grab 5', funded by the National Lotteries Charities Board, aims to develop a nationwide school-based campaign to increase fruit and vegetable consumption in 7-11 year olds, with a focus on low-income groups. The project will work with local partnerships such as Health Action Zones, Education Action Zones and the Healthy Schools Initiative and encourage children to eat fruit and vegetables by complementing curriculum work with practical activities. A process and outcome evaluation of the pilot scheme is planned.

Concerns have been expressed about the impact of the gradual erosion of food preparation and cooking skills on future nutritional health, since practical skills have been replaced by a focus on technology in the national curriculum. This is of particular concern because, in the past, school has been the prime non-domestic source of cooking skill development (48,49). To address this, cooking skills clubs have been established and evaluation into their impact is underway.

8.6.2   *Workplaces*

Workplaces are considered to be potentially useful settings in which to improve the health of the employed adult population because they have existing channels for communication, provide easy access to a relatively stable number of adults, and offer a cohesive working community, which can provide peer support or pressure. A review of workplace health promotion interventions concluded that "a sustained programme based on principles of empowerment and/or a community-oriented model using multiple methods, visibly supported by top management, and engaging the involvement of all levels of workers in an organisation is likely to produce the best results." (50,51). It suggested that the following features characterise successful workplace health promotion interventions:

- participation
- executive support
- shared responsibility
- integration into the organisation
- variety of content
- variety of method
- tailored to meet staff needs
- comprehensive coverage
- sustainability
- monitoring and evaluation

Few workplace interventions addressed entire population groups. Mostly, they involved a screening or health risk assessment and subsequent counselling sessions (38). Some incorporated an environmental approach by influencing work-site catering provision. The review (38) found examples of effective interventions in both manual and non-manual working populations, and found that effectiveness was not influenced by participant age, gender, socio-economic status, or the size of or nature of the business of the company. Individual screening and counselling interventions seemed to have a greater effect than group-based activities, or workplace-wide activities, at least in the short term. However, another review (50) found that healthier eating had been encouraged by targeted provision of information, such as point-of-purchase labelling of healthy food choices in workplace cafeterias, and by computer-generated personalised nutrition advice.

8.6.3   Food outlets

Food outlets include commercial organisations such as food manufacturers, retailers, caterers, not-for-profit food providers such as community shops or food co-operatives, fruit and vegetable box schemes, and community cafés.

In commercial retail outlets, the most common intervention involved signs at point of choice. Other interventions used video education and feedback on purchases or a supermarket tour (38). The supermarket-based interventions had an impact on food purchases, at least for the duration of the intervention. Interventions based in the catering setting showed a beneficial effect on food choice. Point of choice and environmental manipulations were found to be promising approaches (38).

Little evidence exists in relation to the effectiveness of not-for-profit food providers such as community cafés and food co-operatives or initiatives designed to increase access to fruit and vegetables such as community growing schemes. An evaluation of a community café suggested that, although the café achieved its aim of providing a meeting place for people who lived locally, it was not possible to determine whether or not the café was successful in providing cheap good-quality food because of the difficulties in defining the term 'quality' (52). Evaluations of community-owned retailing, such as food co-operatives, suggest that they have a positive impact on increasing availability of fruit and vegetables in areas that lack local affordable supplies. They enabled people to try new foods at affordable prices, and developed the confidence, self-esteem and skills of those community members involved in organising the initiative (53,54) An evaluation of a community growing scheme suggests that such initiatives may offer similar benefits to community members as do food co-operatives (55).

Evidence relating to the impact of farmers' markets comes from the USA, where they have existed for nearly two decades. It has been suggested that they boost local economies, offer support to farmers in a difficult economic climate, benefit the environment by linking local growers with local consumers, and offer consumers fresh healthy produce at competitive prices (56). However, evaluation is required to establish their effectiveness in the UK.

Research into the effectiveness and sustainability of local food projects was carried out by McGlone *et al.* (57), who defined local food projects as 'a range of initiatives that work with, or are generated by, low-income communities' (p2). They suggest that, at their most basic level, food projects are needed, to help people on a low income to overcome existing physical and economic barriers to obtain an adequate, healthy diet. A series of factors, shown in Table 8.I, were considered to be relevant to the success or failure of a project.

TABLE 8.I
Factors affecting the sustainability of food projects

Facilitate	Hinder
Reconciling different agendas	Opposing agendas
Funding	Instability of funding
Community involvement	Meeting limited needs
Professional support	Lack of support
Credibility	Changing agendas
Shared ownership	Exclusively owned
Dynamic worker	
Responsiveness	

They conclude that, if local food projects are to work, they need to have the following characteristics:

- flexibility
- community ownership
- patience
- committed back-up
- access to funding that is not short-term and not focused only on innovation.

8.6.4   General community settings, e.g. Health Action Zones

Health Action Zones (HAZs) are partnerships between the NHS, local authorities, voluntary and private sectors and community groups. They have been established in areas of the UK with some of the highest levels of deprivation and the poorest levels of health to tackle health inequalities and modernise services through local innovation. HAZs have been given responsibility to develop and implement a locally sensitive health strategy that cuts inequalities and delivers measurable improvements in public health, health outcomes and quality of treatment and care. The HAZ approach is underpinned by a series of principles shared by those involved in health promotion activities: achieving equity, engaging communities, working in partnership, engaging front line staff, taking an evidence-based approach, developing a person-centred approach to service delivery and taking a whole systems approach [source: http://www.haznet.org.uk]. Twelve of the 26 HAZs have objectives relating to improving nutrition in their localities. A variety of initiatives is being developed and implemented to improve access to and availability of healthier foods. These include projects to support breastfeeding and healthy weaning practices, food co-operatives, cafés, breakfast clubs, cooking skills training, community gardening and box schemes, training community food advisers, and work with local food retailers. The Health Development Agency has commissioned reviews of local projects to promote healthy eating and increase fruit and vegetable consumption across England. An aim of these reviews is to identify ongoing evaluations that will contribute to the evidence base around effectiveness.

8.6.5   Clinical settings: one-to-one interventions

As trusted sources of health information, health professionals are in a unique position to promote healthy eating. However, there are a limited number of interventions in the primary care setting that address entire population groups, and very little information relating to interventions targeting lower socio-economic groups or minority ethnic groups (38). The primary care studies provided some of the most consistent evidence in the Roe review, with modest but sustained impacts on blood cholesterol level. While there has been some debate on the cost-effectiveness of one-to-one interventions, an economic analysis of two large studies of nurses provided health promotion advice, and concluded that such interventions were relatively low-cost and therefore the small health gains were still relatively cost-effective (58-60). A lack of evaluations relating to group classes, interactive computer software or videos in the primary care setting has been noted (38), and a need for better knowledge and skills amongst primary care personnel relating to healthy eating has also been identified (40).

8.6.5.1   Reducing blood cholesterol

The average blood cholesterol levels in the UK are much higher than is desirable for cardiovascular health (61). While drug treatment is effective, the public health problem will only be solved by changes in population diet (62,63) Systematic reviews have found that one-to-one advice about a cholesterol-lowering diet (that is, advice to reduce fat intake or increase the polyunsaturated to saturated fatty

185

acid ratio in the diet) leads to a small reduction in blood cholesterol concentrations over 6 or more months (64-66).

8.6.5.2   *Reducing body weight*

Weight reduction can lead to important health gains. For example, a systematic review (67) found that a reduction in body weight in people who were overweight or obese and also had raised blood cholesterol led to a reduction of blood cholesterol. A systematic review (68) examined the effects of weight loss on blood pressure in people with hypertension. Combined data from six trials that did not vary antihypertensive regimens during the intervention period found that reducing weight (most diets led to a weight reduction of 3-9% of body weight) reduced mean systolic and diastolic pressures by 3 mm Hg (95% CI 0.7 to 6.8 mm Hg) and 2.9 mm Hg (95% CI 0.1 to 5.7 mm Hg), respectively.

A combination of advice on diet and exercise, supported by behaviour therapy, is probably more effective in achieving weight loss than either diet or exercise advice alone (69). A low-energy, low-fat diet is the most effective lifestyle intervention for weight loss. Weight regain is likely, but weight loss of 2 to 6 kg may be sustained over at least 2 years (70). Strategies that involve personal contact with a therapist, family support or multiple interventions, or are weight-focused appear most effective, but the resource implication of providing long-term support may prevent routine implementation of maintenance programmes (71).

8.7   Conclusions

What we eat is important for our health, but also important for our social functioning and our personal feelings of wellbeing. It is not surprising, therefore, that it is difficult for an individual to change the way that he or she eats, and even more difficult for outsiders to change the diet of individuals by external interventions. There have been changes in diet in the UK over the last 25 years, but it is not clear that these changes have been made in pursuit of a healthier diet, rather than convenience, perceived fashion, or for other reasons. In this chapter, we have discussed how the principles of health promotion are relevant to nutritional health, and have described some of the ways in which nutritional health promotion may be approached.

There is a great shortage of research on the effectiveness of nutritional health promotion and in particular on the effect of interventions other than one-to-one clinical interventions. As with many other aspects of health promotion, the evidence base for nutritional health promotion is still relatively weak. However, there is considerable activity in this area, and more evidence will undoubtedly become available.

8.8   References

1.   WHO. Ottawa Charter for Health Promotion. *World Health Organisation for Health and Welfare*, Ontario. 1986.

2.   Badura B., Kickbusch I. Health Promotion Research – Towards a New Social Epidemiology. *WHO Regional Publications, European Series No. 37.* 1991.

3.   Bennett P., Hodgeson P. Psychology and Health Promotion, edited by Bunton R., McDonald G. *Health Promotion. Disciplines and Diversity*, Routledge. 1995, 23-41.

4.   James W.P.T., Trehearne W.P. Healthy Nutrition, Preventing Nutrition Related Disease in Europe. *WHO Regional Publications, European Series No. 24,* 1998.

5.   Elliott L., Denny C., Martinson J. Blair warns US of trade war. *Guardian*, September 7th 2000.

6.   Zantonski W.A., McMichael A.J., Powles J.W. Ecological study of reasons for sharp decline in mortality from ischaemic heart disease in Poland since 1991. *British Medical Journal*, 1998, 316, 1047-51.

7.   Committee on Medical Aspects of Food Policy. Annual Report, *Department of Health*, 1999. www.doh.gov.uk/pub/docs/doh/coma99.pdf.

8.   Lakshmi A.V., Maniprabha C., Krishna T.P. Plasma homocysteine level in relation to folate and vitamin B6 status in apparently normal men. *Asia Pacific Journal of Clinical Nutrition*, 2001, 10 (3), 194-6.

9.   Ward M. Homocysteine, folate, and cardiovascular disease. *International Journal for Vitamin and Nutrition Research*, 2001, 71 (3), 173-8.

10.   Bostom A.G., Jaques P.F., Liaugaudas G., Rogers G., Rosenberg I.H., Selhub J. Total homocyteine lowering treatment among coronary artery disease patients in the era of folic acid-fortified cereal in grain flour. *Arteriosclerosis, Thrombosis and Vascular Biology*, 2002, 22 (3), 488-91.

11.   Food Standards Agency. Board decides against mandatory folic acid fortification. 2002. http://www.food.gov.uk/news/newsarchive/62488.

12. Mittlemark M.B., Hunt M.K., Heath G.W., Schmid T.L. Realistic outcomes: Lessons from community-based research and demonstration programs for the prevention of cardiovascular disease. *Journal of Public Health Policy*, 1993, 14 (4), 437-62.

13. Bracht N. Health Promotion at the Community Level 2: New Advances. *Sage Publications.* 1999.

14. Pill R. Issues in lifestyle and health; lay meaning, in Health Promotion Research – Towards a New Social Epidemiology, edited by Badura B., Kickbusch I. *WHO Regional Publications, European Series No. 37*, 1991, 187-212.

15. O'Brien T., Freemantle N., Oxman A.D. Wolf F., Davis D.A., Herrin J. Continuing education meetings and workshops: effects on professional practice and health outcomes. *The Cochrane Library Issue 1*, 2002.

16. Baldwin C., Parsons T., Logan S. Dietary advice for illness-related malnutrition in adults. *The Cochrane Library Issue 1*, 2002.

17. Bury T. Getting research into practice: changing behaviour, in *Evidence-based Healthcare; A Practical Guide for Therapists*, edited by Bury T., Mead J. Butterworth Heinemann. 2000, 66-85.

18. Bunton R., Murphy S., Bennett P. Theories of behavioural change and their use in health promotion: some neglected areas. *Health Education Research*, 1991, 6 (2), 153-62.

19. Murcott A. Understanding life-style and food use: contributions from the social sciences. *British Medical Bulletin*, 2000, 56 (1), 121-32.

20. Shepherd R., Social determinants of food choice. *Proceedings of the Nutrition Society*, 1999, 58 (4), 807-12.

21. Lind J. An inquiry into the nature, causes and cure of scurvy, in *The Challenge of Epidemiology. Issues and Selected Readings*, edited by Buck C., Llopis A., Najera E., Terris M. Pan American Health Organisation Washington, 1988.

22. Bowling A., Research Methods in Health, Investigating Health and Health Services. *Open University Press*, 1998.

23. Peberdy A., Evaluation Design, Promoting Health Promotion, Knowledge and Practice (2nd edition), edited by Katz J., Peberby A., Douglas J. *Open University Press*, 2000, 292-310.

24. De Vries A. Planning and evaluating health promotion, in *Evaluating Health Promotion*, edited by Scott D., Weston R. Cheltenham. Stanley Thornes, 1998, 95-112.

25. Noack H., Conceptualising and measuring health, in Health Promotion Research – Towards a New Social Epidemiology, edited by Badura B., Kickbusch I. WHO Regional Publications, *European Series No. 37*, 1991, 85-112.

26. Chapman S., Lupton D., The Fight for Public Health, Principles and Practice of Media Advocacy. *BMJ Publishing Group*. 1996.

27. Needham G., Oliver S. Involving service users, in *Evidence-based Healthcare: A Practical Guide for Therapists*, edited by Bury T., Mead J. Butterworth Heinemann. 2000, 85-105.

28. Charles C., Gafni A., Whelan T. Shared decision-making in the medical encounter: what does it mean? *Social Science Medicine*, 1997, 44, 681-92.

29. Boyd O.J. Food health and income chapter VIII, Nutrition at different income levels, in *Poverty, Inequality and Health in Britain 1800-2000; A Reader*, edited by Davey Smith G., Dorling D., Shaw M. The Policy Press. 2001, 186-96.

30. Krebs-Smith S.M., Kantor L.S. Choose a variety of fruits and vegetables daily: understanding the complexities. *Journal of Nutrition*, 2001, 131, 487-501.

31. Orbach S. *Hunger Strike*. London. Penguin Books, 1993.

32. Department of Health. Health Survey for England 1999. *Department of Health.* 2001.

33. Guttmann N. Public Health Communication Interventions, Values and Ethical Dilemmas. *Sage Publications.* 2000.

34. Donkin A.J.M., Dowler E.A., Stevenson S.J., Turner S.A. Mapping access to food in a deprived area: the development of price and availability indices. *Public Health Nutrition*, 2000, 3 (1), 31-8.

35. Marshall T. Exploring a fiscal food policy: the case of diet and ischaemic heart disease. *British Medical Journal*, 2000, 320, 301-5.

36. James W.P.T., Nelson M., Ralph A., Leather S. Socioeconomic determinants of health: the contribution of nutrition to inequalities in health. *British Medical Journal*, 1997, 314, 1545.

37. Acheson D. Independent Inquiry into Inequalities in Health. *London Stationery Office*. 1998.

38. Roe L., Hunt P., Bradshaw H., Rayner M. Health promotion interventions to promote healthy eating in the general population: A Review. London. UK. *Health Education Authority*. 1997.

39.   Brunner E., Cohen D., Toon L. Cost effectiveness of cardiovascular disease prevention strategies: A perspective on EU food based dietary guidelines. *Public Health Nutrition*, 2001, 4 (2B), 711-15.

40.   European Union. Nutrition and diet for healthy lifestyles in Europe; science and policy implications. Proceedings of the European Conference, May 18-20, 2000, Crete, Greece. *Public Health Nutrition*, 2000, 4 (2A), 337-434.

41.   Glanz K. Progress in dietary behaviour change. *American Journal of Health Promotion*, 1999, 14 (2), 112-7.

42.   McArthur D.B. Heart healthy eating behaviours of children following a school-based intervention: A meta-analysis. *Comprehensive Pediatric Nursing*, 1998, 21, 35-48.

43.   Tedstone A., Aviles M., Shetty P., Daniels L. Effectiveness of interventions to promote healthy eating in pre- school children aged 1-5. *Health Education Authority Effectiveness Reviews*, 1998. www.hda-online.org.uk/html/research/effectiveness. html.

44.   Lister-Sharp D., Chapman S., Stewart-Brown S., Sowden A. Health promoting schools and health promotion in schools: Two systematic reviews. *Health Technology Assessment*, 1999, 3 (22).

45.   Leather S. *The making of modern malnutrition: an overview of food poverty in the UK*. The Caroline Walker Trust: London. 1996.

46.   Department of Health. *National Health Service Plan*. Stationery Office London. 2000.

47.   Sustain Project. *Grab 5, Welcome to the Grab 5!* Action pack website. Funded by the National Lottery Charity Board, 2001. http://www.sustainweb.org/g5ap/index.htm.

48.   Sustain. Get Cooking! National Food Alliance, *Department of Health and BBC Good Food*, London. 1993.

49.   Lang T., Caraher M., Dixon P., Carr-Hill R. Cooking skills and health. *Health Education Authority*, London. 1999.

50.   Peersman G., Hardan A., Oliver S. Effectiveness of health promotion interventions in the workplace; A review. *Health Education Authority*. 1998. www.hda-online.org.uk/html/research/effectiveness.html.

51.   Ginsburg M. An appraisal of workplace health promotion for the British Heart Foundation. *Oxfordshire Health Promotion*. Oxford. 1998.

52. Kaduskar S., Boaz A., Dowler E., Meyrick J., Rayner M. Evaluating the work of a community café in a town in the south east of England: reflections on methods, process and results. *Health Education Journal*, 1998, 58, 341-54.

53. Price S., Sephton J. *Evaluation of Bolton's Food Co-ops*. Community Healthcare. Bolton. 1995.

54. Ostasiewicz. *Evaluation of Tower Hamlets Food Co-ops*. Tower Hamlets Food Co-op, London. 1997.

55. Hussein & Robinson. *Gardening for health: evaluation*. Heartsmart and Bradford Community Environment Project, Bradford. 2000.

56. Friends of the Earth. The Economic Benefits of Farmers' Markets. *Friends of the Earth Trust*, London. 2000.

57. McGlone P., Dobson B., Dowler E., Nelson M. *Food Projects and How they Work*. York Publishing Services Ltd for the Joseph Rowntree Foundation, York. 1996.

58. Wonderling D., McDermott C., Buxton M. Costs and cost effectiveness of cardiovascular screening and intervention: the British Family Heart Study. *British Medical Journal*, 1996, 312, 1269-73.

59. Langham S., Thorogood M., Normand C., Muir J., Fowler G. Costs and cost effectiveness of health checks conducted by nurses in primary care: the Oxcheck study. *British Medical Journal*, 1996, 312, 1265-8.

60. Wonderling D., Langham S., Buxton M., Normand C., McDermott C. What can be concluded from the Oxcheck and British family heart studies: commentary on cost effectiveness analyses. *British Medical Journal*, 1996, 312, 1274-8.

61. NHS Centre for Reviews and Dissemination. Cholesterol and coronary heart disease: screening and treatment. *Effective Health Care*, 1998, 4 (1), 1.

62. Hooper L., Summerbell C.D., Higgins J.P.T., Thompson R.L., Clements G., Capps N., Davey Smith G., Riemersma R.A., Ebrahim S. Reduced or modified dietary fat for prevention of cardiovascular disease. *The Cochrane Library*, Issue 2, 2000.

63. Dwyer J.T. Diet and nutritional strategies for cancer and risk reduction, Focus on the 21st Century, *Cancer*, 1993, 72, 1024-31.

64. Tang J.L., Armitage J.M., Lancaster T., Silagy C.A., Fowler G.H., Neil H.A.W. Systematic review of dietary interventions trials to lower blood total cholesterol in free-living subjects. *British Medical Journal*, 1998, 316, 1213-20.

65. Brunner E., White I., Thorogood M., Bristow A., Curle D., Marmot M. Can dietary interventions change diet and cardiovascular risk factors? A meta-analysis of randomised controlled trials. *American Journal of Public Health*, 1997, 87, 1415-22.

66. Clarke R., Frost C., Collins R., Appleby P., Peto R. Dietary lipids and blood cholesterol: quantitative meta-analysis of metabolic ward studies. *British Medical Journal*, 1997, 314, 112-17.

67. Denke M.A. Review of human studies evaluating individual dietary responsiveness in patients with hypercholesterolemia. *American Journal of Clinical Nutrition*, 1995, 62 (2), 471S-477S.

68. Mulrow C.D., Chiquette E.A., Angel L., Cornell J., Summerbell C., Anagnostelis B., Grimm R. Jr, Bland M.B. Dieting to reduce body weight for controlling hypertension in adults. *The Cochrane Library*, 1998, Issue 3, 2002.

69. Glenny A.M., O'Meara S., Melville A., Sheldon T.A., Wilson C. The treatment and prevention of obesity: a systematic review of the literature. *International Journal of Obesity*, 1997, 21, 715-37.

70. NIH (The National Heart, Lung, and Blood Institute). Clinical guidelines on the identification, evaluation, and treatment of overweight and obesity in adults. *National Institute of Health*, Bethesda, Maryland, 1998. www.nhlbi.nih.gov.

71. Health Development Agency. *Health Development Agency Evidence Base*, 2002. www.hda-online.org.uk/evidence/eb2000/corehtml/intro.htm.

INDEX

Additives, control of, 172
Adolescents, nutrition in, 37-62
Adult nutrition, 91-117
Advertising, influence on young people, 40
Ageing, nutrition during, 118-39
Alcohol, consumption by the elderly, 121-2
  during pregnancy, 77-8
  effect on incidence of CHD and stroke, 109
  increasing risk of breast cancer, 9
  pre-pregnancy, 67
  role in cancers, 115
Allergies, prevention in infant through maternal diet, 79-80
Anaemia in childhood and adolescence, 6-7
  in the elderly, 135
  risk in young people, 51
  through iron deficiency, 53
Animal fat, recommendations to restrict intake, 8
Anorexia nervosa, 41
Atopic disease, link with infant nutrition, 32
  protection by breastfeeding, 21
Auto-immune disease, link with infant nutrition, 32
B group vitamins, DRVs for, 93-4
  requirements in the elderly, 124
Blood cholesterol, need to reduce, 185-6
Blood lipids, of men and women – findings of NDNS survey, 99-100
Blood pressure, in the elderly – findings of NDNS survey, 129
  of men and women – findings of NDNS survey, 101

Body mass index, of men and women – based on NDNS survey, 99, 100
Body weight, during pregnancy, 67-8, 85
  in pre-pregnancy stage, 64-5
  in the elderly, 123
  reducing, 186
Bone loss, effect of high-protein diet, 10
  effect of high-salt diet, 10
Bread, changes in pattern of consumption over last century, 5
Breast cancer, as diet-related disease, 9, 115
  reduced risk through breastfeeding, 17
Breastfeeding, 16-24
  effect on mother, 17-8
  possible hazards, 233-4
  versus formula feeding (Table), 25
Bulimia nervosa, 41
Caffeine, during pregnancy, 79
Calcium, contribution to bone density, 10
  DRVs for adults, 95-6
  importance during pregnancy, 76
  to avoid osteoporosis, 113
Calcium intake, in young people, 47
  inverse relationship with hypertension and stroke, 110, 111
Cancer, role of diet, 107
  diet-related, 9-10, 113-6
Carbohydrate, in mother's milk, 22
  DRVs for, 93
Carbohydrate intake, in the elderly – findings of NDNS survey, 127-8
  of men and women – findings of NDNS survey, 100
  of young people, 45

Cardiovascular disease, as diet-related disease, 7-8
  link with infant nutrition, 32
  link with obesity, 7
  role of diet, 107, 108-11
Caseins, in mother's milk, 20
Catering outlets, health promotion activities, 179
Child health, steps to improve, 57-9
Childhood obesity, 41-4
Chloride, DRVs for, 96-7
Chronic diseases, link with infant nutrition, 31-2
  risk factors, 107-16
Cis n-3 and n-6 polyunsaturated fatty acids intake, in young people, 45
Clinical settings, for nutrition interventions, 185
Colon cancer, diet-related, 114
Colorectal cancer, as diet-related disease, 9
Colostrum, importance of, 16
  nutrients in, 18
Community, health promotion activities, 178
Complex carbohydrates, influence on serum cholesterol levels, 109
Copper, intake in young people, 47
  requirements, for adults, 97-8
Coronary heart disease, influenced in prenatal life by maternal nutrition, 11
  role of diet, 108-10
Cows' milk, 24
Dairy products, changes in pattern of consumption over last century, 5
Dental caries, in young people – link with sugar consumption, 56
Diabetes mellitus, link with obesity, 32 link with infant nutrition, 32
  link with obesity, 7
Dietary Approaches to Stop Hypertension trial, 110-1
Dietary consumption, patterns based on NDNS survey, 98-102
Dietary fat intake, in the elderly – findings of NDNS survey, 127-8
Dietary fibre, findings of NDNS survey, 100
  influence on serum cholesterol levels, 109
Dietary patterns, clusters – findings of NDNS survey, 103-7

clusters among UK elderly – findings of NDNS survey, 131-3
Dietary records, of young people (Table), 38
Dietary Reference Values, for adults, 91-8
  for energy, 92-3
  setting of, 153
Diet-related cancers, 9-10
Diet-related problems in the UK, 6-10
Eggs, changes in pattern of consumption over last century, 5
Elderly, nutrition for, 118-39
Energy, DRVs for, 92-3
Energy demands, during lactation, 83-4
Energy intake, in the elderly – findings of NDNS survey, 127
  in young people, 41-4
  of men and women by region – findings of NDNS survey, 101
  of men and women – based on NDNS survey, 99
  of men and women by socio-economic status – findings of NDNS survey, 102
Energy requirements, during pregnancy, 69-73
  for the elderly, 119
Environment, impact on health, 12
Erythrocyte Glutathione Reductase Activity Coefficient, to assess riboflavin requirement, 93-4
Estimated Average Requirements, for adults, 91-2
European Union French Presidency Initiative, 160
Farmers' markets, 183
Fat, DRVs for, 93
  in mother's milk – nutrients in, 18-20
Fat intake, increasing risk of colon cancer, 9
  of men and women – findings of NDNS survey, 99
  of young people (Table), 44
  recommendations for lowering, 7-8
  role in colon cancer, 114
Ferritin levels, in young people, 51
Fibre intake, as possible cause of decreased risk of colon cancer, 9
  of young people, 46
Fluids requirements, for the elderly, 121-2
Folate, importance during pregnancy, 53-4, 82

link with CHD, 109
policy on adding to food, 172
Folate status, of young people, 47
Folic acid, importance pre- and peri-
pregnancy, 66, 75-6
Food allergy, protection by breastfeeding, 21
Food choice, factors affecting, 177
in young people – social influences, 40-1
Food distribution, policy making, 149-53
Food intake, during pregnancy, 74-5
Foodborne diseases, during pregnancy, 78-9
Formula feeding, versus breastfeeding
(Table), 25
Formula milks, 24-7
Fruit and vegetable intake, regional and social
differences, 55
Fruit and vegetables, advantages in young
people, 52
changes in pattern of consumption over
last century, 5
government advice on intake, 39
recommendations for increasing intake, 8
role in cancers, 115
role in reducing risk of breast cancer, 9
Gestational diabetes, 85
Glucose tolerance, improved by physical
activity, 111
Grazing, in young people, 40
Growth reference charts, for infants, 30-1
Haemoglobin levels, in vegetarians, 51
Health Action Zones, 184-5
Health behaviour interventions, 173
Health promotion, 170-92
Health promotion interventions, 173-6
evaluating, 174-5
Heart disease, effect of high sodium intake,
96-7
High-density-lipoprotein cholesterol, inverse
relationship with CHD, 109
High-protein diet, increasing bone loss, 10
High-salt diet, increasing bone loss, 10
Human development, periods of transition
(Fig.), 3
Human life cycle, main stages, (Fig.) 2
Human nutrition, approaches to, 1-14
over the last century, 4-6
Hypertension, as diet-related disease, 7-8
effect of high sodium intake, 96-7

link with diet, 110-1
link with obesity, 7
Immunocompetence, lowered in the elderly,
135
Infancy, nutrition in, 15-36
Infant feeding, 15-6
International Conference on Nutrition, 158-9
Intersalt Study, 110
Iodine, importance in pregnancy, 54
Iodine intake, in young people, 47
Iodine requirements, for adults, 97
Iron, importance in pregnancy, 53
Iron deficiency, in adolescence, 6-7, 52
in the elderly, 125
Iron intake, in young people, 47
Iron requirements, for adults, 97
Lactation, nutrition in, 63-90
nutritional demands during, 83-4
Lactoferrin, in mother's milk, 20
Lactose, in mother's milk, 22
Lactose-free milk, 25
Listeriosis, danger during pregnancy, 78-9
Lower Reference Nutrient Intakes, for adults,
92
Lysozyme, in mother's milk, 20
Macronutrient densities, among UK elderly –
findings of NDNS survey, 133
Macronutrient intake, in young people, 44-6
Magnesium, DRVs for adults, 95-96
intake in young people, 47
Malnutrition, in the elderly, 135-7
Maternal fat, changes during pregnancy (Fig.),
72
Meat, changes in patterns of consumption
over last century, 5
Media, influence on young people, 40
Metabolic rate, during pregnancy (Figs), 71
Micronutrient densities, among UK elderly –
findings of NDNS survey, 133
Micronutrient intake of the elderly, 123-5
of young people, 47-53
Milk, changes in pattern of consumption over
last century, 5
Mineral intake, of men and women – findings
of NDNS survey, 100-1
of the elderly – findings of NDNS survey,
128
of young people 47, 49, 50 (Table), 52-3

regional and social differences, 54-6
Minerals requirements, for the elderly, 121-2
Minerals, DRVs for adults, 95-8
  requirements in the elderly, 125
  RNIs for adults (Table), 96
Mother's milk, 18-23
  constituents in – compared with cows'
    milk and infant formula (Table), 19
National Diet and Nutrition Survey, findings
  on elderly, 125-34
National Diet and Nutrition Surveys of British
  Adults, 98-107
Necrotising enterocolitis, in preterm infants –
  protection by breast milk, 31
Neural tube defects, importance of folic acid,
  66
  resulting from poor folate status in
    pregnancy, 54
Niacin, assessment of status, 94
Nitrogen, non-protein – in mother's milk, 21
Nitrogen balance studies, to set adult protein
  requirements, 93
Non-insulin-dependent diabetes mellitus, as
  diet-related disorder, 8-9
  influence in prenatal life by maternal
    nutrition, 11
  role of diet 107, 111
Nutrients, during pregnancy, 74-5
Nutrition, in infancy, 15-36
  in school children and adolescents, 37-62
Nutrition-related problems in the UK, 6-10
Nutrition Forum (UK), 160
Nutrition interventions, effectiveness of,
  177-86
Nutrition policy initiatives, European, 157-60
  UK, 160-2
Nutritional problems, of the elderly, 134-5
Nutritional status, of the elderly – findings of
  NDNS survey, 128-9
Nutritional stress, in prenatal life, 11
Nutritional targets and recommendations,
  153-7
Obesity, as major risk factor for certain
  diseases, 7
  in adults – dangers of, 112-3
  in children, 41-4
  in men and women – findings of NDNS
    survey, 99

increasing risk of breast cancer, 9
increasing risk of colon cancer, 9
infant, 28
influence in prenatal life by maternal
  nutrition, 11
link with CHD and stroke, 110
post-partum, 85
pre-pregnancy, 64-5
Oral health, in young people, 56-7
Osteoporosis, as diet-related disease, 10
  as measure of calcium deficiency, 96
  effect of diet, 113
  problem in the elderly, 135
Ovarian cancer, reduced risk through
  breastfeeding, 17
Overweight, pre-pregnancy, 64-5
Peer pressure, in young people, 40
Phosphorus, DRVs for adults, 95-6
Physical activity, importance in young people,
  41-4, 52
  reducing the risk of colon cancer, 9
  reduction in – leading to obesity, 7
  role in improving glucose tolerance, 8
Plant foods, role in cancers, 115
Plasma iron levels, in vegetarians, 51
Plasma total cholesterol, in young people, 45
Policy making for nutrition, 140-69
Post-partum nutrition and nutritional status,
  83-6
Post-partum obesity, 85
Potassium, DRVs for adults, 96-7
  intake in young people, 47
  inverse relationship with hypertension and
    stroke, 110, 111
Potatoes, changes in pattern of consumption
  over last century, 5
Poverty, impact on health, 12
Pre-eclampsia, effect of obesity, 85
Pregnancy, energy requirements, 69-73
  nutrition in, 63-90
  teenage, 81-3
Pregnancy-induced hypertension, effect of
  obesity, 85
Pre-pregnancy nutrition, 64-7
Preterm milk, 25
Primary care, health promotion activities, 178
Processed food, increase in purchase and
  consumption over last century, 6

INDEX

Protein, DRVs for, 93
  in mother's milk – nutrients in, 20-1
  intake of men and women – findings of
    NDNS survey, 100
  intake of the elderly – findings of NDNS
    survey, 127
Protein requirements, for the elderly, 120
Public health policy, 171-2
Reference Nutrient Intakes, during pregnancy
  (Table), 75
  for adults, 92
  for lactation (Table), 84
Respiratory allergy, protection by
  breastfeeding, 21
Riboflavin intake, of young people, 47
Riboflavin requirements, assessed by
  Erythrocyte Glutathione Reductase Activity
  Coefficient, 93-4
Salmonellosis, danger during pregnancy, 78-9
Saturated fat intake, effect on total cholesterol
  level, 108
  link with hypertension and stroke, 110
  of young people, 45
  recommendations for restricting, 7-8
  role in cancers, 115
School children, nutrition in, 37-62
School meals, free, 152
Schools, health promotion activities, 178,
  180-1
Selenium requirements, for adults, 97-8
Semi-skimmed milk, recommendations to
  increase intake in young people, 58
Serum cholesterol, in men and women –
  findings of NDNS survey, 100
Seven Country Study, of link between diet
  and CHD, 108
Snacking, leading to obesity, 7
Social circumstances, effect on morbidity in
  adulthood, 11
Social influences, on food choices of young
  people, 40-1
Sodium, DRVs for adults, 96-7
  intake in young people, 51
  link with high blood pressure, 53
  link with hypertension and stroke, 110
Soya milk, for infants, 26
Starch, as possible cause of decreased risk of
  colon cancer, 9

intake of young people, 45
Stroke, influenced in prenatal life by maternal
  nutrition, 11
  link with diet, 110-1
Sugar intake, of young people, 46
Supermarkets, health promotion activities,
  179, 183-4
Supplements, during pregnancy, 77
Teenage pregnancy, 81-3
  nutrients needed, 53-4
Thiamin, adult requirements, 93-4
  deficiency in the elderly, 124
Trace elements, DRVs for adults, 95-8
Veganism, dangers of in young people, 41, 51
  risks in infants, 29
Vegans, need for vitamin D supplements
  during pregnancy, 77
Vegetables, in reducing risk of colorectal
  cancer, 9
Vegetables and fruits, advantages in young
  people, 52
  changes in pattern of consumption over
    last century, 5
  government advice on intake, 39
  intake – regional and social differences,
    55
  recommendations for increasing intake, 8
  role in cancers, 115
  role in reducing risk of breast cancer, 9
Vegetarianism, in teenagers, 41, 51
  link with anaemia in adolescence, 6
  lower rate of CHD, 109
  lower risk of colon cancer, 114
  lower risk of diabetes, 8-9
  lower risk of NIDDM, 111
  need for vitamin D supplements during
    pregnancy, 77
  risk in young people, 52
Vitamin A, adult requirements, 95
  during pregnancy, 78
Vitamin B_6 requirements, for adults, 94
Vitamin C, intake in young people, 52
Vitamin C requirements, for adults, 94-5
  requirements in the elderly, 124
Vitamin D, requirements during pregnancy,
  76-7
  requirements for the elderly, 120-1, 124

Vitamin deficiency syndromes, in the elderly
  (Table), 123
Vitamin intake, of men and women – findings
  of NDNS survey, 100-1
  of the elderly – findings of NDNS survey,
  128
  of young people 47, 48 (Table), 52-3
  regional and social differences, 54-6
Vitamin requirements, for the elderly, 120-1
Vitamin supplements, for the elderly, 125
Vitamins, DRVs for, 93-5
  in mother's milk, 22-3
  RNIs for adults (Table), 95
Weaning feeds, 27-9
Weight gain, during pregnancy, 67-8
Welfare Food Scheme, UK, 151
Whey proteins, in mother's milk. 20
WHO European Office Action Plan for Food
  and Nutrition Policy, 159
WHO International Code of Marketing of
  Breastmilk Substitutes, 26-7
Workplace, health promotion activities, 178,
  182
World Food Summit, 159
Zinc, adult requirements, 97-8
  importance in pregnancy, 54
  intake in young people, 47